PELICAN BOOKS

THE PELICAN HISTORY OF GREEK LITERATURE

Peter Levi, a classical scholar, archaeologist and poet, was born in 1931. He has translated two works for the Penguin Classics: Pausanias's *Guide to Greece* (in two volumes) and *The Psalms*, as well as a translation of Yevtushenko (with R. Milner-Gulland) for the Penguin Modern Poets; and he is the editor of *The Penguin Book of English Christian Verse* and the Penguin Classics edition of Johnson's *A Journey to the Western Islands of Scotland* with Boswell's *The Journal of a Tour to the Hebrides*. *The Light Garden of the Angel King*, his account of his travels in Afghanistan, is published in the Penguin Travel Library. In 1984 Peter Levi became Professor of Poetry at Oxford University.

PETER LEVI

The Pelican History of Greek Literature

PENGUIN BOOKS

Penguin Books Ltd, Harmondsworth, Middlesex, England
Viking Penguin Inc., 40 West 23rd Street, New York, New York 10010, U.S.A.
Penguin Books Australia Ltd, Ringwood, Victoria, Australia
Penguin Books Canada Ltd, 2801 John Street, Markham, Ontario, Canada L3R 1B4
Penguin Books (N.Z.) Ltd, 182–190 Wairau Road, Auckland 10, New Zealand

First published by Viking 1985
Published in Pelican Books 1985

Made and printed in Great Britain by
Richard Clay (The Chaucer Press) Ltd., Bungay, Suffolk

For Deirdre

'The Reader will find here no Regions cursed
with irremediable Barrenness, or bless'd with Spontaneous Fecundity,
no perpetual Gloom or unceasing Sunshine;
nor are the Nations here described either
devoid of all Sense of Humanity,
or consummate in all private and social Virtues ... He will discover,
what will always be discover'd by a diligent and impartial Enquirer,
that wherever Human Nature is to be found,
there is a mixture of Vice and Virtue,
a contest of Passion and Reason ...'

from the Preface to *A Voyage to Abyssinia*,
by Father Jerome Lobo,
a Portuguese Jesuit,
translated by Samuel Johnson (1735)

CONTENTS

CONTENTS

INTRODUCTION

There is usually something to be said for the expression of a lifetime's passion. And probably it is only after a lifetime that one can make sense of literary history for oneself. Some scholars found colonies and create empires of knowledge. Others, perhaps the best, leave only two or three great monuments of a life-work, two or three editions or commentaries. Some put their whole scholarly power into teaching. And there are those who spend a lifetime just trying to make sense of their material, burrowing into it like moles or crawling about all over its surface very patiently, like snails.

After rather such a useless and unproductive lifetime, with no empire opened, no colony flourishing, no great scholarly monument and not many pupils, one is justified in expressing to the best of one's ability what sense one has made. It will be useful to many readers, more now than ever before, I imagine, to know what Greek literature contains and what it is like, to understand it as history and to experience some of its attractions. Even specialized scholars may find a one-man *tour d'horizon* refreshing or amusing. Its only authority is that of personal conviction. It depends massively on other people's work, but it is never based on second-hand opinions, though it often records more opinions than my own. It is a personal book in the limited sense in which taste and reading are personal. They become more so the older one gets. When I was younger I would have written more freshly but more wildly, and even less accurately.

The purpose of this book is first to record the writings of the ancient Greeks, then to describe them, to offer short samples and to show what the writers were like. It is not long enough to be comprehensive, but it claims to be a critical history. That means it is subjective, and pays attention to whatever I thought important. I do not think I have strayed very far from the normal educated opinions of my own generation, and I hope I never stray without warning the reader from the opinions of scholars on scholarly matters. Of course, nothing has been so worked over as the Classics, but scholarly and critical opinion do shift all the same. This book is for now. I have attempted to feed a hungry curiosity about Greek poetry and prose which arose rather recently and is widespread. When traditional classical education came close to foundering, a new readership arose that wanted Greek poetry for its true nature and on its merits, and Greek prose in the same way, without any reference to education. I greatly sympathize with that curiosity and that hunger.

Still, it is not always easy to answer a simple question or meet a simple demand. Greek is inevitably a learned subject, though its difficulties in the past have been grossly exaggerated. Even if one sticks close to the texts one cannot quite avoid the learned industry of classical studies, though one can often escape more lightly than our teachers used to admit. The lists of further reading I offer are minimal, but most of the absences from those lists are deliberate. I have mentioned only the few books I found most helpful, and avoided discussing whatever a sensible reader could afford to ignore. I have tried to stick to the text, and to be honest.

Any history of literature will raise questions about comparative importance. Since such a small amount of ancient Greek literature survives, compared to what once existed, there is a further problem about fragments and absences. Where we have complete plays, I have said very little about tantalizing fragments. I have concentrated on what has survived in bulk, but paid some attention to those mutations and transformations that seem important, however little evidence we have for them: the origins of the prose romance, for example, and the Alexandrian poems about fishermen. There are almost, but not quite, equally important kinds of poem I have virtually ignored: Alexandrian poems about the stars, for example. It is a question of literary merit, which is unpredictable, and may raise any kind of writing to sudden greatness, and even if merit is lacking in what survives, a question of the momentum of literature and of later influence.

But I have not traced every Greek origin of every European influence; we shall be concerned with good writers and great writers and what sets them in perspective, and with little else. I do not think many readers, if they knew the field, would complain at what I have left out, except that I have failed for lack of space, and by concentrating on literary value, to record the interesting mass of Greek technical and medical writings. Yet it is essential to grasp that throughout the archaic and classical and Hellenistic periods of Greek, as they are called, a crowd of ghostly figures whom we scarcely know are thronging on the edges of the works we study. From time to time, one must name them. It may be that literature has no history. There is only history, and literature is part of it. Certainly the history of literature is not just a string or succession of great writers or surviving writers. But the great writers really are paramount, and they illuminate everything else; it is to read them that one learns Greek, and I have concentrated on them. The greatest Greek writers, on a Shakespearean scale of greatness, are Homer and Plato, I think.

In the course of writing this book, I felt I was learning a good deal, much of it by now already forgotten or pushed to the back of the mind, but most of it, I hope, embodied in the book. One of the problems was pace. After endless pondering and futile note-taking, I saw that I must put the whole thing on paper in some form in about a year or else abandon it. A slower pace would have obvious advantages, but would be self-defeating, since one might easily spend ten years on each of these twenty chapters. Since I have already passed a lifetime teaching and rereading the Classics, and come to that point of life where one forgets more quickly than one can learn, the book seemed to be a matter of now or never. I reread a lot of Greek literature in the evenings while I was writing. The longest pause was on Plato; I found myself reading some of Plato, Aristotle, Plutarch and even Xenophon for the first time. My own tutor, who could write better Latin and Greek verse at fifteen than I have ever written, read the whole of ancient Greek literature in seven years and then gave it up and became a doctor. But I have found the repertory of Greek writers is inexhaustible by a serious reader with other interests in an average lifetime. While I wrote, I seldom found reason to alter any seriously considered opinion, however conventional, about what was, or was not, great literature. Greatness is something anyone can see at once, though the judgement of past centuries is a less reliable guide than one imagines. As for the shape of Greek history, and the shape of the history of Greek literature, I was both alarmed and pleased to rediscover the other day that my innermost feelings about the subject correspond rather closely with those expressed by Louis MacNeice in *Autumn Journal*.

About some problems I changed my mind more than once. Even since finishing this book, I have found that I believe less than I did in the truthfulness of Herodotos, and a little differently about his dates, but I have let the chapter stand. The alternative would be complete rethinking and rewriting of chapter after chapter – in fact, another lifetime. Some problems I left aside because I saw no solution. What is the point of discussing the Acts of the Apostles only in terms of thorny and intricate controversies? To discuss them helpfully would take much more space than the subject deserves. How can one fit all that can be known from comparative literature into one chapter on Homer, or from social anthropology into the fifth-century chapters? What is the point of talking about Hieronymos of Kardia, in whose eyes the nomads were heroes of freedom, since we lack his writings?

I paid too little attention to the traditional association of certain styles and even dialects with particular genres, I suppose because I do not really understand it. In lyric poetry it may have something to do with musical style, as well as the prestige of great originals. I think I have stressed insufficiently the poverty of our evidence for early philosophers. We know them only through later eyes, and we are lucky if we have one complete and genuine paragraph of their writings. The same is true to a lesser degree in other areas of Greek literature. We do better to stick as far as possible to what we have most of, and to the best of that. I wish I had space and leisure to deal with Marcus Aurelius and Julian; they open new perspectives I could not follow. But every generation has to explore the storerooms for itself, and every generation finds its own treasures that others had neglected. Every reader who has time will find them.

For a comprehensive discussion of the whole of this subject, down to the last nook and cranny, one should still consult Albin Lesky's *History of Greek Literature* (1966) or the new *Cambridge History of Classical Literature*, Volume One (1984), which is more reliable and up to date, but not always as full or as readable. For a clear, succinct account of most of the known facts about the more important writers and phenomena, one must still use the *Oxford Classical Dictionary*.

My own book has a less academic purpose: to give a short, lucid description in easy, continuous prose of most of ancient Greek literature, showing differences, explaining relationships, briefly discussing dates and developments, conveying by a little use of translation the qualities of the best Greek poets and prose writers, and setting them in the context of history and of life.

Although I have been lucky enough to work for many years in Oxford, where I was also a student, and to have had invaluable help from those who taught me and from colleagues, I do not feel it would be decent to name the great men to whom I am most indebted, since the numerous shortcomings of this book, of some of which I am conscious, are mine alone. Thoroughness is hard to combine with simplicity and depth. But I must express my gratitude to Pauline Hire, for access to books, and to Nigel Wilson, who kindly agreed to question the more questionable sentences I had written, and made a number of valuable suggestions, including the truth about baby lobsters. The inevitable trouble with such a long book (which at the same time is not long enough for its subject) is that, whatever one may imagine before writing, or after having written, the scale and balance are substantially determined by small problems, and not by large considerations. Historians of literature are often villains; they are not quite historians and not quite critics, and not quite in command of their subject. There is no excuse really except stubborn affection for the Classics, and a certain sense of what happened.

Peter Levi
St Catherine's College
Oxford

8 January 1984

BOOKS FOR GENERAL REFERENCE

Particular references are given at the end of each chapter.

Cambridge History of Classical Literature, vol. 1 (Greek), 1984
N. G. L. Hammond, *History of Greece*, 2nd edition, 1967
A. Lesky, *History of Greek Literature*, 1966

M. Nilsson, *Greek Popular Religion* (in some editions, *Greek Folk Religion*), 1940
Oxford Classical Dictionary, 2nd edition, 1970
Oxford Introduction to Greek Literature, 1985
C. M. Robertson, *Shorter History of Greek Art*, 1981
C. A. Trypanis (ed.), *Penguin Book of Greek Verse*, 1971

Penguin Classics include excellent translations of many Greek books.

· 1 ·
HOMER

No one knows quite how old the Greek language is. The Myceneans in the Late Bronze Age certainly knew Greek, but whether, as most scholars used to believe, they brought the language with them when they entered what we now call Greece, probably from central Europe, not long before 1600 B.C., or whether they learnt it later from the natives or the art-loving and magnificent Cretan kings whose place they were to take, remains to my mind uncertain. Professor Chadwick, perhaps the greatest modern authority on the subject, thinks that Greek developed inside Greece.

The earliest evidence we have of the Greek language comes from the clay tablets on which treasury and palace records were inscribed in two syllabic scripts called Linear Script A and B, towards the end of the Bronze Age, about 1200 B.C. These tablets sometimes survived by being baked hard in the fires that destroyed the palaces. Linear Script A has not yet been deciphered, but almost no living archaeologist or philologist now denies that Linear Script B is a representation of the Greek language. A similar but independent syllabic script was used in Cyprus, which gives rise to similar but independent scholarly problems. Those are outside our scope here.

From the eleventh century B.C. to the eighth the Greeks seem to have been illiterate, and the older treasury records of the Mycenean palaces contain no poetry or continuous prose, not even hymns or the legends of the gods. So Greek literature begins effectively with Homer and Hesiod, when their works were written down in the new alphabetic script that the Greeks learnt from the Phoenicians. But in the long period of nearly four thousand years during which the Greek language has retained its identity, it has suffered transformation after transformation. The words for king, bronze, olive, parsley and god have not altered in any of them down to this day, and the alphabet is still the classical alphabet. What has altered most seems to be pronunciation. We can manage the consonants, and we know something about the farmyard vowels, though even here a touch of scepticism is in order: a gun goes off 'bang!' in English, but 'pan!' in French, yet in Chinese I understand 'pan!' is the bark of a dog, which is 'bow wow' in English, transliterated as 'vgaoo, ooaoo!' in a modern Greek translation of Shakespeare.

We know that Greek poets took seriously the length or shortness of syllables, but that may be an adapted system from another language; it can never have been an exact rule in spoken Greek that all short syllables were equally short, and every two of them precisely equal to one long syllable. We must beware of taking the evidence of poetry too literally. Homer can draw out a short syllable and make it as long as he chooses, like any ballad singer. We lack in ancient Greek a sense of the living language to measure against poetry. In this matter a knowledge of modern Greek is just as confusing as Nordic ignorance, because the accent on ancient Greek words, which in modern Greek is an accent of stress and has sometimes shifted, was an accent of musical tone or pitch down to several generations after the time of Christ. The only analogy I know for such a pitch accent is in Chinese, which is little help. What is worse, the pitch accent cannot have collapsed into a stress accent overnight, but we are not now able to reconstruct any stage of that long process.

And yet we develop a strong feeling for Greek prose and poetry, and some discrimination of their sound values, even reading them as crudely as we do. And little by little, our understanding has improved. The old public school pronunciation of Greek before 1914 made a rousing and unashamedly English noise. We have at least got beyond that. Careful attention to sound values in the chorus of Aristophanes' *Frogs* reveals a different poetry and a subtler joke. The boyish frogs of my own schooldays in the 1940s have turned into the genuine article. 'Brékekekéx, Koáx, Koáx' has become 'Brekekeke-e-ex, Koa-a-ax, Koa-a-ax'. It is possible to make further observations which go a long way to explain how it comes about that our sense of poetry and verbal music does not in practice cease to function when we read ancient Greek. Indeed, the pitch accent of ancient Greek meant that every delicate shade of expression must be conveyed by small words which in English we translate as an inflection of

the voice, a shrug or a gesture. We can therefore understand Greek
with unique precision.

The rhythms of prose and the metres of poetry in classical Latin
and in Greek were based on the repeated pattern of long and short
syllables. Our own prose rhythms and traditional metres are based
on similar patterns, but in terms of stressed and unstressed syllables.
Yet in Latin, and to a growing extent in Greek as the pitch accent
altered to a stress accent, the pattern of stressed accents also existed;
it was in contrast or in descant with the long and short pattern,
so that they never coincided. You could not have *Fórtia córpora fúdit
Aías* in a Latin poem. And in English, long and short syllables exist;
Tennyson once claimed he knew the classical 'quantity' of every
syllable in our language, except for the word 'scissors'. In English
stressed verse – in Shakespeare's sonnets, for example – quantity and
stress are in descant; they never or almost never precisely coincide
for as long as a line. So the subtle rhythms and counter-rhythms
of ancient Greek correspond curiously closely to those of English,
and all the more so because not having any pitch accent ourselves,
we inevitably impose a stress accent when we read Greek, however
conscious we may be of quantities.

In Latin we can trace the adaptation by an illiterate people of an
alphabet not designed for their language, and the slow adaptation
of Greek metre and all the Greek techniques of poetry, at first roughly,
for centuries with a certain strong awkwardness, and then with
perfect suppleness in the generation of Virgil and Horace. In Greek
both of the same processes apparently took place. A full study of
Homeric Greek suggests that even the hexameter, Homer's long line,
was not perhaps originally native to Greek. Perhaps no metrical
system is precisely native to any language: poetry is a formal
behaviour of language; it is controlled and learnt. The discipline and
apprenticeship of orally transmitted poetry, to judge from Irish and
central Asian examples, was always severe. What the Muse inspired
was memory, not verse technique.

It is possible that Homer's hexameter was adapted from habitual
combination of two lyric lines. Lyric poetry, at least in the form of
work-songs, is certainly older than Homer; it goes back to the earliest
level of primitive song, and for all we know to the contrary it may
be pre-human. The hexameter Homer uses apparently transmits a

few phrases and combinations of words that go back to the Bronze Age, but the origins of the hexameter itself are not necessarily so ancient. When the metrical rules and characteristic line of an oral tradition of heroic poetry alter, not every phrase is lost and many are adapted. That process can be clearly seen at work in the Serbian epic tradition, and to some extent in medieval Greek. In the eighth century B.C., when Greek literature first began to be written down, we can sense the pressure of adaptation on the alphabet, but heroic verse already existed. We begin without warning to overhear a conversation that had been going on for a long time; it is nearly over when we begin to listen.

Another feature of Homeric poetry which ought to be made as clear as possible in advance is the problem of mixed dialect. This has occupied scholars for many decades. Since the first full and scientific decipherment of Linear Script B as Greek by Ventris and Chadwick, which was substantially complete in 1952 and which identified the Linear B language as 'a Greek dialect ancestral to Arcado-Cyprian' (one of the ingredients and probably the oldest ingredient of Homeric Greek, an ingredient of which something had already been reconstructed independently of poetry), a case has been built up for the existence of dialects even in Mycenean Greek. So far as they can be known, they were less marked than the very strong dialect differences in classical Greek, which the later Greeks in their quarrelsome and subdivided world, dispersed among islands and mountain valleys like the Swiss cantons, took to be marks of racial as well as national divisions.

Homeric Greek contains Aeolian – that is, Thessalian and northeast Aegean dialect forms – for instance, a long *a* in the dual form of the name *Atreida*, meaning 'the two sons of Atreus', and in the genitive singular *Aidao*, 'of Hades', and *Atreidao*, 'of the son of Atreus'. The basic dialect is Ionian, which is Athenian and south-east Aegean Greek. The Aeolian forms occur where Ionian Greek had no equivalent word, or no metrically equivalent form. The Aeolian word for goddess is *thea*, and that occurs because Ionian has only *theos*, a god of either sex. Ionian has no dual form, and in Ionian 'of the son of Atreus' would be *Atreido*. It is as if Aeolian Greek poetry had been adapted into Ionian Greek. These dialects, and the racial mythology that went with them, certainly existed by Hesiod's time, which is not very different from Homer's. Since we know that Homer uses many inherited archaisms, and since Aeolian forms often correspond to the Greek of Linear B, it is tempting to suppose that was where Homer got them from, but not all Homer's Aeolian words are Mycenean: not, for example, *pisures* for four. At least some Aeolian forms are guaranteed by their metrical position in the text of Homer. The study of Greek dialect history is still in the melting-pot, but the mixture of dialects in Homer refuses to vanish.

In a long oral tradition of poetry, in which every performance is a new work of art, such a mixture of dialect is not surprising. Poets travelled, and poems also travelled from mouth to mouth. Similar admixtures of dialect can be found in the *Chanson de Roland*, of which the Oxford manuscript records an Anglo-Norman version, and even in the text of Chaucer, who was not an oral poet. The epic poetry of the central Asian Turkish tribes has penetrated the poetry of the Tajiks, who speak Iranian, through bilingual singers. Dialect contamination occurs in so many epic traditions, even where it falls short of the movement of a poem from one language into another, that we ought to assume that this phenomenon is the rule and not the exception. It tells us little about the Greek epic tradition except that it was old and wandering. About the *Iliad* and the *Odyssey* it tells us nothing. The admixture of dialect in the traditional language of poets was surely older than those poems.

Scholars have argued since the eighteenth century about the nature of Homeric epic: whether at least the *Iliad* was composed by one individual poet and written down or dictated or substantially dictated by him, or whether Homer's works are a mass of traditional, popular material, roughly flung together and shaped at a late stage when the creative fire had died down. Is the *Iliad* a Bronze Age poem, a Dark Age poem, or an eighth-century poem? It does after all contain some famous contradictions. Dinner is eaten twice on the same evening. A dead man reappears at his son's funeral. In the *Odyssey* a spit of olive-wood to put out the one eye of the Cyclops glows red-hot as if it were an iron spit. All these examples suggest impromptu adaptation. Several episodes suggest reworking and new intepretation. Some limits can be set to these disturbing questions at once.

The division of Homer into twenty-four books for each poem, which neatly uses up all the letters of the Greek alphabet, may have been tidied up by Alexandrian scholars in the third century B.C., but the division itself evidently goes back to the poet who devised the *Iliad*. The work of the greatest of Alexandrian scholars was very conservative. We know from many scraps of contemporary papyrus something about the wild errors he weeded out of the text. The more one studies Aristarchos, the more one respects his work. The episodes that may once have served for particular recitals or derived from separate stories are not difficult for us to pick out, but the unity of the *Iliad* is real, and repays intense study. Its first and last books are intimately connected, as we shall see. The poet who shaped a traditional material that was very old into the *Iliad* did so with a strong hand. He was still capable of working with all the techniques of orally transmitted poetry, but he was conscious of the whole of his poem throughout. The contradictions are relatively trivial, although certain details are awkward to explain. The reshaping was one man's work. And after all, the differences between illiterate and literate composition are smaller than scholars suppose. Every poet imitates to some extent, otherwise his work would not be recognized as a poet. Every poet has learnt a language of poetry. Imitation and adaptation, memory and imagination, are closely interconnected in all poetry.

The language of Homeric epic is full of 'formulae' as the scholars call them: adaptable phrases as much as a line long, but usually shorter than that, which fit together like pieces of jigsaw for a variety of purposes. The repertory of these phrases is thought to be traditional, like the 'word-hoard' of Anglo-Saxon poetry, and epic poems have been dated, and ranked as more or less 'genuine', according to the relative quantity of 'epic formulae' in their texture. The trouble with this procedure is that scholarship moves scientifically and mechanically. The mechanical analysis, the counting and classification of these phrases, produces a most mechanical view of poetry, which is not desirable. But the urge to discount mechanical procedures is even less desirable. The *Iliad* uses many more formulae than the *Odyssey*, which is interesting. It does not mean the *Odyssey* is less genuine in any way. It does not even show it was written later, which we may believe on other grounds, or by a different poet. Nor does the operation of these repeated phrases detract in the least degree from Homer's originality as a poet, any more than Alexander Pope's inherited language and controlled metre reduce his different greatness. Homer's language is subtle, inventive and bold. The *Iliad* is a poem, not a problem. It is one thing for the Greek king to say 'There shall come a day when holy Troy will be destroyed', but quite another for Homer to give the same sentence to Hector, about to die for nothing. Often in the *Iliad* a word or a phrase without tragic resonance is echoed with overtones of doom (cf. Macleod, p. 25).

But before discussing the *Iliad* seriously, I must do my best to tidy up another old and mechanical problem, that of its date. Most of the passages in the poem supposed to indicate a date are unreliable. The only phrase of 'epic formula' that can be verified in Mycenean Greek is said to be *xiphos arguro-elon*, a silver-studded sword, but time and ingenuity will surely produce others. The drilled infantry tactics that occur in the *Iliad* two or three times seem to have existed by 725 B.C., but not much earlier. It is probably significant that between 725 and 700 ancient tombs began to be opened and the dead worshipped as noble ancestors; some of them were given Homeric names, though no one knows whether Homer's influence led to the tomb-worship or the tomb-worship lies at the root of Homeric mythology. In Homeric poetry, writing is scarcely known, almost magical, rather as in Serbian epics a letter is called a book and messages are delivered by birds. That is not surprising. It is much odder that riding on horses was an accomplishment that amazed Homer, although he says so much about chariots. We should think perhaps of a place, rather than a date, at which riding was nearly unknown.

There are at least two objects in the *Iliad* which certainly belong to the Bronze Age: a cup belonging to Nestor (11.632) and a helmet made of boar's tusks (10.261). Either could have been turned up by the plough or discovered in a tomb at any time. The enormous body-like shield Ajax carried was an even stranger piece of anti-quarianism; the archaeologists maintain that it would have been obsolete before the Trojan war, but Homer of course was not an archaeologist. As for the Trojan war itself, there was only roughly such a war, and in those days the sea-shore was nearer to Troy than it is now or was in Homer's time. Mycenae, where Homer's Agamemnon ruled, and where in Homer's own time or close to it he was worshipped as a god, really was once the greatest and most magnificent castle in Greece, and the seat of great kings. But in general Homer has the political structure of Greece in his poem, its architecture and some of its geography wrong. Still, the only two lines in the *Iliad* that archaeology suggests are spectacularly late, perhaps as late as the fifth century B.C., are about the collecting up of the bones of the dead and taking them home to the dead man's children (11.632). Aristarchos wanted to cut out those two lines, but his argument is not conclusive.

Arguments about early and late features of language have often turned out to be fruitless. The terms early and late are at best relative, and we lack evidence for absolute dates in the development of Greek. The subject is a battlefield where the dust has not yet settled. Personally, I accept the recent findings of Richard Janko, which I will discuss in the next chapter. Apart from the many indications, some of which I have suggested, we have one knock-down argument about the date of Homer. For some reason it has dropped out of recent discussion, but it has the merit of being scientific. Homer's sailors navigate by stars, to which he refers in detail. They can see no pole star, so they steer by the Great Bear, who is not of course motionless, but at least 'never bathes in the streams of Ocean', never dips below the horizon. His relation to other constellations makes it possible to calculate true north. The heavens alter slowly; what is called their Great Year has a day of seventy years and a month of two thousand. The Great Bear began to sink below the Aegean horizon in the course of the ninth century B.C. At that time the pole star had not been visible in the Aegean for several hundred years.

It has been suggested that Homeric poetry was not purely oral, not impromptu poetry created in performance. That involves a misunderstanding of oral poetry, which is not of its nature impromptu, only constantly adapted in performance, as we know from the way in which Irish bards were trained. It also underestimates the powers of poets. The theory is that Homeric poetry is dictated poetry, a special category between illiterate and literate, on the model of the twentieth-century Yugoslav poetry collected by Milman Parry. 'The poet sings and the professor writes,' as one of his bards gleefully dictated. The model can be criticized until it falls apart, but the scope of the organization of the first two and the last two books of the *Iliad* certainly suggests written poetry. That would place Homer in the eighth century when Greek began to be written. Navigation by the stars would not have altered, and only the line about the Great Bear would be a hundred years out of date. Nor would the Great Bear have dipped often at first, or for long. In our own northern sky of course, the Bear still never sets. Homer's phrase about the Bear occurs both in the Iliad (18.489) and the Odyssey (5.275).

It is not possible to put Homer much later than the eighth century, because he soon begins to be quoted and adapted and in the end even illustrated like a strip cartoon. Wilamowitz, a scholar of striking brilliance and some perversity, hit on the eighth century during the 1920s; earlier scholars put Homer a hundred years earlier. The late eighth century has become popular; it is a working hypothesis which would now be hard to abandon as it fits the known facts rather well. The great religious and athletic meetings of the Greeks began in that century. Clearly, Homer is a traditional poet, his poetry is the last distillation of the Dark Ages from 1100 to 700 B.C. We may guess, but do not know how long a development may lie behind them. Unless the towering body-shields of Ajax and of other heroes are a freakish invention or an archaeological discovery, as I am inclined to imagine, then the tradition was very long indeed. What we know of the fragments of epic poetry after Homer suggests that in the seventh century a sharp decline of standards took place, less sharp in the Homeric hymns, but sharp in the handling of long epics. That may be merely by contrast with Homer's individual genius. Wilamowitz placed Homer in the centre of a process by which generations of poets led up to him and later generations of poets altered and spoiled his poems. They were ruined masterpieces only a great scholar could rebuild. But there are very few traces of spoiling in the works of Homer, and the Iliad in particular depends utterly on its final touches. They create its moral meaning and its poetic momentum.

Finally, one should consider the length and purpose of the Iliad and the Odyssey. 'Je veux lire en trois jours l'Iliade d'Homère,' says Ronsard to his servant. It is not an idle wish if one reads fast, though twenty-four evenings is a more usual pace. If one removes the framing books, the first two and last two, the action of the Iliad occupies exactly three days; it is curiously suggestive that it also takes three rather full days to recite. In Book 1 Achilles is angry for eleven days and in Book 24 the gods have resisted Zeus eleven days; the plague lasted nine and so did the lament for Hector; Book 2 and the second last book each record a two-day ceremony of burial and a pause from war. It happens that the festival of Apollo on his holy island of Delos lasted for three days, and there were other such festivals. The Homeric *Hymn to Apollo* fixes the origin of the Delian festival early enough for Homer. Twenty-four books suggest twenty-four hours, and that may be an ancient division, but the conception of three eight-hour days is compelling. In the *Iliad*, singing is a princely accomplishment, as it is in late romances, but professional singers, who are sometimes blind, are treated with great respect and listened to with pleasure or with tears. The singer Demodokos is an honoured visitor. Singers in Homer are not precisely court poets, but they do sing about recent events, like ballad singers down to modern times. The fact that their poems are never long may be deceptive. We are given by chance in *Beowulf* a fine but a brief story of just this kind, which also existed as a full-scale, monumental poem, of which just twenty or thirty lines survive in the Finsburgh fragment.

And who was Homer? The social position of poets is likely to have varied greatly from century to century. The eighteenth-century example of the blind Dunvegan poet and harper Roderick Morison is instructive. He was trained in Ireland in one of the last bardic schools. The young Macleod found him in Edinburgh and lured him to Skye. He held a lucrative plot of land, but not rent-free, from the Macleods, until he quarrelled with them over the dangerous subject of Jacobite loyalties. After that he wandered the roads in summer from house to house. As late as the fifth century B.C., Pindar, the lyric poet, travelled very widely in the Greek world; he depended on commissions, and his relations with his patrons and with cities were not always easy. But Homer ignores his contemporaries. His mighty undertaking does suggest a quiet corner, a strong demand for his work, perhaps for his actual performance, and some degree of peace, even though his work records a terrifying experience of life. Odysseus and the swineherd seem to speak with his mind when they tell their stories. 'Great griefs give a pleasure in later life, when those tell them who suffered greatly.' 'You lead a good life, you have your food and drink,' says Odysseus to the swineherd, 'but I have been wandering about through many cities and settlements of men.' But for what is deepest, most genuine and tragic in Homer's mind, one must look closely at the poetry of the *Iliad*.

Its texture is full of interwoven beauties and ironies that seem to react on one another and yet have a separate existence, like the scales of a salmon or a mackerel where the flashing silver and black and the other subtler colours appear to play not on the individual scales but over the whole fish. The reason for the difficulty of analysis is that Homer's Greek is largely paratactic: sentences are loosely organized and phrases loosely strung together; they are not fully syntactic, they are not thoroughly and lucidly organized logically or even rhetorically, though they have a pre-rhetorical rhetoric of their own. To feel the power of this style in English, one should read the account of Falstaff's death in Shakespeare's *Henry V*. The moral impersonality of Homeric narrative depends on it. So do the intimacy and directness of Homer. Without paratactic construction Homeric irony would not exist, and the immense repertory of small phrases and variable half-lines could not be so swiftly applied. The secret of Homer's art is his paratactic power. That is the coherence of the fish-skin.

So the Trojans kept watches; but infinite panic held the Achaians, companion of cold fear, with grief unbearable all the best were struck. As two winds arise on the fish-haunted sea, Boreas and Zephyros, and they rush down from Thrace, suddenly they come, and the dark wave is confused together, and it sheds much seaweed out of the salt sea, so was their spirit divided in the breasts of the Achaians. And the son of Atreus, with great grief struck at heart, wandered to the clear-voiced heralds, commanding them to call each man by name to assembly, not to cry out, and he laboured with the first. (9.1 ff.)

The speed and impetus of this style carry you swiftly. The small puzzles and contradictions that clear syntax would iron out are no disadvantage. Then notice the tension between noise and silence in this passage, and the irony of the barren and unresponsive sea, which is only the fishing-ground after all, but now it separates the Achaians from home, and fear is chilly, and this is night. I am not sure what the seaweed is doing, but I am certain its role is crucial. The metaphor of the winds and the sea, physically obscure as it is, draws the reader or listener fully to imagine for himself something only lightly or obliquely related to the action. In this way he is drawn into the process of imagining the entire poem as it moves. The metaphors in the *Iliad* make it a 'do-it-yourself' poem; that is an important characteristic of performed poetry.

The metaphors are not just ornamental, they are not virtuoso passages attached to the text by a single point of likeness, and they are not just appeals to everyday life. Ajax is beaten back as children beat a donkey out of the crops, but heroes leap like lions into the sheepfold, and the Greeks had never seen a real lion. (That is why lions in Homer fail to roar, which as a matter of fact makes them all the more sinister.) By leaving the listeners each free to work their own imaginations, Homeric poetry achieves more than precise description could do. The great spear of Achilles gleams like the most ominous star of autumn. One is drawn into full imaginative working life. The same with the two winds on the fish-haunted sea: in real life no one has ever felt two winds at once, but the slight obscurity adds to the force of these verses.

And in this way, paragraph by verse paragraph and episode by episode, the texture of the poem is built up, with fluent changes of tone and movements of ironic contrast. Homer knows the effects of paratactic composition and exploits them. These compositional habits have been explained as devices of impromptu composition and as aids to the gasping memory; they are never merely mnemonic, and composition was never merely impromptu. Performance was adaptation, it was a continuous rethinking and feeling; performance was always a revision. Bartlett, the Cambridge psychologist, has pointed out that remembering is a process not of reproduction but of reconstruction, which depends on selective perception. That is particularly true of unwritten poetry. The *Iliad* is full of digressions, of long and floating themes. Yet they are intricately woven into one another; this compositional habit is as conscious, and as consciously exploited, as the paratactic stream of phrases.

The repeated epithets, which do so much for the formal structure of Homeric verse, 'bronze-shirted Achaians' and 'fish-haunted' or 'barren sea' and 'helmeted Hector', awaken an appetite which they satisfy. Once again, their effect is to draw the listening imagination into nothing less than a world. The same is true of repeated themes, the battle, the duel and the death. In Homeric verse there are only fifteen or twenty things that can happen in a battle. They exist in different combinations or very occasionally in one full-scale conflict. Their constant, formal repetition is terribly convincing; in a way, they are the entry music of death. Some of the repeated themes, the variations of death, are very ancient; like the themes of folk-tales, they lie close to the sources of all Homeric narrative. The champion in battle, the two noble brethren, in primitive poetry two kinsmen, in Homer two loving heroes, in the poetry of Aischylos physical lovers, the young man who dies before his father, the end of the blood feud, the assembly which is played on like long grass in the wind, the love scene whether of gods or men, the feast and the games, and the unequal battle: all these themes are adapted in a thrilling variety of ways.

Early in the *Iliad* Diomedes plays the champion's part of absent Achilles. But Hector is also a champion. Only the death of the greatest champion will make Achilles hero of heroes, and death at Achilles' hands is Hector's inevitable fate. So meanwhile we learn a great deal about heroes, in many variations. The two loving heroes also occur in several examples, but I believe only to illuminate the climactic case of Achilles and Patroklos. The death of Hector is the end of a blood feud that arises from the pathetic death of Patroklos. It gives Patroklos a dignity and meaning. Hector among others dies before his father; his fall is like the fall of Troy. Hector's death is mighty. 'Great he lay and greatly fallen, forgetful of his horsemanship.' But the most moving death of a son in the *Iliad* is that of Sarpedon, son of Zeus, and Sarpedon's burial by Sleep and Death, swift messengers, is all the more moving for the self-echoing quality of the verse. Sarpedon really had a tomb where he was worshipped, far away from Troy, as a divine hero. In order to explain away his death at Troy in another tradition, Homer is pushed to this marvellous invention. Zeus is unable to save his own son.

And Zeus the cloudmaker spoke to Apollo: 'Arise beloved Apollo, clean the dark blood, take Sarpedon from the spears, and bearing him far away, wash him in the streams of the river and anoint him with immortal ointment, and put immortal clothing on him, and give him to swift messengers to carry, to Sleep and Death twin brethren, who will lay him swiftly down in the rich country of broad Lycia: there his brothers and his kin will give him burial with a mound and a pillar, for that is the due of the dead.' So he spoke and Apollo was not deaf to his father. He went down from the mountains of Ida into the dreadful battle-noise, and at once lifting up godlike Sarpedon from the spears he took him far away and washed him in the streams of the river, and anointed him with immortal ointment, and put immortal clothing on him, and gave him to swift messengers to carry, to Sleep and Death twin brethren, who laid him swiftly down in the rich country of broad Lycia.

We should remember that the heroic poet's audience are older than the heroes he commemorates; I think the *Iliad* was written by an old man for the old. 'Happy is any man since who can beget such sons ... Their defiance will live after them, in every land where there are men to hear.' That is the Norse poet of *Atlamal*. In the *Iliad* another son recalls his father's advice in famous words: 'To be always a champion and do better than all others, and fight always in the front rank.' The pathos of the advice would not be lost on an audience of fathers (cf. also *Iliad* 5.152 ff. and 11.328 ff. and 6.445–6).

The *Iliad*, like most archaic Greek poetry, is based on a moral system quite unlike our own, which survived in a ragged form until yesterday in southern Italy, in Spain and even in parts of Greece. It is not a philosophy, but the pure expression of a social organization now lost. To a greater or lesser degree, all epic poetry, all genuine heroic poetry, expresses this same world-view. Honour is the greatest good, shame the worst evil. Kings rule by prestige, expressed and determined, as other social relations are expressed, by the giving and accepting of presents. Obligations are absolute, particularly blood-vengeance, but also war as a competition of honour. The laws of hospitality are binding and elaborate. Such a system is intended to prevent wrong and war; yet it leads inevitably to war on the margins of a given society. Piracy cannot be prevented, and Helen was stolen by a foreigner. Typically, women are at the bottom of the trouble, but it is also women who reward the brave with pleasures and lament the dead. Lamentation is woman's poetry and preserve; an imitation of it has touched the *Iliad*, and altered or created its meaning. Men do at times, on the great funeral vases of the eighth century, take part in lamentation, but not, I think, in the dirge.

Achilles knows he is doomed to die young. He is said to have 'chosen' youthful, glorious death. If he hesitates, that is a dramatization of his choice: to be a hero and die young. In fact the society of the *Iliad* is one in which the absolute social obligation to heroism is breaking up; one may consider that it was felt in the eighth century much as a boy of sixteen considers absolute moral obligation, or as a young officer considered patriotism and courage in 1914. The *Iliad* was a conservative force in a changing world. Imaginatively, the individual hero is beginning to feel the griefs of freedom, although the structure of the poem is given and one is not really free to abdicate from heroism – or only free enough to give a tragic resonance to one's destiny. Achilles will accept and lament. The heroes are toy soldiers, but they bleed. The gods and men know human life is grievous. It is this core of mixed feelings that generates the plot of the *Iliad*, and many details of its poetry.

The Trojan war has lasted nine years and will last ten. The *Iliad* is only an episode; the hellish sufferings of war extend forwards and backwards beyond this poem. The war seems to have lasted so long only because the Trojans refused to come outside their walls and fight. Once Achilles meets Hector Troy will fall, because Achilles is the absolute champion and truest hero. Achilles' victory will be dramatic only if it takes some winning, and if Hector also is shown to be a very great hero. So Achilles must be put – must put himself – out of action, while Hector has his hour of championship. Only a fine point of honour could keep Achilles from battle-honour. He must quarrel, and with a king divinely sanctioned, so that Achilles is inhibited from killing the king. For three days Achilles sulks, and in those three days almost the whole *Iliad* takes place.

But the great hero's offended honour must be implacable, so the embassy sent to him and the promises made are useless. The only thing that can move him is an absolute obligation of blood-vengeance for Patroklos, his brother by adoption. The death of Patroklos is brave and foolish, like so many deaths in the *Iliad*. In a sense the *Iliad* is his memorial as much as Hector's. So Achilles kills Hector, and his rage is still implacable against Hector dead: to deprive your dead enemy of burial was the extreme of heroic anger. But Homer knows that the absolute hero is also magnanimous. His affronted honour can yield the dead body, though only if Hector's father begs for it. Through Priam's agency Achilles is able to show compassion. It may well be felt that Priam is by far the more tragic figure, and that Hector if not Priam is the true tragic hero of the *Iliad*. Of course, Homer is perfectly conscious of that irony. Achilles is too terrible to be liked, but he is a splendid and breathtaking figure all the same, just as gallantry and its physical arms are splendid in the *Iliad* – 'but he crashed as he fell, and his weapons clanged around him'. The *Iliad* is crammed with such ironies, and Homer has exploited them all deliberately.

Some of them come to the point of formal paradox in Homeric verse. 'All day the men contend in grievous war', as if it were their daily work. The sea is 'dark as wine', it is 'the sea that gives no vintage'; its barrenness is in contrast with a happy life, but it is implicit that men do travel the seas. The watch-fires on the Trojan plain like summer stars, that Tennyson and Pope both so well translated, are in ironic contrast with the truth of the war. The word 'bridge' leads us into an emotional ambush.

> And these all night upon the bridge of war
> Sat glorying; many a fire before them blazed:
> As when in heaven the stars about the moon
> Look beautiful, when all the winds are laid,
> And every height comes out, and jutting peak
> And valley, and the immeasurable heavens
> Break open to their highest, and all the stars
> Shine, and the Shepherd gladdens in his heart:
> So many a fire between the ships and stream
> Of Xanthus blazed before the towers of Troy,
> A thousand on the plain; and close by each
> Sat fifty in the blaze of burning fire;
> And eating hoary grain and pulse the steeds,
> Stood by their cars, waiting the thronèd morn.

Through the champing of the horses we feel the multitude of the soldiers, and the impersonal fineness of the dawn breaks over this passage with a deadly irony. The shepherd looks up with gladness, but he would look down from his mountain with terror at these fires. The ignorant, beautiful horses chew their grain, knowing nothing except that daybreak means work. Elsewhere in the *Iliad* there are constantly recurring ironies about the death or fall of the great and godlike, the cowardice or weakness of the fine and beautiful, the pity, woe and dreadfulness of war, sometimes lightly and sometimes fully stated. The famous metaphor of Ajax beaten back out of battle like a donkey beaten out of the crops is only one of these ironies stated in reverse. Ajax is ugly, stubborn and formidable. Nestor is old, wise and eloquent, but the Achaians are generally grim and silent, the Trojans are vocal and brilliant, because the Trojans are losers. The texture of the *Iliad* is woven through again and again with pathos which seems objectively and quite impersonally stated. It is none the less deliberate. The godlike impersonality of Homer and his godlike intimacy belong to the essential weave of epic poetry, but Homer is not at all impartial. Indeed, he has difficulty in controlling the partialities of his gods and in making their behaviour coherent. The *Iliad* is innocent of nationalism; the Trojans talk in the same phrases as the Greeks; war is something suffered by actors and victims alike.

Conflict is among other things an entertainment, and the laughter of the gods at club-footed Hephaistos, and of men at the thrashing of Thersites, harshly as they strike us, do not exclude ambiguity of feeling. Perhaps the worst thing about the gods is their likeness to Homer's audience; they can weep, they are enthralled by tales of old sufferings, they can take sides and show compassion and pay the tribute of full attention, but whenever they choose they can transfer their attention elsewhere, be busy about their private affairs, or be absent on long visits to the just Aithiopians whom the gods love. That the conflict of the gods themselves is entertainment for Zeus probably only reflects its entertainment value for the audience.

> With a great crash they fell together, broad earth groaned,
> great heaven trumpeted, and Zeus enthroned
> heard on Olympus, his dear heart rejoiced
> with laughter seeing gods meet in conflict.   (21.389)

There is something voyeuristic about the gods in their relation to mankind, but also about us in our relation to the gods. This arises inevitably from the poet's relation to his listeners; one should not make heavy weather of it, since it is far older than the *Iliad*. In general in the *Iliad*, the gods bring nothing about; they are only a metaphor for what might well have happened anyway. They add a sense of fate, of a dramatic order of nature. A defeated hero escapes in the dust-cloud of the war, a weapon hits the mark, the king is much disturbed by dreams, some true and some deceiving. Divine motives are like human motives, but in a world of their own, not always related to ours. The gods are sometimes terrible, usually beautiful, always impressive. Homer makes jokes about the gods, some of them unexpected. The gods are in contrast with mankind, and the comparison of the first and the last books of the *Iliad* suggests that, morally, men are fractionally taller than the gods. The gods of the *Iliad* have an interest in justice, but justice of a limited kind.

In Book 14 Zeus has to be removed from the action, to allow the fortunes of war to swing a little and to prevent Hector from annihilating the Achaians before Achilles comes to meet him. The protection of Zeus has to be suspended. Zeus cannot quarrel with himself, he must sleep. The sleep must be magical and long-lasting. So Zeus is overcome by the pleasures of love, which are greater for him than those of war. Homer has great sympathy with this, as one can see in the ambiguity of his treatment of Paris with Helen, but of course that is not an attitude permitted to human heroes. For them one omen, one flight of birds is best, to fight for one's country, and die doing it. Indeed, one of the most moving tensions in the *Iliad* lies in the relation of Hector to his family, his father, his wife and his child. He is not able to avoid war as Paris does, or to choose love before dignity, as Zeus does (14.345 ff.):

> Gazing he spoke, and kindling at the view,
> His eager Arms around the Goddess threw.
> Glad earth perceives, and from her Bosom pours
> Unbidden Herbs, and voluntary Flowers;
> Thick new-born Violets a soft Carpet spread,
> And clustering Lotos swelled the rising Bed,
> And sudden Hyacinths the Turf bestrow,
> And flamy Crocus made the Mountain glow.
> There golden Clouds conceal the heavenly Pair,
> Steeped in soft Joys, and circumfused with Air;
> Celestial Dews, descending o'er the Ground,
> Perfume the Mount, and breathe Ambrosia round.
> At length with Love and Sleep's soft Power opprest,
> The panting Thunderer nods, and sinks to Rest

In this passage of uncharacteristic luxuriance, made even grander, less like a Greek mountain in spring and more like a scene in the Royal Opera House, by Pope's admirable translation, one can see description functioning as Homeric metaphor functions. What it covers is the act of love. Descriptions on a smaller scale in the *Iliad*, a golden ornament or a grove of elm trees, often have the same symbolic and mysteriously refreshing power. 'Level with his horses held the other horses, that drew their chariots with a marvellous noise, and before them Apollo lightly dashed down the banks of the great ditch with his feet, kicking the piled earth down into the ditch ...' (15.353 ff.). The feet of the galloping horses cover the awkwardness of the god kicking over the clods. Pope's translation is seductive, but it does disguise and transform the nature and texture of Homeric poetry. Homer's language is not as noble and swift and uneccentric as Matthew Arnold thought it was. (Arnold was confused by his worship of Wordsworth and perhaps by some resentment of Tennyson.) But an inner simplicity is essential to Homer, and it will be useful to consider the same passage (14.345 ff.) in the Lang, Leaf and Myers version of 1887, two years after Arnold's death:

So spake he, and the son of Kronos clasped his consort in his arms. And beneath them the divine earth sent forth fresh new grass, and dewy lotus, and crocus, and hyacinth, thick and soft, that raised them aloft from the ground. Therein they lay, and were clad with a fair golden cloud, whence fell drops of glittering dew. Thus slept the Father in quiet on the crest of Gargaros, by sleep and love overcome, with his bedfellow in his arms.

Pope is more richly but less sharply erotic than Homer. And how simply and effectively in Homeric verse one thing echoes another, spoken or unspoken. When Poseidon goes to war and the sea echoes on the shore, the sea is not quite an attribute and need not be a metaphor: it is part of an insistent suggestion; it contributes to the force of a powerful, cumulative context. The drops of glittering dew falling on the mountain play just such an obvious part in the love scene. The crude likeness of the flowers to a bed is clear but unspoken. In a later epic imitation, the flowers are a sweet-smelling dress for Aphrodite, and poetry is degraded to a decoration. Here, the invincible god 'by sleep and love overcome' (Sleep and Death are twin brethren) is named only as the Father on the crest of Gargaros, with his bed-fellow (unnamed because the majesty is his) in his arms. Small wonder that Pope makes him 'the panting Thunderer'; as usual, the elements of Homer Pope has selected for exaggeration are not as foreign to Homeric poetry as they might seem. The texture of Homeric verse repays extremely close attention, and even the classic English trans-lations of Homer repay close comparison.

The irony of Zeus overcome is in itself slight, but the contrast of this scene with what is coming and what has passed in the *Iliad* is stark and heavily ironic. The *Iliad* is about honour and about death; it is, therefore, deeply about the experience of life. Heroic life is tragic life. It is not set, as the Greeks imagined and late scholars assumed, in an earlier society, in a precise historical past, but in an imagined world distilled from life, in conditions of great purity and clarity. Its material is mostly battle and death, in which the poet controls every detail he chooses with a vivid realism. But the commanders and great heroes control the course of battles, and Zeus controls the whole unfolding action, only so far as the poet consciously controls the entire mass of his material. In this the poet's best instrument is his control of speed. He can linger on a detail or a string of metaphors that read like a repertory of alternatives, or he can exhaust every twist and turn of a long digression. He can switch attention to heaven. But he can also be as swift and as deadly as the heroes are, pausing only for a line, only for a word, to give death its element of lamentation. A name is enough. The formality and dignity of the *Iliad* are a matter of repetition. But throughout these tragic and terrible verses, the attention constantly comes to bear on tiny details as subtle as the shimmering of light or the shivering of leaves in a short story by Chekhov.

The *Odyssey* is agreed on linguistic grounds to be a little later than the *Iliad*. If Homer wrote them both, it was an interesting and a strange development, since in the management of plot the *Odyssey* is more ambitious and a little unsteady in technique. The poem shifts about more between places, following the fortunes of persons; it is dotted with numerous flashbacks and stories in miniature and episodes isolated from one another. The basic device of the return of Odysseus is one that occurs also in central Asian poetry, in the tales of *Dede Korkut*, and in general the *Odyssey* is closer to folktale in many of its themes than the *Iliad* is. Many of the apparently later features of the *Odyssey* may be explained by this difference of kind, this difference of poetic tradition, and scholars have argued quite soberly that the same Homer may have worked in both traditions. Once you have admitted the mastery of the poet of the *Iliad*, what is beyond him? I would be pleased if I could accept this argument, but the opposite question has equal force. In a tradition of poetic texture magnificent and as closely knitted as this, why should we assume there was only one great poet? The earliest written tradition that knows of only one Homer, though it can name a number of lesser and later epic poets, goes back to the sixth century B.C., when we are told that the manuscripts of Homer were collected and reorganized by Peisistratos the governor of Athens, and by Polykrates of Samos.

The analogy with *Dede Korkut* is very striking. In that poem the hero has been away for sixteen years imprisoned by enemies. Sixteen years in this epic seem to be based on the time it takes a son to grow to maturity. The wanderings of Odysseus were equal to the whole Trojan war over again, but not enough adventures were recorded to cover that time, so he lived in love seduced by the nymph Kalypso in a cave. The Asian hero returns in disguise on the wedding-day of his betrothed; he rises through the social ranks one by one, just as Odysseus shelters with a swineherd, fights a beggar and enters as a guest. Both heroes bend a mighty bow; Beyrek the Asian shoots the bridegroom's ring, Odysseus shoots through the rings on the tips of twelve axes. The *Dede Korkut* version goes back at least to the ninth century A.D., so we are forced to believe either in an influence of the *Odyssey* on the nomads of Asia or vice versa, or in a common source. The latter solution is distinctly easier. Adventures at sea and among islands are a simple way for the island Greeks to supply the lost years, and all the more easily if, as it appears happened, the *Odyssey* has borrowed some adventures from an older poem about the Argonauts, the first human sailors. This argument has the great advantage of explaining why the *Odyssey* divides so oddly into the adventurous journey and the return and revenge of Odysseus, which read like different stories. The nomadic poet of *Dede Korkut* knew the desert, but not the sea or the islands.

When the *Odyssey* was composed, the Greeks already had their common athletic festivals and common oracular shrines; their communications were a spider's web. The *Odyssey* has an obvious connection with Greek exploration of the Mediterranean, perhaps with the commercial and colonial expeditions of the eighth century B.C. and the stories they brought back. The home of Aiolos, god of winds, was on the island of Lipari, off the Sicilian coast, and the Cyclops, who exists in folk-tales all over the world, seems to have been a Sicilian monster. But myth is very difficult to date, and folk-tale impossible:

it exists only in constant transformations and adaptations. The piracy in the *Odyssey* and the dominance of Phoenician ships suggest the Late Dark Age, but the *Odyssey* is about the sea imagined on dry land, and similar stories even in recently recorded Greek folk-tales have the same quality, the same authenticity. The difference is the scale and sweep of Homeric narrative, its nonchalant continuity of realism, the texture of the verse itself, the irony and darkness it has in common with the *Iliad*, which do summon up the ghost of a single poet. The character of Odysseus in this long poem is a mature creation, quite unlike his role in the episodes of the Trojan war. The concentration of one goddess on one hero and his son opened new possibilities for poetry. In the *Iliad*, Athene was every hero's helper and a goddess of war. Where the gods show such development, we are justified in supposing that human beings have altered just a little, though from the point of view of poetry the loss of the turbulent contrasted gods of the *Iliad* may be thought to outbalance the gain.

Both the *Iliad* and the *Odyssey* are about the breakdown of a moral order thought to be natural and divinely sanctioned, and about the restoration of that order. Both poems are extended not only in their number of verses but in a comparably vast range of detail, of poetic or aesthetic effect, and of life in the world. Both explore many moral paradoxes by irony and contrast. In both poems the physically glorious lives of the great and the fineness of natural things form an undertone; darkness and death form another. In the *Odyssey*, in the indoor battle which begins the hero's revenge, the same techniques of poetry, the repetitions and the ironies, are used with other words and other material than the *Iliad*, and with quite another effect.

The arrow-point pierced his delicate neck right through. He swerved to one side, and the cup dropped as the shaft went home. A thick jet of blood gushed from his nostrils; he suddenly kicked the table from him and spilled all the food upon the floor; the bread and roasted meat were befouled with blood ... He fell down sprawling and writhing over his table, and spilled on the floor his food and his double-handled cup. He struck the ground with his forehead in agony, and with both legs he kicked the tall chair until it rocked; and dimness descended on his eyes ... The goddess took the semblance of a swallow, and speeding upward she chose a settling-place on the roof-beam of the murky hall.

That is Walter Shewring's very precise translation. The tall chair
is a detail which might occur in the *Iliad*. The ominous swallow on
the roof-beam of the murky hall operates as metaphors operate: it
invites the listening imagination to create size and darkness.

In some ways the *Odyssey*, with its didactic gods and its domestic
massacres, is a grimmer poem than the *Iliad*. The resolution is violent
and scarcely convincing. One revenge killing provokes another and
the characters seem doomed by the obligations of heroism to perpetual civil war. 'They began to turn back towards the city, eager
to save their lives. But Odysseus, with a terrible cry, gathered himself
and swooped upon them like an eagle from high in air. Then Zeus
sent a thunderbolt from heaven. Reeking, it fell ...' And yet how
else, without violating those rules of honour which guaranteed the
order of society and underlay all epic narrative, could one redesign
the end of the *Odyssey*? Should Telemachos have died in the battle?
Poetry belongs to losers, and all heroes are losers. Odysseus is half
hero, half the tricky man, the cunning disguiser, the everlasting
survivor. He is like the Wanderer and the Seafarer in Anglo-Saxon
poetry, moving through a mythical but otherwise a similar world.

Greek and Anglo-Saxon poetry are not the same, of course, and
the differences are instructive. The strong rhythms of Anglo-Saxon
suggest a stringed music of melodious vigour; the Homeric hexameter
is a long line that can often in different ways suggest the sea itself.
'Ship stood in haven ring-necked, icy and eager, a lord's boat', when
Beowulf travelled. The ship's qualities were his, it might as well be
his horse. The *Odyssey* is slower, more in love with the ship's
behaviour, when Telemachos captains his first ship.

> Swift to the shore they move: along the strand
> The ready vessel rides, the sailors ready stand.
> He bids them bring their stores; th'attending train
> Load the tall bark, and launch into the main.
> The prince and goddess to the stern ascend;
> To the strong stroke at once the rowers bend.
> Full from the west she bids fresh breezes blow:
> The sable billows foam and roar below.
> The chief his orders gives; th'obedient band
> With due observance wait the chief's command:
> With speed the mast they rear, with speed unbind

> The spacious sheet, and stretch it to the wind.
> High o'er the roaring waves the spreading sails ...

The adventures of Odysseus himself at sea are more dramatic; he sails even on rafts and his best ships are wrecked. He reaches home by the skin of his teeth in spite of the anger of Poseidon. His final end will be to wander over the earth with an oar on his shoulder, until he finds a people who mistake it for a thresher's shovel: a people that is who have never seen the sea, the Arcadians it seems. Not one of his companions came home alive. 'We made our gloomy way to the ship on the sea-shore, weeping without restraint.' The meanderings of the journey were unending, like the circles of an *Inferno* that has no guide. And yet what gives the *Odyssey* its powerful attraction is surely the freshness of island after island and adventure after adventure. One would think that Odysseus, naked and alone on an unknown coast, befriended by a kindly princess who had luckily come to do her brothers' washing at a stream near by, would be the climax, but the most thrilling episode of all is the first day on his native island and the night spent with the swineherd.

In a sense, this is the meaning of the *Odyssey*: the return to the real world and the restoration of its heaven-ordained order. The true Odysseus is a peasant, not a king: the audience of the poem know more about peasants than kings. So Odysseus after his first night of lovemaking and story-telling in his own palace set out again 'to the wooded farmland to see my father', who lived on his own land with farm servants and an old Sicilian slave-woman. The hero found the old man foully dressed like a labourer, working at the earth under his fruit trees. The contrast of rough clothes, hard work, good farming and good-heartedness with courtly behaviour, luxury and meanheartedness is certainly intended. The theme recurs. Odysseus now has for companions the cowherd, the swineherd, his son and his father. In the final recognition scene of many, Odysseus meets the old family of farm servants, one old man and his six sons. This is his whole army to cope with the coming vendetta. Such a story has to be popular poetry, not court poetry. When the Serbian empire fell to the Turks in the fifteenth century A.D., and the patronage of the old nobility ceased to exist, the old Serbian poetry underwent a transformation. Old stories and old institutions were understood only in popular terms, and popular drinking habits and village relationships subtly altered the old material. In the *Odyssey* we have a world in which Achilles would not have been at home, though he would, of course, have preferred it to death; Achilles is the brave and dangerous man who dies young, Odysseus is the man of experience whose triumph is survival. Both types exist in many traditions. Achilles having made his choice is envious in the underworld of the life of peasants (*Odyssey* 11.489–91).

The sea itself is a powerful and multiple symbol, and it is also real. The multiple resonance of real things, and the mirroring of great themes in smaller events and phrases are common to the *Iliad* and the *Odyssey*. Chapman's translation still conveys something of that quality: 'They boarded, sat, and beat the aged sea.' Even Pope's elaborate formality does not quite drown it. Here is a scene in interesting contrast with the love scene of the gods in the *Iliad*. It is a tale told in the underworld.

> Thick, and more thick they gather round the blood,
> Ghost thronged on ghost (a dire assembly) stood!
> Dauntless my sword I seize: the airy crew,
> Swift as it flashed along the gloom, withdrew;
> Then shade to shade in mutual forms succeeds,
> Her race recounts, and their illustrious deeds.
> Tyro began: whom great Salmoneus bred;
> The royal partner of famed Cretheus' bed.
> For fair *Enipeus*, as from fruitful urns
> He pours his watery store, the Virgin burns;
> Smooth flows the gentle stream with wanton pride,
> And in soft mazes rolls a silver Tide:
> As on his banks the maid enamoured roves,
> The Monarch of the deep beholds and loves;
> In her Enipeus' form and borrowed charms,
> The amorous God descends into her arms:
> Around, a spacious arch of waves he throws,
> And high in air the liquid mountain rose . . .

One can almost hear the sea, and yet throughout the amazing grandeur of this story one can still hear the spurting of the blood. The shifting and terrible images of the underworld beget this glittering transformation scene of Poseidon in love, which, unusually for a

Greek myth, does not end in tears. And yet the sea in this story, and its lesser image of the silver stream, is deliberately different from the terrible waters Odysseus has crossed. What it has in common is the god it hides. The sleeping of the sea conceives monsters.

> Wide o'er the waste the rage of Boreas sweeps,
> And night rush'd headlong on the shaded deeps ...
> Nine days our fleet th'uncertain tempest bore
> Far in wide ocean, and from sight of shore:
> The tenth we touch'd, by various errors tost,
> The land of Lotus and the flowery coast.
> We climb'd the beach, and springs of water found ...

What is refreshing in the *Odyssey* is its expression of simple and vigorous human appetites. What is more deeply satisfying in it is deeply entangled in the miseries and dangers of the long story, the sadness of Odysseus and the terrible momentum of his homecoming, lit, as it were, by the lightning-strokes of Zeus. One would be justified, perhaps, in reading this long poem only for its surface brilliance and variety. But at a deeper level the satisfaction of the *Odyssey* is hard to disentangle from the recurring motifs and images that are mirrors of its meaning. Men are foolish, strangers are dangerous, the anger of the sea is obscure and implacable, Zeus is hard.

The *Odyssey* is technically, and by the latest reliable studies linguistically, more developed and later both in time and in process, than the *Iliad*. Among the new techniques, its attempt to cut between different scenes and persons, or different themes of the same story, are not all equally successful, though there is nothing in the *Odyssey* quite as absurd as the two heroes in the *Iliad* who are discovered isolated on the edge of a battle, because the battle moved on and the heroes kept their position where Nestor told them to stand many hundreds of verses ago. The constant development of the devices of fiction is among the clearest marks of true Homeric poetry. The language of the *Odyssey* contains archaisms, rather as illiterate ballad poetry does, but the *Odyssey* shows no traces of 'literary' composition.

Something should be said also of the surviving fragments of epic poetry which the ancient Greeks rightly thought to be post-Homeric.

The only named writer of these poems sometimes said to be earlier than Homer is Eumelos; we have splendid lines by him, but terribly few. His interest in the Black Sea and the Dnieper, and what small linguistic evidence we have, are said to suggest the seventh century, but ancient scholars put him earlier. What once were called his works may be an amalgam of authentic poems and forgeries of various dates. Maybe his only authentic work was a hymn to Apollo at Delos. This and the other writings once attributed to him connect him with the wars of Sparta against Messenia, which certainly survived in thrilling and picturesque legends, but which equally certainly did really take place. Almost all the rest of Greek epic poetry was about the Trojan war; so the coincidence of great antiquity, epic poetry and real, recent events in Eumelos make one long to know more about him.

We have five lines from an epic about the battle of the gods and the Titans. Homer in the *Odyssey* speaks of the deeds of gods and men as the subject of epic, but the gods in Homer are suspended in ironic contrast with humans, as we have seen. We may even laugh at the gods as they do at us. In the *War of the Titans* we know that Zeus danced, 'the father of gods and men danced in the midst of them', and that the god 'brought the race of mankind to righteousness, revealing oaths and holy sacrifices', so the poem was evidently intended both to delight and to instruct. We have a little more of an epic about Thebes, in which the action of the gods was most severe. Homer refers to this Theban story as he does to many others of which we have later versions. We have noticed that the sea episodes in the *Odyssey* probably owe a great deal to a lost epic of the Argonauts, the story of the first ship and its magical quest. But the fragments of old epics that happen to survive mostly set out to supply a background to Homer: the outbreak of the Trojan war, the homecomings of the heroes, the fall of Troy, and the story of the next generation.

We have just enough evidence of this kind to measure the impact of the *Iliad* – it was overwhelming. Its language was eastern Greek Ionic with an older Aeolic, north-eastern base or heavy influence. Mainland Greece seems to have had an epic tradition of its own, but after Homer that was overshadowed by his language. Hesiod's family settled in Boiotia, and probably carried with it the Ionian epic language, which through his own poems as well as through Homer's took root there. The epic tradition took a long time to die. Even though the Homeric poems were first officially recorded by Peisistratos of Athens in the sixth century, yet by 500 B.C. we hear of forgeries of Homer. There is little or no sign of any genuine epic composition, with or without the use of writing as an *aide-mémoire*, after the Persian wars, although when the first generation of professional literary scholars purified and restored the text of Homer in the third century B.C. in Alexandria, the versions that were circulating, and which survive to this day on pieces of papyrus, were often extremely wild.

Imitation is a tribute of a kind. All poetry emerges from memory of poems and of a language; it adapts what it knows, and invention is always a kind of adaptation. The special techniques of epic poetry are linked essentially to memory, to organic adaptation, and above all to performance. Homer calls on his Muse only as a goddess of memory. There is no doubt that Homeric poetry shows extraordinary powers, and to us the personality of the poet is slow to emerge from our impression of his adapted style and inherited language. And yet Homer is unique even among epic poets. After poetry had become a scholarly entertainment, the kind of 'epic' that began to be composed was less direct, less serious; it was an intellectual game. But it was still a tribute to Homer, in its way. The *Aeneid* embodies a delusion about the nature of great poetry, and being so great or so nearly great a poet, Virgil comes close to imposing that delusion on us. The *Iliad* and the *Odyssey* are simpler and more subtle.

We grasped the stake with its fiery tip and whirled it round in the giant's eye. The blood came gushing out round the red-hot wood; the heat singed eyebrow and eyelid, the eyeball was burned out and the roots of the eye hissed in the fire ...

Dawn comes early, with rosy fingers. When she appeared, the rams began running out to pasture, while the unmilked ewes around the pens kept bleating with udders full to bursting. Their master, consumed with hideous pains, felt along the backs of all the rams as they stood still in front of him. The witless giant never found out that men were tied under the fleecy creatures' bellies ...

This narrative style, understated in prose but very well caught by Walter Shewring, is neither baroque in the manner of literary 'epic', nor ornamental as folk-tales usually are. It is strong and supple and full of devices. It can change pace or direction or mood from phrase to phrase.

> You that I love best, why are you last of all the flock to come out through the cavern's mouth? Never till now have you come behind the rest; before them all you have marched with stately strides ahead to crop the delicate meadow-flowers, before them all you have reached the rippling streams, before them all you have shown your will to return homewards in the evening; yet now you come last. You are grieving surely ...

It is as if the whole of reality with all its ironies were the subject of Homeric poetry. And it is as if poetry were the natural language of mankind.

DATABLE TRACES OF HOMER

(i) INFLUENCE OF HOMER ON LIFE

The religious worship of heroes before 'Homer'	Odysseus on the island of Ithaka: early 8th century Akademos at Athens: even earlier
Burial of the dead in imitation of Homer's heroic funerals, which took place only in areas conscious of Mycenean ancestry, that is Cyprus, Euboia and Attica	At Salamis in Cyprus by 750 B.C.
Traces of the worship of heroes at genuine Mycenean tombs, in Argos and Messenia as well as the consciously 'Mycenean', non-Doric-speaking areas (Eumelos was Messenian)	Begins soon after 750 B.C.
Graffito on a cup from a Euboean grave on Capri, with a joke about 'Nestor's vast cup' (*Iliad* 11.623–7)	About 720 B.C.

(ii) EPIC IMITATIONS OF HOMER (ALL FRAGMENTARY)

Aithiopis by Arktinos of Miletos *Fall of Troy* by the same writer	Said to be a 'pupil of Homer'
Kypria by Stasinos of Cyprus	Said to be 'Homer's son-in-law'
The Little Iliad by Lesches of Lesbos	Before Terpander of Lesbos (?), that is, before 675 B.C.
The Homecomings of the Heroes by Agias of Troizen	Alive and well in 628 B.C.
Telegoneia, the next generation, by Eugammon of Cyrene (a Spartan colony in North Africa)	Alive and well in 566 B.C.

BIBLIOGRAPHY

M. Arnold, *On Translating Homer*, 1862
C. M. Bowra, *Tradition and Design in the Iliad*, 1930
C. M. Bowra, *Homer*, 1974
H. M. and N. K. Chadwick, *The Growth of Literature*, 1932
N. K. Chadwick and V. Zhirmunsky, *Oral Epics of Central Asia*, 1969
J. N. Coldstream, *Geometric Greece*, 1977
E. R. Dodds, *The Greeks and the Irrational*, 1951
J. Griffin, *Homer*, 1980
J. Griffin, *Homer on Life and Death*, 1980
R. Janko, *Homer, Hesiod and the Hymns*, 1982
G. S. Kirk (ed.), *The Language and Background of Homer*, 1964
S. Koljevic, *The Epic in the Making*, 1981
P. Levi, *The Greek World*, 1980
H. Lloyd-Jones, *The Justice of Zeus*, 1971
C. Macleod, *Homer: Iliad XXIV*, 1982
C. Macleod, *Collected Essays*, 1983
P. Mazon, *Introduction à l'Iliade*, 1948
G. Murray, *Five Stages of Greek Religion*, 3rd edition, 1935
G. Murray, *The Rise of the Greek Epic*, 4th edition, 1934

M. Parry, *The Making of Homeric Verse*, 1971

A. Pennington and P. Levi, *Marko the Prince*, 1984

W. C. Scott, *The Oral Nature of the Homeric Simile*, 1974

M. Ventris and J. Chadwick, *Documents in Mycenean Greek*, 2nd edition, 1973

S. Weil, 'The Iliad', in *Intimations of Christianity among the Ancient Greeks*, translated and edited by E. C. Geissbuhler, 1957

2

HESIOD
AND THE HOMERIC HYMNS

Between Homer and Hesiod there is a vast gulf. The *Odyssey* follows the *Iliad*, and Hesiod's *Works and Days* follows his *Birth of the Gods*. It has always been convenient, for those who were concerned to trace a moral and even a theological evolution and a social development through the early poetry of the Greeks, to treat these poems as four stages of that development, but the truth is not so simple. Hesiod is a poet of a different kind, but still a traditional poet working by the techniques of orally transmitted poetry, and his language is an adaptation of the Homeric language. Martin West has suggested that the *Birth of the Gods* may even be earlier than the *Iliad*, and if that could be demonstrated it would not have any very bewildering social implication. But a very rigorous recent study of the linguistic evidence by Richard Janko has made an interesting case for leaving these four long poems in their traditional order, and I shall follow the outline he traces.

The problem is not as dusty or unimportant as it may sound. In Homeric epic human beings are free to make decisions, but only just free. Achilles conforms to the code of honour which is absolute and unquestioned in his society, unless Homer by dramatizing the consequences of choice may be thought to offer the beginnings of a question about it. Odysseus in the eleventh book of the *Odyssey* makes a deliberate moral choice of how to behave in a battle, though here again the choice is to conform. The received morality is the framework of these poems; it is not precisely their subject-matter, but we get a strong impression of its nature; in the *Iliad*, Socrates would have been treated like Thersites, just as in Athens he drank hemlock.

But there really are differences of moral thinking. In the *Iliad* Zeus is responsible for the evil in men's minds, as well as the good, but in the *Odyssey* men deserve their punishment: they are responsible for their own wickedness. And they are 'god-fearing'. I am disinclined to see any of this as a great theological or moral advance. It probably represents no more than two different strains of proverbial wisdom. Popular proverbs often contradict one another, and Homer's intimate sense of moral reality is not a theory. One ought not to place much emphasis, for example, on the explanation offered by a later epic fragment, that Zeus is good because he caused the Trojan war to relieve the evils of over-population. Here as elsewhere, Zeus and his justice are a simple reflection of village reasoning.

Hesiod, particularly in the *Works and Days*, argues fiercely as a villager about justice and about bribe-eating kings. Given the difference of his subject-matter, his world is bound to seem centuries apart from Homer's, and in the *Works and Days* he is speaking as an individual, referring to the circumstances of his own life. He names his village, a poor place on the northern slopes of Helikon, and describes it in memorable terms as 'Askre, awful in winter, miserable in summer, and no good at any time'. But Homer speaks impersonally. It is like the difference between Deuteronomy, a chronicle with deliberate moral meaning, and the prophecy of Micah, whom Hesiod in some ways resembles. And even long after Hesiod, one can find in Solon, the poet and lawgiver of Athens, a sense of justice and, as Hugh Lloyd-Jones has pointed out, a sense of Zeus which goes back to the *Odyssey*. Solon wrote around 600 B.C., but his concern is like Hesiod's with the justice that should rule disputes among a peasant people. That was an ancient theme: even in Homer, the legendary King Minos rules in the underworld as a judge among the dead, to decide their disputes.

Richard Janko (see p. 46) puts the *Works and Days* in the mid-seventh century, not an impossible date but a late one for what little we know of the life of Hesiod and the mysterious 'bribe-eating kings'. Still, given that the *Odyssey* is a late-eighth-century poem, and the Hesiodic *Birth of the Gods* has to be fitted in between them, he has little option. Whether Hesiod himself really wrote all the works attributed to him is unknowable, but there is no doubt of the relative dates either of Homer's or of Hesiod's poems: we have two series, two traditions, two named poets. Hesiod gives us his own name. The *Birth of the Gods* and the *Catalogue of Famous Women* are earlier than the *Works and Days*. The *Iliad* is earlier than the *Odyssey*. Homer does

seem on linguistic grounds to be earlier than Hesiod. The time-scale
remains obscure. But Janko has used about twenty different criteria,
each of them showing a gradual change of linguistic usage between
the *Iliad* and later poetry. Every one of them argues for the same
relative dates. They are not changes in the style of poetry but in
the Greek language.

Hesiod's father had emigrated from Kyme in Asia Minor, one of
the richest of the north-eastern cities of the Greeks, which appears
first to have flourished in the shadow of the brief and brilliant
Phrygian kingdom. Midas, the famous rich king of Phrygia, was
pushed out of Cilicia by the Assyrians at the end of the eighth century,
and his kingdom fell to an invading nomadic tribe called Cimmerians
not long before 670 B.C. His wife was a Greek from Kyme, and he
was the first foreigner to give an offering, a splendid throne, to Apollo
at Delphi. In the ruins of Gordion, his city, an ivory plaque represent-
ing a Greek cavalry soldier has been found, so it is not improbable
that he employed Greeks. But culturally the stream of influence west-
wards was far stronger than any Greek influence in Phrygia, and
the later date we are now using for Hesiod suggests that his father
may have left Kyme when Phrygia fell, and that the oriental influences apparent in Greek art in the seventh century may embody
some of the images and ideas one can trace in Hesiodic poetry.
Hesiod's Aphrodite, for example, has Asian origins, and his *Works
and Days* has a lot in common with Eastern 'wisdom literature'.
But although Hesiod's poetry adapts the Ionic, eastern style of Homer,
it seems that Homer's style had spread swiftly and in an earlier generation, so that even if Hesiod learnt to compose purely from mainland
examples his models would still have been Homer's poems.

He found himself in Askre for reasons we shall never know. If I
am right to imagine his father was a refugee, as well as being a
merchant (*Works and Days*, 631–40), then the connection of Kyme
in Asia Minor with Kyme in Euboea, from which its founders had
sailed, was probably an important link. How one became a poet in
the ancient world is also mysterious. Askre is very close to Thespiai
and to the shrine of the Muses of Mount Helikon. Hesiod tells us
he was a shepherd and received his calling as poet and prophet on
that mountain. The *Works and Days* refers often to a quarrel with
his brother Perses over their inheritance. Perses seems to be real,

and the quarrel real, though Perses alters as the poem proceeds, and is mostly a creature of context. He is there to be berated and advised about morality and agriculture, two subjects closely connected in primitive religious thought.

Martin West, who as editor has recently devoted more thought and deeper research to Hesiod than this poet had perhaps ever received before, describes the strong personal character that emerges from the poems as that of 'a surly, conservative countryman, given to reflection, no lover of women or of life, who felt the gods' presence heavy about him'. There is certainly something gnarled about his utterances, and sometimes in the texture of his verse. But he has a grandeur and an originality which are thrilling, and which no later poetry has quite recaptured. We have an impressive translation of his *Works and Days* by Chapman, who shares his surface qualities. Otherwise there is not much to tempt an English reader except a smooth, dull eighteenth-century version by Thomas Cooke (1728), known in his day as Hesiod Cooke, and now remembered if at all only for his place in Pope's *Dunciad*. Yet the hymn to the Muses with which Hesiod opens his *Birth of the Gods* is magnificent:

Begin and sing the Muses daughters of Helikon, who keep the great and holy mountain Helikon, and dance soft-footed round the water-spring of the violets and the altar of the mighty son of Kronos. They have washed their soft bodies in Permessos or the Horse's spring or holy Olmeios and set up their dances on the summit of Helikon, dances of beauty and attraction, stamping swiftly. From there they went, hidden in deep air, moving at night, uttering their lovely cry, praising Zeus in song ...

So far, this is at least as able as any of the hymns to the gods in Homeric language that were written in Hesiod's generation or at any later time. It is a polished, ornamental invocation, and not at all gnarled. It is noble and sensuous. A little later, Hesiod describes his calling:

It was they who once taught Hesiod his beautiful song, as he grazed his sheep under holy Helikon. This is the speech the goddesses said to me first of all, the Olympian Muses, daughters of sovereign Zeus: 'Hedgeside shepherds, base shameful creatures, nothing but bellies, we know how to say many false things like real things, and we know when we wish how to tell the truth.' So they spoke, the clear-talking daughters of Zeus, and

they gave me a staff, a branch of flourishing laurel, a fine one they cut,
and breathed into me divine utterance, to cry aloud what shall be and what
was. And they commanded me to sing the birth of the blessed ones who
for ever are, and to sing first of them and ever last of them. But why speak
around the rock and the oak? Begin then, sing the Muses who praise their
father Zeus in song, delighting his mind in Olympos, telling what is and
shall be and what was.

In both these passages I have skated over some difficulties of interpretation. The violets are an adjective, but in Greek 'violet-looking'
sounds very like 'good-looking', both words are conventional and
they are often apparently confused. But a goddess existed called the
Violet-crowned, so maybe the violets belonged to the goddess of the
spring; its water can hardly have been violet-coloured. I am not sure
whether the 'deep air' (literally 'much air') ought to be deep mist
or cloud. The phrase about the rock and the oak is an obscure proverb.
It has attracted a mountain of learned commentary, but no one really
knows quite what it means. It does represent an interesting intrusion
of Hesiod's craggy rusticity into a formal passage. Typically of
proverbs in archaic verse, its function here is transition to a new
phase of the poem. Fables and proverbs enter deeply into the stuff
of Hesiod's mind and of his verse style, though they are less apparent
in the *Birth of the Gods*.

The hymn to the Muses continues for 115 lines. 'From the Muses
and far-shooting Apollo come singers over the earth and harpers,
from Zeus come kings. Happy is he the Muses love, sweet utterance
streams from his mouth.' The ancestry of the gods in their generations
follows. Some of the stories have a savage violence, but even at the
worst they have also some stark grandeur. 'The sweetness of utterance' is never abandoned, and Hesiod will often linger in phrases
of remarkable beauty on one god or another. Even his lists of names
are melodious: Proto, Eukrante, Sao, Amphitrite, Eudore, Thetis,
Galene, Glauke, all Nereids, all mermaids. Some have survived in
English as eighteenth-century ship names. The mating of the gods
also has a forceful and cumulative beauty. 'One was mortal, two
immortal and unageing, but it was with the one that blue-haired
Poseidon lay, in a soft meadow and spring flowers'; 'Tethys bore to
Ocean whirling rivers, Nile and Alpheios and deep-whirling Eridanos';
'Theia bore the great Sun and the bright Moon, and Dawn, who

shines on all earthly men, and on the immortal gods who hold broad heaven, when she was brought under in love by Hyperion.' The underworld and its gods are fully and resonantly treated. The matings of goddesses with men are stated less numerously, and those of gods with women even less. The poem tails off with what is usually thought a much later list, but the join is hard to find and the date and authorship of these closing lines are impossible to establish.

The *Works and Days* is better known to most readers and more easily subdivided, but here again not all the connections of thought are obvious. Hesiod was a public poet; we know that he crossed over into Euboea to compete at the funeral games held for Amphidamas and won the tripod for a poem in praise of the gods: perhaps his *Birth of the Gods*, or the shorter hymn to Hekate, the underworld goddess, which it embodies. He never otherwise crossed the sea (*Works and Days*, 650–57), and he dedicated his tripod at the sanctuary of the Muses of Helikon. So he was not one of the wandering reciters or chanters of epic poetry, like the family called Homeridai, Homer's children, who were based on Chios. But he knew poetry of many kinds, and sewed together his material from many sources. The patchwork is curiously hard to tear apart, and it is better to take the text we have as all 'Hesiod', and shrug our shoulders at the exceptions. At the end of the *Works and Days*, for example, we seem to have lost another section which circulated in the ancient world as a separate poem on the omens read from the flight of birds.

Our text ends, 'Blessed and happy he who knows all these things and works unblamed by the immortals judging the flights of birds and avoiding sins.' We must accept that these linking devices were an ordinary resource of poets: they do not always mean one poet has taken over another poet's work, or linked two old poems together. That does sometimes happen, notably in the Homeric *Hymn to Apollo*, and in an alternative last line of the *Iliad* which links it to a new epic. Instead of 'So they prepared the tomb of Hektor the tamer of horses', it reads 'So they prepared the tomb, and there came an Amazon ...', introducing the *Aithiopis*, in which Achilles and the Amazon fight. The unity of the *Works and Days* is easily subdivided by a superficial analysis into the invective and advice to Perses, with a number of separate stories and fables, advice to farmers and about ships, and notes about the calendar. The miscellaneous and fragmentary, proverbial character of some of the advice is, I believe, deliberate. It is a claim to antiquity and authority, an identification with recognized country wisdom. On the level of poetry, by that subtle interweaving of textures and accumulation of context which is the essential procedure of poetry to this day, but perhaps in no other way, the *Works and Days* works very well indeed. They present a world.

> ... because easily he diminishes the mighty and raises up the obscure, and easily he straightens the twisted and crops the mighty, Zeus high thunderer who dwells in the high houses. Hear, see, attend, and direct judgements with justice; and I would say some truth to Perses. There was not only one race of Quarrels, but there are two on earth ...   (*Works and Days*, 5–12)

It would be hard to invent a passage that links the *Birth of the Gods* to the *Works and Days* more strongly, or a stronger statement of Hesiod's profound theme. The doctrine of the two kinds of Quarrel or Conflict, one good and one bad, was not an original invention, though in the *Birth of the Gods* Hesiod neglected it. It appears significantly in the *Iliad*, in the description of the shield of Achilles Hephaistos made, on which all human life was represented, good and bad, peace and war. The second of the two Conflicts

> Zeus set in the roots of the earth and made her much the better for mankind ... For the gods have kept life hidden from mankind, or easily in one day you would work to have enough for a year though you were idle, and hang the rudder in the hearth-smoke at once, and the labour of oxen would perish, and of long-labouring mules. But Zeus hid it in rage of heart when clever Prometheus deceived him; he thought up sad dooms for mankind, and fire he hid, but once more the good son of Iapetos [Prometheus] stole it for mankind from wise Zeus, deceiving Zeus who delights in thunder, in a hollow reed.

Fables and meanings are intricately mingled, and Hesiod's serious, rumbling undertone moves on through mythology without real interruption. It would be a mistake to think him primitive: the Greeks were not 'primitives' in the seventh century, but much of the interest of their art and literature is their intelligent and even sophisticated ways of dealing with primitive material. They were still very close to their own cultural roots, and Hesiod was closer than most. Nor are all his stories mythological.

Now I tell a fable to kings in their wisdom: this is what the hawk said to the pretty-throated nightingale, carrying her high in the clouds in the grasp of his talons, and she wailed pitifully pierced by the crooked claws, and he spoke to her in power, 'Poor creature, why do you speak? One much stronger has you, wherever I shall take you, singer though you are; I shall make you a dinner or let you go, as I choose. Fool it is who wants a fight with his betters, he loses the match, and suffers pains as well as the shame.' So spoke the swift-flying hawk, that long-winged bird.

Hesiod is often read for his philosophy of labour, and for the astonishing insights he offers into the mentality of the Greeks. One should remember all the same that this is a poem, meant to be heard rather than read and to be known by heart, and that Hesiod's use of his material is highly ambivalent. We have a number of huge collections of Greek proverbs, some used in different senses, and some better still, not used at all by famous writers. They deserve more careful study than they get. Even Hesiod's throw-away lines are not quite as throw-away as they look. Why does his hawk say it might let the nightingale go? Whose side is Hesiod on? What about the word for singer, which is also the word for a poet? The precise wording is what makes the image at the end of the hawk, that long-winged bird, unforgettable. Similar observations might be made about Hesiod on ploughing, and about 'Get a woman, a bought woman not one to marry, one that will follow the plough'.

Many individual lines in the *Works and Days* have for us a special freshness and strangeness, not to be found even in Virgil's *Georgics*, that magnificent adaptation which has brought just a whiff of Hesiod into so many European libraries.

When the Pleiades fleeing before the fearful strength of Orion fall into the misty sea, then the blast of all sorts of winds rages; at that time keep ships no more on the wine-dark face of the sea, but remember and labour at earth as I tell you. Draw up your ship on land and prop it with stones on all sides, to withstand the power of the wet blasts of the winds: and pull out the sea-plug, so that the storm-rain of Zeus does not rot it. Store all the gear in your house, stowing in good order the wings of the sea-going ship, and hang the well-made rudder over the hearth-smoke. Wait for a seasonable sailing until it comes, and then drag your swift ship to the sea and put in a cargo, to bring profit home, as your father and mine, you great fool Perses, sailed in ships in search of a good living.

This poetry is not as homely as it looks.

Probably the most famous episode in all Hesiod's poetry is the myth of the Golden Age. It was, of course, an old story retold. Hesiod has put in a special age of heroes, who hardly fit into the structure of the myth:

First of all the Olympian gods created the golden age of mankind. They lived in the time of Kronos who was king in heaven, and passed their lives like gods with untroubled spirit, without pains or grief, no miserable old age came upon them, ever the same in their hands and feet they delighted in festivals, and died as if sleep overcame them. All good things were theirs, the life-giving earth bore crops in plenty and to spare on its own, and they of their own will in peace lived off the fields with many good things. But when earth had covered that generation, they are the divine beings, by the wisdom of great Zeus, the good, the earthly ones, the guardians of mortal men, the wealth-givers, that is their kingly privilege.

In the silver age men were children for a hundred years, but later they behaved badly. The third age was bronze; they were immensely strong, and worked in bronze, and lived in bronze houses, there being no iron. 'And they died at one another's hands, and went to the vast house of cold Hades nameless, and black death took them, defiant as they were, and they left the shining light of the sun.' The heroes who followed were better; they were the demigods, the heroes of narrative poetry, who died in war at Thebes, 'struggling over the flocks of Oedipus', or at Troy, 'beyond the great gulf of the sea, for Helen'. Now they live in the islands of the blessed. 'And would I did not live with the fifth age but died before it or was born later: because this age is iron.' The lamentation that follows is a powerful attack on an unnatural and warlike age; it recalls the last part of Shakespeare's *Henry VI*.

Other poems were attributed to Hesiod as well as these, and we have a rather full set of fragments of one of them, the *Catalogue of Famous Women*. It has great interest as a collection of mythology, but I do not believe it could possibly be by Hesiod. It proceeds calmly and levelly through an endless mass of material, perfectly and smoothly organized. It is well executed and often attractive, but it is not the work of a great poet. The level it attains is that of William Morris, or of Drayton's *Polyolbion*. Beautiful as it is, one would hardly learn Greek to read it, although if its fragments were the only Homeric or sub-Homeric poetry that survived, we would certainly marvel, and be thrilled and charmed by them. Among many beguiling stories I get pleasure from that of Periklymenos, 'blessed, to whom Poseidon earthshaker gave gifts of every kind: sometimes he appeared among the birds as an eagle, sometimes he was recognized, a wonder to behold, as an ant, at times again in the glittering tribes of bees, at times a dreadful snake implacable ...'. He was caught and killed at last as a bee, standing on the chariot of Herakles. Athene had been his ally, but he offended her. Among even less likely 'Hesiodic' poems was one about the prophet Melampous, who acquired the gift of animal language by having his ears licked by two grateful young serpents that he rescued and brought up.

Richard Janko (as we have seen) dates the *Catalogue* before the *Birth of the Gods*, even though a mention of Kyrene seems to date it after 630 B.C.; neither date seems to me absolutely impossible, but one must note that his argument about Kyrene reads like special pleading. If we accept that the *Catalogue* is early, the Kyrene story could be a later intrusion, like Latinus at the end of the *Birth of the Gods*. The *Shield of Herakles*, a bad and bloodthirsty poem of 480 lines, appears to be late on linguistic grounds, and neither its merit nor its subject-matter, a baroque fight in which only two blows are struck, tempt one to put it any earlier. We are dealing with the end of a tradition, a decline from gold to silver, silver to bronze, bronze to iron. All the poems are in hexameter verse, they all derive from the same Dark Ages, and they all show Homer's influence. It may be that poetry about the gods survived longer as a living tradition. The poems called the Homeric Hymns, the longest of which are narratives, or contain long narratives, date from several centuries; the best of them contain some of the finest early Greek poetry we have. The art of verse narrative took a long time to die out, but after Hesiod's time the scale of what survives was smaller; the more pretentious poets, the ones who supplied the gaps in the Homeric poetry of the Trojan war, were not apparently the best.

The arguments about the precise dates of 'Homeric' hymns, which are all certainly post-Homeric, are complicated by questions of mutual influences, and the influence on this or that work of Hesiod. Some of the arguments that scholars have elaborated are over-clever, and to my mind full of special pleading. The worst case is the *Hymn to*

Apollo, in which a hymn to Apollo of Delos, which claims to be by 'the blind poet of rocky Chios', that is, by Homer, is followed by one to Apollo of Delphi, joined to it by the briefest of links. They appear to have been linked, the link as it were forged, by a poet called Kynaithos of Syracuse, working at the end of the sixth century B.C. for a festival held by the grandest patron of the age, Polykrates of Samos, who like Peisistratos at Athens, formed a collection of Homeric texts. But both these hymns are splendid, and both are respectably ancient.

The Delian hymn probably belongs to the middle of the seventh century, and looks like the work of one of the early Homeridai, the family of poets to which Homer also had belonged. The Delphic hymn can be roughly dated by a war to the 580s. We surely owe the survival of both these fine poems to Kynaithos. The other principal hymns from our collection are one to Aphrodite, which is contemporary with Hesiod but perhaps of less merit than some others, one to Demeter, late seventh century, which is perhaps Athenian and certainly the masterpiece of a great poet, and one to Hermes, of the late sixth century but still a fine poem, probably Boiotian. Lastly one should not forget a rather short hymn to Pan, which I have always thought was composed about 500 B.C., and which I take for the very last Greek poem of real merit that shows traces of Homeric technique. It is a charming and lively work, but only forty-nine verses long. We possess in all thirty-three hymns, and they almost all contain very attractive verses. But here I will concentrate on the best. Once again, Chapman made the classic translation, which is probably one of the sources of the odes of Keats. Shelley translated the *Hymn to Hermes*.

The *Hymn to Demeter* tells the foundation story of the sanctuary of Eleusis and the Eleusinian mystery, which was an important part of Athenian religion. The mystery has to do with the growth of corn, the death and rebirth of the year, the birth of a son and of an ear of corn; its symbolism is grounded in earth and underworld, darkness and light. The poem contains these same elements, but the verse is not at first sight mysterious except from time to time on a grammatical or scholarly level, like most archaic verse.

But go my child and obey, and do not be too grudging with Zeus of the thunderclouds; create a life-giving crop swiftly for mankind. So she spoke, and Demeter of the fine wreath did not disobey, and at once she sent up a crop from the clodded fields. And all the vast earth bristled with leaves and flowers.

The verse is essentially narrative, with some subtlety of texture and a few bold and simple psychological touches which belong to story-telling art, not just to poetry. The story unfolds in nearly five hundred lines, with sustained dramatic excitement and great beauty, but it ends predictably; it is a hymn after all, and it is not long enough to have any structure comparable to the *Iliad* or the *Odyssey*.

The hymns depend on Homer's heroic narratives, but no such hymn in an earlier generation could ever have given rise to Homer's vast creations, whose roots are in heroic story-telling and in the lamentation of the dead. The poetry of the hymns is Homeric only on a small scale. It is curious that among the features it shares with the *Iliad* is an addiction to long lists of place-names. In Homer we have a list which has encouraged and at times misled generations of archaeologists, giving all the Greek cities that sent ships to Troy, with the numbers of men and a few well-chosen scraps of information. The *Hymn to Demeter* traces Demeter's wanderings in search of lost Persephone in great detail. The *Hymn to Apollo* traces Apollo's road to Delphi, the Delian hymn gives Apollo's empire and refers to Leto's wanderings. Even the *Hymn to Hermes* gives one of these journeys. The habit survives in Aischylos, in the *Agamemnon*, where we get a list of all the beacon-fires that were lit to pass across the Greek world the news of the fall of Troy. As poetry, these passages are wonderful, particularly in the *Iliad* and Aischylos, and to an un-travelled audience they must have been thrilling entertainment.

Some rather later inscriptions on stone at Delphi have recently led to suspicion that the unity of the Greeks was somehow preserved through the Dark Ages in certain sanctuaries where Bronze Age cities were remembered. That is unlikely for many reasons, and I can no longer believe as I once did that Homer's list derived from a Delphic or a Delian list; the opposite is far more likely. But this problem brings us to the heart of the Greek festivals of the Early Archaic or Geometric Age, that is, to the earliest influence of Homer, at just the time when the great festivals of the Greeks at Olympia, at Delphi and elsewhere, began to be founded. The national identity of the Greeks depended historically on Homer. The cult of the heroes spread swiftly even among Dorians who made no claim to Mycenean descent. Geographically, the identity of the Greeks centred on their international shrines. One can find traces of that feeling in the *Odyssey*; it is strong in the Homeric hymns. They are not to be dismissed as the competitive propaganda of holy places.

Beginning I sing fine-haired Demeter dreadful goddess, she and her daughter of the fine ankles whom Hades took, and wide-watching deep-thundering Zeus gave, separated from Demeter of the golden blade and glittering crops, as she played with the deep-breasted daughters of Ocean, picking flowers, the rose and saffron and the pretty violet, on a soft meadow, and iris and fritillary, and narcissus that Earth by the plan of Zeus grew as a trap to give pleasure to the Receiver [Hades], a glimmering and wonderful thing, that struck awe into all who saw it, immortal gods and mortal men. Out of its root it grew a hundred heads, and at the powerful smell all heaven above and the whole earth laughed, and the salt swell of the sea. In wonder she stretched out both hands to take the pretty toy, and the broad earth gaped open ...

The mixture of beautiful and sinister among the flowers, and the sense of imminent tragedy in these lines convey strongly a number of Greek country attitudes that have persisted to this day. What a perfect introduction to the entrance of the Demon King. Demeter's golden blade has worried a number of scholars; it may be a sword and not a sickle, and she borrowed the epithet from Apollo, but going so closely as it does with the glittering crop, it works admirably. If instead of glittering crop one ought to translate gleaming fruit, as is possible, it still works very well. Everything in these lines is shimmering. It is possible that the sky and earth and sea glittered rather than laughed; the word has both meanings.

A reader of ancient Greek poetry cannot afford to brush aside small difficulties of this kind. Attention to them can reveal the stuff or texture of the verse. When Persephone was stolen away she gave a great cry,

calling on Zeus her father, the most high and most good. But no immortal and no mortal man heard her voice, nor the gleaming-fruited olive trees, except wicked-hearted Hekate of the shining head-dress from a cave, and the lord Helios, Hyperion's bright son, as the daughter called on Zeus her father; but he was apart from the gods in a muttering temple, receiving fine sacrifices from mortal men.

This passage has been attacked by scholars as an irrelevant elaboration added by some later poet, because a few lines later Demeter does in fact hear her cry out, 'but no god or man wanted to tell her the truth, and no bird'. It is possible that the 'gleaming-fruited olive trees', effective as they are to modern taste, are a mistake; several bird-names would fit with hardly a change of a letter in the text; only the gleaming fruit would have to be altered. The interest of these connected problems is not in their solution, but only that in considering them one learns something about the poetry. For better or worse, one is forced to enter into the poet's workshop.

The mythology of this poem is full of magical folk-tales, but it is told with a disarming simplicity and seriousness; as a narrative it is irresistible. Nicholas Richardson, whose edition of it contains the only satisfactory scholarly commentary on this or any other of the hymns, notices interesting alternations between gravity and gaiety in the story, and in general a graceful and harmonious quality that belongs to visual art in the same period. He notices a number of ironies and jokes, which are certainly deliberate. Demeter disguised as a nurse in her wanderings has thrust a baby into the fire to make him immortal. Someone spots her and complains, and the old lady is furious and flings down the baby on the floor, grumbling about mortal folly. When the young women of the house pick the child up, it just goes on yelling. 'Its spirit was not appeased, for far inferior were the nurses who now held him.'

The Homeric hymns very often deal with the birth and childhood of gods; the incidents are often humorous, and the tone playful, but there is also a terrible and barbaric streak underlying the playfulness which is to be found in folk-tales everywhere. The striking feature about the hymns is their balance of qualities. Shelley neatly caught the tone of the baby Hermes inventing the lyre by killing a tortoise for its shell.

> The babe was born at the first peep of day;
>   He began playing on the lyre at noon,
> And the same evening did he steal away
>   Apollo's herds; – the fourth day of the moon

On which him bore the venerable May,
    From her immortal limbs he leaped full soon,
Nor long could in the sacred cradle keep,
But out to seek Apollo's herds would creep.

Out of the lofty cavern wandering
    He found a tortoise, and cried out – 'A treasure!'
(For Mercury first made the tortoise sing).
    The beast before the portal at his leisure
The flowery herbage was depasturing,
    Moving his feet in a deliberate measure
Over the turf, Jove's profitable son
Eyeing him laughed, and laughing thus began:-

'A useful godsend are you to me now,
    King of the dance, companion of the feast,
Lovely in all your nature! Welcome, you
    Excellent plaything! Where, sweet mountain-beast,
Got you that speckled shell? Thus much I know,
    You must come home with me and be my guest;
You will give joy to me, and I will do
All that is in my power to honour you.

'Better to be at home than out of door,
    So come with me; and though it has been said
That you alive defend from magic power,
    I know you will sing sweetly when you're dead.'
Thus having spoken, the quaint infant bore,
    Lifting it from the grass on which it fed
And grasping it in his delighted hold,
His treasured prize into the cavern old.

Then scooping with a chisel of grey steel
    He bored the life and soul out of the beast ...

The *Hymn to Aphrodite* is almost entirely about her love affair with Anchises and the birth and rearing of Aineias, who rules Troy after the Trojan war. A noble family at Skepsis, not far from Troy, still retained the title of kings and claimed descent from Aineias in historical times. The narrative of this hymn has the charming surface and the essential triviality of court poetry, though the song the poet Demodokos sings after dinner in the *Odyssey* about Aphrodite and Hephaistos is not dissimilar. The *Hymn to Pan* is lighter still, but brisk and amusing, and from its formal structure one might think it ancient.

> Speak Muse with me of the dear son of Hermes, goat-footed, two-horned lover of clattering, who wanders over the wooded ravines where the nymphs dance, and where they tread the crest of the sheer rocks, calling on Pan the herd-god, gleaming-haired and shaggy, the lord of every snowy summit, the heights of mountains and the rock-roads.

The narrative is short, almost cursory, like the briefest stories in Homer; it is the story of the birth of the god. The hymn is a breathless celebration of hunting and wild life, and more than the others it shows a lyric influence.

Lyrical Swinburne translated a very much later offering to Apollo, newly discovered in his time; it was found inscribed on stone at Delphi. His original was in lyric metre, and dates from the second century B.C., but he makes it infinitely more rhapsodical. His thrilling and insistent rhyme scheme makes far too much of a lyrical gallop without meaning; to my own taste even Chapman's rhymes are out of place in the earlier hymn, as Swinburne's are here. Still, it is worth seeing how things progressed over the centuries, and what became of the tradition of hymns in a later age; it was swamped in false lyricism. Swinburne's version does underline this fact, and perhaps after all it hardly exaggerates the decline of poetry.

> ... Ye that hold of right alone
> 　　All deep woods on Helicon,
> Fair daughters of thunder-girt God, with your bright
> White arms uplift as to lighten the light,
> 　　Come to chant your brother's praise,
> 　　Gold-haired Phoebus, loud in lays,
> Even his, who afar up the twin-topped seat
> Of the rock Parnassian whereon we meet
> 　　Risen with glorious Delphic maids
> 　　Seeks the soft spring-sweetened shades
> Castalian ...

This is horrible, is it not, and neo-classic in an oppressive sense? The contrast with the ancient 'Homeric' hymn I mentioned before is very great:

I will remember and not forget Apollo the archer, at whom the gods in
the house of Zeus tremble as he comes, they leap up as he approaches close,
all of them from their seats, when he draws his glittering bow. Leto alone
remained beside Zeus whose delight is the thunder. She unstrung his bow
and shut his quiver, and took the bow with her hands from his strong
shoulders, and hung it on his father's pillar from a golden peg, and she
led him and seated him on a throne. And his father gave him nectar in
a golden cup, saluting his dear son, then the other gods sit down, and great
Leto rejoices because she has borne a strong archer son. Rejoice, blessed
Leto, because you bore splendid children, the lord Apollo and Artemis re-
joicing in her arrows, her in Ortygia, him in rocky Delos, lying towards
the long mountain, the Kynthian hill, close to the palm tree by the stream
of Inopos.

This is unexciting, but it has a clarity and a subdued sparkle, the
true archaic surface qualities, as the *Catalogue of Famous Women* has.
The Delphic part of the Homeric *Hymn to Apollo*, which is later, seems
to me far better and a fine poem. 'And so farewell, son of Zeus and
Leto; I shall remember you again in yet another song.'

BIBLIOGRAPHY

(i) HESIOD

Theogony, edited with commentary by M. L. West, 1966
Works and Days, edited with commentary by M. L. West, 1978
Works and Days, edited with commentary by T. A. Sinclair, 1932; reprinted
    1966
Fragmenta, edited with Latin notes by R. Merkelbach and M. L. West, 1967
Oxford Classical Text, edited by F. Solmsen, R. Merkelbach and M. L. West,
    1970
Principal Works, edited by F. A. Paley, 1883

(ii) HOMERIC EPIC FRAGMENTS

The principal Homeric epic fragments are included in vol. 5 of the Oxford
    Classical Text of Homer
Epiconum Graecorum Fragmenta, edited by G. Kinkel, 1887

(iii) HOMERIC HYMNS

Homeric Hymns, edited with commentary by T. W. Allen and W. R. Halliday,
    2nd edition 1936; reprinted 1963

Inni Omerici, edited with Italian translation and commentary by F. Cassola, 1975

The Homeric Hymn to Demeter, edited with commentary by N. J. Richardson, 1974

Collectanea Alexandrina, edited by I. U. Powell 1925, includes the second-century-B.C. hymn to Apollo

3

EARLY LYRIC POETS

Lyric poetry and folk-poetry existed before Homer. If proof of that were needed, Homer mentions them; he even quotes a work-song for harvesters. But all that survives of them today is a bewildering profusion of fragments, quoted in later antiquity, and some rather scanty scraps of papyrus; their quality is dazzling, but we have extremely few complete poems. Nor is it obvious that lyric poetry made any progress, whatever that would mean, or that any clear progression or evolution can be traced. Song is primitive, and the birds have their languages. But poetry is an activity and a language, a set of gestures, always taking place in the shadow of history, and by recalling what we know of that history, we shall understand poetry better.

If the *Odyssey* is an early-seventh-century poem, then Archilochos was Homer's younger contemporary. Kallinos, Tyrtaios and maybe Semonides wrote in the time of the *Works and Days*, and almost all the Greek lyric poets wrote their songs while the Homeric tradition we have just followed through the hymns was unexhausted. Most of them lived in the seventh and sixth centuries B.C.; several were long-lived, so that Anakreon (575–490?) could have known Sappho or Alkaios, yet he lived to hear the early work of Aischylos. Alkaios was born probably about 620, when Archilochos, who died young, was hardly ten years dead. When the world is moving fast, ten years may be a long time: Milton was born in Shakespeare's lifetime and Pope soon after Milton's; the senior English poets at present were born before the deaths of Thomas Hardy and Robert Bridges. The Greek world of the eighth and seventh centuries was expanding physically and exploding politically, but in other ways it altered less fast than we imagine. Only in the fifth century and in Athens was development of every kind unbelievably swift. The last great lyric poets, Pindar, Bacchylides and Simonides, lived on into that world, where they were the last spokesmen Homer would have recognized.

I have chosen not to separate poets of the earlier age – the archaic world so-named after its remarkable sculpture – by the usual distinction, according to their metres. The later Greeks did class them by metre; the nine lyric poets, recognized as classic in the third century B.C. – nine poets corresponding to the nine Muses – were Alkaios, Sappho and Anakreon who wrote personal songs, and Alkman, Stesichoros, Ibykos, Simonides, Bacchylides and Pindar, who wrote choral songs. Writers of elegiac couplets, which were sung at one time to the music of the flute, rather like Spanish *coplas*, and those who used metres with an iambic basis, often for satiric and sharply precise purposes, were differently classed. These distinctions have their use, but the subject-matter of many of the poets and the undertones of their poetry overlap; it seems vital to understand from the beginning which of them were and were not contemporaries.

The dates of these poets have in most cases been bitterly disputed. I have no space to argue each one fully; the dates I use are more or less acceptable to most modern scholars, and some are certain. The famous nine all wrote for the music of stringed instruments, and sometimes the flute as well. The number of strings increased during our period, probably in competition with the more numerous notes of the flute; the strings had no fingerboard or keyboard. But flute and lyre go back to the Bronze Age; they appear in Crete on the Hagia Triada sarcophagus, and in the *Iliad*. Iambic poetry had a special stringed instrument of its own, perhaps a late development. It sounds like 'slamming out the three basic chords' on a guitar.

Archilochos of Paros (675–635?) lived in the age of colonization and colonial war of which transmuted echoes haunt the *Odyssey* and (more faintly) the *Works and Days*. He was the bastard of a noble family on Thasos. Iambic poetry, which was his skill, developed in the cult of Demeter; it was humorous and brisk. In his hands it was also vividly personal, highly sensuous, and full of realistic assurance. His love poetry is impressive for its laconic beauty and great strength; every word is chosen, and yet his verse has the suppleness of real speech. He conveys a stronger and more intimate sense of personality than any other ancient Greek poet, and to judge by his recently discovered seduction poem, with its swift and perfectly controlled changes of tone and its stinging images, the ancient critic was right who called him the greatest Greek poet after Homer.

He liked love and he liked drink, but in war, at sea and in trouble he was an anti-heroic poet and a cheerful pessimist whom real soldiers or real adventurers might find sympathetic. 'Look Glaukos, the sea is already stirring up deeply into waves, and cloud standing up straight over Tenos: a storm sign. And fear suddenly strikes'; 'Don't rejoice too much when you win, don't lie down at home and groan when you lose; enjoy your joys and grieve over your sorrows not too much, understand what rhythm has a hold on mankind'; 'I don't like a big commander or a strutting commander or one with glorious whiskers or a clever shave; give me a little one, knock-kneed, firm on his feet, and full of heart'; 'Some tribesman has my shield which I left intact beside a bush unwillingly and saved myself. What do I care about that shield? Let it go; I can get another one as good.'

> I am a servant of the King of War
> and learnt the lovely gift of the Muses.

or again:

> My kneaded bread is on my spear, on my spear wine
> from Ismaros; I lean and drink it on my spear.

In some ways Archilochos is overshadowed by epic poetry; one might almost say he inhabits a crevice in Homer. Even in love, this is distinctly mannish poetry, though it is not philistine. The same or worse can be said of much of the poetry of his age, and can be seen in the paintings on drinking-cups and pots, because these are the songs and instruments of the drinking-party, the evening dinner where men dined and entertained one another alone. Sappho's poetry is limited in the same way, but limited to a world of women. But Archilochos treats women with gentle affection and directness, and in his long seduction poem with irony as well; even his cruelty is ambivalent, his attitudes are those of Odysseus but his poetry is sharply autobiographical. 'She held with delight a sprig of myrtle and a fine flower of the rose, and her hair shadowed her shoulders and her brow.' Even an impersonal dedication written by Archilochos is personal. 'Alkibie offers to Hera the holy veil of her hair, on reaching honourable matrimony.' Archilochos and his attitudes deserve

a book of their own, few as his fragments are. 'O Zeus, Zeus father,
yours is the power of heaven, you see the works of mankind, right
and wrong, the sins and the justice of animals are your concern.'

Here is the seduction poem. My translation is feebler than Archilochos and less crisp, and I have had to guess at some missing words.

'... but if you press and your heart drives,
a girl in our house longs to be married,
beautiful, gentle, virgin; and I think
her beauty is flawless. Consider her.'
So she said to me, and I answered her:
'Daughter of noble, good Amphimedo,
whom the vast earth has covered over now,
young men know many god-given delights
outside the holy thing, and one will please.
And you and I will plan this with the god
in quietness when your black dress is gone.
I will obey what command you give me,
inside your gates, behind the border wall;
do not be grudging to me, friend, I'll keep
to the long garden grass. Neoboule?
Let someone else have her. She has ripened,
her virgin blossom has dropped away,
and her grace gone. She knows of no Enough,
she is mad now and beyond measure.
Let the crows have her. Let me not suffer
by having such a woman for my wife
as pleasures my neighbour. I want you much more.
You are not unfaithful, not deceiving,
she is more sharp and makes herself men-friends.
I fear she might in her hot eagerness
bear me blind early puppies like a bitch.'
So I spoke to her and took the girl
and laid her among blossoming flowers,
I covered her over with my soft cloak
and took her neck between my arms;
she stopped crying and the fawn fled no more,
and I stroked her breast gently with my hands
and she showed me her fresh unprinted place.
Enfolding her whole beautiful body
I loosed my bright strength, stroking her fair hair.

Kallinos lived in the middle of the seventh century, about the same time as Archilochos. He wrote his poetry in continuous linked couplets; his subject was bravery and war. He did for Ephesos in troubled times what Tyrtaios, his slightly younger contemporary, did for Sparta. His morality is stern, but his verse is vivid and invigorating. 'A man should fling a last spear as he dies. It is an honourable, shining thing to fight for earth and children and your wife.' The style of Tyrtaios is not dissimilar, but he introduces a somewhat ornamental epic colouring which suggests that these songs were intended as entertainment for the elderly as well as exhortation for the young.

> I would not remember or account a man for speed of foot or wrestling, not if he had the size and strength of a Cyclops and outraced the Thracian North Wind, not if he was better built than Tithonos, richer than Midas and Kinyras, not if he was more kingly than Pelops son of Tantalos and had the honey-sounding tongue of Adrastos, and all glory except for bravery and strength; for no man is good in a war if he does not go on daring when he sees bloody slaughter.

Kallinos and Tyrtaios may be closer to the true mind of the Greeks of their age, but Archilochos is more companionable, and Homer gains immensely over these fierce poets by the ironies and the pathos of narrative art.

Semonides, in the second half of the century, quotes a line of Homer in a poem of linked couplets, and he has some sense of Homeric pathos. Indeed, his tone in this poem begins to explain the sense we now attach to the word 'elegy', the metre of the couplets.

> One finest thing the man from Chios said: The generations of men are like the generations of leaves. Few mortals take that in through their ears and stow it in their hearts. Each man has hope, which is connatural to young men's hearts. Until a mortal attains the lovely flower of his age, he thinks many vain thoughts in his empty mind. He has no thought of ageing or dying, nor in health any idea of pain. Fools, whose mind goes that way, not knowing that the time of youth and of life is short. Learn this and to the end of life endure in soul, enjoying the good things.

This wisdom is not perhaps very deep, but enough for an after-dinner song.

Semonides is more famous for an iambic poem of which we have more than a hundred lines, brilliantly and fully treated by Hugh

Lloyd-Jones as *Females of the Species*. Semonides mocks a series of types of women in terms of the creatures they resemble and their dominant passions: the lazy sow, the nasty vixen, the barking bitch, the dangerous ocean, the patient, undiscriminating ass, the ferret with nasty habits, the luxuriating mare, the tricky monkey and the excellent bee ('She stands out among all women, and a godlike beauty plays about her. She takes no pleasure in sitting among women in places where they tell stories about love. Women like her are the best and most sensible whom Zeus bestows on men'). The animal fables of Hesiod and the free speaking of Archilochos make all this unsurprising, and less original than it used to be thought, and the archaic tendency to lists is something of which one can have enough, but taken lightly Semonides is a pleasing poet for an hour or two. One would only wish for an ancient Greek woman's poem on men whom Zeus bestows on women. Indeed, sometimes one wishes Penelope *had* written the *Odyssey*, as Samuel Butler maintained.

The sweetest, the most autumnal of the elegists was Mimnermos the Kolophonian, who was probably in fact from Smyrna, where he was born about 2,500 years before George Seferis. He lived in the later seventh century. Roman allusions to his work make one sad we have so little of it. His personal love poetry lives only as an influence. He also treated mythology, history and war. Kallimachos, a fine critic, thought his short poems were best. But the best that survives is nothing but fragments of a passionate philosophy of life. Maybe the statues of the kouroi, with their simple sensuality, their restrained strength and their secret smiles, are thinking about poems by Mimnermos.

We are like the leaves the flowering season of spring breeds, suddenly increasing with the sun's rays, and like them we delight in the flowers of youth for an inch of time, knowing neither evil nor good from the gods. But black Doomspirits stand around us, one holding the end of nasty age, the other of death. The fruit of youth is a moment, as the sun shines over the earth; but as soon as that moment finishes, at once dying is better than living. Many evils come to the heart. Sometimes the house is crushed and the painful labours of poverty arrive, another man loses his children, in desire of whom he goes under earth to Hades. Another has heart-devouring illness. There is no man to whom Zeus does not give many evils.

Is this poetry sententious? But it is remarkably clear-eyed.

A piece of one of his war poems is so remarkable one cannot but mention it. Alas, we do not know who was the soldier he celebrated.

That was not like his bravery and lordly heart as I learnt it from my elders who saw him, smashing the dense squadrons of the Lydian cavalry on the Hermian meadows, a man with an ash-shafted spear. Pallas Athene would not at all have faulted the grim gallantry of his heart, when he rushed among the front of the fight in the whirl of bloody war, dodging the biting weapons of his enemies. No man ever was better to frequent the labour of violent battle, when he walked there like the sun's beams.

This surely is in its way Homeric. Mimnermos is writing about reality, but he has also understood a lot about the *Iliad*. When he writes about the Sun's car, 'winged and golden, on the surface of the water', crossing from west to east every night, Mimnermos is as good as the best of the Homeric hymns. 'For the Sun has pain all his days, and there is never any relief for his horses and him, when Dawn with a rose in her fingers leaves Ocean and climbs up into the sky.'

Ancient poems and poets were traditionally classified according to their metre because every metre was thought to entail a special area of subject-matter and a special tone. That is more or less true of iambic verse, which tended to be satiric, invective or public speaking of some kind, but Archilochos wrote in several different metres, and the same themes wandered from poet to poet and from form to form among the Greeks, just as they have done in more recent European poetry. The poetry attributed to Theognis, for example, is a collection of verses composed at any time between the late seventh century and the fifth; the poems are all rather short, consisting of single couplets or continuous couplets, lasting at the longest about thirty lines. They include a few lines by Mimnermos, Tyrtaios and others. They are elegantly phrased pieces of accepted wisdom and popular philosophy, sometimes cracker-barrel philosophy. 'I do not long for wealth or pray for it: may I live with no trouble on little'; 'Hope is one good goddess left to men: the others have deserted us for heaven; Faith is gone, great goddess, and Modesty, and the Graces have left this earth my friend. There is no faith and justice in sworn oath, and no one venerates the deathless gods ...' Gloomy as they often are, and personal as some of the advice seems, being addressed to a boy called Kyrnos as Hesiod addressed his brother Perses, these poems appear to be drinking songs, and some of them are lively, a few charming. Mostly, they suffer from their inescapable likeness to the mottoes in old-fashioned Christmas crackers. In their true social context, they trod a tight-rope of sobriety and gave pleasure by doing so.

All the same, it is worth lingering for a moment over Theognis, not only because mediocre and bad poetry, particular anthologies of banal verse, can sometimes tell us more about a past age than its great art, but also because one can see in such a collection how by simplicity and boldness or even by a kind of chance honesty, in an age when everyone could sing, great poetry or sharply imprinted poetry stood out from what was merely conventional. Theognis offers some rather subtle tests in literary criticism which professional scholars have been known to fail. Unfortunately, it is not easy to reproduce the same variation of quality in translation. 'You are a horse, my boy, you ate your oats, as soon as you got into my stables and found a driver of desires, good grass, and a cold water-spring and shady groves.' I take these impressive lines to be symbolism not quite amounting to *double entendre*: they are crisply and boldly stated. But this other couplet, evocative as it is, seems in Greek more threadbare. 'Whoever does not love horses and boys and hounds, his spirit never shall have peace.' One can follow the mind of a Greek of this class and of this historical moment through a number of innocent twists and turns by reading the poetry attributed to Theognis. We know it was popular, if only because an ancient painting has survived on a fifth-century drinking-bowl that shows a drinker singing Theognis after dinner; the words are written above his head. Theognis became part of entrenched upper-class culture as the excellent but uneven works of Surtees have done in English.

But my personal favourite among the lyric poets of the great age is Alkman, composer of choral lyrics, which he wrote for festivals of the Spartan gods at a time when Sparta was still an innocent and rustic place. He lived in the second half of the seventh century B.C., and lived to be old. The stories about his life and origins that have survived are not at all reliable; probably he was a Spartan, who lived and died in the craggy shadow of Mount Taygetos. His poetry conveys more than most the quality of his life and its simplest attraction. When the gods meet at night for their festivals, they enjoy a village feast; the verse is both tough and luxuriant.

Often on the crests of the mountain, when the gods enjoy their shining festival, you carried a gold vessel in your hands, a great bucket such as the shepherds have: your hands filled it with lionesses' milk, you made Hermes his huge and perfect cheese.

There is something attractively vigorous about Alkman; even his wildest exaggeration never shatters the mystery. How stellar and lunar and full of glimmer this night festival is, and yet how perfectly homely. Alkman wrote the original of Goethe's *Über allen Gipfeln*:

> The crest of mountains and the river-courses sleep,
> the crags and the ravines,
> all creeping tribes the dark earth nourishes,
> beasts of the wild and peoples of the bees
> and monsters in the deeps of purple sea,
> and all the tribes of the long-winged birds sleep.

The world he imagines has an almost magical strangeness, and a still more mysterious tranquillity. One would like to know the context of this sleepy fragment; it was almost certainly religious. An amusing and, I think, irresistible conjecture of George Huxley places another of his fragments at a girls' diving or swimming festival of which we know very little, on the south coast of Sparta in Alkman's old age. The poet speaks as an ageing bird who prays 'to fly away over the blossoming spray of the sea's waves, among the flock of halcyons painless in body, sea-purple holy bird'. When the male halcyons grew old, the legend said that females crowded round and carried them on their wings. Many mythical creatures and remote peoples wandered about on the edges of Alkman's poems. He wrote about the Skiapods, who lie in the shade of their enormous single foot as if it were an umbrella. (Maybe they began as wearers of snow-shoes or skis? An equally unlikely story about a beast called the Shadow-tail, *skioura*, gives us the English word squirrel.)

The most mysterious of all his fragmentary poems is also the most substantial, the *Partheneion*, the *Virgin-song*, for a night festival of Artemis. The words of the poem were divided between rival groups or choruses of young girl dancers. We know he also wrote marriage-hymns; he appears to have written often for girls, and his sense of this ritual combines intimacy and solemnity.

There is a vengeance of the gods.
Blessed is he whose day
is passed in happiness
without weeping. I sing
the light of Agido:
I see her as the sun,
the witness that it shines.
The leader of my dance will not
let me give praise to her or blame to her.
Herself is glorious as if
you loosed in meadow-grazing herds
a strong horse that will take his prize
with the ringing of his hooves,
a horse from rushing dreams.
Look and see: this horse
from Venice. But the hair
of Hagesichora
my cousin is blossom
of the purest gold.
The silver of her face,
how can I make it plain?
is Hagesichora,
second in beauty after Agido,
a horse of Scythia
runs with a Lydian:
because the Pleiades
at dawn arising like
the star of Sirius
compete with us who carry in the plough.

The ritual remains obscure, and the meaning of some verses is impenetrable. The Dawn-goddess is celebrated: the plough and the stars and horses are enigmatic. Was there a star chorus and a horse chorus? The meaning is intricate, and the language as densely interwoven as that of Andrew Marvell's flower poems. If we understood the ritual, the poem would certainly be much clearer, but that would not alter Alkman's special qualities as a poet; they are always the same.

And he shall give sweet-stewed allseed,
and white sweetcorn and harvest of the comb.

Most ancient cooking sounds more or less disgusting. The eighteenth-century French Encyclopedia remarks with some justice that the *Iliad* is a great poem in spite of the awfulness of the food in it. But this tiny bit of Alkman has the same charm as his grander poems. Among the scatter of useless knowledge about him preserved by later scholars we hear that he called the jaws chewers, wrote about breast-shaped ritual cakes (the same kind of cakes survived in Sicily as late as Il Gattopardo), and called quinces sparrow-apples. Other fragments are full of flower-names or the names of villages and hills, or they pause at a gold ornament like a flower, or 'Rhipas, mountain blossoming with woods, breast of black night'. Some of his poetry, though not all, grew up in the nourishing shadow of Homer; he wrote hexameter lines, cursed Paris, wove affectionate verses around Odysseus – all this, no doubt, from a Spartan point of view. A line about Ajax fighting Memnon suggests a knowledge of post-Homeric epic poetry; that is not surprising. In his beliefs he was provincial and outside the mainstream. His Muses were as natural as flowers or dew-fall, they were the daughters of Earth and Heaven; they were older than Zeus.

  Because we have so little of his work, and such short bits and pieces, it is permissible to think less well of Stesichoros, a younger contemporary of Alkman, although as an influence he had a main stream importance. Still, his conceptions were strong, and he does represent a half-way house between epic and dramatic poetry. He wrote narrative choral lyrics. He lived from about 632 to 553 B.C., mostly at Himera in Sicily. Many of his subjects were epic: Helen, the Sack of Troy, the Homecomings, the funeral games of Pelias, the Calydonian boar, some Theban stories, some adventures of Herakles, and the *Oresteia* in two parts. But naturally, given his date, he often gave new turns and new incidents to the old stories. He told the stories (even in a choral lyric) as if he were making them up fresh. He was popular for more than a hundred years, perhaps for his music. Sokrates in prison is supposed to have heard a man singing Stesichoros in the street, and learnt the song from him. Wonderful stories were told in late antiquity about Stesichoros, and strange poems attributed to him, but picking about among what is genuine we shall have less excitement, there being so little of it. His 'serious Muse', as Horace calls it, has, all the same, inspired some fine sculpture and vase-painting which does survive.

> And Helios, Hyperion's son, stepped down
> into the golden cauldron till he came
> beyond ocean to deeps
> of night holy and black,
> to mother, noble wife and his dear sons,
> and walked into the grove in shadows of laurel
> on foot the son of Zeus.

This is not quite straight narrative, but such a style might sustain a long story, as we are told that Stesichoros did. It is hard to distinguish the archaic sparkle and fairy-tale charm of this story from his personal style. The strange grove has laurel trees because they belong to Apollo and the sun. The sun's cauldron has to be golden; the simple folk-tale was once meant to explain how the sun returns to rise in the east every morning. Stesichoros embroiders it in this poem or another to explain the journeys of Herakles. One can see from a more recently published fragment how much he owes to Homer, but how, by isolating and slightly embroidering what he admires, he alters its nature for the worse. He takes from the *Iliad* the famous simile of the dying warrior whose head droops like a rain-beaten poppy. He exaggerates both the ghastliness and the pathos of epic narrative by his rhythms, though the verbal beauty survives and spreads like a coloured stain.

> There seemed to come a snake with bloodied head,
> from whom appeared the king Pleisthenides.

That is an evil dream, but when Stesichoros speaks of 'myrtle foliage, crowns of roses, and wreaths of plaited violets', his style is essentially the same. It is the same again in his famous apology to Helen, when he withdrew the insults of an earlier poem, having been stricken blind, so we are told.

> That story is not true.
> You did not go in the fitted ships.
> You never came to Troy's towers.

Even the comparative originality of Stesichoros as a story-teller is not surprising. Sicily was a world of its own in such matters and as late as the fifth century B.C. the painters of Athenian pottery were capable of continual innovation. So far as we can judge from the short fragments, Stesichoros had a certain romantic warmth even as a story-teller. His eye gleamed with invention. It was Helen's ghost or spirit or double that went to Troy, not real Helen. Agamemnon's wife dreamed of him as a bloody-headed snake, and she and she alone murdered him. Elektra and Orestes recognized one another as adults because she had a lock of his childish hair. Some of the re-touching of mythology was powerful. He was the first recorded poet to tell of the birth of Athene, who sprang fully armed from the head of Zeus. The severe grandeur of the stone sculptures from the Heraion of Foce del Sele, now kept at Paestum, probably gives a more truthful impression of his poetry than any recitation of the striking epithets that he invented: 'delightless' meaning sleepless, 'hollow-hoofed' of a horse, 'silver-rooted' of the river Guadalquivir, because it runs down from the silver mines, 'steep' of the underworld, 'midnight' of a star, and 'five-guarded' of the night, divided into five watches, perhaps. Stesichoros apparently invented or introduced into poetry from south Italian dialect the word 'midnight': not a contemptible contribution to our repertory.

Musically, Stesichoros was credited by Greek scholars with the elaborate triple structure of Greek lyric stanzas, which with some variations was basic to later lyrics and odes, as the structures of Ronsard and Ben Jonson and Spenser became basic in English poetry. Alkman repeats a single stanza form. The triple structure of Stesichoros was of two stanzas commonly called strophe and anti-strophe, the second being the exact formal repetition of the rhythms of the first, with a third, added, complementary stanza. The series of three could then be repeated indefinitely. The *metra*, or basic rhythms of which these stanzas were composed, were elaborately interwoven, and to this day they are easier to follow by ear than they are to analyse in metrical terms. Indeed, the names of the metrical units are often Alexandrian and probably unauthentic. Sometimes they are modern. But each poet had his favourite *metra*, and every poem had its own stanza forms, which were in most cases an original musical composition, like a modern song. We have no way of knowing just how elaborate musical composition or stanza form could be before the use of writing. It may well be true, on the analogy of plainsong, that lyric poetry grew more elaborate in form when poets learnt to write, but that music lost a native freedom.

From the metrical point of view, Stesichoros is well on the way towards Pindar.

One might hope for an answer to this difficult question by looking closely at folk-song and popular song. Its metres are simpler and its structure is far less complicated, and the poems are shorter. But one of its most memorable kinds of stanza, down to the end of the sixth century in Athens and later, is something we first meet as the stanza of Alkaios. The rhythm of simpler work-songs seems to underlie it. Alkaios and Sappho, though they wrote in Lesbian dialect, were still admired and loved in fifth-century Athens; they occur on vase paintings as beautifully severe figures, singing their poems. Yet they had lived in a very different world, in the last twenty years of the seventh century and early in the sixth. They are thought to have invented a number of famous forms of stanza for personal lyric poetry, and perhaps did so. Their personal songs are often, though not always, expressions of deep personal emotion; their rhythms have a subtle simplicity, an immediacy, which in choral lyric after Alkman is rarely to be found. They were close relatives, and it may be that the perfect control and musical lucidity of their poems belong to a tradition and a society more than to their own genius. Their poetry is often intensely personal. Their island of Lesbos was already famous for the music of Terpander, whose lyre of seven strings became a standard instrument; he probably adapted it from the Lydians. The obscure Arion who rode on a dolphin's back was another musician from Lesbos.

The ethos of Alkaios is that of his world. He was a Lesbian nobleman, conscious of heroic values, active in battle and in politics, conscious of Homer. His hymns are less grand, less objective, and more personal than the Homeric hymns, but equally intended to give delight. They were not intended for public festivals. His gravity and personal commitment, in politics like those of Shakespeare's Wars of the Roses, and his deep and spirited joyfulness in celebration, inspired Horace to revive lyric poetry, and through Horace this obscure, archaic island nobleman inspired the Latin poetry of the Middle Ages and the vernacular poetry of the Renaissance. Even in fragments of a few stanzas he is still fresh, still impressive. His poetry smells of vine-leaves and the sea. He treats mythology with freedom and elegance. He could also be dramatic in love-poetry and at times luxuriant, at other times almost Homeric in his darkness of tone.

He had more than one might think in common with Archilochos, but his rank was higher, his life different, his poetry more formal.

... Run for a sure harbour. Let no soft idleness grip us, for a great prize is clear to be seen. Remember our old labour. Now let a man stand his ground. Let us not shame our good fathers who lie under the earth ...

> Come to me over sea from Pelops' Island
> strong sons of Zeus and of Leda:
> show yourself to me, be friendly Kastor,
> and Polydeukes,
> who go over the wide earth and all
> seas on swift-footed horses,
> and easily rescue men from death
> and its coldness,
> leaping on the crest of the fitted ships
> shining far away, running on rigging,
> carrying light in the difficult night-time
> to the black ship ...

These are feelings and prayers one might easily match in Archilochos, but Alkaios is prouder and much more formal, more aesthetic. The heavenly twins, whose home is the Peloponnese, are riders on white horses; they are also St Elmo's Fire, which glitters in the rigging of ships in bad weather. Unfortunately, the rhythms on which this poetry hangs are not possible to reproduce. The best Alcaics in English are probably Tennyson's poem to F. D. Maurice, but the Isle of Wight is not the same thing as ancient Lesbos.

They say that once, O Helen, a bitter remedy for evil deeds came to Troy and its children from you, and Zeus burnt holy Ilion with fire. It was not to such a marriage the glorious son of Aiakos called all the blessed, taking the tender girl from her halls to the house of Cheiron, and loosed the girdle of the pure maid, and the love of Peleus and the best of mermaids flowered, and in a year she bore a son, strongest of demigods, happy driver of chestnut foals, and over Helen the Phrygians and their city perished.

This curious fragment has the common tendency of oral and archaic story-telling in prose and verse to travel in a circle, ending where it began. Achilles was the son of Peleus and the Nereid or mermaid Thetis; he was brought up in a cave by Cheiron the centaur. His mother's wedding, at which the gods were guests, was a famous story which had its dark side: it was popular in painting as well as in verse. But this strange lyric is evidently more personal. It is not clear quite how Alkaios applied his story. Was this part of a marriage-poem or a love-poem? He could write gently and sensuously, about soft-handed girls washing their thighs in the river Hebros, 'finest of rivers running out into the purple sea', and about scent poured 'over my much-suffering head and over my grey-haired chest'. Almost every fragment of Alkaios offers a fresh and sharp insight into his mind. Few ancient poets define themselves as clearly. His poems about drink and celebration are admirable, bold and clear, but the fragments are mostly short, and they do not translate well.

Let's drink: why wait for the lamps? Daylight is a finger ...

Zeus rains down, and a big storm drops from the heavens, and the water-channels have frozen ... Overwhelm the storm, pile up fire, mix the sweet wine generously, and put a soft cushion under your head ...

This is the origin of Horace's ode about Soracte (1.9).

Drench your lungs in wine, because the star is circling and the season hard and all things thirst from the heat: the cicada sounds off sweetly from the foliage, pouring out a dense shrill song from his wings, now that summer blazing ...

This is a lyric version of a few lines of Hesiod (*Works and Days*, 582–588). It is of some interest that the *Works and Days* of that apparently embittered small farmer were so popular in Lesbos. Alkaios referred often in his poetry to his life, and it is tempting to trace his history, though even the historian Herodotos failed to do so with accuracy. His brothers fought in his childhood against the most powerful family in their city. Alkaios in his day fought later tyrannies, but his motives are always personal. His ally Pittakos became governor by popular election, and Alkaios went into exile. He visited Egypt. At one time he fought against Athens in the battle for Sigeion, a fortress town on the straits, built of the stone of Troy. Alkaios lost his shield, though he survived. His brother fought under the King of Babylon. He was on good terms with the Lydians.

Sappho's poetry is lamplight in a room or moonlight in a garden, compared to that sunlit world, but her fortunes like his included exile, and like the rest of the Lesbian aristocracy she had eastern connections. Her poetry was written for a women's world of refined senses and intense personal passions. Professor Page let his complicated judgement tilt, on the evidence of one fragmentary sexual word on the torn edge of a mutilated papyrus, to the view that she was in the modern sense 'Lesbian'. Sir Maurice Bowra defended her heavenly purity and the visionary beauty of her verse. They may both have been right, but Page less probably. Sappho's society and her personality were utterly unlike anything we know. She was a married woman, certainly a love poet to women, and she wrote marriage-hymns. One must forget the ninetyish cult of Sappho's fragments and the coarse-grained probing of academic persons, and try to read her as herself alone. By coarse-grained, I mean such probings as the interpretation of a line of Horace on Sappho in the underworld, *questa puellis de popularibus*, 'lamenting over girls of her nation', as if it meant 'they were Lesbians in more senses than one'. That occurs in the standard English commentary on Horace's odes (1978). It probably represents the present orthodoxy about Sappho, which I find anachronistic and unacceptable. It disregards social context.

> My muse, what ails this ardour?
> My eyes bedim, my limbs shake,
> My voice is hoarse, my throat scorched,
> My tongue to this roof cleaves,
> My fancy amazed, my thoughts dulled,
> My head doth ache, my life faints,
> My soul begins to take leave ...

Sir Philip Sidney made this version at a time when Sappho's verse might have gone well into English, but in his day very few poets knew enough Greek, and Sidney himself seems not to have known the original, but only a later prettification of the poem. The original has been somewhat starkly translated by William Carlos Williams.

> Peer of the gods is that man, who
> face to face, sits listening
> to your sweet speech and lovely
> laughter.

It is this that rouses a tumult
in my breast. At mere sight of you
my voice falters, my tongue
is broken.

Straightway, a delicate fire runs in
my limbs; my eyes
are blinded and my ears
thunder.

Sweat pours out: a trembling hunts
me down. I grow paler
than dry grass and lack little
of dying.

This is underwritten; Sidney comes closer to the tone: 'It flutters the
heart in·my breasts ... my eyes see nothing and my ears boom, a
cold sweat grips me.' But Sappho can speak at times with some
grandeur; Alkaios is her cousin in verse technique as well as by blood.
Thomas Hardy translated a fragment that conveys her power.

Dead shalt thou lie; and nought
Be told of thee or thought.
For thou hast plucked not of the Muses' tree:
And even in Hades' halls
Amidst thy fellow-thralls
No friendly shade thy shade shall company.

The untranslatable quality of these poets, which Hardy comes close
to capturing, is the way the living rhythms of their voices play both
with and against their stanza forms. 'Stars around the noble moon
hide their gleaming form again when she is most full and shines
on the earth ...' In a prose version nothing emerges of Sappho but
her crispness of language, and perhaps a sense of her silver-gilt
colouring, her cool diction.

Come from Crete to this pure shrine; it is a graceful orchard of fruit trees,
and altars smoking with frankincense, cold water sings among the apple
boughs, and all this place is overshadowed with roses, trance drops down
from the shimmering leaves, the horse-breeding meadow has blossomed with
spring flowers, the wind is breathing honey ... Pour out your nectar gently
in golden cups, O Cyprian, intermingle it with our festival.

The Cyprian is Aphrodite. I am not sure why she is coming from Crete.

Sappho's love-poems sometimes have a mythological framework. Helen's story gives substance to a splendid poem for Anaktoria, 'whose lovely step and the glittering sight of whose face I would prefer to all the chariots of Lydia and the infantry in arms'. That poem begins, 'Some say an army of horsemen, some say infantry, some say ships are the noblest sight on the dark earth, but I say what one loves.' She could even, on occasion, write narrative verse with much less than usual of her native Lesbian dialect and with epic overtones of rhythm; one about Hektor bringing Andromache home to Troy as a bride has survived. It reads like a more lyrical type of Homeric hymn. The impossible attempt to translate her is almost irresistibly tempting, though it may not much extend our sense of the kind of poet she is.

... like a goddess recognized, and in your music most rejoiced, but now splendid among Lydian women, as the rose-fingering moon when the sun has set outdoes all stars, and light takes over the salt sea and the flowering fields, and the fine dew falls, roses open and soft weeds and flowering sweet clover.

It is difficult not to translate Sappho with Victorian oversweetness. Her poetry is indeed full of a pure, natural sweetness, and full of longing. The way the moonlight works in this poem to express the distance of her lost friend as well as her personal quality and the natural quality of love is remarkable. Sappho can command a lightness as well as a seriousness of tone, and many tones within one poem. Viewed in retrospect, in comparison with later Greek history and literature, let alone with our own, she has a remarkable innocence and warmth.

> Coloured-throned immortal Aphrodite,
> deceiving child of Zeus, I beseech you
> do not afflict me with griefs and troubles,
> goddess, in my spirit,
> but come hither, if ever other times
> you caught my voice from a distance
> you heard me and left your father's house
> of gold and came,

harnessing your chariot, and your beautiful
swift sparrows drew you above dark earth
densely fluttering their wings out of the heavens
through mid-air,
and suddenly arrived, and you, O blessed,
smiling with your immortal face,
asked what I suffered now, and what
I called for now,
and what I most wish to happen now,
raging in spirit; whom shall I persuade
to love you once again, who is it now
wrongs you, Sappho?
Because if they run they will soon follow you,
and if they refuse presents they will give them,
if she doesn't love, she will soon love you
even unwilling.
Come to me now again, and set me free
from bad anxieties, and what my spirit
desires to be, make be, and you yourself
fight on my side.

The form of this pleasant prayer can be paralleled from later prose inscriptions on stone from a temple on Samos, but the mixture of confidence, playfulness and personal pain is inimitable. The poem is made of gossamer, made of nothing, and although I have translated line for line, I have not attempted to convey its lively rhythms. Its variation of syntax within a given stanza form, its coherent, lucid progression and its prepared climax must be apparent. However closely based it may be on popular speech and song, this goes far beyond folk-song. Its strength is in its delicacy.

Alkaois and Sappho were almost exact contemporaries of another aristocrat involved in the politics of his city, Solon of Athens, the lawgiver. Like Pittakos, the friend and enemy of Alkaios, he came to power by the consent of a people weary of tyrannies, noble families in conflict, and revolutionary war. He ruled with powerful equity, and expressed himself in verse, very likely in actual speeches made in verse. Pittakos was also credited with six hundred lines of political verse, which have not survived. Solon's speeches survive among his poems, and his ability both in elegy and in iambic verse is astonishing. He owes something to Tyrtaios. He is very different from Alkaios, more objective in purpose and understanding, and impersonal in motive. His verses also have a more dramatic quality and a gravity of eloquence that seem to arise from their context in real life. Solon and Pittakos were famous sages: Alkaios, much as we may love him, was not. I have translated Solon's couplets as well as his longer and shorter iambic lines all as rather rough blank verse, in order to emphasize his strength more than his dexterity.

> I come as messenger from Salamis
> with words of poetry to be my speech ...

Scholars have found it hard to believe that a politician in a national emergency could possibly begin a real speech with this couplet. But we have seen how long the tradition of chanted and recited verse lingered on after the invention of writing. Poetry is heightened and controlled language, and around the year A.D. 600 even in Athens there was no other so heightened or so closely controlled. All we need quibble about is the precise occasion of these speeches. What was the occasion of first performance of the poems of Tyrtaios? Solon's words suggest that his at least were really delivered to the Athenian people. He is not speaking in generalities.

> Our city shall not perish by God's fate
> or the mind of the blessed, immortal gods
> because a great-hearted, well-born watcher,
> Pallas Athene, guards it with her hands.
> Mad citizens want to ruin this great city
> persuaded by corruption of riches,
> and the unjust mind of their leaders; certain
> for them great sufferings follow great pride.
> They cannot hold their greed, cannot govern
> this present happiness which lies in peace ...
>
> ... And one of them steals from another,
> they do not keep the sayings of Justice
> who silent knows what is and what shall be,
> as time passes she comes and shall avenge.

That is the poetry of moral wisdom. It has a preaching intonation. This is not the first example of it in Greek, nor is Greek the only ancient language in which it can be found.

> The strength of snow and hail comes from a cloud,
> the thunderstroke from glittering lightning,
> from great men comes the ruin of cities,
> we drop by ignorance into slavery.

The critic Diodoros remarked centuries afterwards that he spoke like an oracle. In another poem of couplets, which can hardly be a speech, he prays to the Muses, the daughters of Zeus and Memory. He asks the gods for wealth and good repute, to be sweet to his friends and bitter to his enemies, an honourable figure to his friends and a terrible one to his enemies: to have wealth but not get it unjustly, because justice always follows. Zeus sees the end of all things, and Zeus is as sudden as the wind at sea. This is an old-fashioned and clear morality. Politically, Athens was in turmoil, and Solon's practical activities began a movement which brought democracy to birth in the end, but as a poet he represents something older than his own generation. Even the sensuous couplet about loving boys 'at the lovely blossoming of youth, the beautiful thighs and the sweet mouth' recalls old Theognis at least as closely as any later poet. His power is in the poetry of political and social justice, and best in his iambics.

> For this I called the people together,
> why did I cease before it was achieved?
> Be my witness in the justice of Time,
> greatest mother of the Olympian gods,
> black Earth, whose boundary-stones
> I once removed when they were often fixed,
> and who was then a slave, and is now free.
> I brought home many who were sold away
> to Athens built by gods, to their country,
> sold away justly or unjustly,
> or fleeing by necessity of debt,
> who could no longer speak Athenian,
> so far they wandered, slaves, fearing their lords,
> whom I set free . . .

Some suggestion survived among later writers that Solon had written other kinds of poetry as well. Plato even pretends that the story of Atlantis the lost island came by word of mouth from Solon, but that is an unlikely attribution. Martin West's suggestion, that the story came from Egypt closer to Plato's own time, is a good one.

Solon's wanderings as a sage had become legendary, but they are not part of his true biography.

Until this point, the poets after Homer we have discussed have lived all over the Greek world and its islands, and several have moved from city to city. In the second half of the sixth century Polykrates of Samos and his court were a magnet for poets. The Persian threat was more and more serious, and when Polykrates was murdered by them and the east began to shut down, Athens took over his role, so that towards the end of the century Theban Pindar went naturally to Athens to learn his trade. Poetry remained international, as we shall see. But in his day, the brilliance and the gaiety of the court of Polykrates had an importance. His great restored sanctuary of Hera, the Heraion of Samos, was the most splendid piece of architecture the Greeks had ever seen; its original (560–550 B.C.) was the beginning of their wonderful temples. The flourishing season of Samos was a springtime of the arts in some ways; in others it was an Indian summer. Polykrates lasted ten years or so (532–522).

Ibykos came to Samos, though he was born on the straits of Sicily at Rhegion (modern Reggio di Calabria), and he died there; he is said to have refused the dictatorship of his city; he was famous as a poet before Polykrates came to power, and he may even have come earlier to Samos; the island had a rich past but a violent recent history. His narrative poetry followed the track of Stesichoros, with whose work his was sometimes confused. His rhythms were simple and charming; his language was a mixture of his own local Doric, a few deliberate archaisms copied from epic poetry, and just a colouring of Lesbian dialect in honour of Sappho and Alkaios. He wrote love-poetry – that is, love-songs – of extraordinary freshness and a certain Sappho-like elaboration, addressed to boys. There existed no social convention in his world for any heterosexual kind of love-song. Marriage was linked to property and alliance, it was not subject to the free play of passion or of art.

In the songs of Ibykos, names were mere excuses for poems; sharp and attractive natural images imprinted themselves on the air in an endless succession, just as the images of mythology did in his narrative poems. The name of Polykrates himself was scarcely more than a dedication: '... And you, Polykrates, shall have glory ever-lasting, as by my song and by my glory.' Ibykos was a professional.

> In spring the Cretan quinces
> wet with the streams of rivers
> in the Virgins' uncut garden
> and shoots increasing under
> shadow of branches flourish but my love
> never sleeps ...

Within his chosen limits, Ibykos is an excellent poet. We have heard some of his metaphors before, but not all of them. Love with blue eyelids pitches him into the net of Aphrodite. 'Ah how I fear his onslaught, as a prize-winning chariot-horse in old age unwilling goes to contest with the swift wheels.' Coloured birds on the topmost leafy branches preen in his poetry; a boy was 'brought up by Aphrodite and Persuasion with fine eyelids among flowering roses'. In mythological narrative heroes like Siamese twins are born from a silver egg. He dealt with the rape of Ganymede by Zeus and the rape of Tithonos by Dawn. His Achilles married Medeia in the Elysian fields. His Diomedes married Hermione and was made immortal like the Dioskouroi. His Hektor was Apollo's son. The glamour of the *Iliad* to poets like Ibykos ensured the utter falsification of its spirit, as well as the slavish imitation of such wooden features as its archaic grammar, which at times they exaggerated. It was Ibykos who had Helen take refuge in a temple of Aphrodite and Menelaos fling away his sword for love: a theme appropriately handled by Rupert Brooke.

But one should not look for ten o'clock at midday. Taken as he is, in his pitifully small handful of fragments, Ibykos is a pleasing and surprising poet. When I came fresh to Greek lyric poetry, he was one of my favourites. He is not a deep writer, but his immediacy increases his enchantment, even in fragments of a few words.

Anakreon was another such poet of simple rhythms and personal love. He lived to be eighty-five and to admire the early lyrics of Aischylos. He was born in about 575 at Teos on the Asian coast; when it fell to the Persians in about 540 B.C., the refugees sailed across to Abdera in Thrace. When Anakreon was summoned to Samos by Polykrates in about 532, he was already famous as Ibykos had been. When Polykrates died, Hipparchos summoned him to Athens. Anakreon's songs were immensely popular, and widely imitated three hundred years later or more. The imitations are neglected nowadays, though they have great merits quite different from the star quality of Anakreon. He was the last great composer of solo songs, a professional musician in whose work the songs achieved a light simplicity and sharpness. His poems are the easiest of all to follow.

> I clasp your knees, deer-shooter
> chestnut-haired child of Zeus
> Artemis, goddess of wild beasts ...

The language and the images of his poems are seldom more perplexing than these simple lines, though his music is delightful and too subtle to reproduce, and he has a rhythmic and syntactic elegance.

> O Lord with whom Eros
> and the blue-eyed Nymphs
> and purple Aphrodite
> go playing, and you roam
> the high crest of mountains:
> I clasp your knees, so come
> kindly to me and hear
> a prayer full of grace:
> give Kleoboulos good
> advice, make him accept
> my love, Dionysos.

Anakreon's poems have a dandy quality. One can see how they appealed to the court of Samos, and one can see also how it came about that when aristocratic society crumbled this sort of poetry more or less ceased to be written. Only the less ambitious elegiac couplet survived with self-renewing force for century after century. Anakreon had an inimitably light touch. 'I am in love with Kleoboulos, I am mad about Kleoboulos, I gape at Kleoboulos.' Kleoboulos becomes a complete declension, but love is always present indicative, here and now. 'Gold-haired Eros hits me with a purple ball, provoking me to play with a pretty-sandal girl; but she comes from well-built Lesbos, doesn't like my hair for being white, gapes at another girl.'

> O boy with the girlish look,
> I follow you, you don't listen,
> and you do not know you hold
> the horses of my soul.

There are a few traces of other rhythms and some of more serious subjects, even a little wisdom and one or two references to politics. 'I would not want the horn of Plenty, nor to reign a hundred and fifty years as king over Cadiz'; 'Poseidon's month and the wild storms ...' But Anakreon's most striking poems are those that find fresh metaphors for love. A girl rolls her eyes and runs from him like a Thracian pony. Another flutters like an unweaned fawn that its mother deserted in the forest. Eros is a blacksmith who hammers the poet and dowses him, or Eros is a boxer. Anakreon is never a hero.

> My temples now are grey, my hair is white:
> my grace of youth is gone, my teeth are old,
> and little time of my sweet life is left:
> therefore I whimper, fearing Tartaros,
> Hades' cave is terrible, awful
> the road down, those who go do not come home.

Anakreon is attractively human in all his moods. The aged teeth are a particularly telling phrase. The powerful elegance of the last two lines of this poem are beyond my ability to reproduce in English. Anakreon is not just an easy but a very memorable poet. After one has been reading him, one's head will be full of his rhythms for a long time. We are told he died at Athens by choking on a grape-pip. Who knows? He went 'unde negant redire quemquam'.

In the archaic Greek world, professional poetry overlaps with amateur and occasional poetry of many kinds, the usual occasion for verse being death or dinner. If one had imagined among the swarm of poets a progression of poetry, a kind of graph, from resounding Homer to intimate Anakreon, or from sharp Archilochos to sweet-and-sour Anakreon, it will be a corrective to consider Hipponax of Ephesos, a poet of about 540 B.C., famous for his deadly invective, the angriest and most interesting of Greek satiric poets. He is as lively as Archilochos; his iambic verses are under fine control, far more so than Juvenal's verse in Latin, and as much so as Villon's in French, although we have very few fragments long enough to make this judgement possible. He was an influence on the joke invectives of Horace, but Horace's clever imitations do not equal the original.

Hipponax is outspoken and precise. He uses words that were common in spoken language but are rare in literature, and it was interest in these difficult words that endeared him to ancient as it does to modern scholars. He mixes a smattering of Lydian and Phrygian into his Greek. That could be why his work has survived mostly in short quotations, but failed in the mass to pass the prejudices of classicizing critics in late antiquity. And yet Herodas and Horace knew him, and even the Byzantine scholar Tzetzes. He certainly used some unusual words. 'Sindian cunt,' he says, heaven knows in what context, and 'Hermes dog-strangler, friend of thieves, come and curse', and 'mother-lover Boupalos', and 'They drank from the milking-pan, she had no cup, the boy fell in and smashed it'; 'I came in the dark to Arete with the heron of good omen, and I was folded.' The apparently undirected vigour of these phrases would no doubt fall into place if we had Hipponax in longer pieces.

> He at his ease in flowing quantity
> day after day ate tunny, honey, cheese
> like any eunuch out of Lampsakos,
> he ate up the inheritance, must dig
> the mountain rocks, eat ordinary figs
> and barley cakes which is the bread of slaves.

The mess of honey and cheese is a special dish. In another piece about food, preserved like the first for the interest of its gastronomic vocabulary by Athenaios, he has someone 'not chewing up gamebirds and hares, nor toasted cheese smothered in sesame, nor fried bread soaked in honeycombs'. A less talented writer of the period, called Ananios, wrote an entire poem about the food of the seasons. Almost nothing of it survives except a memorably gruesome passage about the meat of hare, dog and fox. Hipponax prays to Hermes in a swift patter.

> Hermes, dear Hermes, Maid's son, Kyllenian,
> I beg you, being so very freezing . . .
> . . . give Hipponax a cloak, a little shirt,
> and little sandals, little furry boots
> and sixty bags of gold . . .
> You never ever did give me a cloak,
> thick for the winter to keep off the frost,
> you never hid my feet in thick fur boots
> that might have stopped my chilblains from breaking.

The Greek word for chilblains is excessively rare in literature, yet it must have been common in life. Hermes is called dog-strangler because he slew the monstrous dog Argos which Zeus set to guard Io, but there was also a disease of dogs called the strangles, which everyone must surely have known by name.

> Zeus, father, Sultan of Olympian gods,
> Sultan of silver, why not give me gold?

The word I translate as Sultan is Lydian (*palmys*), and the text of this fragment has often been questioned, but this reading appears to make sense of a kind. The outrageousness of Hipponax and the persona of poverty are hard to separate.

> Wealth never, as he is extremely blind,
> came to my house and told me, Hipponax,
> I have three hundred silver bits for you
> and many other things. He has slow wits.

We have parts of one or two prolonged curses by Hipponax, more sustained than any we know by Archilochos; they are on unsigned scraps of papyrus, but the metre and the language are right and seem to carry the mark of the master.

... Let the top-knotted Thracians have him, and there let him go through many evils, eating slaves' bread, frozen stiff, with plenty of seaweed on his whiskers and teeth clattering, lying like a sick dog by the edge of the sea ... this let me see: the man who wronged me and trod oaths underfoot, once my friend.

It is rather hard to say whether the passing recollection of Homer in some of the wording of these lines is a stiffening or a parody: probably both. Hipponax was by no means incapable of charm. He wrote of 'the black fig, sister of the grape'. One would not at all understand the sixth century B.C. if one left out Hipponax.

I will discuss some early philosophers and their writings in the next chapter. Some of them were essentially poets, and their interests and verses overlap with those of a poet like Hesiod or a sage like Solon.

SOME LOST OR VERY FRAGMENTARY POETS
OF THE ARCHAIC AGE

Anonymous Kolophonian (?) poet: *Margites*, an early parody of Homer in mixed metres, story of a fool (7th century?)

Polymnestos of Kolophon: poet and musician (7th century)

Aristoxenos of Selinous (Sicilian): iambic poet who influenced Epicharmos (late 7th century?)

Asios of Samos: comic or satiric elegiac couplets (late 7th century?)

Echembrotos (Arcadian): lamenting flute music and sad verse (7th to 6th century)

Periander of Corinth: one of the seven sages, said to have written couplets (7th to 6th century)

Ananios (Ionian): on the food of the seasons, satiric poet (6th century)

Sakadas of Argos: poet and musician (early 6th century)

Demodokos of Leros: satiric elegiac and iambic verse on places (6th century)

Phokylides of Miletos: said to have written couplets (6th century)

Panyassis of Halikarnassos: high-minded literary epic (late 6th century)

BIBLIOGRAPHY

C. M. Bowra, *Early Greek Elegists*, 1938

C. M. Bowra, *Greek Lyric Poetry*, 2nd edition, 1961

C. M. Bowra, *On Greek Margins*, 1970

A. R. Burn, *The Lyric Age of Greece*, 1960

D. A. Campbell (ed.), *Greek Lyric Poetry* (selection), 1967

T. J. Dunbabin, *The Greeks and their Eastern Neighbours*, 1957

T. Hudson-Williams, *Early Greek Elegy*, 1926

L. H. Jeffery, *Archaic Greece 700–500 B.C.*, 1976

R. Lattimore, *Greek Lyrics* (translations), 2nd edition, 1960

D. L. Page, *Sappho and Alcaeus*, 2nd edition, 1959

D. S. Raven, *Greek Metre*, 1962

M. L. West, *Studies in Greek Elegy and Iambics*, 1974

4

PRE-SOCRATIC PHILOSOPHERS

By the beginning of the fifth century B.C. – that is, in the prelude to the classical age – with the generation that fought and beat the Persians as boys, and later established direct democracy at Athens, we begin to have abundant evidence of written literature, even though most of it is still fragmentary and survives only in quotations, some of them meagre. We must now either mix verse and prose, if we pursue a single theme like history or philosophy, or mix up a variety of subjects if we attempt to catalogue decade by decade. I am strongly committed to a clear chronology, because without that literature has no history, and even lyric poetry makes only an unreal sense. Chronology does reveal a certain progression and isolates areas of confusion, and literary criticism makes better sense if it is historically based; these are the axioms of this book. But as written prose emerges in Greek, it represents a variety of intellectual activity which ought probably to be treated together. Natural science, medicine and philosophy, the criticism of myth, the investigation of origins of cities, customs, families and the universe itself, and the beginnings of the writing of history, are part of a single picture. The old relationship of moralizing and philosophy and solemn verse and entertaining stories, let alone natural science, affected philosophers as late as Plato and Aristotle. Some of the intellectual baggage that was transferred from verse to prose in the archaic period was not unpacked for a very long time.

We must therefore overshoot in this chapter those stricter limits of chronology and also of subject-matter which in later chapters devoted to individual writers it will be easy to preserve. Nor is it within the possibilities of my treatment to give a full and clear exposition of the intellectual outlook and philosophy of every writer. Excellent and thorough studies of the early Greeks as thinkers already exist, and will be found listed in the bibliography to this chapter. My interest is more in what kind of writers they were, and how or why they should be read. There is no doubt that, taken together, what are called the pre-Socratic philosophers give a dazzling impression of the emergence of intellect, of wide speculation, thrilling criticism and fascinating detail. Their Egyptian and oriental influences are by no means sufficient to explain them. The Ionian Greeks were the seed-bed of European intellectual life. Yet we know of no origins of Greek thought, only of the beginnings and the progress of written literature. A full treatment of pre-Socratic Greek thought should really begin, though few of them do, with the vigorous intellectuality of Homer and of Hesiod.

The activities of Levantine sages come to notice only in the sixth century B.C. Anaximander of Miletos seems to have been born in 610 B.C. and died in 545, at the time of the fall of Sardis to the Persians. Thales of Miletos apparently predicted the eclipse of 585 B.C., and was definitely older than Anaximander, perhaps by ten or twenty years, so he was probably born around 625 B.C. He was Phoenician by remoter ancestry and anecdotes connect him with King Kroisos of Lydia. Pherekydes of Syros, one of the obscurest and most teasing of these early figures, lived at about the same time, in the days of Alyattes of Lydia in the earlier part of the century, or more probably a little later. Thales left traces of his activity in politics, in the attempt to set up a federated state of all the Ionian east Greek cities, in the diverting of rivers, the geographical problems of the Nile, and in astronomy, in the study of eclipses, which he based on Babylonian records, of the solstice and of the stars of the Wain or Little Bear, a constellation the Phoenicians are said to have noticed as navigators. Thales wrote no book except perhaps a navigational star-guide which appears to have been two hundred lines of verse. It is easy to see how Thales, in the great commercial city of Miletos, could draw on Babylonian, Phoenician and Egyptian knowledge at once, and how much the increasing unification of the world contributed to create an intellectual melting-pot.

It was an age of navigation, and Thales believed the surface of this world floats on water like a raft at sea. Water is the origin and perhaps even the material of all the transformations of our world. Earthquakes and landslides come of the tossing of the sea beneath us. Everything is alive, and magnetism is a living force; the physical world is full of forces or gods. Anaximander, his pupil and maybe his kinsman, pursued the same subjects with increasing precision, and he certainly wrote a book, though we have little enough of it. He advanced geometry, devised a schematic map of the earth's surface, and introduced a joker into the pack of words used by the early thinkers by calling the first material of all things the 'unlimited', the 'infinite'. Yet his language was much closer to myth than to metaphysics; it was admirably pregnant. 'All the heavens and all the worlds in them come to be from the one limitless element: and the source out of which all existing things come to be is the same into which they are also resolved, by necessity, as they pay penalty and retribution to one another for their injustice according to the assessment of time.'

As the statement of a profound belief about how the universe works, how time proceeds, what underlies all theology and all morality, and how one season and one material yields to another, this saying of Anaximander can hardly be bettered, but its resonant diction is closer to poetry than to prose. It belongs to the literature of wisdom, not to the technical and precise language of logical analysis. It has an effective sublimity which later philosophers constantly tried to recapture, but which escaped them. It is bold, and it is both subtle and simple. Even in poetry, such language was not going to outlive Aischylos. His universe was strung together by mathematics as if by music: the earth was like the floating slice of a stone column, three times as wide as it was deep; and the distances of all heavenly bodies suggested similar proportions: the sun's fiery mouth was the same size as earth, but its body was twenty-seven times the width of its mouth, the stars nine times and the moon nineteen times the earth's surface. Thunder was 'smitten cloud' and lightning was the bursting of the wind through cloud. The sun was drying up the earth's water, and the wind turned the sun. The first men came out of the bellies of fish; life came from mud by the sun's heat.

Pherekydes of Syros may have lived a little earlier or a little later than Anaximander, but his language was even more closely like that of myth, although his book was speculative, and in prose. It began 'Zeus and Time and Chthonia were for ever ...' He was imagined later as having been a travelling wonder-worker in many different areas of Greece. There is no doubt about oriental influences on his thinking, but the ancient suggestion that he read the secret books of the Phoenicians need not be taken very literally. His description of the physical generation of gods is detailed and primitive, but apparently allegorically intended, or partly so, like other mythology. We have on a fragment of papyrus his account of the marriage of Zeus; its prose is even simpler than one would expect, and its charm fresher. Prose story-telling must have been like this for many centuries.

... they make him his dwellings, many and great. And when they had finished all this and possessions of servants and serving-girls and everything else needed, when that is all ready they make the wedding. And when the third day of the wedding comes, then Zeus makes a robe, big and beautiful, and on it he embroiders Earth and Ocean ... [wishing] your marriage to be ... I honour you with this. And so be glad and be with me. They say this was the first Unveiling, and from this came the law for gods and men. And she replied and took the robe ...

It appears from other fragments that Zeus spread out the robe flat on the branches of a great oak tree that was winged and immortal, and the robe is the surface of the earth. Pherekydes is a sage of irresistible oddity, but had he written in verse, we would have been pleased to enjoy him in a more relaxed way. As it is, one must recollect that the obscure origins of Orphism (with all things born out of an egg) belong to the same period, and Pythagoras himself, who lived in the second half of the sixth century, and whose influence was enormous, had some very odd doctrines indeed.

Pythagoras was a mathematician, perhaps a wonder-worker; he was born in Samos, went into exile in Italy, lived in Kroton and died in Metapontion after a political failure. He wrote no books, and his disciples, who lived as a community and included at least one woman, Theano, who became famous, kept much of his teaching secret. He taught the kinship of all living things, the transmigration of souls, the need for sobriety and abstinence and as many ritual observances as Hesiod's or more. 'Stir not fire with iron'; 'Wear no ring'; 'Hands off beans'; and so on. Beans may mean voting counters, so some form of democratic politics may have been prohibited. The alternative ancient explanation, for which I retain from boyhood a certain affection, is that beans cause the breaking of wind, and wind is spirit, spirit is soul, so eating beans causes the dispersal of the soul. On a more serious level, Pythagoras was the source of a metaphysical system of Limit and Unlimited, which I by no means understand, and of a purely mathematical explanation of the world, things being ultimately numbers or functions of number: an intuition as fruitful as it was striking.

Anaximenes of Miletos followed Anaximander in the second half of the sixth century, and Alkmaion of Kroton followed Pythagoras in the early fifth. One activity of these sages overlaps with another, and some go far beyond literature. A religious sage like the legendary, undatable Epimenides the Cretan had something in common with Pythagoras and Pherekydes, and something else with Onomakritos, a forger of holy writings employed and then banished by Hipparchos the tyrant of Athens. Many but not all the sages were active in politics. They all accumulated legends like barnacles. Strange characters who hardly belong to literature at all crowd here into the margins of its pages.

Xenophanes of Kolophon, who lived his long life from about 570 to 475 B.C., might have stood with Mimnermos and the other archaic poets, since he wrote in verse, or equally with the first historians like Akousilaos, since he did handle history. The traveller Skylax, who served under Dareios I in the late sixth century, wrote a description of a southern journey between the Indus and the Arabian gulf, and some lost anonymous writer who stands behind the *Ora Maritima* of Avienus described the coast from Tartessos to Marseille at about the same time. Aristeas of Prokonnesos, who was probably early enough to influence Alkman, wrote a verse account of real and imaginary peoples in central Asia and in the wonderlands beyond; I speak of him only here because, fascinating and extraordinary as his poem seems to have been, we know him almost only as an influence on much later writers, as we know Pythagoras and Thales. The influence of Aristeas ripens into visibility only in the later fifth century B.C., with Herodotos. And yet his *Arimaspeia*, his largely legendary account of the far north, must have been roughly contemporary with the *Odyssey*.

Anaximenes followed Anaximander; at least that is how ancient scholars sorted them out. He wrote in 'simple and economical Ionic speech', according to later Greeks. He refined his master's (or was it his contemporary's?) teaching, to a point where the primal and basic stuff of the universe was air, rarefied or condensed into everything: into fire, wind, cloud, earth and stone. The opposites, rare and dense or heat and cold, are the principles of generation, heat and cold being the product of rarefaction and condensation. He was plodding on, or stalking energetically, towards the foundations of natural science. But it is important to remember that for Anaximenes air was a force, a god – an infinite and immeasurable and ever-moving god – a conception which greatly shocked Cicero, though it appealed to St Augustine. His earth was as flat as a lid or a table, and its lack of thickness kept it from blowing about. The stars were nails or flakes or petals of fire, and his heavens turned above the earth like a cap or a dome. His sun sank below hills and the sky twisted round until sunrise, but nothing sank below the surface of earth. All this has a naive and pleasing ingenuity, and the variety of the opinions of the sages adds to the pleasure they give; but I doubt whether one point of view is always more clever or closer to truth than the last.

Alkmaion of Kroton, the successor of Pythagoras, has left few fragments. He was convinced, as they all were by the year 500 B.C., of the importance of opposites and oppositions; bodily health was balance, the right mixture of heat and cold, hunger and nourishment, and so on. The soul being divine is always in motion, like sun, moon, stars and heavens. Men die 'because they cannot join beginning with end'. Alkmaion was interested in the brain, and seems to have been a consciously original writer. But the principal contribution of Alkmaion and the Pythagoreans is said to have been to mathematics. They believed 'the elements of numbers to be the elements of all things, and the whole heaven to be a musical scale and a number'. Mathematics is not part of literature, so I do not feel bound to analyse these views, to trace their Babylonian origins, or to discuss calendar mathematics or metaphysical oppositions. But universal music has a resonance here and there in the contemporary poetry of Pindar.

Xenophanes of Kolophon offers a relief from these speculations. He knew Kolophon before it fell to the Persians, but lived most of his long life in eastern Sicily. He wrote in verse denouncing Homer and Hesiod for the lies they told about gods. Homer had become a textbook and as a textbook was provoking reactions. The work of Stesichoros shows that such criticism was not unique, and the increased fastidiousness of Pindar and of later writers proves that the case Xenophanes made was a strong one. But Xenophanes was something of a curmudgeon. 'He is said to have held contrary opinions to Thales and Pythagoras, and to have rebuked Epimenides.' He was a nobleman, and he recited his own songs. He is said to have written long poems about the foundation of Kolophon and the colonial city of Elea (later Velia near Paestum); if he really did so, he ranks as an early historian. He composed in elegiac couplets, in Homeric hexameters, and in mixed metres, and he appears to have invented a new satiric genre. His interest in natural science hardly goes beyond common sense, and a certain hostility to theologians. The wilder speculations of his contemporaries did more to advance physics and astronomy, but Xenophanes is easier reading.

He attacks Homer and Hesiod for dedicating or 'making over to the gods whatever is culpable in men: the thieving and lechery and cheating', and all mankind for imagining gods who eat and dress, and speak, and look, and are born like themselves. 'Ethiopians have black, snub-nosed gods, and Thracians have blue-eyed, red-haired gods.' I doubt whether these observations were as startling to the Greeks as scholars have sometimes imagined. 'If cattle and horses and lions had hands, or drew with hands, or did such works as men, they would have drawn the shapes of gods like them, horses like horses, cattle like cattle, and made their bodies like the ones they have.' This amusing and all but clinching argument remains as poetry a rather awkward offering. When Xenophanes puts forward his own view of God, his verse is still heavily constructed, and less sublime than the prose of other sages.

> One god, the greatest among gods and men,
> unlike in mind or body to mankind ...
> Ever still he remains and is not moved,
> nor is it proper he move here or there,
> but untroubled shakes all by thought of mind ...
> All of him sees, all thinks, all of him hears.

His force as a critic was greater than his perception as a philosopher or his power as a poet. The earth, he thought, was of indefinite or infinite thickness. The sun was a concentration of burning clouds, moving on an infinite course, 'but seeming to move in a circle because of the distance': the sun was a fresh one every day, there were infinite swarms of suns. Cloud, wind and all rivers came from the ocean, and all things came from earth and water. He argued from the marine fossils of Paros, Malta and Syracuse that time is cyclical; life is blotted out every so often and water dissolves the earth into mud. A new beginning follows, 'and this foundation happens for all the worlds'. Here again, his common-sense observation of fossils is more exciting than the use he makes of it. Something similar can be said of his sharp observation and yet less interesting argument about the limits of human knowledge. 'If god had not begot yellow honey, they would have called figs sweeter than they do.' We have only two long fragments of his poetry, one about sobriety at the feast and one about the worth of wisdom and the worthlessness of athletes and horses by comparison. They are lamentably dull. He was not a great poet or a great philosopher, only an 1890s bicycling rationalist in home-woven plusfours: high praise in the context of 510 B.C.

His contemporary Herakleitos of Ephesos is more attractive, if only for the sharpness and proverbial ingredients of his style. He wrote about nature, politics and the gods in a style probably closer to the real and witty speech of the eastern Greeks than even the traditional story-telling style of Pherekydes of Syros. 'The sea is the purest and filthiest of all water'; 'We must follow the common thing: reason is common but most people live as if they had a private mental process'; 'I prefer what you can see and hear and learn'; 'The way up and down is one and the same.' Philosophers have found the piecing together of doctrine from remarks like these a tantalizing and impossible task. It has been suggested more than once that Herakleitos never wrote a book at all, and that these sayings of his were rammed together higgledy-piggledy by his disciples, but eccentric as his book doubtless was, Herakleitos does seem to have written it in a deliberate way, in an age when prose discourse in writing was a new experiment.

He liked paradox. It was his philosophic weapon, his habit of style, and no doubt the expression of his character. It is probably best to consider his language as that of rustic wisdom. 'Everything runs,' he said, 'everything flows'; and 'You can't get down into the same river-water twice.' God is day, night, summer and winter, and all opposites. God alters as fire alters by the name and smell of what it burns. Reality hides. God thinks everything is good and beautiful and right, but we think right and wrong are different. One has the sense of a powerful mind, a genuine personal presence, in reading Herakleitos. It is humiliating in a way, that this great feat of self-expression in prose and in philosophy occurred so early in our history, and has so seldom been equalled since – probably never until Montaigne. He is as tough as hobnails. 'One must understand that war is common to all things, and justice is strife, and all things come to be according to strife and necessity.' There is an echo of Anaximander in these words, but Herakleitos takes things further. 'War is the father of all things and the king of all things; some he has made gods and some men, some slaves and some free.' He knows the world and he has read Homer with bitter irony.

His world was terrifying. Ever-living fire was its one element, and the sea and earth were quenched fires, reabsorbed finally into fire. The stars were cups of fire feeding on the bright exhalations of the sea. 'The Sun shall not overstep his limits, or else the Furies, the servants of Justice, will seek him out.' The sun of every day is new because its fire is renewed by fresh exhalations of the sea. Does he mean the glittering of waves, or the light-mist on the horizon? The soul of man was also fire, arising out of moisture and extinguishing itself into moisture. Sleep blocked away the soul from the world-fire; virtuous souls returned alive to the living fire. The rituals and beliefs of religion were ridiculous, though they might point towards truth by mistake. But Herakleitos had his conventional side. 'The people should defend law like a city wall'; 'The best choose one thing in place of everything, everlasting glory among men: but most people are glutted like cattle'; 'Character is a god over every man.'

Parmenides, Zeno and Empedokles worked in the fifth century; they were born respectively about 510, 490 and maybe 485 B.C., but all these dates are uncertain. Parmenides and Zeno were old Pythagoreans who broke away; Empedokles appears to have studied a number of philosophers. Parmenides and Zeno came from Elea, and Empedokles from Akragas, now called Agrigento. Zeno was a sharp arguer whose logical paradoxes are still entertaining and worth thinking about; had he lived later, he might in time have written *Alice in Wonderland*. But Parmenides and Empedokles must detain us longer, because they were both poets of a strange and rather new kind. In them 'philosophic' poetry became an instrument and style of its own. They adopted all shreds of sublimity they could master; they tried to adapt Homeric verse, but failed altogether to master its suppleness. They preferred grandeur to lucidity. They used image and allegory with a simple woodenness which in the end is impressive.

It is tempting to call Parmenides a terribly bad poet, or to suggest he was so bad that he stumbled into originality. That is not quite right. Aristophanes in the *Birds*, in his parody of an Orphic poem about the creation, shows a certain feeling for the kind of verse that must lie behind the pretensions of Parmenides.

> Out of the houses of Night the Sun's daughters
> brought me to light, and pushed away their veils.
> There are the gates of Night's road and of Day's,
> stone frames the doors and the threshold of stone.
> They in high air are warded by great doors,
> and vengeful justice holds the keys of both.

One can easily see how this is made up of scraps of old poetry, rags and tatters of Homer, and pieces of philosophy from as far back as Anaximander. In the heaven of Homer, the Seasons or the Hours roll back the gates of the Sun; but this is allegory of a more laborious kind. Parmenides is at his worst about the 'is-not' and the 'is', a subject of which he exhausts the possibilities both of philosophy and of grammar. Yet there is no denying the resonance of these knotty sentences.

> Thou canst not know non-being, nor perceive
> nor speak it, for to think is as to be ...
> Coming to be is quenched, and death unknown.

It is all a trick of course, all a riddle. The old folk-tradition of riddling philosophy, taken up into great poetry by Hesiod and into philosophy at least as early as Herakleitos, reaches a formal apotheosis in Parmenides. These riddles are solemn; they are not meant to be entertaining. The sage is wearing his charlatan's cloak. Reality is one motionless sphere. 'One thing is thinking and the thing that's thought.' In the centre of all circles of fire and air stands 'the goddess who steers all things, and begins all works of nasty birth and begetting, sending female to mix with male and male with female'. Would the world have done better to remain inside its Orphic egg? If one is ever tempted to criticize Greek culture or our idea of it as Athenocentric, Parmenides will be a corrective. But no doubt the local scale of the schools of philosophy does mirror their unimportance. Some sparks from the burning cities of the east Greeks had lighted fires in Italy and Sicily. Two Pythagoreans from Kroton or Tarentum travelled to Phlious in the Peloponnese, not a big place, and it was there that Pythagoreanism lingered on a hundred years.

Empedokles was a different figure altogether. He was famous as a doctor, active as a democrat, and Aristotle says he was the inventor of rhetoric; that must mean that he taught Gorgias, and apparently began the first movement to control the rhythms of prose as strictly as verse rhythm. His two great poems, five thousand verses altogether, were *On Nature* and *The Purifications*. He was sometimes credited with medical writings and tragic poetry, but wrongly it appears. He was not without an unsober aspect; he seemed to claim to command wind and weather, and strange stories were told about his death. One of them inspired Matthew Arnold. Empedokles inherited from Orphism or from Pythagoras the idea of love as the great force of the universe. His verse was compounded from stale crumbs of Homer, but it was sometimes as remarkable as his perverse intelligence.

> Hear first the four roots of all things that are:
> bright Zeus, life-bearing Hera, Aidoneus
> and Nestis whose tears water human springs.

He seems to mean Fire, Air, Earth and Water, Aidoneus being Hades. His universe is a sphere, but poetry improves it.

> For there the Sun's swift limbs are not discerned
> nor is the shaggy strength of earth, nor sea,
> but self-equal all ways and limitless,
> steady, enveloped in dense Harmony:
> one sphere rejoicing in pure solitude.

The history of the world was an endlessly repeated cycle ruled by Love and Strife alternately.

> On Love gaze with thy mind and be not dazed,
> for she is known inborn in mortal limbs,
> through her come loving thoughts and mutual work,
> her name is Aphrodite and Delight.

That is at least an improvement on Parmenides. The astrophysical views of Empedokles are less convincing however. He knew the moon was a reflective surface and thought the sun itself was just a concentrated reflection of the blue dome of heaven. It is not recorded what he thought about shadows. As for human evolution, the earth took in water and fire, and 'there arose white bones divinely fitted by joints of Harmony'. Earth, fire, water and brilliant air came together, 'and anchored in the perfect harbours of the love goddess ... Hence came blood and all the shapes of flesh.' Limbs wandered about alone, and when they joined they were monstrous. Mankind emerged by the survival of the fittest and the separation of the sexes after some obscure earlier sexless phase. Being compounded of all elements and forces, we are able to perceive the four elements and the two forces. 'The gentle, immortal stream of innocent love' is central to his writings; in his golden age there was not Zeus or Kronos or Poseidon, but only Aphrodite, queen of the world, which

> With consecrated statues worshipped her,
> with painted creatures and confused perfumes
> burning pure myrrh and scented frankincense,
> poured streams of tawny honey on the ground:
> altars not wetted with sheer blood of bulls,
> but this was the worst horror of mankind,
> to tear out life and then eat the good limbs.

The transmigration of souls was in his doctrine a wandering hell of banishment from element to element; it was the punishment of bloodshed and false oath suffered by demigods, and it lasted thirty thousand seasons.

> The might of air will drive him into sea,
> the sea will spew him up on to dry land,
> earth flings him to the rays of the hot sun,
> and sun into the eddies of the air.

> Each one receives him and will cast him out,
> and of these I am one, fleeing the gods,
> wandering man who trusted raving Strife.

It is hardly surprising that this powerful poet, the most powerful preaching voice since Hesiod perhaps, had an influence beyond his own city. I have lingered a little over his work because of its relevance to better known writers, including Plato, Pindar, Aristophanes and, in Latin, Lucretius. His use of allegory and his inventive mythology are quite free of inhibition, and his thoughts are bold. One can sense in him in spite of his provincial quality a kinship with classical Athenian intellect.

The last of the pre-Socratic sages who are best dealt with here is Anaxagoras of Klazomenai, who lived from about 500 to 428 B.C. He belonged in Athens to the circle of the young Perikles, as an attack on whom Anaxagoras was sued and in the end exiled for denying the divinity of the sun and moon. He wrote only one book, but according to Plato's *Apology of Sokrates* it was easily and cheaply available in Athens many years after his exile. He wrote in simple prose, in short clauses loosely linked, in the archaic Ionian prose style. 'All things were together, infinite in quantity and smallness ... All things being together, nothing was visible because of their smallness; for air and fire covered everything, and both were infinite.' He combines sublimity and simplicity, like earlier writers:

Other things have a share of everything, but intellect is infinite and self-governing and not mingled with anything; it is itself by itself alone ... And all that would be and all that was, all that is not now and what is now and what will be, all these things intellect has set in order: and also this circulation in which the stars and sun and moon and the air and fire circulate and separate.

We do not need to pursue his scientific views or his philosophic arguments, or even the political significance of his trial, into great detail. It is sufficiently interesting that prose of this kind was being read at Athens throughout the second half of the fifth century. His views of the details of nature were rational, original, and full of errors by our standards, but at the time there is no doubt they were thrilling. Sun, moon and stars were red-hot stones, the stars passed below the earth, the sun was bigger than the Peloponnese. He was interested in seeds and in eggs. His contemporary Philolaos of Kroton realized earth spins on its own axis. His younger contemporary, Demokritos of Abdera, born about 460 B.C., either invented or elaborated from the work of Leukippos of Miletos, whose writings and date remain obscure, the theory that everything in the universe consists of atoms. The repercussions of that theory belong to another subject and a later age. Protagoras got into trouble at Athens for agnosticism about the gods, even in the age of Perikles. In the fifth century, the Homeric gods had plenty of fight left in them.

In a medical treatise in Ionic dialect *On the Sacred Disease*, for instance, which sets out about this time to show that epilepsy has a physical mechanism and is not a kind of divine invasion to be cured by chantings and purgations, the writer attacks 'wizards and purgers and wandering quacks and charlatans' whose treatments and diagnosis are itemized.

And if they mimic a goat and if they roar or get spasms on the right, they say the mother of the gods is to blame. If they utter rather sharply and loudly they compare that to a horse and say Poseidon is to blame. And if some dung appears, as often happens under pressure of illness, they name it after the Queen of Hell, or if it is rather frequent and thin like birds, Apollo of flocks. And if he foams at the mouth and kicks out with his feet, Ares is to blame.

This treatise is more earnest and severe than my quotation shows, though its prose stye continues mostly the same, far more primitive than that of Herodotos. Its point is that the world is one thing, equally divine and equally subject to science.

That the laws of nature are uniform and may decently and success-fully be investigated by us is perhaps a theological axiom or one that emerges from the conflict of theology and criticism; it is based on a respect for the universe. Plato has Sokrates in the *Phaidros* ask his disciple whether one can understand the soul without first understanding the universe: the young man replies that according to Hippokrates of Kos one cannot even understand the body without first understanding the universe. Hippokrates was a doctor and a theorist of empirical medicine, who has been credited with a vast variety of early and late Greek medical writings. I do not believe we possess a word by him, but that does not mean the earlier 'Hippokratic' writings are uninteresting. Their solutions, as in the case of epilepsy, are often incorrect, but their arguments, and their touches of generality, are enthralling.

This disease seems to me in no way more divine than the others, but it has the same nature as other diseases and the same cause as every disease. And it is curable, and no less so than the others, at least such as are not strengthened by long time so as to be more powerful than the remedies applied. It begins as other diseases do from bodily inheritance.

The thought, being a little more subtle and complex here, has produced a more coordinated syntax, though my translation slightly exaggerates its complexity for the sake of clarity. Throughout this short treatise we find touches of the same universal views. The divine is pure and purifies. Man is delicate, particularly in the womb. One must keep an eye on weather: 'To old people the worst enemy is winter.' The south wind, the Meltemi or the Sirocco, makes things 'dull instead of bright, hot instead of cold, wet instead of dry'. The machinery of phlegm, of veins and of the whole external world is thought to be very simple, and explanations still refer to Ionian theories: 'All things are divine and all things are human.'

This has been thought of as an early work of the writer of *Airs, Waters and Places*, or as the work of that writer's pupil. They are closely connected, and such phrases as 'moisture is in all things' and 'offspring is bodily, moist from the moist and diseased from the diseased' occur in both. They may be written, I believe, by two disciples of Hippokrates himself, but if so the author of *Airs, Waters and Places* had the better mental equipment. I take *On Old Medicine* to be too late to interest us in this context. *Airs, Waters and Places* discusses a number of points of environmental difference and their effects: wind and water in particular, and then the contrast between Europe, Africa and Asia. Here the unification of the world is at work once again, but this treatment is still a curious mixture of empiricism and prejudice. Water from the rocks is bad and overheats for theoretical reasons. Rain-water is the lightest, sweetest, finest and clearest of all, for equally theoretical reasons. But then suddenly 'This is how to find out' and 'My proof is this', even though what he is demonstrating is the viciousness of ice-water and snow-water.

The treatment of Asia as a medical environment is a good piece of continuous prose, better knit than the *Sacred Disease*, and yet as simple. The writer knows about cheese from mares' milk, and the number of wheels and the subdivision into rooms of a nomad wagon, but his idea of central Asia is not equally detailed in other ways.

The sun comes most close at the end of his course, when he approaches the summer solstice, and then for a little while he warms them and not much. Airs blowing from hot parts do not reach them except rarely and weakly, but cold airs blow forever from the north and from snow and ice and great waters. They never leave those mountains, they make them hard to live in. By day great fogs cover the plains, and in those they live, so that winter lasts for ever but the heat only a few days, and not much of it. For the plains are high up and bare and not crowned with mountains, but yet they slope from the north. Wild animals are not big there, but such as shelter underground.

This is a rationalizing writer. He attempts to explain temperament by political regime, to explain Amazons, to explain what sound like tattoos: they existed in order to cauterize the excessive moisture of a cold country away from the right shoulder, in order to increase the ability to throw javelins. Nomads grow fat and squat because they fail to swaddle their babies and sit about all their lives on horses, which is a sedentary life. Can this possibly be the voice of the islander Hippokrates? Doctors were usually itinerant. 'The Scythian race is tanned by the cold, there being no sharpness of the sun. Their whiteness is burnt by the cold and becomes tan.' He is surely equally at sea about male impotence contracted by too much riding, which leads he says to transvestism and role-changing unless it is cured by letting blood from the ear. Social explanations such as a modern anthropologist could furnish, for example candidacy for the post of shaman, utterly elude him. His medical argument is equally naive; he argues that since this happens to the rich, it is yet another proof that gods, who he presumes are grateful to the rich, have nothing to do with the matter. 'They always wear trousers and sit on horses most of the time, so they do not touch their private part with their hand, and from cold and weariness they forget desire and sex and never move a muscle until they are unmanned.' It is no surprise that he thinks Europeans superior, if only because geography and climate make them so. 'Bravery and endurance would not be naturally innate in such souls, but law could produce them', is the best he can say of Asia.

Periods and movements do not come neatly to an end. A curious ragbag of fragments must be thought of as the sediment of the Archaic Age. Panyassis of Halikarnassos, a poet of a kind, who produced respectable and much admired epic verses about Herakles, was a contemporary of Hekataios, historian and geographer, one of the most talented of early prose writers and one of the most influential. By the end of the sixth century, in the days of Panyassis, Akousilaos of Argos was already producing genealogical epic material in prose. Even later, towards the end of the fifth century, Antimachos of Kolophon wrote a Theban epic as well as a long, sad, love elegy, full of eastern stories. He was defeated in a contest of poets on Samos called the Lysandreia after the Spartan Lysander, by an epic poet otherwise quite unknown to us, called Nikeratos. Antimachos was the first editor of Homer whose name we know. Kritias, an anti-democratic Athenian nobleman who died in a street battle at the end of the century, wrote a lot of elegant, deadly dull verse about the customs and inventions and politics of different Greeks, almost a hundred years after Hekataios had done it in prose. He favoured Sparta, loved Anakreon and hated Archilochos whom he thought low. He wrote unreadable hexameter poetry as well as some uninspiring tragedies for the Athenian stage. His prose has whatever charm attaches to conservative simplicity, but in his verse, where allegory and science faint into insignificant metaphor, Ionian speculation has come down in the world.

> ... thunder's dread thumps,
> the star face of the body of heaven,
> noble artwork of Time, that wise craftsman,
> whence comes the sunstar's shining anvil-stone
> and the wet rains march out towards the earth.

Hekataios wrote a guide to the known world, and also a book about genealogies of great families descended from heroes or gods, including his own. His younger contemporary Herodotos was somewhat scornful about that (2.145). Hekataios was opposed to the disastrous Ionian revolt against the Persians in 500 B.C.; he must at that time have been a mature and influential citizen. He was also, as E. R. Dodds pointed out in *The Greeks and the Irrational*, the first person ever recorded to have thought the gods funny. Homer is almost an exception to this observation, but not quite.

The fragments of Hekataios are delightful and often record strange information. He wrote with the simplicity and clarity of folk-tales. He imposed reason where he could, but he recorded mythology with a confident purity of tone. 'I write this as I think the truth dictates, for it seems to me that Greek stories are numerous and ridiculous.' But he then tells us how a dog gave birth to a stick which became a fruitful vine, and therefore the king named his son Shoot, whose son was called Vine (Phytios and Oineus). He tells also of a talking ram and a dreadful snake in a cave at Tainaros called the Dog of Hades because whoever it bit died of poison at once. In Egypt, he knew of a floating island holy to Apollo, and he seems to have known of Stonehenge, 'a circular temple of the Sun', in the middle of the island of Britain. Delphi was in the centre of his world-map. Ocean, according to Hekataios, married his own sister Tethys and begot three thousand rivers, of whom Achelaios was the oldest and had most honour. His remoter landscapes are dramatic: 'mountains high and densely forested, and in the mountains huge thorns', and 'both mountains and plain overgrown with wild woods, huge thorns, willow and myrtle'. His Paionians in north Greece 'drink beer and anoint with oil of milk', which must surely mean butter – a custom for which the rancid Burgundians were famous in later centuries. Had the works of Hekataios been fully preserved, they would have greatly cheered up classical studies.

BIBLIOGRAPHY

F. M. Cornford, *From Religion to Philosophy*, 1912, reprinted 1957
H. Fränkel, *Early Greek Poetry and Philosophy*, 1975
W. K. C. Guthrie, *Greek Philosophers, Thales to Aristotle*, 1950
E. Hussey, *The Presocratics*, 1972
G. L. Huxley, *The Early Ionians*, 1966
W. Jaeger, *Theology of Early Greek Philosophers*, 1947
W. H. S. Jones (ed.), Loeb edition of Hippocrates, 4 vols., 1923–31

W. H. S. Jones, *Philosophy and Medicine in Ancient Greece*, 1946

G. S. Kirk and R. E. Raven, *The Presocratic Philosophers*, 2nd edition (with M. Schofield), 1983

R. Pfeiffer, *History of Classical Scholarship*, vol. I, 1968

M. Robertson, *History of Greek Art*, 1976 (shorter version, 1981)

The much-needed and most useful study of Orphism by Martin West (1984) appeared too late for me to use it.

· 5 ·
PINDAR

The Archaic Age flowered late. A certain heaviness had clung to Greek sculpture until the middle of the sixth century. Suppleness and vigour in the visual arts increased very greatly towards the end of the century, and the great age of architecture began then mostly, one must admit, under the last dictators and the doomed nobility. The choral poetry of Pindar is technically more complex, grander in conception, more shimmering in surface detail, than anything that can have preceded it. Of course, every technique of his is rooted in earlier poetry, but in his celebrations of victories at the games he combines the freest use of mythological examples, splendid and solemn prayers, and impressive sensuous ornament, with monumental weight.

His influence on European literature, through Ronsard, Hölderlin and Gongora, and in our language Ben Jonson, Gray, Wordsworth, perhaps Milton, and certainly Cowley and Dryden, has been enormous and fruitful. We owe to him, even in the dog-days and decline of the ode, the words and the whole idea of 'Rule Britannia'. But Pindar's poetry is like a snowstorm. He has seldom been thoroughly understood. Of the poets I have mentioned, all are separated from Pindar by rhythmic simplification, and all but Hölderlin by the use of rhyme. Only Gongora is as difficult to follow at first reading; but once it is more deeply read, Pindar's poetry becomes swift, delightful, varied and thrilling. Something of the brilliance of the festival itself and the excitement of victory shows through his verses. He likes grandeur and believes in the physical effect of blood and breeding in dogs, horses, aristocrats and athletes, perhaps in the divine or heroic – let us say the half-divine – origins of families. His myths of bravery, strength and beauty are convincing. His poetry is full-blooded and impetuous, but his principal quality is awe.

Many kinds of poetry were crumbled together to make the humus in which his verse grew. His narrative can be full or swift, lyric or epic. It is always selective and exactly controlled. At times he uses the special tones of oracles and proverbs. Indeed, his most splendid and monumental verses can swivel round a transitional phrase, often a proverb, as a taxi used to swivel round a sixpence. What appear to be solemn warnings are sometimes only stage thunderclaps, introduced for their proverbial resonance, so that lightning will seem to play around the head of a ruler and a patron. Pindar is a close contemporary of Simonides of Keos and of Aischylos; they have similarities and contrasts of great interest, which I do not think have been quite fully explored. But most scholars and most historians would probably agree that the difference between the Archaic and the Classical Age lies somewhere between Pindar and Aischylos. Pindar's patrons were mostly the great and noble all over the Greek world; most Greek poetry was in some sense occasional; its nature was determined by the nature of its performance, and the Athenian democratic theatre differed greatly from the international four-yearly athletic festivals of the Greeks, even more so than the lonely grove of Olympia differed from Athens.

Pindar was born noble in 518 B.C. at Thebes, and died in Argos around 438 B.C. A great deal has been written in this century, in German by Wilamowitz down to the twenties, and in English by Sir Maurice Bowra, about the details of Pindar's life and relationships as they appear in and between the lines of his victory poems. At this stage of the game, it is better to consider his poems objectively, as individual works of art. The foundations of this kind of study were laid partly by Bowra himself, whose work is still the best introduction to Pindar, and whose translation makes coherent sense of the poetry, but more effectively by Elroy Bundy in the early sixties. Bowra was inclined to think Bundy's slim volumes were a work of genius, but they appeared too late to influence him except in his Penguin translation of the complete odes.

Pindar was a professional poet throughout his long life. The odes, the celebrations of victories at the games, are the first substantial corpus of Greek poetry that we have after Homer, Hesiod and the Hymns; but the fragments of his other poetry are also much more plentiful than those of earlier lyric poets. He wrote love poetry; 'I, because of the goddess, am gnawed by the heat, and melt like the wax of holy bees, when I see the youth and the fresh limbs of boys.' He wrote some athletic celebrations not to be found among his collected odes. He wrote hymns to the gods for shrines and cities, and special paeans to Apollo. 'Iee! Iee! Now the all-fulfilling Year and the Seasons, daughters of Justice, have come to the horse-whipping city of Thebes, with a garlanded feast for Apollo.' For Apollo as an agricultural god, which is not his usual role, one can find some confirmation in the festivals and month-names of Athens, but it is not certain that this fragment does give him a role of that kind. It represents a moment in the calendar and that may be all.

Pindar's paean for Abdera begins 'Bronze-breastplated Abderos, son of the mermaid Thronia, and of Poseidon, from you I derive this paean for the Ionian people.' The sense of occasion is evident, and Pindar's vast repertory of local and family mythology follows from that. Pindar's religious poetry is splendid, and less complicated because more impersonal than his athletic celebrations, which are essentially concerned with family, with the athlete's father even if he is dead, with his blood in which the sacred water of some special spring may flow, and with the wealth, the physical prestige and peak of glory of the family, and with its future. For Pindar, as for generations of Greeks before him and many after him, honour and glory and physical prowess and victory go closely together. Honour is a public, not a private matter. Its opposite is public shame, or un-celebrated obscurity. The nearest he comes to the cult of conscience, guilt and inwardness, to the sporting values of Christian cricketers and the Protestant work ethic, is a solemn quotation from Hesiod (*Works and Days*, 412) at the end of the sixth Isthmian ode: 'Trouble is an aid to achievements.' Solemn morality was an inherited part of grandeur in poetry by Pindar's time.

He wrote dithyrambs, an Athenian form of choral lyric with dancing in honour of the gods. They were essentially narrative: Herakles in the underworld, or Cerberus, for the Thebans, for example. A dithyramb for Athens calls on all the Olympian gods to join the dance, and after a ritual compliment to Zeus passes on at once to Dionysos, to whom dithyramb belongs even at Thebes. His divine invocations splendidly invoke the gods themselves celebrating. He

wrote processional chants for sanctuaries, and choral, ritual songs for
young girls.

> For provident Apollo comes
> mingling immortal grace with Thebes;
> I shall belt on my robe and swiftly bring
> in my soft hands a noble wreath of bays.

Some of the images and phrases that follow are charming, even
thrilling; one has the sense of a crescendo poet playing diminuendo.
But the innocence of Alkman's girls and of his gods has departed
from the earth. Pindar composed other poetry for ritual dances, and
some pure praise poems for his kings and great nobles. One can almost
sense that before its history closes the ode will encompass Tennyson
on the burial of the Duke of Wellington, and Thomas Warton on
George III bathing in the sea at Yarmouth. But Pindar's verses are
still attractive ornaments and full-blooded poems. Phrases like 'the
yellow tears of the green incense tree' come as easily to him as they
did to the young Milton. 'Come Cyprian lady into this your grove,
to the hundred-limbed company of young girls.'

We have all too little of Pindar's grave lamentations for the dead.
They summon up a wonderland of the dead. Wonderlands were
always a theme of Pindar's, and an element in his early athletic odes.
As a theme of Greek poetry they were traditional, but Pindar's
handling is special, and became deeper and more moving as he grew
old. His mystical, other-worldly side is hard for us to grasp, and
perhaps it ought not be taken in isolation. There had been visionary
poets before him, and his claim to actual visions was simple and
literal. If the 'I', the first person of his poetry, means in the eighth
Pythian Pindar himself, then one of his last poems, written at seventy-
two, recorded in passing an encounter with the divine hero Alkmaion
on the road to Delphi; Alkmaion's shrine at Thebes was beside
Pindar's house. He can speak soberly of the dead, but mystically as
well. 'The body of all men falls to overwhelming death, but an image
[or a ghost] of life is left alive, for that alone is from the gods.' His
wonderland of the dead, or of the blessed heroes, is far stranger.

> In nights like ours for ever
> and a sun like ours in their daytime
> the brave win a life without labour.

They do not put out their hands
to trouble earth or sea for an empty living.
Close to the most honoured of the gods
those whose pleasure it was to keep their word
pass days without weeping.
The others carry
a burden that should not be looked upon.
And they that have endured three times over
life in this world
life in the other world
go by the road of Zeus
to the tower of Kronos,
where Airs, the Ocean's daughters,
are blowing round the Island of the Blest,
and the flowers are gold
on earth blazing in bright trees
or water-nourished,
with these they twine their hands and these they weave;
severe Rhadamanthys is their lord
whom father Kronos keeps
to be his counsellor,
near the almighty height of Rhea's throne.
Peleus is there, Kadmos is there,
the mother of Achilles took him there
when she by praying moved the heart of Zeus.

It is as if for Pindar even Zeus has to be seen in terms of his father, Kronos, the god of the Golden Age. But his religious feelings are serious. 'Happy is he who having seen those things goes under earth: he knows the end of life, he knows the god-given beginning.' In his athletic poems the gods are in contrast to mankind. What they give is wonderful and delicious, but it will not last, and the gods are terrible as well. The achievement of one athlete on one day is all the more moving because of this divine machinery, and because of the brevity and the limits of his joy. This undertone of sadness or of emptiness is an essential ingredient in Pindar's athletic poetry. The effect of the presence of gods on the poems is multiple, it works both by connection of several kinds and by separation.

The odes are further complicated by a riddling quality. Pindar apparently assumes a huge knowledge of the characters in traditional stories. He embroiders or mediates the stories instead of telling them straight. Nestor, for example, is introduced simply as 'the Messenian'. Hippolyta trying to ensnare Peleus by trickery 'won the help of her lord, master of the Magnesians', who gets named a few lines later. Often enough the myths were locally popular, and they may at times have been requested in the commission for an ode. But the movement of syntax can also be complex and headlong, and the sentences frequently overrun the stanza, and even the series of three stanzas. There can, therefore, have been hardly a pause between stanzas; the music and singing must have been continuous. Indeed, it is hard to see where Pindar's chorus ever drew breath. The listener is drowned and lost in the strong flow of the poem, which slows down only to finger a phrase or an ornament.

> Go, sweet song, out of Aigina,
> and carry news of Lampon's son,
> Pytheas tough and strong,
> wreathed at Nemea in the all-in fight,
> who has not yet the summer in his cheek,
> the mother of the soft down on the grape.

Down on the cheeks and pubic hair separated boys from men. The records of Greek games make it clear that adolescence occurred later in ancient times than it does today. Pytheas was not fully mature, but he was already strong enough to win the all-in fighting at Nemea. That was in 485 B.C. His brother won at the Isthmus in 484 and again in 480, in the same alarming event. Pytheas had also won the boxing. Pindar's celebration ode in 480 refers to the battle of Salamis, but allusively. The Aiakidai, patron heroes of Aigina, are said to have appeared to the Greek fleet as it sailed out against the Persians. Pindar refers only to the heroes and the city itself; the battle is not precisely described.

> Now can the city of Ajax testify
> once more in battle
> by seamen raised up high,
> Salamis in the deadly thunderstorm
> of Zeus, hailstorm of death
> over unnumbered men.
> Drench thy proud words in silence:

> Zeus orders everything,
> Zeus lord of all: and in lovely honey
> these honours welcome joy of victory:
> let a man struggle and labour, let him learn
> of games from Kleonikos and his sons.

The metaphors in this early work of Pindar's are not continuous but cumulative. Is 'drench thy proud words in silence' meant to refer to rain or springwater or the sea? Each metaphor influences the next by the building up of a context, but one is not meant to linger or question these images: the storm, the hail, the drenching silence and, above all, the honey pass swiftly. Molten or flashing gold, incidentally, which I take to include honey, is one of Pindar's favourite images and metaphors. The poem begins with the Mother of the Sun 'because of whom men prize gold in its great strength', and the racing of ships at sea and chariots on land 'in the swift eddies of racing'. The battle of Salamis was a great victory, and Pindar gives full play to the strength and ferocity of the Aiakidai, Homer's heroes. But Salamis ended in a bloody massacre. 'Drench thy proud words in silence' is not only a transition; it is a deliberate and effective pause. When he wrote this poem at the age of thirty-eight, Pindar was at least on the edge of being a great poet.

His transitions are usually to be explained by the special mix of subject and image appropriate to a particular family and place. They were not always graceful, sometimes they were intended only to wind unexpectedly into some new surprise. As recently as 485 B.C., at thirty-three, he had invoked silence much more clumsily.

> ... child of a goddess whom the Sand-maiden
> bore where the sea-waves break.
> Of that wrong hazard I am shy to speak
> and how they went from that fair famous isle,
> what fate drove off the brave from land of vines:
> I cease: it is no gain
> always that truth should show
> her face and never flinch:
> silence can be the counsel of the wise.
> My purpose is to praise
> wealth and strong hands and war dressed in iron:

dig my pit long, from here I make my spring,
lightness is in my knees,
the flight of eagles hovers across seas,
and graciously to them
the lovely chorus of the Muses sang
on Pelion, Apollo among them
swept his hand on his seven-tongued strings at will,
and with his golden quill ...

The shyness and the heavy change of subject cover or rather advertise the fact that the Sand-maiden's child Phokos was treacherously murdered by Peleus and Telamon, holy heroes, who then had to leave home rapidly. Pindar moves on to the wedding of Peleus and Thetis, of which the Muses sing. The boy for whom the poem was written came from Aigina, so local stories were called for. But the pretence of changing subjects in midstream, which Pindar also uses elsewhere, and which seems intended to hold audiences agape – that is to add an immediacy, as if this highly technical and complex poetry were an impromptu performance or an amazing conversation – is to modern taste too coy a trick. And although one can sense how the sea journeys of Peleus and Telamon fit in with the Sand-maiden and the breaking waves, and the light knees echo strong hands and lead to the spring and the swoop and the sea and Apollo's hand like the eagle's swoop, yet the long jump is surely an unintentionally gross intrusion, a gratuitous image? Perhaps because it appears to us absurd in itself? Sublime poetry has to be full of amazing detail, it lives on surprise, it can topple over terribly easily. The fault is tactical. But what of the entire strategy of transition? Is it not somewhat jejune? Pindar's piety pushes him into it, we must suppose. He cannot criticize Peleus or Telamon. Still, my point is that when Pindar was older he managed these things more gently, less jerkily.

It is hardly surprising that his first obviously very grand and great poem was written for the magnificent Hieron of Syracuse, when Pindar was forty-two, for a victory in the Olympic horse-race. His odes are not in chronological order as we have them, but this extraordinary work was placed by ancient scholars as his first Olympian, though he had already composed for an Olympic victory for a young athlete when he was hardly thirty (the fourteenth). Olympia of all inter-Greek festivals had the highest prestige, and at Olympia it seems to have been horse-races and chariot-races that brought the greatest glory. Athletes in Pindar's day were thought to have almost divine powers; they were like reincarnations of Herakles the man-god, and even their statues could do miracles. But Pindar had no doubt of the immense and overriding glory and sweet success of horse-breeding kings. For Hieron of Syracuse he wrote a masterpiece.

When Sir Philip Sidney, for whom poetry is a divinely inspired fiction, the mirror of an ideal beauty, wrote that 'it is that faining noble images of vertues, vices, or what else ... which must be the right describing note to know a poet by', he might almost have had Pindar in mind. But Pindar, like most poets, entangles his poetry continually with the surface phenomena of this planet, and his gods and his other world are not an absolute beauty, but a projection of life, a recognized truth and an accepted fiction. Moralizing about divine power and justice is a separate matter for Pindar, and it is expressed in a different tone from his glorious and embellished narratives of the gods. In the first Olympian ode, all these things come together.

> Water is noblest, gold as glimmering fire
> glitters at night beyond wealth of the great:
> if you will turn to sing
> of games, O my dear heart,
> look for no hotter shining star
> than the day's sun in the high air,
> nor better than the Olympic gathering,
> whose famous hymns arise
> dressed in the wits of the wise,
> chanting Kronos' son to them that come
> to the rich blessed hearth of Hieron
> who holds the rod of equity
> over sheep-cropped Sicily,
> reaping the heads of virtues as of grain,
> in music's feast illustrious ...

These words are Pindar's introduction; he has already swept across a stanza break after the word Hieron without pausing, but he has scarcely reached cruising speed. The word I give as 'noblest' is *aristos*; it has that connotation, but it also means 'best'. The word I give as 'virtues' also means achievements, acts of valour and gallantry and championship: *aretas*, related of course to *aristos*, and in English to aristocracy. This poem is all the more untranslatable for being so brilliantly sustained at the level of wit as well as poetry; all its surprises and climaxes are calculated. He goes on:

> where we crowd to play
> round that beloved table. Therefore take
> down from its peg the Doric lute
> if Pisa's grace
> and Pherenikos' filled thy mind
> with sweetest thought,
> when by Alpheios' banks he ran
> unspurred his body sped the racecourse length,
> mingles his master with his strength,
> that king of Syracuse horses delight,
> whose fame glows bright
> in Lydian Pelops' sturdy settlement:
> whom the strong Earth-shaker loved,
> Poseidon, when ...

We have crashed another stanza barrier between strength and the king of Syracuse; Pisa is a lost ancient city that left its name to Olympia; Pherenikos is a racehorse, whose name means Bringer of Victory. Jockeys are never mentioned in these poems, and of trainers only the athletes who trained their kinsmen or their sons. 'Lydian Pelops' sturdy settlement' is the Peloponnese, and the Olympic festival is his gathering. Poor Pelops as a baby was served up for dinner to the gods by his father Tantalos, and greedy Demeter ate a piece, so the gods put him together again with an ivory shoulder. Poseidon's affair with Pelops followed. Pindar flirts disapprovingly with this intimidating group of stories. The famous ivory shoulder was on show in the shrine of Pelops in the Olympic grove in Pindar's time. The temple of Zeus had not been built.

> ... whom the strong Earth-shaker loved,
> Poseidon, when
> old Klotho drew him from the clean
> bowl with his shoulder gleaming ivory.
> Many are miracles, mortality
> speaks at times beyond the true:
> embroidered tales deceive
> with painted make-believe.

*

> Grace makes all sweet delights of men,
> gives honour, makes believable
> often what was incredible,
> and days to come are wisest witnesses.
> Proper a man should speak well of the gods,
> the less his crime.
> I shall speak of you, son of Tantalos,
> other than those before me in old time.

Pindar goes on at once to tell the story of Tantalos and his 'most innocent' banquet for the gods, at which Poseidon fell for Pelops and carried him away on golden horses to the house of Zeus, just as Zeus carried off Ganymede. Pindar has inherited from earlier poetry both his mythology and his habit of criticism, but both are highly selective. Ganymede carried off by Zeus is the subject of a famous statue, old in Pindar's day, made of painted terracotta, which, when its colours were fresher forty or even twenty years ago, was the most brilliant small object in the Olympia museum; but its colours have faded since its excavation. Ganymede as an image not only excuses Poseidon's behaviour but lends him glamour and youth. Pindar ended his tenth Olympic ode in about 474 B.C., two years later, with these words about a boy boxer:

> whom by the Olympic altar I saw win,
> beautifully built
> and at that age which once
> warded off shameless death from Ganymede
> with the Cyprian goddess.

But in the first Olympic ode Pelops disappears from earth for a time, only in order to explain how the envious neighbours invented the story of his being eaten. This theme of the search for the lost boy comes from the Homeric *Hymn to Aphrodite*, where it belongs to Ganymede. Tantalos was honoured by the gods.

> And yet he could not stomach his fortune,
> he came to harm:
> the mighty rock which Zeus hung over him
> which he for ever longs to ease away
> and is exiled from joy.

His sin was stealing the immortal food and drink of the gods. Pelops

was therefore reduced to mortality, and at once we are back with
the story of his youth and marriage. He prayed to Poseidon.

> When he came into sweet blossom of youth
> down darkened on his chin,
> his thought rose to the bride waiting for him.

Poseidon gave him winged horses and a chariot of gold, and Pelops
raced Oinomaos at Olympia, and won his daughter for a bride. 'She
bore him princes, six sons eager in courageous virtue.'

> Now in the splendour of
> sacrifices of blood
> he mingles by the ford of Alpheios,
> his tomb is busy by
> the crowded holy place, and the glory
> of the Olympic daughters looks from far
> in Pelops' racing ground
> where speeding feet contest the length,
> and bold courageous height of strength.
> The winner all his days
> shall breathe serene delicious air
> after the games: the good things of each day
> come best to men: I crown
> my man with horse music
> and with Aeolian song.

The Olympic daughters are the Olympiads, the four-year cycles of
the games. Horse music meant a special tune associated with the
heavenly twin riders, Kastor and Polydeukes. Hieron is praised for
hospitality, for knowledge of good, a sort of connoisseurship of virtue,
honour and the arts, and for power; the god (unnamed) guards him,
and Pindar hopes one day 'if the god desert thee not' to praise him
for a chariot victory by the hill of Kronos at Olympia, the one event
more glorious than mere racing, four horses being more glorious than
one. Hieron did win it in 468, but Pindar was not commissioned.
This poem ends solemnly with proverbial warnings to kings that
underline Hieron's greatness.

> One man is this way great and one man that:
> kings are the crest and height,
> look never beyond that,

> forever in this world walk on the height:
> may I keep company
> as much with victory,
> to be in art a beacon to all Greeks.

Pindar is of all poets an expert in sudden boasts, in the sudden climax and the dramatic alteration of tone. This long and remarkable poem is framed between Olympic boasts, and as usual or almost usual, Pindar's exaltation of his own art adds to the glory of the winner, it does not detract. This is essentially a poetry of performance; hence the need for continual excitement, breathtaking brilliance, constant surprise. His gods are awe-inspiring in their beauty and strength, but above all in their suddenness. 'Beside the grey sea in darkness, alone, he prayed the heavy-booming Trident-lord: and he appeared beside his feet: he said . . .'

For Theron of Akragas, a Sicilian ruler even more magnificent in his day than Hieron, Pindar told the story of the journey of Herakles to the Danube and the country beyond the north wind in pursuit of the doe with golden horns; he brought home trees to shade the Olympic grounds. The doe was magical; Pindar seems to suggest she was offered to Artemis by the nymph of Taygetos, the Spartan mountain, in place of her own virginity, when Zeus required it. The nymph became one of the Pleiades. The story is briefly, allusively handled with a series of twists and turns, and the poem ends with a number of deliberate recollections of the ode for Hieron, surely by request. In another poem for Theron, Pindar referred at some length to Oedipus and the saga of Thebes, from whose heroes Theron claimed to draw his blood. That theme suddenly modulates into the wonder-land of the dead, a passage I have already quoted. That in turn modulates into praises of Achilles and an interesting self-defence.

> He threw Hektor down,
> Troy's unconquered, unshaken column,
> handed Kyknos to death,
> to death the Ethiopian son of Dawn.
> The quiver at my arm
> has many swift arrows
> that whisper to the wise:
> but to the crowd must be interpreted.
> He knows whose blood can tell

> unlearned fools babble,
> two crows caw
> in vain against the holy bird of Zeus.
> Hold thy bow to the mark ...

It appears from ancient commentaries, and it seems not improbable, that the cawing crows who criticized Pindar for allusiveness and gnarled difficulty were the two excellent professional poets Simonides and Bacchylides, whose work I will treat in the next chapter. They were kinsmen, and rival professionals to Pindar, and in Sicily at the time. The legendary rivalries of poets before Pindar are not based on convincing evidence, though Hesiod's winning a tripod at Chalkis leaves no doubt that contests of poets did take place. But this professional competition for great commissions to which Pindar refers must have been to the poets of his day a basic fact of life. Pindar was professionally very successful indeed. He could afford at the end of his life to criticize even the mighty city of Athens, in the years leading up to the Peloponnesian war and the shaking to pieces of all Greece. He had personal connections in very many cities; the glory he gave was highly valued, and he was an honoured guest.

For Telesikrates of Kyrene, who won a race in armour, Pindar told the tale of Kyrene the herd-girl who wrestled with lions, and who

> let her sweet bedfellow
> sleep briefly brush her eyes
> before day broke.

Apollo bedded her and she bore Aristaios, hunter and shepherd, whom Earth and the Seasons made immortal. 'His name shall be Zeus and holy Apollo, delight of them that love him.' Most of this story is put into the charming and prophetic mouth of Cheiron the centaur, who gives Apollo advice. The poem was performed at Thebes and contains Theban saga as well as praises of Delphi. It ends with the Kyrenian legend of Alexidamos, who won his wife by running a foot-race – modulating, it seems, into a wedding hymn.

> He took the virgin princess hand in hand,
> led her through Nomad riders in their host.
> With rain of leaves and flower wreaths

> they pelted him.
> Many the wings of victory
> that he had won.

Sometimes Pindar is compelled 'by the rules of song' to break some story short, or so he says. Sometimes he promises to tell it another day. The truth must be that he controls his torrent of words very precisely. He is skilled at very short as well as very long sentences, and the variety of his handling, even within one poem, is part of his attraction.

I fear I may have made him sound at times like second-hand Yeats; he is really more like Spenser, but with far greater variety of tone. The poem where he most closely approaches epic, and best shows his difference from epic, is probably the fourth Pythian ode, which he wrote for Arkesilas of Kyrene, a chariot winner. The poems for horse-breeders are often richest in myth, not only because these men were the greatest patrons, but because their role in the games was less personal. He tells for Arkesilas the story of the Argonauts, which he leads into by the lesser odyssey of the origins of Kyrene and the colonization of Africa. The thin connection of blood is that Arkesilas derived his from an Argonaut, but the stories image one another. Yet Pindar spends most of this long ode on prophecies and pre-liminaries. As the Argo finally sails, another long passage records the prayer of Jason. These details are not static, they are enthrallingly told:

> The Captain on the stern
> held in his hand
> a cup of gold,
> called on the Father of the sons of heaven:
> Zeus, his spear the lightning-flash,
> on the swift rush of waves and on the winds,
> the nights, and the sea's roads,
> serene days and beloved homecoming;
> assenting thunder answered out of clouds
> and tearing through them flashed the bright lightning.
> And the heroes breathed courage again ...

Just a few verses more and witchcraft begins, the Argonauts having got through the clashing rocks to land, and into the presence of

Medeia. The rest is a mixture of exotic and charming. Jason ploughs his furrow straight with fire-breathing oxen, with undertones of an athletic event and a suggestion of winning a bride. He wins 'the fleece that glitters with the matted gold'.

> To that strong man his friends
> held out their hands
> and gathered grass to crown him with,
> and they caressed him with sweet words:
> the wizard offspring of the Sun
> told him where the gleaming Skin ...

The poem ends with an allusion to Damophilos, a kinsman of the king exiled for conspiracy, whom Pindar knew and for whom he pleads, though in tactfully riddling terms. Given the variety of ingredients, the coherence of this ode as a poem is remarkable. Its episodes are subtly and thoughtfully balanced. Maybe its African undertones hold it together.

> Atlas still wrestles with the sky,
> but Zeus immortal set the Titans free.

It is these single, sharp images, as much as the long river-rumble of Pindaric poetry, so much more easily followed by ear than by analysis, that linger in the mind.

His mixture of variety and coherence can be paralleled in the multiple subjects of archaic art, laid out in long friezes and some-times in layers of friezes like cartoons in a newspaper. One imagines that Pindar drew on things like the Chest of Kypselos at Olympia, and not only on written sources. What about the crown of grass? Is that country observation or Kyrenian custom? Atlas still wrestling with the sky is an unforgettable image of a mountain, but to Pindar Atlas was more giant than mountain. He is a poet of ancient mythology, not of Wordsworthian nature. He has the impetuous flow of Swinburne or Dylan Thomas, but with masterly restraint, and very much more to say. Each of his odes is an elegant solution of a different set of technical problems.

Probably the most famous of all his images is the eagle of Zeus, in the first Pythian ode, written in 470 B.C. when Hieron won the chariot race in the valley below Delphi, a poem performed in Sicily.

Delphi is still haunted by eagles: this one is the pet hawk on the rod of Zeus.

> Lute of gold, Apollo's pleasure
> and the flower-haired Muses' treasure,
> which the dancing foot
> hears and splendour starts,
> whose command the song obeys
> as you spin out and advance
> in the prelude of the dance:
> extinguishing the eternal fire
> of the sharpened thunderstone,
> and on the rod of Zeus the eagle sleeps
> down his side drooping his swift wing,
> of winged things king:
> you have poured out a cloud that darkens eyes
> over his crooked head,
> sweet bolt on his eyelid:
> he dozes and he heaves his supple back,
> caught in quivering song.
> The brutal war-god leaves
> his harsh and pointed spear,
> consoles his heart and rests,
> arrows of music can enchant
> the gods' daemonic minds,
> Apollo's skill enchants, and Muses with deep breasts.

These lines are followed by darker ones, with hardly a break, but only an alteration of tone. The things that Zeus hates listen to the Muses with horror and fear. Monsters under water and under the earth tremble, and Typhos the hundred-headed monster on whose shaggy chest Sicily lies is one of them, 'whom the pillar of heaven holds down, white Aitna, which all the year through suckles its biting snows'. We have modulated through landscape back to Hieron, founder of the new city of Aitna, where this poem was performed. The volcano had very recently erupted, and Pindar proceeds to handle that magnificent spectacle as if he were an eyewitness, which he seems not to have been. Typically of the divided mind of the archaic Greeks, and of his own mastery of many tones, he faces his subject with perfect directness, even though he frames it (before and after his description) with heavy mythology and a prayer to Zeus. Pure founts of unapproachable fire belch from the mountain's depths, its rivers pour down glowing smoke, red flame rolls in the dark 'and into the deep, level sea throws the rocks roaring'. The giant, creeping worm throws out fire-fountains. No other age of the world would have given us so grand a volcanic eruption in verse, and with so little nonsense; no poet but Pindar, unless Dante, in whose verse realism and the divine equally intermingle and equally draw apart, may be the one exception. I had written this chapter before reading the 1982 lecture by Hugh Lloyd-Jones, and I am delighted to see that we arrived at the analogy with Dante independently.

NOTE

A good way of testing Pindar's personal quality and his individual technique is to compare the fifth Olympic ode, which is an imitation written by someone else in Sicily under his influence, with Pindar's genuine work. It celebrates the same winner as the fourth Olympic ode, and it seems to celebrate the return home of Psaumis to Kamarina in 448 B.C. It is very strictly planned, with one short triple unit to the nymph Kamarina, one to Pallas Athene and one to Zeus. It contains a mixed metaphor of worse than Pindaric obscurity, about a river that 'welds swiftly together the high-limbed avenue of well-built halls', whether with mud or timber or otherwise no one knows. This ode is simpler and more jejunely planned than even the simplest of Pindar's celebrations, and it is less intricately woven together as a poem. Its use of proverbial maxims is a fumble: 'If men prosper, their townsmen think them wise' is neither a climax nor a transition; it recalls the most bathetic choral comments of Athenian tragedy. 'If a man waters healthy happiness ... let him not seek to be God' is a ridiculous pastiche. At its best, this ode sounds like an English adaptation of Pindar by someone like Gilbert West or Abraham Cowley. Yet it was accepted and treasured in its day as Pindar's poems were, and at least one scholar, Didymos in the first century B.C., believed Pindar had written it. But Didymos was a compiler, not a literary critic or a poet.

BIBLIOGRAPHY

C. M. Bowra, *Pindar*, 1964
C. M. Bowra, *The Odes of Pindar* (translation), 1969
Elroy Bundy, *Studia Pindarica*, 1962
G. Huxley, *Pindar's Vision of the Past*, 1975
H. Lloyd-Jones, 'Pindar', *Proceedings of the British Academy*, 1982

6

SIMONIDES, BACCHYLIDES
AND FOLK-SONG

Simonides lived from about 556 to 468 B.C. Although he was an older contemporary of Pindar, it is better to treat him after Pindar has already been considered in detail, because Pindar's poems have survived in far greater quantity, and Simonides, in spite of his seniority, his excellence and his influence, is a shadow by comparison. What we have of his work must continually be set against Pindar's for illumination. Before he began the wandering life of a professional poet, he was apparently choir-master of Apollo's temple on the island of Keos, in sight of Sounion. It may roughly be true that the new and brilliant temple architecture of the Greeks went with that new choral music and poetry which had increased so greatly by the end of the sixth century B.C. Simonides wrote paeans for Apollo and dithyrambs for Dionysos; in both cases the aim was to include lyric narrative, which was thought of as an amusement, a toy or delight of the gods. They would listen to choice poetry as they would like to own fine ornaments in their sanctuaries. The relevance of the narrative was secondary or immaterial. The stories poets told, like the stone friezes of the Delphic treasuries, were television serials for the gods, art galleries for mankind. Simonides also wrote choral lamentations for the dead and choral praises; as Ibykos adapted themes of Lesbian lyric verse to choral poetry, so did Simonides adapt the poetry of ritual lamentation, which must have been folk-poetry, and older than the *Iliad*. And he wrote drinking-songs and epitaphs of couplets, to be inscribed on stone or engraved in bronze: another kind of folk-poetry that had grown up in the shadow of Homer. He appears even to have written curses to be performed chorally.

Simonides was summoned to Athens by Hipparchos some time after 527 B.C. He was extremely successful in Athenian competitions as a composer of dithyrambs, a kind of poetry in which narrative brilliance had overwhelmed ritual meaning, rather as operatic settings overwhelmed the Roman liturgy in the eighteenth century. In one of the dithyrambs of Simonides, the hero Memnon gets buried in Syria: it is hard to attach this to Dionysos. The successful rival he seems to have displaced was called Lasos of Hermione, of whose work we have only a few somewhat ordinary lines, and references to such characters as the Centaurs and the children of Niobe. When the Athenian tyrants fell, Simonides moved to Thessaly; he spent the Persian wars in Athens, and he died in Sicily. In Thessaly he wrote celebrations of victory in the games, praise poetry and dirges for the royal families. Many epigrams and aphorisms gathered around his name, anecdotes smothered his memory like ivy; even reforms in the Greek alphabet came to be attributed to him. But the genuine fragments give a rather clear impression of his poetry.

As early as 520 he wrote for Glaukos of Karystos, a boy boxer at Olympia, born almost within sight of Keos, 'Not Polydeukes strong would have raised his hands to him, nor Alkmene's iron son' – Herakles, that is. These are undoubtedly high terms to praise a young lad, but no one seems to have objected, and one catches a glimpse of spirited good humour. Simonides seems to have been a highly original and influential poet, and the poetry of athletic celebration may owe a great deal to him and his aristocratic patrons. He was a dexterous professional, who for a fee could transform a team of mules into 'daughters of storm-footed horses'.

His melancholy was lucid and chilling. The rhythms are convincing, but the poetry is untranslatable, being made of simple words like the Common Prayer funeral service. 'Short is the strength of men, unfulfilled their cares, in a short age trouble on trouble, the same inescapable death overhangs them, since both good men and whoever may be wicked have this one equal inheritance.'

On another occasion he put the same thought not quite as conventionally.

> Being man say not what tomorrow is,
> nor seeing a happy man how long he shall be that,
> the motions of a long-winged fly are not
> so rapid as he is.

The fly sounds like a mosquito, but the point is his whizzing not his buzzing. Alkman's birds and Hesiod's hawk are 'long-winged'; can it have come by poetic convention to mean merely swift? I had supposed the destruction of coastal cities by mosquitoes and malaria was unknown to the Greeks at this time; whatever the truth is about that, the long-winged fly is nicely ominous.

The Thessalian praise or drinking-song Plato quotes in his *Protagoras* is selected for its views on morals, which may not be very seriously intended, but they have some interest: if only because they widen the repertory of heroic and convivial sentiment beyond expectation.

It is difficult for a man to become truly good with his hands and his feet and his mind, built four-square and faultless ... Nor does what Pittakos said ring well to me, wise as he was, that it is hard to be good. A god alone would have that privilege, a man has to be bad some way, in the grip of unbeatable circumstance ... but I have found and tell you this: I praise and love all who willingly do nothing shameful, but not even the gods can fight with necessity ... a man that knows justice profiting a city and is not too helpless is sound, and I shall not blame him, for the generation of fools is infinite. All things are good in which is no disgrace.

These views were not meant to be criticized abstractly; they have the function of Pindar's moral views. Probably someone is being excused, maybe for losing a battle in war or politics. Could this poem possibly be about taking the wrong side in the Persian wars?

In a few long fragments, Simonides stands out as a purely and undatably lyrical poet: 'Above his head infinite birds wing, and out of blue metallic water leap up fish with music's beauty and the song.' These lines are supposed to have something to do with Orpheus. 'They say that Virtue lives in unclimbable rocks And keeps her holy ground Not seen by human eyes Unless heart-eating sweat Streams from within: And they come to the summit of courage.' The high view of morality comes from Hesiod (*Works and Days*, 289–92); the word Virtue could equally mean courage, the quality of an athlete or an aristocrat; it is an objective, not a psychological word. Wilamowitz, to the fury of later scholars, mended a damaged place in the poem by making Virtue 'keep the holy dances of the rapid nymphs'. His suggestion seems to me jolly, although unlikely. He also wanted the brave to come to the summit by courage (literally, by manhood), not the summit of courage (or of manhood), but it is important in translation to keep nineteenth-century school overtones out of this poem. The word means courageous strength, not 'manliness'; it means being built four-square.

We know that Simonides understood the brevity of praise and the crumbling of monuments, and the fact that he has thought through the meaning of his poetry must surely be what makes it so moving. In the two long fragments he is very precise, and in the epigrams his couplets are bitten off short. He railed in verse against Kleoboulos of Lindos, a Rhodian and one of the Seven Wise Men who included Thales, Solon and Pittakos, for claiming in hexameter verse that the tomb of Midas, a bronze maiden, would last for ever. Did Kleoboulos really write the bronze-maiden poem? The earliest Greek verse epitaphs are recorded only in the late seventh century, and the earliest bronze statues that fit this poem existed no earlier; this is a long inscription, and it sounds like a sizeable statue. Still, perhaps it is worth translating the poem attributed to Kleoboulos as well as the answer by Simonides.

> I lie on Midas' grave, a maid of bronze.
> While water runs and the tall trees have leaves
> and suns arise and shine and shining moons
> and rivers flow and the sea beats the shore
> I will remain on this lamented grave
> and say to passers-by, Midas lies here.

The epitaph circulated, perhaps it was not really inscribed anywhere; Midas was a king of Phrygia and a friend of Delphi; he died by suicide in 696 B.C., but if this tomb with its poem and its bronze girl ever existed, it might be a hundred years later, I suppose. The story is terribly suspicious, and yet Simonides certainly knows the earlier poem.

> Who in his right mind would praise Kleoboulos,
> who to eternal rivers and the flowers of spring
> and to the sun's flame and the golden moon
> and the sea's turning has opposed a stone?
> All things are weaker than the gods. A rock
> can break in human hands:
> this was a fool's saying.

We shall see that these stern and vigorous verses are relevant to his own epitaphs. One of the most admired and longest pieces of Simonides is a solo aria, or part of one, about Danae and Perseus. Zeus in the shape of a golden shower of rain enjoyed Danae, and the infant Perseus was therefore thought to be her bastard by an unknown lover. She and her child were sent to sea in a wooden box, but they both survived, which is another story. The lines Simonides devoted to her have a softness of incision and a delicacy; they are utterly unusual for early Greek poetry as we have it, and without parallel even on the stage, at least until Euripides. This pathos is hard to translate into English, and the touches of archaism and cliché in Simonides make it even more difficult. It is the musical rhythms of the original that appeal, and the strange diction, the deliberate originality within a stiff convention, as with the long-winged fly:

> When in the painted chest
> the breathing wind
> and shifting surface of the deep
> struck fear in her, with not unwetted cheeks
> she flung round Perseus her loved hand
> and spoke: O child, how I suffer
> while you sleep
> and suffering lay your drowsy head
> on joyless planks bronze-riveted
> in blue night-gleam, dark air:
> and care not that the deep
> salt water sprays above your hair,
> nor for the wind's call,
> lying in your purple shawl,
> beautiful face.
> If terrible were terrible to you
> then you would turn your tiny ear.
> I say sleep, child,
> let the sea sleep,
> let unmeasured evil sleep,
> let some change of mind
> from you Zeus father come.
> If my prayer is rash
> and is not just forgive.

A word like 'bronze-riveted' is used to give epic and ominous tone: Ibykos in a piece with Homeric overtones calls the ships at Troy 'many-riveted'. It was necessary to quote this piece at some length, because we have so little ancient poetry of precisely this kind. In language it belongs to an awkward age, unsure of its convention, and in a way false, as if poetry and mythology had suffered from over-production. It prefigures tragedy and the classic restraint, the classic passion, of the next generation. Yet Simonides has never heard of rhetoric; in musical terms his poetry is perfectly genuine, as crisp and as light as a leaf. It may well be that my criticisms are over-refined or simply wrong. But the other substantial lyric poem we have by Simonides is a celebration of the Spartan dead after Thermopylai. The subject could hardly be more real. It was written for performance at Sparta, at a monument newly built, a divine heroic shrine, almost a temple. We are not to think of a modern war memorial; this is a king's tomb, a saint's tomb, but without the dead bodies.

> Of those who died at the Hot Gates
> their fate is famous, their death beautiful,
> their tomb an altar,
> their lamentation is our memory,
> they have praise not pity,
> and such a winding-sheet neither decay
> nor all-victorious time shall ruin.
> Holy to courage, this has a householder:
> the honour of Greece; Leonidas is witness,
> king of Sparta, who left one ornament:
> his courage, and a glory everlasting.

These are noble words, but is the theme not somewhat fully stated? Is the poet's problem about what he dare say, what he must say, about the precise status of the dead and about the lamentable absence of their bones, not all too apparent? But this poem is a splendid device, and it is good to be on sure ground about its authorship, because it explores a dramatic boldness and powerful, clipped wording that recur in a number of poems of the same wars whose attribution to Simonides has in recent years been quite widely questioned. It appears to me there are no substantial grounds for denying that Simonides wrote the best of these other poems; we know that some of them he certainly wrote. In a number of cases we have no absolutely hard evidence; it becomes a question of his unique personal style, and of interpreting Herodotos. Simonides was certainly imitated. So a scholarly doubt became a question, a question became a fashion, and a fashion became a scholarly game. I would wish to accept more attributions to Simonides than most recent scholars.

This small point of difference has great importance, because it is the epigrams that give him teeth as a poet. Indeed they make him, or if he did not write them, a group of unknown writers, unique in European history in the laconic gravity of his commemoration of the dead. We have splendid tomb epigrams attributed to several great poets before his time, and some of the epitaphs inscribed on stone which archaeology has recovered are as moving, but the Persian wars have added something to the poetry of Simonides. The excellent epitaphs of Anakreon are empty gestures compared to these. 'The Athenians, champions of the Greeks at Marathon, laid low the power of the gold-ornamented Persians' is not genuine Simonides; it is boastful in the wrong way, and it frigidly adapts two themes from Homer: the Trojan who dies in spite of the gold ornaments in his hair, and the duty to be a champion, a fighter in the front line. Compare the genuine style of Simonides in the first of these poems:

> This is the memorial of famous Megistias,
> whom once the Persians killed at the crossing of Spercheios,
> a prophet, who well knew then the approach of Death-spirits,
> yet did not presume to desert the chiefs of Sparta.

> The earth of glory has covered those who here died
> with you, Leonidas, king of Sparta's wide dancing floor,
> having met in war the strength of a multitude
> of arrows and swift-footed horses of the Persians.

> If to die beautifully is the greatest part of courage,
> to us of all men Fortune granted this:
> active to crown Greece with freedom we lie here
> with praise unageing.

> Tell them in Lakedaimon, passer by,
> we obeyed their orders and here we lie.

Herodotos tells us that Simonides inscribed a memorial to the prophet at his own expense: they were old guest-friends. But can he have written both the second poem and the last? If I must abandon one, then I abandon the second. The strange phrase 'earth of glory' strikes a Simonidean note, like the strange 'night-gleam' in the Perseus poem, but the whole epitaph is perhaps lamer; it lacks economy. The last couplet I have translated has in Greek by some alchemy of word-order the grandeur of a roll of thunder. Herodotos distinguishes this, with some other Persian war poems, from the epitaph for Megistias, but only because that monument was paid for by Simonides personally. He will, therefore, have signed it. The others, being state tributes, will not have been signed. 'O stranger, tell the Spartans that here we lie having carried out their commands', or 'obeyed their words', has a chilling brevity; we know of no Spartan poet capable of so perfectly expressing the grim in-souciant gallantry of the Spartans at Thermopylai. We know of no one but Simonides. His style hinges often on a simple word: as on the word 'once', or 'once upon a time', in the epitaph of Megistias.

Simonides was older than Pindar, but his kinsman Bacchylides was younger, and a lesser artist. Short of consulting the ancient critic Longinus, who is excellent here as elsewhere, one can scarcely do better than sum him up as Sir Richard Jebb did in 1904, soon after the first publication of the great Bacchylides papyrus. 'He has a value for mythology, enhanced by the fact that (unlike Stesichorus and Pindar) he did not originate or innovate. He excels in picturesque narrative: he has much grace, much charm. And he enlarges our conception of Greek lyric poetry in the fifth century just because he is a minor poet.' Bacchylides wrote between the late 480s and the early 460s; he was a professional poet, and Simonides was his mother's brother. Apart from some important commissioned work for Hieron of Syracuse, his patrons tend to be local, from the island of Keos, from Phlious near Nemea, from Aigina or Athens. One poem was written for a Thessalian for a local horse-race, one for Metapontion in southern Italy where he claimed a blood connection. His circle was far narrower than Pindar's. He liked now and then to use words like 'soft-stepping' and 'erotic-limbed'. His rhythms are musical, but not powerful. His stories are introduced without any obvious relevance, and the passages of moralizing in his work tend to banality.

But Hieron liked him greatly. Ancient critics acclaimed him as one of the nine great lyric poets. As a young man, I recollect preferring him to Pindar, and hearing Sir John Beazley, who was as much a master of Greek poetry as he was of painted pottery, express the same view. I think now there was something Victorian about his glamour; those aesthetic views about Greek art which I once felt were my own, but which really I had learnt at school, were rooted in a ninetyish, almost decadent sensibility, in which Beazley, who had been a friend of the poet Flecker, and a contemporary of C. C. Martindale who wrote *Goddess of Ghosts*, had grown up. But Bacchylides really is charming. He is a deliberately easy poet, which makes a pleasant change. One would like to have his love poems, which are lost. He is lucid, simple, obviously beautiful; those are gifts it is oddly easy to underestimate.

His meeting of Herakles and Meleager in the underworld is a fine set piece, in which he mingles emotions like a dramatist. In one of his Theseus poems, he does use some dramatic conventions, at least to the extent of a change of speakers. One thinks of the famous lyric origins of tragedy, but this Theseus poem is hardly more than dramatized monologue: it is like the Easter Sequence of the old Roman liturgy, changing persons without a change of voice. 'Dic nobis, Maria, quid vidisti in via? Angelicos testes, sudarium et vestes, sepulcrum Christi viventis et gloriam vidi resurgentis.' One dramatizes the event by carrying on an imagined conversation with an eyewitness. In the poem by Bacchylides, old King Aigeus of Athens is talking to some unnamed witness of heroic deeds of Theseus as Theseus approaches Athens. Theseus was the king's son, and the climax ought to be his recognition, but the poem is incomplete, and Bacchylides cannot be trusted not to let a story drop as suddenly as he takes one up.

Here Bacchylides is celebrating an Olympic victory of Hieron.

> ... Thrice happy he who got from Zeus
> the grandest privilege of Greece:
> who knew he should not hide
> the tower of his wealth
> in the black cloak of dark.
> The temples throng with ox-roastings,
> and the lanes throng with hospitality.
> Golden shines the glittering

> of the worked tripods that stand
> before the temple where the Delphians follow
> through the great grove of Apollo
> beside Kastalian streams.
> To glorify the god, the god,
> is the best wealth.
> Lord of horse-taming Lydia
> when Sardis to the Persians fell,
> vengeance fated under Zeus,
> Kroisos was guarded by the gold-
> sworded Apollo ...

Why this Delphic story at Olympia? According to Bacchylides, when the Lydian king attempted suicide by having himself burnt alive, 'Zeus with a black cloud put out the tawny flame' and Delian Apollo carried off the old man to the wonderland that lies beyond the north wind, because in life he gave the world's most generous presents to Delphi. The story was illustrated by an admirable painter on a vase that has survived. Its relevance is clear, however oddly Delphi is introduced here.

Bacchylides copies Pindar, but the imitations are more eccentric than the originals. Archaic story-telling in prose and verse often moves in circles; it likes to end where it began, as in this case with Apollo's sanctuary at Delphi, to which Hieron, like Kroisos, had been magnificently generous. But this habit of ring-composition, as it is called, is looser-jointed in Bacchylides; his language also has the vices of its virtues, being less intensely interwoven than Pindar's. His best poem is perhaps the story of Theseus diving for a ring to the sea-bottom, into the underwater kingdom of the sea-goddess Amphitrite, in order to prove his identity. We have an illustration of this scene by Euphronios, one of the greatest of vase-painters, on a pot in Paris, and another on the François vase in Florence, and we know that it was painted on the walls of the Theseion of Athens by Mikon in the fifth century. It is surely true that Bacchylides was a particularly visual poet, and it may be that the visual arts had a special influence on him. That would explain the sense he conveys of being an aesthete even at the suicidal fire.

It would follow reasonable convention either now or on an earlier page than this to discuss Korinna, a woman poet from Tanagra near

Thebes who wrote in dialect and was remembered later as Pindar's rival. We have pieces of two very jolly poems apparently by her, one of them a singing contest between two local mountains, Helikon and Kithairon, and the other a local topographically based legend about the river Asopos, whose daughters were seduced by gods. I cannot believe either of these could possibly be earlier than the Alexandrians, to whom we shall come. The metrical technique looks Alexandrian. The thick dialect can be paralleled then; so can the folk-song motif of the mountains, and the obscure mythology of the Asopos. Personified mountains are at least in Greek visual art a rather late convention. The text of these poems as we have it cannot be earlier than the late third century B.C. If there really ever was a Korinna, it is likely enough that her works were lost; they never reached the Alexandrian library. What we have is a talented, amusing pastiche of about 200 B.C. But while I feel sure of this, I also feel that these pastiche poems are much better than the surlier critics will allow, so I shall recall her name later among Alexandrian poets. The task of translating her is beyond me.

Another cause that merits a limited defence is to be found in another woman lyric poet, Praxilla of Sikyon near Corinth, who lived in the early or middle fifth century. She apparently wrote dithyrambs, one of them about Achilles, but the very few lines we have of hers are narrative hexameters, the metre of Homer and the Homeric hymns. She was locally famous, as the woman poet Telesilla, to us equally obscure, was famous at Argos. Praxilla was mocked for three rather good lines about Adonis, which were condemned for bathos. Indeed, the lines are preserved only to explain the proverbial phrase 'Sillier than Praxilla's Adonis'.

> I leave the sun's light which is the noblest,
> and then the shining stars and the moon's face,
> then the ripe cucumbers and fruits and pears.

Sikyos, the ancient Greek for a cucumber, is linked to the placename Sikyon, and Adonis, after all, was a garden god. Time has turned us against much that was admired by the ancient Greeks, but it has made this slight poetry more pleasurable. Praxilla is also credited with one or two minor contributions to the collection of Athenian after-dinner songs which has survived by quotation. These songs are in simple metres, sometimes Lesbian songs; they are undemanding and yet sparkling. 'Pallas Triton-born Queen Athene, set up this city and this people, keep away troubles and divisions, and untimely deaths. you and your father'; 'Health is best for mortal man, second to be born beautiful, third to be innocently rich, fourth to be young among friends.'

A certain sentimentality intrudes: in Athens 'to be young with' also means to celebrate, to have a party, with someone, and the same word means 'noble' and 'beautiful' or 'well built'. But in Greek the attractive rhythms of the latter poem make it acceptable, just as the music might alter the sense of a German student song. And one of these stanzas is an admirable lament for the dead. Interestingly, it is written from a purely aristocratic point of view, though the lost campaign was fought as early as 515 B.C., by the family of the Alkmeonidai against the tyrant Hippias after the murder of Hipparchos by Harmodios and Aristogeiton. This assassination became in retrospect the symbol of liberation and democracy, but in the Leipsydrion poem the Alkmeonidai only lament for their dead. 'Alas, Leipsydrion, betrayer of your friends, what men you destroyed, good fighters and well born, who showed then who their fathers were.' Leipsydrion was a small mountain fortress.

Harmodios and Aristogeiton were celebrated in a number of single-stanza poems and variations which sometimes get construed as a single mutilated work, but wrongly so. The number of variations is no more than a mark of their genuine popularity. 'Dearest Harmodios, you never died, but they say you are in the Isles of the Blessed, where swift-footed Achilles is, and the good son of Tydeus, Diomedes.' The mythological treatment of Kroisos by Bacchylides was written within a generation, less than seventy years after the real event. This Athenian song was composed even sooner after its event, perhaps thirty-five years after. Statues of Harmodios and Aristogeiton stood in Athens, inscribed by Simonides, before 480 B.C.: 'And a great light broke over Athens.' The head of the army, the *polemarchos*, had to sacrifice annually at their graveyard memorial, as if they were divine heroes, demigods. It is not clear when that cult began, and not clear whether the memorial really contained their ashes or bones. I assume not, since Harmodios was cut down at once by the dictator's bodyguard, and Aristogeiton died nastily after torture. The regime

survived them by several years. Is this song meant to explain the
religious worship of one whose bones were nowhere to be found?
Its phrasing is most guarded. 'You never died' fails to convey the
particle *pou*: 'it seems' or 'I guess' you did not die. 'But they say'
removes the song still further from assertion. One is saying what
one would willingly believe, and no more. Achilles seemed a historical
character to the Greeks.

> O dear Harmodios you never died:
> they say you are in the islands of the blest
> with swift-footed Achilles and great Diomedes.

In yet another version Hipparchos, who was assassinated, is named
as the tyrant. That is not true: Hippias was the tyrant and Hipparchos
was only his brother. The plot was to kill Hippias, but it misfired.
These songs contain the confusions of propaganda and of corroding
time. All the same, ramming them together as one poem (all but
one incomplete stanza which we know only from Aristophanes),
Wordsworth as a young man translated them effectively in the spirit
of 1790.

> And I will bear my vengeful blade
> With the myrtle boughs arrayed,
> As Harmodius before,
> As Aristogiton bore,
> When the tyrant's breast they gored
> With the myrtle-banded sword,
> Gave to Triumph Freedom's cause
> Gave to Athens equal laws.
> Where, unnumbered with the dead,
> Dear Harmodius, art thou fled?
> Athens says 'tis thine to rest
> In the islands of the blest,
> Where Achilles swift of feet
> And the brave Tydides meet.
> I will bear my vengeful blade
> With the myrtle boughs arrayed
> As Harmodius before,
> As Aristogiton bore,
> Towering 'mid the festal train

> O'er the man Hipparchus slain,
> Tyrant of his brother men;
> Let thy name, Harmodius dear,
> Live through heaven's eternal year;
> Long as heaven and earth survive
> Dear Aristogiton, live;
> With the myrtle-banded sword
> Ye the tyrant's bosom gored,
> Gave to Triumph Freedom's cause,
> Gave to Athens equal laws.

I have altered 'myrtle-branded' to 'myrtle-banded', conjecturing that a mistake of the pen or the printer has confused Wordsworth's intention. Or can he have thought 'myrtle-branded', which seems to me unintelligible, might have the sense of 'myrtle-brandished'? The principal fault of his version is a failure to detect the intimacy of the Greek, but this deficiency has a compensating advantage, and his poem is a formal republican hymn, splendidly resonant and spirited. Some of the poems in the same Athenian collection are little jokes, others as light as snowflakes.

> Would I were a beautiful ivory lyre,
> and beautiful boys carried me to the dancing-line.

> The sow has one acorn, but wants to get another,
> I have one beautiful girl, but I want to get another.

> Drink with me, celebrate with me, love with me, wear a
>   garland with me,
> Go crazy with me crazy, be sober with me sober.

They are like Spanish *coplas* or Cretan *mantinades*, songs which are essentially impromptu and which one can hear fresh on the lips of their makers to this day. They are short, traditional variations, responses to a challenge to sing. No doubt they depend on wine and atmosphere, but then they flare up like fireworks for a moment or two, and one is glad of the stroke of fortune that preserved them. They are the last leavings of a tradition that goes back to Homer. When Hermes created the first lyre from a tortoise, 'then the god sang a fine chant, making it up as he went along, like lads who dare each other at a revel: the tale of a god and a sandalled nymph. And as he sang one thing, he had the rest in his mind.' Some of the Athenian songs still have a narrative residue. Some have a named author, though the names leave us little the wiser. They are on the edge of folk-song in spite of their literary influences. In the history of Greek literature, a work of art, a song or a tune by Alkaios or Alkman, could be so popular as to live for centuries, and become something close to folk-song.

We have some genuine folk-songs and work-songs of the ancient Greeks. 'Grind mill, grind; Pittakos had to grind, though he was king in great Mytilene' and 'Send a big sheaf, send a sheaf' are working chants where the rhythm of work dictates the metre, as in 'Long John, he's long gone', a rail hammering song. At this stage of human development the rhythms of work underlie the rhythms of dancing and of music, and the simplest *metra* of Greek lyric poetry are audibly based on them. We even have the words of a few ancient children's games, like modern counting rhymes or skipping rhymes. 'I shall hunt a brazen fly. You will hunt, you will not take.' Some of the words have the same surrealism, the same unexplained or lost meaning that the Opies have studied in modern children's games.

> Tortoise, what are you doing in the middle?
> I spin wool and saffron of Miletos.
> What was your offspring doing when he died?
> He leapt into the sea from white horses.

Is the tortoise a turtle, and are the white horses a riddle for the waves, as they might be in English? A sea-turtle might bring what a ship might bring from Miletos. But the four lines retain their freshness and their strangeness: one is glad to be defeated by them.

One ancient folk-song offers an astonishingly close analogy with the children's collecting songs of nineteenth-century England, indeed of most of nineteenth-century Europe, including Greece. A Cornish version, used on the Monday before Shrove Tuesday, goes like this.

> Nicka, nicka, nan;
> Give me some pancake and then I'll be gone.
> But if you'll give me none
> I'll throw a great stone
> And down your doors shall come.

The formula is more briefly stated in the children's cry on the eve of Hallowe'en, 'Trick or treat', which used to be common in

Wisconsin and is now to be heard again in the English villages where perhaps it began. The ancient Greek version comes from Rhodes. As a folk custom it appears to have survived the Middle Ages and the Turks.

> The swallow has come, has come,
> bringing fine seasons
> bringing fine harvest
> white on his belly
> and black on his back.
> Hand us a fruit cake
> from your rich house,
> and a can of wine
> and a net of cheese.
> Swallow wants some crusts
> and some polenta.
> Shall we go or shall we get it?
> Yes, if you give it. If not we won't stop.
> We'll take your door-frame or your door,
> or else your wife who sits inside,
> she's small, we'll carry her easily.
> As you give so may you get.
> Open up. Open the door to the swallow.
> We are not old men, we are little children.

This sinister and charming piece deserves a moment's attention because it indicates that the roots of poetry were in popular imagination and in folk-song as much in ancient times as they are today. Greek being if not a dead at least an utterly transformed language spoken by rather few Europeans, it is all too easy to take too academic a view of even the early origins of literature, and to forget the common language and the experience of life on which poetry must have drawn. We have just a few snatches of popular and anonymous poetry, but we ought to take them into account. The great master-pieces to which we shall soon turn were trees that grew in a wood, they were not 'miracle-bred out of the living rock' as one is tempted to imagine.

> Where are my roses? Where are my violets? Where's my lovely parsley?
> Here are your roses. Here are your violets. Here's your lovely parsley.

Those are the haunting words of a popular dancing game, a folk-dance. The words are still haunted by the ghost of their music, much more so than great poetry maybe, because the music was simpler. Only in the lyrics of Aristophanes, of all educated poetry, do we catch the tone again.

Finally, here is an aubade, like 'Amorous Sylvie' in English. This is Lokrian; I am not able to date it, and I am inclined on scattered evidence to call it a folk-song. It was obviously a dramatic popular love-song of the kind all nations have; it was never part of 'literature', properly so-called. It was a local dialect poem, or an imitation of one, but I am inclined to think it genuine.

> O what's the matter? Don't betray me please,
> get up before he comes,
> he'll do you some great harm
> and me poor wretch.
> Day has broken.
> Can't you see the light at the window?

Here we could be in almost any century. The progression of poetry is not a question of a succession of ages, but of what is thrown up from many different levels into the constantly changing formal structures which history and social history determine, and of what is thrown up from many levels into the work of an individual genius.

BIBLIOGRAPHY

C. M. Bowra, *Greek Lyric Poetry*, 2nd edition, 1961

A. R. Burn, *The Lyric Age of Greece*, 1960

D. A. Campbell (ed.), *Greek Lyric Poetry* (selection), 1967

R. C. Jebb, 'Bacchylides', Proceedings of the British Academy I, 1904

R. C. Jebb (ed.), *Bacchylides*, 1905

F. G. Kenyon (ed.), *The Poems of Bacchylides*, 1897

P. and I. Opie, *Lore and Language of Schoolchildren*, 1959

P. and I. Opie, *Children's Games in Street and Playground*, 1969

D. L. Page (ed.), *Lyrica Graeca Selecta*, 2nd edition, 1975

M. Platnauer (ed.), *Fifty Years (and Twelve) of Classical Scholarship*, 1968, pp. 72–3 and fig. 6

7

AISCHYLOS

Greek tragic drama had many elements of ritual and was performed only at festivals of Dionysos. A chorus of twelve Athenians, fifteen in the second half of the fifth century, with two or three actors, wearing archaic masks and a dress that became more elaborately stagey as time went on, enacted an epic or heroic story with dancing, about which the little information we have is probably misleading, and with original music sung by the chorus between scenes. Three tragedies were normally performed in a series, all by one poet on one day, and they ended with a lighter-hearted offering called a satyr play, which we shall consider separately. So the story might be divided into three parts, which is what happens in the *Oresteia* of Aischylos, the only complete trilogy, as they are called, to survive. There are exceptions to almost every rule I have mentioned.

Scenes of violence occurred always off-stage; that is probably due to a highly formalized acting tradition. Prometheus chained and Ajax falling on his sword are exceptions to this rule, and there were others. Morality was severe and proverbial. The tragic momentum of events, the sense of tragic necessity and of tragic consequences, the conception of the hero as a man challenging nature or the gods and hungry for calamity, the working of curses and fulfilment of prophecies, the ironies and the intense seriousness of Greek tragic poetry, all derive from epic. Tragedy is an urban substitute for epic poetry; epic poetry already dramatizes, it is already tragic in the loose sense of the word. The speeches of messengers, which remained an essential feature of tragedy, were virtuoso performances of verse narrative; they can even be lies, tales told almost for their own sake, like the lying story Odysseus told the swineherd.

Tragedy is an Athenian art. It was first performed in the market-square of Athens, with a cart as a background; probably the actors came in from the country to honour the god in Athens. Performances were not without touches of realism, which seem to have increased with time, but the style of the ancient productions, the sense of theatrical time and the pace of development of the plot, appear to have been determined by music, by the chorus with its movements and counter-movements. The effect was immensely grand, and the physical background mattered very little. When the round theatre of Athens was built under Perikles, it was essentially a circle cleared for dancing and marked by a ring of big stones, much like a threshing-floor, with room for the audience on wooden benches in a hollow of the hillside. The stage, even in its minimal form of a platform with the simplest architectural background, came even later, I believe. A rocky outcrop on one side intruded for many years into the acting space and was evidently useful to producers.

The technique of the Athenian dithyramb, the choral celebration of Dionysos to which Pindar and Bacchylides and Simonides contributed, had an influence on the tragic poets, and they on it. The *Suppliant Women* of Aischylos, not a very early play, is like a dithyramb scarcely modulated into drama. But the dithyramb went on to develop in its own way, becoming heavier and more elaborate, with cascades and detonations of musical figures. On late-fifth-century tragedy like that of Agathon it was an appalling influence. Music altered, poetry altered, and the tragic chorus lost its way. As Plato taught later, when music alters the state itself suffers metamorphosis.

Not all tragic stories end badly, though they almost all entail calamity for the hero. The gods impose a solution, usually awe-inspiring rather than attractive. But they have a polytheistic, secular streak. They are strongly rooted in Homeric epic. These are not divine moral spectacles like a Noh play. Tragedy in the sense of tragic theatrical performance, which raises special expectations of a tragic climax from its first words and opening tones, and fulfils them by the action it represents and the force of its language, was a Greek invention. European dramatic tragedies derive from it. There is something complete about a tragedy, and one can see why Aristotle wrote that by the end of the fifth century B.C. tragedy had 'attained its nature'. It existed as a public spectacle at Athens by about 500, and within its hundred years we can trace a development, an extension of dramatic means and devices, an accumulation of excitements, something like the life-cycle of a flower, an expansion and a withering but hardly an evolution.

It was a public art, supported by the state and organized as a competition for public honour and a prize, so we should expect a headlong competitive development from year to year. Sometimes we do sense something of the kind, particularly in the bold devices of Aischylos and the elaborate dramatic effects of late Euripides, but rich as our surviving material is, it remains insufficient to make this the most useful approach to the plays; the complete plays we have are scattered over a century, and they are nearly all by three poets: six or perhaps seven by Aischylos, seven by Sophokles, seventeen by Euripides, the anonymous *Rhesos* and one satyr play. This does not reflect the relative success of the tragic poets in the theatre, or their real merit, but rather the taste of later antiquity for the rhetorical flair and emotional warmth of Euripides, and perhaps for a certain operatic extravagance in his late plays, into some of which extraordinary lines and even scenes were introduced after his death to tickle the declining taste of a later age. In the same spirit pageants and processions were introduced into revivals of Aischylos in the fourth century or later. There was no official collection of the texts of Aischylos, Sophokles and Euripides until the late fourth century. And when all this is said, the survival of more than a basic collection of nine Euripidean plays has been a freak of chance.

Tragedy in its genuine life was bounded by the social and political changes that utterly transformed the city and society of Athens in the course of the fifth century. It flourished in the confident youth of the Athenian democracy, though by the Persian wars in 490 B.C. Aischylos was already producing plays, and theatrical festivals were already an institution. Throughout that century, democracy extended and state-regulated patronage increased. The rich were selected to compete for honour in mounting the tragedies just as they were directed to build and equip ships. The last great tragic poets died about the time of the fall of Athens at the close of the century, and when Athens revived, the new tragic dramatists appear from their surviving fragments to have been minor poets of comparatively small talent. It may also be relevant that a new code of values then prevailed. The noble and rich were no longer so anxious to compete for glory, because wealth was measured no longer in prestige but in coined money. Perhaps the influence of professional teachers of rhetoric and sophistry, and the new zest for philosophy, may have blasted tragic poetry at the roots, but that is very doubtful.

The truth probably is that the deaths of Sophokles and Euripides in 406 not only marked the end of an age in the Athenian theatre but made that end inevitable. Euripides and Sophokles were the greatest poets alive and they were very old men. The only other promising tragic poet of whom we know anything at that time was Agathon, born about 448 B.C., who went away to Macedonia with Euripides as the shadows darkened in Athens, and died soon after him. Anyway, his verse appears from the criticism of Aristophanes to have been terribly overloaded and overembellished. His choral poetry was no longer relevant to the rest of the drama; it was an independent 'poetical' interlude. That is the climax of a process one can see at work earlier in the century. It is more interesting that Agathon is said to have dropped mythology, which was already subjected to surprising variations by Euripides, and to have based at least one tragic production on an original fiction.

The classic form of the tragic drama was less stiff than we are inclined to think, and innovation must always have been an essential element in dramatic effect. The theatre does not generate pure art-forms, because its origins are mixed. Most of the speeches were in iambic verse, a technique the Athenians had mastered at least as early as Solon. But the choral lyrics had an archaic colouring and some touches of traditional lyric dialect. The actors at certain moments sang lyric arias and there were lyric scenes and lyric conversations. The poets composed their own music; one would greatly like to know how they taught it to the actors and the chorus.

The dance movements seem to have been traditional and austere. Tibetan sacred dances filmed some years ago by Prince Peter of Greece are said to furnish an analogy, but the treatment of dancers in Greek vase paintings gives at least a strong if static impression of flowing and acceptably beautiful movement. All modern attempts to recreate the ancient tragic conventions in the theatre have failed more or less disastrously. The ritual origins, and, if such a phrase makes sense, the ritual meaning of tragedy (Can the meaning of an ancient ritual ever be so precise? Is it ever articulate?) have often been probed in vain. We sense only their shadow, and we can point only to groups and families of ideas and institutions which the pressure of dramatization has brought out now here, now there on the surface of the text. Almost all we have is the words, and in the Greek tragic theatre the words were extremely important. From the remotest seat at Athens or at Epidauros, one can hear every tragic whisper.

Perhaps it is worth saying what little more can be said about ritual. The Greeks were both a pastoral and an agricultural people: they had gods who arose from growth and the year's cycle, and gods who were encountered in wild country. Their stories were a dense abundant mass of folk-tales interwoven with simple religious practices and with the great epics. One way of ending a tale told to a child at Athens, as we say 'and so they lived happy ever after' and Greeks today say 'and we live happier than them', was 'and so the story came true'. Many tragedies of Euripides have a similar ending, and the fulfilment of obscure prophecy enters deeply into the narrative sense of Sophokles. It is such simple forms of narrative and of poetry, including Homer's, that give tragedies their atmosphere of ritual coherence. To pick out and dramatize a single story is to unify and to formalize it. Once that is done in front of an audience, then the audience judges the story more objectively than it would judge an epic. We come more critically to the behaviour in *Murder in the Cathedral* than to that in *Paradise Lost*. In the theatre every audience is a critic. It judges a version of its own institutions, it judges the mythical history and meaning of Athens, it judges even the judging gods. Drama is an initiation, as it had always been.

The traditional history of Athenian dramatic festivals began with Thespis under Peisistratos in the late thirties of the sixth century. He came from Ikaria, a village near Athens with a sanctuary of Dionysos where the god is supposed to have given the vine to Ikarios, who was then murdered by drunken villagers and honoured as a divine hero: an active ghost who needed to be placated, who acted much like a village saint in southern Italy in the last century. We know little about Thespis or in what sense he 'invented' the tragic drama or devised or introduced its conventions, but there is no doubt about his real existence and public performances. The text of his plays that circulated later and of which we do possesss a few lines is credibly reported to have been a forgery. The ancient lists of festivals and

winning poets inscribed on stone do not pretend to go back beyond
510 B.C.; they record the state patronage of the democracy. Most
of the early recorded names are obscure to us.

Choirilos, who was writing by 520, composed an *Alope*; she was
a local Athenian heroine, who bore to Poseidon his son Hippothoon,
one of the ten heroes after whom the Athenian tribes were named
under the reforms of Kleisthenes at the very end of the sixth century.
One would like to know the date of his *Alope*. Phrynichos, who won
his first prize around 510, wrote as Aischylos did about the daughters
of Danaos, about the fate of Meleager (a Homeric story), and about
Alkestis, as Euripides did. In his *Fall of Miletos*, he dramatized
contemporary history. Miletos fell to the Persians in 494 B.C. He was
fined heavily for reminding the Athenians of their griefs. In his
Phoenicians he treated the more acceptable modern subject of the
defeat of the Persians at Salamis. Some almost conclusive, or at least
highly probable evidence connects both these productions with the
policy and patronage of Themistokles. The *Phoenicians* must have
been the ·model for the *Persians* of Aischylos, whose patron was
Perikles. Some notes on the plot of the *Persians* tell us that Phrynichos
opened his play with a eunuch reporting the defeat of Xerxes while
he set out thrones for the royal council of Persia, presumably the
chorus. The two plays have virtually the same first line, but
Aischylos altered the eunuch's iambic verse to a lyric chant, and
set his own scene at the tomb of Dareios where he intended to produce
a ghost. Phrynichos' handling seems naive and free and perhaps less
solemn, less intensely dramatic.

We have hardly enough of the work of Aischylos to trace his
development as a tragic poet. Until the recent discovery of an ancient
record that gave some exact dates, scholars assumed that the
Suppliants with its simple, apparently 'primitive' structure, and its lack
of dramatic action, must be very early. Yet similar observations might
have been made about the first two thirds of the *Agamemnon*, in which
nothing much happens but the distant fall of Troy. Both are the
opening plays of trilogies. Aischylos begins slowly and with poetry,
he establishes an epic dignity and depth, and an entire past, an
entanglement of myth and inheritance and consequences. He raises
the most serious issues early and plainly. The air shivers with
thunderbolts before the first rumble of thunder. The *Suppliants* was

produced in 463 B.C., in competition against Sophokles. It may of course have been the revision of an old text; it might even owe something to Phrynichos. But both in art and in literature, the Archaic Age lasted longer than we were brought up to believe, and the classic moment was shorter – less than a lifetime.

A similar problem of incomplete evidence overshadows recent discussions of the *Prometheus*. Oliver Taplin has offered strong and honest reasons for rejecting its authenticity. Mark Griffith has subjected it to intense scrutiny, and by a masterly accumulation of arguments from language, structure, verse technique and so on, builds a far more convincing case than previously existed that there is something wrong with the *Prometheus*: that it was falsely attributed to Aischylos. Seldom has such a stern view been so widely and strongly supported; nor have I seen any published criticism full enough to demolish his thesis. And yet I still think Aischylos wrote the *Prometheus*, a masterly play, and I believe some other pockets of muttering and resistance hold out against what is now the victorious view.

It is not possible for anyone but a great expert fresh from years of specialized study to marshal the full case against the valuable work of Mark Griffith, or in anything less than a long article. Briefly, my own case would be that he puts too much pressure on features thought to be unique, given what a small proportion of the plays of Aischylos survive. A papyrus fragment of Aischylos discovered since he wrote has already removed one such example. Then, I doubt the value of accumulation in arguments of this kind: it would take a huge number of oddities to make a doubt, and no number of mere doubts can make a conclusive case of forgery, particularly in the case of so surprising an author. The only knock-down arguments are linguistic, and by those I was not convinced. Griffith himself puts more weight on style and structure, and his case is strong. But with greater inward diffidence than I have well expressed, I must treat *Prometheus Bound* as the genuine work of Aischylos. I am inclined to put down its oddities to its being an older play reworked.

But we should begin any serious study of Aischylos with the *Oresteia*. In three tragedies he enacts the murder of Agamemnon by his wife on his return from Troy, the revenge murder of that murderess and her lover by Agamemnon's young son Orestes, and the pursuit of Orestes by the Furies, his judicial absolution at Athens, and the conversion of these terrible goddesses by Athene to become the underground protective powers of the earth of Athens. The story is based on Homer, on a number of local religious cults and the stories told about them, and on the physical survival of the ruins of Mycenae. Something is made of the alliance of Athens with Argos against Sparta, gratuitously from the point of view of the plot; Athenian institutions are given heavenly sanction; there are resonant and solemn sentences about society and its links, and conservative sentences about public morality, but the political colouring of the last play, which is democratic, is not the whole message or principal momentum of the trilogy. It is only one of the moral perspectives that open at the end like partings between clouds. A tragedy is played out, a curse is reversed, natural order is restored, a family saga unfolds, and from all of it, from all history and mythology, the fall of Troy, Agamemnon's murder, Apollo's action, and the quarrel of the older and the younger gods, Athens arises like Haydn's 'new-created world'.

The story arose from a typical family-revenge saga, with consequences and repetitions spilling over from one generation to the next. It is curious that Agamemnon's wife was orginally one of three disastrous sisters, Nemesis, Helen who caused the Trojan war, and Klytaimestra who murdered Agamemnon. In epic poetry of many traditions, and Norse saga, it is women who cause trouble. But Aischylos is almost unconscious of the origins of the curse, which goes back to the obscure Pleisthenes; his characters are figures in a web already woven long ago. At different moments different moral aspects of the story are exploited. Agamemnon had sacrificed his own daughter to the gods, he had looted Troy, he was a proud king and he trod on purple; he brought home the prophetess Kassandra to be his mistress and his slave. But the whole moral weight of this tragedy rests on Klytaimestra.

She is a terrifying and isolated heroine. Her lover enters as almost an afterthought, and plays an even smaller part in the second play. Is he there to take some share of guilt away from her, or just because the story was after all Homeric? In Homer he was much more important. The watcher on the roof at the beginning of the *Agamemnon* derives perhaps from the watch kept on the tower of

Aigisthos in the *Odyssey*. Homer's Agamemnon had left a family retainer, a poet and singer, to watch his queen, and Aigisthos had put this poet on a deserted island to die. Aischylos drops that motif. He concentrates on the murderous queen. The technique of his verse is a simple and bold strength, a cumulative power of rather bare but bold imagery, and an ability to make familiar things the most ominous of all: the buzzing of bees, the procession of serenaders, the family guest, cattle, a purple cloth. The *Agamemnon*, like *Prometheus*, makes a powerful effect out of a strange feature of archaic poetry that can be traced through the longer Homeric hymns to the *Iliad*: the long, geographic catalogue in verse. The same device occurs in the *Cyclops* of Euripides. From beacon to beacon across the entire Greek world, flame answers to flame, 'because the city of Troy has fallen, so says the messenger of fire at night'. The naming of the beacons is iambic, like a messenger speech; it is the first long speech of Klytaimestra. Aischylean character is a projection of dramatic grandeur and simplicity, and a function of bold, simple action; it does not exist for its own sake. Even its subtleties are bold and simple: Kassandra's death scene, for example. But Klytaimestra is unforgettable.

We have more than one serviceable English version of the *Oresteia*, including a posthumous and unrevised but very powerful version by Robert Lowell. The most useful is the clear translation by Hugh Lloyd-Jones, with lucid, unpretentious introductions to the three plays in which every word is well weighed. Oliver Taplin's commentary on this and all the plays in his *Stagecraft of Aeschylus* is a new foundation for Aischylean studies, and one of the most serious and interesting contributions to the understanding of the Classics to have appeared in English for many years. But it is a positive advantage not to have read most modern discussions of these famous plays, and not to have seen most modern productions. Aischylos is a poet of great dramatic grandeur, but he is terribly simple. Even the simple building that formed the background of the stage did not exist until late in his career, when Perikles set up the theatre of Dionysos. The *Oresteia* is the masterwork of his old age; it was produced in 458 B.C. But one should notice that we have none of his early work. The earliest is the *Persians* in 472. The *Seven Against Thebes* and the *Suppliants* belong to the sixties, and the *Prometheus*, supposing that to be genuine, later still, it seems.

Lowell's version catches an appalling epic severity in the early chanted lyrics of the *Agamemnon*. Aischylos uses rhythms that recall Homer's, and his omens owe more to old poetry than to life.

> I know the omen of the angry birds
> hurled Agamemnon and Menelaus
> like a spear at Troy – two thrones, one mind!
> Two eagles came to our kings,
> one white-tailed, the other black.
> They lit on the spear-hand of the palace.
> Everyone saw them. They killed a hare.
> Her unborn young were bursting from her side.
> Cry death, cry death, but may the good prevail.
>
> Then Calchas, the prophet of the army, cried:
> 'The eagles are the sons of Atreus feasting
> on the hare. In time our armament
> shall fall on Troy, and butcher its rich
> herds of people, but let us fear
> the gods lest they loosen the iron claw.
> There's a goddess, who
> is sick of the eagles' banquet. She pities
> the unborn young and the shivering mother.'
> Cry death, cry death, but may the good prevail.

One by one, Aischylos plays a series of strong cards at the beginning of this trilogy, and gradually they come together in the mind. His Justice is fearful and his Zeus is stark. One was taught at school that this poet was a powerful and liberating theologian; but nothing is liberating in Aischylos except his poetry; he hardly adds to the repertory of things said about the gods, except in his powerful wording: and that indeed is liberating. The translation I offer is verbally accurate, but misses his solemn musicality.

> Zeus, whoever Zeus may be, if he
> is pleased so to be called,
> by this I speak to him:
> I find no likeness though I weigh
> all things in the scales but Zeus,
> if I must truly throw
> useless weight from my mind.

And now not even he who once was great
who with his fighting courage swelled,
he shall not be spoken: he once was:
and he that was born then
was thrown and he has gone.
Who gladly cries Zeus champion
will hit the centre mark of thought:

who has put men on the road to be wise
by the authentic law
to learn by suffering,
and painful memory drips
like sleep into the heart
and those unwilling have learnt to be wise;
maybe the blessing of those gods by force
throned on the dreadful steering-bench.

The second stanza refers to the grandfather of Zeus and to his father. This is not a climax of the play, and by no means the only attitude to Zeus or to the gods that Aischylos suggests. It is just one of the astonishing series of set pieces with which he sets a mood, and transforms a squalid domestic killing repulsive to Athenian citizens into an action of awe-inspiring horror. The murder is followed by bitter mockery, and Kassandra's death adds a further dimension. The revenge of Orestes in the second play is set among powerful scenes of grief and of prayer, and at its climax he runs away in horror, pursued by the invisible Furies. In the third play the Furies are visible. They are old and terrible women who snuffle like dogs. The legend that they caused a real panic in the audience and that pregnant women miscarried is based only on the text of the play, which really is frightening. Lowell catches their tone.

This smell of blood is sweet and comforting;
her blood flows over the place he stands on.
Nothing will wipe it away.
His hands cannot be clean,
until his lifeblood has joined his mother's.
Drop by drop, we will suck it from him.

The closing scene which reverses the nature of the Furies is a triumphant and to my mind convincing piece of poetry. As a spectacle it must have been spare but magnificent, and one must assume that its music made it overwhelming. Oliver Taplin has done much to strip away irrelevant and undramatic spectacles from the plays of Aischylos; he has even removed one to which I admit with shame I was once attached: Zeus in a lost play weighing the souls of two heroes in the balance. But what remains has all the greater power. We must acknowledge that the resolution of the *Oresteia* was both musical and visual; those elements exist in the text only in ghostly form. It was Aischylos, we are told, who added the second actor, thereby inventing full dramatization, and in old age adapted the third from Sophokles; and it was Aischylos who invented the trilogy. But no later poet used the chorus so fully or with such effect, and the *Oresteia* is the only complete trilogy we have.

We must face some of the problems of *Prometheus*. Some scholars have dated its spectacular effects as late as the forties or the thirties. To begin with, Force and Hephaistos chain Prometheus to a rock at the ends of the earth, by the decree of Zeus, because he befriended mankind and stole, as Force says to Hephaistos, 'your flower, brightness of all-working fire' to give it to mankind. Critics dislike the vindictive and all too human Zeus of this play, but we lack its resolution in which Prometheus was set free. It is as if we lacked the transformation of the Furies. The simple and bold quality of the conception has been dismissed as Wagnerian grandiosity, wrongly in my view. When the gods desert Prometheus, he speaks and chants alone for forty lines. He is comforted by the winged Okeanides, daughters of Ocean, the chorus of this play. There is a foolish controversy about how they arrive 'with quick wings convoyed by swift-carrying airs'. In a winged cart perhaps? Eduard Fraenkel dismissed this as the *Okeanidenomnibustheorie*, and wished to substitute elegantly designed individual wheeled chairs sprouting wings from their hubs like flying invalid chairs, which he found beautifully drawn on an Athenian vase. Oliver Taplin speaks with scorn of the chorus descending on strings like pantomime fairies. But all this is taking a dramatic poem with ridiculous literalness. The flight through the air was only in words, like the premature births that the Furies caused. No doubt it was musical also. It coincides, or nearly so, with a fashion for sculptures of flying figures on temple roofs at Athens. But the chorus in my production would enter like any other chorus.

The daughters of Ocean are followed by Ocean himself, mounted, it seems, on a griffin. I think the mechanical animal flew but not the actor. Most of the play consists of long discussions, and yet its effect is dramatic, even in the modern theatre. It is like a restrained thunderstorm, and its ending is the coming of the bird that must consume Prometheus. He has not submitted to Zeus, and one's sympathies are with him. Of course, there is bound to be a compromise; we are told only that Prometheus knows a secret. The secret apparently was that Thetis, with whom Zeus proposed to couple, was fated to bear a son mightier than his father. When Zeus was told the secret, as must have happened in a later play, he married off Thetis to Peleus, and she bore Achilles. Otherwise Zeus would have been overcome by his own son as he overcame his own father, and as his father overcame his grandfather. The same violence of succession was traced in the *Agamemnon*, in pointed contrast with the story of Orestes. In *Prometheus*, Hermes is the messenger of Zeus.

> You, sophist, overbitter to your harm,
> sinner to gods and honour of mortals,
> you, thief of fire, I speak to you.
> The father bids you tell of what marriage
> you boast, that shall fling him out of power:
> and this without riddles, and word by word.
> Prometheus, put no double roads to me.
> You see Zeus has no softness for your kind.

Prometheus in chains is still a formidable god. Suffering is objective and the gods are legendary. Prometheus no more owes an inward or a spiritual submission to Zeus than any human being does to any Greek god. One must not impose Christian views either on Prometheus or on Zeus. They both fight for their honour, which is to them a supreme value, as it is to archaic Greek society; that is an assumption not a statement of the play. Its centrepiece is the prophecy of the wanderings of Io, tormented with a gadfly by Hera because Zeus loved her. This treatment of the ends of the earth and the mythical Asian countries where she must go is not only thrilling in itself, though as Fraenkel pointed out the lines have no intention of geographical accuracy; it is also in keeping with the fundamental conceptions of the play, the wisdom and knowledge of Prometheus, and the origins of our world.

... there storm-driven by many wandering ways,
 but understand that in the future time
 that sea-gulf shall be called Ionian,
 and for mankind your journey's monument.

It is as if the Greek world were being created. She has already been told that on the banks of the Nile Zeus will touch her and give her peace. She will be the mother of the race that will come to Argos in the *Suppliants*. Herakles will be a descendant of hers. She plainly has a certain amount in common with Prometheus himself, and she weaves his action into the future history of mankind. I am inclined to believe, although hesitantly, that the idea of human progress was not unknown to this writer. I find the play a strange and surprising, but also a splendid entertainment.

Its authenticity has been doubted on and off since the 1850s. Its oddest feature of all is its ending in storm and earthquake and air and şea stirred up together, the thunderbolt of Zeus and the cry of defiance. I do not think we need imagine any Wagnerian sinking into the earth. That misconception is in no way authorized from the text; it seems to have arisen from an ancient scholarly note that 'the thunder breaks and Prometheus disappears'. We should think of words and of music, not of literal stage machinery. The same is true I suppose of the fire and earthquake in the *Bacchai* of Euripides. But I have no idea how Prometheus got off the stage. I wish at such moments that I could agree with Mark Griffith.

Seven Against Thebes is one of the finest and most sadly neglected of the works of Aischylos. This was the last play of a trilogy, the fulfilment of a curse and the third stage in the family saga of Oedipus and his father. Seven companions have come to fight against the city of Thebes because the two sons of Oedipus have quarrelled. The action when it comes is swift. 'O proud destroying Death-fates and Furies, that have consumed the race of Oedipus, from stem to stern.' The chorus play a less important part than usual except in lamentation. Fifth-century critics noticed in this tragedy only the presence of war, 'Ares, the Killer, and blood-loving Fear'. This presence is indeed real, and in an atmosphere we can neither recapture nor perhaps imagine, those clashes of arms must have had great power. We know that many of the audience had experience of war, and we should remember the contemporary Megarian gravestone of a man who 'broke off his spear seven times in the body, and lived an innocent life'. Aischylos himself fought at Marathon, and that battle was the only boast he recorded in the epitaph he wrote for his own grave.

As the play opens the king broods and a messenger reports as his brother and his enemies approach. He encourages his people and the chorus of citizens broods in its turn. Then in a series of short formal scenes, separated each time by five lines of their comment, a messenger describes the seven champions, and seven times the king answers. This austere structure takes us more than half-way through the play. The crucial narrative role of this messenger is unique in tragedy; the structure of the play is an innovation of simple originality. Aischylos handles the formal structure of plays with the same freedom he handles everything else.

> The curse of Oedipus has boiled over,
> visions and phantasms of sleep come true.

The messenger reports the death of the king and his brother at one another's hands. 'So the one god was common to them both, he has extinguished their unhappy race. And we have ground both to rejoice and weep.' As for the quarrel over Thebes, that nightmare is over. 'And they will have what earth they get for grave, carried by father's prayers to evil fates.' The tragedy finishes in lamentation.

Its ending has sometimes been thought inauthentic, but the verse is fine, although it appears that some degree of mangling has taken place, and it is obscure whether the dead brothers will be buried without any further trouble: that is, without the further quarrel Sophokles made famous in his *Antigone*, and the new generation of catastrophe that the audience also knew. I am inclined to think that in the closing play of a trilogy Aischylos would so end the action, and a number of verses indicate that he so intended. The final scene, in which a herald commands burial for the king and non-burial for his brother, and is then defied by Antigone, the whole matter being bundled up in under fifty lines, must surely be inauthentic. The power of this play is in its bare simplicity, and in narrative verse. But the revised ending referring to later events in the saga has been made with skill. One longs only to know what verses it may have dislodged.

Few perhaps, as this play is thirty lines longer than the *Furies*, another closing tragedy.

A. F. Garvie wrote a spirited defence of the *Suppliants* of Aischylos fifteen years ago, and Richmond Lattimore has thrown light on it as a story. Garvie's defence is an explanation of the consequences for critics of its late date, which is thought to destroy the opinion that this was primitive, archaic work. He maintains that the important role of the chorus of suppliants, who are, as it were, the true heroines of the play, was a deliberate integration of the chorus into the action. Whether this is true or not, we can make no sensible conjecture about originality of structure in the *Suppliants*. Lattimore, whom Taplin follows and amplifies, points to a story pattern of which we have four other examples, including works by Sophokles and Euripides. In these plays, suppliants have come as refugees to a foreign city, and the powers of that city will then protect them. Ritual supplication has an important resonance in Greek life, and a prolonged resonance in literature from Homer onwards, but these stories are public and political: they are about refugees. Both visually and dramatically the *Suppliants* depends on this fact.

The suppliants, the daughters of Danaos, are fleeing from the threat of a forced marriage in Egypt to the sons of Aigyptos, whom one version of the legend records that in the end they married and murdered. They are said to have been punished in the underworld, but in Argos they were venerated as heroines, being, it seems, identified with the prehistoric burials at Prosymna near the temple of Hera, and as mothers of the Dorian race. They come to the altar to make ritual supplication in good order. Danaos looks for a protector, and the king arrives. The women pray in more and more impassioned lyric verse. But once again Danaos spies out the land, the suppliants flutter, and an Egyptian mission arrives with a herald to recapture them. The king rescues them with soldiers – including, it appears, chariots, the reality of which even Oliver Taplin accepts, though I am still inclined to resist it. The acting area must by now be somewhat thronged, and scholars have found a speaking part for the Egyptians, but unnecessarily and I think wrongly. These were not real crowd scenes, and Gilbert Murray's suggestion, that this play had three conflicting choruses, led by Danaos, the king and the herald, is not acceptable. He is as simple and bold in conjecture as

Aischylos in composition, but wrong. The suppliants themselves remain central, and all attention concentrates on them. They are the waves on which winds play, and the altar is the rock. Rescue ends the play, and we know less than is often suggested about the rest of the trilogy. The story that Hypermestra, the only one of the daughters of Danaos not to murder her husband, was tried and acquitted at Argos, summons up an echo of the end of the *Oresteia*; it might refer to a treatment by Aischylos.

The speeches, particularly the lyric arguments of this play, have a passionate eloquence, and the enactment does not lack dramatic momentum. The only exception is a passage so badly mutilated that scholars have thought it deliberately barbarous, and given it to a chorus of Egyptians. But the effects of poetry are cumulative, they are a building up of context, and simple dramatic structure suits them well.

> Worship the common altar of these Lords,
> and like a flock of doves in purity
> crouch here in fear of hawks that wing together,
> that hate your blood's kin and defile your race.
> How can a bird that eats a bird be pure?
> Mated unwilling with a man unwilling
> how is one to be pure? Dead and in hell
> one would not fly from it, having done this.
> Another Zeus judges all ravellings
> down there, and gives last justice to the dead.

His special power is not theological or moral; it is poetry, it is to dramatize. Only a scholar alone at his desk could think of it as undramatic. Gilbert Murray's vision of a ghostly ballet is much more illuminating. The lyric passages are more untranslatable the better they are, and Greekless readers must simply accept that some things about Greek tragedy will remain mysterious if one does not know Greek – and some even if one does.

One may turn with relief to a play less vexed by criticism and mutilation, to the earliest complete tragedy to survive by Aischylos or anyone else, the *Persians*. One of the most thrilling things about it to our sensibility is the sympathy it inevitably shows with the enemy. The *Iliad* is about Achilles, but its climax is the lamentation for the dead Hektor. The Persians by their outrageous pride, the sin so

resented by villagers whose community it threatens, and therefore
so resented by their gods, and above all by the Greek gods in the
aftermath of the age of tyranny, have incurred a terrible punishment
on a personal and national scale. Aischylos fought at Marathon, and
he sounds like an eyewitness of the sea-battle at Salamis. But his
sympathy, the enlivening force of his dramatization, is not confined
to the formal implications of a tragedy, nor to a tragical rhythm in
history or in these events. It descends into detail, in the Persian
messenger's account of the battle.

> And when the light of the sun had perished
> and night came on, the masters of the oar
> and men at arms went down into the ships;
> then line to line the longships passed the word,
> and every one sailed in commanded line.
> All that night long the captains of the ships
> ordered the sea people at their stations.
> The night went by, and still the Greek fleet
> gave order for no secret sailing out.
> But when the white horses of the daylight
> took over the whole earth, clear to be seen,
> the first noise was the Greeks shouting with joy,
> like singing, like triumph, and then again
> echoes rebounded from the island rocks.
> The barbarians were afraid, our strategy
> was lost, there was no Greek panic in
> that solemn battle-song they chanted then,
> but battle-hunger, courage of spirit;
> the trumpet's note set everything ablaze.
> Suddenly by command their foaming oars
> beat, beat in the deep of the salt water,
> and all at once they were clear to be seen.
> First the right wing in perfect order leading,
> then the whole fleet followed out after them,
> and one great voice was shouting in our ears:
> 'Sons of the Greeks, go forward, and set free
> your fathers' country and set free your sons,
> your wives, the holy places of your gods,
> the monuments of your own ancestors:
> now is the one battle for everything.'
> Our Persian voices answered roaring out,

and there was no time left before the clash.
Ships smashed their bronze beaks into ships;
it was a Greek ship in the first assault
that cut away the entire towering stern
from a Phoenician, and another rammed
timber into another. Still, at first
the great flood of the Persian shipping held,
but multitudes of ships crammed up together,
no help could come from one to the other,
they smashed one another with brazen beaks,
and the whole rowing fleet shattered itself.
So then the Greek fleet with a certain skill
ran inwards from a circle around us,
and the bottoms of ships were overturned,
there was no sea-water in eyesight,
only wreckage and bodies of dead men,
and beaches and the rocks all full of dead.
Whatever ships were left out of our fleet
rowed away in no order in panic.
The Greeks with broken oars and bits of wreck
smashed and shattered the men in the water
like tunny, like gaffed fish. One great scream
filled up all the sea's surface with lament,
until the eye of darkness took it all.
I could not tell the whole tale of that harm,
not if I strung words together ten days.
Understand one thing well: that on one day
there never died so many men before.

THE QUEEN: How great a sea of evil has broken
on the Persians and all the Asian race.
MESSENGER: Understand this: the evil is not small,
such a catastrophe of suffering
had come on them it struck another stroke.
THE QUEEN: What fortune could be worse hostile than this?
Say what disastrous thing you mean that brought
even a greater evil on our men?
MESSENGER: The most high-natured and high-spirited
and bravest Persians and most nobly bred,
in whom their lord had highest trust always,

THE QUEEN:
MESSENGER:

> died by an infamous, inglorious death.
>
> **THE QUEEN:** O misery, O evil! O my friends!
> Tell me what the death was by which they died.
>
> **MESSENGER:** There is an island beside Salamis,
> a small isle, a bad anchorage for ships:
> dancing Pan is the god of the island
> and lives there on the edges of the sea.
> There he set them to kill those agile Greeks
> reaching the island from their ruined ships,
> and save their friends out of the arm of sea,
> ill foreseeing what the future would be.
> When the god gave the Greeks the sea-battle
> that very day they walled their bodies up
> in brazen armament, leapt from their ships,
> and ringed the island in one metal ring,
> so that our men had no way they could turn.
> Then they smashed them with rocks thrown with their hands,
> and deathly arrows flew from the bowstring,
> At last they rushed them in one breaking wave,
> battered and butchered their unhappy limbs,
> until they all wasted away their lives.

It is clear enough that Aischylos wishes to record the great glory of the Athenian victory. It is also noticeable that he introduces the god Pan, whose entry into Athenian life is associated with Marathon. Centuries later, the geographer Pausanias found 'no statue of any skill on the island, only some wooden idols of Pan which are more like *objets trouvés*'. Was there really some fishermen's cult, of which Aischylos had private knowledge, or did he invent the Pan connection? Was there a statue later that the Romans took away before Pausanias wrote? However that may be, Aischylos allows a special fate to these Persian noblemen, though he might have invented their rank. It is made clear that they deserved their fate, and when he sees it Xerxes howls with grief. And yet in their death the poet pities them, just as he does those who died in the water. 'I saw the Aegean sea blossom with dead', he wrote elsewhere.

The queen's conversation with her messenger occurs early in this tragedy. Aischylos reserves not only his climax but even his principal characters. In a theatre of only two or three actors, that is an almost inevitable technique. The queen is not the wife of Xerxes, but his mother, the widow of Dareios, as the chorus made plain at her entry. She is 'bed-mate and mother of the Persian god'. The news of Salamis strikes her, therefore, with special power; it is followed by a long musical lamentation, interrupted by the queen's command to call up the god or ghost Dareios. The twenty-four lines of her speech are among the strongest and most dramatic in this tragedy; they are a poetry of darkness and magic that neither Marlowe nor the Jacobeans could outdo. The central scene of the play is between the ghost and the old queen, but its climax is still to come, with the entry of Xerxes. All his verses are chanted or sung, and the end of the tragedy is his lyric conversation with the chorus. One of the most interesting things about the whole play is its economy of theatrical means.

Aischylos wrote eighty plays or more, and fragments of many of them survive by quotation or on the rags and tatters of papyrus which come to light every year. We know he wrote about the Argonauts, the death of Ajax, the birth of Dionysos, the legends of Aitna in Sicily, and the fates of Kallisto and Oreithyia. In the *Myrmidons*, the *Nereids* and the *Phrygians*, he handled the central material of the *Iliad* itself. His Achilles quarrelled with splendid bitterness. He and Patroklos were lovers, an innovation that shocked a less creative and more merely scholarly generation of later Greeks. The Nereids were his mother's companions who brought him his arms; perhaps only Aischylos would have hit on such a chorus. In the third play Achilles was shown wrapped up in his grief and silence for a very long time. The play was sometimes called the *Ransoming of Hektor*; the Trojan chorus must have addressed him for a long time in vain. It is clear that the poet handled the most famous scenes in epic poetry with bold freedom. There is a clarity and strength of conception in his structures, here as in the *Persians*, that goes beyond small adjustment or adaptive subtlety. Of all his lost trilogies this is the one most scholars most regret.

In late antiquity Aischylos was thought of as the greatest of all writers of satyr plays. We have only a few fragments, admittedly moving and funny, of his satyr play the *Netfishers*, though we have much of the *Trackers* by Sophokles, and the whole of the *Cyclops* by Euripides. Aristotle and his circle believed that these plays with a

chorus of satyrs were the original Greek dramas and the source of
tragedy and comedy. In tone, those we have are humorous and at
times pathetic; they have a pantomime quality, and they parody their
plots. In a fragment of Aischylos, when Prometheus brings fire from
heaven hidden in a fennel stalk a satyr kisses the pretty flower and
singes his beard. One satyr play or its equivalent was played at the
end of every trilogy; the same author wrote all four plays.

The satyrs are always a bit lost. They have got separated from
Dionysos, and they are childish as well as wild, sexually as in other
ways. In the *Netfishers* they fish up the infant Perseus in his box
from the sea. One cannot reconstruct the whole plot, but the
characters include a king's brother called Net, and an Old Man of
the Island, maybe a god, maybe Silenos, the disgraceful old father
of the troop of satyrs. The island is Seriphos. Net is the name of the
fisherman in the folk-tale, to which Aischylos has added the satyrs.
'Come along my love, my duck, my darling,' they say to the child.
'Popopopopopopo.'

> Come along quick to the children.
> Come nicely to my nursing hands, my dear.
> You will have weasels to play with,
> and fawns and baby hedgehogs,
> and sleep in one bed with mother and father.

There is a certain sexual by-play here, because the mother is Danae
the beautiful, and the 'father' is surely Silenos. The child was
fascinated by the perpetual erections which the satyrs wore as a stage
dress, held on by a kind of bathing trunks. 'What a cock-lover the
little fellow is,' remarks a satyr. If to any readers it should seem bizarre
that Aischylos was the master of this genre, they should consider
the broader comic scenes of which Shakespeare is still the unequalled
master in our language.

Greek tragedies are short by modern standards. They are coherent
individual poems, separate poetic systems. When they were organized
as trilogies, which was not always, the three plays were deliberately
varied from one another; the sex and nature of the chorus and the
pace and structure of the tragedies differed deliberately. The contrast
of the satyr play, with its inventive intrusions of the lost satyrs into
a myth and a place not associated with them, and with its consequent

comic freedom, adds another dimension. The whole performance lasted a long morning, it appears. When a comedy was added to the celebrations later in the fifth century, the comedy was played after lunch. The audience of Aischylos, earlier in the century, passed one whole day during the festival week with that mighty poetry reverberating in their ears. Timing, the artificial, controlled time of a work of art, and pace and variation are a large part of his skill. Morality, catastrophe and human character, which so fascinate us, are hardly more than aspects of his overriding musical technique in dramatic poems: they are the roll of drums, the blare of trumpets. He is essentially dramatic.

One of the most illuminating ways of visualizing the theatre of Aischylos, though it goes beyond the bounds of literary history, is to study the compositions of the great black-figure vase-painters of the late sixth century, and the red-figure painters of the late sixth and early fifth. It is in the rhythms of this dense and yet economic art, more than in representations of the actual subjects of his plays, that one can discover something like the spirit of Aischylos. One can also find sometimes a remarkably uninhibited handling of mythology. The spirit of the satyr plays is represented very fully.

But Aischylos is a poet, and to understand him we must read his words. No verse drama in English is anything like his. No historical moment and no society will ever again be like his. Even within the fifth century, the generation that fought at Marathon was recognized to have been unique. When Aischylos died, a decree was made that anyone applying to produce a play of his should be granted state patronage, and he is said to have won many prizes posthumously: a situation that Aristophanes reflects in the *Frogs*. Aischylos remained an overwhelming presence to the Athenians, all the more so perhaps as his poetry became to them an expression of the unrepeatable past, before things went wrong, before the age of the Parthenon. When Aischylos died, Sokrates was still a child, and Aristophanes had not been born.

THEATRICAL HISTORY

Before 570 B.C. Kleisthenes of Sikyon transferred the 'tragic chorus' from the cult of the hero Adrastos to that of Dionysos.

About 534 B.C. Thespis added an actor, probably using iambic verse, to the 'tragic chorus' in Athens. He perhaps altered formal face-painting to the use of a mask. Tragic masks reflect very late sixth-century fashions.

About 500 B.C. Pratinas of Phlious introduced or reintroduced satyr plays to Athens. Phrynichos introduced masks for women.

After 498 B.C. Tragic performances transferred from the market-place to the sanctuary of Dionysos (some wooden seats had collapsed). The move may have been as late as 460.

Early 5th century Aischylos introduced two actors in costume.

488/7 Comedy was added to tragedy.

In the 460s Sophokles introduced a third actor. He increased the chorus from twelve to fifteen.

About 460 B.C. The first background building for actors, a simple one, now untraceable, was constructed. The development of scene-painting followed, dress became grander and finally the theatre itself more elaborate.

449 B.C. Prizes began to be offered for actors. Mechanical devices increased.

440 B.C. Comedy spread to a festival of its own.

About 432 B.C. Tragedy spilt over into that festival also.

After 420 B.C. The new musical style led to virtuosos aria and the detachment of the chorus from dramatic enactment. Agathon introduced pure fiction.

In the 4th century Tragedy spread all over Attica and all over the Greek world. (Aischylos had already written plays in Sicily, and Agathon and Euripides in Macedonia.)

Late 4th century The first big raised stage and permanent stone architectural background, at first very simple, were built for the revivals of fifth-century plays under Lykourgos.

THEATRICAL FESTIVALS

This list is not of equal authority throughout, and differs here and there from the opinions of Pickard-Cambridge.

Country Dionysia (Christmas season)	Village rituals, chants and processions. Small town performances of popular tragedies and comedies, and some at Eleusis and Piraeus, from the late 5th century on.
Lenaia (January–February)	Comedy (from 488). Tragedy (from 442) with some curtailment in wartime. Transferred from Dionysos in the Marshes to the new theatre after about 460.
Anthesteria (early March)	Competition for actors to be chosen for the City Dionysia (?)
Great or City Dionysia (March–April)	Day one: Parade etc. in the Odeion of Perikles (from the 440s on). Day two: Dithyrambs (ten). Day three: Five comedies (from 486) Cut to three in wartime and the special day cancelled. Days four, five and six: Three tragedies and a satyr play daily. Day seven: Prize-giving

BIBLIOGRAPHY

M. Bieber, *History of the Greek and Roman Theater*, 1971

A. F. Garvie, *Aeschylus' Supplices*, 1969

M. Griffith, *The Authenticity of Prometheus Bound*, 1977

R. Lattimore, *The Poetry of Greek Tragedy*, 1958

R. Lattimore, *Story Patterns in Greek Tragedy*, 1964

A. Lebeck, *The Oresteia*, 1971

H. Lloyd-Jones, *The Justice of Zeus*, 1971

H. Lloyd-Jones, *The Oresteia* (translation), 1979

R. Lowell, *Prometheus Bound* (translation), 1969

R. Lowell, *The Oresteia* (translation), 1978

L. MacNeice, *Agamemnon* (translation), 1936

A. W. Pickard-Cambridge, *Dramatic Festivals of Athens* (revised by J. Gould and D. M. Lewis), 1968

A. Podlecki, *The Political Background of Aeschylean Tragedy*, 1966

O. Taplin, *The Stagecraft of Aeschylus*, 1977

A. D. Trendall and T. B. L. Webster, *Illustrations of Greek Drama*, 1971

8

SOPHOKLES

Sophokles lived nearly all the years of the fifth century, from about 496 to 406 B.C. Euripides was only ten or eleven years younger, and died in the same year, but we have no play by Euripides before 438 (his *Alkestis*); he won no more than five successes in his lifetime, and as a dramatist he was a late starter. But Sophokles performed as a boy among the dancers who celebrated Salamis, and at first he acted in his own plays, beginning at twenty-eight in 468 B.C., before the *Oresteia*. He played the tragic musician Thamyras, who was struck blind, and a beautiful princess in a story from the *Odyssey*, or so we are told. He also wrote paeans, elegies and odes, as well as his tragedies, and in dramatization he shows great technical versatility. Still, it is a reasonable conjecture that we have nothing by him earlier than his *Ajax*, written in the fifties or later, then nothing until the *Antigone* (possibly about 442), the *Women of Trachis* (perhaps in the thirties), *Oedipus the King* in the early twenties, *Elektra* probably later, *Philoktetes* in 409, and *Oedipus at Kolonos* written in extreme old age, produced posthumously, his masterpiece I think. Because of the gaps in our knowledge, the idea of a progression from Aischylos to Sophokles and then Euripides hardly makes any sense. Most of the Sophokles we have is later than our first Euripides, and the influences were probably mutual. The *Women of Trachis*, with its long prologue and its theme of passionate love, may easily owe something to the younger writer. It is hard to know: the same age and city and audience nourished them both.

Aischylos fought for his country more than once, and Euripides took a minor part in public life once or twice, but Sophokles had a public career. Aischylos was well-born, but Sophokles was rich.

His father was an armourer and ran a workshop. Euripides was said to be low-born. Sophokles was a treasurer of the empire in 443, twice at least a general, once with Perikles against Samos and once with Nikias, and one of the commissioners appointed to govern Athens after the Sicilian disaster. He was a friend of Herodotos, and a friend of the admirable poet Ion of Chios, of whose work we have much too little. In the theatre he won twenty-four times, which appears to include ninety-six of his hundred and twenty-three plays: a very successful lifetime. He held the priesthood of a healing god, and entertained in his house the holy snake of Asklepios; that is, he was instrumental in the founding by a certain Telemachos of the first Athenian public hospital, the Asklepieion on the south slope of the Akropolis. After his death he was worshipped as a hero under the name Dexion; he was an official of the older medical sanctuary of the Helper, but he seems to have encouraged the take-over by Asklepios.

This surely has an important bearing on the problem of his attitude to pain. No tragic poet is so bleak, no fifth-century writer has a tragic sense so extreme, as Sophokles. His *Philoktetes* is the tale of a man in anguish for ten years from an incurable snake-bite. Admittedly, here as elsewhere in his last plays, the tragedy covers a divine mission. But one is interested and pleased to learn that outside poetry, Sophokles was concerned with a healing sanctuary. The plague at Thebes in the opening scene of *Oedipus the King*, or rather, *the Tyrant*, is not scientifically described; it is like no plague that ever was on sea or land. But that is because it is a curse, and the audience must read it as a curse from the gods, like the formula of cursing reversed into blessings at the end of the *Oresteia* of Aischylos.

Sophokles is a poet of the years when reason and hope were dominant: his life was bounded by the Persian wars and the fall of Athens, but those years of something like scientific rationalism were bounded also by the triumph of democracy and the failure of Athens at war, or perhaps the decline began with the plague at Athens which Thucydides so scientifically described. They were the years of Perikles and his circle, when Protagoras 'cannot feel that the gods exist or do not exist, nor what their shape is, for many things hinder true knowledge, the obscurity of the subject and the brevity of life', and when the same philosopher proposed a philosophy of human progress through law and reason and morality. Anaxagoras, the friend of Perikles, discussing the proverbial Greek question whether men would do better by not being born at all, a proverb of which Sophokles made deadly use in tragic poetry, said one would choose to be born 'in order to study the heavens and the whole universe'.

These philosophers were more like nineteenth-century Unitarians than like the gleeful sages of the French enlightenment. In his doctrine of unwritten laws in the *Antigone*, and his view of the nature and history of man, Sophokles sometimes seems to be grappling closely with their ideas. In the thirties, when technical treatises began to be written on numerous specialized subjects, Sophokles seems to have written one on theatrical technique. 'There is no *techne*, no art or technique,' wrote a medical writer, 'which does not exist.' Logic and rhetoric, based on a study of human beings as well as on language, flourished in his time. He uses less sophistry than Euripides, but as much rhetoric. Yet having said all this, one must accept that the mythological and theological world of the plays of Sophokles is coherent and uncompromising. Poetry was the life of his soul, I suppose, his refuge and his expression. He wrote tragic poetry with passionate conviction, coolly manipulating the structure of the stories in order to reveal what was most terrible: Oedipus self-blinded and self-exiled, his wife hanged and his children cursed, Herakles burned alive.

The construction of his tragedies is always lucid, although they differ greatly from one another, and so is the momentum of his thoughts, although his verse style is often mannered in iambic speech, and compressed and rather exotic in lyrics.

> Look, here Orestes is, who by device
> was dead, and by device was saved alive.

These lines follow a long and gripping set piece in which the lying story of the death of Orestes was told in great detail. In the *Antigone*, the same kind of formalization is carried even further.

> ... no sweet or bitter story since that time
> we were two sisters of two brothers robbed,
> killed on one day each by the other's hand.

The familiar stories have been boiled down almost to the condition of riddles. The strength of these verses expresses the very marrow of tragic form, the marrow of folk-tales. How much more analytic than Aischylos he is about the Furies, and yet with no loss of power.

> O Furies, dreadful children of the gods,
> who see all murders of the unjustly dead
> and see all beds of marriage that are robbed,
> come now, help now, avenge our father killed.
> Send me my brother home. I can no longer
> carry the weight of grief I am to bear.

In Sophokles, tragic poetry is more dramatic than in the loose sense poetic. 'Cut out the poetry, Watson,' remarked Sherlock Holmes, and T. S. Eliot said he had been trying to do that all his life. In the same sense Sophokles in his iambics cut away every undecorous ornament, although he retained a range of tones and of pace. His most powerful effects are simple, but always within a closely interwoven and dramatic context, like lying words in Shakespeare. He distinguished three stages in his own development, an early grandeur, followed by a harsh and technically mannered style, and then the best and most adapted to character. That seems to refer only to the verbal texture of iambics, and it is probable we have no examples of the two earlier stages as he distinguished them, but the sense of this progression does fit the verse we have. The adaptability to character does increase, and the harsh mannerism does seem to have been a suppressed temptation in his verse.

The action of his *Ajax* is strange at first sight. Ajax has been driven mad, recovered his wits, and killed himself from shame, from affronted honour, soon after line 865, but there are 555 more verses of the play. The material they treat is the dispute over the hero's burial. To modern taste this is bizarre, unworthy argument, and I recollect that as a schoolboy I found these pages an anticlimax. But to the Greeks the burial of the dead was a matter of central importance, and it often gave a motive to tragedy, particularly during war. Ajax was a very great hero at Athens, because he came from Salamis, and the influential clan or society of Salaminians worshipped him. His temple and a black wooden statue stood in the ruinous city of Salamis in the age of Hadrian, but they are hard to date. He certainly received worship as a divine hero at Athens, and his grave at Troy was a landmark. His suicide had been a favourite theme in art for two hundred years. One must accept the meaning of this play for the Athenians, to whom Ajax was tied not by the accident of birth alone, but by his importance after death. Sophokles like Aischylos is localizing the general epic poetry of the Greeks, implanting it and rooting it in Athens.

Structurally, the bridge between the two parts of the play is the arrival of Teukros, the faithful friend and half-brother of Ajax, just too late to prevent the imminent suicide, and his insistence on a decent burial, almost a placation of the dead man. The madness of Ajax was the action of Athene herself; we are told in her opening dialogue with Odysseus that she saved Odysseus and the sons of Atreus (who commanded the Greeks) from murder, when Ajax felt himself dishonoured by the award to Odysseus of the arms of Achilles; she drove Ajax to attack cattle. The opening scene is as awful as a village vendetta.

> He is inside that hut, and now his head
> drips with his sweat, his hands with blooded sword.

When Athene calls Ajax out, he believes she has helped him, he will give her 'spoils from this hunt, all gold'. His vengefulness is as unpleasant as the mockery of the goddess. Even Odysseus pities him. His disturbed sailors speak at once of sea-washed Salamis. One should remember that the Athenians backed their claim to ownership of Salamis with a line of the *Iliad* in which Salaminians and Athenians sailed to Troy in one regiment. It is noticeable that we are invited to pity Ajax by Odysseus, by the chorus and by his wife Tekmessa, but that Athene speaks austerely and proverbially of the punishment of pride.

> Because one day bends and raises again
> all human things, and those whom the gods love
> are modest, and the gods hate evil men.

I do not know how seriously we are meant to meditate on these parting words: they are like the formal rhyme that ends a scene in Shakespeare. But what they express is part of the moral bones of this and every tragedy. It is necessity, it is the irreconcilable, which we single out as tragic. In this play, the death of Ajax will bind him mysteriously closer to the Athenians: heroes are the dead, worshipped as if they were ghosts. It would be frivolous to consider that a happy ending, but it does offer a new and religious dimension to the audience. The tragical hero is slowly revealed, first through Athene, then through Tekmessa begging the chorus for human help, once again as if this were a village world, and then through lyrics Ajax sings himself, hating the Trojan coast and longing for home.

> Now what must I do, hated by gods,
> and loathsome to the army of the Greeks,
> and hateful to all Troy and to these fields?
> Shall I go home, desert this anchorage,
> leaving these kings, and cross the Aegean sea?
> How can I look into my father's eyes?

Tekmessa fails to comfort him with a decorous and restrained speech, as analytic of 'what one should say' as the verses I quoted earlier about the Furies. The chorus longs for home, 'O glorious, sea-beaten, happy Salamis ...', and meditates the grief of his parents. Ajax speaks again.

> Long extending, immeasurable time
> brings unknown things to light and buries all,
> and there is nothing not to be foreseen.

As his mood intensifies, his thought simplifies. Is not this lucid expression of what such a character might reasonably feel – that is, a character who is precisely the projection of a story, just a figure in an enactment and no more – possibly what Sophokles meant by language adaptable to character? The heavy grandeur of the first line is no more than a choice of tone. The self-analysis of Ajax in the following lines is terribly effective. Typically of the riddling reductions of stories that so attract Sophokles, Ajax has a sword given him once by Hektor.

> When I have come to an untrodden place
> I shall hide this weapon that I most hate
> where it shall not be seen by any man,
> let night and Hades have it underground.

He is speaking to the sailors, and it is clear from many hints that he deceives them. They call in relief on Pan and Apollo, and on Zeus.

Ajax disappears, a messenger reports the arrival of Teukros in the camp and a fatal prophecy about Ajax. Tekmessa rushes off to get help. A little more than half-way through the play Ajax makes his final speech of fifty-one lines. He had never intended not to die.

> The killing edge stands where it would cut best
> if there were time to reason over it,
> the gift of Hektor, of all foreign men
> most loathed by me and the most hated sight.
> And it sticks in the enemy Trojan earth,
> all fresh-ground with a steel-eating whetstone.
> I set it in and dug it well around
> to be most friendly with swift death to me.
> So far is put in order. Then you first,
> Zeus, as is fitting, bring me your aid now.
> I do not ask a favour lasting long.
> Send me some messenger to take away
> my evil news to Teukros, let him first
> lift my body from this fresh-running sword,
> and let no enemy spy me out first
> to throw my body to the dogs and crows.
> Zeus, I ask this of you, and now I call
> conducting Hermes, take me underground,
> easy-footed and swift,
> when I break my side open with this blade,
> I call the helping, always virginal
> and terrible and long-stepping Furies
> who see all things suffered among mankind:
> see how I have been ruined by these kings.
> May they be evilly dragged to evil
> and utter ruin as the Furies see
> how by self-murder I must perish now.
> Come O you rapid, punishing Furies,
> taste blood, take the whole army of the Greeks.
> And you that ride up steep heaven, O Sun,
> when you shall see the land where I was born,
> tell my old father and my sad mother
> the tale of my curses and my last fate.
> O miserable, when she hears that news,
> she will fill up all that city with shrieks.
> No use the vain lamenting of these things:

> the matter must be done and swiftly done.
> O Death, Death, come to me, visit me,
> I come to you, there I will speak to you.
> And you, O brightness of this shining day,
> and you, the riding Sun, I speak to you:
> this last of times, and never more again.
> O light, O holy ground of my home earth,
> Salamis, rock of my father's hearthstone,
> and glorious Athens, and my neighbour race,
> and springs and rivers and the fields of Troy,
> farewell to you, all that have nourished me.
> This is the last word Ajax cries to you,
> the rest I'll speak in Hades to the dead.

Nothing could be clearer or better organized or more black. The characters of Sophokles have a complete conviction in their speeches because they are expressions of a story, precisely thought through. They are persons passionately but impersonally created, almost like figures in an allegory. Their cries are like the cries of birds, their gift of human utterance appears almost magical. There are perhaps greater speeches in Greek, but this is a fine one. I have not been able to convey in translation the power of individual lines, but I hope to suggest, line for line, the progression from tone to tone, including the fit of brutal rage and of course the eery solemnity. The rest of the play is not an anticlimax. Odysseus contributes a moral wisdom that was new to the Greek theatre (1332ff.). Through Tekmessa's grief and the indignant sadness of Teukros the drama unfolds, until Sophokles has demeaned Menelaos and even Agamemnon, though not Odysseus, in order to build up the Salaminians. The last of the few choral lyrics that occur late in the play ends: 'What pleasure is left to me, what pleasure now? Where the forested and sea-washed promontory threatens the water, under the jutting cape of Sounion, to speak to holy Athens.'

With *Antigone*, it is important to make clear the climax of the action, because modern liberal scholars, captivated by the heroine's intransigent virtue and defiance, have misread the play as her tragedy alone, in which case the action ends early and the melodramatic events of the last scenes are an unnecessary elaboration. But this is also the tragedy of Kreon, who defies the gods and natural laws and is ruined, just as Antigone defied authority and perished. We should leave aside for a moment our own excitement about the humanism expressed here and there in this play. Let us even assume that Sophokles may share it; still, *Antigone* is a tragedy, and humanism is only one of the motive forces of its conflict. This becomes easy to see if one watches the unravelling of the plot.

Oedipus had two sons and two daughters. The two sons have killed one another; Kreon (a general name given to a number of rulers in mythology), the uncle and brother-in-law of Oedipus, is in command of Thebes. The two daughters are Antigone and Ismene, a weaker sister like Elektra's weaker sister. Kreon's son Haimon is engaged to marry Antigone. Kreon forbids the burial of one of the brothers, Polyneikes, as the aggressor, which he was. Antigone resolves to pay him the due of the dead, Ismene will keep her secret but will not help. The chorus are elderly citizens full of proverbial wisdom and human feelings: they are no one's mouthpiece exactly, and they are anonymous, a quality that gives power to some of their utterances, here as in *Oedipus the King*. Antigone carries out her plan, not once but twice. Sophokles wrings the last drop out of the situation. First 'she sprinkled thirsty dust and sanctified'. Kreon has the corpse flung out, it is guarded at a distance because it stinks, Antigone returns and is caught renewing the rites of the dead. She defies angry Kreon, and dismisses Ismene's pretence to have helped her. Haimon pleads furiously but in vain. Antigone laments her fate in lyrics with the chorus, and Kreon has her walled up. Teiresias the prophet, whom Kreon defies, brings fearful prophecies and warnings. Kreon repents too late: Haimon has killed himself and died cursing his father, and Antigone has hanged herself. Eurydike, Kreon's wife and Haimon's mother, imitates his suicide. Kreon's fate is to live on.

In this tragedy, love is a forceful theme. It is among other things the tragedy of a pair of lovers, and Antigone's love of her brother, even Ismene's for Antigone, are woven into its texture. Antigone laments her unfulfilled love, Kreon's unnatural behaviour centres on denying the rights of the lovers, and Antigone greets her tomb as a bride-chamber. I think it must be assumed, though scholars have occasionally denied it, that an Athenian audience believes automatically in the burial of the dead, and that although Antigone's action is seen through the guard's description as sad and terrible, and attended by convulsions of nature, no one in Athens would question her right and duty to bury her brother. This is the working out of a saga and a family curse. Kreon is deluded, maddened or blinded by the gods. 'Do not kick the dead,' says Teiresias, but Kreon would not hear his persuasions.

One would very much like to know how much of this plot Sophokles made up. Haimon is a name in the *Iliad*, where Maion son of Haimon is one of the young men of Thebes. But the story of Antigone and Ismene which proliferates later into many versions, is not known to be older than the fifth century. The disputed burial of Polyneikes and the death of Antigone are apparently creations of the tragic theatre. Ion of Chios wrote in a dithyramb that both sisters were burnt to death in the temple of Hera by a son of Eteokles; one is not told why. The story of the curse on Oedipus and his family grew downwards through generations. In the earliest epic poems about Oedipus, there were no children of the incestuous marriage, though the two sons doomed to quarrel did appear in the Theban epic that lies behind the *Seven* of Aischylos. An attempt by W. Burkert to trace an origin of the deadly rivals in eastern art is not really helpful: versions of the same theme can be traced back through Dark Age art to the Myceneans, the theme is a folk-theme, like that of Balin and Balan or Sorab and Rustam.

The burning to death may be a local legend that means Antigone and Ismene were divine heroines transformed as Herakles was. That would explain the persistence of their names in Theban topography. But I am inclined to think that Sophokles invented the young lovers and the suicide of Kreon's wife. The verse technique of this tragedy shows great assurance, and so does its conscious manipulation of structure, with sparing and telling use of choral lyrics and contrast of characters.

> It was like this. When we came to the place
> carrying out your terrible commands,
> we swept away what dust lay on the dead
> and stripped the corpse naked of covering,
> and took our station high up on the rocks
> not be struck by any stench of it.

The Greek is more concrete and syntactically denser than my

version, but I mean to convey its swiftness as the opening of a narrative. Antigone's argument with Kreon is, of course, in quite another style.

> It was not Zeus proclaimed your laws to me,
> nor Justice, sister to gods underground,
> who gave humanity such laws as those;
> I did not think your proclamations
> (being human) so strong as to overrun
> the sure, unwritten statutes of the gods:
> which do not live today and yesterday,
> but always: no man knows their origin.

The choral lyrics in *Antigone* are in contrast to this sharp eloquence, and they seldom carry the dramatic action further forward until late in the play. But Sophokles uses them with precision to carry forward the tragic progression of thought and of feeling. After the great rage of Kreon, while the guard goes to bring back Antigone for her scene of splendid argument, the chorus modulates the mood in words too often taken out of context. Fine as they may be, one should notice their dramatic use as well as their sentiment. The guard has been terrified and horrified by Kreon.

> Many things are monstrous, none
> is more monstrous than a man.
> He crosses grey sea-water in
> the roaring waves and the storm-wind ...

One might as easily translate 'terrible' as monstrous, but the point certainly is that man is unnatural and masters nature and 'Earth, most high goddess'. Man provides and is never without devices – except that he cannot avoid Hades. He hopefully progresses now to evil, now to good, 'crossing the earth's laws and the oath-bound justice of the gods'. This phrase is perhaps deliberately obscure. He builds his city high, but the unrestrained man with whom wrong dwells is an outcast, a man without a city. Once again, it remains ambiguous whether Kreon or Polyneikes (probably) or Antigone is intended. When Antigone appears as prisoner, the chorus is appalled. But the background of thought and feeling against which argument takes place has already been constructed, and the wavering world-view of the chorus makes the clear speeches that follow all the more dramatic. Sophokles plays his aces coolly.

These lyric themes recur, and they do much to bind the whole tragic poem together. In the next lyric interlude the storm rages worse than ever: I suppose these are the verses Matthew Arnold remembered on Dover beach. After Haimon's scene with Kreon, the chorus cry out to love.

> Eros in battle unconquered,
> Eros god of animals,
> night visitor in the soft cheeks of youth,
> wanderer above seas and among sheep-folds,
> whom no god can flee from,
> and no mortal man ...

It is curious how the theme has been transformed. By some trick of half-conscious memory, one retains the sense that Eros is perhaps lawless and terrible, and obscurely identical with the human spirit. In the long interlude so introduced, the chorus of old men and the lamenting Antigone sing antiphonally. 'Unwept, unfriended, with no wedding song, I am led down by the receiving road. It is no longer lawful I should see the holy eye of light. And no friend groans over my fate unwept.' Between her dying speech, which follows, and the prophecy of Teiresias, the chorus sing how Danae even in a prison of bronze, even in a tomb-chamber, had her lover. But fate is terrible, or monstrous. No wealth, no war, no tower, no blue-painted sea-beaten ships can escape it. The mythological examples become more frightening as the themes transform into blacker and blacker colours. Towards the end of the play, before the final scenes, the chorus pray wildly to Dionysos, a deeper and a darker god than Eros.

> Dancing leader of the fire-breathing stars,
> master of night voices,
> born son of Zeus appear ...

Dionysos of course does not appear, only the climax of the tragedy appears. The ironies of this play are intimately interwoven.

The *Women of Trachis* is a dramatization of the death of Herakles. It was prophesied he would rest after his labours and prophesied he would die by the centaur he killed, whose blood impregnated the shirt his wife gave him when he came home expecting rest. She thought it was a charm to win back his love. Herakles has himself burned alive to be rid of the burning pains of the poisoned shirt. We must assume that the audience knew Herakles was a god, not just a hero, but the happy ending is utterly concealed: it is simply not to be found in the text, which is a tragedy so appalling as to be awe-inspiring. Aristotle is thought to have said that tragedy is a purgation of the passions by terror and by pity. That would be true of the *Women of Trachis*.

An interesting translation of this tragedy by Ezra Pound, which is rather accurate, and once or twice even corrects mistakes made by Sir Richard Jebb, throws light both on the play itself and on Pound's own poetry. Herakles makes his son Hyllos swear to burn him.

> The dead beast kills the living me,
> and that fits another odd forecast
> breathed out at the Selloi's oak –
> Those fellows rough it,
>   sleep on the ground, up in the hills there.
> I heard it and wrote it down
>   under my Father's tree.
> Time lives, and it's going on now.
> I am released from trouble.
> I thought it meant life in comfort.
> It doesn't. It means that I die.
> For amid the dead there is no work in service.
> Come at it that way, my boy, what
> SPLENDOUR,
>
>   IT ALL COHERES.

[*He turns his face from the audience, then sits erect, facing them without the mask of agony; the revealed make-up is that of solar serenity. The hair golden and as electrified as possible.*]

In a footnote, Pound observes that 'This is the key phrase, for which the play exists.' It is indeed, in his translation, the innermost marrow of the tragedy, and he has grasped better than academic critics 'the main form of the play, and how snugly each segment of the work fits into its box'. That is perhaps his privilege as a great poet. But the precise phrase he chooses is not in Greek a separate sentence, and it will not sustain the weight he puts on it; it is little more than a phrase meaning 'Since all this clearly fits'. And yet he is right about this new understanding by Herakles being the key to the play. He is only wrong to succumb to the temptation to import into the text and action of the play a solar serenity which lies beyond it. In his own late poetry Pound wrote, in *Canto* CXVI,

> I have brought the great ball of crystal;
>   who can lift it?
> Can you enter the acorn of light?
>   But the beauty is not the madness
> Tho' my errors and wrecks lie about me.
> And I am not a demigod,
> I cannot make it cohere.

Herakles accepts a death that relieves him of overwhelming pain, and his last words are a choking back of pain. He is ready to quarrel with Hyllos, and binds him to obedience with a fearful oath. 'Swear by the head of Zeus who fathered me.' 'I swear, and Zeus is witness to my oath.' As an acting part, this Herakles must have been immensely demanding. The part is short but climactic: he appears singing or chanting, at verse 983 of a tragedy 1,278 verses long. There are no deep alterations of character possible within the conventions of Greek acting, but there are certainly deep disturbances, and rather swift alterations of tone. Herakles has to express a seizure of pain in the middle of a long iambic utterance. Sophokles was deeply interested in theatrical technique, and a guild or society of theatre people that he founded seems to coincide with the first organization of professional actors, around the middle of the century. The rhetorical force, the comparatively subtle psychology, and the analytic, epigrammatic quality of his writing combine to make a formidable texture. Whoever discusses Sophokles must feel he is dealing with someone more intelligent than himself. The technical mastery is most obvious where Aristotle found it, in *Oedipus the King*, in which the principal part is by modern conventions almost unactable. Modern naturalism smothers the continual variety of tone.

The problem goes deeper. Tycho Wilamowitz, the son of the great scholar, a young scholar himself of brilliant promise who was killed at Ivangorod in October 1917, argued in a posthumous book that a certain intellectual incoherence, a moral discontinuity, can be traced in the tragedies of Sophokles. My own view is that Sophokles was clear-headed and precise in the dramatic structures he imposed on his stories, that the poetry he wrote very exactly expresses that structure, and that the most striking thing about him is his eye for the bones of a story, his sense of a tragical progression. The weakness of my position is that it entails the axiom and method that the unity and progression of the plays is real and waiting to be traced.

Yet the momentum of the action is not always obviously consistent with the progression of thoughts and feelings, at least at first sight. A full analysis of the *Women of Trachis* reveals more problems than I have discussed, although I think they have solutions. Herakles in the *Women of Trachis* is encrusted with greatness, goodness and wickedness, like some vast old ship's figurehead dragged from the sea encrusted with barnacles. He is too big for the moral system of the play, he is half a god, his virtue is that he has obeyed Zeus. His stature is superhuman rather than morally admirable. He is mythical, a figure in a story casting a shadow. A tragedy is a poem about heroes, an enactment, not a pure moral allegory. But the theatre is a magnifying glass, and one cannot avoid judging both the heroes and the gods, and Sophokles knows this. His Herakles is unlike his Athenian Theseus.

There is no doubt of the lucid coherence of Oedipus in *Oedipus the King*, a man fated by birth to murder his father and marry his mother Iokaste, exposed as a child and secretly brought up abroad, who did unknowingly what he was fated to do. In the action of the tragedy he is king of Thebes, and swears to remove a plague or curse by rooting out the source of pollution. He inquires relentlessly, and discovers his own history too late. He must carry out the punishment with which he cursed himself. His wife commits suicide, he blinds himself and is sent into exile alone. Yeats has translated the last lyric.

> Make way for Oedipus. All people said
> 'That is a fortunate man';
> And now what storms are beating on his head?
> Call no man fortunate that is not dead.
> The dead are free from pain.

These closing lines of the text may not be really by Sophokles, and Yeats in this laconic version has perhaps improved them, but they sum up the sort of proverbial wisdom that the chorus, intellectually daring only in despair, often does express. This play resounds once again with the fulfilment of dire prophecies, and Kreon plays a political, somewhat detestable part, consonant with his character in *Antigone*; Teiresias plays almost the same part. Proverbial wisdom is not what one believes with the whole of one's mind, maybe, but an inscribed stone at Athens recording the expedition of Tolmides in 447 and a lost battle tells us of just such an enigmatic prophecy fulfilled. Indeed, it commemorates the fearful truth of an oracle more than it commemorates the dead. My impression is that Sophokles more than half believed in such things, and most of his audience much more than half.

And yet he manages the mechanics very coolly. Sophokles is famously the master of dramatic ironies. There is a moment in mid-tragedy when Oedipus is full of hope and the chorus sings a pastoral celebration, because Oedipus must be god-born on the mountain of Kithairon. Lyrical false hope is a device Sophokles uses elsewhere. It prolongs and increases the tension: the audience knows it is irony; it will plunge him deeper into despair when the moment comes. Musically, it offers a variation of tone and a relief, a contrast. Psychologically, it admirably conveys the instability, the suppressed fear, and the increasing hysteria of Oedipus. The gods have him in their grip. Ancient critics called Sophokles the lengthener of agony. Oedipus in the end understands that he has been carefully ambushed by Apollo, and so do the chorus.

> Ah! Ah! Everything came true.
> O light, may I look my last on you.
> Born where I must not be: and then bedded
> where I must not! murdered where I should not.

It is impossible for me to reduce these verses to their true, riddling tightness. But Yeats translated the sadder, slower chorus.

What can the shadow-like generations of man attain
But build up a dazzling mockery of delight that under their touch dissolves again?
Oedipus seemed blessed, but there is no man blessed amongst men.

Oedipus overcame the woman-breasted Fate;

He seemed like a strong tower against Death and first among the fortunate;
He sat upon the ancient throne of Thebes and all men called him great.

But, looking for a marriage bed, he found the bed of his birth,
Tilled the field his father had tilled, cast seed into the same abounding earth;
Entered through the door that sent him wailing forth.

Begetter and begot as one! How could that be hid?
What darkness cover up that marriage bed? Time watches, he is eagle-eyed,
And all the works of man are known and every soul is tried.

Would you had never come to Thebes, nor to this house,
Nor riddled with the woman-breasted Fate, beaten off death and succoured us,
That I had never raised this song, heart-broken Oedipus.

Even in these long, breathing sentences, the verbal texture of Sophokles and his syntactic agility are closer to Donne than to Yeats. If one were to desire an entire book about *Oedipus the King*, that would not be a study of problems or of hidden beauties and strange coherences; it should be a simple commentary, following through the powerful eddies of the language over the lucid, rocky course of tragic dramatization. The situation of Oedipus is like one of those old philosophic problems of which Louis MacNeice observed that one has only to uncork them to set the paradoxes fizzing. They are a mask of course for secret fears common to mankind.

Elektra is the treatment of a theme we not only know that Aischylos handled, but we have his *Libation-bearers*, the second play of his *Oresteia*. When I came fresher to this subject, I preferred Sophokles, but as I grew older I became disinclined to that view, maybe because no single play full of devices can equal the tidal surge of the whole *Oresteia*. The Orestes of Sophokles returns and plans his revenge, Elektra cries out with sorrow from the palace, not knowing he has come. She is ill-treated and comes lamenting to her father's tomb. The queen dreams about an ominous, overshadowing tree. Elektra persuades her weak sister to pray for Orestes. She then confronts the queen as fiercely as Antigone confronted Kreon. Her hope and the queen's fears centre on the vengeance of Orestes. We then hear the news of his death, false of course, delivered at the palace, with a brilliantly lifelike and quite fictional description of a chariot-race.

But strange offerings are found on Agamemnon's grave. Still, Elektra believes the lie, and prepares to take her own deadly revenge.

Orestes arrives with an urn of the ashes of Orestes, and at last, painfully and slowly, they recognize each other. The queen's murder followed by that of her lover is the climax of the tragedy. Its psychological and dramatic subtleties are over, and the action itself, so long delayed, is almost outside them. Throughout what we know of the career of Sophokles, the dramatic interplay of the characters has been more and more closely enmeshed, and here it reaches admirable complexity with no loss of pace; the tragic structure is still clear. If Elektra has a more evidently dark side than Antigone, that follows simply from the inherited plot.

The angry Orestes in this tragedy speaks often with epigrammatic bitterness, even to his sister.

> Leave out all those unnecessary words,
> do not like a bad mother preach at me
> of how Aigisthos in my father's house
> takes all and scatters all and squanders all.
> Telling that story would wear time away.
> Show me what fits me in this present time,
> where we shall hide and where we shall appear
> to wipe away their laughter by this road.

The narrative of the chariot-race functions as the car-chase does which old producers used to introduce into the second-last reel of films. It is a tense story leading to a death. It both distracts the audience from tension, being an exciting story well told which they know is a fiction, and at the same time symbolizes the tension and increases it. From the point of view of dramatization, it is necessary to convince the queen that Orestes is dead, to lull her and to make the climax more powerful. The story needs to be detailed and convincing, as in fact it is. Few tragic iambic speeches are much longer than fifty verses, but this is eighty-five.

> This I was sent for, I will tell it all.
> He had gone to the famous all-Greek games
> to join the contest for the Delphic prize.
> He heard the loud proclaiming of that man
> who is the herald that must judge them first,

and entered shining, struck awe in the world,
coupled his nature with the course and held
victorious acts and honour in his hand.
I tell you little where I could say much,
I never knew that man's action, his strength.
Know only this, that when the pentathlon
in all of its five contests was proclaimed
he carried off the honours of all five;
he was proclaimed citizen of Argos,
his name Orestes, Agamemnon's son,
whose father led the army of the Greeks.
So far so good, but when a god does harm
no man is strong enough to run from it.
This man, on the next day, when rapid feet
of horses try their contest in the sun,
entered there among many chariots.
One was Achaian, and from Sparta one,
two Libyans harnessed their chariots,
he with Thessalian horses was the fifth,
the sixth with chestnut foals Aitolian ...

The audience is expected not only to have national prejudices, but to know something about the breeds of Greek horses. We have evidence that the cavalry of Athens used more than one breed, Thessalians being one of the favourites. To breed horses, and to own and enter them for the chariot race which was the most popular spectacle of the games, was the height of aristocratic grandeur. The narrative, which has more enjambement of verses, and moves a little more rapidly than my version, is too long to reproduce at its full length. It runs its sparkling course more and more swiftly towards the death. One of the drivers is 'the ninth from Athens builded by the gods', later referred to as 'the skilled Athenian'. The race begins at a bronze trumpet, in a crash of hooves and a cloud of dust. When Orestes falls, his horses scatter, 'and all the throng of men lamented him'. In its way, this set piece is as much an eyewitness record of a Greek chariot race as the description of the battle that Aischylos wrote. Neither of them has any rival even in the prose histories of Herodotos and Thucydides.

Philoktetes was bitten by a snake on Lemnos, and stank and screamed so badly he was marooned there on the way to Troy. But the Greeks discovered that Troy must fall to the bow of Herakles, in the hands or by the means of Neoptolemos son of Achilles (the prophecy being vague), and Philoktetes had that bow. So Odysseus masterminded the plan to induce Philoktetes, by fair means or foul, to return to the Greek army. Young Neoptolemos told the marooned soldier the Greeks had come to take him home if he handed over the bow. He then repented, returned him the bow, and insisted that home was where Philoktetes, still suffering, must be taken. Herakles then appeared and persuaded Philoktetes to go willingly to Troy, because suffering leads to glory. It will be seen that Sophokles has here so overweighted his delaying devices that the dramatic machinery breaks down, and the ending, the only possible ending, is a bizarre divine apparition. And yet it works. Herakles is massively reinforced by the sense that 'so the story came true'.

Surprising as it may be, various versions of this story were handled by Bacchylides, Pindar, Aischylos and, in 431, Euripides, who made his play a conflict between honourable vengeance and honourable loyalty to the Greeks. Both Aischylos and Euripides had a neutral chorus of Lemnians, but Sophokles made Lemnos a desert island. The most memorable element in his tragedy is the fiendish suffering of the hero, expressed throughout the action, sometimes in lyrics but sometimes not, and the power of sleep, which is his only relief, and is prayed to as the god Sleep, whose winged head in bronze in the British Museum seems the embodiment of these verses. There is a saving touch of Asklepios about the god Sleep.

The moral problems of the play are not capable of brief or simple resolution, but one must note that everyone has some right on their side. Only Neoptolemos is admirable, but only Neoptolemos is wrong, within the framework of this tragedy. So would a morality we recognize as decent break up the structure of Greek tragedy, given free play? It seems that it would, because tragic form depends on inherited stories of which a merely moral view can make no sense. Poetry can make sense of them, but poetry contains many elements unresolved. And every retelling of a story and every dramatization of it makes fresh sense of it, for better and for worse. The poetry of *Philoktetes* is magnificent, and the play is not as broken-backed as I have made it seem. One should keep one's eye not on Neoptolemos but on Philoktetes himself and his mysterious calling.

Oedipus at Kolonos is an even stronger treatment of the vocation to suffering. The Greeks' words for holy and for taboo show in their history a fascinating shift of meaning from what is accursed, untouchable and set apart to what belongs to the gods, what is protected, what is sacred. Anthropology provides numerous examples of this status. Those 'afflicted by Allah' are under his special protection. Oedipus is a blind, wandering beggar with prophetic powers, guided by his daughter Antigone and seeking the place where he is doomed to die. This place will be holy, it will protect the country where he dies. There were several reputed graves of Oedipus, just as there were several graves of Iphigeneia, a potent heroine. Sophokles sets the death scene at Kolonos, a little hill outside Athens with a sacred grove, easily visible from the Akropolis. He was born at Kolonos. When he wrote this play, Athens was on the point of destruction by the Spartans. The poet makes the generosity of Theseus, protector of refugees, and the mysterious and awe-inspiring death of Oedipus, and the holy god-protected trees of Kolonos, a guarantee that Athens will survive. This underground current of Athenian feeling in the play is very strong.

Its essential structure is the one that Lattimore pointed out in the *Suppliants* of Aischylos: supplication, protection, threat and rescue, all dramatized here with interacting characters and tense action; but its climax is death, the ultimate protection and the end of suffering. This play is in some ways comparable to *King Lear*, and conveys the same terrible sense of tragic wisdom. Whatever meaning that phrase has, it has it in this tragedy. Sophokles had died before it was produced.

Yeats translated it for the Abbey Theatre in 1934, close to the height of his powers. His version of the last three lines is right, though it is not quite literally accurate. 'Raise no funeral song. God's will has been accomplished.' The threat to Oedipus in the course of the action comes from Thebes, and from the past. Kreon has imprisoned Oedipus in the palace, and refused him his self-exile, but Oedipus has escaped; Kreon tries to recapture him and gets repelled by Theseus only at the last moment, threatening war. (Thebes was a Spartan ally in the fifth century.) Polyneikes appears on his way to fight his brother, which was the action of the *Seven Against Thebes*, but Oedipus curses them both. Throughout these scenes, Oedipus becomes more and more terrible, like a prophetic Lear, but with a passion rooted in the saga and in the curse on his house. 'The gods know that my wrongs can strike, that my revenge shall not be in words.' He is gentle only to his daughters. The chorus echoes his thunderous solemnity.

Endure what life God gives and ask no longer span;
Cease to remember the delights of youth, travel-wearied aged man;
Delight becomes death-longing if all longing else be vain.

Even from that delight memory treasures so,
Death, despair, division of families, all entanglements of mankind grow,
As that old wandering beggar and these God-hated children know.

In the long echoing street the laughing dancers throng,
The bride is carried to the bridegroom's chamber through torchlight and
  tumultuous song;
I celebrate the silent kiss that ends short life or long.

Never to have lived is best, ancient writers say;
Never to have drawn the breath of life, never to have looked into the eye
  of day;
The second best's a gay goodnight and quickly turn away.

This translation is very loose, it is a meditation on compressed phrases, a teasing out of implicit themes. But it conveys the momentum of the play and of its choral lyrics better than one could hope to do otherwise. It is arguable that Greek tragedy is not translatable except into Latin; some of the Renaissance Latin translations are very fine and even accurate. The involvement of Yeats with Sophokles was always in terms of his own Irish preoccupations. A note in the Variorum edition of his plays says of the sacred wood at Kolonos, 'I saw the wood of the Furies was a haunted wood like any Irish haunted wood.' They are not quite the same, and we shall see how that affected his brilliant version of perhaps the most brilliant of all tragic lyrics. But the wandering blind beggar, and even the olive 'which gave Athenian intellect its mastery, miracle-bred out the living rock', do for better and worse recall Ireland, and 'Galway rock and cold Clare rock and thorn, wherein the gazing heart doubles its might'. The verse texture of Sophokles is denser and its colouring is a darker black.

The choral lyric about the grove at Kolonos is not only one of those moments of relief and contrast that occur in many of his tragedies. The grove is almost a character in this play, almost the principal character. It is a holy place, untrodden by human beings, silent, therefore, and echoing. It is clear from close reading of the text that Sophokles carefully builds it up as a presence from the beginning.

> 'Blind old man's daughter, Antigone,
> to what country, what people, have we come?
> ... Put me by the gods' groves and sit me down.'

> 'Father, unhappy Oedipus, I see
> the city's crown of towers is close by.
> I think this place is holy, full of leaves
> of laurels and of olive and of vines,
> and nightingales swift-winged make melody.
> Bend your limbs here on this rough-surfaced rock.'

The first Athenian to come by warns them that the place is sacred and forbidden, 'not to be touched or dwelt in: it belongs to the dreadful daughters of Earth and Darkness'. It is the place Oedipus has been looking for, the grove of the Eumenides, the Furies of the *Oresteia*. It has been suspected that some of the religion of this place may be an invention of the poet, but it is much more likely to be local belief; Sophokles knew these trees. Tragedies are woven out of the expectations of their audience, and the Athenians were more familiar with Kolonos and its rituals than the audience of Shakespeare's *Lear* with Dover cliffs. The Athenian tells Oedipus what gods are worshipped at Kolonos, and we have independent evidence of most of them. Oedipus prays to the goddesses in the wood. It is perhaps important to notice, since we are not polytheists, that to the Greeks all their landscape is sacred landscape. The descriptions we have of it are not just aesthetic even if they seem so.

Even their painted landscapes, which show an almost Chinese delicacy, are full of temples and stray altars and fenced sacred trees. The inhabited earth is god-haunted, and even the wilderness of mountain and forest has its own gods. The sacred map of ancient Athens and its close surroundings as we know them would be a crowded one. One of the cults that has defeated Yeats in this play is that of Zeus Morios, who protected the oldest Athenian trees. They were so ancient as to be sacred, god-given, the first trees and original gift of the gods, and the councillors of the Areopagus sacrificed under their branches once a month, completing the twelve trees in a year. One cannot pack such things into a verse translation. When Sophokles wrote, the groves of Attica were vulnerable to the Spartans: the holy trees that Zeus and Athene watch over are an important part of the background of the tragedy.

The choral lyrics that celebrate Kolonos occur nearly half-way through this long play, when Theseus has offered Oedipus his protection in spite of the threat from Thebes which Ismene has reported. Apollo's prophecy is already known that Oedipus dead will protect Athens, that the Thebans will come 'in arms and you will blast them from the tomb'. Theseus is undeterred by any threats.

> Be comforted, and if without my will
> Apollo sent you, I praise Apollo.
> And yet I know that without me my name
> will guard you and you shall not suffer harm.

At this point the chorus break out into their lyrics, though as soon as these four stanzas of song are over, Kreon will appear like a stage demon; he will take Antigone, to be rescued later, and Oedipus very nearly will suffer harm. Still, for the moment the sacred wood dominates the theatre, in its bright aspect now as in its terrible aspect later.

> Come praise Colonus' horses, and come praise
> The wine-dark of the wood's intricacies,
> The nightingale that deafens daylight there,
> If daylight ever visit where
> Unvisited by tempest or by sun
> Immortal ladies tread the ground
> Dizzy with harmonious sound,
> Semele's lad a gay companion.
>
> And yonder in the gymnasts' garden thrives
> The self-sown, self-begotten shape that gives
> Athenian intellect its mastery,
> Even the grey-leaved olive tree
> Miracle-bred out of the living stone;

> Nor accident of peace nor war
> Shall wither that old marvel, for
> The great grey-eyed Athene stares thereon.
>
> Who comes into this country, and has come
> Where golden crocus and narcissus bloom,
> Where the Great Mother, mourning for her daughter
> And beauty-drunken by the water
> Glittering among grey-leaved olive trees,
> Has plucked a flower and sung her loss;
> Who finds abounding Cephisus
> Has found the loveliest spectacle there is.
>
> Because this country has a pious mind
> And so remembers that when all mankind
> But trod the road, or splashed about the shore,
> Poseidon gave it bit and oar,
> Every Colonus lad or lass discourses
> Of that oar and of that bit;
> Summer and winter, day and night,
> Of horses and horses of the sea, white horses.

The nightingales of Sophokles sing among wine-purple ivy; it is not extravagant to imagine that they were the closest nightingales to Athens. The gymnasts' garden is the grove of Akademos nearby, where Sokrates talked; Sophokles refers to its gods but never names it. His chorus say they never heard of such a tree as an Athenian olive growing in the Peloponnese. Yeats has reversed the order of the second and third stanzas. The 'abounding Cephisus' is today best not visited, but it can still be seen in a memorably beautiful old photograph, in the *Pictorial Dictionary of Athens* by Travlos. The discoursing lads and lasses sound like a local catechism of initiation; that is a possible reality, but it is not in the text. The final lines of the Yeats version surely owe something to the Elgin marbles: once again his colouring is brilliant and justified, because Poseidon was god of ships and horses and patron of the riders on the Parthenon frieze, but this climax covers a confusion in the text of Sophokles, who is saying something about a ship, that 'follows the hundred-footed Nereids', of whom there were fifty. The translation by Yeats may not be exact, but only a pedant would despise it.

From this moment the tragedy dives into a thunderstorm and the

speeches of Oedipus become longer and increase in power. His cursing
of Polyneikes is particularly awful. Oedipus has appealed to Justice
'enthroned beside the ancient laws of Zeus'. I have translated his
iambics into verse; Yeats gives them in prose.

> Be gone, be spat out, be unfathered,
> baddest of bad, understand these curses
> I call on you, let your spear never take
> the earth you were bred in, never come home
> to hollow Argos, only kill and die
> by that same hand that you were exiled by.
> I curse, I call the dark ancestral hell
> of Erebos to carry you away,
> I call on the goddesses of this place ...

One must add after such a quotation that this play is not empty
of reason or common morality, mostly from Antigone. But now
Oedipus is ready to die. Herakles in the *Women of Trachis* is superhuman as soon as he is named. The tragic grandeur of Oedipus has
increased so that pity turns to awe. The curses are over and his verses
take on a silver tone.

> And I myself shall guide you to the place,
> grasping at no man's hand, where I must die.
> And this you shall not name to any man,
> neither where that place lies, nor whereabouts;
> this will defend you more than regiments.

Oedipus is the riddle-solver; perhaps death is the Sphinx. The blind
man will lead, the dead man will defend, the cursed man will bless,
the man dogged by curses and oracles has unravelled his own fate
and he must search out his grave, which is a holy place, his sanctuary.
This shamed, dishonoured and blinded man will be hidden. Verses
play for the last time over these paradoxes.

> We must go now, the god presses me.
> Children, come so far, I will lead you now,
> you were your father's guides and he is yours.
> Go now, and do not touch me, leave me go,
> I must find out my holy grave alone
> where fate is that the earth shall hide my bones.
> This way, walk this way, here. I am led on

> by Hermes and the goddess underground.
> O light unseen, which once was light to me,
> now you touch my body for the last time.
> At last I go to hide my end of life
> where Hades is. But most dear of strangers,
> live happily and in prosperity,
> you and this country and your company,
> and in your good fortunes think of me dead.

The longer account of the death itself comes in almost the last verses of the play, in a full-scale narrative by a messenger lasting eighty verses. It is pleasing to think that almost the last poetry Sophokles wrote was a dramatic innovation, though it owes something to plays by Euripides, as other parts of the play also do, including the humane character of Theseus and the saving role of the heroic dead. Readers of the Yeats translation should be warned that his emphasis on love in his prose version of these lines is wrong.

> We wept a little. When we ceased to weep
> and no lamenting was heard any more,
> there was a silence. Suddenly a voice
> called out to him. On every head of ours
> the fearful hairs with terror stood on end.
> The god cried out many times, many times,
> Oedipus, come, come. Oedipus, come.
> Why delay? You have lingered a long time.
> And when he knew that the god cried to him,
> he spoke to Theseus to come close to him,
> then when he came he said, O my dear friend,
> give me your hand's old faith to my children
> and you to him my dears, and promise me
> you never will desert them willingly.

No one but Theseus knows in the end how Oedipus died. The climax of the tragedy is an absence. The teller of the story saw only Theseus shielding his eyes from some terrible sight.

> It was no burning lightning of the god
> nor any storm that swirled out of the sea,
> that carried him away at that moment.
> It was some convoy of the gods or some
> befriending chasm of unlighted earth.

> In his passing he was not lamentable
> he was not suffering disease in pain,
> but wonderful, if ever human was.

The sisters lament with the chorus for a short time, then Theseus reappears to speak his last, chanted lines. 'Cease lamentation, children. Where the favour of earth and night lies, one must not grieve. They will be revenged.' In a few words he as it were seals the grave with secrecy and solemnity. The last verses of the chorus mean 'Cease now and raise no further lamentation. All this is ordered.'

So ends the last tragedy Sophokles wrote. One has the impression that we have seen only glimpses of his range and his development and his amazing powers. But in the *Oedipus at Kolonos* he had 'attained his nature', as the form of tragedy did in his life-work. The fragments of his lost tragedies fill a thick volume, but his work makes the case strongly, if it needed to be made, that one should study complete plays even at the cost of neglecting fragments. The *Trackers*, his satyr play of which a substantial part survives, is closely based on the Homeric *Hymn to Hermes*. One is pleased that he liked that; it is perhaps the only thing he has in common with Shelley. But his verse technique in the *Trackers* is less powerful, perhaps because it does not embody the strong paradoxes and tensions of his tragic stories.

The fragments we have of the lost plays of Sophokles are a fascinating and rewarding study, though of course they are tantalizing. In his *Aletes*, the son of Aigisthos tyrannizes at Mycenae after a false report of the death of Orestes among the Taurians, where he was rescuing his lost sister Iphigeneia. Elektra, believing Iphigeneia is her brother's murderess, makes to attack her with a blazing torch: an interesting variant on conventional recognition scenes. The *Odysseus Pricked* is an even stranger tale of the later generation of a famous family. Odysseus is murdered by Telegonos, his lost son by Circe: recognition came too late. In *Phineus*, Asklepios heals blindness. In *Teukros*, the old father of Ajax grieves.

> How empty the delight I had, my son,
> when you were praised as living. In that dark
> the Fury fawned. I was deceived in joy.

There are many memorable lines among the fragments, including the proverb 'Under the stone watches the scorpion'. Some old reconstructions are bizarre or incredible; it is not quite possible to believe in his *Statue-bearers*, in which the gods abandoned Troy, carrying their statues, although he does seem to have treated this ominous event in verse one would like to have. Shakespeare and Cavafy got the theme of 'The god leaves Antony' ultimately from those lost lines. Among the shorter fragments, one is pleased to have one from *Thamyras*:

> The strings of zithers and plucked instruments
> and the sweet wooden music of the Greeks.

We know that Sophokles wrote a *Phaidra*, possibly intended to rival an early Hippolytos play by Euripides; his *Theseus* pursued the same theme of the terrible consequences of erotic passion, and to judge by its influence must have been unforgettable. In his *Niobe*, into which W. S. Barrett has recently fitted some freshly discovered verses, the gods are shown in the act of murder. It remains curious that although Sophokles has attracted the work of great critics, they have so often found it difficult to get under his skin. There is something enigmatic about him, which was once taken for tranquillity and mature restraint. I do not discover that quality in him. His poetry is sometimes linguistically hard to unpick, and it is subtle as language, and often on fire with passionate excitement. His complexities are deeply thought as well as felt. It is strange that a poet should emerge as a personality only at the age of ninety. And yet I feel that *Oedipus at Kolonos* is the key to Sophokles. He was a nearly exact contemporary of Perikles, and remembered Athens before the Persians came.

SOME DATES IN THE LIFE OF SOPHOKLES

496/5	Birth of Perikles and Sophokles
490	Aischylos fought at Marathon
480	Salamis. Sophokles danced in the celebrations
472	Aischylos' *Persians*
469	Birth of Sokrates
468	Sophokles defeats Aischylos in the theatre. Death of Simonides

458	*Oresteia* of Aischylos
456	Death of Aischylos
454	Treasury of Delos moved to Athens
450	Trial of Anaxagoras who escaped from Athens
444	Protagoras drew up for Athens the laws of a new colony, Thourioi
443	Sophokles is imperial treasurer
441	*Ode to Herodotos*. Euripides wins a tragic prize
440	Sophokles is general with Perikles. Stays with Ion of Chios
438	Death of Pindar. Parthenon consecrated, Euripides' *Medeia*
431	Peloponnesian War begins
429	Death of Perikles from plague
428	Euripides' *Hippolytos* wins tragic prize
420	Sanctuary of Asklepios at Athens founded
413	Sophokles is a commissioner after the Sicilian disaster. Euripides writes an elegy for the dead
409	*Philoktetes*
406/5	Death of Euripides
406	*Oedipus at Kolonos* written. Death of Sophokles
404	Fall of Athens
401	*Oedipus at Kolonos* produced at Athens

BIBLIOGRAPHY

C. M. Bowra, *Periclean Athens*, 1971

R. Carden, *The Papyrus Fragments of Sophocles*, 1974

K. J. Dover (ed.), *Ancient Greek Literature*, 1980

S. C. Humphreys, *Anthropology and the Greeks*, 1978

H. Lloyd-Jones on Tycho von Wilamowitz and on Reinhardt in *Blood for the Ghosts*, 1982

K. Reinhardt, *Sophocles*, 1979 (German original, 1933)

T. von Wilamowitz, *Die dramatische Technik des Sophocles*, 1917

R. P. Winnington-Ingram, *Sophocles*, 1980

W. B. Yeats, 'King Oedipus' and 'Oedipus at Colonus' in *Collected Plays*, 1952

9

EURIPIDES

Euripides was, verbally and mentally, an agile poet who cultivated the extremes of passion. His building-blocks, and those of part of the work of Sophokles, were not characters but scenes, and the passions of his characters seem to have interested him only in terms of scenes. Aristotle taught, and critics have rediscovered from him, that ancient tragic drama represented actions rather than persons; it enacted stories. Euripides does this, not so much with stock characters, which traditional mythology and masked actors were bound to impose, as with stock scenes: the confession to the confidant, the recognition scene, the furious rational argument, and so on. In the end he was manipulating these scenes and situations with so many surprises and variations and *coups de théâtre* that the stories all but fell apart under the strain. But his poetry is electric and he is intensely dramatic. If to be dazzling is the wrong quality for a tragic poet, that is the worst criticism one can make of him.

We have precise dates for eight of his surviving plays. He first had a tragedy performed at the Great Dionysia in 455, but his first competitive success was in 441. He had only three or four other successes in his lifetime, although he wrote ninety or so plays. The tragedies we can date are the *Alkestis* in 438, *Medeia* in 431, *Hippolytos* in 428 (a success), the *Trojan Women* in 415, *Helen* in 412, *Orestes* in 408, and the *Bacchai* and *Iphigeneia in Aulis*, both first produced in Athens after his death. The *Phœnicians* is somewhere between 412 and 408, and if the *Rhesos*, which survives among his plays, were really by him, which it is not, it would have to be extremely early. But in small elements of iambic verse technique, particularly in the freedom of substituting two short syllables for one long one, the tragic poetry of Euripides shows a curiously even development. Metrical freedom increases with mathematical regularity throughout his career. It is therefore possible to give approximate dates for all his surviving plays, and scholars of this subject have conspired to do so. With Aischylos and Sophokles we have insufficient evidence for a framework like this, and no mechanical criterion. Metrical freedom seems from what small evidence we have to decrease in the plays of Aischylos throughout his career. Dating the plays of Aischylos by their style has led to shaming mistakes. But in the special case of Euripides even the hardest-headed of critics agree that the method seems to be justified. It was discovered by the Polish scholar Zieliński in 1925.

Intellectually, Euripides was a modernist, and his tragedies often contain progressive or modern-sounding opinions. It would be a mistake to put great weight on these isolated utterances, since tragic poetry is an impersonal art. It is too easy to be confused by the comedies of Aristophanes, in which Euripides is constantly satirized, into thinking one can place him as a corrosive or subversive thinker, almost a trendy and a charlatan. I therefore propose not to take comic criticisms into account at all, until we come to consider comedy as a whole, although the temptation, because here at last we have a writer in a critical context, is very great.

As a poet he showed originality. P. T. Stevens has traced in him an interesting use of popular speech, and he was an inventive lyricist. The story of Athenian prisoners singing his choruses in the quarries of Syracuse is probably true. Still, it is clear enough that Euripides belonged more fully than Sophokles did to the atmosphere of the intellectuals we scornfully and perhaps wrongly lump together as 'sophists' in the late fifth century. His personal theology remains obscure to me, though he entertained a variety of ideas in this as in other matters. His Athenian patriotism is undoubted. It is unclear exactly why he went away to Macedonia in old age, when Athens was near its fall.

He died there. There was a story that he was torn to pieces by the king's dogs. That looks like a characteristic piece of Greek mythification, but if one considers the kind of mastiff they probably were, then it does seem a perfectly possible accident. Another picturesque detail that stern scholars reject is that he used to write poetry in a sea-cave on the island of Salamis. I recollect an artificial grotto for the grave of a dead dog at Prior Park, overlooking Bath, put up by Pope. We were told as boys that he used to write his poetry there. Such a myth arises easily. And yet the sea-cave is no more unlikely than the ruined tower at Stanton Harcourt where Pope translated Homer, or the peculiar haunts of many other poets. If it were true, it would be interesting that he wrote outside of Athens; but likely enough, the pleasing detail is based only on some lost verses of a play. One might as well say that Sophokles had felt homesickness at Troy. In 440, he might have done, but then the *Ajax* was probably already written. Poetry is based on the experience of life, but from fifth-century tragic poetry one cannot reconstruct that experience except in the broadest terms.

Alkestis was performed in 438 when Euripides was already within sight of fifty, a mature poet and clever dramatist, a tragedian of at least eighteen years' standing. It was not exactly a tragedy: it seems to have been played instead of a satyr play, and it was tragic with comic touches. It contains a resurrection from the dead, and it has a pantomime quality which is as admirable as it is unexpected. The simplest *coups de théâtre* are the most effective. Apollo has given Admetos, who was once his kind employer during a spell on earth, the privilege that on his fated day someone may die in his place. The *Alkestis* opens with an encounter between Apollo and Death. Alkestis dies for her husband like a real tragic heroine, but then Herakles arrives at the house, and after being well entertained by Admetos, he ambushes Death and beats him up. If this seems a ridiculous piece of buffoonery, one should remember the legend of the Olympic boxer who beat up the ghost or heroic apparition of one of the sailors of Odysseus, rescued a girl and drove the ghost into the sea. His name was Euthymos and it happened in the 470s, at Temesa on the Italian coast. The story was told at Olympia, but Temesa had a painting of the event. And one might remember the medieval treatments of the Harrowing of Hell.

So Alkestis is rescued, and after various devices and subterfuges, all ends happily. The dramatic construction is light-hearted, and deliberately naive, but the *Alkestis* is admirably dramatic. The intermingling of gods and men and the allegorical Death, the true gods of the dead being too serious for parody, belongs to a level of folk-tale and popular narrative of which we have all too few examples. Solemn tragedy ought not to blind us altogether to its

existence. The chorus of *Alkestis* are villagers. One should add a note
about the story. Apollo had served his spell on earth because Zeus
imposed it as a punishment. And why? Because Apollo killed the
Cyclopes, the metal-smiths of Zeus. And what did he do that for?
Because Zeus killed Asklepios with a thunderbolt, for raising a man
from the dead. As Death enters in *Alkestis*, Apollo identifies him:

> I must not be polluted in this house.
> Now I see Death, the high priest of the dead,
> who comes to take her to the house of Hell.

The temptation to translate this into the terms of a play like *Everyman* is irresistible. At key moments the formality becomes absurd, as
it does in the English mystery plays. 'Not willingly, but goodbye my
children.' 'Look at them, look.' 'I can no longer live.' 'What, do you
leave me?' 'Goodbye.' 'I perish.' 'Admetos' wife is gone, she is no
more.' This is followed by an aria sung by a little boy. Tragedy is
a mixture of musical and spoken words, and that is the original
meaning of our word, melodrama. Small wonder that such a genre
tends to extremes of passion and surprise. The extravagance of
Euripides in his late tragedies can be traced back to the *Alkestis*
and to his strong sense of a popular form. As for the verse texture of
this play, it is a stiff but intellectually less tense form of the tragic
verse we so admire.

> We are mortal and must have mortal thoughts;
> as for the solemn and the frowning brows,
> to all of them if you take me for judge
> life is not life but merely misery.

The constant playing on words, and the somewhat artificial
resonance of iambic verse against which the language plays in a
series of cascading variations, are a style which is not impossible
to imitate, and Euripides may be accused in his verse texture of
self-imitation. But he is sometimes in a short passage hard to
distinguish from Sophokles, as some disputed fragments show. His
verse is a capable machinery in which the god or the ghost is not
always present. When it is, then Euripides is a great poet. If we had
the whole of his fascinating *Telephos*, produced like *Alkestis* in 438,
we might date his greatness that early. After *Alkestis* comes *Medeia*,

in 431. He was in his early fifties, and the theatre already knew something about the sustained passion of tragic heroines. But Medeia, the oriental sorceress, is magical in more senses than one.

Medeia fled from home with Jason her lover, who then married the daughter of Kreon of Corinth, causing her furious rage and pain, here expressed off-stage in lyric verse. When she appears her torrent of iambic eloquence starts slowly, in reasoned conversation with the women of Corinth. The element of popular language in this play is particularly strong.

> They say we live a life not perilous,
> tranquil at home while they contend with steel;
> in this they reason wrong: I should prefer
> to stand three times to arms than bear one child.
> But you and I are not on one standing,
> you have your city here and father's house
> support of life and loving company,
> I am deserted, townless, insulted,
> and from my barbarous land stolen away,
> I have no mother, no brother, no kin
> to be my fellow in catastrophe.

These arguments are central to Greek feeling, however modern they may appear. They are folk-wisdom and go back to prehistory. The undertone of women's protest and perhaps of sympathy for slaves sharpens them, of course, to an Athenian audience and to us, but they belong to the situation of the play. Kreon has exiled Medeia with her children, and their confrontation is stormy, but she wins a day's grace. When he leaves the stage, she meditates murder.

> And I have many deadly ways for them,
> I do not know what to try first my dears,
> whether to burn the bridal house with fire
> or thrust in through her stomach some sharp blade,
> entering in silence where their bed is.

The choral lyric that follows has a coolness and great beauty. It begins, 'The streams of holy rivers backwards run, and justice and all things are overturned. The thoughts of men are devious, the gods' faith does not hold out now.' It ends by lamenting over Medeia in very much the terms of her own speech. She then encounters Jason himself, in a firework display of articulate passion on her side, and almost convincing argument on his. The play proceeds as a series of these meetings between two persons. Aigeus the father of Theseus (Medeia had a later connection with Theseus in mythology) appears in a sub-plot only half developed; he does little to further the action beyond offering her a future, but this utterly alters her mood to one of triumph.

> O Zeus, Justice of Zeus, Light of the Sun,
> now I triumph over my enemies,
> it will come, we have walked into that road.
> Now my hope stands to have justice on them.

From this point her vengeance unfolds. She pretends reconciliation, sends her children with deadly presents so that Kreon and the new wife die in anguish, and finally murders her children. The legend of Medeia is a long one, full of magic herbs and murders; in this play she is the very spirit of vengeance; the furious, wronged woman has mounted to a height of passion which is not human, she is a spirit of rage, and one remembers that she was a famous witch. She is fire and air, her other elements she leaves to baser life. The dragon chariot of the Sun, her grandfather, carries her off, spitting defiance at tragical, ruined Jason, who lives on as Kreon does in Sophokles' *Antigone*. She was affronted and insulted, and there is no moral measure we can usefully apply to the dreadful result. This was a folk-tale, it was not fiction. It reveals Euripides as an awe-inspiring tragic poet, and that no doubt is what it was meant to do.

His *Hippolytos*, three years later in 428, is, I think, a much greater play. Even its moral machinery is more interesting, and it has an economy and even a restraint we may agree to call classical. It is worth noticing that Euripides had already presented a *Hippolytos*, with a more passionate and flagrant Phaidra and a dumb-struck hero hiding his face for shame, which was unsuccessful. The diminished or controlled fire of the second *Hippolytos* won a prize. Between the two stands surely the lost *Phaidra* of Sophokles, in which the heroine was almost certainly virtuous, believing that Theseus was dead and she was a widow. The tragedy of 428 begins with Aphrodite and ends with Artemis. One would greatly like to know whether they appeared in equal dignity and glory. It is possible that Aphrodite spoke her prologue from the stage, because most prologues are human. Since the conclusion belongs to Artemis she appeared as a goddess from above the action. The tragedy consisted of their conflict.

Hippolytos was an unripe boy who liked to hunt and worshipped Artemis, but he fatally neglected Aphrodite. To ignore any god is a traditional sin for which Greek heroes in stories pay dearly. Phaidra, wife of Theseus, desired his son Hippolytos, in this second *Hippolytos* as in the earlier play. But now the scene is Troizen where Hippolytos was brought up. Phaidra fell for him when he came to Athens for the games, but now Theseus and Phaidra visit Troizen and she is feverish with love. But she tells no one except an old nurse; the audience has to be told by Aphrodite. A complicated intrigue of misunderstandings occupies most of the play. The nurse tells Hippolytos, swearing him to secrecy. Hippolytos believes, forgivably I think, that this is just Phaidra's device to let him know. He speaks furiously to Phaidra. She believes he will tell her secret and hangs herself for shame, leaving a note for Theseus to protect her good name by accusing Hippolytos of rape. Theseus curses his son, Poseidon responds with a monster that causes a chariot smash, and Hippolytos, who has kept his promise not to tell, is carried in dying. Artemis appears and tells the truth to Theseus, and Hippolytos dies tranquilly and somewhat virginally on stage. The creaking vehicle of this story, based half on ritual and half on folklore, becomes in the hands of Euripides a convincing and a moving tragedy.

Its characters are powerfully sketched in a few lines, like the best of restrained Greek drawing in the visual arts. Phaidra's debate with herself is perhaps touched by moral philosophy, but I am not speaking of great psychological subtlety or of modern acting techniques, only of what can be conveyed in a few words.

> I have at home certain bewitching drugs
> of love that only now rise to my mind,
> which neither shamefully nor harmfully
> will cure this fever if yourself are brave.

Love-magic and poisons belong to women, and in tragedy as in folk-tales they often go wrong. The word I translate as drugs had 'love-charm' as its original meaning, but by now it meant any kind of magic: Orestes in the *Oresteia* referred to Apollo's oracles persuading

him to matricide as 'the drugs of this resolve', though that may be
a daring Aischylean reversal of familiar things into ominous meanings. The person characterized so clearly in the sinister verses of
Euripides is the old nurse. Hippolytos himself is drawn with precision
in his very first prayer to Artemis.

> O goddess, I bring you what I have made:
> a twisted wreath picked from pure meadow-ground
> where no shepherd ever grazes his flock,
> no steel has ever come, the bee in spring
> passes across the untrodden meadows,
> Virginity guards them with sprinkling streams.

The word I translate as Virginity means modesty, shame, and
respect, but its meaning is very strong in Greek, and is at the root
of this play. It is a moral imperative, like innocence, more than a
virtue. It is half of the system of shame and honour, disgrace and
glory, by which the Greeks lived, at least until the fifth century, and
which social anthropologists have studied. In 428, Hippolytos was
an old-fashioned young man. His last words paint the same picture.

> I shall be firm. I am dying, father.
> Cover my face up swiftly in your robe.

The choral lyrics of this tragedy are as memorable as its cleanly
chiselled iambics.

Eros, Eros, who drips desire on eyes, bringing sweet favours to the soul you
storm, never come to do me harm, nor out of season. Not the thunderbolt
of fire, nor the stroke above the stars is like Aphrodite's which Eros son
of Zeus flings from his hand. In vain, in vain, by Alpheios, and Apollo's
Delphic shrine, the Greeks pile up the slaughtered meat, yet we do not worship
him, Eros tyrant-king of men, who holds the key to Aphrodite's rooms ...

The choral poetry of Euripides has an oblique relevance to the mood
of the action, but in its way it guides by delay and formalization
of thought and feeling the otherwise rapid momentum of his
tragedies. And it is beautiful. The only academic lecture I have ever
heard which was moving in its beauty was largely about the lyric
poetry of this play. It was given by Gilbert Murray in extreme old
age; alas, I remember hardly a word of it. Since 1964, ten years
after that lecture, the commentary by W. S. Barrett has made

Hippolytos one of the best known and best understood of all Greek tragedies.

The great Wilamowitz believed he could trace the spiritual development of Euripides. The *Children of Herakles* has been grouped with *Andromache* and the *Suppliants* in a cluster of patriotic tragedies – one should add the fragments of *Erechtheus* – and dated accordingly. G. Zuntz, a scholar capable of wild mistakes who all the same occasionally wrote well about Euripides, wanted to put the *Children of Herakles* in 430, because the prophecy of Eurystheus in the play, that Attica or at least part of it would be protected from Spartan invasion, was soon going to be proved untrue. This is a variation on a brilliant argument by Wilamowitz, who dated this tragedy on similar grounds after 430, when the threat was imminent, but maybe as late as 427. The technical arguments, which Wilamowitz had not known, point to 425. In such a case it is probably foolish to be absolutely bound by them; one should allow a little variation within a few years. But Zuntz is forced to make a careful rearrangement of the historical evidence, and to reject Thucydides in order to establish his own date of 430. He is wrestling with the lordly and casual ghost of Wilamowitz, here as elsewhere. This is certainly a wartime play. Beyond that, the truth is obscure, although Zuntz might well be right.

The children of Herakles are suppliants at the altar of Zeus at Marathon, pursued by their father's enemy Eurystheus. Demophon, son of Theseus, offers protection, and Iolaos, the old companion of Herakles, defeats the herald of Eurystheus in argument. The chorus are humane Athenians. Battle follows, and Athens wins it, through the noble action of a girl, one of the children, who sacrifices her life, and was worshipped in the fifth century as Makaria, the nymph of the spring of Marathon. Athens is aided by Hyllos, son of Herakles, and his army.

Eurystheus is captured, and brought before Alkmene, the aged mother of Herakles, who had fled with her grandchildren. Small wonder that in a line which has needlessly puzzled Zuntz and Gilbert Murray, when she asks how Iolaos did in the battle, she is told 'his youth has been renewed', since he and she belong to the same generation; but this is not a phantom or a miraculous apparition interpolated by actors, it is surely only a metaphor. Alkmene demands the death of Eurystheus, but agrees to hand over his corpse for burial. In return for this magnanimity, Eurystheus offers a prophecy of Apollo that his dead body will protect Attica.

This tragedy is short, but full of problems. Our text is incomplete. Worse, Makaria disappears from the text prepared to die, but we hear no more about her death and nothing about her worship. Wilamowitz thought we had the play in a shortened version made for a later revival. As for Eurystheus, we know from Strabo that he was buried at the temple of Athene Pallenis in Gargettos, which is the modern Ieraka. This identification has been certain since 1942. Pallene is a different town, identified in the same year at the modern Stavros, admittedly not far away. Buried at Gargettos, or even at Pallene, Eurystheus could not protect the coastal plain as Wilamowitz argues, but only the approach to Athens itself by the pass between Hymettos and Pendeli, near Ayia Paraskevi, still a bottleneck of traffic. The argument of Zuntz, that in 430 the Spartans took precisely this route, is misconceived, because they were moving in the opposite direction, from the plain of Athens to the seaside. Eurystheus is supposed to protect Athens itself, and that hope is undatable.

The tragedy of *Hecuba*, dated perhaps by a reference to the Delian festival in 426 or 425, centres on yet another furious woman. Priam's widow sees her daughter Polyxena carried off to be slaughtered at the tomb of Achilles, and discovers that her last surviving son Polydoros has been murdered for gold by his foster-father, Polymestor, king of Thrace. She and her women obtain the neutrality of Agamemnon, entice Polymestor into their tent, and there stab him blind and murder his children. The prologue is the ghost of Polydoros, and this, even more clearly than *Medeia*, is a revenge tragedy. It is powerfully written, and given its contradictions of place and a certain lack of logical unity in the plot, skilfully put together. Polyxena dies nobly, and her horrible fate is made almost acceptable and inevitable, compared to what follows. The prologue had already made that clear.

> For Peleus' son appeared out of his grave,
> holding back the whole army of the Greeks,
> who steered for home over the sea-levels,
> demanding my sister Polyxena
> dead on his grave to love and honour him.
> He will get it, his friends will give it him.

It is worth noting that human sacrifice was abhorrent to the Greeks in historical times, although it did take place, with ritual cannibalism, in one remote sanctuary in the mountains of the Peloponnese, at Lykosoura; there is some evidence for a ritual of human scapegoats; and Herodotos speaks of the three prisoners slaughtered or torn to pieces before Salamis. But at a level below that of civilized poetry, human sacrifice was a fascinating element in folk-tales; Homer accommodates it, although by terrible exception, and there are occasions in the *Iliad*, as Emily Vermeule has put it, 'when the soldiers feel like joining the dogs in dissecting the enemy', though the gruesome threats of head-hunting are only ornamental. Hecuba in the *Iliad* would like to pluck out the entrails of Achilles and eat them raw, and the goddess Hera would like to eat men alive like a demon in the popular Greek underworld, but Zeus hates these excesses. Furious revenge in Greek feeling is the privilege of mothers, and that is dominant in Hecuba's role here, while the human sacrifice on the grave of Achilles is just something out of a ghost story. The Greeks had been opening Bronze Age graves for propitiation and worship since the eighth century. They were doing similar things in central Athens in the fifth. It may be that like the *Ghost Stories of an Antiquary* by M. R. James, these fearful stories began from archaeology of some kind.

The play is full of reasoning as well as passion. When Polyxena dies, Hecuba muses on the origins of constancy of soul or nature. Is aristocratic or excellent quality bred into children or is it educated? As Albin Lesky remarked, 'Hardly anywhere else is it so conspicuous that the problems which motivate Euripides are forced out in places where they achieve a curious effect.' One might cite equally the odd outburst of Medeia on the loneliness of intellectuals, but 'motivate' is too strong a word for these preoccupations. These tragedies have a momentum of their own. They are not intellectual problem plays, but thought expresses feeling in a tragic progression.

> And this to have learnt well
> is to know shame by ruling-lines of good,
> and in these matters the mind aims in vain.

Hecuba will die howling, she will turn into a dog. The blinded king knows this from Dionysos, prophet of the Thracians. The tragedy ends in furious dialogue between the king and Hecuba, without divine intervention, and Agamemnon concludes it in a few words, more ominous than he intends.

> I see the wind shaking the sails for home;
> good fortune sail with us to that country:
> and may we find good fortune waits at home,
> now we are loose of all our troubles here.

Elektra is the only tragedy of Euripides we can compare with full, surviving treatments of the same theme by Aischylos and by Sophokles. It used to be wrongly dated to 413 because of a reference to ships in the Sicilian sea, but such a reference is not so easily datable, and we should follow the arguments from verse technique, and put it earlier, even at the cost, if it is one, of allowing Euripides a wide artistic range within a very few years. It is not even objectively certain whether Sophokles or Euripides produced an *Elektra* first. Here Elektra is in a farm on the border of Argos, the prologue is by a peasant, and the chorus are country neighbours. Aigisthos hid Elektra from suitors and planned to murder her, for fear she might bear a child to avenge her father. Klytaimestra, 'her savage mother', saved her, but Aigisthos to lessen his fear married her to a peasant. Kypris means Aphrodite.

> If a man with authority had her,
> he'd rouse Agamemnon's murder from its sleep,
> and justice come home to Aigisthos then.
> But Kypris knows I never shamed her bed,
> she is a virgin still as she has been.

This prologue is powerful, and one is in the mood of a bloody revenge tragedy from the beginning. Elektra also defines herself strongly from her first appearance. She has gone out for water as an excuse to be out of doors, which under Greek social conditions a woman would need.

> O night of blackness, nurse of golden stars,
> through whom I take my vessel on my head
> and make my way down to the river-springs,
> not driven to it by necessity
> but for the gods to see how I am wronged,
> I wail for my father to the high air.

The chorus invite her to a country festival of the gods at the famous Heraion of Argos, a country temple. When Orestes and his friend Pylades approach the farm, she sends to an old shepherd, Agamemnon's old servant, for food to entertain her guests. The play does not suffer in any way from these touches of rustic realism, though no doubt they may derive from satyr plays. But the strong contrast with Sophokles suggests that Euripides comes later, and is writing a counterblast. The shepherd plays a vital role in the recognition scene. This scene contains criticism of the recognition scene in Aischylos, which scholars find a shocking intrusion, even an interpolation, but one cannot put it beyond the whim of Euripides. The vengeance follows step by step; Aigisthos is cut down at a country sacrifice, and Klytaimestra is lured to the farm with a false report that Elektra has a child. Their confrontation is dreadful. Elektra rages but her mother is merely sad; she admits her crimes, and they have not made her happy. Elektra takes her indoors to her death. The messenger's narrative of the death of Aigisthos had been grim enough, since he died at a moment of innocence, hospitality and sanctity.

> We found him in the water-fed gardens
> cutting the tender sprigs of myrtle-shoots.

But when Klytaimestra dies the children are struck by horror.

> Take her, cover my mother in her robes
> and clean her wounds. She bore two murderers.

These verses are not in iambics but in a prolonged lyrical exchange. Kastor, with his brother Polydeukes, immediately appears, and expresses a stern view of what has been done.

> She suffered justice but you did it not.
> And Apollo, Apollo – he's my lord
> and I am silent. Wise: for you unwise.
> We must praise it. But now you must perform
> all things that Fate and Zeus decree for you.

Elektra must marry Pylades and Orestes go to be tried in Athens. The instructions are very detailed and cover the ground of numerous stories. The judgement of Euripides through Kastor about the plot of the *Oresteia* is not untraditional except in its laconical expression and perhaps in its emphasis. 'Wise as he is, he gave an oracle unwise for you' is not contrary to the sense of many generations about Apollo's oracles.

Andromache, which perhaps ought to be dated about 425, before *Hecuba* and the *Suppliants*, was not liked by ancient critics; we are even told by an ancient scholar that it was never performed in Athens. Modern critics have followed the hint. Hektor's widow, Andromache, is a suppliant at the altar of Thetis, mother of Achilles, in Thessaly where Neoptolemos carried her off. His wife Hermione and her father Menelaos have plotted to ruin Andromache and her child by Neoptolemos. But Peleus, father of Achilles, defeats Menelaos in a rather one-sided argument, and the villainous Spartan king withdraws. The chorus consists of local women, sympathetic and helpless. Hermione fears her husband's return, but at this point she is suddenly carried off by Orestes. We hear from a messenger how Orestes had Neoptolemos killed at Delphi; this death was legendary, though not the detail. The tragedy, which already has a lament by Andromache in elegiac couplets, finishes in laments for Neoptolemos, and a final appearance of Thetis, who foretells a happy dynastic future for the Molossians, for whom this play, a piece of wartime diplomatic propaganda, was probably intended. I must admit to a great affection for it. Sophokles also wrote an *Andromache*, probably set at Delphi, possibly earlier than this one.

In our tragedy, Andromache disappears at line 765 and Hermione at line 1047; the last 238 verses concentrate on dynastic history. Euripides is fitting the great figures and famous stories of the Greeks into the history of the Molossians, as he so often and so significantly does into that of the Athenians: and this is why his *Andromache* is so particularly episodic. One modern critic sees it as a subtle psychological study of Hermione, which it is not; another cleverly centres it on Andromache by returning her to the stage, where her annihilating silence is the point of whatever is said about the dead Neoptolemos. The ingenuity of the theory is misplaced. P. T. Stevens suspects the whole momentum of the tragedy may lie in the awful consequences of war: 'all the result of one unhappy war'. The war is certainly like a curse, and Euripides enters closely into its consequences, as Aischylos so forcefully sketched them in the Kassandra scene of the *Agamemnon*. But the application of these sub-epic events to a dynasty seems to me the true reading, and the only one that explains the faults as well as the virtues of the tragedy. Thetis is splendid.

> For I who should bear children with no tears
> lost the swift-footed son I had by you,
> Achilles whom I bore the best of Greeks.
> Therefore I come to order: you obey.
> Bury Achilles' son who here lies dead,
> take and bury him by Apollo's hearth
> to shame the Delphians, his grave shall tell
> his violent murder by Orestes' hand.
> The woman prisoner Andromache
> shall settle here among Molossians
> with Helenos in happy marriage-bed,
> and her son here, last blood of Aiakos.
> Molossia shall see king follow king
> in long inheritance of happiness ...
> I will relieve you of all human harms,
> I will make you an undecaying god,
> and in the house of Nereus afterwards
> you shall dwell on with me, god with goddess.
> And you shall walk dry-footed from the sea
> to meet your most dear and my most dear son
> Achilles on the island he lives in
> by the White Rock beyond the Euxine Strait.

The *Suppliants* is another of those Euripidean tragedies which deliberately expressed Athenian wartime feeling. The right date must be about 424. The myth had been handled by Aischylos in his *Eleusinians*. Theseus of Athens intervenes to secure the burial of the seven dead heroes who fought against Thebes. The chorus consists of the mothers of the dead and their attendants. They are suppliants at the altar of Eleusinian Demeter, where the ancient road crosses the hills from Thebes. The prologue is by Aithra, mother of Theseus. When Theseus is ready to refuse Adrastos, the defeated king of Argos, Aithra turns his mind to the miserable mothers, who are begging for the bodies of the dead. He praises humanity and intelligence against Adrastos, and then freedom and democracy against a Theban herald. But he must enforce his position by battle, and he does so: the messenger's speech in this play is a battle narrative.

The weight of tragedy is in ceremonial lamentation over the dead, whose funeral speech Adrastos then speaks. Who dare say today that this is untragical? It is the sadder for being impersonal, until Adrastos names the names, and clearly enough the Athenians will have felt it with its many national references more closely than we do. But when Adrastos has spoken, Euadne, one of the widows, flings herself on to the pyre that burns her husband. This scene is expressed in lyrics of great dignity; it is less operatic than a modern reader might foresee. The children of the dead end the story with a procession of the urns of ashes, and a fresh dirge in which their voices join. Athene arrives to impose an oath on the hero Adrastos that Argos will be loyal to Athens.

It is some of the details that wrench this play almost out of tragic form, towards national drama of another kind, and which produce the most memorable moments, though as music and as lyric poetry its conclusion must have been impressive in the theatre. I include here the abstract and granite praise of courage in the funeral speech.

> Wonder not, Theseus, at the words pronounced,
> how at those towers these men dared to die.
> From being bred not cowards comes a shame,
> and that man who is bravely exercised
> shames to be less: because courage is learnt,
> as a child learns his speech and things untaught,
> and what is learnt is hopeful to survive
> into old age. Train up your children so.

The foundation for this view has already been placed by Theseus, not Adrastos, early in the play.

> They say men's evils mount above the good,
> but I maintain the opposite of that:
> men get more good than evil comes to them;
> if not we would have never seen the light.
> I praise whichever of the gods set firm
> our life above the bestial and foul,
> putting the understanding into us
> and then our tongue the messenger of words ...

The speech is a long one, ranging over much of the situation of mankind. It is oddly echoed and amusingly parodied in the *Cyclops*, as we shall see. It must have been a philosophic set piece. This bright-eyed view of humanity makes a darker blackness of the end of the play, because its message is surely that the brave die. If one asks whether this is a play about men or about women, one begins to see a deeper level of its tragic feeling. The brave speeches of the men are all set against a presence of mourning women. That is the point of Euadne, more courageous than the dead heroes, and more alone. It also adds meaning to the procession of boys. They want to be like their fathers and avenge them in battle. They will go the same way. 'Train up your children so.'

The *Trojan Women* belongs to 415, and it paints an even more calamitous picture of the consequences of war. Hecuba, the widowed queen, suffers in it every painful calamity of the famous legends that can be crammed into one play. It is the Trojan play to end Trojan plays. Only the slaughter of Polyxena, because that had been already treated so fully, hardly figures in this treatment. In his series of three plays in 415, Euripides showed first the youth of Paris and the seed of destruction, then the story of inventive Palamedes, who was betrayed to death by Odysseus at Troy, and finally this succession of episodes under the ruined walls. In verse that alters with brilliant effect from scene to scene, he delivers a series of hammer-blows. They are linked only by lamentation, with a faint compassion from the Greek herald, and a few strangely nostalgic lines about the holy land of Greece. At times Euripides fills the air with fire and brimstone, at times the formal clang of the verses sharpens his meaning, and sometimes his rhetorical patterns overspill like waterfalls.

> O throne of Earth and thou whose seat is earth,
> hard to be known whatever thou mayest be,
> necessity of nature, mind of man,
> Zeus, I pray to thee, who leads on mankind
> in justice by a road not to be blamed.

> O mortal fool who will pull cities down,
> temples and holy places of the dead,
> and make all those a desert, and then die.

> To bring her where she shall be put on board . . .

> Lead me, who walked soft-footed once in Troy,
> lead me a slave where earth falls sheer away

> from rocky edges, let me drop and die
> withered away with tears. Never say now
> that happy was happy until we die.

The prologue is by Poseidon, who reveals to Athene what storms he has in store for the Greeks. The captive women wail together over their future. Talthybios the herald comes to tell them how they must be divided. Hecuba belongs now to Odysseus. Kassandra sings mad and beautiful prophecies of vengeance, but she must go to Agamemnon. Hecuba spells out her wrongs, 'what things I have suffered and shall suffer, all for one woman and for one wedding'. Helen is still what Aischylos called her, 'Helen, Hell of ships and Hell of cities'. Andromache laments in her turn, and then comforts Hecuba.

> Mother, hear the best thing that I can say,
> and let me put delight into your thoughts.
> Not to be born and to die are the same,
> dying is better than to live in grief.
> Happy men falling to unhappiness
> wander in spirit from prosperity,
> but spirit dies and does not know its wrongs,
> no more than if it never saw the light.

Andromache is told her young child is to die. Menelaos with Helen faces Hecuba. The confrontation is one of long, impassioned argument. Helen's defence is the story of Paris and Aphrodite. She is a prisoner, firmly gripped, and Menelaos intends to kill her. I do not think that variations on the old legends as late as 415 should be checked against Homer: they were many and conflicting, and an audience in Athens expected new ones. Helen is present to give pain to Hecuba, and I do not find her speech indecent or inappropriate, though Lesky calls it 'a striking example of the sport with the mythical tradition which was inevitable when it was no longer taken seriously'. This is not sport but passionate rhetoric, as the phrase 'Paris, that torch of bitter fire' suggests.

> So where Greece was lucky, I was ruined,
> I am bought for my beauty, insulted
> by those who should with flowers crown my head.

It is true that Helen uses many tricky and exaggerated arguments, but her passion is not feigned and not laughable. T. C. W. Stinton has degraded these verses in his analysis; it is untrue, though his translation makes it sound true, that 'the form in which argument and counter-argument are cast suggests a tone almost of burlesque'. Still, it would be improper to ignore the doubts of capable critics even where one does not share them. My point is that these are two raging, furious women. Their lucid clarity in argument should not blind us to that. As the tragedy ends, Hecuba receives the dead body of Hektor's and Andromache's child, who was flung to his death from the battlements. The order comes to sail, and Troy burns. 'Let's run into that fire.' No one does so. The tragedy finishes in lament.

In 412, Euripides presented his *Helen*. It was the first of the amazing constructions, with their elaborate catastrophes and reversals, which include most of his late work. In 412 he was probably over seventy, but the fecundity of his dramatization was still increasing. Not Helen but her phantom or her cloud-shape went to Troy. An old Greek sailor asks in this tragedy, 'And did we labour ten years for a cloud?' Helen was in Egypt but her protector the old King Proteus is dead, and his son Theoklymenos wants to wed her. She has taken refuge at the tomb of Proteus, where she acts as prologue. Teukros arrives on his way into exile, full of bad news including the death of Menelaos. She sings, and the chorus enter singing in reply. 'Winged women, virgin daughters of Earth, Sirens come to my laments, with Libyan flute or pipe or strings ...' She tells the Greek women her troubles in a long speech.

> Other women by beauty fortunate
> live out their lives; by beauty I perish.

The chorus suggest she goes to ask Theonoe, the old king's daughter, 'child of the son of the sea-Nereid, who knows all things' whether Menelaos really is dead or not. They sing again, and Menelaos arrives alive while they are indoors consulting Theonoe. He wishes he were dead, and says so in elaborate language: 'O Pelops who at Pisa raced horses with Oinomaos once, I wish that then, before you made a banquet for the gods, I wish your life had ended among gods, before you got my father Atreus, who then in Aerope's bed begot my brother Agamemnon and myself, a famous couple ...' I am not able to praise these lines very highly, but they are in the mood of this joyful tragedy. He talks things over with an old woman,

Helen emerges, and recognition occurs after a short dialogue peppered with lines like 'You rightly name a most unhappy man', and 'Hekate of lights, send kindly ghosts.' It is all elegantly done, and would be dramatic if it were not so ornamental.

A messenger tells Menelaos that the ghostly Helen, the one he got back from Troy, has gone up into heaven.

> Your wife has gone into the folded air,
> she has ascended, hidden in heaven,
> leaving the solemn cave where we kept her,
> saying, 'Unhappy Phrygians and Greeks,
> who by device of Hera died for me
> beside Skamander, thinking Paris had
> Helen between his hands who had her not ...'

Here one must confess to enjoyment of a kind. The play is so full of surprises and so honest about it. If one is not yearning for something else, this is excellent entertainment. Perhaps by 412 one had got past facing the worst, and distraction was in order. The *Iliad* itself has such moments. Here Helen and Menelaos chant together for a while. Then Menelaos discusses the truth with the old sailor, his messenger, whose speeches are in all cases enjoyable. But the king is going to murder these strangers, and escape requires intrigues and devices. They are successful in the manner of a light adventure story. No harm comes to anyone. Theoklymenos would have killed his sister, but the gods forbid him. And is all this a tragedy? In the formal, modern sense, certainly not. But the Greeks called it one, and it uses many tragic techniques for its own legitimate purposes.

The *Herakles*, or *Herakles Mad*, marshals the new abundance of devices for a tragical theme. The tragedy is a mighty one. In its verse technique, in some passages, it is clear that Euripides archaizes, something which one often suspects even when he is most original, but which is usually hard to verify. Perhaps it is all part of his restlessness, as it was of the vitality of Picasso, to take from unexpected places and continually to transform. This tragedy is Athenian, in that it reintroduces the humane Theseus, a well-known character to readers of this chapter so far. The prologue is by Amphitryon father of Herakles. To him appears Megara, wife here of Herakles. She and the children are suppliants at the altar of Zeus in Thebes. Lykos, grandson of an old king of Thebes, has killed Kreon, and proposes to slaughter all the family of Herakles, while that hero is performing his dreadful labour in the underworld. The aged Theban chorus are as helpless as usual. Lykos threatens fire, but Herakles returns and saves his wife and children at the last moment.

Not the last moment of the play: the loving family are now established as characters and ripe for the kill. Iris, the messenger of the gods, appears with Frenzy or Madness while Herakles is indoors offering sacrifice. The dramatic force of this scene cannot easily be grasped without reference to the *Marginalia Scaenica* of John Jackson, who greatly sharpens the text. We hear from a messenger how Herakles goes mad, and murders his family. This speech is in full and telling detail. His father escapes only when Athene throws a rock at Herakles. The doors are opened and we see him tied to a column of the house. He wakes from his madness and wants to die. But Theseus, whom he rescued in the underworld, persuades him he must live and suffer. He is now stricken and without resource. He goes away to find sanctuary in Athens, leaning on Theseus. One must add at once that Euripides did not invent the story. The legends about Herakles include much awe-inspiring violence, and Hera was his enemy. 'And Hera now will put fresh blood on him.' He sees the gods clearly in the end, though the framework of the play says otherwise.

> I say the gods are not adulterous,
> and I have never thought their hands were bound
> nor that one god mastered another one;
> a god rightly a god can have no need –
> those things are miserable poets' tales.

The *Phoenicians* was a tragedy in which poetry for once fulfilled Pater's prediction by aspiring after the condition of an operatic libretto. It would be severe and foolish to say it is not a success. Eduard Fraenkel has shown how fine a play underlies appalling corruptions and interpolations. The drama has been made more dramatic, falling men whirl in mid-air like fireworks, and the ghosts of old plays about Oedipus haunt this one. Yet as in all these late works of Euripides, the action, complex as it is, has been precisely calculated; each episode, each dissolving situation, leads to the next through a symmetrical set of reversals like the figures of a dance. Whatever merely adheres to the text of this play like a gross ornament, whatever is gratuitously dramatic without function, is suspect. The tragedy, with its foreign chorus, is baroque from the first line, though even these opening lines have been attacked recently as inauthentic.

> O thou that cut'st thy road through heaven's stars
> riding a chariot jointed with gold,
> O sun, on thy swift horses whirling flame ...

And by line eleven we are certainly in trouble. Iokaste is introducing herself and her ancestry, clearly and in detail, but someone has added a needless verse that hangs by the skin of its syntactic teeth, about Kreon. It is a useful lesson that passages of this kind attracted the interpolations of actors. Iokaste, by the way, has survived the blinding of Oedipus. Later in the play we have several irrelevant verses about the burial of Oedipus at Athens, as if everything about him had to be crammed in wherever it could be fitted. These are short examples of persistent problems: the plot of *Antigone* and even a verse from *Oedipus the King* invade this text mercilessly. The ending is utterly corrupt.

After Iokaste has explained the situation, Antigone on the city wall watches the battle of the seven against Thebes. Polyneikes, the exiled, aggressive brother of the legend, enters the city in a diplomatic attempt to settle the conflict by negotiation, but Eteokles, the brother in possession, the wicked natural man of the first book of Plato's *Republic*, refuses to yield, and battle must follow. Kreon is told by Teiresias that victory depends on the sacrifice of his son. Kreon wants the boy to run for it, but the boy prefers to die. The seven fail to take Thebes and the brothers prepare a duel. They kill one another, and Iokaste kills herself over the corpses. Kreon now exiles Oedipus, who was indoors, and forbids the burial of Polyneikes, Antigone resolves to bury him with her own hands, she breaks off her engagement to Haimon, and means to follow her father.

These variations and this *tour d'horizon* of Theban myth, constantly supplemented by the chorus, who are Phoenician slave women on their way to Delphi, are not introduced only for the sake of novelty. The tragedy is cumulative. The late antique analysis of its plot rightly remarks that 'This tragedy is most tragical, has many persons, and is full of numerous pungent sayings.' But the objection to Antigone on the wall as irrelevant and Polyneikes the diplomat as unfunctional do not hold water. She sings on the wall, and this tragedy is meant to be enveloped in music. It is a pity that we lack a full modern commentary on the *Phoenicians* that would properly sort it out. We have in English only the short, sometimes very intelligent commentary by A. C. Pearson (1909). It is impossible to deal here with the literary problems of the play, because they are rooted in many vexed questions of technical scholarship. Albin Lesky wished to accept the contradictions of the text on the grounds that this tragedy is an omnium gatherum. That is a counsel of something more futile than despair. The *Phoenicians* is a thematic rearrangement meant to dramatize the whole Theban saga with a single impact. That is why the exile of Oedipus is reserved for its ending. Its unity depended heavily on its spectacular succession, which leaves one no time to ask questions, and on its music, which was probably exotic and certainly fresh. I wish that in the early eighteenth century someone had translated it to music by Handel: though the true music of Euripides might sound to us more like a Cretan or an Albanian folk-song.

Ion is another essentially lyrical play but its musicality is far lighter, and its plot of intrigues and devices closer to *Helen* than it is to the *Phoenicians*. Ion son of Apollo and founder of the Ionian race is a boy sweeping out the temple at Delphi and scaring birds; he is ignorant of his birth in Apollo's cave at Athens, but this play is about his recognition. The prologue is lyrical, sung by the boy Ion. It catches an echo very rare in fifth-century tragedy of the sort of poetry that neo-classic, romantic writers imagined to be classical. It also perfectly summons up dawn at Delphi just as it still is.

> Now the sparkling chariot
> and the horses of the sun
> glitter on the extended earth,
> and the upper air on fire
> puts the stars to flight.
> Now the untrodden mountain crest
> of Parnassos glittering
> takes the touch of dawn
> for the race of men.

Smoke of unwatered frankincense
mounts into Apollo's roof,
the Delphic priestess takes her throne
at the tripod of the god,
crying to the Greeks she brings
the same words Apollo sings.
Servants of Apollo, go
to that silver spring below,
fetch holy dew, Kastalian water,
and enter to the Delphic shrine.

A chorus of pilgrims from Athens arrive to visit Apollo's temple. They are thrilled to recognize statues of gods and giants and 'Look, Athene, my own goddess.' The plot unfolds itself bit by bit, like a dance to the music of some pleasant harpsichord. Childless Xouthos and Kreousa of Athens, Ion's mother, inquire of Apollo about having children. Kreousa and Ion have a verse conversation of complicated ironies. Apollo tells Xouthos that Ion is Xouthos' son. Kreousa is furious about this bastard, having lost her own baby, and tries to murder Ion at dinner with poisoned wine, but the attempt fails. This is reported in a messenger speech worthy of the most talented thriller writer, a verse masterpiece of technique squandered on a fiction. The old man who was Kreousa's instrument confesses, she flees to the altar, Ion threatens her, and the Pythian priestess produces a little box of proofs of his identity. What about that for a dramatic recognition scene? Athene appears in majesty, decrees the future and explains Apollo's plot.

But when this threatened act was opened up,
he feared your death through your own mother's plots,
and hers by you; devices rescued all.
And so in Athens would this silent lord
both this your mother then have recognized,
and you, got by Apollo upon her.
But to end this, and the god's oracles,
why I harnessed these horses, listen now.
Kreousa, to the country of Kekrops
take up this boy and go, and seat him there
in the monarchic throne ...

I hope I have translated these involved verses not incorrectly. In the end Xouthos will get children and a future, and 'Apollo has done all things well.' Euripides has in this play preferred mystery to his usual clarifying prologue, but the workings of his providence are still labyrinthine. The happy ending fits these final explanations better here than the ending of a dark tragedy would fit such a late un-ravelling of the plot. 'I praise Apollo though I did not praise,' says Kreousa. 'I praise your change that now you bless the god,' says Athene. Kreousa and Ion then go off godlike to Athens in Athene's chariot. I take the chariot to be a device to isolate them from poor old Xouthos. He has not spoken since dinner-time, but he must surely be 'this silent lord'. The poetry of this play has a faultless, silver-gilt quality throughout.

Iphigeneia went to the Taurians as Helen went to Egypt, rescued by Artemis and leaving her ghost to a more tragic fate, and there are other similarities between the plays. Even some lines and phrases are the same. As late as 1950, it was still argued that *Iphigeneia among the Taurians* was an earlier play than *Helen*: the opposite view depends on trusting the argument from smoothly gradual develop-ment in verse technique. Iphigeneia, priestess of Taurian Artemis, a barbarous version of the goddess, speaks the prologue. Orestes and his friend Pylades arrive: he is still troubled by a few of the Furies, in spite of his acquittal, and Apollo has told him to capture the statue of Taurian Artemis, to which the local Asians sacrifice strangers, and bring it home to Attica. The chorus are captive Greek girls who sing nostalgic songs about home. They do little else. A shepherd reports like a messenger how Orestes had an attack of his frenzy and the two adventurers were captured. Iphigeneia wants to save one to get a letter to Greece. A conversation of entangled ironies turns into a scene of mutual recognition, and brother and sister rival one another in self-sacrifice, just as Helen begged Menelaos to flee alone but he resisted.

The rescue device is a purification of the statue at the sea-shore, and a second, even more exciting messenger speech tells how they fought their way to freedom. We are not only approaching the begin-nings of romance, but also prose story-telling, which took a great deal from verse narratives like these, and could still learn from them, maybe. In a divine appearance fascinating to historians of religion, Athene decrees the worship of Artemis at Brauron, an initiation sanctuary of young girls and one of the most venerated holy places in Attica; its worship existed also in Athens, in the shadow of the Parthenon. Iphigeneia is not only an epic heroine; she was once a Mycenean goddess, whose name appears on the tablets recording offerings. This is not the only legend about her to suggest that some vestige of human sacrifice was thought to cling to her. Even at Brauron, Athene says, 'Some blood must be shed', but the human sacrifice is no more than a persistent theme of folklore, and one is not bound to credit that it really happened. This macabre theme is surely what underlies her own sacrifice by Agamemnon at Aulis: that would have arisen easily as a narrative explanation of why she accepted human deaths in her worship. But one cannot date the development of the folk-tale, and to fifth-century tragic poetry these grim conjectures are only marginally relevant. Iphigeneia's cult reflects the atmosphere of Brauron.

> ... there when you die be buried, and be brought
> presents of robes of fine embroidery,
> which women who in childbed lost their lives
> left in their houses. And I order these
> Greek women to be sent home from this land ...

In his seventies, in 408, Euripides wrote his *Orestes*, the greatest of his tragedies of this kind, rich in resonance and dense in complexities. Luckily its case is difficult but not desperate, partly because Vincenzo Di Benedetto, who had attended Fraenkel's seminar on the *Phoenicians*, produced in 1965 a detailed commentary on *Orestes*, a tragedy of comparable surprises. Lesky speaks of 'repeated new twists' which 'made it a hit on the stage', as if that were disreputable. But trivial analysis too easily trivializes late Euripides. The tragedy is imaginatively, genuinely and deeply abundant. It is to Sophokles as a garden of melons is to a tree of crisp apples. They are very different writers who influenced one another both by attraction and by repulsion, but one must not look for austerity of structure in a poetry built on other principles.

Elektra speaks the prologue, with Orestes lying in a coma beside her. Her explanation of affairs is dramatic in an unexpected way.

> It is not terrible to utter this:
> there is no suffering nor god-sent grief
> but the nature of man carries its weight.

> They say that blessed Tantalos – I have
> no quarrel with his luck – the son of Zeus
> goes wandering, bearing upon his head
> that stone which rears above him through the air.

This is poetry thoroughly philosophized. The stone of Tantalos, here and later in the play, is the sun: a combination of ideas not to be found before Euripides, though it may not be his invention. The image is starkly strange, and the sentence a beguiling one. Yet it only serves to introduce in a fresh way the old familiar list of the ancestors of the house of Atreus. One is meant not so much to be impressed as fascinated by such verses. The first scene is one of argument and intrigue between Elektra and Helen, who was sent home under cover of night for fear of stoning. Orestes has been terribly ill since he murdered his mother, and Elektra tells the chorus of women to walk softly as they approach. Orestes is wailed and lamented over, then he wakes; the mutual love shown on the stage between the hero and his sister is unique in surviving tragedy, and it has that pathos of which Euripides was the theatrical master. There is a higher percentage of popular speech in this than in any other tragedy of Euripides, some of it in the intimacies of this scene. Elektra and Orestes are being boycotted in Argos, and on this day they may be formally condemned to death by stoning. The only hope is Menelaos, who is expected. The stoning motif sets this tragedy more solidly than most in village reality as Athenians must have known it.

Menelaos comes, knowing already from the sea-god Glaukos, 'a truthful god who stood close in my sight', of his brother's death. It seems he may intervene in Argos, but Tyndareus, the father of the murdered queen, also arrives. The tendency of the later Euripides to produce old survivors of earlier generations in these plots, like Iokaste still alive in the *Phoenicians*, does not arise simply from epic continuity or a wish for novelty. It expresses an essential density of life: even in epic poetry tragedy is by its nature family tragedy. Sophokles learnt that lesson from Homer, and lonely Ajax has his Tekmessa, and thinks both of Teukros and of Telamon his old father. In the *Orestes*, at the old man's entry in mourning, the hero is plunged into shame and despair; Tyndareus greets Menelaos kindly as a kinsman, but the sight of Orestes is too much for him.

> What! does this mother-murderer, this snake
> glimmer his baneful lightnings, whom I loathe?

The furious old man has his way, as even the slightest acquaintance with village feuding systems and obligations to vengeance should teach one that he must. Menelaos withdraws and Orestes must save himself, with the aid of his friend Pylades. That is just as it would be in Calabria or southern Greece today, and those ancient critics led by Aristotle who thought Menelaos was needlessly unvirtuous have underestimated the proper authority of Tyndareus. Orestes now pleads his own case to the Argive assembly, and we hear the proceedings through messenger. If there were any doubt about the Athenian appetite for lawcourts and rhetorical arguments, this narrative should quiet it. Orestes has some support, but angry citizens are too loud against him, and he and Elektra are condemned to suicide. Pylades wants to die with them, but brother and sister are so close in affection that he hardly yet counts.

> Shall we not rightly die both by one sword,
> and one tomb keep us both, one cedar box?

But with Pylades the rescue operation begins. Their device is to 'kill Helen and make Menelaos grieve'. Elektra adds the idea of taking young Hermione, Helen's daughter, as a hostage against the likely results. Helen had sent her off early in the play by Elektra's advice to take offerings to Klytaimestra's tomb, but now they catch her. The account of how the murder attempt misfires and Helen escapes by divine magic is given in an aria by a barbarian slave escaping from the knives. An old misunderstanding has led some scholars to exaggerate the operatic atmosphere of this event, by having him jump off the roof, as if 'between the roof-top and the ground, he music sought and music found'. But we need no longer trouble about that hypothesis. He describes what obviously was not enacted, his route of escape by climbing along an entablature and down a column. His language is elaborate, and apparently deliberately barbarous, presumably to excuse the exotic music which Euripides was determined to introduce. His narrative when it comes is quite clear all the same.

The conclusion must after this be spectacular. Orestes with his sister, his friend and Hermione appears on the roof. Menelaos rages below, but agrees to intervene to save them from the mob. Orestes

at once tells Elektra to fire the palace. Menelaos yells to the mob
for help and for the blood of Orestes. In the full heat of this action,
which takes a very few lines, Apollo appears to give his solution.
Helen appears as a goddess. Pylades can marry Elektra, and Orestes
can go to Athens, get acquitted there, and marry Hermione.
Menelaos can get another wife, though Wilamowitz wanted to wipe
out that verse as an improper suggestion, and no one knows what
other wife he found. I am for removing it. Menelaos comes later into
Apollo's speech, where he is told to leave Orestes king in Argos, and
'Come and be king over the Spartan land, your wife's endowment.'
He agrees, and says, 'O Helen, child of Zeus, I envy you, who shall
dwell in the rich house of the gods. To you, Orestes, I my daughter
join, may you have good of this, and so may I.' It is all far too operatic
for Menelaos to be thinking of another wife. And as if this were really
a play about villagers, he does seem to prefer money.

The *Bacchai* is a posthumously produced tragedy written in
Macedonia. It is probably the greatest play Euripides wrote. It is
genuinely tragic and terrible, and treats the central themes of
irrational forces and of religion. Its verse is of great beauty, but its
attitude is unbending. The chorus of Dionysos' followers sings lyrics
as exquisite as any he ever wrote, but otherwise it almost never
speaks. Thebes has denied the god's divinity, and this is the story
of his revenge, and the tragedy of Pentheus king of Thebes, who
is torn to pieces by the Bacchai.

> 'I bring you him who put to ridicule
> me and my mysteries. Take your vengeance.'
> And as he spoke one flash of dreadful light
> struck at the earth and struck against heaven.
> The air was silent. The wooded ravine
> held all its leaves silent. No creature called.

It may easily be that the majestic and uncompromising quality
of this play is the inherited mark of a lost play of Aischylos. But
it is also Euripides at his best. The prologue is by the god, and he
sets his tone at once.

> I am Dionysos, the son of Zeus,
> I come to Thebes, where Semele bore me,
> made pregnant by the fire of the lightning;

> I have altered my god's shape to a man's
> by Ismene's water and Dirke's springs.
> I see my thunderblasted mother's grave
> here by this dwelling, and the ruined house
> that smoulders from the living flame of Zeus ...

The songs are clear, and they reveal from the beginning the serious sanctity of this worship, its liberation of women, and its ominous violence. This type of religious cult belonged to the margins and the wilderness of Greek states, but by the end of the fifth century it was on the march to the heart of cities, and all the more powerful for being rejected. E. R. Dodds has thrown much needed light on these themes, both in his exemplary commentary on this play and his *Greeks and the Irrational*. But one can no longer maintain that the religion of Dionysos was a missionary religion: new evidence has shown that the Myceneans already knew him as a god. Euripides sets his play in the unknown country of prehistory and legend, though its message was modern. It is about a trap set by the gods as deliberately as the devices of rescue in slightly earlier plays.

> Women, the man is standing in a trap:
> he will go to the Bacchai, and there die.
> Your work now Dionysos ...

Pentheus is a traditional tragic tyrant: brutal, violent, suspicious, and uncontrolled. Dionysos is a human moral agent by stage necessity, but he is also a force as absolute as Aphrodite. His effect depends on individuals. The chorus of worshippers are like Athenians idealized, not like those women he drove mad.

> The god will not enforce a moral mind
> in women over love, but in nature
> this must be looked for: in divine frenzy
> she who is moral shall not be destroyed.

I regret my pitiful translation 'moral', which sounds particularly mealy-mouthed in these words of Teiresias, but if it had more force it would be very close to the Greek meaning. André Rivier in an essay on Euripidean tragedy says that 'The revelation of an area lying beyond our moral categories and our reasoning is the fundamental fact on which the tragedy of the *Bacchai* rests.' Indeed, Euripides does not argue much or moralize much in this play, in the sense that the characters do not, but 'beyond moral categories' is a modern idea which Euripides would associate with tyranny and barbarism. E. R. Dodds makes the more appealing suggestion that Macedonia, the wild countryside, and the old story, 'released some spring in the aged poet's mind, re-establishing a contact with hidden sources of power which he had lost'. The poetry of this play is certainly full of passionate exaltation.

Its first human characters are Teiresias the prophet, Kadmos his friend, and King Pentheus. As they discuss the crisis of the women and the new cult which Teiresias and Kadmos mean to join, Teiresias foresees where the arrogance of Pentheus will lead. Dionysos is brought in as a captive and with powerful irony answers an interrogation.

> PENTHEUS: First I shall cut away those wanton curls.
> DIONYSOS: My hair is holy. It is of the god.
> PENTHEUS: Then give me that pine-wand out of your hand.
> DIONYSOS: Take it from me yourself. It is the god's.
> PENTHEUS: I shall fetter your body in a cell.
> DIONYSOS: The god himself will free me when I will.
> PENTHEUS: When you call him with those frenzied women.
> DIONYSOS: He is near, he sees what I suffer now.

The imprisonment ends in fire and earthquake during some wild singing from the women in which the goddess Earthquake is invoked: a power whose Greek name is redolent of a poet like Aischylos. Then the vengeance starts. Pentheus is lured in disguise in women's dress to see the women at their orgy. We have two magnificent messengers' narratives, the first to tell Pentheus the truth about the wild and beautiful worship of the women, the second to record the catastrophe. No narrative in Greek is much more powerful, and nowhere in tragic poetry is there so strong a sense of wild landscape. It has an almost Chinese intensity and bareness. It is very untypical. After the frenzy, the coming-to. Agaue returns, as she believes, weary from hunting on the hills, carrying her grisly trophy.

> KADMOS: And whose head do you carry in your arms?
> AGAUE: A lion's, so the hunting women said.
> KADMOS: Think clearly. Quickly look it in the eyes.
> AGAUE: Ah, what do I see? Why do I hold this?

KADMOS: Take a clear look and you will find that out.
　AGAUE: I see the worst of grief and misery.
KADMOS: Well, does it look to you like a lion?

What she is carrying is her son's head. This slow awakening, which takes many more lines than I have translated, is the grimmest passage in the tragedy. The appearance of Dionysos does not take place until this scene has had time to sink well in. His decrees are not light. After much violence and suffering, Kadmos and his wife will become immortals 'in the land of the blessed', but the women are exiled. They recognized the god too late.

When Euripides died, pieces of an unfinished or disordered tragedy were found in his papers and worked up into something playable by his son or nephew or grandson. The tragedy was then crudely altered for some later production. *Iphigeneia in Aulis* is a terrible mess. But there is no doubt he wrote some of it. The choral lyrics at verse 1036ff. are excellent, and pieces of dialogue between Agamemnon and his wife look genuine, though even there one finds strange intrusions: a few lines added to increase pathos, where Iphigeneia goes to die with her little brother Orestes hiding under her skirts like the spaniel of Mary Queen of Scots, and a very awkward introduction by Klytaimestra. The play has two prologues, one grafted into the other, and its conclusion is certainly not authentic. As it stands, a long, unskilled messenger speech reports the sacrifice of Iphigeneia, with Artemis substituting a deer at the last moment. But a short quotation that happens to survive from the original makes it clear that Artemis stopped the action at an earlier stage, and foretold the business of the deer at the sacrifice, probably in her closing speech.

The chorus gives a very long, quasi-epic account of the Greek fleet and its heroes in metrically oversimple lyric verse. Is this a duller version of Antigone on the walls of Thebes, or a much less dramatic, uncomprehending attempt to imitate Euripides? On the other hand, the play has scenes of Euripidean multiple irony which are well conceived. It is a playground for textual criticism, though the bones of a fine tragic poem are still to be encountered among the rubbish. Gilbert Murray's suspicion of very late tampering with this text is perhaps unjustified, since the false verses he thought so late do not observe the special Byzantine rules for iambics.

The *Rhesos* is another matter. It is a complete, full-blooded and picturesque adventure tragedy, but it is not by Euripides. It transfers the tenth book of the *Iliad* about night raiding to a lyrical setting, with choral night alarms, a very attractive dawn song based on a folk-song theme, plenty of meaningless sub-plots that lead nowhere, and some exciting killing. It has no philosophic element, and no epigrammatic verses. Rhesos is the son of a Muse, who describes too casually how she begot him; he is king of Thrace and comes to support Hektor at Troy, but he does not survive one night. *Rhesos* makes pleasant reading, but it does not read like a fifth-century production.

> Immortal horses by immortal sires
> they bear the raging son of Peleus,
> they were the gift of the colt-breaking lord
> Poseidon of the sea to Peleus.

If these incompetent verses, which are in some ways worse in Greek than in English, are by Euripides, one would be most surprised. But this play is enjoyable all the same, if one skims lightly over it; it is all of the same texture, and very lively.

No other fifth-century tragic poet except Agathon merits more consideration, and no other, to judge by their miserable fragments, in the fourth century. A Strasburg papyrus has preserved a big piece of a lyric treatment of a tragic theme from the late fifth or fourth century; it is philosophized poetry, a counterblast to tragic poetry and a denial of tragic necessity. It has no very high literary value, but one is interested to know that such poems were written and circulated. But Agathon is the same charming young poet we shall encounter fresh from his first theatrical success, in the *Symposion* of Plato, so we are prejudiced in his favour. He was a mannered and aesthetic writer, who treated his choral odes as a kind of interval without reference to the progress of his plots, to an even more pronounced degree than Euripides. The action of his plays was full of complexities, as one might expect from late Euripides, and in one tragedy he invented not only some but all his persons and events, here at least outdoing his master. Yet one suspects he still shared the Euripidean addiction to variations on stock scenes.

The fragments of the lost plays of Euripides are often substantial. His influence, which their survival reflects, was, after his death, immense down to Byzantine times. The fragments show that in his

Telephos, produced with *Alkestis*, he had already invented a wounded king disguised in rags, creeping into the Greek camp at Argos and threatening the child Orestes. In his *Cretans*, another relatively early play, his plot revolved around Pasiphae falling in love with a bull that Poseidon sent up from the sea. His *Erechtheus* was performed about 423, when the Erechtheion was begun on the Akropolis in the ruins of the Mycenean palace. It deals with a mythical battle for Athens, and with a fascinating cobweb of religious cults on the Akropolis.

> And I command he shall in this city
> have his own holy place walled round in stone,
> and shall be named for him who struck him dead:
> Poseidon, terrible, and have his name,
> but called Erechtheus in his people's rites.

In *Hypsipyle*, about the time of the *Phoenicians*, son rescues mother after adventurous intrigues. In *Archelaos* we have fragments of a late play that Euripides wrote in Macedonia for the king's pleasure.

> Danaos, father of the fifty girls,
> leaving the noble waters of the Nile,
> who fills himself from the dark-blooded stream
> of Aithiopia, when snow dissolves,
> and the sun drives his team through upper air,
> came to Argos and built his city there ...

The voice is still familiar and beguiling, however overloaded with ornament, and it is still perfectly clear. The geography is in nice contrast with that of Aischylos, who was thrilled by the Nile but less knowing. It was in Aithiopia that the Phaethon of Euripides fell to earth and scorched the desert.

Finally we should pause over his satyr play, the *Cyclops*. It is written in relaxed tragic verse, and the plot is light and adventurous until it stings one with a grotesque climax, when the Cyclops has his eye put out. But the chorus of satyrs are sad as well as jolly. The Cyclops defending his way of life is a sympathetic parody of arguments to be found elsewhere, both in tragedy and in philosophy.

> Wealth, little man, is the god of the wise.
> The rest is fine words and pretentiousness.

> I bid my father's headlands of the sea
> go fly away. Why should I pretend?
> I don't fear Zeus' thunderbolt, my friend,
> I don't see Zeus as stronger than I am.
> That's all I care. Do you want to know why?
> Then listen here. When he pours out the rain
> I have a dry shelter under this rock,
> I dine on a roast calf, I dine on game,
> I lie back and I wet my belly well,
> drink milk by the bucket, and screw my cloak,
> and fart thunder as Zeus makes thunder.
> And when the Thracian wind comes with the snow
> I wrap my body up in pelts of beasts,
> and make my fire up, snow don't worry me.
> Earth produces grass by necessity
> whether it likes or not, and fats my flock.
> I sacrifice to no god but myself
> and to my belly here, to this great god.

In this happy, muddy, pastoral world, the satyrs are lost, and yearning for their lost god Dionysos. 'The loud god, the ivy-crowned, the desirable god, is the one I long to see, and leave this desert of the Cyclopes.' In some moods I find this satyr play more moving than a tragedy, at its simple level.

It is not easy to sum up the works of Euripides. They are very various, but always pointed. He had a closing formula, sung as the chorus withdrew, which he used many times.

> Many the transformations of the gods:
> and many things they judge as we do not:
> and what appeared was not what was fulfilled;
> the god found his way through the unlikely.
> And that was how this matter concluded.

These lines represent the mental processes of the chorus to the point of travesty. But this impenetrable tragic mask invites by its restraint some further penetration. It has been felt in the past that Euripides by his irreligion or anti-religion somehow invites a religious response, but that is a wild argument. He is neither irreligious nor exactly challenging. The only thing fresh and sharp in his horror stories is the momentum he gives them, which is usually tragic. And one must add the lucid cobweb of his language, in which one is caught in the end among his thoughts. We know far more about his feelings than about his thoughts.

> There is a vengeance touches underground,
> and touches all living mankind.
> The mind of the dead does not live,
> yet it has an immortal moral part
> that blows into this world's immortal air.

If to think freely makes one a free-thinker, that is what he was, but if one doubts his passionate feelings about the gods, one should reread his *Herakles* and his *Bacchai*. And yet he was fully an intellectual in the modern sense, he lived by intellect, and he was a great, a chaotic and stormy poet. For such a personality, polytheism offers more space than the religions of our own childhoods.

As an artist he was restlessly active. Let us seek out obscure local stories. Let us adapt famous stories. Let us revive the omniscient prologue. Let us reshape the climax by introducing an omniscient god in mid-air, *deus ex machina*. Let us make the chorus purely lyrical. Let us dramatize lamentation. Let us do away with the chorus. Let us use a standard final lyric that fits all situations. Let us never allow two situations alike. 'He was drawn,' wrote Wilamowitz, 'by a fatal necessity, an innate quality, whose truly daimonic power he had sung: we know and see the best but do it not. It was he who showed Medeia complaining about the wise intellectual struggling against envy and malice. He was in need of praise. Sophokles got first or second prize, but Euripides had drunk philosophy to the dregs, yet almost no response came except the laughter of Aristophanes.' Overstated perhaps, and romantic, but well put. One should remember that Sokrates admired Euripides, and that when he died, Sophokles brought in his own chorus robed in black, in mourning for him. It is hard to get at the truth about his character.

DATES OF SURVIVING TRAGEDIES OF EURIPIDES

438	*Alkestis*
431	*Medeia*
428	*Hippolytos*
	Children of Herakles
	Elektra
	Andromache
	Hecuba
	Suppliants
415	*Trojan Women*
412	*Helen*
	Phoenicians
	Herakles
	Ion
	Iphigeneia among the Taurians
408	*Orestes*
(406	Death of Euripides)
	Bacchai
	Iphigeneia in Aulis

Of the fragments that I discuss, *Archelaos* belongs to 408 or 407, *Erechtheus* to 423 or just earlier, the *Cretans* before 430, *Telephos* to 438.

The *Cyclops* is hard to date. I take the *Rhesos* to be very late, and not by Euripides.

BIBLIOGRAPHY

C. Austin (ed.), *Nova Fragmenta Euripidea*, 1968

W. S. Barrett (ed.), *Hippolytos*, 1964

G. W. Bond (ed.), *Hypsipyle*, 1963

A. P. Burnet, *Catastrophe Survived*, 1969

J. D. Denniston (ed.), *Elektra*, 1939

V. Di Benedetto (ed.), *Orestes* (Italian commentary), 1965

E. R. Dodds, *The Greeks and the Irrational*, 1951

E. R. Dodds (ed.), *Bacchae*, 1960

J. Jackson, *Marginalia Scaenica*, 1955

R. Lattimore, *The Poetry of Greek Tragedy*, 1958

D. L. Page, *Actors' Interpolations in Greek Tragedy*, 1934

P. T. Stevens (ed.), *Andromache*, 1971

P. T. Stevens, *Colloquial Expressions in Euripides*, 1974

T. C. W. Stinton, *Euripides and the Judgement of Paris*, 1965

E. Vermeule, *Death in Early Greek Art and Poetry*, 1981

R. Warner, *The Medea* (translation), 1944

V. von Wilamowitz-Moellendorff, *Analecta Euripidea*, 1875 (reprinted 1963)

R. P. Winnington-Ingram, *Euripides and Dionysus*, 1948

G. Zuntz, *The Political Plays of Euripides*, 1955

· 10 ·

ARISTOPHANES

One cannot help suspecting that of all the marvellous arts of the Athenian democracy in the fifth century, it is Aristophanic comedy rather than tragedy or music or painting or architecture or sculpture or even political organization or philosophy, which I take to be arts of a kind, that most intimately expresses Athens. How complicated the necessary historical and social conditions were which gave rise to it. It expresses a society in headlong process of social change, and comedy itself swiftly changes. Aristophanes started work in the theatre only in 427 B.C. as a very young man. He was born in the last glorious peacetime before the war with Sparta, while the Parthenon, which was the end not the beginning of the achievements of Athens, was still being built. Athenian comedy already existed; it was part of his birthright.

It was as conventional as tragedy, equally a theatre of poetry, and a moral, teaching theatre, but contemporary. Its verse, and its moral authority, distinguish it from every modern imitation. Its range was astonishing, from pure as well as low lyrics and high comedy, through knock-about farce and obscenity to vulgar jokes. The key to this range is fantasy; in the theatre of Aristophanes a hero has his triumph because fantasy triumphs. The gods are amiably thumped, but not on the whole more unkindly treated than they are in tragedy. Theatrical illusion, whatever that means in Athenian terms, was constantly ruptured, but that is because comedy was a conspiracy with the audience, a joke from beginning to end. Invective was common, and caused personal and political trouble for the writers, so that within the career of Aristophanes we notice his sharp arrows much blunted, though they were never quite discarded even by Menander a hundred years later. The traditional chorus was a group of Birds or Clouds or Frogs or any other freakish creatures, and their appearance in costume was a big moment. The last chorus like that we hear about in the fourth century was in a play called the *Caterpillars*.

The origins of comedy, ancient or modern, are a matter of folklore. It seems to begin with vigorous choral dancing in animal disguise. The formal patterns of alternation between lyric and chanting or between lyric and verse speech suggest the formality of a dance of another kind. The comic conflict, as in Euripidean encounters of Right and Wrong Argument, or summer versus winter, or St George and the dragon, must go back further than I feel any need to trace it. The final celebrations in Aristophanic comedies, with rousing chorus, as in a modern pantomime, are also apparently ancient: they belong among celebrations and festivals which were seasonal. The swift, episodic succession of scenes towards the end of the plays belongs to simple rustic comedy anywhere, but in this case to rustic comedy as it was early in the sixth century, maybe. Comedy existed in some form in many places. Megara claimed its origin, so did Sicily, and Doric farce and comic choral performance outlived the Athenian theatre of the fifth century. That retained its salty sexuality and its ritual erections when the theatre of Athens had tamed itself and become middle class.

Comic choruses appear in Athenian vase-painting from the sixth century; these spirited representations are not meant to be exact, but to be souvenirs of a famous performance. We have young men in armour on older men dressed as horses, dancers dressed as mad birds, riders on ostriches, riders on dolphins, and so on. We also have fat, padded, phallic dancers. Early in the sixth century, they attend on the entry of drunken Hephaistos, tricked by Dionysos into heaven – a subject already treated by the Sicilian Epicharmos. Throughout the development of comedy, the surviving visual evidence is richer than it is for tragedy. But the early examples belong more to folklore than to theatrical history. The dancing and singing chorus and the simple ritual drama were widespread in Greece. Even Sparta had its drama of celebration, violence and retribution, about the stealing of fruits and cheeses. In late-sixth-century Athens, one of the subjects was the effect of drink.

Megarian comedy belonged to the Megarian democracy in the early sixth century. The Athenians claimed an original comic poet called

Susarion, said in fact to be a Megarian, but these claims are insubstantial. Epicharmos of Syracuse, on the other hand, though he lived into the late 470s and perhaps later, was probably older than Pindar and Aischylos, and we have numerous titles and some solid fragments of his comedies. Unfortunately, many of them survive as quotations by Athenaios, whose interest in obscure details of eating and drinking habits they all too grossly reflect. The same theme survives with admirable rustic vigour in Aristophanes, but taken out of context the fragments of Epicharmos are not as attractive as one might hope.

They have a liveliness, and a breathless comic style that reflects peasant language. Comedy, like tragedy, has its messenger speeches, but in Aristophanes they are often connected together by 'and ... and ... and then ... so then ...' They are paratactic, not syntactic, like Shakespeare's description of the death of Falstaff, and none the worse for that. Epicharmos was already producing parodies of epic, of religion in his *Delphic Visitors*, and of accepted military values. The theatre of Aristophanes was so bound up with parody of tragedy that it was in many ways parasitic on tragic poetry. One is meant to laugh both with and at the peasant view of every solemn institution. But Aristophanes in his own way was a remarkable and an admirable poet.

The Athenian state took over responsibility for comedy at the Great Dionysia in about 487 B.C.; and from 440 B.C. comedy became part of the winter festival of the Lenaia. It had a chorus of twenty-four, which at a central point in the comedy addressed its chant to the audience directly to make a moral or political point, and at times to speak personally for the poet, who might be a member of it. This is what Aristophanes inherited and what pushed comedy towards being a personal, political vehicle like sophisticated political cabaret. That did not last long: such movements in the theatre never do, because the audience does not last even one generation. The theatre of Aristophanes in all its circumstances was the creation of an audience and a moment, and of course of a poet. One should not try to explain it by its ancient ritual formulae, but as a mixture that altered and remade itself as Athens altered.

Still, comedy and its audience were in most ways solidly conservative. Democracy was not to them a new idea, and the power of Athens was already tilting towards a decline, as many of them must have suspected. And they liked the animal choruses, the carnival aspect of the theatre. They enjoyed simple mockery and amusing fantasy, and the Flies, the Goats, the Ants, the Fishes, the Nightingales and the Bees. Kratinos wrote a comedy with a chorus of satyrs. I have never myself seen anything in the theatre much more enchanting than the *Birds* of Aristophanes in a college garden thirty years ago. But inside and outside the theatre time is unfortunately a one-way process.

The first Athenian comic poets we can place securely are Chionides, who won in 486, and Magnes, who won in 472, but they belong to the prehistory of this art: their plays seem to have been only three hundred lines long, and mostly choral. Of Ekphantides we know only that he claimed to scorn coarse Doric jokes: yet another theme that had a long life. Kratinos, most brilliant of the lost comic writers, was an older contemporary of Aristophanes, but it is better to deal first with the only complete fifth-century comedies we have.

We have nine fifth-century and two later plays of Aristophanes; the first to survive complete is the *Acharnians* in 425 B.C., after six years of war and several of plague, and four years after the death of Perikles. In his lost *Banqueters* of 427 an old man had two sons, one brought up traditionally, the other on rhetoric and sophistry. In his lost *Babylonians* of 426 he attacked the politician Kleon, who was a nasty piece of work by all accounts: Kleon threatened him furiously in reply. The Acharnians are villagers. We know little about Acharnai except that it boasted a fine temple of Ares, an unusual god, which was later removed bodily to Athens, and that 'the gods they worship are Apollo of the Street and Herakles, they have an altar of Athene of Health whom they call Athene of Horses, and they call Dionysos and Ivy the same god'. The hero Dikaiopolis, whose name means Just City, is wonderfully rustic. He hates being cooped up in Athens by war, and longs for his own farm.

From his first lines, Aristophanes shows a casual and apparently effortless command of iambic verse, looser than tragic verse but quite equally controlled, which the tragic poets might have envied and which defeats all translations.

> How I eat out of my heart, eat it away,
> I enjoy little, so little, four things:
> my sorrows are what sand the sea gargles ...

But the sand the sea gargles is all one word, which is unexpectedly placed, perfectly timed, and somehow extremely funny. These long, invented words are an important weapon in this poet's armoury. They are not translatable. What this language with many differences most resembles is the language of Shakespeare's comic rustics, which no living writer can aspire to imitate. Worse still, most of the continual string of jokes are about politics or the theatre; for a modern reader without Greek they would need an exhausting commentary, although I have seen them brought alive even in a classroom, and one can sense the life in them before one catches every nuance. The first episode after the monologue of Dikaiopolis, who 'groans and yawns and farts and scratches and considers' as he waits for the people's assembly to begin, is a parody of the reception of ambassadors. The assembly dissolves at a drop of rain, and the Spartan Amphitheos arrives, chased by Acharnians.

> I came here with an armistice for you,
> but old men from Acharnai smelt it out,
> horny old men, hearts of wild holly,
> hard-shelled old men, old Marathon men ...

The chorus are charcoal-burners from the Parnes range that rears up behind Acharnai. Their lyrics carry along the comic plot, and include numerous jokes. By now we are settling down to humour not only of caricature with verbal wit, but also of situation. Dikaiopolis decides to celebrate the country Dionysia, which he does with a ramshackle phallic procession, which is not only a comic *coup de théâtre*, but moving somehow as well as funny. One begins to see what powers of lyric poetry may be lurking in Aristophanes. He makes Gilbert and Sullivan seem the thinnest of gruel. The hostile chorus are won over to the hero's side, an ancient procedure of comedies, and a romp with Euripides as a comic character follows. Dikaiopolis then addresses the audience.

> ... since Comedy also knows right from wrong,
> what I shall say is terrible, but right.

Kleon will not tell lies about me now
for slandering this state in foreign eyes.
We are in the Lenaion, just ourselves,
there are no foreigners and no tribute
and no allies from the allied cities,
we are ourselves, threshed wheat of this city,
since I call foreigners chaff of the state.
Of course, I hate the Spartans utterly
and may Poseidon god of Matapan
earthquake their houses on to all their heads.
I lost my vineyard, my vines were cut down,
but between friends, as we are all friends here,
why do we blame the Spartans about that?
Our own men – and I did not say the state,
remember that, I did not say the state – ...

He is going to blame the aggressive economic sanctions taken by
Perikles against Megara. This is not exclusively a peasant's point of
view, though Aristophanes puts it in a countryman's mouth. The
wealthy had probably more to lose by Spartan raids on the countryside than the peasants. But one must leave the disentangling of the
precise political positions of Aristophanes to historians and social
historians. Here he wants peace, and my limited aim is to show as
far as I can the various interwoven textures of the *Acharnians* as
a play. This quotation was a rather sophisticated political speech,
the more effective for being lightly but definitely in character. Perikles
'thundered and lightened and stirred up all Greece, and passed decrees
written like drinking-songs: let them be banished from market and
earth, and from the sea and from the continent'. The hero then
encounters the angry general Lamachos, the chorus admits his
victory, and remarks 'let's get down to the anapaests', the traditional
metre in which chorus speaks to audience. Their subject is at first
the same as the hero's political speech, then it extends into respect
for old men and social morality; they name names, and praise a
political rival of Perikles.

There follows an appealing farce in which a Megarian tries to
smuggle piglets. An informer gets short shrift. He is finally swopped
with a Theban for a basket of eels. A festival is announced. A farmer
has lost his cattle, a bridegroom wants to stay at home and make

love, Lamachos wants to go to war. These episodes are swift, and the verse they are written in makes them swifter. It pauses only for parody. One's head reels from the abundance and the vigour of these farcical scenes, and from their swift succession. A messenger tells us Lamachos is ridiculously wounded. Half-way through this account he breaks into a parody of tragic messenger narratives.

> O glorious eye, I see you the last time,
> I leave the light and I no longer live:
> so saying, fell into a water-ditch ...

The play ends in joyous mockery of Lamachos, with the chorus chanting victory for our hero; things appear to end here for no reason except that it was time to go home. If I have expounded the action at tedious length, that was to show what kind of framework, if any, Aristophanes inherited.

Next year came the *Knights*, with a similar but not the same structure. It opens with a scene between the two complaining slaves of an old man called People. This old gentleman has been taken over by a new slave, the Paphlagonian – that is, Kleon. What is to be done in a household turned upside down by this new slave?

NIKIAS: The best for us to do as things are now
is grovel at the idol of some god.
DEMOSTHENES: What idol? Where? Do you believe in gods?
NIKIAS: I do.
DEMOSTHENES: What evidence have you for that?
NIKIAS: 'For I am hateful to them.' Is that right?
DEMOSTHENES: You convince me, but look at it like this,
shall I explain things to the audience?
NIKIAS: Why not?

This is the same world of tragic parody and of calmly stepping into roles or out of them, a habit still to be seen among modern comedians. The explanation to the audience is a kind of messenger speech about People. The two slaves find their champion in the Sausage-seller: the useful French translation of Aristophanes by Hilaire Van Daele calls him a *charcutier*, but he is not as refined as that, only an honest market-man. Hardly has he met the Paphlagonian when the chorus of Knights, or riders, fills the stage. Being in a comedy they are comic, but in life these are the young Athenians who inherited wealth; they provided their own horses. They are the riders of the Parthenon frieze, and Alkibiades was one of them.

Choruses usually go for someone, and these go for the Paphlagonian. He appeals to the audience, to 'old men, old magistrates, brethren of the wage', that is, to the elderly members who were coming to depend, or thought to depend, on the small, regular state wage for sitting on juries and tribunals. Money value was a new thing in the fifth century, but it utterly altered people's lives in the course of a hundred years after coined money began to circulate freely. In wartime under siege, when the easier rustic economy was impossible, as the old social bonds altered, and as no one could afford to distrust money, this process became feverish. It has been admirably explained by K. J. Dover in his *Greek Popular Morality*, an important aid for making sense of Aristophanes.

The odious Paphlagonian gets intellectually and farcically trounced in a succession of metrical chants and music until half-way through the play, when the chorus addresses the audience. Aristophanes deals in a few lines each with older comic poets: Magnes who could turn his voice to a lute-player, a wing-flapping bird, a louse or a frog, but in old age lost his habit of mockery and so fell out of favour, and Kratinos, rolling things along like a river in spate, whose songs were so popular until he took to drink, and Krates, apparently a more sparse and delicate and much less favoured writer. After this set piece, so precious to us, and in itself amusing and spirited, the chorus break suddenly into an unforgettable lyric.

Lord of horses, Poseidon, whose pleasure is the hoof-beat of bronze-jangling horses, and the neighing, and the blue-nosed, swift, tax-gathering warships, and the contest of youthful men glittering in their chariots and smashing them, come to this dance, O golden trident, O Sounion-praised, dolphin god, O son of Zeus from Cape Geraistos, and most dear to Phormion and to Athens, of all gods at this time ...

Phormion has just won important naval victories. 'Bronze-jangling' may be wrong: the word is literally 'bronze-banging', and Van Daele will not go beyond 'galop sonore comme l'airain'. But I take it the horses were unshod, but harnessed and armed. There is a second stanza of this lyric to come, after another long choral chant to the audience as citizens.

The second chant is the praise of old men. 'We mean to praise our fathers, because they were men worthy of this earth and of Athene's robe, who in battle on foot, and in the breaking of ships, were everywhere and always victorious, and an ornament to this city.' The chant is sixteen lines long. The second stanza of the hymn of the Riders follows. 'O Pallas who keeps this city, O goddess of this most holy country, greatest of all in war, in poets and in power, come and dwell with us and bring our fellow Victory in campaign and in battle, the companion of our dances, who fights with us against our enemies. Appear, come now, because you must by every art give these men victory, now if ever.' Another chant with the praise of horses, and we return to the Sausage-seller, and a longer messenger speech by him, about the Paphlagonian in conflict with the Riders.

Paphlagonian and Sausage-seller then have their quarrel out on stage, and People comes on to decide the conflict. It lasts a long time, and demonstrates remarkable resources of comic invective. When it ends we get a second, shorter minuet of chants to the audience and of lyrics, a defence of satire and a charming story about the conversation of the warships, who are women, as one would expect. People is converted and his youth is somehow renewed for a marriage with Armistice.

By 423, when the *Clouds* appeared at the Great Dionysia, an armistice was being negotiated. Athens had suffered some defeats, and the mood had altered. It is possible that Kleon had shut Aristophanes up, but that is obscure. At any rate, the *Clouds* is about philosophers, and Sokrates is much mocked in it. We know from Plato's *Symposion* that the poet and the philosopher were extremely close friends. Maybe it was safer in that year, at least at the Dionysia, to mock one's friends: the humour is broad but very funny and not savage, there is even an element of reverence in it here and there.

But it was no use. Kratinos rose from the past, and produced a winning comedy, Aristophanes was beaten into third place. His comedy must have been brilliant. I have heard Eduard Fraenkel sigh that of all the treasures buried in the sand of Egypt what he most yearned for was the *Bottle*, by Kratinos. The old poet introduced himself as a hopeless old profligate, whoring after boys (who were a chorus of Wine-cans), who finally got converted to return to his old wife Comedy. As a comic construction this has admirable possibilities, and we have no doubt of the poet's powers. Horace spoke of 'Eupolis atque Cratinus Aristophanesque poetae', and other writers of old comedy, with great affection and respect. They were his masters in that poetry which Pope imitated in English.

The *Clouds* opens with an Athenian father, sleepless at dawn.

Eeooo. Eeooo. O Zeus almighty, how long the nights are: endless! Will it never be day? I heard the cock crow long ago. The slaves are snoring. They never used to. Curse this war for all manner of things: now I can't even punish my slaves. Even this fine young man here, he doesn't wake at night, he lies farting, all bundled up there in five blankets. Well, if you like, let's wrap up and let's snore. But I can't sleep, I eat my heart away with the expense of stables and the debts, because of my son here, with the long hair, riding his horses and driving his teams, he even dreams horses: I perish, watching the moon move to the twentieth. The interest is galloping . . .

The son wakes and the household stirs, and the old man decides to go to thinking school, to learn the new sophistries for himself. A pupil bemuses him and Sokrates appears. 'I walk on air considering the sun,' he says. 'I never understand things in mid-air, except by mingling my intellect and subtle thought with air, which is the same.' Even the Sokrates of Plato says somewhere 'Nothing is more in mid-air than the gods': the more one knows about Sokrates, the funnier this play becomes. This solemn and dotty Sokrates prays to Air, and to the Clouds, who then appear.

> O everlasting Clouds,
> let us reveal our dewy glorious selves,
> come from Ocean, deep-echoing father,
> to the high mountains shaggy with forest,
> gaze on the distant peaks
> and on all fruits and watered holy earth
> and the loud babble of godlike rivers
> and the deep sounding and the babbling sea:
> because the unwearied eye of heaven shines
> with stony glittering beams.
> Shake off the shady drift
> of our immortal form and we shall see
> all earth with our far-staring eye.

If there is a certain reminiscence here of the chorus in *Prometheus*, it is probably deliberate. Aristophanes does at times deliberately recall earlier lyrics and earlier music that the audience loved. The address to the audience in the *Clouds* is about his own poetry and about politics, and the formal quarrel or debate is between Right and Wrong Argument. The rest of it is a string of more and more farcical episodes between Sokrates and the old man.

> STUDENT: Does the gnat sing forwards or backwards, then?
> STREPSIADES: What does Sokrates say about the gnat?
> STUDENT: He maintains that the inmost gut of gnats
> is narrow, by which slender waist the air
> runs violently outward through the arse;
> then, where the hollow and the narrow meet,
> the bottom buzzes from the force of wind.

This sort of nonsense will have done Sokrates little harm. Sophistry and perverse morality are severely handled, but so did Sokrates severely handle them. The austere and solemn teachings of the Clouds late in the play may perhaps owe something more to him. They turn out to be traditional-minded divinities, and not new-fangled ones. Aristophanes is a witty poet and an amusing philosopher, not just a script-writer for television comedians, though he could do that as well.

In 422, his subject in the *Wasps* was old men crazy about sitting as judges of the people's courts. They are a chorus of Wasps, and the comedy is about a conflict of generations. It is highly instructive, but one must not take it too literally. The play opens with two slaves discussing the affairs of the house. The son, called as it were Anti-Kleon is trying to keep his crazy father, called as it were Pro-Kleon, locked up at home, to get over his mania. The old man tries to escape by the chimney disguised as smoke, and other such pranks. His son convinces the chorus, and then consoles his father by letting him try two dogs in the case of the stolen cheese.

The accusing dog stands for Kleon, the defender for general Laches, a friend of Sokrates who in real life had been prosecuted by Kleon. The trial of the dogs is very funny indeed; the defendant gets acquitted by mistake. Son proceeds with father's education by training him how to behave at dinner. The old man behaves disgracefully, steals a flute-girl, and challenges the audience to dance. 'I envy the old man his good luck, having so altered his dried-up ways and his style of life. But now with the new lessons he'll have a big fall into luxury and soft life. Maybe he wouldn't like that, because it's hard to change your nature which you have for ever. But it has happened to many: seeing other people's views they've altered their ways.' This chorus of the old men is in nice contrast with a narrative of his awful behaviour: deliberately, of course, though it shocked some scholars into an inclination to move its position in the play. Read fast, the play works well, and the old man's conversion to merriment is an acceptable climax.

The *Peace* is a triumph of fantasy on a greater scale than anything so far. It was played in 421, a few days before the Peace of Nikias was signed. The *Wasps* had been presented during an armistice that did not last long. It was wrecked by Kleon and the Spartan commander Brasidas, both of whom were killed in the campaign that broke it. The Peace of Nikias was more serious, and more popular in Athens and at Sparta than in some other Greek states. Aristophanes was beaten into second place by the *Flatterers* of Eupolis, but the *Peace* is both spectacular and funny. Two slaves are looking after a giant dung-beetle, on which their rustic master, who calls it Pegasos, wants to visit Zeus to complain about the war. This seems to be a joke version of some machinery used in the *Bellerophon* of Euripides. Hermes tells the old man the gods have flown away high up in disgust, and War is king and keeps Peace in a deep pit. War is going to crunch up the cities of Greece with a pestle and mortar. But Terror, the servant of War, is unable to find the tools, because Kleon and Brasidas are dead. So War goes indoors to make instruments, and the old Athenian summons a chorus of Greeks to rescue Peace. As they pull her out, Harvest and Festival appear beside her and Hermes shows them all the road to earth.

Hermes has given in a comic narrative chant an amusing travesty of Athenian history ('O most wise farmers, you must understand my words, and you will see how Peace perished . . .'), but Peace and Harvest and Festival never speak; they are a silent allegory. The address to the audience is a long boast about the poet, with some charming lyrics. 'Muse, push away wars, and dance with me your friend, who seal the marriages of gods, the feasts of men and festivals of the blessed: which was your business from the beginning . . .'

The dung-beetle is left in heaven, Peace is enthroned, and the rest of the comedy is a series of episodes. Naked Festival is given to the Council of Athens, Peace gets offerings, a fraudulent interpreter of oracles is repulsed. In another address to the audience Aristophanes speaks of peasant celebrations, with unsentimental gluttony and a strong feeling of their vigour. He was born in the city, but Athens was a country town about the size of Lewes or Oban. This choral chant or poet's chant has some technical interest also, as it reports conversation with questions and answers of marked realism. In the last episodes of this extremely happy play, the sickle-maker praises the old man, the armourer complains, a boy has to unlearn epic poetry, and it all suddenly ends in a wedding song for the old Athenian.

> Be silent all, and bring a bride out here
> to give wealth to the Greeks and a good crop,
> and wine in plenty, figs to eat,
> and our wives to be fruitful,
> and all good things we lost,
> just as we used to have,
> and shining steel to cease.
> Come out, woman, to this field,
> beautiful as you are,
> lie with me beautifully.
> Hymen, O Hymenaios!

In 414 that mood had altered. The peace had not lasted, and Athens had sent to Sicily a huge expedition which was soon to fail utterly. The atmosphere of the city was hysterical, with mysterious sacrilege followed by fear and ferocious inquisition. The *Birds* of Aristophanes is a fantastical play. A citizen and his friend have left Athens.

> We're flying away from home with both our feet,
> not that we hate our city, not at all,
> that great city born to be happy,
> that general provider for all men.
> But the crickets sit singing on the twigs
> a month or two, Athens sings for ever,
> singing away their lives in the lawcourts.

They are off to consult a mythical hero who was turned into a bird. The plot of the play is the building of the city of the birds. It is fantasy laced with satire. It is more lyrical than anything the poet had written in the past, and its great set piece, an aria in which the hoopoe summons the other birds, with some use of bird-mimicry such as possibly a bird-snarer might use, is an amazing extension even of his powers. This is the first animal chorus we have from Aristophanes, apart from the *Wasps*, who (alas) are more melodious in the Vaughan Williams overture than in the Greek text. Nor has Aristophanes lost his sharpness: in this play he hits out at Sokrates, at Gorgias the writer of melodious prose, and at some politicians.

In the first hundred lines the heroes have met the hoopoe's servant and then the hoopoe himself. His appearance involves a joke about the *Tereus* of Sophokles. They agree together to build what will become Cloud-cuckoo-land.

> Epopopoi. Popoi. Popopopoi. Popoi.
> Io, Io, ito, ito,
> hither my feathered brethren come
> who dwell in sprouting hollows of the farms,
> ten thousand tribes of barley-eaters,
> races of seed-gatherers,
> swift on the wing uttering your soft song,
> and in furrows dense
> twittering on the clod
> in voices of delight
> tio tio tio tio tio tio tio tio
> you that in the orchards haunt
> underneath the ivy branch
> and on the mountain and on the wild olive and in the hill bushes
> fly to my call
> trioto trioto totobrix.

The song is much longer, and in Greek it is a single, perfectly sustained, virtuoso passage of onomatopoeia. It is metrically thrilling in its variations. One must remember also that Greek verse is quantitative, so that although this whole aria has numerous short syllables (not one long syllable in the third-last line of what I have written), probably to fit the new flute music, yet the 'o' in 'ito' and the 'i' in 'totobrix' are long. It is really impossible to convey to Greek-less readers the quality of this song. The arrival of the Birds is both comic and lyrical. They are hostile at first and need to be won over, but a chanted scene persuades them that even the gods depend on birds: they can blackmail the gods.

The first long choral address to the audience is a cosmogony: an account of the creation of a type that belongs to the rather mysterious cult of Orpheus. This is the earliest fully surviving example; the Orphic hymns we have belong to the Roman empire. It is bird-oriented and it has some jokes in it, but this passage is of great beauty, like the solemn teachings of the *Clouds*, parody as it is.

And if you can believe that we are gods, your prophets shall be Muses, seasons, airs, winter and summer and a touch of frost, we shall not run off proudly to the clouds, to sit there as Zeus does, we shall give you, and to your children and to their children, health, wealth, long life and peace, and youth and laughter, dances, festivals and milk of birds; you will weary of good things, you will all be so rich.

Bird-milk is proverbial for unreality. The lyrics that follow between chants are even more untranslatable than the invocation of the birds, and as full of bird-noises, of which my own favourite is tio tio tio tinx.

In swift episodes a priest with solemn ritual language, a poet who speaks in quotations, a soothsayer, the town planner Meton and two other noxious Athenians arrive and are driven away. The second set of choral chants follows, in which the birds make laws and discuss Athenian politics. A messenger announces the building of a wall by the birds, and another warns of trouble from the gods; the gods send Iris their messenger to threaten; now human beings want to become birds, and after a new succession of episodes, Prometheus arrives to help, followed by Poseidon and Herakles and a Thracian god unable to talk Greek. Suddenly the birds have won, and a messenger brings Sovereignty herself. The play ends with a wonderful, solemn wedding-hymn, and a procession of victory. The Athenian is the bridegroom and dances with the goddess.

So far as we know, Aristophanes had written no play between the *Peace* and the *Birds*. That may be a mere failure of our limited evidence. In the *Birds*, he has not gone back to his intimate quarrel with the Athenian people about politics and the war. He has taken the allegorical triumph from the middle of the *Peace*, and constructed an entire play out of gleefully humorous and fantastical comedy of situation. The episodes are present in rich succession, more rapid than before, but hemmed in by lyrical stanzas and by the bones of a unified plot. Perhaps his greatest gift was that of sheer fantasy, sheer lyrical and comic invention. Still, the play came second again, and its mood was not repeated. After the Sicilian disaster of 413 Athens began obviously to lose the war.

There was a second version of *Peace*, in which Agriculture was a character, and perhaps in these years Aristophanes wrote a lost *Farmers* and a lost *Seasons*. But to return to surviving plays, in 411 he presented *Lysistrata* at the Lenaia in midwinter, and the *Thesmophoriazousai*, which I shall call the *Festival of Women*, at the Great Dionysia, in early spring. In both plays his existing interest in women flowered. The *Lysistrata*, if it is viewed alone, seems to be a fascinating, lonely cry about the position of women in his world, but anyone interested in social rather than literary history, supposing the two to be different, would do well to observe the roles of women in the earlier works of Aristophanes in more detail than I have presented them. Lysistrata was well discussed by Nigel Wilson in an article in *Greek, Roman and Byzantine Studies* in 1982. It is clear at least that women, like farmers, want peace, and that Peace and Harvest and Festival and the Muse are female, and Athene matches Poseidon; even Sovereignty is a woman, Agricultural cults are based on sexual union and fertility, and the real Athenian marriage ritual spoke of ploughing and of fruitful seed. In these two comedies the chorus are women, and they have taken over: a situation only slightly less fantastical in Athens than that of the *Birds*.

In *Lysistrata* the women refuse sex unless they get peace. Lysistrata, probably the parody of a real high priestess of Athene, has called a congress of women, and after some uncertainty they turn up from all over Greece, wickedly and amusingly characterized. A chorus of old men opposes the chorus of women. The jokes in this play are hilariously funny. Having found his situation, Aristophanes exploits it and develops it remorselessly until one's ribs ache. Rather freely translated, it has been extremely successful in the modern theatre. It contains strange touches of pathos, so that one is sorry for the person one is laughing at, which are clearer in the performance than on the printed page, and a rather strangely moving choral lyric about the obscure myth of Melanion. Both the halves of the chorus are sarcastic exaggerations by the poet of prejudiced views of well-known stories.

> Let me tell you a story
> I heard when I was a little boy.
> A young man called Melanion ran away from marriage
> and went into the wilderness
> and lived among the mountains.
> He hunted hares and trapped the bears,
> and had a dog,
> and never came home, and sulked his life away:
> he hated women, so do we, just like Melanion.
>
> Let me tell you a story too
> against Melanion's.
> There was Timon well defended
> by a trackless wilderness,
> flung out there by Furies,
> and there he lived from hatred
> and cursed the wickedness of men:
> like us, he hated wicked men
> but he loved the women.

The theme of misanthropic Timon was not new in the comic theatre. But one sees suddenly that what is being said and felt here and in one or two of the episodes is parody of a kind, and that Aristophanes in the theatre must have demanded a subtle, immediate conflict of feelings. This is knock-about comedy which is not merely knock-about. It exaggerates gently the inherent division of feelings that even a Punch and Judy show arouses. Even the thick dialect of the Spartan woman, much mocked throughout this play, comes into its own at the end, when she sings what is obviously a beautiful hymn to the Muse of the Spartan mountain Taygetos, praising 'Sparta, whose care is the dances of the gods and the beating of the feet beside Eurotas, and the shaking hair of the Bacchai'.

The *Festival of Women* is another matter. It involves a women's revolution of a quite different kind. The feast of the Thesmophoria was indeed a women's holy day in which men had no part. It was an autumn feast of Demeter, in which women set up tabernacles of branches, and pigs (for centuries a symbol of fertility in the Middle East) were offered with seed corn to the goddess who would bless the crop. The comedy has little to do with this cult, and virtually nothing to do with politics. It is about the superiority of women, and it satirizes Euripides and Agathon rather heavily. It particularly exploits the recent plays of Euripides. Euripides is a character from the first scene, in which he takes a relative to call on Agathon, whose lyrics are almost oversweet, and even whose servant talks like a poetry machine. Agathon's first lyrics are sung antiphonally as it were, with a chorus, though Agathon sings both parts. They are being parodied for their wandering and perhaps impromptu music. It is infuriating but true that one cannot quite discern the beautiful or conventional from the ridiculous in this scene. I cannot avoid feeling that Aristophanes after an initial musical parody shows admiration for Agathon in these lyrics, but I may be wrong.

This is a comedy without a full hero. The women of Athens are plotting revenge on Euripides, so he means to dress the pansy-looking Agathon as a woman and get him into the Thesmophoria to hear the plot. Agathon refuses, so Euripides shaves and singes his kinsman. The women complain of the poet, but the kinsman points out he might have said worse on the subject of women. He is caught, and grabbing a baby which turns out to be a wineskin he takes refuge at the altar. The women chant the defence of women. 'If we're bad why marry us? If you find us out of doors you go raving mad: you ought to be happy to be rid of us.' The kinsman and Euripides adopt various Euripidean devices of rescue, but this ends with Euripides arrested by a policeman. Finally, a truce is agreed, and a prostitute gets round the policeman. The comedy closes: 'We have played enough, it is time for us all to go home. May the gods of this day give us the reward of their favour.' Alas, this cheerful, clever piece means less to us on the printed page than it should, because it is so bound up with parodies of Euripides, which for our benefit require annotation; in production it has sometimes been an immediate success, at least in Oxford college gardens.

After the *Festival of Women* we have no complete play until the

Frogs in 405: in some ways a sad play, but yet with the last traces of the fireworks and haunting beauty of which Aristophanes had been capable. The three great tragic poets were dead, and Dionysos in despair has to adventure underground to find the best of them, to bring him back to earth. He hears, as gratuitously as other lyric scenes in Aristophanes, the singing of the blessed spirits in the Elysian fields, and has trouble with a chorus of frogs in the Stygian marshes. In a comic but not wholly unserious contest between Euripides and Aischylos, in which the verse techniques of both are mocked, Aischylos wins. Sophokles is too sweet-natured to take part. The slave of Dionysos on this journey is an enterprising and amusing figure, humanely caricatured on the whole, though humour about slaves is trivial as ever, and lowbrow.

> DIONYSOS: Do I, Dionysos, son of Jugofurine,
>   march and sweat and let him ride?
> SLAVE: What about me?
> DIONYSOS: You're carrying nothing.
> SLAVE: I carry this.
> DIONYSOS: How do you?
> SLAVE: It's heavy.
> DIONYSOS: Isn't it on the donkey that you're on?
> SLAVE: Not if I carry it, by Zeus no.
> DIONYSOS: You're being carried, how are you carrying?
> SLAVE: I don't know, but I know my shoulder hurts.
> DIONYSOS: If you say that donkey's no use to you,
>   then pick the donkey up and carry him.
> SLAVE: Ach, why didn't I volunteer for sea?

Slaves who volunteered as rowers were made free after a naval victory that year. This matter crops up again in a choral chant, where Aristophanes says, 'I am not against it, I applaud it, it's the only sensible thing you've done.' The two adventurers, underground now, encounter Herakles and a dead man and finally Charon, helmsman of the ferry of the dead, who we know as a grizzled old figure on funeral vases. Dionysos has to row across Styx. He is bewildered by the rhythm of rowing, and more so by that of the frogs, but at last he learns to chant in time with them. The 'ex' and 'ax' are long syllables.

Brekekekex, koax, koax,
brekekekex, koax, koax.
Children of the marshy springs,
chant together in your hymns,
hear my music while I sings
koax, koax.

This scene is untranslatable really. It is funny, fantastical and
aurally brilliant, and not long enough for one to tire of it. The play
as a whole, and another lost play by Aristophanes about rescuing
old-fashioned Painting or Art from the underworld, owe something
to the *Towns* of Eupolis, a rival of Aristophanes active in the twenties,
and perhaps still alive, though he died at sea at some time in this
war. In the *Towns*, the quest in the underworld was to find a great
national leader, and the conclusion was to raise Perikles from the
dead. His play was produced probably in 412, but things had gone
too far by 405 for political fantasy of that kind. Now even the theatre
seemed to be doomed, let alone the military forces of the state. But
the *Frogs*, in its lugubrious way, is a cheering and interesting
production. The frog chorus is utterly original, the chorus of the
blessed must have been eery and thrilling, and the critical scenes are
full of lively intelligence. The choral chant contains a splendid compliment to Kratinos, dead for some few years, whom Aristophanes
acknowledges as master of the verse of comedy. Its political message
is said to have earned an encore.

His criticism of Euripides and Aischylos here is almost wholly about
their verbal texture. The main instrument is parody, both of themselves and one another, by both characters, with gleeful lyrics from
the chorus and ridiculous interjections by Dionysos. Translation cannot easily convey these subtleties all at once. Aischylos is attacked
but in the end valued for the solid weight of his words, Euripides
is mocked for some slippery, glittering expressions and for a habit
of syntax by which almost any can is easily tied to the tail of his
usual type of opening sentence: 'When Kadmos from the city of Sidon
came, Agenor's son ...' and so on. A lot of this criticism is deliberate
buffoonery, intended only to amuse, but the impression given is that
in the end Aristophanes really reveres Aischylos, at whom he
certainly smiles for his epic vocabulary, but that he finds Euripides

irresistibly funny, over-clever and slapdash. On the other hand the addition of 'tophlattothrat, tophlattothrat' between lines of Aischylos is also devastating. One can mock Tennyson, a lesser poet than Aischylos I suppose, in the same way, and yet greatly admire his work.

There is a problem about the chorus in this play. Did the frogs fling off their frog costumes and transform into the happy souls? Or were there two choruses, one not seen? There are no frog noises once Dionysos has crossed the marshy river, so maybe the frogs were only an episode. Yet they give their name to this comedy, so they ought to be its true chorus. The play won first prize. Were they, as frogs, ever visible? Were they a throwback to the old days of animal choruses, which Aristophanes introduced just from nostalgia, just for fun, when something more solemn had become usual? At any rate, the chorus at the end of the play are not frogs, because the king of the dead says, 'Light now your holy lights and go with him, with music and with hymns.' The Birds were certainly birds, though the Wasps were only men. It is sad not to know if the frogs were really frogs. We have very little evidence of animal choruses at Athens any later than the Frogs.

Aristophanes survived the fall of Athens and the civil war. He is to be found in the early fourth century taking a normal part in the politics of the restored democracy. But the theatre, like everything else, had altered vastly. His next play was in 392, the Assembly of Women, in which the women of Athens take over the apparatus of state, establish communism and abolish marriage, the rule of sex being first come first served, with priority to aged and ugly women. The play ends in a public feast. How serious is this joke? Of course it is enacted as funny, but this is philosophized fantasy, and similar ideas are recorded in the Politics of Aristotle and the Republic of Plato a little later. This comedy is not without some grain of a half-serious idea, though only a grain. He is mocking political philosophy. But the verse, for better and worse, is smoother than before, the humour is more robust than the language, there are few lyrics, the fantasy is less fantastical, and the choral music has withered away to a series of interludes for which no words are recorded, a central performance with formal chants, and a closing song of a few uproarious lines.

This play and the last we have, Wealth, are the only surviving examples of a transitional style (and yet is not all theatrical art transitional?), which ancient critics called Middle Comedy. But the *Assembly of Women* stands at the very beginning of that process. The principal pair of lyric arias is divided between a boy's serenading love-song, a touching and amusing mixture of popular themes, and a girl's song of anxiety for a lover, which parodies and sets off his. The final episode about a young lover whose bodily services are disputed between old women has the same quality as some scenes in *Lysistrata*: the humour is not as obvious or as cruel as it looks; if well enacted it would nicely confuse one's sympathies, and that is the intention. The comedy is not without real references to the politics of the moment, but scholars like to trace a shift from political to social criticism, which had certainly begun to take place now if not long ago. This play contains some deadly remarks about money values.

> Now let me say something to the judges:
> let the wise ones remember my wisdom
> and jokers treat me kindly for my jokes ...

Was the young Aristophanes not more confident about the role of his comedies? Twenty-five years ago he had written that 'therefore what we say must be excellent, because children are taught by schoolmasters, but to the growing young the poets speak'. But one must not exaggerate the difference: the competition always depended on judges, and I do not find any evidence that the moral reasoning of Aristophanes in his poetry had altered. His tone was subtler, that was all, and the range of dramatic representation in some ways extended.

The *Ploutos* (*Wealth*) was produced in 388. Wealth is blind and seeks a cure; he is sent by Delphic Apollo to Athens to be cured by Asklepios, and his slave describes this cure in one of the best narratives – I think the best – that this poet ever wrote. But the practical result of the cure, shown in farcical episodes, is appalling. The old woman loses her young gigolo, the priest of Zeus the Rescuer starves, and so on. The comedy ends with Wealth installed 'where he used to live', in the treasury in the west end of the Parthenon. We hear of torches lit and a procession, but there are no lyrics, only a final couplet.

> We must no longer linger, but go up
> to the west end, and singing follow them.

They must have sung, and they must have sung words, but probably those of a traditional hymn, something popular and old-fashioned, not written or composed for this occasion. The reason may surely be that the music of the day did not work well in the theatre. If the long example we have of the awful dithyrambic poetry of the fashionable composer Timotheos, with whom Euripides is supposed to have collaborated, is anything to go by, Aristophanes preferred clearer and simpler rhythms than any that could be mated with the new music. Some critics prefer to think that the choral interludes separating the five parts of *Wealth* were only dances with wordless music, but that is more than we know. At least at the end of the play the chorus sang, and the old atmosphere of celebration came for a moment to life. Otherwise, the peasant chorus retained only a toehold in the action.

The humour of the narrative about Wealth being cured is simple, but its language is more complex than usual. A slave is being questioned by a woman.

> WOMAN: Poor man, were you not frightened of the god?
> SLAVE: Yes, by all gods, I was, in case he got
> in first with his ribbons into the pot:
> the priest told me beforehand about that.
> When the old women heard the noise I made
> she raised her hand and so I gave a hiss
> and then a good bite like a holy snake,
> and so she snatched her hand away again
> and lay down in her blankets dead quiet
> farting worse than a ferret out of fear.
> So I took my pull at the offerings
> and when I had enough I went to sleep.

From this low level of humour the speech gradually modulates through the mysterious Cure and Healing, who blush and hold their noses, to some political jokes about how the god cures named public figures, then through the naive comments of the woman, to another mood.

WOMAN: O what a patriotic god, and wise!

SLAVE: So after that he sat down beside Wealth
and first he felt the head of the old man,
then he took up a clean piece of linen
and tied it round his eyes. Then Healing
covered his head up in a purple cloth
and all his face. The god clucked and clucked
and two great snakes slid out from the temple
in supernatural length.

WOMAN: Beloved gods!

SLAVE: In silence they slipped underneath the cloth
and licked at his eyelids, or so I thought,
and before you could drink ten cans of wine
Wealth stood up madam, able to see:
and there I was applauding with delight;
I got my master on his feet, the god
vanished into the temple with his snakes.

There is still a grain of mystery at the heart of the comedy, and the level of humour is still boldly unashamed of itself. No effect lasts longer than a line or two – in fact the speed of comic verse seems to have increased – and yet the momentum of the whole scene is cumulative. One should add that the same is true of the whole play, which is perhaps why the criticism of society in *Wealth* appears to cut deeper than elsewhere. The comedy is as funny, but the sadness is sadder. The other great set piece in the play is a defence of poverty, industry and self-help; its arguments are brushed aside, but I am not sure that Aristophanes treats the ideal of Wealth in the Parthenon with much conviction.

Aristophanes left two posthumous plays, and the Alexandrian librarians knew forty-four of his works altogether. One of the posthumous comedies had a seduction in it and a recognition scene which later critics saw as a foretaste of late comedy; the other was a parody of tragedy. It is curious that 386 B.C., when an inscribed stone tells us that at last the tragic festival began to produce revivals of older plays, may well be the date of his death. In the course of the fourth century, theatrical performance spread all over the Greek world. We have rather full records of its organization at certain centres, in particular at Delos. There were new poets and fresh plays, but nothing we know about them suggests that they are worth a long discussion here, until we come to Menander, who needs a chapter of his own. Still, Euboulos in his handful of fragments, and Mnesimachos, in a caricature of Philip of Macedon as an iron-eating savage, show real talent, and Epikrates and Ephippos attack the philosophers in a way that interests (or ought to interest) the historians of philosophy. The Muses had not all forsaken Athens. The lights did not all go out when Aristophanes died. Probably what seemed to later antiquity and still seems to us the overwhelming brightness of the fifth century, which makes the fourth century a place of shadows by contrast, is largely an effect of the political nostalgia of the later Athenians. But we are forced to base our conclusions on what has survived.

In Aristophanes we have not only a writer but a process, and many reflections of an uncontrollable real world outside the theatre. The texture of his plays is too rich and various to be easily pinpointed, and too precisely calculated as language to be well conveyed by translation or even the most successful modern production. In Renaissance tragedy we have at least a tragic language we feel and understand, but Renaissance comedy, wonderful as it is, flowered out of a gift from the Romans and from Menander; it does not attempt the range of Aristophanes. It does not sting so often like a bee and it makes less honey; it is also (in Italy at least) more obscene but less vulgar than Aristophanes. The social bonds of his world have long ago dissolved. What is most admirable in Aristophanes within that world, which today we need scholarship to reconstruct, is his perfect timing, his precision. 'Do not let sleep, life's honey, flood your eyes.' His mankind consists of 'creatures of shadow, children of the leaves', but they are more awake than we are, and who would need to sleep if he had such waking dreams? It is important that the theatre was open for less than a week and only twice a year, and every play had one performance only, and the whole of Athens saw it.

Kenneth McLeish has written much that is worth thought about Aristophanes, including this: 'Like Aeschylus, he rarely philosophizes, rarely explains: philosophy and explanation vibrate in the words themselves. In both artists, the polished intellectuality and elegant pattern-making of Sophocles or Euripides are replaced by rawness, illogicality, feeling itself. Our interest focuses not so much on the forces at work on man as on man himself.' I am not sure whether all of this is true, but it is certainly worth thinking about. Personally, I am inclined to think that I like Aristophanes because he so loves everything I most value, including poetry.

> The graceful thing
> is not to sit
> by Sokrates and talk
> and cast aside the Muse
> and all the great matter
> of the tragic art.

He wants more poetry and fewer philosophers. In particular he wants another Aischylos. Was he wrong? Might Sokrates not have felt deeply that he was right?

Last of all one should record the curious fact that what is possibly or even probably the gravestone of Aristophanes, showing a fine stone relief of a sad poet with two grinning comic masks, survives in the hands of the local council at Lyme Park, Stockport. It was a chance find brought home from the Grand Tour; the name is missing, but the date is right.

BIBLIOGRAPHY

K. J. Dover, *Aristophanic Comedy*, 1972

J. Henderson (ed.), *Aristophanes, Essays in Interpretation*, 1981

K. McLeish, *The Theatre of Aristophanes*, 1980

C. Prato, *Euripide nella critica di Aristofane*, 1955

F. H. Sandbach, *The Comic Theatre of Greece and Rome*, 1977

G. Sifakis, *Studies in the History of Hellenistic Drama* (with a full bibliography), 1967

G. Sifakis, *Parabasis and Animal Choruses*, 1971

A. D. Trendall and T. B. L. Webster, *Illustrations of Greek Drama*, 1971

Note: Among modern English commentaries on the Greek texts, K. J. Dover's *Clouds* (1968), D. M. MacDowell's *Wasps* (1970) and R. G. Ussher's *Ecclesiazusae* (*Assembly of Women*) (1973) contain material useful even to Greekless readers.

HERODOTOS

We have overshot the fifth century, because it was desirable to treat theatrical poetry closely together. Aristophanes started writing only in the twenties, though comedy as an art began much earlier. Herodotos the historian was dead by 420. He had lived about sixty years, and he is the first substantial Greek prose writer whose work survives, and Sophokles in the late forties has been thought to show precise knowledge of his writing. Herodotos was apparently a professional story-teller of some kind, a prose entertainer, though many scholars dislike the idea. His written work, which is largely an account of the Persian wars, certainly shows numerous traces of an oral technique, and its rag-bag quality here and there might easily arise from its being his stock-in-trade. The hard evidence for his being paid vast sums as a 'professional lecturer' is not as hard as it seems however. He was certainly a friend of Sophokles, who wrote him a poem, and apparently in Athens in the forties, in the Athens of Perikles, while the Parthenon was being built.

He was a kinsman of Panyassis the late epic poet. His great predecessor, Hekataios, wrote firstly about peoples and secondly their history, but Herodotos wrote firstly about the history of one war, and secondarily the peoples it involved. His second book, which is about Egypt, harks back to the older method. He came from Halikarnassos, and by blood he was partly Karian. He left Halikarnassos for ever at a time when that unhappy city, modern Bodrum, a settlement with remote Doric origins, had been wrenched by civil war. A tyrant ruled who was grandson to that Queen Artemisia of whom Herodotos gave his account in the Persian wars. Panyassis was killed and Herodotos withdrew to Samos, so the unreliable story goes, and although Herodotos and his friends won in the end, he never settled at home again.

Whether as a story-teller, or more likely a merchant, or both, Herodotos seems to have wandered a long way. We have a dedication with his name scratched on it from Naukratis, the Greek trading settlement on the Nile estuary, and he is known to have been in Samos, in Athens, and more than one part of Egypt, both before 460 so it appears, and certainly after 449, also at Gaza and Tyre, at Babylon, in what is now southern Russia, up the Dnieper perhaps as far as Kiev, in Thasos, in Cyrenaica and Crete, and of course at Delphi.

Small wonder he became a professional teller and then writer of tales. But the journeys cannot be precisely traced or more than loosely dated. Some scholars view them sceptically. We are told, probably by guesswork, that he was born in 484 B.C., which makes forty years before he crops up in Athens. The cup found at Naukratis fits his visit there in the early forties. His story of the Persian wars, organized later by librarians into nine books named after the nine Muses, ends with the naval action at Mykale and the capture of Sestos in north Greece in 478 by Xanthippos, the father of Perikles. Herodotos, it must not be forgotten, wrote about what was rather remote, not about the events of his own adult lifetime. So far as Athens is concerned, he wrote as a Periklean, and when he left Athens it was to go as a colonist to Thourioi, a city founded under the influence of Perikles, on the east coast of the toe of Italy. Thourioi replaced the ruins of Sybaris, and was built in 443 B.C. Herodotos lived on there until at least 430, and it may well be in Sybaris that he composed his written history. His grave was there, though the epitaph recorded from it is not authentic.

The last events he records are mentioned in his later books, and took place in 431 and 430. He knows about the Theban attack on Plataia (7.233), the expulsion of the people of Aigina (6.91), the invasion of Attica (9.73) and the execution of envoys (7.137), which he puts in to conclude the story of a vengeance of the gods against Spartan heralds. His account of a chariot dedicated 'on the left as you enter the Propylaia of the Akropolis' is not so helpful. This monument was destroyed in 480, then renewed; fragments of its inscribed base have been found, but where it stood in his day and when it was put there remain a problem. It will almost certainly have been moved when the new Propylaia, the formal entrance built under

Perikles, was built between 437 and 432. But it is not safe to conclude that Herodotos came back to Athens at that time and saw where it then was.

He quotes its inscription, and many other inscribed stones from the Persian wars, and he clearly used written sources as well, where any existed, but almost all his information appears to come from personal questioning of witnesses and from traditional stories. He is informative about whatever a travelling merchant would know, from local produce to means of transport and the navigability of rivers. He has special information about all the places we know he visited: that is almost always how we know of his visit. Some later Greek writers say he used written sources rather fully, but the details almost never confirm these remarks. He did use Hekataios, and just possibly his own contemporaries like Xanthos the Lydian and Hellanikos of Lesbos who were younger, and Charon of Lampsakos, but except for Hekataios the evidence is inconclusive; it is certain he did not use them much or know their work well, and nor do we. He may or may not have used lost works at whose existence only the deepest scholars have guessed.

It remains interesting and quite likely that from Hekataios he learnt something of the vastness and complexity of the world, and the power and achievement of Persia, but in Athens he understood, probably for the first time, what Marathon and Salamis meant. What makes him the first serious historian is his combination of great scope and precise focus, his imaginative power as a story-teller and his rationalism, his concern with the truth. A sanguine critic might expect such a writer in the generation of Sophokles. But there was no Herodotos before Herodotos, and in his own lifetime he had no rival in scope or in precision of detail.

His digressions are numerous and entertaining, but they are pinned in place by relevance of some kind. Even the vast mass of his description of Egypt has its point. It is an appendix to the invasion of Egypt by Kambyses, and it helps to build up the clash of the Persian superpower with Greek rocks. His tragical stories are as precisely placed as his relieving anecdotes. His writing reveals complicated patterns of symmetry and contrast and matching series of stories, and he likes to tell his tale in a circle, winding his way round again to what introduced it. These are the techniques of an oral story-teller. He can balance his emphasis on a shift of word-order as a ballet dancer can balance on the points of his shoes. He is conscious of the contrast of long phrases or words against short, of assonance and of word-play, yet nothing is obtrusive in his language; it flows as brilliantly along as the sea in summer. He learnt something from the Athenian theatre and more from folk-tales. One can find in him, as J. D. Denniston pointed out, a Homeric habit of thought, a tragic momentum and sense of climax, and abundant comedy. He writes with a wonderfully loose wrist, and yet with exact control.

There are some muddles in his writing, at least as we now have it. He promises to tell some Assyrian stories, but we never hear them and he never wrote them. They might have balanced his treatment of Egypt: in that case they are a sad loss. His account of the dead kings of the Pyramids seems to have got out of place, not as a seventeenth-century English historian wrote, 'because my spaniels had got in among my papers', but more likely because of his attempt to iron out a confusion of Egyptian chronology. Chapter 124 of Book 2 and what follows it ought to come after Chapter 99, but, as he said, he depends on what the priests told him, and he has obviously had trouble with them, and with his notes. In Book 7, he promises to tell us later why Athenades of Trachis happened for the wrong reason to kill the loathsome Epialtes who betrayed the Greeks at Thermopylai, 'but the Spartans gave honours to Athenades all the same'. We never do get told, but this is hardly a great matter.

Herodotos thinks Homer is an acceptable witness for prehistory, and he accepts a mythical framework for the remoter past. He or some earlier writer already has it sorted out into generations, as the tragedians have. Indeed for Euripides it was already a game to produce surprising contemporaries as it were out of a hat, and such a game depends on its rules being known. Herodotos understands that much of civilization came from the east, including more of religion than Athenian tragedy would admit. 'Everyone,' he says of his personal mystical instruction in Egypt, 'knows the same about divine matters.' He understands that the Dark Ages were full of migrations; he is particularly keen on the foundation of the Dorian race in southern Greece by the return there of the children of Herakles, and on the Ionian migration to the Levant. Only Athens is allowed to be herself alone, because he learnt her prehistory from the Athenians. He does rationalize about religion. The priestesses at Dodona 'murmur like doves' instead of interpreting real birds, and 'the Thessalians themselves say Poseidon created the channel where the Peneios runs, which is quite probable, because anyone who believes that Poseidon shakes the earth and the chasms caused by earthquake are the work of that god would say if he saw this one that Poseidon made it: the parting of the mountains being the work of an earthquake, as it appeared to me'.

In historical times he likes to give the origins of all his information. Given two stories, he likes to tell both, and usually, though not always, to abstain from any conclusion, though he is capable of altering the balance by a considerable weight of irony. This impartiality, and his liking for eyewitnesses, sometimes greatly impressed scholars in the past, though Plutarch attacked him in a mildly interesting but perverse pamphlet. On the whole it is surprising how reliable he is, wherever his work can be tested archaeologically, though it would not of course be safe to rely on every detail. The gods are active in many events, and individual heroes are fully celebrated. His curiosity is amiably childlike, so that no ancient and perhaps no modern historian is more entertaining. But throughout his work fate is rigorous, chance is perverse, oracles are slippery and Zeus punishes. And after all his meanderings, his work comes to a climax like a long-expected thunderstorm, and it ends in triumph.

He certainly learnt, as I have said, from tragedy and comedy, but also more importantly from those folk-tales and forms of story and those sayings that dictated many values to the Athenian theatre. The strain of humane sadness and compassion in his writing, which often goes unremarked among brighter surface qualities, has its roots there. 'I wonder whether to exterminate the Lydians. At present I think I behave like one who kills the father but spares the sons.' In another context:

'Go home and do not blame yourself. Pride is an awkward inheritance. Do not heal harm with harm. Many prefer common sense to justice. And many in the past have lost their father's inheritance by seeking their mother's. Tyranny is a tricky thing, it has many lovers; he is old and past his youth; do not give away your good.' She told him all the persuasive arguments her father had taught her, but he answered that he would never come to Corinth until he knew his father lived.

This persuasive princess argues like a character in Euripides, yet her proverbial language is that of the chorus. In two or three more sentences the story (3.53) comes to an appalling climax.

As for the influence of folk-tales and animal fables, a type of story of which Hesiod, Archilochos and Aischylos already provide evidence, they are to be found everywhere in Herodotos, but mostly in speeches.

A flute-player saw fish in the sea and so he fluted, thinking to draw them on to land. When he was cheated of this hope, he took a net and caught a great quantity of fish and drew them out. Seeing they were jumping he said to the fish, 'Don't dance for me now; when I played the flute you wouldn't come out and dance.'

This is a Persian king refusing to accept a surrender. Even the famous story of Gyges, who saw the queen naked by the king's connivance, which so shamed her that she had him kill the king, is a folk-tale of some kind. In the heady days when it was first discussed, a piece of a play about Gyges found on a scrap of papyrus was thought to be a fifth-century tragedy. The likeness is remarkable; Herodotos concludes his tale as a tragedy might with a settlement by the Delphic oracle. But the dramatic fragment was a late one. The essential tragic form had existed in stories, in this case an eastern story, before the tragic theatre at Athens began.

It was shown beyond serious doubt by Joseph Fontenrose in 1978 that much of what we used to think we knew about the Delphic oracle's replies to the questions of the Greeks has passed through the forms of folk-tales. They include riddles, proverbs and magic behaviour by animals. The originality of Fontenrose's work is that between the area of legend and mythology where we place the oracle's answer to Oedipus, and the area of history, where the replies are certainly historical and can sometimes be verified in numerous ways, there exists a huge mass of doubtful stories, and he has enormously extended the area of doubtfulness. It includes more or less everything Herodotos says about oracles. There is no doubt of the importance in life of Apollo's great shrines, nor of their real influence, but their importance in the theatre and even in Herodotos is quite another matter. It is a reflection of folk-stories. Scholars used to suggest that Herodotos used a special source, a book of Delphic oracles, but that theory is out of fashion now. He was a story-teller, and the oracles of Apollo played as much part in traditional story-telling as the activity of Zeus, usually to point an irony. The story of Kroisos of Lydia is an excellent example. The oracles Herodotos quotes read like legends, not like any real Delphic replies that we know: they do not come from Delphi but from a long tradition of stories about oracles.

His stories are sharply pointed. What the king of the Aithiopians said to the Fish-eaters about Persian luxuries is typical of a kind of insight and a traveller's irony which give pleasure to this day.

Give the king of the Persians this bow and tell him, the Aithiopian king advises you, when the Persians can easily draw a bow of this size then they should come and fight the long-lived Aithiopians, who greatly outnumber them: and until then he should thank the gods for not putting it into the heads of the sons of Aithiopians to conquer any land beyond their own. So he handed over the bow, and taking the purple dress asked what it was and how it was made. When the Fish-eaters told him the truth about sea-purple and about colouring, he said they were deceiving people with deceiving clothes. Then he asked about the gold, the twisted collar and the bracelets. The Fish-eaters explained the decorations, but the king laughed, and thinking they were fetters said we have stronger fetters than those. He said the same about scent as he did about the dress. When he came to wine and found out how to make it he was delighted, and asked what the Persians ate and what was the longest they lived. They said they ate bread, and showed him dough-mixing, and told him eighty years were the longest life. The Aithiopian said he was not surprised they lived so short a time if they ate shit, and it would be shorter still without the wine.

His political views are clear; he never holds them in reserve. He disapproves of tyranny and believes that the gods punish it. The successor to Polykrates of Samos refuses to be tyrant, 'because I did not approve of Polykrates lording it over men like himself, nor do I approve of anyone else doing the same'. The Persians 'enslaved' cities, not only 'lorded it over men': they were insufferably arrogant. All the same he admits their truthfulness, their loyalty and their courage. They are defeated through barbaric indiscipline and lack of skill in arms. That estimate does not seem improbable. He believes that the energy of the Athenians came from their freedom. That is the central insight of many later historians also; it is very hard to resist, and in the generation that fought the Persian wars I am disinclined to resist it. No doubt there were other factors, such as a new consciousness of power, a pride in the past and in Athens that had been cultivated with innocence and success by great families and great artists, a deep horror of barbarism, and a close, still almost untouched, almost primitive social organization, with the values implicit in Homeric poetry. Of most of these he has some inkling, but there are other factors we can now judge better from our own analysis of the world and its history.

He is realistic, all the same. He notices weakness and treason even in Athens, and he disapproves of ruthlessness even in wartime. But he lets Athenian speakers put their case strongly: 'our most ancient nation, we who alone have never ceased to be truly Greeks, one of whom [Menestheus] Homer the poet records as the best man at Troy to marshal and arrange an army', and in another speech 'who alone of all the Greeks fought man to man with the Persian and in that great task overcame and conquered forty-six nations' at Marathon. His own opinion, which he argued carefully (7.139), and in language which was closer to that of a history lecture than these trumpet-calls of Athenian pride, was that Athens really had saved the whole of Greece by her action. If they had fled from their country or surrendered to Xerxes, there would have been no resistance at sea, the wall at the Isthmus would not have lasted long, Sparta would have lost her unwilling allies, and one by one the cities would have fallen, 'even if they had performed great actions and died nobly'. It is always tempting to overthrow optimistic interpretations of history, but the view Herodotos takes of the central events of his writings seems to be justified. Plutarch thought he was unfair to Argos and Corinth, which is likely, and hard on Sparta, which I doubt. But Plutarch also thought he was mean about the degree of the Athenian victory at Marathon, which is absurd.

One should compare his argument about the effect of the Athenian resistance to Xerxes with his laconic account in an earlier book of the fall of Ionia.

Only these among the Ionians would not tolerate slavery, and departed from their own countries, but the other Ionians except for Miletos offered battle as those who departed had done, and fought bravely each for his own country, but they were defeated and taken, and they remained on their own territory, and whatever was imposed on them they carried out.

The strength of his account of the war lies in his knowledge of its historical beginnings. With all its strange details and counter-currents, it was to him a single process. Had he lived another twenty years, he might have come to a sadder view of Athens. Probably we owe our Athenian sympathies to the date of the death of Herodotos, and therefore indirectly to the circle of Perikles. Herodotos wrote not a history of Athens, but one of the Persian war and the struggle for Greek freedom. That is what shows Athens in a glorious light.

His own pride is not unlike Athenian pride. He had Karian blood, but he identifies that with the people of the Greek islands who ruled the seas under the legendary Minos of Crete. The Karians are in fact a non-Greek Anatolian people, but their ancient home in the islands was a widely held idea. Thucydides thought he could demonstrate it archaeologically; Aristotle found their traces in the Argolid and Pausanias at Megara. The interest of all this to us is only in the self-definition of Herodotos. He was not a racist, and he knew the mixed society of Greek cities, but he did think he was Greek and not barbarian, and he was proud of that.

In a more naive way, he was proud of Samos. 'I have spent rather long over Samos, because the three greatest works of all Greece are there', a tunnel through a mountain that carried an aqueduct, built by a Megarian, the enormous breakwater of the harbour, and 'the greatest temple of all the temples we have ever seen, the architect of which was Rhoikos of Samos. That is why I have spent rather long over the Samians.' The temple of Hera was a colossal building more than a hundred metres by fifty, surrounded by a double colonnade, triple at each end, in fact a young forest of stone pillars. But it was not finished. The temple built by Rhoikos had been destroyed by the Persians. What he saw was an even grander temple, the temple to end temples, commissioned by Polykrates after 530 B.C. The harbour breakwater was also that great man's work.

On the whole, Herodotos likes to attach history to the stories he knows about individuals. These stories may often eddy from intrigue to intrigue, but they are usually moral in some way. That is why he intrudes the longish tale of Masistes, brother of Xerxes, into the last stages of his work. Masistes is introduced quarrelling with a Persian general, whom he called worse than a woman, but the point, which takes some time to emerge, is that meanwhile Xerxes fell in love with the wife of Masistes, and the consequences were fearful. Masistes retired to raise a rebellion in Afghanistan, with his sons and his men. 'But Xerxes, finding out what he was going to do, sent an army against him and killed him on the road, and his sons and his army with him.' These few pages are not only a tale of Persian intrigues, but an essential hint of the vengeance that hangs so thunderously over the Persians. Xerxes died through just such an intrigue in 465, too late to be part of this history, but the story of Masistes shows with consummate scorn which way the Persians were headed.

At Salamis, he gives a fine role to Artemisia the queen of Halikarnassos, fighting on the Persian side. No doubt that is for local patriotic reasons, and not from any Homeric impartiality, but it is worth considering his account of this battle for several peculiarities of structure. In the build-up towards it he gives full councils of war on both sides, secret plans, and the 'oracles of Bakis', which were pure folklore, or at best the product of some god-drunk shepherd. 'I cannot contradict these prophecies as untrue, as I do not want to give the lie to those who maintain them definitely, in a matter of this kind.' When the arguments in council were over, 'much wrestling with words', the Greeks got ready to fight. 'Dawn appeared, and they mustered the men to go on board.' Themistokles spoke to them 'and ordered them to go into the ships'.

They embarked, and the warship came from Aigina, from its mission to the Aiakidai, that is, the sons of Aiakos, divine heroes one of whom was Achilles, whose help this ship brought.

Then the Greeks brought out all their ships and at once the barbarians attacked. The other Greeks backed water, but Ameinias of Pallene, an Athenian, pulled out and rammed. The two ships tangled, and were unable to separate, so the others helped Ameinias and joined in. The Athenians say that is how the fighting started, but Aigina says the ship that went to the Aiakidai was first. And it is said that the vision of a woman was seen and shouted a command that all the Greek camp heard: 'Sirs, how long are you going to back water?'

Herodotos then explains the line of battle, discusses the desertion of a few Persian Greeks by secret arrangement with Themistokles, and goes on to assure the reader, 'I could record many names of captains who took Greek ships', but he mentions only two Samians, and how they were rewarded, one with the tyranny of Samos and the other with a vast territory. 'But most of the fleet at Salamis was smashed, by Athenians or by Aiginetans, because the Greeks fought in order and in formation, but the barbarians without order or intelligence, so that something like this was bound to happen to them.' All the same, he says the Persians did far better that day than in earlier action, being both inspired and terrified by the presence of Xerxes. One can see in all this that the historian's feelings were mixed. As for his truthfulness, we know that Aigina won the prize for courage in this battle. As for the vision of the lady, we know of a number of other signs and omens Herodotos has not recorded: an owl of Athene, a white dove of Aphrodite, a divine snake and so on.

He then moves to the long episode of Artemisia's performance in battle and the impression it made on Xerxes, and finally a short account of the carnage, and what Xerxes thought about that. Herodotos has dutifully recorded the Greek victory, but his history of it is by no means what one might expect. He dwells mostly on what is disputed, or what by special knowledge he can add to what his first readers would already know. He has given us enough speeches in the council of war, so Themistokles at dawn says little. 'His words consisted wholly of the better and the worse contrasted in the nature and the circumstances of mankind.' Freedom or death, perhaps? But as Herodotos puts these words, they sound like the rhetoric of the mid-century; in fact they sound like the views of a contemporary Athenian, and that is no doubt where he got them. He does not write as if he had ever seen a battle at sea. Even the truthful sound of the Athenians backing water might be deceptive; if they were so disciplined in their tactics, backing water might be a crucial tightening of ranks. But it is clear that Herodotos intends to be scrupulously truthful.

Herodotos plunders any official list and every inscribed stone he can find. He knows the provinces of Persia and the inscription on the victory tripod at Delphi. He has dates of some kind for Persian, Egyptian, even Median kings, however and wherever they were calculated. He knows of Persian bilingual inscriptions and has a few words of Persian. We have already referred to an inscription on the chariot-base on the Athenian Akropolis, though the fragments as we have them make one doubt whether he transcribed the verses himself. But he is not an assembler of evidence in any scientific way. He has no library to speak of. Nor is he an antiquary. He knows of Tiryns and Mycenae only as modern fortified towns. In his opening chapters, in pursuit of the traditional arguments about who started wars between Europe and Asia, he takes a higher hand than even Euripides with the old material. Jason stole Medeia, so Paris stole Helen. He is making sense of a kind of the mythological tangle, but is this any more than a game? My own suspicion is that Herodotos treats these stories unseriously because they offer no criterion of truth, and they are not fresh.

In search of freshness, with an ironic mixture of credulity and incredulity, he is willing to chase after Aristeas to that wonderland in the north where the one-eyed Arimaspoi fought the griffins for their gold (4.13). Aristeas was possessed by Apollo, but Herodotos made no such claim. He did not even believe the Arimaspoi were one-eyed. What he is really after is the geography of Russia and an explanation of the wave beyond wave beyond wave of nomadic peoples that Russia generated. The most surprising thing about Herodotos on nomads is his accuracy about customs he could not possibly have understood. His explanation of the mysterious disappearances and returns of Aristeas are less convincing, just because there he has more to reason about. Among the nomads he simply repeats what he has heard, and modern research has often found him right. Aristeas

in the seventh year returned to Prokonnesos and composed the poems now called *Arimaspea* by the Greeks, and having done so disappeared again. But I know he visited the Metapontines in Italy where I have lived, two hundred and forty years after the second disappearance, as I calculated in Prokonnesos and in Metapontion. The Metapontines say he appeared to them and told them to build an altar of Apollo in their country under his name and stand his statue beside it. He told them Apollo came to their country alone of all Italian Greek peoples, and that Aristeas as he now was had followed the god, though at that time, when he followed him, he was a crow. When he had said that, he disappeared, and the Metapontines say they sent to Delphi to ask the god what this man's ghost really was. The priestess ordered them to obey the ghost and things would go better for them. They did what they were told, and now they have a statue called Aristeas beside Apollo's statue, and laurel bushes grow around it. This statue is in the market-place. That is enough about Aristeas.

The reader will see by now that Herodotos tells one whatever he happens to know, or thinks he knows, but that somehow it all fits into the prodigious scheme of his single work, which is about Europe and Asia, and their war. He wants to compose a prose epic. On the whole, he is somewhat laconic about religion; he has no wish to make enemies on the subject. The crow is Apollo's holy bird, and the only faint lifting of an eyebrow Herodotos allows himself is (unless I am imagining it) in the puzzled tone of the Metapontine question to Delphi. The Delphic reply, by the way, is in perfectly correct form, and likely to be authentic. The laurel bushes somehow add to one's pleasure in this story – their timing is perfect – but I doubt if irony is intended. Herodotos has been there, he wants to assure us that he is an eyewitness.

He has an attractive tale of the choosing of the king of Persia. The choice lay between seven noblemen. They agreed to settle it by a sign from heaven. They would all mount their horses next morning, and whichever horse whinnied first as the sun rose, its rider would be king. As a method it sounds bizarre to us, but signs of just this kind were highly respected by the Greeks. There was an oracle functioning as late as the second century A.D. in the Peloponnese, where the message of the god was whatever words one first heard when one left his sanctuary. Whatever is in the hands of chance is in the hands of fate, and therefore in the hands of the gods. The Spartan army used to camp wherever a sacred animal lay down to rest for the night. 'But Dareios had a clever groom', who tethered his horse's favourite mare outside the town, and when the light of day appeared the riders rode out, and his horse whinnied and raced ahead. 'And as it whinnied, lightning flashed from a clear sky and thunder was heard. And they leapt down from their horses and worshipped Dareios.'

This comes after a long argument between the seven noblemen about what is the best constitution, democracy, oligarchy or monarchy: to put it into the mouths of Persians is surely to intend a joke. The horse is light relief. Herodotos' art is a story-teller's art: he can use a sign from heaven in more ways than one, as he can use an oracle. In the horse story, he means to leave us wondering. He means also to leave Dareios wondering. Elsewhere, even a lesser divine intervention like a dream can be a climax. After Marathon, the Persians sailed on to attack Athens, and a shield was seen on the hills flashing in the sun as a signal to their ships. Herodotos then gives us ten whole chapters about the family history of the Alkmeonidai, the noble clan who had supported democracy in its infancy. He begins indignantly:

It is amazing to me, and I do not accept the story, that the Alkmeonidai then flashed a shield by arrangement to the Persians, as if they wanted the Athenians under barbarians and under Hippias: they who have shown themselves worse haters of tyranny even than Kallias, or at least as much. Kallias was the only Athenian, when Peisistratos lost power, who dared to have his possessions auctioned, and who devised everything else most hostile against Peisistratos.

The ten or eleven lines of text that follow this sentence are a mysterious addition, not written by Herodotos but by a close student of his style, probably more than two hundred years after his death. They give a lot of information which is detailed and perhaps true about Kallias. But their main interest is that they demonstrate how enthusiastically Herodotos was read and how intimately relished. His influence on later writers has been much underestimated in the past: as late as the Roman empire he was not only popular for his amusing lies but imitated for his style. This raises the problem of his dialect. It used to be taken for rather pure Ionic, though some of the Ionic forms are distinctly odd, and if, as we now know even more clearly from a new analysis of Herodas, the literary interest in artificial dialects, like the false Doric in which Theokritos wrote, extended also to Ionic in the Alexandrian period, we must now begin to admit that Herodotos has not survived in exactly his original form. He may even have written in Ionic without being a native speaker, simply because that was expected of those who told prose stories. If so, his case would not be unique. The lines in question here (6.122) show an alarming ability to infiltrate the text. One cannot foresee what a full modern study might reveal, though it is certain enough that substantially our text of Herodotos is genuine. It is a relief to observe that the false chapter is missing from the best manuscripts.

His defence of the Alkmeonidai continues. 'They were illustrious in Athens from their beginnings, but from the time of Alkmeon and Megakles they became glorious.' This is connected with the story of Lydia and the origins of the Persian wars. The historian's position is taking shape: the clan had always hated tyrants, and they became wealthy by playing a trick on Kroisos, who laughed at it. They spent money on racing chariots at Olympia; in the days of honour as a supreme virtue that kind of spending would be applauded. We are then told at great length the story of the suitors for the daughter of Kleisthenes, which ends with Hippokleides from Athens, most aristocratic of all these splendid noblemen, drinking a great deal and dancing the dances of Sparta and of Athens, and finally standing on his head on the table and dancing upside down. 'You have danced away your marriage,' said Kleisthenes. 'Hippokleides don't care,' he replied.

The girl, who was called Agariste, got married to Megakles, and from their union was born that Kleisthenes who established the artificial tribes and democracy in Athens, and took his name from his mother's father. He and Hippokrates were the sons of Megakles, and Hippokrates had another Megakles and another Agariste, named after her grandmother: she married Xanthippos, and being pregnant saw a vision in her sleep; she thought she gave birth to a lion. A few days later she gave birth to Perikles by Xanthippos.

No introduction of a famous name could be grander or more dramatic, and this, of course, is what the whole digression about the Alkmeonidai was leading up to. It was a story of noble lineage, matrilinear one notices, and aristocratic ethics, and carried a political message, all of which comes together in the last two words: Perikles son of Xanthippos.

It is worth noticing that Kallias was even richer than Perikles and probably anti-democratic; his wife was one of the Alkmeonidai and his sister was married to Kimon, rival and enemy to Perikles. As for the dream, such stories were common, and Aristophanes in the Knights (424 B.C.) has a parody of an oracle that 'a lion shall be born in sacred Athens, and fight a crowd of midges'; the art of Herodotos as a teller of tales is to make effective use of such commonplace sayings and pieces of folklore, which somehow transform him and which he transforms. He has certain skills in common with Montaigne.

Some of his stories are terrible, and their sudden twists are grim, 'because always the gods are envious and bitter to taste'. When Harpagos ate the flesh of his own child,

when he appeared to have had enough to eat, Astyages asked him if he liked the dinner. Harpagos said he liked it greatly. Then they brought the covered dish with the head and hands and feet of his son, and told him to uncover it and take what he wanted. Harpagos obeyed and uncovered it and saw the remains of his son. But seeing it he did not break out, he remained in control of himself. Astyages asked him if he knew what game he had eaten. He knew, and he said, 'Whatever the King slaughters is very good.' With this reply he took up the rest of the meat and went to his house. There, I suppose, he meant to embalm and bury it all.

It is not only the deadly coolness of this story that makes it so terrible. The climax is an intrusion of informality, which somehow makes everything worse. When Herodotos says 'There, I suppose ...' it ceases to be a Greek story about Persians and becomes real. This sort of literary skill is surely intuitive, not contrived. Yet it has something in common with the conclusion of tragedies. The last sentence is an irrepressible intrusion of humanity.

The battle of Plataia, the final defeat of the Persians in a full-scale confrontation of land forces, is naturally one of his set pieces. We are given preparations on both sides rather fully, including an embassy to Sicily which entails an account of Greek affairs in the west and of the struggle with Carthage. Herodotos traces a war, but what he gives us is a world. The battle itself he describes in great detail. As usual, honours are scrupulously awarded, but emphasis is perhaps another matter. Before the main battle with its precise tactics, the Persian cavalry under Masistios, 'who had an Isfahan horse, gold-bitted and beautifully decorated', attacked across the plain. The Persian riders jeered at the Greeks, and no one would face them except 'three hundred picked Athenians under Olympiodoros son of Lampon' and some archers. The archers are serfs or foreigners, but this whole story hinges on them. The three hundred picked Athenians are a suspiciously heroic and traditional number, as at Thermopylai, Syracuse (Thucydides 6.100), and elsewhere. But Olympiodoros was father of the prophet Lampon, one of the commissioners for the founding of Thourioi, friend of Perikles and of Herodotos.

Yet the story is honestly told and terrifying. As the Persian cavalry advanced in ranks with Masistios leading, one of the nameless archers hit his horse between the ribs; the horse reared up in pain and threw him.

When he was down the Athenians attacked him at once. They took his horse and killed him fighting, though at first they were unable. He was armed like this: he had an inner breastplate of fine gold workmanship and over his body-armour he wore a purple dress. Striking at the breastplate they accomplished nothing, until someone realized what was the matter, and stabbed him through the eye. That is how he fell and how he died.

One fears he means through the eye-slit of a helmet. The body-armour of Masistios was kept for six hundred years or more in one of the sanctuaries on the Athenian Akropolis, though if Herodotos had seen it, and if he wrote for non-Athenians, one would expect him to have said so. This story is Homeric.

After the death, two armies fight over the body which the killers have stripped. Then the Persian army wail and lament for the dead man,

cutting hair from their heads and their horses and their baggage animals and howling insatiably. And all Boiotia echoed with their lament, at the death of that man who after Mardonios was best thought of by the Persians and by the king. So the barbarians in their own way honoured Masistios, but the Greeks were greatly cheered, having received a cavalry charge and thrown it back.

The story being over, Herodotos alters tone, returning to tactics. The despised archer who brought the great man down would probably have been equally despised in the *Iliad*.

Scholars in the past have argued whether Herodotos really finished his great work, or whether it simply tails off. The references to events late in his life which I have already considered make it clear enough that he continued to revise, and to add new material. We are not certain how he spent his last years, and ancient biographies are terribly unreliable. It is sometimes thought, though without hard evidence, that he revisited Athens, and it is impossible to disprove the late Greek tradition that he spent his old age in the court of Macedonia, although Thourioi claimed his grave. To compare the Crimea first with Attica, and then, 'for those who have not sailed by Attica', with the heel of Italy, does not suggest that he expected his readers to be Athenians (4.99). A. Bauer in 1878 launched, among other opinions, the view accepted by R. W. Macan in 1908 and by How and Wells in their standard commentary of 1912, that the last three books of Herodotos were written first. I am sceptical about these arguments, and certain that the dissection of Herodotos into layers of altering opinions superimposed on one another is a fallible process. No doubt the whole history is patchwork, and one can identify some of the larger and even some of the smaller patches. But one cannot produce a history of changes of feeling out of it. If I am right to believe that Herodotos was a public performer, even an entertainer, then his work was at first intended to be heard, not read: it depended on immediate attraction; Thucydides criticizes him for these qualities. It is hard for us to know when he added what to his repertory, or how many times his material was reworked.

So the question whether his work was unfinished loses its meaning. The last book by no means merely tails off. It ends with a story in the usual pendant form, which is calculated for its unexpected climax. The Greeks have taken Sestos, which commands the Hellespont, that narrow strip of sea which separates Europe from Asia. It was the key to the sea of Marmara and therefore to the Black Sea. It was opposite Troy. The taking of Sestos by the Greeks is as good a point as any to conclude the history of the war. Then comes the pendant. The Persian Artayktes had plundered the shrine of Protesilaos, the divine hero who was the first Greek ashore at Troy and first to die. Artayktes took this dead hero's sacred land for an estate, and used his temple for a harem, making love to his women in it. The Greeks captured Artayktes; they refused an enormous ransom; they crucified him at the place where Xerxes had crossed over his bridge of boats into Europe, and stoned his son to death in his sight.

'And it was the grandfather of this Artayktes who was crucified who first expounded to the Persians that argument which they took up and brought to Cyrus.' The Persians had little territory and that little was rough. Why not get themselves a better? What could be finer than ruling many people and all Asia? Cyrus agreed to this action, but gave a warning. 'They must be ready not to rule but to be ruled. Soft countries generally breed soft men, the same earth will not give wonderful crops and men brave in battle.' The Persians considered this and understood it, they accepted the warning, 'and chose to rule and live in a miserable region, rather than cultivate the plains and be slaves'.

The view that strong rocks breed strong peoples is as commonplace to us as it was to the Greeks. Thourioi was built on the ruins of Sybaris, a proverbial example of luxury breeding weakness. The doctrine can be found in the Hippokratic work *Airs, Waters and Places*, though that is later than Herodotos. It is implicit in Homer and in much early Greek mythology. But the reversal of expected sense is what makes a thrilling ending to the book. One thinks that the grandfather of Artayktes has done something terrible by starting Persian aggression, and so he has, and the guilt has descended like a curse on the grandson. That is the original connection: that is how the pendant hangs. But Herodotos is unwilling to close his book with this appalling expiation. So he adds the king's answer, as if Persian expansion had never taken place, and ends with an ominous rumble about the choice not to expand. We are back to the major theme of the book, not only to its consciousness of geography, but to choosing not to be a slave. I am unable to convince myself that this is not a warning to the Greeks. We know from the events of his lifetime that it was a warning they greatly needed, and one that neither the Spartans nor the Athenians would take.

BIBLIOGRAPHY

A. Andrewes, *The Greek Tyrants*, 1956

B. R. (Barnabe Rich?), *Herodotus* (translation of Books 1 and 2 only), 1584

J. Boardman, *The Greeks Overseas*, 3rd edition, 1980

J. B. Bury, *History of Greece* (edited by R. Meiggs), 1951

J. Fontenrose, *The Delphic Oracle*, 1978

W. G. Forrest, *Herodotus* (edited in English), 1965

N. G. L. Hammond, *History of Greece*, 2nd edition, 1967

W. W. How and J. Wells, *Commentary on Herodotus*, 2nd edition, 1928

J. E. Powell, *The Histories of Herodotus*, 1939

The Oxford Classical Dictionary on 'Herodotus' and 'Historiography' is particularly useful.

· 12 ·
THUCYDIDES

Thucydides, or in Greek Thoukydides, was the first and the mightiest Athenian historian of Athens. There is an impressive and awkward weightiness about his expressions which are the result of thought. He was quite conscious of technique in his writing, and in the course of a lifetime of work he taught himself what history is. Herodotos wrote about a war, but he also wrote about a process. It is likely that this sense of profound cause and consequence matured rather late in his life. He began to prepare his history from the beginning of the Peloponnesian war; he took part in the war, and being then disgraced and exiled from Athens, obtained his later information from both sides. It was in those twenty years of exile, in the decline of Athenian power, that he ruminated more deeply.

His presentation of contemporary history is strange to us, because it depends so much on impersonated characters and invented speeches, and on explanations in terms of motive. This tradition goes back through Herodotos, who in Books 7 and 8 elaborately balances speech against speech, to Homer. By an austere exclusion of accident and divine action, and by an attempt at impersonality, Thucydides has produced a convincing but a curiously limited narrative. Herodotos could include more of reality. What Thucydides expresses may be limited, but it is profoundly impressive. His brooding gravity hangs above the tangled, overorganized sentences like the spirit of history itself brooding over the face of the waters. He makes mistakes and he has his passions, but he is a powerfully serious writer.

He was born in the early 450s, a little older than Aristophanes, but younger than Sokrates, at Halimous on the coast near Athens. He was one of the young men Perikles set on fire, although by blood he was a kinsman of Kimon and Kallias and Thucydides son of Melesias, the opposition to Perikles. He was rich, with an interest in Thracian gold-mines, which fits his family background. In 430 he caught the plague, but recovered. In 424 B.C. he was an Athenian commander in Thracian waters; he was disgraced and exiled for failing to protect Amphipolis from Brasidas the Spartan – unfairly disgraced, I suppose. He was not recalled until the fall of Athens, and a few years after that he seems to have died; he was buried beside Kimon. No one knows for certain where he spent his twenty exiled years. His work proves in several places that he was still writing after 404, and if his reference to Archelaos of Macedon is justly dated after that monarch's lifetime, then he was still at work after 399. But he clearly intended to end his history in 404. Alas, he stopped writing in mid-sentence at 411 B.C.

Naturally, his work shows signs of uneven revision. The plague is still called the worst Athenian disaster, although we know he thought the Sicilian catastrophe in 413 was worse still. Yet one can argue that Chapters 89 to 118 of Book 1, describing the growth of Athenian power, were written late, since they refer to Hellanikos (1.97.2), whose work was not known before 407 B.C. On the other hand, Books 5 and 8 are unfinished: the episodes are rather loosely sewn together, there are no imaginary full speeches except about Melos, where the speeches are elaborately finished, and in Book 5 documents are quoted word for word, although everywhere else they are reworded. And yet something like a second introduction, and a new beginning, occurs in Chapter 26 of Book 5, as if the entire work had once meant to end in the truce of 421 B.C. This fresh introduction was clearly written after the fall of Athens, and the whole history has been sufficiently reworked to make it read now as if the historian had always known that war really continued throughout the so-called peace of 421–413.

It is not my business to trespass on the specialized problems of Greek history: I am not competent to deal with them. The level-headedness and the reliability of Thucydides have ensured that his text has been worked over in great detail by modern historians. And it is true that his principal purpose was to make a truthful and a monumental record; that purpose overrides purely literary considerations. As a historian we must leave him to the historians. His use of documents has been criticized. I do not know why he omits the tribute assessment of 425 or ignores the Peace of Kallias. We shall consider him here only as a writer and as a craftsman. He insisted, against the example of Herodotos, that he was a contemporary historian, writing from his knowledge, not for a performance, or to make any enchanting impression on hearers, not a teller of tales, but a rather dry, non-anecdotal recorder and analyst. His work was intended to be a 'possession for ever', and in the recurring crises of the world's history to throw some light.

We are told all this in the introduction to Book 1. There is no doubt that he means to measure himself against Herodotos, and to criticize that great man. He stresses the comparative importance of his subject and greatness of his war. The magnitude of suffering is important to him: human progress has led to greater and greater concentrations of power, vaster wars, worse calamities, more suffering. He feels it as tragedy, but he also stresses it competitively. He records here a tidal wave and there the eruption of a volcano (3.89 and 116), because they were great disasters. He fills in the history of his century precisely from 479, from the capture of Sestos, where Herodotos ends. On the whole he leaves aside whatever Herodotos had treated, but in a few passages, for instance, the murder of the tyrant by Harmodios and Aristogeiton, he agrees with the earlier account, more or less, although we know that wildly different stories were circulating. His characterization of individuals owes a good deal to Herodotos, both in matter, in the cases of Pausanias and Themistokles, and in manner.

His elaborate method of chronology and the iron structure that he permits chronology to impose on his writing are an advance on Herodotos but not a completely new departure. In the late fifth century the beginnings of historical science were sprouting everywhere. In the past, history and myth had been organized by generations and genealogies. The inscription of Hieropythos of Chios and the notice of the Philaidai by Pherekydes of Athens show that families in the fifth century could trace their blood back to the eighth or ninth. Hekataios thought fifteen ancestors were not an extravagant number to be able to name. But all this took no account of absolute dates.

In the late fifth century, Hippias of Elis organized and edited a complete list of Olympic champions going back to 776 B.C. Later still, Hellanikos of Lesbos published not only his systematic versions of heroic mythology and studies of foreign peoples like those of Herodotos, but more importantly a list of the priestesses of Hera at the Heraion of Argos going back a long way. He also wrote an early history of Athens, though Thucydides criticizes his fifth-century chronology. About 425 B.C., a list of the archons or governors of Athens was inscribed on stone, no one knows by whom. Can it have been at the initiative of Thucydides? The list goes back to 683 B.C. He had studied and correlated these systems; he would date a year by the archon of Athens, the ephor of Sparta and the priestess of Argos. Still more efficiently, he numbered the years of the war. And since the Greek cities used different month names and kept different festivals, he would indicate a precise time of year by a phrase like 'the wheat being full in the ear'. Compare this new exactness with the biblical Book of Kings, where the writer is content with 'the spring of the year, the time when kings march out to war'. The purpose of the new style is precision and not entertainment. It is meant to be understood in the future, and all over the Greek world.

The momentum of history in his writing is certainly in the loose sense tragic. It is more Homeric than theatrical, as Colin Macleod pointed out. In the Sicilian disaster, it is like a drum-beat. It may be that had he lived to complete his work, this tragical tone would have seemed to express one single process, one vast roar of the sea, as it is wave follows wave separately, and his strict organization by years and by seasons breaks up the material with a variety of effects. There is no doubt that he was conscious of these problems of technique. The height of Periklean glory and the Athenian ideal moment is the funeral speech of Perikles. That is followed at once by the ghastly details of the plague, by which in the end Perikles died. We are not told that, but after the plague and a last short speech by Perikles comes a brief and bitter analysis which leaps forward in time. As it touches on his own attitude to Perikles, to the Athenian democracy and to the process of the war, it should be considered here. I quote the translation by Thomas Hobbes, which with miraculous accuracy catches the very tone and footfall of Thucydides, and the texture of his prose.

For the sense of their domestic losses was now dulled, and for the need of the commonwealth, they prized him more than any other whatsoever

For as long as he was in authority in the city in time of peace, he governed the same with moderation, and was a faithful watchman of it, and in his time it was at the greatest. And after the war was on foot, it is manifest that he therein also foresaw what it could do. He lived after the war began two years and six months. And his foresight in the war was best known after his death. For he told them that if they would be quiet, and look to their navy, and during this war seek no further dominion, nor hazard the city itself, they should then have the upper hand. But they did contrary in all, and in such other things besides, as seemed not to concern the war, managed the state according to their private ambition and covetousness, perniciously both for themselves and their confederates.

Athens under Perikles was 'in name a state democratical, but in fact, a government of the principal man'. None of those who followed him had the same freedom to act. He was powerful in dignity and wisdom, and incorruptible, 'he freely controlled the multitude', and 'having got his power by no evil arts, he would not humour them in his speeches', but those who followed 'applied themselves to the people, and let go the care of the commonwealth'. As he proceeds into detail, the historian's judgement becomes more and more deadly. Yet at the very end of the catalogue of disasters and hopeless courage, he returns to Perikles. He is writing after 404, of course: '... till they had overthrown themselves with private dissensions. So much was Pericles above other men at that time, that he could foresee by what means the city might easily have outlasted the Peloponnesians in this war.'

The slightly awkward, undisturbed deliberateness of his style is a most powerful device. The subtlest intrigue, the longest process or the briefest episode, acquire in his writing an iron mechanism.

But neither had the Corcyraeans any purpose to force entrance by the door, but getting up to the top of the house, uncovered the roof, and threw tiles, and shot arrows at them. They in prison defended themselves as well as they could, but many also slew themselves, with the arrows shot by the enemy, by thrusting them into their throats, and strangled themselves with the cords of certain beds which were in the room, and with ropes made of their own garments rent in pieces. And having continued most part of the night (for night overtook them in the action), partly strangling themselves by all such means as they found, and partly shot at from above, they all perished. When day came, the Corcyraeans laid them one across another in carts, and carried them out of the city. And of their wives, as many as were taken within the fortification, they made bond-women. In this manner were the Corcyraeans that kept the hill brought to destruction by the commons.

Phrases like 'by all such means', and the subordination of the whole dry and clear story to the final sentence, create a bleak and awe-inspiring impersonality.

Thucydides was conscious of the devices used for pleading in court and public persuasion, and when he wishes he uses them, but not naively. He was conscious of the degrading powers of political rhetoric, which he treated with distrust. Colin Macleod has shown in a series of sharp analyses how subtly the historian can make use of these techniques. The debate at Athens over Mytilene and the debate at Sparta over Plataia are parodies carried to the height of tragic art. The two debates probe deeply into how self-interest operates in war. Athens as an empire is checked in the end by fear of its subjects, but Sparta can lose only prestige or alliance, so the Spartans are more utterly ruthless. The hollowness of the speeches is terrifying. It recalls the arguments in tragedy of those who are too strong to need to argue at all. One sees how conventional daily morality is undermined. Self-interest operates so powerfully as to be almost mechanical. Humanity and pity hardly operate. We are told that in war language itself gets corrupted, and in the events and debates that follow we watch that coming true.

In the climax of the Sicilian disaster, the impersonal framework, the lack of rhetoric and also the lack of anecdote give an iron ring to his words. We know of at least one thrilling anecdote about this final battle which Herodotos would surely have included. It is the story of an Athenian cavalry captain, the only leader to get his men clear away; he rode back alone, though the battle was over, and fought until he died. Thucydides leaves it out. Nothing disturbs the framework. No individual can do anything, because it is generals who act, and the whole terrible day is framed between 'And Nicias when it was day led his army forward' and 'Nicias yielded himself unto Gylippus'. Hobbes is unable to translate as restrainedly or quite as impersonally as the Greek demands. The water in the river-bed, for example, in the Greek text, 'was at once polluted but none the

less was drunk muddied and bloodied as it was, and to most was
something to be fought over'.

And Nicias when it was day led his army forward, the Syracusians and
their confederates still pressing them in the same manner, shooting and
darting at them from every side. The Athenians hasted to get to the river
Asinarus, not only because they were urged on every side by the assault
of many horsemen, and other multitude, and thought to be more at ease
when they were over the river, but out of weariness also, and desire to drink.
When they were come unto the river, they rushed in without any order,
every man striving who should first get over. But the pressing of the enemy
made the passage now more difficult: for being forced to take the river in
heaps, they fell upon and trampled one another under their feet; and falling
amongst the spears and utensils of the army, some perished presently, and
others catching hold one of another, were carried away together down the
stream. And not only the Syracusians standing along the farther bank, being
a steep one, killed the Athenians with their shot from above, as they were
many of them greedily drinking, and troubling one another in the hollow
of the river, but the Peloponnesians came also down and slew them with
their swords, and those especially that were in the river. And suddenly the
water was corrupted. Nevertheless they drank it, foul as it was with blood
and mire, and many also fought for it. In the end, when many dead lay
heaped in the river, and the army was utterly defeated, part at the river,
and part (if any got away) by the horsemen, Nicias yielded himself unto
Gylippus (having more confidence in him than in the Syracusians) to be
for his own person at the discretion of him and the Lacedaemonians, and
no further slaughter to be made of the soldiers. Gylippus from thenceforth
commanded to take prisoners.

The information for this laconic but cumulative and terrible record
must have come from an individual. The slaughter was appalling,
but so confused that 'they that were conveyed away by stealth were
very many, and all Sicily was filled with them', and it was surely
one of these escaped Athenians who told Thucydides exactly what
happened. Yet in his account no individual figures except Nikias and
Gylippos; there is a strange, dreamlike inevitability in the sequence
of phrases. And this account is also the end of Book 7. Its true climax
is in the quarries, where his language recalls the plague:

As for those in the quarries, the Syracusians handled them at first but
ungently: for in this hollow place, first the sun and suffocating air (being

without roof) annoyed them one way; and on the other side, the nights coming upon that heat, autumnal and cold, put them (by reason of the alteration) into strange diseases ... Also the smell was intolerable ... And whatsoever misery is probable that men in such a place may suffer, they suffered. Some seventy days they lived thus thronged ... And this was the greatest action that happened in all this war, or at all, that we have heard of amongst the Grecians, being to the victors most glorious, and most calamitous to the vanquished ... Few of many returned home. And thus passed the business concerning Sicily.

His technique here is not difficult to follow. Phrase by phrase, his analysis of what occurred is simple, but it is cumulatively organized and builds up power like a great wave that breaks in an epigrammatic and almost abstract conclusion. Death is not the end, because the dead 'lying together there on heaps' create or increase the stinking smell. Even hunger and thirst are not the end. He caps it with 'And whatsoever misery ...' All this without a trace of false rhetoric, and without any subjective expression of pity, except in the word 'ungently', which in Greek is merely 'roughly' or 'badly'. As for the gods, they appear to be quite absent. Even when the news reaches Athens at the opening of Book 8, it is received with incredulity, anger, fear and grief 'for the loss which both every man in particular, and the whole city sustained' – both personal and material loss. There is still no mention of pity, however deeply it may be implicit.

One should interpret this mood in the light of what we were promised in 1.23. Never before, in any older war, were there destruction and slaughter and banishment on such a scale.

And those things which concerning former time there went a fame of, but in fact rarely confirmed, were now made credible: as earthquakes, general to the greatest part of the world, and most violent withal; eclipses of the sun, oftener than is reported of any former time; great droughts in some places, and thereby famine; and that which did none of the least hurt, but destroyed also its part, the plague. All these evils entered together with this war, which began from the time that the Athenians and Peloponnesians brake the league ...

These are by any Greek standard to be considered as divine convulsions. They mark the anger of the gods, and we are told why. Thucydides does not mention justice or vengeance, but is the theme not implicit? Silence on the subject of the gods is a strong position. His writing is all the more weighty because his embittered and tragical irony has no religious outlet. And yet I cannot believe that the sentence about drought, plague, eclipse and earthquake is not intended to convey the anger of the gods. 'And whatsoever misery is probable that men in such a place may suffer, they suffered.'

At the end of Chapter 23, he tells us that the true underlying cause of the war was fear: Spartan fear of Athenian expansion. Fear is a constant theme throughout his work. It lies behind the unprovoked attack of Athens against Melos and behind the Sicilian expedition. Even the acquisition of empire is a result of fear, or so the Athenian speaker says to the Spartans in Book 1.

So that at first we were forced to advance our dominion to what it is, out of the nature of the thing itself, as chiefly for fear, next for honour, and lastly for profit. For when we had the envy of many, and had reconquered some that had already revolted, and seeing you were no more our friends as you had been, but suspected and quarrelled with us, we held it no longer a safe course, laying by our power, to put ourselves into your danger; for the revolts from us would all have been made to you. Now it is no fault for men in danger, to order their affairs to the best ...

This kind of Machiavellian realism about motives occurs in Thucydides largely in speeches, but we have already seen that the speeches are to be taken together, one against another, and always in a context of power and intention. They are a revealing instrument of political analysis, however barefaced their arguments may be. And one does not have to go far in the modern world to discern that fear is still an important and profound motive.

Not long before his sadly early death in 1971, Adam Parry, who was then a professor at Yale, wrote a short study of great importance, in which he calls the *History of the Peloponnesian War* 'an intensely personal and a tragic work'. Among the examples of personal comment he gathers together, the most forceful have something in common I believe: 'I began writing this history from the moment the war broke out ...'; 'so every kind of bad behaviour established itself in Greece through civil wars, and decency, which is the greater part of nobility, was laughed at and disappeared ...'; in a night battle, 'How can one have clear knowledge of anything?' In all cases the writer is trying to control himself, and considering deliberately the tactics of expression. He showed, as Parry pointed out, 'a tendency to use distancing, "scientific" language at moments where emotion is strongest'. A passionate contempt must surely underlie his observation that of all the prophecies in the whole course of the war, the only one that came true was about its lasting three times seven years.

Parry goes further than I can follow him, in maintaining that in the chapter I quoted for its earthquakes and eclipses, Thucydides maintains that 'Civilization is the creation of power and is splendid and admirable, but it inevitably ends in its own destruction, so much so that this destruction is virtually the measure of its greatness.' The truth is that the historian simply dwells on the unparalleled mightiness of the conflict and its uniquely appalling results, moving on at once to the convulsions of nature and the plague. He does not think civilization 'inevitably ends in its own destruction', but he observes from beginning to end the process of betrayal and corruption and decline. He believes fear is at the root of much of this process. But he thinks that had they remained uncorrupted, or had Perikles lived, the Athenians could have won the war. It is not certain, but entirely possible, that some passages of the famous funeral oration of Perikles, which Thucydides made up, and which echo his phrases in Book 1 about greatness and power, are intended to be a fearful piece of arrogance: to express an arrogance that the gods punished. The best side of Perikles is perhaps deliberately painted in his last recorded speech, in the knowledge of how the dream went bad, how it ended, how (as most Greeks would say) it drew down vengeance.

Evils that come from heaven you must bear necessarily, and such as proceed from your enemies valiantly; for so it hath been the custom of this city to do heretofore, which custom let it not be your part to reverse: knowing that this city hath a great name amongst all people, for not yielding to adversity, and for the mighty power it yet hath, after the expense of so many lives, and so much labour in the war; the memory whereof, though we should now at length miscarry, for all things are made with this law to decay again, will remain with posterity for ever. How that being Grecians, most of the Grecians were our subjects; that we have abidden the greatest wars against them, both universally and singly, and have inhabited the greatest and wealthiest city; now this, he with the quiet life will condemn, the active man will emulate, and they that have not attained to the like will envy.

This is like a ghostly Perikles speaking about the fall of Athens. It was fine for Athens to be so hated, 'For the hatred lasteth not, and is recompensed both with a present splendour, and an immortal glory hereafter.'

The distinction between things said and things done, 'what in action they performed', is important to Thucydides in several ways. It is not only that as a moralist he feels one should judge people by their actions; their words are his invention, and their actions are an essential clue to the degree of seriousness with which some particular speech ought to be taken. The speeches are sometimes composed in deliberate contrast with the actions. Perikles is the great believer in reason and in words: 'We likewise weigh what we undertake, and apprehend it perfectly in our minds; not accounting words for a hinderance of action, but that is rather a hinderance to action, to come to it without instruction of words before.' For better and worse, the Athenians really were a terribly articulate people in the late fifth century. The Spartans distrust this intellectuality in the pages of Thucydides, and no doubt they did so in fact. 'The chances of war are not accessible to reason, they are not predictable.'

But Perikles thought they were. The Spartan Sthenelaidas will have no truck with words, or with reason either; he appeals to war. We know the historian believed that the increasing power of Athens compelled Sparta to make war: in that case, well might the Spartans ignore Athenian speeches. The greatest contrast in all this long history between words and 'what in action they performed' is between the words of Perikles and the fall of Athens. This irony is unquestionably deliberate: one can watch Thucydides adding to it after Athens has actually fallen.

He was an aristocrat with some Thracian royal blood. No one who has not seen the Thracian gold treasures from Bulgarian museums can have a full appreciation of the grandeur of that. The *Rhesos* ascribed to Euripides conveys some sense of it. In politics as a young man Thucydides belonged to the generation that first worshipped Perikles, and was then disappointed by the war. When the direct democracy Perikles had helped to set up became ungovernable, he was a shocked and cold-eyed observer. After the Sicilian disaster, the Athenians blamed those orators who had spoken for the expedition, but not themselves for having voted for it. He writes of their covetousness, and the strength of the position of Perikles, who had nothing to gain from the democracy. He himself remained what in Athenian terms would be called a moderate democrat. It is worth examining his comments on a crisis that occurred late in the war, later than the Sicilian expedition, at a time when the war was not yet lost only because the Spartans 'were most commodious enemies to the Athenians to war withal'.

A council of four hundred had taken power in Athens by force of arms. Apart from murdering, imprisoning and deporting various of their enemies, and putting an end to the democratic chaos that they blamed for what happened in Sicily – a chaos they had worsened by a reign of terror and assassination before they finally took power – these unpleasant people aimed to negotiate a truce with Sparta, but meanwhile to give nothing away. The inner and controlling core of the four hundred wanted peace with Sparta at any price, to be achieved by treachery if necessary, some of the subtler outer members wanted the art of the possible in Athens, and meanwhile the democracy still controlled the fleet in eastern waters. In this catastrophic situation, the intervention of a few highly intelligent men prevented civil war from breaking out. After one lost battle, admittedly an alarming one, the four hundred fled to the Spartans. They were succeeded by a body of five thousand: a sovereign assembly with greatly reduced numbers from the old people's assembly. They were voted in and Thucydides expresses a guarded relief.

The Athenians, upon this news, made ready notwithstanding twenty galleys, and called an assembly, one then presently in the place called Pnyx, where they were wont to assemble at other times, in which having deposed the four hundred, they decreed the sovereignty to the five thousand, of which number were all such to be as were charged with arms; and from that time forward to salariate no man for magistracy, with a penalty on the magistrate receiving the salary, to be held for an execrable person. There were also divers other assemblies held afterwards, wherein they elected law-makers, and enacted other things concerning the government. And now first (at least in my time) the Athenians seem to have ordered their state aright; which consisted now of a moderate temper, both of the few and of the many. And this was the first thing, that after so many misfortunes past, made the city again to raise her head. They decreed also the recalling of Alcibiades ...

By 'temper' he means not mood but mixture. The word 'execrable' is in Greek very strong and includes loss of rights and property, and exile. The Greek text expresses enthusiasm for the new constitution rather more heartily than Hobbes allows.

It is quite clear from this passage that he disliked and disapproved of the full, direct democracy, because it did not work well. This is not a question of class interest or class warfare so far as I can see, but of the efficient prosecution of state business, above all of the war. He had no time for the four hundred, and he still wanted to see Athens democratic and victorious. But the reader may well ask how the Athenians got the number five thousand into their heads. There were perhaps twenty or thirty thousand Athenian citizens. The number five thousand had been on the agenda since before the four hundred took power. The four hundred were chosen by five presidents appointing a hundred men who then appointed three each. The five thousand were due to be appointed probably in some similar way by the four hundred as and when the four hundred should decide. In theory, the five thousand, whom in the event they never named, were going to be a sovereign assembly. To appoint them at once when the four hundred fled was a clever stroke, and to include 'all such as were charged with arms' shows prudence at least. It seems to be crucial that the five thousand were going to elect generals. It must also be recorded that they were chosen from all classes except the lowest; this was a franchise of householders. The five thousand were not to be paid for their service, and they were all over thirty.

It was always the intention of those politicians who, having once been outer members of the four hundred, now became governing spirits of the five thousand, to continue to rule in the full democracy, which in the end they would restore. This process was no doubt greatly hastened by the victorious actions of the democratic fleet under Alkibiades. Democracy was restored and the state was reunified in the summer of 410. Because this happened without a crisis it would perhaps have called for little comment from Thucydides, who died writing about 411. Probably he thought of the five thousand and the democratic government that followed them as continuous. What we lack, since it must have been the key to the final decline of Athens in his eyes, is his last comment on the late career of Alkibiades.

That spirited nobleman was his remote kinsman, and a private fortress in Thrace made him almost a neighbour, if the historian was still living on his own estate. Alkibiades was brilliantly successful overseas until he returned from exile to Athens in 407. His policy was that of a second Perikles, to restore the empire Perikles had built. The democracy and its politicians were equally optimistic. It is hard to believe that Thucydides would not have condemned these policies at this stage of the war. But in 406 Alkibiades lost a naval battle, and at once lost at Athens his usual re-election to command; he retired to Thrace. It would be open to Thucydides to judge the democracy for rejecting him. He himself had been exiled for such a failure. The connection of Alkibiades' recall with his compliments to the five thousand, although Alkibiades did not really return and was not really absolved until 407, does at least tenuously suggest that Thucydides saw Alkibiades as a last hope, a reincarnate Perikles whom the foolish democracy cast aside. In the last pages he actually wrote, Alkibiades is still triumphantly active, and the Athenians 'conceived that their estate might yet keep up, if they plied the business courageously'.

Being so long, and an account of war, the history he wrote is very much concerned with courage and with stamina. To him, courage is an iron quality; he is very much more stoical than Homer, but like Homer he is bitterly ironic. The years of the war are constantly striking their midnight, down to the last note that strikes his own. 'When the winter following this summer shall be ended, the one and twentieth year of this war shall be complete.' He is analytic about courage only in speeches, and it is his triumph that the tough and laconic utterances of the Spartans which are so impressive in Herodotos, and which influenced even the Athenian poetry of the Persian wars, appear in their context here as something less than the reasoned daring Perikles could evoke so vividly. Physical courage is mere heat of the blood, he has no great respect for it, and he is in two minds about bloodshed.

He lay all night at the temple of Mercury undiscovered. The next day he cometh to the city, being a very great one, and taketh it. For they kept no watch, nor expected that any man would have come in and assaulted them so far from the sea. Their walls also were but weak, in some places fallen down, and in others low built, and their gates open through security. The Thracians, entering into Mycallessus, spoiled both houses and temples, slew the people without mercy on old or young, but killed all they could light on, yea, and the labouring cattle, and whatsoever other living thing they saw. For the nation of the Thracians, where they dare, are extremely bloody, equal to any of the barbarians. Insomuch as there was put into practice at this time, besides other disorder, all forms of slaughter that could be imagined. They likewise fell upon the schoolhouse (which was in the city a great one, and the children newly entered into it) and killed them every one. And the calamity of the whole city, as it was as great as ever befell any, so also was it more unexpected, and more bitter.

Interest shifts from what was done to what was suffered. The historian expresses horror in the most conventional terms; he almost deserts objectivity. House, temple, young, old, cattle and even children go down in a lake of blood. But the Thracians are almost his blood-relatives, and horrified as he has been, as phrases like 'without mercy' and 'any of the barbarians' show, he goes on to give the devils their due. The Thebans chased them, and killed some on the sea-shore 'for swim they could not'; those who had boats rowed clear. But then, 'in the rest of the retreat, the Thracians behaved themselves not unhandsomely against the Theban horse-men, by whom they were charged first; but running out, and again rallying themselves into a circle, according to the manner of their country, defended themselves well, and lost but few men in that action'. He stresses suffering, notices tactics and commends coolness. The Thracians are not precisely blamed for barbarity: it is treated like a fact of nature. But two hundred and fifty out of three hundred Thracians died. Blood wipes out blood.

The show-piece of the war and the principal moral story of the history is the Sicilian expedition. Its setting out is described at length:

But the Athenians themselves, and as many of their confederates as were at Athens on the day appointed, betimes in the morning came down into Peiraeus, and went aboard to take sea. With them came down in a manner the whole multitude of the city, as well inhabitants as strangers: the in-habitants to follow after such as belonged unto them, some their friends, some their kinsmen, and some their children; filled both with hope and lamenta-tions; hope of conquering what they went for, and lamentation as being in doubt whether ever they should see each other any more, considering what a way they were to go from their own territory. And now when they were to leave one another to danger, they apprehended the greatness of the same more than they had done before, when they decreed the expedition.

Here as elsewhere, he is lamenting the catastrophe and fore-shadowing it before the fighting began. This, he goes on, 'being the first Grecian power that ever went out of Greece from only one city, was the most sumptuous and the most glorious of all that ever had been set forth before it, to that day'.

The details follow. It was not only greater than the fleet that sailed against Troy, about which he has already put forward firmly dismissive arguments early in Book 1, but as great at least as the largest fleets of this present war. And not only had the state spent, but the private individuals whose honour and whose duty were to equip each warship had 'bestowed great cost otherwise every one upon his own galley, each one striving to the utmost to have his galley, both in some ornament, and also in swiftness to exceed the rest'. The fleet as he says was and was thought to be immensely ambitious. The money it cost one way and another was a huge sum, and the enemy heard all about it 'for the strange boldness of the attempt, and gloriousness of the shew ... and for that it was undertaken with so vast future hopes, in respect of their present power'. By the terms of this description, one knows that the expedition is doomed. And yet this remains a moment of great beauty. As Pindar in his ode about the Argonauts settles suddenly on the long moment of prayer before the ship set out, so here suddenly a silence falls, and we can see in perfect detail, which is never lavished on any battle, the moment of freshness and eagerness: the last moment before the tragedy begins to unfold.

After they were all aboard, and all things laid in that they meant to carry with them, silence was commanded by the trumpet; and after the wine had been carried about to the whole army, and all, as well the generals as the soldiers, had drunk a health to the voyage, they made their prayers, such as by the law were appointed before their taking sea; not in every galley apart, but altogether, the herald pronouncing them; and the company from the shore, both of the city and whosoever else wished them well, prayed with them. And when they had sung the Paean, and ended the health, they put forth to sea.

In spite of the beauty of this translation, Hobbes has had trouble with one sentence. The wine was mixed in mixers, with water as for a dinner, not carried about, and it was not drunk in healths, but 'in cups of silver and of gold they poured it out' as an offering to the gods. Obviously the rowers at the oars can pour nothing, but the soldiers and the captains together poured it as a common offering: that is what Thucydides wants to stress. It is the act of consecration of the entire fleet and the people of Athens, and a moment of unbearably tragic undertones. Within a few sentences, we hear in a speech by the Syracusan Hermokrates, 'For in truth there have been few great fleets, whether of Grecians or barbarians, sent far from home, that have not prospered ill.'

It is only when Thucydides has his Sicilian campaign well started, at the moment when Alkibiades was sent for, to return under arrest to Athens and face charges of sacrilege there, that he introduces a digression of Herodotean proportions about Harmodios the tyrant-slayer. It seems likely enough, as Momigliano suggested many years ago, that this talented piece of antiquarian research was an early essay by the historian which was available ready-made for the position where we find it today. Perhaps it started as an improvement on Herodotos. It is tied to the obscure and evil-smelling intrigues that brought down Alkibiades only by the fact that the people 'were ever fearful, and apprehended every thing suspiciously', and conceived his sacrileges 'to have been committed by him upon the same reason, and conspiracy against the people'. It is a pity we are given this gratuitous discourse about the sixth-century tyranny, where we might have relished a bare and sober analysis, or better still a set of speeches. As it is, the intrigues make no sense and are meant to make none.

The people were 'full of jealousy and bitterness', and suspicious of 'oligarchical or tyrannical conspiracy': they imprisoned indiscriminately and listened to informers indiscriminately. So far as treason is concerned, Alkibiades was an adventurer, and once accused of treason soon committed it. So far as the people are concerned, Thucydides does not treat the low classes with much understanding or much sympathy. They are like a stage army, like the army that perished at Syracuse. Their function is to suffer. Their actions bring trouble on their own heads. He does not really believe in their gods, only in the tragic mechanism which Hesiod calls vengeance.

The history he wrote is unique in its seriousness, and apparently in its truthfulness. Later Greek historians could not imitate the dark and hollow thunder of his prose. By trying to increase the seriousness, they became passionate and dramatic and victims of their own techniques: the truth suffered, and so did literature. His subject-matter was also unique, as he said it was, and knew it would be from the first day of the war. He chose to write about the greatest crisis of the ancient world, and about a war that shook many things to pieces, and about a time in which the world was altering utterly, even independently of that war. He understood something, though not everything, about economics. He came close to being scientific as a historian. Somewhere he remarks that historical research is very like medical research. His ideas about human life and about history were deliberately hidden from us; today they have to be excavated with tact from his writings. But the ideals he attributes to Athens at its best and to Perikles have indeed lived as he said they would. They are admirably thought through and strikingly formulated. They still appear both strong and fresh, as if they were newly written.

BIBLIOGRAPHY

A. W. Gomme, A. Andrewes and K. J. Dover, *Historical Commentary on Thucydides*, 5 vols., 1944 and later

N. G. L. Hammond, *History of Greece*, 2nd edition, 1967

A. H. M. Jones, *Athenian Democracy*, 1960

C. Macleod, *Collected Essays*, 1983

A. Parry, 'Thucydides', *Yale Classical Studies*, vol. 21, 1972

J. de Romilly, *Thucydide et l'impérialisme athénien*, 2nd edition, 1951

J. de Romilly, *Histoire et raison chez Thucydide*, 2nd edition, 1967

G. E. M. de Ste Croix, *Origins of the Peloponnesian War*, 1972

13

XENOPHON

The utter eclipse of Athenian power lasted hardly ten years; by the end of 394 B.C Athens had revived, through the successful device of a surviving admiral called Konon who had held a command since before the Sicilian expedition. He defeated the Spartans at sea, using Persian ships; he then refortified Athens. Thucydides had died, but both Theopompos and Kratippos, whose work is probably what has now surfaced as a papyrus text, the *Hellenika Oxyrhynchia*, independently completed his history in the same detail – with the fatal difference that they both seem to have ended the story with a new Athens rising from the waves. That is a bad and frivolous distortion of what the great historian intended. The only writer to continue his work as he intended was Xenophon, but on a very much lighter scale. Xenophon has taste and intelligence, but there is something incurably lightweight about him.

It is strange that such a variety of works should be written by one man. The truth probably is that he did not write them all, but he wrote most of them. He certainly did not write the *Constitution of Athens* which occurs among his works. Its author was the most bone-headed kind of conservative, anti-democratic, anti-Athenian, and violent against slaves and the poor. He used to be referred to by scholars as the Old Aristocrat or Oligarch, but he is hardly able to string a sentence together. His style is amusingly simple, but not genuinely archaic. This buffoon is highly valued by scholars as a witness and a rare example of the opposition to the Periklean party, and of pristine, pre-sophistic prose. When his argument wanders in circles it is dignified as 'archaic ring-composition'. His pamphlet has even been attributed to great men, and it has been dated in the 420s or in the lifetime of Perikles, even in 445.

The arguments are available, but one need not pause over them long; the pamphlet takes a brief hour to read, and one can make up one's own mind. My own view is that the author was some minor member of the circle of the four hundred, writing between 413 and 411 to promote sedition overseas. 'Il vaut le détour', but one must not take him too seriously either as a political thinker or as a writer. I do not think he is 'our earliest Attic prose', as Bowersock and Lesky believed; Antiphon is earlier, and so is much of Thucydides. An early date for the pamphlet does not stand up to a close reading of it.

Maybe, for those readers with time to spare, this brief matter is worth arguing in slightly greater detail, if only because some historians have argued powerfully for an early date. The political situation in the pamphlet, in so far as it is not fantasy, is too far forward on its road to be pre-war; it chimes with the comments of Thucydides on the crisis of the four hundred and five thousand. The war seems to me to be clearly referred to more than once. The insolence of slaves at Athens was a product of the war, according to Aristophanes. The Greek word *eni* for 'there is', which occurs twice, could be early, but it occurs as late as Plato. The great cities ruled by Athens through fear and small cities through their need could I suppose be early or late, but the emphasis on money values smells late to me, and the concentration of comedy on criticizing the noble, rich and powerful must be later than the early plays of Aristophanes, unless it is just a silly remark. 'That is why they disgrace decent people and drive them out and kill them, and promote the malicious' sounds like some time after Alkibiades and his friends were exiled. (The exile of Thucydides son of Melesias in 443 is too early on other grounds.) Finally, at the end of these boring arguments for which I apologize, I should record that rereading the Old Oligarch straight after all the works I have so far discussed, I was strongly impressed by his use of late Thucydidean arguments mishandled, which suggested a late date, and by the inferiority of his mind and style even to the Hippokratic writings. As schoolboys, even as undergraduates, we found the Old Oligarch refreshing, but one is not laughing with him, one is laughing at him.

Perhaps it is best, having gone so far, to dispose here of some other minor and in certain cases doubtful works of Xenophon before discussing his serious writings and their date. His *Hieron* is an odd little conversation between the poet Simonides, a famous wise man on

whom many jokes and witticisms and clever answers and anecdotes
were fathered, and the famous Syracusan tyrant Hieron. In a spirited
exchange Hieron convinces him that in all the pleasures of life, private
citizens are happier than tyrants, and Simonides gives the solution
that the proper happiness of tyrants is to outdo other tyrants by
making their people happy. This piece of nonsense is argued with
verve, in the kind of mannered prose style that Plato parodies in
the *Symposion*. The arguments are frank, well conceived, and hard-
hitting. It was a display piece, intended for some form of public
performance.

Xenophon's *Agesilaos* is the formal praise of a heroic king of Sparta
who died in 360 B.C. Xenophon deliberately adopts a memorial style.
A modern reader may feel this piece is too exquisitely ornamental,
and that discussing it here we should begin to trace the decadence
of fourth-century prose, before we have considered its best achievements. Yet Plato and Xenophon were born within a year or two
of one another, in 429 or 428. It is only the fact that Xenophon
as a historian followed Thucydides which gives him a priority in this
book, which as a philosopher or an ornamental stylist he would
hardly merit. All the same, the seeds of decadence had been sown
at Athens by the Sicilian Gorgias in 427 B.C., and his suave and
tinkling style was a constant influence on literature, throughout his
long life (483–376 B.C.) and beyond it. Agathon's speech in Plato's
Symposion is a parody, and Xenophon's *Agesilaos* an unhappy
imitation, either of Gorgias or of Prodikos.

He did not so, but confronted and enmeshed with the Thebans, and shield
to shield they heaved, fought, killed, died. And there was no crying out,
no, but not silence either, but such an utterance as is the product of rage
and of battle.

And when at last the battle was over, one could see where they had fallen
together, the earth crimsoned with blood, dead men's bodies, friends and
enemies together, shields thrust through, spears smashed, daggers naked
of their sheaths, some on the ground, some in the body, some still in the
hand.

Enough of this style is surely quite enough. *Agesilaos* is only a
little over thirty pages, but it is too long. Xenophon's *Constitution
of Sparta* is a prolonged hymn of praise to the way the Spartans lived,

by the institutions of Lykourgos, a misty figure to whom much was falsely attributed, and with notable enthusiasm by Xenophon. He even dates the great man in the generation of the children of Herakles. Xenophon is often absurd, and not always sympathetic from a modern liberal point of view, in this treatise; but it is less ornamental than *Agesilaos*, and constantly interesting. Chapter 14 alone was written in 371 B.C., when he was disliking Sparta and longing for Athens. He often writes like a furious, fox-hunting squire, but with a shrewdness and a certain twinkle. His enthusiasm for discipline and physical fitness is part of his character. I do not feel I have ever met the modern equivalent of any earlier Greek writer of any merit, but one feels Xenophon is a character and even a social type one has encountered. Perhaps that makes one like him more than one should. But his Greek at its best has a wonderful clarity and liquidity; he is so easy to read, so intellectually undemanding, so interesting and so courteous to the unknown reader.

The other minor works are *On Resources, Cavalry Command, On Riding* and *On Hunting*. The pamphlet on the resources of the Athenian state is terribly short, a mere seventeen pages, but thrilling to historians and to all students of Greek things who want to go beyond a superficial knowledge. Its discussion of the slave problem is frank and blood-chilling. Xenophon is on the whole a reasonably approachable conservative, but one can see how the Old Oligarch's *Constitution of Athens* got among his books. The point of the resources pamphlet is to show how Athens could be rich enough without imperial aggression.

But if nothing I have said is impossible or difficult, and if by so doing we shall be better liked in Greece, and live more safely in our homes, and get a better glory, and the people will have provision in plenty, and the rich be relieved of the expense of war, and with that great abundance we shall hold festivals even more magnificently than we do today, and fit up temples and restore walls and ship-houses, and give priests and Council and authorities and knights their ancestral conditions, why do we not put our hands to this work at once, and hope even in our own lifetimes to see this city happy and secure?

Cavalry Command, Riding and *Hunting* used to be more widely read than they are today, in that period when classical scholarship was thought to be a preparation for these occupations. It is a pity they are neglected now, since they teach what we no longer know, and they represent an important element in European life for thousands of years, but above all in Greek life and literature in the classical period. One can see from Aristophanes, and from the reference in the last paragraph, that the Knights or Riders represent a precisely defined, rather high social class, and most of Athenian literature seems for better and worse the product of that class, though poetry is as usual more democratic, and the ancient class system was not like ours. That is particularly true of the country. Xenophon on horses and on hunting writes innocently. *Cavalry Command* is a handbook for officers, giving a list of their duties. 'The gods being placated you must enrol Riders, to fill the legal number and avoid diminishing the existing cavalry. If new Riders are not admitted, they will always be getting fewer. Some are bound to retire by age and others fall away in other ways.' He is a practical officer of state, and he gives the details of training horses and men, the parade to the Parthenon (where to gallop and where to rein in), behaviour on campaign, and battle tactics.

His *Riding* is mostly about horses. Horse-trading has evidently not much altered over the centuries, since a large part of this work tells one how not to be cheated, and much of the rest why you should be nice to horses and not show off. He writes 'for his younger friends', and bases his work on an older treatise which most scholars agree has not survived, by a famous late-fifth-century cavalry commander called Simon, who dedicated a bronze horse where the road to the Akropolis slopes steeply uphill at the Eleusinion, with his famous actions engraved around the base. Xenophon's book is full of charming advice. Let the mane grow so that you have plenty to hold on to. Simon used to say a well-shaped hollow hoof rang like a cymbal. Let the horse have a room in your house where you see him often. The fodder in his manger should be as hard to steal as the food in your larder. Approach the horse on his left (as one is still taught). Make much of your horse. A horse's spirits are like a man's temper. In the war you should armour your horse as you do yourself. For you a dagger is better than a sword.

His *Hunting* begins with a curious mythological introduction: a long list of hunting heroes and the odd claim that Zeus and Cheiron the centaur had the same father. To Cheiron, Apollo and Artemis

revealed hunting and hounds. This learned and ornamental introduction, which lasts for three pages, does appear to belong with the rest
of this little book, which is elaborately written throughout, but has
been thought inauthentic. And yet it seems central to Xenophon's
interests, and the educational value of hunting, and the attack on
sophistic intellectuals, do seem to point to him as author. He is mostly
quite practical on hare-hunting, on wild boar and on deer. He writes
less freely than the Xenophon we like best, but being a mannerism,
that might easily have worn off. 'Your netter must have eagerness
for his work and have the Greek language, and be about twenty
years of age, be lightly shaped, strong and of sufficient spirit to master
his tasks and enjoy his work.'

'There are many ways of tracking in a single pack: some bitches
when they find traces go on with no sign, so one does not know
they are hunting, some just wag their ears but keep their tails quiet,
and others keep their ears still but shake the tip of their tails.' I cannot
imagine who else would have written this. He knows hares run in
a circle and have one ear up and one down; he deduces that hares
have one ear heavier than the other, which is a pleasing thought.
On the points of hounds, he is as detailed as one could imagine, much
more so than Shakespeare. He knows that the traces of a hare differ
in summer and winter, and he knows how frost affects a scent. He
reasons about such things constantly, sometimes wrongly, as if they
were the deepest truths of natural philosophy. He gives numerous
hound-names, he knows Indian deer-hounds as well as three Greek
breeds.

As for the intellectuals,

good education teaches one to keep the laws and speak and hear about
virtuous men. Those who devote themselves to labouring and learning
perpetually [at hunting] get laborious lessons and exercises for themselves,
but they also get salvation for their cities. Those who are not willing to
be taught laboriously, but prefer to pass their days in unseasonable pleasures,
are the most weak-natured of all. They obey neither good laws nor good
words, because through not labouring they fail to discover what a good
man has to be like.

Which one learns in the hunting-field? Well, he sees it as the ancient
equivalent of a public school, and preferable to many of those it

was in many ways, no doubt. He concludes by suggesting that the same goes for women. One cannot help liking Xenophon.

He was an Athenian from the countryside, who was born about 428 B.C. As an aristocrat and as an Athenian, he must have had a difficult time as a young man. In 401 B.C., at a bad period for Athens but against the advice of Sokrates, he went as a private volunteer to join a Greek expeditionary force in Asia. Its purpose turned out to be nothing less than the occupation of the throne of Persia. The expedition failed, but Xenophon, who was elected leader, got his army away after a very long march of amazing courage through hostile territory. He then served in Thrace as a mercenary commander, and under the Spartans in Asia in the same way. Meanwhile Sokrates had been executed in 399, and at some time in the early nineties Xenophon was exiled. But he liked the Spartans, who now employed him, and simply continued with his career as a mercenary officer. That was how he met King Agesilaos, and it was under Agesilaos that he served at the battle of Koroneia in 394 against Athens.

The Spartans settled him on an estate south of the river Alpheios, in the wild, god-haunted country beyond Olympia, where the hills are beginning to become mountains. It was near the modern village that used to be called Mazi, before that was resettled ten or fifteen years ago, after an earthquake. In 371, this neutral ground, properly called Triphylia, was taken over by Elis, and Xenophon had to move, first to the Isthmus, then at last back to Athens. His exile officially ended about 368, but he came home only when Corinth expelled its Athenians three years later. In 362 B.C. his son Gryllos died fighting at Mantineia in a battle in which Athens and Sparta were allies. Agesilaos died in 360, Xenophon in about 354.

He began to write history by finishing the work of Thucydides; he cannot have undertaken that before the great man died, and by that time he was abroad, though he is sometimes thought to have used notes Thucydides wrote. However that may be, it is certain that in the three years between 404 and 401, Thucydides in his fifties must have been an important influence on Xenophon in his twenties. To two masters, Sokrates and Thucydides, and to King Agesilaos, Xenophon devoted most of his life. His first work in history was written apparently before 394, and before the larger-scale works of Theopompos and Kratippos. He went on writing history in a series of seven consecutive books, covering almost all the years between 411 and 362; they are called his *Hellenika*. But they are not one thing by any means. In 388 or so, having finished the two books that conclude the master's work, he wrote his *Spartan Constitution*, and a year or two later he started on his personal memoirs of the Asian adventure. He circulated the earlier part of them under the pseudonym Themistogenes of Syracuse, but added the later, angrier part (5.3.7, etc.) under his own name in the 370s, in answer to criticism.

Between the two parts of his Asian memoirs come the first two of his four books of records of Sokrates and I suppose his *Apology of Sokrates*, all written by the end of the eighties. The last two books about Sokrates are usually dated very late in his life, and *Cavalry Command* and *Riding* might equally be late, though one may doubt his having the heart for those subjects after the death of Gryllos. In the early seventies he returned to his history. The years 402–401 he never covered, and the years from 401 to 399 were already covered by his memoirs. So he had now to cover the twenty years from 399 to 379, the first five being active years for him, and the last fifteen spent writing. He wrote about what he knew, which was more about Sparta in those years than about Athens. Most of Book 5, which takes the story down to 375, was written in Corinth in about 369, and the last two books, where his sources suddenly and greatly improve, were written in Athens. The *Hellenika* ends in 362, with the battle in which his son died.

Several of the works of Xenophon are undatable; one can only guess where they fit. His passions were history, hunting, moral philosophy and education, and within this series battle as a theatre of virtue and history as a test of men can almost be reduced to other aspects of morality. But his history has excellent qualities. His continuation of the great war is written with an attempt at impersonality and respect to chronology; but in his very first paragraph, the atmosphere becomes romantic. The Spartan admiral Mindaros 'saw the battle below him as he sacrificed in Troy to Athene'. Xenophon is almost too fine a painter of historic vignettes. Still, one must not complain. The sequence of events is clear and well written.

His reported speeches are not so subtle nor so ample as one might hope: they have shrunk to a dramatic device. The last sentences of his continuation give the not surprising impression that he felt his subject was civil war. Society had been broken, and now it was repaired.

'And having sworn oaths that there should be no malicious re-collection of injuries, even to this day they work together in one political system and the people abides by its oaths.' The oaths are important to Xenophon; one may even suspect that he thought the breaking or keeping of an oath rather than of a social bond was the underlying theme of Thucydides. I make this suggestion because of Xenophon's insistence in 5.4, written in Corinth in about 369, on oath-breaking as the central fact in the rise and fall of Sparta. Having concluded the Thucydidean history of Athens, he was now matching it and outdoing it by adding the rise and fall of Sparta to the rise and fall of Athens. The idea is perhaps too complicated to work well; the analogy is not quite true. Nor was his own view the same in the earlier Spartan books as it was by 369. But the oath-breaking then became central to his explanation of history. Perhaps Agesilaos was his Perikles, but his tone was his own.

One might have much else to say in Greece and abroad, of how the gods do not ignore the impious or the unholy: but now I will say what lies before me. The Spartans, who had sworn the cities would be independent, and who occupied the Theban Akropolis, were first punished only by those they wronged, although never until that time were they overcome by anyone.

The breaking of the oath and the sin of imperialism are taken together. To enslave a city is like enslaving a man, which was punishable at Athens by death if you did it within the state of Athens. One must remember that passionate feeling about the freedom of one's city, and the analogy of subjection with slavery, are not just an abstract confusion or a political idea. The important politics of the Greeks, even the Athenians, were carried on with ideas and motives from outside politics. The motive of the state was always thought of like an individual motive. This point is clearer in Aristophanes than in Xenophon, but in the matter of oath-breaking and enslavement, it is important to realize he is treating a great state like an impious individual.

He is interested in character, and dramatic in his handling of it. The division of opinion about Alkibiades that Xenophon carefully analyses in Book 1 is really a relic of the technique of Thucydides; instead of opposing speeches we get long, opposing opinions. As with the speeches, one is meant to see through some of the arguments at once: 'that being a slave to helplessness he was forced by necessity to serve the enemy, in danger of death every day', and that 'being the only ones left, they were loved by the citizens just because there was no one better left alive'. But this is an effective passage, and it says as much about the people as it does about the hero. He likes heroes, and we owe it to his particular loyalty to Sokrates that in a sudden historic vignette we catch sight of that philosopher at an extraordinary moment of moral integrity in a political crisis:

> Certain of the presiding committee refused to put forward this vote illegally, and again Kallixenos got up and again he made the same accusations. So they yelled to the refusers to speak. And the whole committee agreed in their fear, and put it forward, except for Sokrates, who refused and insisted on doing all things according to the law.

Xenophon is a short-winded author. His seven books of *Hellenika* cover nearly fifty years, but taken together they make only one volume, and not a fat one. His *Anabasis*, the memoir of his Asian expedition, is longer and in its scale more substantial. And it is admirably written, more relaxed than his *Hellenika*, where the solemnity of the historian's vocation overcomes him. It is also packed with surprising details. It is hard to separate his book from the adventure itself, and hard to understand that without a map. His achievement was amazing, and he all but underplays it. He served under leaders like Klearchos, an exiled Spartan who ran a mercenary army in Thrace, but more particularly under Proxenos of Boiotia. The political background to the Persian quarrel is swiftly outlined, and the ominous words follow, that the Persian pretender 'was ready to move up-country'. By the end of 1.6 the *anabasis*, the march up-country, is over, and the fighting begins. By 5.3, the abandoned mercenary army has fought its way to the sea. Klearchos died early, and a Spartan called Cheirisophos was nominally in command; Xenophon writes from his own point of view and stresses his own importance, though not objectionably: but this is probably why he published his memoir under a Sicilian pseudonym. He added the later part under his own name, and the whole work was divided into seven books by some tidy-minded librarian, to match the *Hellenika*.

He reports speeches and the making of decisions fully, and includes information valuable to us about the habits of the inland Asian peoples. His own speeches are highly characteristic. 'But those who recognize death as common to all men and inevitable, and who struggle to die honourably, they are the ones I see as more likely to reach old age, and to have a happier time as long as they live.' 'Until now,' says Cheirisophos, 'I only knew you were an Athenian, but now I praise you for your words and your actions, and I wish we had more like you: it would profit all of us.' That was the night Xenophon was chosen to replace Proxenos. As he first wrote this book, it ended with these words: 'And of the tenth part of the money due to Apollo and Ephesian Artemis, each of the generals took his share to keep it for the gods. Xenophon had Apollo's dedication made and dedicated in the Athenian treasure-house at Delphi, and inscribed his own name and that of Proxenos, who died with Klearchos, because he was his friend.' The last word is not simply affectionate, it implies unbreakable, almost formal bonds of mutual friendship with a foreigner.

Xenophon began the second half of this memoir, which continues the story of the same army, with an idyllic description of his life near Olympia, and his dedication to Artemis. He had left her money in Ephesos with the treasurer, in case of being killed fighting under Agesilaos. This man came to Olympia on religious business and handed it back. 'Xenophon took land and bought it for the goddess where the god chose. It happens the river Selinous runs through this land, and a river Selinous runs by the temple of Artemis at Ephesos. And there are fish in both, and shell-fish: but at Skillous there are beasts of every kind of game that can be hunted.' He dwells on the public feasts he holds at his temple, the local people who come, the hunting of the game by Xenophon's sons and their friends, and the feasting. 'The goddess gives them grain, bread, wine, cheese, a share of the sacrificial animals and of the game.' One wishes he had lived on there, undisturbed and unembittered. If one grants him his changes of style, and the special atmosphere of his *Agesilaos*, he does seem to have improved as a writer as he went on.

His Sokratic writings are so far below the level of Plato's as philosophy that they are overshadowed and neglected works. As entertainment they are charming, and one should not forget that a Greek philosopher is a public entertainer of a kind, at least until the age of Aristotle. His *Apology*, the last speech of Sokrates, was not the first account to be written: there seem to have been several versions, one of them the convincing reconstruction by Plato. Xenophon's claim to special interest is his conviction that Sokrates wanted to die, and deliberately goaded his judges into the death sentence. It appears from Plato that Xenophon's opinion was legitimate. He was also concerned to defend the influence of Sokrates on the young, and here he is obviously speaking from experience. But some of his stories are inventive, however amusing. The Delphic oracle is not likely to have called Sokrates most free, most just and most decent of all mankind, and if it did he would hardly quote it so smugly, still less add 'What about Lykourgos of Sparta? It called him a god.' Through the beard of Sokrates we hear the voice of Xenophon. A strange reference to the hero Palamedes suggests the flickering influence of Prodikos, who perhaps taught Xenophon rhetoric.

His *Memoirs of Sokrates* are an amazing rag-bag. Scholars have argued fiercely whether they were all written as one piece, and therefore rather late in the day, or whether the first two books might be early work, an immediate reply to the pamphlet of a certain Polykrates. We know little about the pamphlet except that it attacked Sokrates, and it is rather the coherence of the second half of the *Memoirs* than any solid argument about the first two that persuades me to accept an early date for the first two books. The third and fourth books deal with questions of how to run a household or a state; they are practical and read like Xenophon. They correspond to late works of Plato, in which Sokrates as a character has been swallowed up and become fiction. The *Memoirs* certainly begin as polemic:

He was always in the open. He went early to the public walks and gymnasia, and when the market-place was full he was openly seen there, and he always spent the rest of the day where he would see most people. And he was mostly talking, and those who wanted could listen. No one ever saw Sokrates do or heard him say anything impious or unholy.

In this strongly worded but slightly beef-witted defence Xenophon does at least honestly confront the lurking suspicion every modern historian must have entertained about Sokrates. He was accused of corrupting youth. It was arguable not just that philosophy had ruined the younger generation, an accusation we have all heard so often we begin to understand its true meaning, but that the particular circle of Sokrates had included some nasty and anti-democratic figures, including Kritias (one of the Thirty) and Alkibiades. Xenophon's answer is that he cannot defend either of these bad men, but that being what they were, it was part of their ambition to see what could be made out of the cleverness or the social prestige of Sokrates. They were before Xenophon's time of course, as Sokratic admirers. Still, it is true as Xenophon says, that they deserted Sokrates for politics, being opportunists. But this defence must surely have been written before the *Symposion* of Plato.

Xenophon knows some things about Sokrates one is pleased to hear, but one is never quite certain whether he exaggerates or from time to time invents. He himself likes moral teaching and decent standards; he is not a profound reasoner. Perhaps Sokrates really was fond of quoting 'With all your might perform what is holy to the everlasting gods', at least to boys like Xenophon, but there is something profound and moving about Sokrates that hardly flits across these pages. The second book is a dialogue with Aristippos designed to teach self-control. The Sokrates who argues has the same tranquil lilt that Plato gives him, and I believe that this book, though not the first, must reflect Plato's literary influence. We have already seen that Xenophon can adopt a style swiftly, and that is what he does here. He even quotes the sophist Prodikos of Keos, a teacher of refinements of language and rhetoric who was famous for an allegory about the choice of Herakles between Virtue and Vice. One can feel at once the influence of another style, that of Prodikos of course, on this passage: 'her body adorned with purity, her eyes with modesty, her shape with decency, her clothing white'.

The attempts that scholars have made to isolate the sources of Xenophon, who as a pupil of Sokrates is not thought deep enough to be acceptable, have had the strange effect of crediting him with a wide philosophical culture. A lot has been written about his copying Antisthenes, and Plato, and even an entire generation of early pupils of Sokrates supposedly simpler-minded than the later ones. But if one accepts that Xenophon knew Sokrates well, as he said he did, then the simple-mindedness is his own, and his unreliability arises from muddle-headedness on intellectual matters. Xenophon was not a deeply intellectual man. It is typical that what he recalled of the philosophy of Prodikos was not his doctrine of the evolution of mankind through great and godlike benefactors who taught the use of fire and metal and grain and so on, nor any of the linguistic subtleties that Prodikos taught, but only the vivid images of Virtue and Vice.

In the later books we hear some arguments that sound far more like Xenophon than Sokrates. Are Athenians as numerous as Boiotians? As well-built and handsome? Kinder? And proudest and most thoughtful and thereby most inclined to risk themselves for glory and for their country? And we have better ancestors. But we lost some battles and instead of them fearing us we now fear them.

'And that is how I feel things to be,' said Sokrates. 'But I think under a good strong ruler the city is better off now. Courageous spirit begets negligence and easiness and disobedience, but fear makes people more careful and obedient and disciplined. One could show this is true from what happens in ships: when they are not afraid of anything, they are full of indiscipline, but when they fear storms or enemies, they not only do all they are told to do, but they keep silent and wait for what is going to be commanded, like members of a chorus.'

Xenophon's philosophic writings are constantly amusing, and interesting for their stray insights, but as philosophy they are below Plato's level, even though as doctrine they have a good deal in common.

Xenophon's teaching about art is at least as strange as the true Sokratic doctrines, but more simplistic.

'O Kleiton,' he said, 'I can see and I know the runners and wrestlers and boxers and all-in fighters you make are beautiful, but what most enchants the souls of men through their vision, the lifelike appearance, how do you work that into statues?' Since Kleiton was unsure and not swift to reply, 'Don't you make them livelier,' he asked, 'by imitating the forms of those who really are alive?' 'Oh yes,' said he. 'So you imitate the hollows and the swellings in bodies, and the compressions and pulls and tensions and relaxations, and make them more like the real thing and more convincing?'

'That's just it,' said he. 'And doesn't it give a special pleasure to the observer if you imitate the effects of bodies in action?' 'Very likely,' he said. 'So you have to make the eyes of men fighting convey more threat, and you imitate the enjoyment in the expression of winners?' 'Very much so,' he said. 'And so,' he said, 'the statue-maker must imitate the actions of the soul through form.'

I doubt whether this crudely realistic view of the passions or operations of the soul conveyed in sculpture would have occurred to anyone in an earlier generation. The very first hint of it is in some of the pediment sculptures at Olympia. Small wonder that the sculptor was 'unsure and not swift to reply'.

Xenophon's *Oikonomikos* is a pair of Sokratic dialogues about family life, the moral code of squires and the management of estates. They are very hard to date: in some ways they suggest the period of peace near Olympia while his sons were growing up, but scholars of the subject are inclined to place them with much else towards the end of his life. One dialogue is with Kritoboulos, the other with Ischomachos. As usual they are rather moral than metaphysical, and they stress the severe, clean-living side of Sokrates. ' "They are slaves," said Sokrates, "to very hard masters, sex, drink, stupid and wasting pride . . ." ' He packs in a lot of elementary information about planting and agriculture, with the complacent conclusion that all this is very easy to learn and everyone knows it, so the difference between the prosperous and the hopeless is between industry and laziness, a moral difference. It is a curious thought today, given the operation of new techniques and of capital investment in modern farming, that this may once have had some truth in it.

The most attractive of Xenophon's philosophic works, and I think to amateurs of all his works, is the *Symposion*, the dinner-party. He imagines dinner in the house of Kallias in 422 B.C.; Plato sets his similar dialogue in 416. Neither is easy to date, and they are certainly related. In Xenophon's dialogue Sokrates speaks of sensual and spiritual love, and so he does in Plato's. Xenophon's party is given by Kallias for Autolykos the all-in fighter, Plato's for Agathon the poet. Xenophon has flute-girls and a mime of Dionysos and Ariadne, Plato's guests decide against flute-girls at the beginning, but suffer a riotous invasion by Alkibiades in love. Can it be possible that on this one occasion the lesser writer gave the greater an idea which he transformed into a masterpiece? Or must we blush to admit that Xenophon so little knew his limitations that he produced a crude imitation of Plato's greatest work? That, I regret to say, is the likely solution. There was a law of diminishing returns about all such imitations in the ancient world. And Xenophon was nothing if not an imitator. Horrified as one must be at the admission of such taste-lessness and such frivolity as his adaptation of Plato here implies, this is still an attractive book. His party is more riotous and the talk more inconsequential, but no doubt Xenophon thought he knew more about parties than Plato did.

> Then harmonizing lyre to pipe the boy played and sang. Everyone applauded him, but Charmides did more. He said: 'It seems to me, gentlemen, just as Sokrates said about the wine, that this mixture of the young boy and girl and the voice singing put grief to sleep and bring love awake.' At this Sokrates spoke again: 'Gentlemen, they're giving us pleasure enough. I know we think ourselves far better than they are. Wouldn't it be a disgrace if being here together we don't try and give one another some profit or pleasure?'

Never was sex more often defeated by words than in the works of Xenophon. This dialogue has its intensely serious moments, as Plato's had, and its idle talk about love.

> 'But the gods who know all things and can do all things are so much my friends that through their care of me I am never out their minds night or day wherever I turn or whatever I mean to do. Through foreknowledge of the consequences of everything, they speak to me in signs, sending messengers of chance words and dreams and omens, about what I should do and what I must not do, and when I obey them I never regret it. In the past I did disbelieve, and I was punished.'

This is Hermogenes speaking. His words might stand for the good side of the Superstitious Man in Theophrastos' *Characters*. They are an unusual extreme of Greek piety, and as near as Xenophon can get to Sokratic mysticism. The success of this dialogue is its mingling of many elements. It ends with a long speech of Sokrates to Kallias, who in Xenophon's time reconciled Sparta with Athens: a well-chosen substitute for Alkibiades.

Xenophon's *Education of Cyrus* is a long and widely ranging work of fiction, full of morality and probably meant to be educative. The phrase about 'shooting straight, riding straight and being straight in all walks of life', which I recall on the lips of an elderly colonial bishop, comes from it. But it also contains plenty of war, a romantic suicide and some exotic colouring. It is on the edge of becoming a novel, a very bad novel indeed. Xenophon is imitating Herodotos it appears, at least in his catalogues of peoples, but if so he often loses touch with his original, and it may be he was subject to some lesser writer's influence. But the last paragraph of Herodotos, about ancient Persian virtue, fits his mood. Only the first of his eight books is about the education of the king: the rest is a very long and quite fictional account of an ideal king. Herodotos has him die in battle, but here he dies at peace in bed. He is not of course the same as the later Cyrus in whose employment Xenophon served in Asia. The work ends with a melancholy glance at the later decline of behaviour, but for once the last part does not appear to be an afterthought.

This long and on the whole awful book had more influence on later writers than any other of Xenophon's writings. Its faults are great length, unconvincing stories and endless moralizing. But if one regards it as an early example of romance – historical fictions being one of the principal taproots of the first romances – then it takes on a new interest. One would have to call it inventive and talented, but terribly uncontrolled. The moralizing is intrusive. 'So while the enemy were said to be approaching but had not yet appeared, Cyrus tried to exercise and strengthen the bodies of his men, and teach them battle-drill, and sharpen their souls for fighting.' He began by giving servants to every soldier, so that they could concentrate on exercises of war, 'for he knew that those who concentrate and put aside distracted attention are the most successful in every sphere'. He took away their javelins and their bows and taught them to fight with the knife, close up. And so on. It recalls the advice of my old cadet sergeant-major, about being 'up and at 'em wi' a trench-knife'.

The romantic suicide is splendidly tragical, and if it were true, as one sometimes fears, that all tragedy even in the fifth century aspires to the condition of vulgar melodrama, then it might have ended with this kind of thing. The king's friend Abradatas has just been killed in battle.

'Has anyone seen Abradatas? I am amazed because he used to come to me often, but now he is nowhere to be seen.' One of the servants answered, 'O Master, he is dead, he died in battle driving his chariot at the Egyptians. All the others except his company turned away so they say, when they saw the strength of the Egyptians. And now,' he said, 'they say his wife has picked up the body, and putting it in the carriage she was driving in, she has brought him here, somewhere towards the river Paktolos. And they say his eunuchs and servants are digging a grave for him on a hill-top, and his wife is sitting on the ground adorned as she was for her wedding, holding his head on her knees.'

This scene with the dead man's head on the bride's lap sounds like real Asian representations, though I know of no example quite so early.

Hearing this, Cyrus struck his thigh and leapt up at once on to his horse and taking a thousand horsemen rushed to the tragedy. He ordered Gadatas and Gobryas to take what fine adornments they could for a dear friend and brave man dead, and whoever had the herds that followed them, he bade him drive cattle and horses and many sheep to wherever he discovered Cyrus might be, for him to slaughter them to Abradatas.

A scene of much sentiment follows between Cyrus and the widow. '"Now he lies blameless dead, and I who encouraged him sit by him living."' And Cyrus remained some time silently weeping, but then he said, "He had the best death, because he died in victory. Take these things and adorn him from me." Gobryas and Gadatas had arrived with adornments many and beautiful.' As the king leaves after a few more tactless remarks, he says '"Only show me to whom you want to be taken."' She answers, '"Be brave, Cyrus, I will not hide from you to whom I want to go."' He departs, she tells the eunuchs to stand aside,

but she told her nurse to remain, and ordered her when she was dead to cover her and her man under one cloak. The nurse beseeched her greatly not to do it, but she made no progress and saw she took it badly, so she sat and wailed. And she took a dagger long prepared and cut her throat, and laying her head on her husband's breast she died. The nurse lamented her and covered them both as she had commanded. When Cyrus heard of

XENOPHON 325

the woman's deed, he came rushing in shock, in case he could help. The eunuchs seeing what had happened snatched up daggers, all three of them, and killed themselves standing where he placed them.

Any writer as interesting as Xenophon is bound to be uneven. Every writer of his generation was transitional, and now they are all in some way lost, except for the unique genius of Plato. The dating of Xenophon's work by alterations of style would be extremely dangerous; even the dating I have suggested by political attitudes is not without perils and paradoxes; nor do I know any safe criterion to decide the question which of his minor works are authentic. He is such a mixture of raggedness and elegance, and such a mixture in every way, that we should accept what the manuscripts give us, and press no inquiry about Xenophon too far. But if the scheme I have sketched is correct, two interesting conclusions emerge. When he settled down in exile, he imitated the occupation of exiled Thucydides, probably consciously. His most elaborate and prettified compositions belong to the years of his return to Athens.

The most influential historians of Xenophon's time were based on Athens, and the first important antiquarian and local historians, whose works are too fragmentary to be discussed here, worked on Athenian customs and institutions. One of these was Androtion, an active politician and orator. Their influence on later ways of writing about the past was widespread and long-lasting. One can hear echoes of their work not only in the circle of Aristotle but as late as the Roman empire and the writings of Plutarch. The earliest serious antiquarian, as opposed to historian, whose work we know, was that Hippias of Elis whom Sokrates somewhat despised. The two most influential historians were probably Theopompos of Chios (born about 377) and particularly Ephoros, an Asian Greek writing mostly after 350. One probably ought to add the name of Timaios, historian of Sicily, whose work preserved in later writers seems impressively thorough.

Theopompos was a dramatic writer in the bad sense of the word. We have some three hundred fragments of his treatment of Philip of Macedon, which was composed, it appears, in fifty-eight books. He concentrated on his hero and his hero's devices. His contemporary Philistos wrote in the same way about the tyrant Dionysios. The decline here from disappointed Thucydides is obviously sad. His historical criticism was acute but unsure. He thought the peace treaty with Persia, recorded by Ephoros for 449 and referred to by Isokrates, was a forgery, because it was written in the Ionic and not the Attic alphabet. The truth is still controversial, but his argument is insufficient. He was a quirky writer, malicious about Plato and heavily dependent on rhetoric. He devoted many pages to a wonderland on the upper Nile beyond Khartoum, the kingdom of Merope, where enough excavation has now taken place to arouse one's sympathetic curiosity. His life was a troubled one; he travelled widely. He was a vagrant court orator and pamphleteer.

Ephoros of Kyme wrote what became the received version of Greek history. It was a universal history, from the 'Dorian invasion' of the Peloponnese in prehistoric times, but without mythical events. He was a stylish writer and a learned one, who drew on many written sources. He was a rationalizing, moralizing interpreter of the past. He wrote a book on style, though his own style was criticized for lack of impetus and lack of fizz. Among those he used were the historian Kallisthenes, a junior kinsman of Aristotle, and the orator Anaximenes. The fragments of all these writers are amusing enough to beguile a winter's afternoon, and thrilling to professional historians, who must still analyse which of them imitates the other, and which may at times be nursing some undiscovered nugget of truth. They do have a place in the history of literature, because they influenced and exemplify its decadence, but none of them seems from his fragments to be a great historian.

Hellanikos of Lesbos, the historian of Attica, who wrote in the late fifth century, is to my mind much more interesting, perhaps just because he was an antiquarian and a gossip. It is no doubt a question of what one wants to know, and of a writer's tone. My own favourite among all fragmentary Greek historians is Charon of Lampsakos, for his fresh and salty, almost primitive style of narrative, in the few sentences we have. He lived in the fifth century, after the Persian wars, and we know all too little about him. His prose is simpler and subtler than that of any fourth-century historian, and quite untouched by oratory or sophism.

DATES (MOSTLY CONJECTURAL)
IN THE LIFE AND WORK OF XENOPHON

429–8	Birth of Xenophon
404	Fall of Athens; return of Thucydides
401	Xenophon serves in Asia
399	Sokrates executed
	(Xenophon exiled)
394	Xenophon serves at Koroneia against Athens
394	Xenophon is settled at Skillous by the Spartans
392	? *Hellenika* 1 and 2
388	*Spartan Constitution*
387–6	*Anabasis*
383	? *Education of Cyrus*
381	*Memoirs of Sokrates* 1 and 2. ? *Apology of Sokrates*
379–8	*Hellenika* 3 and 4
377	Second part of *Anabasis*
371	Xenophon leaves Skillous (Mazi) near Olympia
370	? *On Hunting*
370	Chapter 14 of *Spartan Constitution*
369	*Hellenika* 5 (covering 379–375)
367	? *Symposion*
366–5	Return to Athens
364	? *Hieron*
362	? *Oikonomikos*
361	*Hellenika* 6 and 7 (down to 362)
359	*Agesilaos*
357	? *Riding* and *Cavalry Command*
355	? *Memoirs of Sokrates* 3 and 4. ? *Resources*

BIBLIOGRAPHY

J. K. Anderson, *Xenophon*, 1972

G. Bowersock, *Pseudo-Xenophon*, 1967

E. Delebecque, *Essai sur la vie du Xénophon*, 1957

T. B. L. Webster, *Art and Literature in Fourth Century Athens*, 1956

Note: Bowersock offers strong arguments for an early date for the Old Oligarch, some of them previously suggested by Jacqueline de Romilly, whose authority should carry great weight, in *Revue de Philologie* 36 (1962), pp. 225ff. Felix Jacoby agreed with her, and so do most German historians, under the influence of a dissertation by H. U. Instinsky, 1933. There is therefore a high probability that I am wrong about this matter, but I cannot unconvince myself.

14

PLATO

Nothing in the writing of this history has so refreshed, satisfied and excited the writer of it as a long reading of Plato. Many Europeans have believed that poetry is by its nature superior to prose, and as one reads through the works that survive from the ancient world, one is strongly tempted to agree with them, since the great Greek poets are not only more impressive and memorable, and for most temperaments communicate more immediately than the prose writers, but they are also more intelligent and better organized. The exception of Thucydides proves the rule, because he is victorious in prose through taciturn honesty and laborious awkwardness. But Plato reverses the verdict. His works are about twice the length of Homer's and abundantly full of many different pleasures. They are written with an appearance of easy calmness, with constant humour, parody and variation, they contain unforgettably attractive vignettes of life in the fifth century, and profound and outraged criticism of life.

Admittedly, Plato was a poet, and poetry preoccupied him. He was also a man of the world, and a writer of formidable literary skill. His dialogues were not intended to embody the truth or expound it, but to tease the reader into conceiving of where it may lie. To understand him, therefore, one must enjoy him, and disregard his vast influence on European thought. He cannot be translated into a system of arguments, and his prose style has never been quite captured in English. At important moments he relies on long parables beautifully told, and Sokrates, his principal character, refers constantly, both ironically and with real conviction, to his own ignorance.

The dialogues of Plato are infinitely charming, sharply intelligent, and express an intellectual wisdom not unlike that of Montaigne.

But Plato was not a Platonist, and even if I were competent to do so, it is not the business of this book to trace the precise arguments and shifting positions of every dialogue. They contain numerous lines of reasoning, on some of which professional philosophers in every age including our own have at times put too much weight. His work has, of course, been of always fresh, sometimes fundamental interest to philosophers. But at the same time he is a very great, perhaps an incomparably great prose writer, perfect in a wide range of tones, and the technical aspects of his philosophy cannot safely be disengaged from his prose. In reading Plato, one must follow a multitude of precise and subtle indications built into his language. No other writer is so morally and intellectually searching, no other writer makes so many quiet jokes. Sokrates teases his friends, his opponents and himself, and above all Plato teases his readers.

But the most famous modern criticisms of Plato are well directed and go deep. The constant tendency of his dialogues towards an absolute, the existence of the good and the beautiful in itself, not just good and beautiful things, and the reality of absolute forms, like ideas in the mind of God, are out of tune with modern empiricism. My own view is that Plato's teaching is essentially moral and his reserved belief mystical; but he delights in paradoxes, and his so-called theory of forms has been taken (I believe) too seriously. By putting him back into his historical context we shall dissolve his metaphysical doctrines into sketches and conversations, and understand both his moral disturbance and his intransigent seriousness better. One of the best guides here is Solmsen, in his *Plato's Theology* (1941), and the most fruitfully suggestive introduction to Plato's methods is the introduction by E. R. Dodds to his commentary on the *Gorgias* (1959). Friedländer's great work on Plato is full of penetration and understanding, but it is also bland, suspiciously subtle, and sometimes misleading.

The second modern reason for distrusting Plato is his criticism of poetry and poets, which reaches a climax in his ban against some poets in his utopian *Republic*. Plato was always interested in poetry and often quotes it, though usually he does so in an almost proverbial form, as a traditional wisdom which ought to be examined, whether it is Homer, or 'Sappho the beautiful or Anakreon the wise'. But Plato inherited criticisms of Homeric mythology which he sharpened and to which he added. What he criticized in poets was their theology and their morality. For him and for his Sokrates, who respected the great poets, the question of what we can really believe, and how one can morally speaking live with one's idea of the gods, are more serious than literary discrimination. His remarks are not un-humorous. 'Nothing,' he observes, 'is more in mid-air than the gods.' His criticism of poets is hardly relevant to an age like ours in which the gods have vanished, but his seriousness and his moral logic are indisputable. Christianity has had to face similar criticisms and refine-ments of biblical writers in recent centuries. Plato's view of poets is multiple; it is not properly measured by erecting a line of reasoning into a dogma.

The most serious of all modern charges against Plato has been Karl Popper's, that Plato is a sort of proto-fascist, and an enemy of the open society, an enemy of liberalism. This is a stiff interpretation, but it has a grain of truth. Perhaps it is wrong for the *Republic*, but right for the *Laws*, though even there I have reservations. As a political theorist, Plato is looking for stability, citizen virtue and wise, rather dictatorially wise government. The same tensions and contra-dictions are to be found in Machiavelli for similar reasons. After the youth of Plato and the death of Sokrates – that is, after the fall of Athens – the one overwhelming question that faced thinking Athenians was: What has gone wrong? In the course of the fourth century, the question became even more pressing. As a political theorist, Plato constantly applied moral ideas to the structure of the state. Politically, he accepted much that appears quite unacceptable to us, who live in better times than his. His conservatism must be measured against what was going on in the street. His theories are utopian, but they require a much more precise historical *mise-en-scène* than they get from philosophers like Popper.

One may go further. No political theories ought to be taken seriously that disregard the problem of slavery. The very phrase, 'liberal studies', which derives from Plato, is an intolerable insult to the majority of mankind. It means subjects like music and the immortality of the soul, which only non-slaves, that is slave-owners, have the leisure to consider. The embattled and declining gentry, attempting to defend their standards and impose their ideologies, have not, in most ages of the world, been a pretty sight, though historical and sympathetic imagination may discover exceptions, and at times alter this crude cartoon substantially. But in Plato's *Republic*, the entire city and its utopian structure are only a context and an analogy for the individual man. The momentum of the dialogue is moral, and its principal truths are told in parables. The *Laws* is a very late dialogue written in political despair, packed with experience of the real world. Sokrates hardly speaks in it. I doubt whether Popper has read it quite rightly. I have had great pleasure from it over many years, but then I am not a systematic philosopher, and I have never gone to Plato for my politics. A full discussion of the *Laws* would be an extremely long book, and no one has ever undertaken it. What we need even more than that is a comparison of the *Laws* of Plato with the slightly later *Politics* of Aristotle, to be written by a historian.

There is no doubt that Plato was anti-democratic, by family loyalty as a boy, and by settled prejudice later, and although he despaired of Athenian politics when he took to philosophy as a young man, he was constantly preoccupied by the state and by public morality, so that he made his views clear. He criticized democracy as Solzhenitsyn has done in our own time, because he thought it led to tyranny. He maintains at one point in Book 8 of the *Republic*, not very seriously I admit, that in a democracy even the animals get out of hand. He despises it as 'the supermarket method' (*panto-polion*) of choosing a government. He thinks slaves are born to be slaves and better off as slaves, although he knows that 'the very rich are not good or happy'. This notion of natural slavery has strange consequences. He thinks that whoever is not a slave by nature is somehow not really a slave at heart even in the worst slavish circumstances. This doctrine or this parodox has in our day a serious resonance. In the *Laws*, late in his life, he sees that slavery is a disturbing problem, but he shies away from discussing it fully.

His pupil Aristotle went so far as to believe that all slaves should have freedom in view and be able to earn it. Yet the same Aristotle repeated with no disapproval the view that at least all barbarians are natural slaves. We must admit that even the most intelligent of Greek minds were terribly overshadowed by social and political circumstances. Plato's life-work was a titanic struggle to rescue what he could, and to find a reliable basis for morality and for true religion and for the state. He was not godlike, but only a human being arguing. It is amazing to what a degree he achieved his purpose. Even as an institution, his school for philosophers lasted (with some discontinuity) nine hundred years.

Plato the son of Ariston lived from about 428 to 347 B.C. His mother's cousin was Kritias, head of the Thirty; her brother was Charmides, his assistant. Her second husband was Pyrilampes, who had once been a friend of Perikles. So Plato's family background was upper class, but he was sickened by the events of the dying century, and when Sokrates, to the last generation of whose friends and followers he belonged, was made to drink hemlock in 399, he left Athens and lived for a time in Megara, where Sokrates had other disciples. In the mid-nineties he is supposed to have served in the Athenian army. In 387, at forty-one, he was in Sicily, where he made friends with the ruler of Syracuse, with Archytas of Tarentum, a mathematical philosopher and successful military man, and with Dion, a close kinsman of the ruler by marriage. Plato is said to have been enslaved and then ransomed on his way home. For most of the remaining forty years of his life he taught a school of philosophers in Athens, at the gymnasium among gardens and groves around the old shrine of Akademos, a short walk outside the city walls. He taught beside a shrine of the Muses; when he died in his eighty-second year, he was buried near by.

When Plato was sixty, Athens had secured an alliance with the powerful Syracusans, who were usually pro-Spartan, but next year his friend the ruler died, and Plato was summoned to Syracuse by Dion to produce in the person of the ruler's eldest son the perfect reign of the philosopher king. This enterprise was a disaster, and Dion swiftly lost ground at court. A third visit from Plato in 361, when he was nearing seventy, went even worse. The new ruler was a cultivated young man, who wrote verses and liked philosophers, but he was a weak politician, and ended his life in a long exile at Corinth.

We have a tempting source of information about all this in some of Plato's philosophic letters, which many scholars take seriously, but they are below Plato's usual literary standard, and I follow a tradition that goes back to Richard Bentley in rejecting all thirteen of them as forgeries, including even the three letters which it is still respectable to defend, the third, the seventh and the eighth. But the substance of Plato's biography is not in question; he was famous in his lifetime, and his nephew Speusippos who inherited the Academy, and Aristotle and other pupils wrote about him. We have even a dozen references to him in fourth-century comedy, and Plato and Isokrates figured in a dialogue on poetry by Praxiphanes, which alas has not survived. We have seen that he was imitated by Xenophon more than once.

The philosophic dialogue, with real characters, often a real setting and precisely conceived dramatic date, with remembered or adapted arguments that shade off into invented speeches, is probably Plato's original device; it obscures the boundaries of truth and fiction in the life and thought of Sokrates, his principal subject, beyond the hope of remedy, and some of the same delicate mist obscures the true development of Plato. We all admit that the development and range of Sokrates, who taught but never wrote, are beyond recovery, but even the development of Plato is full of problems, because being historical fictions his dialogues are often hard to date. His characters belong often to a close circle of friendship and kinship, and his earliest readers are surely inside such a circle in a later generation. One can detect numerous private jokes.

Scholars have long agreed, *faute de mieux*, that close analysis of certain small phrases and tricks of speech can establish three groups of dialogues, and even within these three groups offer arguments as to some dialogues being early or late within their group. The seven very short and insubstantial dialogues, and the work called *Definitions*, which follow the *Letters* in editions of his works, as they do in his manuscripts, are not by Plato. One or two of them contain amusing or interesting remarks, but they are the productions of slightly later and much less original writers. Some of the minor dialogues in the main corpus can also be dismissed with more or less certainty: the second *Alkibiades* on grounds of language, the *Hipparchos*, or *Lover of Gain*, as a piece of derivative though not unenjoyable nonsense, the *Anterastai* for similar reasons, though it is worth reading.

Perhaps we should add the *Theages*, though personally I would like to rescue that, and Paul Friedländer, a serious Platonic scholar, accepted both *Hipparchos* and *Theages* as early works. The *Alkibiades*, or *Greater Alkibiades*, is disputed, but worth discussing among genuine works. The *Kleitophon*, as Wilamowitz suggested and Lesky doubtfully agreed, may easily be the work of some rebellious pupil, since it deals toughly with Sokrates; it is only a few pages long, and it lacks the enchantment of real Plato. The *Minos* is also substandard, and contains some sentences too unsubtle to be acceptable. *Epinomis* and the *Greater Hippias* have also been attacked, but not demolished, so they are still worth discussion, though in Brandwood's order of the dialogues (see end of chapter) *Epinomis* like the *Letters* emerges as later than the *Laws*, which would suggest an imitation or perhaps Plato's last genuine work.

Plato had shown interest in philosophy, in what truth underlay persuasion and language, and in what the world is, before he encountered Sokrates. He is supposed to have written tragic poetry, which he destroyed, and contemplated a political career, which he abandoned. Be that as it may, his early interest was attracted by teachings of Herakleitos, which he knew through Kratylos, the subject of possibly his earliest dialogue. His brothers knew Sokrates before he did. Plato had some other philosophic interests also, however it was that he came by them. He shows some influence of Parmenides and Zeno, and some preoccupation with Anaxagoras, Demokritos and Empedokles. He was fascinated by mathematics, and by the mathematical structure of the universe, which he applied speculatively to atomic theory. He knew the earth is a sphere and he considered its geography, once again speculatively. He naturally assumed that what was knowable could all be known by one man, a nourishing illusion that was continued by Aristotle, and revived in the Renaissance with exciting results. Today one branch of science loses touch with another, and one man does not hope to master even the whole of classical studies. Even Plato alone seems to us a very big subject.

The dialogues with dramatic dates late in the life of Sokrates seem to have been written early in Plato's career, and it is possible that his first work was the *Apology*, a version of the speeches Sokrates made to the court at his trial. Numerous versions of that remarkable performance were written; I have considered Xenophon's. We know of half a dozen others, and they went on being composed as late as Plutarch (first/second century A.D.) and Libanios (fourth century A.D.). Plato's is a splendid piece of writing. It is profoundly convincing as a work of art and as a portrait of Sokrates. It is moving, humorous, perfectly serious and clear, and recalls his dead friend with extraordinary restraint, perhaps even with accuracy. 'But now it is time to leave, for me to die and for you to live, and which of us is going to the better thing is unclear to everyone except the god.' As an ironist, as a moral force, and as a saintly and charming philosopher, Sokrates emerges more clearly from Plato's *Apology of Sokrates* than he does from any of the dialogues except the *Symposion*.

In his arguments in the dialogues Sokrates shows the same humorous and quietly defiant integrity. Those earlier dialogues in which, when arguments are over, he claims at last to be a traditional and conservative figure, who knows little beyond his own ignorance, ought to be interpreted with this rock-like and ultimately moral certainty, and with his mystical intuition of the truly good and beautiful, as a silent presence. He is never about to be convinced by the specious persuasions of any of his adversaries. But the dialogue is not a record of debate; it is Plato's method of opening up a subject, his art of persuasion towards the truth.

In the *Gorgias*, for example, an argument about rhetoric has moral implications: it leads to discussion of persuasive power, true and false will, and in the end happiness, the choice of a practical or a considering life, a political or a Sokratic life. This in turn opens out into the difference between pleasure and the truly good, which carries as a consequence the gap between false arts and true arts, with some more discussion of rhetoric, and of music and tragic poetry. Having demolished the pretensions of rhetoric, Sokrates is induced by practical examples to attack Athenian politicians, and show how virtue ought to underlie politics, and how only the philosopher knows it. The dialogue ends with a comparison of human and divine courts.

It will be seen that this movement from superficial to fundamental questions, this spiralling deeper into the subject, is what the whole dialogue is about, what it is for. It must also be obvious that such a sinuous, and yet precisely directed, interweaving progression requires not only great intellectual power and patience from Sokrates, but a pliant and disciplined response from the snakes he charms. In fact this complete control of the progression of each dialogue, which Plato at times can make seem casual, involves him in the least satisfactory feature of the dialogues as fictions. The author is always in absolute control, and he can make his Sokrates oppressively didactic with no rebellion. No doubt in some remote sense that was true to life. In disenchanted moods it is possible even today for the layman used as a philosophic punchball to wonder whether philosophy is anything more than systematized bad manners. And yet Sokrates usually has excellent manners, and the air is alive with jokes. One should not read him too fast; one should not dissect him for ulterior purposes.

The progression of the *Gorgias* shows deliberation. The three stages of the argument are marked by three changes of the person engaging Sokrates in conversation. This will have been clearer to Plato's contemporaries, since here as in most dialogues the first readers will have known who these people were. The *Gorgias*, like numerous other dialogues, is dated by an amusing device: it is meant to take place in the year when a particular boy was at the height of beauty, that is about seventeen. Plato writes for familiar friends and uses such devices quite often. Here I must argue against E. R. Dodds, who thinks the dramatic date of about 420 B.C. is contradicted. His arguments for confusion are all capable of other interpretations: Plato would not have known the date of the *Antiope* of Euripides, nor perhaps the exact date when Archelaos of Macedonia came to power: he was fifteen at the time, and Archelaos had died in 399.

Plato balances many elements of his dialogues in different ways, using them with more and more complexity to open up a theme, and using a marvellous variety of construction to keep his reader amused. Friedländer has traced three stages in Plato's use of myth or fable. This classification is not altogether satisfactory: he gives the *Apology* a rather late date. It is true that the judges in the other world are mythical, and they occur in the *Apology*; so does the device of reported conversation. But I am inclined to attribute some art of myth to the real Sokrates. Story-telling was an ancient art, and even as late as the *Laws*, where fable is little more than the horns of elfland faintly blowing, and where Sokrates has rather little to say, Plato expresses respect for the antiquity of myth. Even sharp Aristotle in his *metaphysics* says 'the lover of myth is in a sense a lover of wisdom'.

Still, there is no doubt that the fables of Plato increased in importance, and in complexity of structural use, as time went on.

In *Protagoras*, a fable of creation and of the origin of politics leads into an argument. In the first book of the *Republic*, which I take to be an early, separate work, the mythical world of the beyond belongs to Pindar; but in the complete *Republic* the fables are a new and thrilling probe into what could not otherwise be said. In *Timaios*, the myth fills the entire structure. In *Phaidros*, minor fables introduce the central fable, with the same deepening and intensifying progression that we saw in the *Gorgias*: only here fable and argument lead into one another. The same is true of the *Symposion*, the dinner-party, the most fascinating of all Plato's literary constructions. Plato's stories are not usually the spearhead of his dialogues, nor are they evasive: story and argument have a constantly varied architecture, they are part of one procedure.

Within the limits of this chapter, it will not be possible to give objectively equal treatment to all the dialogues of Plato. Any study of their interrelations, unless one can accept Brandwood's dating by computer as an objective basis, must risk being made of cobwebs. Apart from Krantor on the *Timaios* in the early third century, the earliest ancient commentaries on Plato were not written before the first century B.C., and although our manuscripts do show signs of Alexandrian critical activity, they did not attract the concentrated attention of the greatest scholars at that time. Plato rather despised antiquaries, and they in turn neglected him. In the restored order we ought now to adopt, the crucial position of the *Timaios* has slightly altered. It now belongs on linguistic grounds at the head of the third group. Scholars used to place it even later, close to the *Philebos* and just before the *Laws*. From there it was rescued in a brilliant article by G. E. L. Owen (*Classical Quarterly* 1953) as the crown of Plato's middle period. That is substantially still acceptable, but contrary to Owen's view, *Parmenides* and *Theaitetos* turn out on Brandwood's calculation to be earlier. The *Symposion*, the *Republic*, the *Phaidros* and the *Timaios* still keep their places at the centre of Plato's life-work.

The *Kratylos* appears less strange than it might when one thinks of it as the earliest dialogue. It begins as a play might do. 'HERMOGENES: Shall we tell Sokrates this argument? KRATYLOS: If you like. HERMOGENES: Kratylos here maintains, Sokrates, that all beings have a proper name by nature.' This is a steep dive into the deep end of philosophy of language, which is central to this dialogue, and recurs in others. The theory advanced is not simply borrowed from Herakleitos; a more general theory emerges. One is not surprised to see Sokrates end by arguing for the permanence of the beautiful and true and good, and against the universal flux of all things. But it is not obvious whether the honours of argument are meant to be more than even; if Sokrates feels triumphant, he is extremely modest about it, and Kratylos accepts that at face value. Plato was already composing with gleeful irony. The entire argument about etymology at the beginning of *Kratylos* is deliberate nonsense, but it does by implicit self-ridicule open up serious matters. This has made scholars feel uneasy, and it does contain rather private jokes. One should learn from it never to underestimate Plato's powers of hidden mockery and parody, or the intimate terms on which his first circle of readers lived. Their relationship with the characters of the dialogues is also intimate.

The last few lines of the *Kratylos* add a little to its dramatic reality: Kratylos is to leave town and Hermogenes will see him on his way. More interestingly, a reference to Euthyphron in mid-argument hints at real life outside the dialogue. Sokrates jokes about his influence. Euthyphron, as we know from the dialogue named after him, was a seer, a respectable profession in the earlier fifth century at least. Sokrates is on his way to inquire into the charges against himself when he runs into Euthyphron, whose sense of purity and justice is so extreme he proposes to sue his own father for murder. The crime is fantastical; it recalls the private speeches of the Athenian orators, and no doubt that is intentional, but even this slight dialogue leads into the deeper question of the holy and the unholy, and whether Euthyphron knows the difference.

It's funny, Sokrates, that you think it makes a difference whether the dead man is one of one's own or not, and not that one should just take care whether the killer killed justly or not, and if he did, let it go, and if not prosecute, even if the killer shares your hearth and your table. Because pollution may occur if you associate knowingly with a man like that, and don't purify yourself and him as well, by prosecuting in justice. The dead man was my dependant, and as we were farming in Naxos he was my serf there. He got angry, when he was drunk, with one of our slaves, and he slaughtered him. So my father tied his hands and feet and put him in a pit while he sent a man here to find out from the sacred office what he ought to do. In the meanwhile he neglected the man tied up – he didn't care about him as he was a murderer – and it was no great matter if he did die. And so he did. He died of hunger and cold and his bonds before the messenger got there from the sacred office. My father and the others at home are furious, because I'm prosecuting my father for murdering the murderer when he didn't even kill him . . .

Is this a parody of a law case, or an unusual insight into daily life in ancient Naxos, or a joke, as the final sentence might suggest, or all three? It is about as outlandish as the problems of language and the flux which in the *Kratylos* lead just far enough into the true territory of Sokrates for us to see a little light beyond our amusement and beyond our bewilderment. 'In leaving now,' says Sokrates finally, 'you rob me of a great hope: that learning from you what is holy and what unholy, I might escape the charge against me, by showing Euthyphron had made me wise in divine affairs, and I would no longer invent or innovate in that area out of my ignorance, and I would live better as well for the rest of my life.'

Euthydemos is a dialogue against sophistry and sophistic arguments, interrupted by Sokratic persuasion to true knowledge and true virtue. But it introduces some sophistications of structure. Kriton asks Sokrates who he was talking to yesterday at the gymnasium, and we meet a whole gang of friends, and then Euthydemos and Dionysodoros, two brothers from Chios, now living in exile from Thourioi, but we circle back to them by way of Kleinias and his crowd of lovers. Beautiful boys are not just part of the gymnasium scenery in the dialogues. One knows their friends and their families, and Plato's readers knew their later histories. The casual realism of settings of this kind is not only an attractive fiction, but it gives a certain social density to the questions that arise.

Sokrates educates, as the dialogues are meant to do. He does so in a golden past, if only in its sunset. One is deliberately given the sense of a moment that would not last. Sokrates is in one sense philosophy itself, in another he is irrecoverable, and those he loved most are now old or dead; Plato writes as a survivor, one of the last generation of disciples. Here it is the two sophists who conduct the conversation: they question first Kleinias, then largely Ktesippos, and finally largely Sokrates himself, with the three debates separated by two Sokratic passages in both of which Sokrates proceeds with the true education of Kleinias. Meanwhile the level constantly deepens and in the end simplifies. The sophists get sillier and more entangled, while Sokrates moves rather undeviatingly towards what is simple and deep.

This structure is strengthened and simplified in the *Gorgias*, a work of lucid perfection, the first dialogue which is not only a great man's work but a great work of art. The introduction is swift and novelistic. In the main body of the dialogue, Sokrates speaks first with the great orator Gorgias, whom one rather respects, then about the same matters with Polos, whom Plato mocks, and last with Kallikles, a wealthy young gentleman about to enter politics in a morally ruthless frame of mind. With each change of person the problem deepens and widens, and the moral chasm yawns open as the implications of the earlier positions appear. Finally Sokrates offers a fable, and a persuasion to true virtue and knowledge. This somewhat iron skeleton is filled in with excellently judged variations of style and pace. It is hardly possible to improve on the treatment of this dialogue by E. R. Dodds, to which interested readers should refer.

It is worth noticing, as Friedländer seems to have been first to point out, that Book 1 of the *Republic* uses the same device of a single theme three times discussed in a deepening spiral. 'We are always circling round the same matter,' as Plato wrote in the *Gorgias*. It is also worth considering that Kallikles, whose later history is unknown, may very likely, as Dodds remarks, have come to a sticky end as a young anti-democrat in the late fifth century, and that he may possibly be, as Werner Jaeger suggested, Plato's might-have-been, his suppressed self, which still haunts the darker parts of the *Republic* somewhere below the surfaces of the pages. Kallikles believed in the rightness of might and the justice of power. But Plato had a vision of the Just City, the state itself infused with Truth, Goodness and Nobility, which he expressed in the *Republic*. Later in the *Timaios* it was a world, a universe possessed by the Good. Later again, in the *Politikos*, it was simply Athens. He felt a contempt for Kallikles which one should remember.

The *Greater Hippias* has been given wildly conflicting dates, but on linguistic evidence we should consider it here – roughly where Friedländer always thought it should go. The dialogue begins without nonsense when Sokrates meets Hippias of Elis, the famous antiquarian savant. The subject is the beautiful. But throughout their conversation Sokrates reports what a third party, whom at first he does not name, might interject, and this mysterious figure scores numerous points at the expense of both of them. In general, Plato is exploring that upward scale of things to which he will give classical definition in the *Symposion*. Here one definition leads to another. The mysterious third person turns out to be Sokrates himself in the final arguments. The circles and returns of the argument are diverting and elegantly conceived. Hippias is not taken seriously: Sokrates runs rings round him. Plato was a copious writer, and this dialogue does not seem to me below his powers or outside his interest, but it satisfies less than what was to come.

Lysis is another minor dialogue. These minor dialogues are often quite short; they are like games of chess all played by the same master, but of unequal merit. Or perhaps they are less deep, go less far than the great dialogues; they are more like games of chess and less like works of art, though all Plato's work has both qualities. *Lysis* is about love. The introduction and setting is a clear depiction of young men in love with one another, hanging about a boys' wrestling school to which they entice Sokrates as a wise adviser who knows their fathers. Sokrates tells the story to no one in particular; as a fiction it is subtly constructed, and the awkwardness and charm of the young men is warmly conveyed. Sokrates speaks at first playfully, then lightly to the boy Lysis, then more seriously to the youth Menexenos. We move from loving behaviour to the moral development of friends, to the nature of what one loves in another, and so on; half-truths abandoned in turn lead towards deeper conceptions. The end is the sudden arrival of family servants with younger brothers in tow, to take all their young masters safely home. Women were not at all free to wander alone in ancient Athens, hence Plato's world of men and boys. Even boys were free within stricter limits than modern homosexuals imagine.

In the *Menexenos*, the serious arguer from *Lysis* has a dialogue of his own. Menexenos was kept out of politics only by illness, and in the dialogue named after him he represents youthfulness, thoughtlessly busy about public life and oratory. All the same, Menexenos was sufficiently a friend to be present at the death of Sokrates. The dialogue is very unusual, since it nearly all consists of Sokrates giving, in a version he attributes to Aspasia the mistress of Perikles, the annual public speech to commemorate the Athenian war dead. What is odder still is that this speech fits a date in the eighties when Sokrates was already dead. The reference to Aspasia is therefore a joke. Indeed, the whole performance is a virtuoso piece of parody. It is an extremely sarcastic imitation of real Athenian rhetoric, and at the same time it is a stylish and moving speech.

This is by far the funniest of Plato's dialogues, and the most savage. The Athenians are praised for their noble origins, all being the children of Mother Earth, and their good luck in having plenty of gods to worship, and for their everlasting constitution 'which some call democracy, and others whatever it may be, which is really perpetual aristocracy with popular approval'. Some serious points are made about freedom and virtue, and the humour of the unserious passages is deadpan. As oratory, the composition is masterly. Plato is doing what orators do, only doing it better, and for a joke. The Athenians are assured that Greek civil war never happened by malice or envy, only by bad luck. They are congratulated for the perfect purity of their hatred of foreigners, and for liberating the king of Persia. Plato's *Menexenos* contains the most powerful pieces of sarcasm about ancient Greek politics that have survived: they cut very deep. Yet much of it is amiable, all of it is sparkling, and some of it is genuinely philosophic.

In the *Meno*, Sokrates meets a grand Thessalian nobleman in the house of Anytos. Meno in later life is recorded by Xenophon as a mercenary general of poisonous awfulness, and it was Anytos who prosecuted Sokrates. In the dialogue itself, Meno is not utterly charmless, nor is Anytos as sinister as one might expect, but we are being shown, as in the *Gorgias*, the wrong principles from which these wicked men had, as it seemed respectably, and as it seemed innocently, set out on their dark journey. The later history of Plato's characters is often meant to be considered as underlying the subjects of discussion. Here the main questions are whether virtue, which also means decency, moral soundness, physical courage and patriotism, can be taught, and how it is that politicians are incapable of educating their own children. The argument proceeds through the refinement of successive definitions. The idea that virtues should simply be listed and discussed empirically, which Aristotle adopted, is considered but discarded. Some sharper remarks and sarcasms in the *Meno* seem to express the same scorn that Plato felt in the *Menexenos*.

Phaido is one of the great old warhorses of European education. It describes the conversations of Sokrates on the last day of his life, and describes his death by poison. As fiction or as biography, it is a sober and most moving document. One loves Sokrates and feels his magnetism more than that of any character in the Greek historians or in tragedy. The women led away weeping and the unemotional gaoler with his rough kindness make the scene poignantly real. I do not believe that on the level of argument and debate we are meant to be overcritical, but the arguments are suggestive and even beautiful. Sokrates dies believing tranquilly that his soul is immortal. However his belief is argued and expressed, Sokrates dying is magnetic to us. He himself is the central 'myth'. In the *Meno*, Plato had already ventured into eternity, and handled the transmigration and immortality of souls in a way I take to be teasing and serious at once. *Phaido* is a fuller statement.

'Were you with Sokrates yourself, O Phaidon, on that day when he drank poison in prison, or did you hear about it from someone else?'

'I was there, Echekrates.'

'What did he talk about before he died? And what was his death like? I should be very very glad to hear. No one from Phleious ever goes to Athens now, and no stranger has come here for a long time from that direction, who could tell us anything precise about it, except that he died by taking poison; no one had any more to say about it than that.'

'Did you not even hear about the trial and how that went?'

'Yes, we were told about that, and we were amazed that it was some time ago, yet he seems to have died long afterwards. Why was that, O Phaidon?'

'It was a stroke of fortune, Echekrates. It happened that the day before his trial the prow of the ship the Athenians send to Delos was garlanded.'

'What ship is that?'

'The ship in which the Athenians say Theseus went to Crete once upon a time with the fourteen boys, and saved them and was saved. They promised Apollo then, so they say, if it came safe home, to send an embassy to Delos every year ...'

The small point may be worth emphasizing that the innermost subject of Plato's dialogues is usually lightly touched in their opening

words, whether it is beauty, virtue, love or death. And it is clear
enough that philosophy for him means teaching: it means education
in goodness. The ship is symbolic in more ways than one, as well
as being real, and Sokrates like Theseus 'saved and was saved', and
Apollo himself makes the last days of Sokrates sacred, a mysterious
god-given gift. The simplicity of these devices somehow adds to the
sense they convey of the seriousness and depth of Plato's writings.
The effect of the denser techniques of modern writing would be less
solemn. It is a great part of Plato's power that what he has to teach
is in the end simple and most serious. The dazzling comedy and
surface texture of some of his writing, and the brilliant abundance
of his arguments, are less central.

Sokrates discusses poetry. He is no poet and no story-teller, he
says. But the readers know that his poetry is his life, and the story-
telling in which he disguises and expresses his final meaning is
masterly. It concerns the duty of life, and the goodness of death.
'We humans are set here at a kind of guard-post, and we must not
run away.' He is not really debating the immortality of the soul or
the nature of the life to come, but Plato is showing how ready Sokrates
was for death, and what beliefs or what truths enlightened such a
man at such a moment. He appeals to Orphic religion and to the
Mysteries, a subject of which we know almost nothing but hints.
Rational objections are admitted, and soberly refuted. On a level of
debate, the procedures of this dialogue can be criticized, but its
progression is masterly, and as a portrait of Sokrates that deepens
and clarifies, it is convincing. One does not end a reading of it
convinced that the soul is like breath or smoke, or that the body
and soul are like an instrument and its music. To the hallowed
Sokratic procedure through concepts and definitions Plato's attitude
is ambivalent and ironic.

Plato's *Krito* is a minor dialogue set like the *Phaido* in prison, and
has something of the same solemnity; in it, Sokrates refuses to escape,
and discusses the sanctity of law. This dialogue is brief: it is a poor
relation of the *Phaido*. As Friedländer has put it, in a sympathetic
but philosophically scrupulous reading of the *Phaido*, 'Wherever the
lines of life are extended beyond all possible experience, Plato in
the solemn language of ancient tradition employs a myth that
complements these lines and reflects back on life itself. Previously

anticipated at the earlier stages of the *Phaido*, the myth finally
becomes autonomous on the largest possible scale.' I do not myself
think that Plato's pupil Aristotle, who was conceptually stricter, and
technically probably a better philosopher, offers any real improvement
on this all too human method.

The *Symposion* is the greatest literary masterpiece of all the
dialogues, and because of its comedy and unpretentiousness, as well
as its wild originality, it is the most readable and acceptable to
modern readers. It is a conversation at a dinner party, in the last
great days of Athens, when Aristophanes and Alkibiades were young
and happy, and the poet Agathon was flushed with his earliest
success. The dramatic date is 416, when Sokrates was fifty-three,
Aristophanes in his thirties, and Plato a boy too young to be present.
The introduction makes it plain that this is a second- or third-hand
account: in fact it is what we had been hoping for, a work of fiction
that liberated all Plato's inventive powers. Nor would it be wise to
underestimate this dialogue as a piece of philosophy.

After dinner, the friends have agreed together to make speeches
in favour of love. Phaidros, as a man of letters and an aesthete, speaks
with literary eloquence and numerous quotations from the poets.
'And with these words I maintain that Eros is the oldest and most
reverend and most sovereign of the gods for the happiness and the
virtue of mankind in life and in death.' The next speech is a piece
of sophistic rhetoric in praise of the idealizing love of boys. It is by
a certain Pausanias, whose language is an exquisite tinkling music
which alas is in the end as soporific as sheep-bells, but the content
of his speech is amusing. Eryximachos, who speaks third, is a natural
scientist and a medical savant: but he is also guyed for his facility
in producing vast and useless general laws which pretend to the
authority of science. Sir Kenneth Dover has noticed in him a
pleasingly absurd resemblance to Teilhard de Chardin. Aristophanes,
who a little earlier was unable to speak because of hiccoughs, is now
warned by Eryximachos to speak seriously.

He begins smoothly, but with sparkling charm. His style is informal,
almost casual, but below the surface perfectly controlled. He gets
funnier and more captivating as he goes on. This, if anything in
Plato's *Symposion*, is a real portrait. Once upon a time mankind had
three sexes: male, female and androgynous. People had four hands,

four feet and two faces, until Zeus split them down the middle for threatening the heavens, and now each of us seeks through the world for our lost half, into which, before we were 'split like flatfish', we naturally fitted. If we behave badly, Zeus will split us again and leave us one leg each. If we are religious and good we may regain our old shape, and meanwhile Eros brings us as close to that condition as we can get. This speech is delivered evidently with a straight face.

'This speech of mine, Eryximachos, was different from yours, so as I asked you, please do not mock it, and we can see what each of the others has to say. Or rather both the others, because Agathon and Sokrates remain.' 'I will obey,' said Eryximachos, 'because your speech gave me pleasure. If I did not know Sokrates and Agathon were specialists in erotic matters, I would greatly fear they might be lost for words, because so much of every kind has been said; but as things are I have good hopes.'

Sokrates tries to engage Agathon in a philosophic dialogue, but Phaidros wants a speech, and a speech he gets. Agathon is elaborately mannered, he talks like the music of a minuet. His Eros is as young and beautiful as himself, and the speech is half joking and half serious. He shows the strong influence of Gorgias, and its concluding sentences are prose poetry. 'Provider of mildness, exiler of wildness, generous in kindness, miserly in unkindness, graciously good, thought of the wise, wonder of gods, ... ornament of all gods and all men, most beautiful and best of leaders, whom every man should follow in noble celebration, joining in the song he sings, that enchants the intelligences of all the gods and of all the human race.' As a stylistic exercise the whole speech is a piece of parody.

Sokrates remarks mildly that all these speeches have been lies. He starts to question Agathon about Eros, and the desire of the beautiful and the good. He then tells of his own instruction by a holy old woman called Diotima in Eros as a way from humanity to the divine. The beautiful is desirable and it leads through human sex to earthly immortality, and through philosophy and poetry to immortality of fame: but love leads in the end to the mystical contemplation of absolute beauty. This is the doctrine that Sokrates has accepted. At that moment Alkibiades bursts into the house with a garland for Agathon, and we come down to earth with a thump.

Alkibiades makes a speech of brilliant, drunken cleverness, not about Eros but about Sokrates as a lover who refuses earthly seduction. The story is funny and very frankly told. Sokrates is praised for a godlike ability to enchant, for complete self-control, simple high-mindedness, genuine mysticism, courage and wisdom. Mysticism is perhaps an exaggerated word, though there are some touches of it in the *Symposion*. Sokrates stood stock-still for a day and night in the open air 'puzzling out something', we are not told what, 'and he stood until it was dawn and the sun came up, then he went away after praying to the sun'. This is at least a symbol of something mysterious.

The party ends as the guests fall asleep. When the recorder wakes again, Sokrates has just finished proving to Agathon and Aristophanes that comedy and tragedy should be the art of one and the same poet. 'Being compelled to this conclusion, and not quite following the argument, they nodded off, and first Aristophanes slept, and then when daybreak had come so did Agathon. So Sokrates, having put them to sleep, got up and went away about his usual business; he washed and went off to the gymnasium, and spent the rest of the day as usual, and having done so he went home again in the evening to rest.'

The *Republic* is another very famous dialogue, built up from a minor one, which survives as its first book, to a huge set piece. Its setting and its characters are full of political meaning. Its arguments are tantalizing and its fables fascinating. It takes place in a house in the port of Athens a year before Plato was born. After a fierce argument about might and right in Book 1, with some suggestion, I think, of destructive and alien ideas in contrast with ceremonial religion and peaceful old age, because we know and Plato knows where those ideas led, he settles down for a long, continuous discussion of the good man and the just city. His utopia is alarming and his metaphysics are intoxicating. It is all an essay in how the state might be governed and man as a citizen governed by the vision of goodness and truth. I must here admit that this dialogue has been partly ruined for me by the need to read it for examinations both at school and at Oxford, so that I still feel coldly about some of it.

But it is surely a masterpiece of writing. It is more constructive than his earlier works; a critic is free either to appreciate or to distrust the great increase of intellectual imagination, of sheer creativity, in Plato's work from this time on. The *Republic* as a work of art, which among other things it is, greatly increases Plato's range and scale. Some elements in the *Republic* derive from the *Gorgias*, but the *Republic* develops them much further. It is subdivided into ten books, not necessarily by the author. The argument flows this way and that, slowly and fully. It cannot be read at a sitting, but if one reads too slowly one loses the thread. The central images of the city and the vision of goodness, which one is supposed to achieve at about fifty, the cave of illusions, and the wonderful and frightening fable of the fate of the soul, are very seriously intended, and yet none of them is to be taken literally. The last part of the work, except for the final myth, does not offer deeper or simpler insights. We have reached the Good in Book 7, but Books 8 and 9 discuss only the degeneration of the state and of the soul of man. Perhaps Plato thought later that his *Republic* was almost too loosely imaginative. It was certainly followed by more severely argumentative works, his *Parmenides* and his *Theaitetos*.

In *Parmenides* young Sokrates with some of the *Republic*'s characters meets old Parmenides and Zeno. This is another fiction, of course, and it is introduced as the retelling of a story told in the past. In the first part, Parmenides criticizes the so-called Platonic theory of Ideas, by which a hierarchy of ideas as of values has greater intensity and reality than the quotidian world of our normal experience. I do not think Plato ever meant more by this notion than to indicate how human beings ought to seek for goodness and truth, and might arrive in their direction. His forms and his Ideas are only one of several ways of expressing what he has to say.

In the early part of *Parmenides*, critics see him as self-critical or as honestly answering objections. The second part of *Parmenides* is a dusty wrestling-ground, a succession of vulnerable metaphysical arguments that lead finally to insoluble conundrums. Here the point to notice is that Sokrates is a silent observer. His presence implies his criticism; it is as important as the silent presence of Anytos for most of the *Meno*. Even Paul Friedländer ties himself in knots over the *Parmenides*, and speaks with gloom of 'the fallacies, some certainly intentional, which are strewn throughout'. The interest of the dialogue was obviously intended to be almost purely technical. It was no doubt a teaching instrument in a school for philosophers. One can get little pleasure from it.

The *Theaitetos* is presented even more starkly. In the introduction the scene is Megara: Eukleides explains to Terpsion how he met Theaitetos being carried ashore and taken to Athens, dying of wounds and dysentery after the battle of Corinth in 369 B.C. Eukleides has a written account of a conversation between Sokrates, Theaitetos and Theodoros, and he reads it. The dialogue he reads has no fictional or dramatic element at all. In ancient times, this circulated without even its introduction; that may have been added, not impossibly by Plato, in memory of dead Theaitetos. We are told he did well in a battle, and that Sokrates in age had met him as a boy and thought well of him. That would make him about forty-five when he died. The setting at Megara must have something to do with mathematical philosophy. Theaitetos really was a distinguished mathematician, though Eukleides is not the famous Euclid, but Plato's host in 399, a friend of Sokrates with an interest in logical paradox that derived from Parmenides. In the dialogue itself, Sokrates is just off to inquire what charge has been brought against him. He remarks how badly philosophers always perform in court.

Theaitetos is introduced in the gymnasium where Sokrates has been talking about him to Theodoros, a mathematician from Kyrene. What is knowledge? What is in common between all kinds of knowledge? One definition is criticized but that does not lead at once to another, as it used to do in the earlier, simpler dialogues. Theaitetos tries to apply a mathematical analogy, he is a lively and excellent pupil; he even looks like Sokrates. The old man is a midwife to his intellectual labour pains. Perhaps knowledge is just sense perception? Man the measure of all things, the world a flux, paradoxes rampant? The arguments are sharp, confusing and numerous, and the boy finds them so.

Sokrates then discusses Protagoras in detail, but even here his role is plainly ironic. The *Theaitetos* is a series of unexpected shower-baths of cold water. It ends, of course, with moral and philosophic knowledge. Its construction is tight, but sometimes puzzling. It is an attempt to embody philosophic education, and in that way to be itself the answer to the deepest questions it handles. In an ironic and deliberately clever dialogue, which dares to mimic the breakdown of argument and conversation at one moment, the reader is meant to learn by example what philosophic knowledge is like and how it is attained. On the level of theory, Sokrates offers many refinements, but no true solution. Is knowledge truthful opinion? How do we learn? Are our pieces of knowledge like birds, some flying about in flocks and some perching alone? True opinion is the object of the best court rhetoric, but knowledge is something else. Is knowledge reasoned true opinion? The soul is not an aggregate of elements, and the good, the true, the Idea which is the object of true philosophic knowledge, has a unity as the soul has. The *Theaitetos* rather reaches this perception than argues this conclusion. Plato believed that knowledge went beyond reasoning.

The *Phaidros* is more easily digested by the average man of letters than the *Theaitetos*. Its setting is pleasant, in idyllic country outside Athens; it discusses the nature and power of rhetoric, of love and of the soul, and mostly consists of three speeches, the second two being by Sokrates. Phaidros has a copy of a sophistic speech by Lysias which he wants to recite but Sokrates makes him read. It argues that lust for a boy does less harm than love. Sokrates thinks it stylish but absurd, but he loves speeches, and Phaidros blackmails him by threatening to cut off supplies, into making a speech of his own. He argues in a sober piece of oratory that such lovers as Lysias are crazy and do harm to their friends. But he says the speaker of his speech is a subtle fellow, and really in love all the time. Sokrates then feels he has blasphemed against love, and offers a speech of recantation. His second speech is about madness, divine possession, the state of lovers, and the immortal nature of the soul, of which, having argued it, he goes on to speak in fables of great imaginative power. From lovers and their souls he moves into high flights of philosophy and mysticism.

The story-telling is as bold in the *Phaidros* as in any of the speeches in the *Symposion*, and the quest is as warmly excited, though the mood and language of this dialogue are less astringent. 'This recantation, dear Eros, the noblest and best we are capable of, is dedicated and done for you, but Phaidros forced it to be said in somewhat poetic language and so on. So in forgiveness of the past and graciousness for the present, kindly and mercifully do not take away my art in love which you gave me, nor cripple me in anger, but grant me even more than now to be honoured by the beautiful.' But the *Phaidros* gets better as it goes on, and its playful tone yields us some pleasant pages. From the nature of rhetoric and the need to base it in true knowledge we move to the methods of Sokrates and their logic, and to other methods. Perikles is highly praised, with the influence of Anaxagoras underlined: a rosier view of Perikles than Sokrates revealed in the *Gorgias*. At the end of the *Phaidros*, Sokrates praises the living word against the book.

'The productions of painting look like living things, but ask them a question and they maintain a solemn silence. The same is true of written words. You might think they understood what they are saying, but ask them what they mean and they just give the same answer over and over again. Anyway, once something is in writing, it circulates equally among those who understand the subject and those who have no business with it. It can't discriminate between its readers. And if it gets badly treated or unjustly abused, it always needs its parent to come to the rescue; it is quite incapable of self-defence or self-help.'

No Greek writer ever wrote a book so close as Plato's to the living word. The variety and abundance of his writings have a missionary intention like that of the living Sokrates: they are meant to be inspiring and life-giving. The *Phaidros* ends with a curiously memorable prayer: 'O beloved Pan, and other gods who are here, grant me to become inwardly beautiful: and whatever I have outwardly to be in keeping with my inner self. May I consider wisdom to be riches. And let me have so much gold as only a sound man could well bear.'

Timaios was the beginning of a vast, unfinished undertaking, a trilogy of dialogues. But the *Kritias*, the second one, remains in an unfinished state, and the third was never written. It was all meant to be a history of the world from creation to political corruption, a cycle sketched in the *Republic*. The main speaker, Timaios of Italian Lokroi, is a Pythagorean. Like most accounts of the origins of the world, this one begins with a myth, but the myth is noticeably Platonic; the creator's action is determined by the eternal Ideas, which he observes and imitates. Plato then plunges us into an honestly intended and most interesting treatment of the mathematical foundations of natural science, a theory of molecules and elemental structure. From this he moves to the physical and spiritual structure of man. Scholars of Plato find this dialogue extremely interesting, and intellectual historians show its enormous influence, yet it is not read today as much as it merits. It is full of extraordinary and powerful conceptions. The *Kritias* shows that Plato was by no means empty of inventiveness at this time, but he abandoned this deeply creative work to write about politics and the dangers of hedonism.

Plato's *Politikos* (*Politician*), uses a clear logical method, which it states in advance, to examine the nature of the statesman. True knowledge turns out to be more valuable than knowing a code of laws. In the *Sophist* he proposes to define sophist, politician and philosopher. One would like to hear this last definition, because so far it has been almost a principle of method for Plato to produce Sokrates himself as philosophy incarnate and the embodied answer to ultimate questions, the motive power of moral education. Readers may feel that was Plato's strength. Sokrates still takes part in these late dialogues, though with more emphasis on his logic than on his humanity, but the promised definition of the philosopher is never given. Was the promise never serious? Was it irony, or an old man's forgetfulness? The interest of Plato in method is underlined by the characters in the *Politician* and *Sophist*; they include Theaitetos and Theodoros and a friend of Parmenides.

Philebos sets out with no nonsense to discuss perception and pleasure. This is one of the continuing leitmotifs of Plato's dialogues, and some scholars have seen in the *Philebos* the end of an evolution, a final statement. I follow the reservations about this view that Terence Irwin expressed. Plato is a less systematic teacher than one might suppose, and his treatment of pleasure is neither one coherent view nor is it a linear evolution. The best clue to his attitude, aside from *Philebos*, is perhaps in the ninth book of the *Republic*, in which the hedonist has to choose philosophy because philosophers have most pleasure. This is a gleeful paradox. There is no touch of Calvinism in the air of Athens; Plato is joking.

The *Philebos* is austerely constructed: it follows the line of more logic and less fiction. Pleasure and perception are subdivided and found inadequate for the good life. The problem of the one and the many shows up yet again in the difficult relation between the One

Idea and the multiplicity of this world in our perception of it. We cannot really track down the good in its pure and single form, only in concrete forms. The dialogue has one interesting literary innovation: a great number of pauses, interruptions of Sokrates in mid-sentence, and resumptions of his sentences. This device is not being used for the sake of realism alone, but to clarify a logical development. All the same, the old repertory of Plato's realistic symbolism is still in use. Philebos, whose English name would be Mr Flowercropper, or Mr Ladslove, hardly speaks; he represents pure pleasure. Pleasure, he says, cannot be expected to give an account of itself. Like Kephalos, the old man in the *Republic* who goes to bed when the discussion gets serious, Philebos is one of Plato's most attractive characters, laconically drawn.

The *Laws* of Plato is a highly original, quite new kind of book. If old men ought to be explorers, Plato fulfils the ideal. The *Laws* consist of twelve books of substantial size. The discussion is in some way related to the preamble he wrote for laws he composed for Syracuse. It takes place in Crete. A Cretan, a Spartan and a nameless Athenian walk from Knossos to the mountain shrine of Zeus, and this is their conversation. It is fuller of experience than philosophy, but it goes deep into the religious nature of law. It will not be practicable to follow all the contents of this enormous work in a few paragraphs. The *Laws* is densely full of interest. Under the criticism of laws runs a deeper stream of frightening speculation about what law is and what man is. The nameless Athenian more and more dominates the argument until he broadens it into the nature of education and of virtue, and the influence of law and reason on the soul.

The *Laws* contains some experimental revisions of Plato's old opinions: on pleasure, for example, and on art. That seems to be due to an acceptance of the experience of life, a diminution of irony, and a new sense of order. But the *Laws* is consciously revisionist. In the *Republic*, gymnastics and music trained the body and soul; in the *Laws* the elementary training is dancing which combines the two. After describing the nature of the state comes a discussion of its decline, as in the *Republic*, but after that again Plato begins a new discussion of a utopian city and how to found it. This reversal has interest as a backward criticism of the *Republic*; the foundation is also different, being based here not on philosophic intuition but only on reason and sober self-control. We are coming close to Aristotle's world. We must follow reason, the soul's own leader, and obey that in us which is immortal. Most of the first laws of the new city are about honour. Honour the gods, your parents, your soul, your body, and bequeath honour to your children. Honour the rules of kinship and of friendship and the laws of the state. Honour strangers and above all else honour those who ask for mercy or protection.

From official organization, with which he fills many pages of details, Plato moves on to theology, with formal arguments against atheism, against the supposed indifference of the gods, and against low or corrupt views of the gods. He then gives his ideal city an appalling control system to protect religious purity; the moral, the political, and the universal and divine order are one in this imaginary state, and he nails them heavily in place. He has been criticized for the *Republic*, and now he exaggerates his paradox. We are not, of course, in Athens, or even in Syracuse, but only in a place imagined on a Cretan mountain-top, which is as close as one can get to the throne of Zeus. All the same, it chills one's blood. At the end of the *Laws*, Plato leads us to the one supreme Idea. 'Maybe,' says the Cretan. 'Not maybe, but truly,' says the Athenian. Most readers have felt at some stage that enough of the *Laws* is enough. But it is worth repeating that most of the interest of this dialogue is in complicated and intermeshing details. Apart from these, the *Laws* is a second attempt to conceive an ideal state, a second and a worse failure, and yet a braver, more radical attempt.

There are other dialogues I have still to discuss, since they are outside the series for which we can be sure of objective evidence for Plato's progress. His *Protagoras* is a splendid portrait of the great sophists, Hippias, Prodikos and Protagoras. It is about the pursuit of wisdom; it contains verbal parody and some pleasing ironies. Protagoras makes two formal speeches, including a myth of creation. He believes that virtue is teachable and education increases the harmony of the soul. This dialogue is evidently earlier than the *Republic*, and some of its characters are shadowy. Each of the speeches is followed by discussion, and the analysis of a poem by Simonides stands in place of a third speech. The dialogue is more attractive as a fiction than it is as philosophy, but it does contain some sharp criticism by Sokrates.

In the *Laches*, fathers consult Sokrates about the education of their sons, and the question what virtue is, which concluded the *Protagoras*, arises swiftly. Plato moves from the old Homeric meaning of the word, physical courage, to strength of spirit, or reasoned strength of soul. Finally he rests his definition on knowledge of what is best. The *Laches* is so animated and full of life it is on the edge of becoming a play. Charmides is a cousin of Kritias and a kinsman of Plato's. He is the hero of his dialogue, full of beauty and talent; he is discovered in the dressing room of a gymnasium, where Sokrates 'undresses' his inner nature. The year is 432 B.C., and Sokrates is just home from the battle of Potidaia. The discussion is about moral soundness. The dialogue is charming and not uninteresting as a life study, but it does not cut terribly deep; it is a small clearing up of problems.

Ion of Ephesos was a performer of Homeric poetry and a pseudo-critical pseudo-expert in the meaning of it. He was virtually a sophist, and too vain even to notice the ironies of Sokrates, who discusses his art and his educative powers in tranquilly destructive terms. Some scholars have taken the *Ion* as a contribution to the philosophy of poetry, but one may reasonably doubt if it was so seriously intended. In the *Lesser Hippias*, the sage has just lectured on Homer; one wishes one had heard him. But the critical skirmish between him and Sokrates does no credit to either of them; it is an irony of history that Plato's idea of clever or true criticism of Homer in this dialogue is now of antiquarian interest only. Aristotle, who ought to know, says this dialogue was genuine. Wilamowitz has argued that in that case it was written in the lifetime of Sokrates, as it plays into the hands of his accusers. But I greatly doubt that. It certainly contains moral paradox, but its circulation was surely at first private. It is not the only dialogue in which Sokrates plays the sophist.

In *Theages*, a gently caricatured farmer brings his son to Sokrates to be educated, and the philosopher leads the young man on to love him, to choose him and to learn from him. Critics have worried that the Sokratic enchantment is unintellectual, merely magical. But the same can be said of most of the best teachers one has observed. The dialogue is a moving one, though without great philosophic weight.

The *Alkibiades* is more seriously constructed, but it offends most modern critics. Still, Xenophon seems to imitate it, and it was greatly respected in late antiquity, so it is likely to be genuine. The dialogue is a tense encounter between Sokrates and Alkibiades alone. In its final pages it hints heavily at the fate of both of them. We ought to concede, here as elsewhere, that part of Plato's purpose is historical fiction or biography. The relationship of the two characters is seen at its crisis and seen deepening: this is even more personal than the *Theages*, and more fully articulate. Usefulness, justice, education and self-knowledge are here treated as dextrously as a hand at cards, and the argument with its patches of brilliance and moments of depth continually reflects the two persons. The meeting of Sokrates and Alkibiades in the *Symposion* refers back to this dialogue with a verbal echo. Indeed, the *Symposion* builds on the *Alkibiades* in more ways than one.

Finally, the short *Epinomis* which follows the *Laws* is reported by Diogenes Laertius, an industrious late Roman compiler of the history of philosophy who is sometimes reliable, to have been written by Plato's secretary Philip of Opous, as an appendix to Plato's *Laws*, which this same secretary published from notes or a rough draft (literally, 'from the wax', which means from notebooks). On linguistic grounds that is an acceptable solution, but it remains an uncertain one. *Epinomis* certainly is an appendix to the *Laws*, and has the same characters, but it may be a way of editing scraps left over from Plato's notes.

It adds little to philosophy, yet it has a simplified Platonic tone that I find credible in his late age.

I do not think men can be blessed or happy, except a few of them: while we live that is what I maintain. But a good hope exists for a dead man to attain all things for which in life one would wish to live as nobly as one can, and to die such a death as I speak of. I am not saying anything particularly wise, but what we all in some way know both in Greece and in barbarous countries, that coming into being is difficult for every creature.

This dialogue discusses gods, stars and other such ultimates. It is thought to show Pythagorean influence. My impression is that it has been little studied. The stars and their influence hold the earthly order of things in place. 'Every Greek should understand our special position ... whatever the Greeks accept from barbarians in the end they render it nobler and more beautiful', because the Greeks are under the special starry influences and care of the gods 'and the therapy of their laws'.

It is possible that Plato wrote one or other of the fine verse epigrams attributed to him. They will be discussed in a later chapter; they are not really relevant to his philosophical writings, except to his acute consciousness of style.

Plato is supposed to have reserved certain all-important doctrines which he taught, but which were for philosophers only, and too important to be committed to general circulation in writing. Aristotle claimed to know about them. No account of these doctrines makes any sense. They sometimes throw light on later Platonists, but never on Plato. He was a highly articulate and voluminous writer over many years, and a famous teacher. The tradition about his unwritten doctrines is extremely unlikely to be true. It may well arise from the mysticism he attributes to Sokrates, from the mysteriousness of mathematics to most Greeks, and from the constant didactic teasing of his dialogues. It is certainly not part of the history of literature, and almost certainly not part of the philosophic activity of Plato.

THE ORDER OF PLATO'S DIALOGUES

Leonard Brandwood, now in the Classics department at Manchester, in an unpublished London Ph.D. thesis written some years ago, produced an order of Plato's dialogues arrived at by a computer. The criteria, some of which were first noticed by Lewis Campbell in his edition of Plato's *Sophistes and Politicus* (1867) and by Blass in his *Ancient Oratory* (1887), are the use of certain small phrases, the avoidance of hiatus, and other quite mechanical tricks of language, which appear to have altered gradually during his life. On such criteria, various progressions had been established and overthrown in the past hundred years. The advantage of Brandwood's results is the comprehensiveness of his test and its objectivity. It is briefly discussed in J. B. Skemp's short book *Plato* (1976); the fact that it has not been fully published is a disgrace to philosophers and to classical scholars. Brandwood does not claim to have settled every question with absolute certainty, but he offers us some objective basis. The order of the dialogues I have discussed would be:

GROUP ONE	GROUP TWO	GROUP THREE
Kratylos	*Republic*	*Timaios*
Euthydemos	*Parmenides*	*Kritias*
Gorgias	*Theaitetos*	*Sophist*
Greater Hippias	*Phaidros*	*Politikos*
Lysis		*Philebos*
Menexenos		*Laws*
Meno		(*Epinomis*)
Phaido		(*Letters*)
Symposion		

BIBLIOGRAPHY

J. Annas, *An Introduction to Plato's Republic*, 1981

E. R. Dodds (ed.), *Plato, Gorgias*, 1959

K. J. Dover, *Greek Popular Morality*, 1974

K. J. Dover (ed.), *Plato, Symposium*, 1980

P. Friedländer, *Plato*, 3 vols., English translation, 1958–69

O. A. Gigon, *Sokrates*, 1947

O. A. Gigon, *Platon*, 1950

J. C. B. Gosling and C. C. W. Taylor, *The Greeks on Pleasure*, 1983

J. Gould, *The Development of Plato's Ethics*, 1955

R. M. Hare, *Plato*, 1982

I. Murdoch, *The Sovereignty of Good*, 1970

I. Murdoch, *The Fire and the Sun*, 1977

K. Popper, *The Open Society and Its Enemies*, 1945

J. B. Skemp, *Plato*, 1976

F. Solmsen, *Plato's Theology*, 1941

G. Vlastos, *Plato's Universe*, 1975

Translations of Plato. The fourth edition of Jowett's translation in a number of massive volumes has had Jowett's mistakes removed. Walter Hamilton's and the other Penguin translations are preferable when available. The *Symposion* has been brilliantly translated more than once, notably by Shelley (recently reprinted in *Shelley on Love*).

15

THE ORATORS

One of the first consciously organized forms of Greek literature with its own clear rules and its own systems was oratory, and the prestige of oratory continued extremely high for even more centuries than this book thinly covers. In the last hundred years, this has come to seem a philistine enthusiasm, popular rhetoric a dangerous taste, and a pedantic insistence on rhetoric in literature the deadly growth of ivy that brought down the temple of the Muses. There is some justice in these prejudices, but ancient oratory and rhetoric, which are two different things, deserve a cooler look however brief. In the days when scholars had a better instinctive grasp of the ancient languages than they have today, they had read the orators much more widely and deeply than we do. At their best, the Greek orators have a powerful force of language, and even a force of human passion, which can still kindle the historical imagination of young people, and which the formal oratory of every great age of literature has imitated.

In the course of time, rhetoric came to mean something florid, something obesely wordy, in our language. Yet the style of the most Tacitean historians is even more closely controlled by rhetoric than those more elaborate styles which also flourished in the Renaissance, let alone the solemn, parliamentary oratory which has flourished since. But rhetoric has always been a matter of taste, a more profoundly personal matter than scholars admit. The English style of the early Royal Society is something Plato would have applauded. On the other hand, we have a letter from a Mr William Woodfall to Lord Auckland, written in 1799, about a speech by the Bishop of Landaff: '... and, I think, his Expressions and mode of Comparison between "the ripe and rich fruit of the British Constitution, Laws, and Government, with the pestilential vapours of the Tree of Liberty, productive only of the Apple of Sodom, fascinating to the Eye, but bitter to the taste, and destructive of all political existence'' equal to anything we meet in Demosthenes, Cicero, or any of the greatest Orators ...' The Bishop's style appears to have been Cicero rewritten in bad taste. Greek rhetoric entered modern history through Cicero.

Cicero in Latin gives the impression of a perfect engine or instrument of expression, with a marvellous range of tones, that was seldom put to any sensible use: there being perhaps little sensible use to which such an ideal instrument could in fact be put. In this he reflects a reality that goes back to the Greek world. In his last years, he wrote with depth and brilliance about the great Roman orators and about the art itself, but his motive was profound regret and nostalgia, the grand art of oratory having perished, so he believed, with the power and importance of the senate in which it was exercised. In Greek life just the same is true, but with notable differences.

Oratory as a fine art arose directly from the conditions of direct democracy. It was the conscious, persuasive manipulation not of a crowd or a mob, but of the sovereign people, either in the people's courts of justice or in its ceremonies or in its assemblies. There is also a pre-rhetorical rhetoric; there are tricks and devices in popular language, and some organization, some oratory, in illiterate societies. The Greeks recognized it in Homer. But the full art of oratory was born and died with the Athenian democracy. Its bad genius or its disgusting element lies in the word 'manipulation', which uses 'persuasion' as a stalking-horse. Court rhetoric lived on, but there is something surreal about it, as about one perfect limb on an otherwise paralysed person.

It has been necessary to postpone the fuller treatment of oratory until now, even though we have observed its beginnings in Solon, in Perikles, and in speeches recorded or invented by historians. That is because history and philosophy have a degree of intellectual and even chronological priority, the great moment of oratory being the age of Demosthenes, the youngest of all the famous ten orators of Athens, except for Deinarchos. This list of ten may well have started as a list of nine that ended with the democracy and had Demosthenes as its last and greatest name (see below). If Deinarchos had been added to show how after maturity comes decadence, the addition would have been well conceived.

Sophistry, political philosophy, the art of persuasion, rhetorical tricks and traditional public speeches are all intermingled in the diverse origins of fifth-century oratory. The spread of literacy meant that one could write a speech for another, and that a skilled man, even a skilled foreigner, could offer for money a speech that an Athenian could use in court. The sophists offered to teach the art of persuasion. Their stock-in-trade was to argue any case in either direction. That is what infuriated Plato, though he was deeply imbued with rhetorical skill and not at all guiltless of paradox. It has always seemed to me in fact that the silly, rather innocent paradoxes and boring cleverness of the sophists derive from philosophers like Parmenides and Herakleitos.

But political philosophy is a less innocent subject, and the result in real life of the political sophistry that Plato opposed in dialogues like his *Gorgias* was indeed appalling. Gorgias himself was a sophist with a respectable interest in rhetoric, that is, in the formal organization of prose and prose rhythm; he is said to have maintained in philosophy the paradox that nothing exists, and if it did we would not know it. The *Helen* of Gorgias is a joke, as he tells us in the last word. It is a dull and ornamental joke. Plato treats Gorgias quite well, and is also supposed to have admired Isokrates; Lysias, who is rather gently attacked in the *Phaidros*, was perhaps no enemy, since as a boy he is present with his father Kephalos and his brother Polemarchos in the first scene of the *Republic*.

Kephalos was a foreigner from Syracuse, the sophist Thrasymachos came from Chalkedon, Hippias came from Elis, Gorgias came from Leontinoi in Sicily. The first written books of rhetoric were by the Syracusans Teisias and Korax, of whom we know little, but Teisias taught Lysias. It is supposed to have been Gorgias who set Athens on fire with the new art. But Gorgias first visited Athens, as an ambassador only in 427 when Perikles was already dead, and Thucydides was already writing. The characteristic style of Gorgias was not unlike Agathon's parody in the *Symposion*. The devices he systematized are often to be found in earlier prose, particularly in the solemn language of early philosophers, but his own influence has been immense.

The style of Gorgias can be easily enough learnt. Diluted with the true rhythms of the spoken language, and mingled with the momentum of passionate truth-telling, this style lies behind Demosthenes and Cicero and Clarendon and Dr Johnson and Abraham Lincoln. Gorgias combines perfect musicality with a crispness of his own, even at his fullest. In our world, the theory of rhetoric has sunk to the level of Hints on After-dinner Speaking: vary tone and pace, end memorably, flatter your audience and so on. But Gorgias was a radical stylist, and his deliberate intention was to raise prose to the condition of a fine art.

That was for better and for worse. Everything he wrote was a *tour de force*, it was an exhibition, it was useless. By hindsight we can see that the greatest prose, Clarendon's or Lincoln's or even Sir Thomas Browne's, has always been written under a certain practical pressure. The praises of Helen by Gorgias, and the praises of reason which they contain, and his *Defence of Palamedes*, are ornamental and clever, like Agathon's speech in the *Symposion* but with less humour. Gorgias, like Perikles before him, composed a funeral speech for the annual ceremony of the Athenian war dead, but it was no more intended for real delivery than the one in Plato's *Menexenos*; he was not an Athenian citizen. To make a display object of a speech for the war dead recalls some lines of W. H. Auden.

> Exiled Thucydides knew
> the empty, meaningless words
> important persons speak
> over an empty grave,
> the habit-forming pain,
> the enlightenment driven away:
> we must suffer it all again.

A quite significant proportion of what we have of Greek oratory had in fact little practical purpose. The speech of Andokides against Alkibiades seems to have been written long after the event. We have already observed Plato's facility in composing speeches. Several short speeches of Antiphon are arguments in imaginary cases for the instruction of his students. Lysias and Demosthenes both wrote speeches about love, which must have been intended only to give private pleasure, though they may possibly reflect a fashion among real lovers for learning from the orators how to plead. 'He that woos his mistress in Roman fashion deserves to lose her,' Dr Johnson remarked, but where love itself is a game with no outcome, the ritual of courting may have an independent life. The Athenian orators wrote imaginary letters, and a variety of display pieces, as well as exercises for students. Even the state speeches of Isokrates were pamphlets meant to be read, not real speeches meant to be delivered.

The subject is further confused by the habit the orators had of adding artistic touches and even new material to real speeches after their delivery. Demosthenes did that in his speeches against Aischines. One must remember that the law system of Athens allowed no appeals, and a speaker who was defending his position and his career in politics by a speech that would be circulated might well wish to add new arguments after a trial or a debate. It is worse still, from the point of view of history of literature, that the authenticity of ancient speeches is rather often doubtful: under the famous names of ten orators we have the work of many, some of them perhaps unknown to us even by name. This confusion goes back at least to the Alexandrian librarians, who catalogued a speech that attacks Demosthenes as a speech by him, and to the circle of Aristotle, who was assured by the adopted son of Isokrates that his father had never written a court speech in his life, and replied that the booksellers had bundles of them.

The list we have of the ten orators of Athens was certainly in existence in the first century B.C., but it does not represent an edition or even an anthology of their works; they survived haphazardly in most cases. It is an odd list: it contains non-Athenians and omits Perikles, though at least fragments of his speeches have survived. The list seems to date the art of oratory from the generation of Gorgias and his influence, although the early comedies of Aristophanes reveal a tradition of oratory already well established, and in many ways like the art that the sophists and theorists of language are supposed to have influenced.

The number ten is arbitrary, and one would expect from the Alexandrians the number nine, as with the nine lyric poets, the nine Muses, and the nine books of Herodotos. But the tenth and last of the orators was Deinarchos, a Corinthian, an enemy of Demosthenes who prospered 'when all the great orators were dead or exiled, and no one else was left worth mentioning', as his ancient biographer notices. He lived well into the third century B.C., and under the monarchies of that time one can easily imagine him being added to the list. He was a pupil and a friend of Theophrastos, Aristotle's pupil. If a list of nine existed before his name was added to it, then the youngest orator on it would have been Demosthenes. To see his work as the climax of the Athenian art of oratory, and his death as part of the tragic catastrophe that destroyed that art by destroying its basis in freedom, would offer a valuable insight. But Aristotle was Alexander's tutor, and Theophrastos lived as he could; one would not expect them to set quite so high a value on Demosthenes.

The oldest orator on the list is Antiphon, a famous right-wing politician of the upper class, and a teacher of the art of argument, who died in the troubles of 411, in which he took a prominent part. He composed court speeches for others, but seldom or never delivered them, until his own trial, at which he was condemned to death after a masterly defence recorded by Thucydides and greatly admired by Agathon. Antiphon was born about 480 B.C., so that he must have been in his fifties before Gorgias visited Athens. His vocabulary was grand, his prose highly controlled in its rhythms, and his composition balanced. He may easily have been an influence on Thucydides. The artificial cases he argued will appear jejune to modern readers, at least in their argumentation. They deal with a death by mistake from a javelin thrown by a boy in a gymnasium, and so on. The speech on the murder of Herodes, who disappeared on shore where his ship had anchored for the night, is more substantial, and has interesting political overtones. The speech on a producer, who killed a boy singer with a drug meant to improve his voice, is bizarre but apparently real. Some fragments of Antiphon may well be by an anti-Sokratic sophist of the same name and generation.

The sweetest thing for any man, gentlemen, is never to run danger of bodily harm, and in a prayer that is what one would pray for; but if one were compelled to danger, then there still remains this, which I think has greatest weight in such a case: I mean, to be conscious that one has done no wrong, and if a tragedy should occur, that it should occur without guilt and without shame, by a stroke of fortune and not by wrongdoing.

It is proper to recall, gentlemen, both the mentality of my adversaries and the way they are approaching things. From the very beginning, they have not dealt with me as I have with them.

This is measured language; it sounds like a man one would take seriously. But he is, as they all are, an orator who knows the tricks of the trade. And this is a world in which every charlatan makes the same claim to be an honest man. Still, Antiphon's voice is compelling, if only because of his generation, rather as most English prose of the right period is compelling. For the ancient critic Dionysios, his prose had a desirable austerity, with 'separate words firmly planted in strong positions, and clauses well divided by pauses'. This style 'does not usually aim at composed periods as an artificial framework, but if it should drift into periodic style, it still seems to carry the mark of spontaneity and plainness'. The persona of the plain man unused to public speaking was an essential weapon of Greek political oratory. Antiphon's style shows few of the linguistic mannerisms and devices of later oratory. Whoever his speakers are, they all take the same tone.

Lysias offers formidable problems. Augustan critics chopped away half the speeches attributed to him, and Sir Kenneth Dover, in a strenuous study published in 1968, demolished a number of others. I take Lysias to have lived from about 459 to about 380, but even this is disputed. His father Kephalos the Syracusan was a friend of Perikles and knew Sophokles in old age. Lysias went for a time to Thourioi, apparently as a boy of fifteen, but had to leave that colony and returned to Athens. Dover's arguments are cogent, and have the merit of disentangling the origins of a confused biographical tradition, but they involve a dramatic date for the *Republic* which one must doubt. We must accept the first festival of Bendis to be precisely dated by an inscription, and that gives the *Republic* a secure dramatic date. Plato uses the festival of Bendis, just before he was born, as deliberately as he uses Agathon's victory in the *Symposion*, to date his dialogue. This means that one must be content not to understand when Lysias returned to Athens. Dover points out that the first datable speech of Lysias we know, the twentieth, can be dated with high probability to about 409 B.C., and the last two, the tenth and twenty-sixth, to 384/3 and to about 382 B.C.

The critic Dionysios believed that the authentic style of Lysias was rather unmistakable because of its extraordinary charm, but no modern scholar would be quite so bold. Dover has made a number of more objective, mechanical and arguably more reliable tests, though as he goes on to point out, the relation between the Athenian client and the foreign advocate, Lysias, whom he consulted, may often have been complex. The advocate could not control the alteration or even the distribution of any writing that passed out of his hands. So it ought not to surprise us that mechanical tests show sometimes more, sometimes less, of genuine Lysias from one speech to another and from one passage to another of the same speech. This difficult situation is the result of his immense popularity as a writer, to which Plato is a witness. Dover has shown that the same problem exists with Demosthenes. In our own language, can one be sure of distinguishing Kipling from authentic George V, whose speeches he wrote?

All this has peppered with ifs and buts any judgement we can make about the works of Lysias and his colleagues. All the same, his style is lucid and attractive. His pleading of a murder case which in French law would have been a *crime passionnel* makes excellent reading to this day. A speech was a performance; it was among other things an entertainment to be valued on its aesthetic merits, even more so in its circulated version than in its moment of delivery. The elegant defence of a cripple in Speech 25 is an example. Aristophanes makes it plain how enjoyable Athenians found the procedures of the courts. I have found the same to be true in modern times. In the famous murder speech, Dover has some doubts about the likely treatment of witnesses, and it looks as if the speech as we have it has in fact been smoothed and a little altered after performance, but in substance this does appear to be an authentic piece of lawcourt drama. Dover's doubt does not go deep or extend far.

The one speech we can say with certainty is the work of Lysias alone is his twelfth, and this is the basis for what unshakable knowledge we have of his authentic style. His brother Polemarchos was murdered by the Thirty, and in 403 Lysias opposed the application of a general amnesty to Eratosthenes, who was responsible. Lysias himself had fled to Megara when his brother was arrested. The speech is damning and bitter, but terribly clear and cold. In narrative Lysias runs swiftly like a fire in stubble, but in appeal and in political denunciation he is powerfully eloquent. He speaks with vehement moral force. His final words are: 'I have finished. You have heard it, seen him, suffered him. You have him: now judge him.'

Lysias is credited with only two court speeches on this scale. The other is the prosecution of Agoratos, a slave's son and an informer, apparently an extremely sinister figure. It was argued before a jury, and long after the crimes were committed, so it was not a murder trial; that would have been before the supreme court. But the tone here is different from that of the attack on Eratosthenes. This reads as a private cry for vengeance; it is passionately scornful. One notices with some alarm that the prison scene, in which wives and mothers and sisters visit the condemned men and hear their solemn demand to be avenged, is very like a similar scene in the speech of Andokides on the Mysteries. These set pieces of emotion had a long life in the Athenian courts. One should recall the pleasing parody in the *Wasps* of Aristophanes.

As an ornamental writer in his funeral speech, Lysias is musical and plays his solemn game with many impressive phrases, but he is a little like Lancelot Andrewes, of whom it was said that he played with his text like a jackanapes in the pulpit – 'Here's a pretty thing', and 'There's a pretty thing'. Lysias on the Amazons: 'They were looked on as men for their valour, not as women for their nature, for they were thought to go beyond men in spirit more than they fell short in appearance.' On the Athenians: 'They thought it a mark of freedom to do nothing under constraint, of justice to assist those who were injured, of fortitude to die if it were necessary, in defence of freedom and in defence of justice.' And again: 'They thought it virtue to chastise a living enemy, but demeaning to be brave against the bodies of the dead.' There is something too mechanical about Lysias and his style, as if his words could be spread over anything whatsoever, like butter. But he was a true friend of Athens and of the democracy.

Andokides lived from about 440 to about 390. He was an upper-class Athenian who got into trouble over a scandal involving sacrilege in 415 B.C. He confessed, alienated his friends, and became a merchant abroad, but in 411 he made a miscalculated move to return, and he was maltreated by the Four Hundred. He also went to prison in Cyprus. He made another attempt to be reinstated at Athens in 410, but returned in the end only under the amnesty of 403. In 400 he was prosecuted again for the old scandal; we have his speech *On the Mysteries* from that trial, and a prosecuting speech has survived among the works of Lysias. In 392 he was sent to Sparta to negotiate peace, spoke *On the Peace* in Athens, was promptly prosecuted yet again, and disappeared finally into exile.

This unlucky man was sneered at by ancient critics for looseness and disorganization in his speeches, but such blame is also praise. The effect of his speeches is that of natural warmth, and if they lack artificial sparkle, one can find plenty of that elsewhere. He was admirably unprofessional as a speaker, and he had a narrative gift that might in other circumstances have made him an important writer. But as things are, when someone told Herod of Athens under Hadrian that his name ought to be added to the ten orators, 'At least,' he replied, 'I am better than Andokides.' By the standards of the age of Hadrian, he was right. But how did Andokides get into the ten in the first place? Kritias, his contemporary, had as many admirers and similar politics, so why Andokides and not, for example, Kritias? Jebb suggested that the reason was his historical interest and the details of his scandal. Dionysios hinted at an interest in the evidence Andokides offers for Athenian dialect.

Isokrates has been greatly praised as a serious political intellectual; it appears that Plato half approved of him, and historians ever since have drawn on him. But the court speeches that have been attributed to Isokrates are not, or at least are never completely, authentic, and his political style is undeniably slow-moving. He intends his style to be quietly cumulative, but one may find it turgid. 'Seeing, O Nikokles, that you honour your father's monument not only with the number and with the beauty of your offerings, but with dances and with music and with athletic contests, yes and with races for horses and regattas for ships ...'; '... so that Xerxes and his encampment sailed over dry land and marched on foot over the sea, he chained the Hellespont, he channelled Athos'. This style is not vigorous, its figures are only for display. Even his sarcasm against kings is lethargic, and his spurs are blunt.

'But remember your worst accusation against the Spartans, that to give pleasure to the Thebans who betrayed Greece they destroyed you who did good to Greece. Do not let this evil now be said against your city, nor these insults in place of the glory you now have.' Too much has been sacrificed for the roundness of every sentence, and the long succession of such sentences is somniferous. Ancient criticism already noticed in him too constant and too ostentatious an effort to heighten the grandeur of his themes. In the time of the Roman satirist Lucilius, Horace's great predecessor, Isocratic style meant pretentiousness. What has been praised in Isokrates has usually been an enthusiasm for literature and a certain largeness of view. If Plato had never written, we might admire Isokrates more. Cicero owes him a great deal.

He lived ninety-eight years, from 436 to 338 B.C. He made rhetorical education respectable, and his pupils included Androtion, Ephoros and Theopompos the historians, and Hyperides and Isaios the orators. None of them, one must admit, is in the highest class of greatness. He was educated by sophists and by anti-democrats, and he was born rich. He believed in a united Greece, and was interested in its cooperation with Philip of Macedon, but without any precise programme. Indeed, his politics, like his prose style, were a closely woven tapestry in which lights and shadows tailed off into each other. His solution to the pressing social problems of the Greek cities was to transform the revolutionary class into a bourgeoisie. He wrote against democracy, but only in one work with any heat, and then at a time when Athens was badly upset by the Social War, the rebellion of the allies in 357–335 B.C. G. L. Cawkwell in the *Oxford Classical Dictionary* gives an admirable and pungently written historical account of Isokrates.

Isaios, his pupil, lived from about 420 to 350 B.C. He is therefore the first of the ten orators to be younger than Plato. He was probably a foreigner, and the speeches he wrote were all meant to be delivered in cases of disputed inheritance. His earliest datable speech was the fifth, in 390, or if that date, which Sir Richard Jebb argued for, is wrong, then not before the seventies. His latest datable speech is at the end of the fifties. He seems to have been preserved for his skill in argument and lucid organization of his cases. He lacks charm, all the same; it has usually been those with a deep interest in Athenian law or in forensic ability who have enjoyed reading him.

His language is less pure and less finely calculated than that of Lysias. He soars into the poetic and drops into the vernacular, un-deliberately, I think, in both cases. Isaios himself may, of course, possibly not be responsible for this apparent unevenness; nor is smoothness necessarily the virtue ancient critics thought it was. Still, he has a momentum. 'When Chairestratos sailed for Sicily, I then foresaw all the dangers that were to come, yet at these men's prayer I sailed with him and suffered with him, and we were taken by the enemy ...'

Lykourgos lived from about 390 to about 324 B.C. He was a states-man on almost a Periklean scale, though in his own lack-lustre century of Athenian history that has not given him the reputation he deserves. He was a financial official for many years with mysteriously wide powers about which we know too little. He greatly increased the revenues of Athens and raised big sums of money from private citizens. He completed the arsenal, rebuilt the theatre, built docks, improved harbours, and apparently greatly increased the navy. He had the first official collection of the works of Aischylos, Sophokles and Euripides deposited in the record office, and their statues placed in the theatre. He was an anti-Macedonian Athenian patriot, and one of the first names on Alexander's black list. He prosecuted often in cases of corruption, once for defeatism and once for treachery. But we have only one genuine speech in full: the prosecution of Leokrates for treachery.

Critics have treated him unfairly. His long quotations from the poets had a deep significance that more than compensated for the disproportion of his compositions. For him and in his time, earlier poetry was the soul and identity of Athens, and in quoting it he appealed to that identity. His severity in prosecution is part of the same picture. 'Things have come to such a pass now that any man who takes the risk and accepts the ill will of defending our common interest is not thought of as a patriot, only as a trouble-maker ... I have not brought this case out of private enmity, but because I thought it shameful ...' It is hard at such a distance of time to make a case for the sincerity of any political prosecution, but some case can be made for Lykourgos.

As for his awkwardness of style in comparison with Isokrates, that may be a virtue. He has even been accused of negligence because he fails to avoid hiatus. That is a late and perhaps over-refined criterion of elegance. Plato conformed more to it as he grew older. But Lykourgos, unlike the more admired orators we have discussed already, was a real political speaker. His style, or what we have of it, is effective. When he speaks of courage he is not inflated but inspiring. Even when he uses the tricks of the trade, he does it soberly and powerfully. 'Be assured that every one of you, as he casts his vote now in secret, will make his own thoughts apparent to the gods.'

Aischines is famous as the political enemy of Demosthenes. He was a clever speaker and a rather successful politician; the times were on his side. But even the three speeches of his that survive do so only for the historical light they throw on Demosthenes, who as an orator was incomparably greater. I have the impression that in the past thirty years the star of Aischines has been rising, partly because of the growing consciousness of scholars that Athenian oratory and politics were a very tricky business, so that the enemies of a great orator deserve a slightly more sympathetic hearing. But his attraction is still largely historical; he is more readable than ancient critics thought he was, and his place in history really does make him worth study, yet one cannot put his praises any higher. He lived from about 397 to about 322 B.C. His political quarrel with Demosthenes erupted in 346, when Philip of Macedon was moving south. It ended in 330, when he failed in a prosecution directed against Demosthenes so badly that he was fined and lost his right to bring such prosecutions. He retired to Rhodes, where he taught oratory.

It would not be possible to describe the quarrels of Aischines and Demosthenes in sufficient detail to make sense of them without explaining the whole history of their times. What was at issue was not simple, and it ought not to be pictured in terms of black and white. As an orator whom one reads, Aischines is hardly convincing. He was a handsome retired actor, and that may be the clue to him. In 336 B.C., the great Alexander himself used an actor as ambassador. Aischines claimed, as most orators did, to speak impromptu and to know no tricks. He claimed not to be an educated man, though he prided himself on quoting poetry, and on the antique gravity of his physical stance. He had a wonderful voice and boasted of it, and, as Jebb wrote of him, 'a certain fluent vehemence'. Jebb went on to accuse him of 'profound want of earnest conviction and of moral nobleness. It is not the occasional coarseness of his style, it is the vulgarity of his soul that counteracts his splendid gift of eloquence.' That is going too far for most modern taste, but Jebb has a point, all the same. It is best to concentrate on the empiricism of Aischines, a poor weapon to oppose to the passionate and continuous art of Demosthenes, but not in itself a dishonest one. They clashed for the last time in front of a jury of a thousand or so, not counting spectators. It was the trial of the century. Aischines was nearly sixty, and if the entertainment he offered was intellectually substandard, it was good theatre all the same.

Now the flood of royal gold has floated his extravagance. And even that is not enough. No amount of money will last long against the demands of vice. In a word, he gets his living not by his resources but by your dangers. And yet what are his qualifications in power of mind or language? A clever speaker and an evil liver ...

I do not find the final invective of this speech, with his enemy aping the Goddess of Persuasion, and the dead of Marathon and of Plataia uttering voices of lamentation from their graves, as powerfully grand as Jebb found it, but nor do I think that the last sentences are quite as bathetic as he finds them. 'O Earth and light! O influences of goodness and of mind, of that education by which we learn to distinguish between noble and shameful things, I have done my duty and finished. If the accuser's part was played well, and adequately to the offence, then I have spoken as I wished; if not, yet I have spoken as I could ...' The trouble with Aischines is that he lacks talent. He is a ham actor.

In the case of Hyperides, we owe a great deal to papyri which are relatively recent discoveries. He turns out to be far better than one might have expected; Jebb noticed his quality in 1893; he was excited by the papyrus fragments, and rightly so. Hyperides lived from 389 to 322; he was thirty when Philip of Macedon moved south, and implacably anti-Macedonian. After the death of Alexander, he led Athens into a war in which the Macedonians were bottled up for a time at Lamia. The Athenian general Leosthenes was killed, and Hyperides spoke at the state funeral of the war dead: the last after-light of freedom and the last solemn music of Athenian oratory make this appear a masterpiece almost beyond its merits. It really is very fine, and finest in its plainest sentences.

We do not owe tears to their fate, only great praise to their action. They did not come to old age among men, they have a glory that never does grow old, they have been made blessed perfectly. Those of them who died childless have left an inheritance to the immortal praises of all Greece; those who have left children have left a trust to the guardianship of a country that loves them. There is something more. If to die is to be as if we have never been, then these men have passed from sickness, pain and everything that troubles life on earth; but if there is any feeling in the world below, if, as we imagine, the care of a divine providence extends over it, then it may well be that these men, who came to the aid of religion in the hour of its imminent desolation, are most precious to that providing power.

There is certainly an influence of Isokrates in these grand phrases, but also of the form itself, a tradition going back to Perikles, and a certain touch of show oratory. But ancient critics valued Hyperides most highly for quite another style, a lightness of touch and a pleasing attractiveness of which we still have little evidence. Dionysios remarks that he 'hits his mark neatly, but seldom lends grandeur to his theme', and yet this modest precision appears nowadays as a greater virtue than sublimity. Hyperides does, in fact, use the grandest of organ-stops, in a passage of his funeral speech where he raises up the ancient dead to greet the new dead. What is compelling about this aged trick is that he carries it off without bombast or inflation of language, without self-consciousness. He is the extreme opposite of Aischines. Even the exclamations of Hyperides are in a way simple, though they are hard to translate effectively into English. They are a relief from a long-drawn-out emotion, like the light foam of a heavy wave. 'A noble and a wonderful undertaking. A glorious and a magnificent self-sacrifice. A soldiership transcending peril, that these men offered for the sake of Greek freedom.'

The most formidable Athenian orator was Demosthenes. The smouldering momentum and the solid crescendo of his speeches, the range of his tones, the second-nature quality of his devices, make him a great artist, if any orator ever was. He mingles simplicity with complication, and the natural rhythms of speech with a vastly extended formal music: musically, Gorgias is like an innocent spinet or an early harpsichord, Isokrates is still as formal as flute music by one of Bach's children, but Demosthenes is like Beethoven. In terms of real music, that would not necessarily be progress, but in terms of oratory it is. In fact the tones and the phrasing of Demosthenes are what all later oratory has attempted to recover. They are audible, with individual differences, in English political oratory.

Sir Richard Jebb praises his lighter gifts as if he were a Cambridge don in the late Victorian age. 'He is adroit with the weapons of irony. His jokes are not jarring, ill-bred, or importunate. When he does pull people to pieces, he does it neatly, with much humour.' But Demosthenes is more formidable than that. Sir Kenneth Dover has shown up the savagery of his deliberate tactics. Demosthenes at his most powerful is a compound of many talents and devices, all of them terrifying.

He lived from 384 to 327, and died by suicide on the island of Poros, with the Macedonians not far behind him. He was the architect of resistance to Philip, and his speeches have been the inspiration of the statesmen of free nations ever since; notably of Pitt and of Churchill. The numerous private speeches that survive under his name contain a number of highly entertaining, lighter court arguments, and often cast welcome light on Athenian life. If Demosthenes had never entered politics, these would still rank him above Isaios and, I think, above Lysias. He would still be one's favourite Athenian orator, if not the greatest, most solemn pamphleteer. But as things are, Demosthenes is almost beyond comparison the greatest of the ten. Burke, Churchill and Cicero have less than his powers. But just as in most cases only a poet can translate a poet, so perhaps only an orator can translate an orator. There is something dusty and didactic about the translations we have of Demosthenes. A Greekless reader might grasp more of his essential quality by carefully considering his English equivalents than by stumbling through translations. Indeed, the same might be true of a number of Greek writers, except that they have no such close English equivalent.

His father was an armourer and a relatively rich man; his grand-father was an architect and his uncle a priest of Pandion; the whole family were people of substance. His mother had Scythian blood, which in terms of temperament was perhaps like Celtic blood in England. He was seven when his father died and had to sue a few years later for his inheritance. The best guide to this complicated story is by J. K. Davies in *Athenian Propertied Families* (1971). It is likely enough that young Demosthenes consulted Isaios, but less likely that Isaios was his teacher. The story that a famous political trial thrilled him as a boy is also likely enough. He became an advocate, he wrote speeches for money and advised clients. But the mass of speeches that go under his name contain at least one (58, *Against Theokrines*), which in fact attacks Demosthenes, and Demosthenes himself apparently wrote speeches on opposing sides of the same dispute, though not in the same court action, at least once. It is hard, there-fore, to know how seriously to take any individual performance attri-buted to him except for the great political speeches. But it is important to realize that he was thoroughly familiar with every trick and device of his shocking trade.

In 355 or 354, at twenty-nine, he entered politics. He did so through political trials, of a kind that played a huge part in the political life of Athens, and had done for a long time. His moment was the aftermath of the war with the allies. One of his first speeches was a fierce attack on the historian Androtion, the pupil of Isokrates, on a question about taxes, and involving a deliberate lack of energy over increasing the navy. Soon afterwards, in a speech against Timokrates, he re-used some of the same material, and reproduced it almost word for word. For better and for worse, he was a professional. His speeches to the people's assembly on increasing the number of persons liable to ship tax, and on an alliance with Arkadia against Sparta, are on technically precise matters that take historians some time to explain. The same is true of his court speech against Aristokrates, which he wrote for a friend, and which dealt with Thracian affairs. In all these tangled matters, the political force and meaning of his speeches are clear. He was an old-fashioned, one might say romantic Periklean, Athenian patriot. What made him a great orator was the course of history, beginning with the increase of Macedonian power in the fifties.

His speeches on the northern city of Olynthos, which Philip first threatened and then swallowed, and his invectives called the *Philippics*, are full of sombre rhetoric. They are frightening and convincing. Even a milder passage has a deadly ring to it.

Do not for one moment imagine that the same things are going to satisfy Philip as satisfy his people. His aim is glory, his ambition is glory. His road is the road of action and of risk accepted: his purpose is the greatest renown in all the history of the kings of Macedon: and he prefers that to security. But his people do not share in those ambitions, they are broken with marching and counter-marching from one end of the country to the other, they are oppressed with wretchedness, they suffer continuous hardships. They are taken away from private occupations and all personal business, and whatever opportunities chance does allow them amount to nothing, because every port in the country is shut up by the war . . .

By a simple alchemy, a closely argued analysis has taken on a powerful rumble, with a few flashes of lightning. The force of his speeches depends on these muscular arguments: it is not just a matter of moving perorations, and the speeches are not symphonic compositions. But beneath their surface one can constantly hear the ghostly noises of more formal composition. The difference from the music of older rhetoric is chiefly that his speeches have a syntactic music and syntactic rhythms, and therefore a lucidity, a rational inevitability, more fundamental than the verbal music of Gorgias. It is apparent even in the quality of his sarcasm: 'What Aischines ought to do is not speak with his hand unemployed, but represent the people with his hand unemployed'; '... You and your friends in their rank, all great tall men, all fine breeders of racehorses; I am not a strong man, I admit, but I am more devoted to you than they are.'

Of his most powerful passages I can arrive at no adequate version, because their syntactic organization is at once elaborate and clear, and the musical rhythms of his sentences precisely outline it.

But at Athens, after Philip has not only ... at Athens it is safe to speak for Philip. And some who were poor are now suddenly rich, and some who were nameless and obscure are now suddenly famous and known, but you are the opposite: you who were glorious are now inglorious, you were wealthy and now you are destitute. The wealth of this city is alliance, it is loyalty, it is good will; and of these things you are now destitute. Because you cared so little, he is prosperous, he is great, he is terrifying at home and overseas, but you are deserted, you are beggars, you are distinguished for poverty and contemptible for your provision.

Demosthenes continued to use the lawcourts for his political purposes, as did his opponents. He was a strong pleader and knew it. He would have recourse rather easily to law: for example, in his case against Meidias, a personal quarrel apparently settled out of court, we have the undelivered speech he must have circulated. As an ambassador he was unsuccessful, and he made less impression on Philip than he did on his home ground. His political line is thought by historians to have been more slippery than appears if one reads only his speeches and his official life. But there is no doubt that his speeches are a great monument to the love of liberty. It is a pity that his funeral speech in 338, after the fall of most of Greece to Philip, has not survived.

Deinarchos is a lesser figure. He fell often into the trap of the long sentence that loses momentum, and even in his more pointed remarks one can hear only harsh and croaking harmonies. Also he exaggerates rather blatantly, and his tone is insufficiently varied. 'This demagogue, O Athenians, this man worthy of death by his own admission if he is proved to have accepted anything from Harpalos, has been clearly so convicted ...'; 'For the wickedest man in the city or rather of all mankind, Aristogeiton, has come to be judged in the court of Areopagus, for truth and for justice.' Demades was a rogue politician of the same period and party, famous for wit. The speech that we have is probably not by him. He was an old oarsman, and a naturally forceful speaker. He led the pack against Demosthenes and Hyperides; he was responsible, therefore, for their condemnations and their deaths. He was executed in 319 for treasonable double-dealing with the Macedonians.

Papyrus fragments have contributed here and there to our massive and confusing evidence for the Greek orators. They offer among other things some excited narrative of a conversation, probably fictitious, in a court case of theft, which is not unlike the narrative of comedy, only less skilful. They offer some bits of an attack on Hyperides by Aristogeiton, a speech in praise of glorious military death that deals with the courage of Achilles and seems to echo philosophy, and some new pieces of writers like Antiphon and Lysias. But it is the anonymous fragments and the less competent speeches on the margins of formal oratory that contribute most.

The art of oratory was ragged at the edges; the fragments are a battle of vehement voices and a patchwork of styles. Apparently fewer orators and fewer speeches were worth preserving for their special merit than the mass of material which at one time was preserved. 'He left them unburied, an act more terrible than tomb-robbing. Those that loot the dead do not compel their bodies to lie unburied, they hide them in the earth. But this man saw to it they had no burial at all.' The exaggeration and the pitiful rhetoric of such a speech as this are counter-productive, as the orators, when they claimed to be unskilled in oratory, understood. All rhetoric, and all oratory but the greatest, are counter-productive.

To put this in terms of information theory, the ratio of signal to noise among the Greek orators is terribly low, and their entropy, the amount of energy wrapped up in their works which is unavailable for effective use, is wastefully high.

BIBLIOGRAPHY

F. Blass, *Die attische Beredsamkeit*, 1874–93

J. K. Davies, *Democracy and Classical Greece*, 1978

K. J. Dover, *Lysias and the Corpus Lysiacum*, 1968

K. J. Dover, *Greek Popular Morality*, 1974

J. E. Hollingsworth, *Antithesis in the Attic Orators*, 1915

R. C. Jebb, *Attic Orators*, 2nd edition, 1893

G. Kennedy, *The Art of Persuasion in Greece*, 1963

D. M. MacDowell (ed.), *Andokides, On the Mysteries*, 1962

E. Norden, *Attische Kunstprosa*, 1921

Oxford Classical Dictionary: see under individual orators; entries written by
    G. Cawkwell, 2nd edition, 1970

Note: The article on 'Prose-rhythm' in the *Oxford Classical Dictionary*, by
K. J. Dover and W. Shewring, gives technical information on rhetoric and a
specialized bibliography beyond the scope of this history.

16

FOURTH-CENTURY POETS

Poetry in the fourth century becomes difficult to follow, perhaps just because the fifth century was later defined as classical, and poets after 400 were neglected and survive only haphazardly, but also, I think, partly because many of the new poets were foreign, and therefore not seriously collected at Athens. We know little about Achaios of Eretria, Aristarchos of Tegea or Ion of Chios, although they were successful tragic poets in the fifth-century Athenian theatre, and even less of Neophron of Sikyon, to whom belongs the nasty distinction of introducing the torture of slaves to the tragic stage. These writers appear to have been smoother and more monotonous than the great poets they jostled for attention, in spite of the occasional wildness of their plots. An exhaustive list of them would pay diminishing returns.

In the course of the fourth century the interplay between literary arts was to become subtler and more intense. Aphareus and Astydamas were pupils of Isokrates, and Theodektes of Isokrates and Plato, but nothing that survives among the scraps of our evidence suggests that what they learnt did them any good as tragic poets. We do know that comedy influenced philosophy, and vice versa, and as comedy still had a life to come, and remained the greatest popular art form, that is a more important relationship. In the fifth century, Epicharmos of Syracuse produced in his own country brilliantly executed plays a little like Athenian comedies. Mr and Mrs Reason were two of his characters, but they seem to have fought like Punch and Judy. Alas, we know little about this lively battle. Sophron of Syracuse, who was later much admired by Plato, wrote popular comedies, called 'mimes', about low life. The fragments are scanty but vigorous. In the most pleasing, witches try to draw down the moon.

At Athens, the comedy that followed Aristophanes tended more and more towards fictions about real life, although the farcical treatment of mythology also remained popular for a long time. It is hard to judge dead jokes, but those of Euboulos (405–335?) do seem extremely dead. Jokes about Euripides continued long after his death, and jokes about gluttony and anti-heroic heroes continued popular. The mysterious touch of poetry, both low and high, which never quite failed Aristophanes, all but deserted the comic theatre in the next generation. Still, something survived, though not it appears in the burlesques. The truth probably is that poetry came and went, with the same flickering lightness that used to be part of London panto-mimes. And somehow it entered into the heart of fiction. The development of comedy in the fourth century was the development of plot. The verse at its best was smooth and harmonious: and as the prestige of philosophy increased, comedy developed a stronger moral bite. The chorus withered away, not at once and not without revivals, until it had become an entertainment unconnected with the plot, a musical punctuation. Burlesque of tragedy or myth continued longest in southern Italy, where the works of Rhinthon more or less correspond to an amusing series of grotesque vase paintings that have survived.

Anaxandrides of Rhodes (400–349?) introduced into comic fictions a type of plot that depended on rape, and therefore on bastardy and amazing recognition scenes in later life, and plots that pivoted on love affairs. Given the powers of Fortune in fourth-century belief and literature, and indeed in fourth-century experience of life, his comedies must have been elaborate exercises in the writer's role as a divine providence, something that affected all romances and all later comedies. It has earlier roots, of course, particularly in Euripides, a wizard-like deviser of fates in his late tragedies. It might also owe something to Agathon. But most of our fragments come from anthologies of moral wisdom; they do not stray far beyond elegance and sonority.

Alexis of Thourioi is supposed to have lived a hundred and five years, from about 375 to 270 or so. He was another elegant and urbane writer on the whole. His plots seem to have dealt with love affairs and confidence tricks, and very occasionally (fifteen out of 140) with mythology. His verse rattles along with creditable comic speed: he is a better orator than most of the orators. Timokles, who wrote late in the fourth century, appears to have been an old-fashioned figure. He descended to burlesque, as Alexis did, and he satirized Demosthenes and Hyperides. He wrote one comedy about a famous local homosexual, whom he presented as Orestes pursued by hag-like aged whores instead of the hag-like Furies.

We have observed the decline of lyric poetry, of which a papyrus text of the *Persians*, an oratorio by Timotheos, offers sad proof. Euripides is supposed to have written the prologue. The influence of drama is evident in these oratorios; tragedy was to Timotheos a malign godmother. In his *Birth Pangs of Semele*, the screams of the heroine were produced with realism. (Lightning consumed her to ashes as she gave birth to Dionysos.) In his *Nauplios* he rendered a thunderstorm on the flute. His Odysseus lamented while the monster Skylla ate up his sailors. This is the sort of writer who makes 'baroque' an insulting word. He wrote in free verse. His contemporary Philoxenos of Kythera was one of the unluckier Greek poets. He worked as a slave in Sparta, and later in the quarries of Syracuse, for too trenchantly criticizing the tragic verse of the ruler Dionysios. Philoxenos was a much-loved poet, and his *Cyclops*, in which the rustic giant hopelessly woos the Nereid Galatea, seems to have pleased Theokritos. The idea of a one-eyed giant singing a solo to the lyre naturally invited parody, which it received, and no doubt the dithyramb, the choral oratorio, was too far gone in his day (436– 379), but Philoxenos shows a true aesthetic sense, and a certain genuine freshness.

The reader may grudge all these shadowy figures even their few pages of commemoration. But hidden somewhere among the verse of this period must lie clues to the big alteration in sensibility, probably a social and historical, not really a literary matter, that divided the fifth century from Menander, and still more so from the Greeks of Alexandria. In the comedy of Menander, something like a bourgeois world held up a mirror to itself. Alexandria was a city of opulence and of poverty, where poets were court officials, and where freedom was only an idea. It is joined intellectually to the earlier writings of the Greeks by a thin trickle of genuine poetry, and by two obscure writers: Kritias the politician and poet, and Antimachos the antiquarian poet.

Kritias was a writer of less merit than importance. His fifth-century dramatic verse was not impressive. His elegies for Alkibiades and to Plato's brothers are lost. His *Constitutions in Verse* may have in-

fluenced Plato and others. Verse was to him just a gentlemanly skill.
His long fragment about Anakreon seems to come from a poem about
the history of literature. The boring and didactic side of his writings
was the seed of the future. Verse was often going to be like his in
Alexandria. Kritias was dead by 403, and it might have been incredible to an observer in that year that Kritias stood for the survival of
the Muses. But belief withered, freedom was lost, literature became a
game, and book-learning hugely increased.

The second of these odd figures, Antimachos of Kolophon, wrote at
the turn of the century. We know rather little about his true merits,
but some of the Alexandrian poets admired him. He seems to have
embellished his treatment of epic themes with lyric and tragic influences. He studied and imitated Homer assiduously; he was perhaps
the first learned poet in the sense in which Virgil and Milton were
learned. 'Literary epic' was his invention more than anyone else's. His
poetry was meant for an educated audience. His long elegy *Lyde*,
which dealt with tragic love affairs in mythology, and was supposed
to echo Mimnermos, had a powerful influence as late at least as Ovid.

It is a relief to turn to the trickle of genuine poetry. We have a huge
hoard of epigrams, tiny poems written in a few couplets; what
survives is an anthology of anthologies, named, after the manuscript
of its final form, the Palatine anthology, and covering more than
fifteen hundred years of these poems, with many false and a majority
of doubtful attributions. In addition we have a few similar short poems
from other stray sources and from papyri, and a substantial number
inscribed on stone. The earliest of these short poems date from before
the fourth century. Gow and Page have sorted out the Alexandrian
and the Roman strata of the Palatine manuscript, but it remains
important to establish what pre-Hellenistic poetry was like.

These little poems have many origins and purposes: they derive
from the epitaphs and the drinking-songs, the dedications and love
messages of an earlier age. Many of the poets who composed them in
the fourth century wrote other works which are now lost. We catch
in the epigrams just an echo of comedy, of satyr plays, of a lost lyricism
or of private life. They are intensely personal, and they seldom pretend
to achieve the plain universality of Simonides. Their fault is to become
precious, which their coexistence in anthologies somehow exaggerates. But their musical language is exquisite – they transmute and

refine the possibilities of poetry – and their small scale, their infinite and infinitesimal variations of diminuendo, express a sensibility as moving as anything to be found in Greek literature. They are the opposite of oratory, and yet more perfectly calculated. In the shadow of the baroque in late antiquity, only the arts of privacy flourished, and the artifice of poetry increased. The sad prettiness of the Tanagra statuettes is a world away from the tough-looking working women in Boiotian figures a hundred years earlier.

Plato, meanwhile, had spoken of the individual soul. 'Even in life, what makes each one of us to be what we are is only the soul; and when we are dead, the bodies of the dead are rightly said to be our shades or images; for the true and immortal being of each one of us, which is called the soul, goes on her way to other gods, that before them she may give an account.' One might well retranslate those words into a Greek epigram, but they come from the *Laws*. Several of the best couplets that we have are supposed to be the early poetry of Plato. The attributions are doubtful at best, but whoever wrote them in his name was a genuine poet. 'Star, you were the dawn-star among the living: dying you are the twilight star among the dead.' Shelley has translated these lines better but a little floridly as an epigraph to his *Adonais*. One should note that the Greeks knew that the morning and the evening star are one and the same; in this couplet and another, Star is a boy's name. 'Star, you are watching the heaven's stars: would I were heaven, looking at you with heaven's eyes.' These short poems are made of nothing, they are the merest wit or fancy, yet their almost bodily elegance makes them indestructible. It is true to say that the rediscovery of Greek epigrams underlies nearly every single one of the renaissances of European poetry, in Italy and France and in England, and as recently as Ezra Pound.

The perfect lyric cadence of these poems in Greek, which like other great innovations in poetry became a manner and a box of tricks that anyone with an ear and a memory could acquire (as Homer learnt his art) must owe something to the practice and revival of archaic lyric poetry. The choral lyrics of the victory celebration of athletes had been pruned away to simple couplets as early as Euripides. Among the early Hellenistic poets who learnt their art in the fourth century, some were scholars, many were women, and nearly all were famous for their lyrics and their lyric inventions.

From Phalaikos comes the lyric form of Catullus on Lesbia's sparrow, from Asklepiades come two of Horace's lyric forms. As for the women, Hedylos of Samos was a son and grandson of women poets; Anyte of Tegea, an Arkadian lyric poet, wrote the first gentle epigrams about animals and the first bucolic or pastoral epigrams. Moiro was a scholar's wife and a poet, Nossis wrote couplets and also probably lyrics. Erinna of Telos near Rhodes has been rightly classed by C. A. Trypanis as one of the best fourth-century poets, though she died at nineteen. Her poem *The Distaff*, written in the dialect of her island, is an unselfconsciously pure and delicate lament for her dead girlfriend Baukis. It was famous in its day, and we know it now through quotations in later writers, but also through a papyrus that gives fifty lines of it. It cries out to be translated by a woman poet.

Of course, public poetry continued to be written, and to be inscribed on stones.

> Pausanias my father raised this stone
> for Hagesipolis his loved son
> whose courage Greece applauds.

The last word includes the meanings of unanimous agreement and applause. The style is deliberately archaic, severe and in the modern sense epigrammatic, but this is a king of Sparta dedicating a statue at Delphi in 380, though the stone that survives is a later copy. Here is another state epigram about twenty years later, from the statue of Epaminondas at Thebes.

> This came from my counsel:
> Sparta has cut off the hair of her glory,
> Messene takes her children in:
> a wreath of the spears of Thebe
> is the garland of Megalopolis:
> Greece is free.

But when one comes to the poem Plato is said to have written for Dion, who died in 354 B.C. at the age of sixty-two, one is in another universe. The Dion poem is a piece of make-believe from the same workshop as Plato's letters. All the same, it may well be a fourth-century poem, and it certainly pretends to be one. 'For Hecuba and all the wives of Troy the Fates determined tears shed from their birth;

for you, Dion, noble, victorious, the gods poured out abundance of hoping; now you lie dead, honoured in your country: Dion who drove my heart mad with eros.' This is a private poem, a scholar's or a minor poet's; having become literary, poetry has ceased to be interesting really, but it retains a certain artifice of tension, a technical pleasure. So much for the bad side of the fourth-century literary movement.

Many of the poems about writers, that began to be written about the time the works of Athenian tragic poets were collected, have a sparkling freshness. Maybe this was the only passionate truth these literary or scholarly poets were capable of, except, of course, for the dominant Alexandrian note of sexuality, with its lamentable, or as some think liberating indifference as to object. The feeling for the romance of writers rather than for their works took on the intensity that literary biography often has today. People were looking for salvation from poetry. The boasting of the fine arts had already reached a high pitch by the time of the painter Parrhasios, whose subtle, almost unearthly paintings are perhaps reflected on the Athenian lekythoi of the very late fifth century. He was from Ephesos, though he worked in Athens. His were the first small-scale paintings to be collected and used by later painters.

> My hand explored the last limits of art,
> I tell you this, a truth you may neglect,
> the boundary is set, no man will pass.
> Yet everything human is imperfect.

The authenticity of this may be doubted, but another couplet is recorded from a painting of Herakles by Parrhasios at Lindos.

> Now you see him, exactly as he came
> to me Parrhasios often in a dream.

This last translation is by Peter Jay. It is not surprising that his Herakles should be dreamlike; his rival Euphranor remarked that the Theseus of Parrhasios had fed on roses, but his own on beef. It was a boastful world. The purely literary epitaphs, at least the later ones, have often an appealing intimacy which drowns out the boasting.

> May supple-footed theatre-growing ivy
> always be dancing on your glittering
> monument, godlike Sophokles:
> and your grave be sprinkled by bull-begotten
> bees and run with Hymettos honey,
> like Athenian wax tablets for ever,
> and your hair crowned with ivy for ever.

This is by Erykios, contemporary with Virgil and Horace. It has a despairing note, the distance of Sophokles is godlike, his grave perhaps neglected, and certainly picturesque; even Athens and Attica are distant. Every type and variation of these short poems had a long development and, of course, they became intimately interwoven. When one strives to disentangle the precise course of every tributary, the result will inevitably be as pedantic as the necessary method.

But the smell of dust that overhangs Hellenistic poetry is partly a result of scholarly activity, not wholly of the admittedly literary quality of the original. These are brief poems and subtle variations, and one should read few of them at a time. The genuinely fourth-century poems scarcely break the bounds of a laconic severity, and they are like inscriptions, meant to be read alone on some ruined stone, like the tombstone of Yeats. Severe as they are, they have all the intensity of romantic poetry, as one can see in a sober version by Peter Wigham of a poem by Perses.

> Artemis,
> This Zone, this Breastband and girlish frock
> Take, votive, from her whom you delivered,
> In her tenth month, of a most harsh childing,
> Timaessa.

In the work of Anyte of Tegea, intimacy somehow creeps into the formality of her lines as warmth creeps into the corners of a room. She is a transitional poet, but I think a very great poet, even on this minor scale.

> To shock-haired Pan and the nymphs who protect the cow-byres
> Theodotos the loner set up this his gift
> Under the look-out peak. Because they gave him ease,
> Worn out in the parching summer, protending,
> In their hands sweet water.

Or this on a hound, for a grave imagined overgrown or for no grave at all:

> And you too perished long ago, by a bush with matted roots,
> Lokrian bitch, swiftest of whelps delighting to give tongue –
> A speckled-throated adder coiled about
> Your light-moving limbs such a corroding poison.

These versions were made by John Heath-Stubbs with Carol Whiteside. Every century since the Elizabethans has found some way of translating Greek couplets, and this is one of the closest modern styles. Alastair Elliot has been equally successful in a translation of the undatable Diotimos, who seems a later poet, to judge by the dramatic complication and the multiple irony of his poem.

> Homing at dusk – the snow falls on them – cattle
> Drift by themselves into the shed.
> Look, still beside the oak Therimachos sleeps
> The long sleep: laid to rest by fire from heaven.

J. W. Mackail, an aesthete with a powerful nose for truffles, had already noticed this poem in 1890. His prose version is: 'Unherded at evenfall the cattle came to the farmyard from the hill, snowed on with heavy snow; alas, and Therimachus sleeps the long sleep beside an oak, stretched there by fire from heaven.' In his critical introduction he has 'the cattle coming unherded down the hill through the heavy snow at dusk, while high on the mountain side their master lies dead, struck by lightning', which is perhaps a preferable rendering in English. But one must not think that words as literary as 'homing' and 'evenfall' are unknown to these poets; on the contrary, they relished them. They were admittedly less sentimental than we are about farmyards, but they had strong feelings about all nature. The translation of Greek epigrams depends on minute details and on a curious combination of extreme subtlety and perfect clarity.

This sense of the landscape and the country and its gods is not far below the surface of the *Difficult Man*, the only complete play to survive by Menander. We have a surprising number of recent additions to his works, all from papyrus, and the *Difficult Man*, the first of the new crop to appear nearly thirty years ago, is not the finest. But its setting is interesting. The god Pan emerges from a cave of the nymphs in the centre of the stage. This is an innocent and rustic world, and Pan is a divine providence of the peasants, but he needs to work at it. On one side lives the Difficult Man, a type rather than an individual, with his daughter, and on the other his ex-wife with her son and a slave, the minister of intrigues. This setting is quite artificial. The village is known, but it was miles from the cave of Pan. The play enacts a conflict and a reconciliation, with sudden wealth to spare, and a climax of feasting and dancing to flute music. It depends on Athenian laws and customs about marriage and inheritance. Menander's comedies were acted in Athens, but they preyed for subject-matter on the countryside, which he treated cavalierly, as much as they did on philosophy, and on tricky law cases. He was fast and funny at his best, and capable of swift changes of tone and of verse texture. He lived from about 342 to 290 B.C.

This is probably the best place to notice the philosophies alternative to Plato's, since they are relevant to every aspect of the intellectual history of the fourth century, even though they left no great literary monuments. The Cynics had followed Diogenes of Sinope (about 400 to 325) and his pupil Krates of Thebes in ascetic simplicity of life, criticism of all illusions, limitation of wishes, and casting away of shame. The strong point of Diogenes was his caustic criticism of bourgeois life, but he survived as a legend rather than a book. The Stoics in the next century borrowed his fire. But Epicurus (341–270), the founder of another powerful and attractive philosophy of friendship, mutual loyalty, and withdrawal from public life, was a fellow-student of Menander as a young man at Athens. These are all philosophies of personal withdrawal, in which the individual is a refugee from the world. The influence of Aristotle and his pupils is no doubt of even greater interest, and we have his books; but he must wait for a chapter of his own. When Menander and Epicurus were students at Athens, Aristotle was in exile of a kind as a Macedonian supporter; they were taught by his pupil Theophrastos, one of whose works has some importance for the development of comedy.

His *Characters* is the brief delineation of thirty character-types, such as the Superstitious Man, the Rustic and the Flatterer. The characterizations are in terms of behaviour; they are highly amusing in places, mordantly conceived, and not long. They certainly owe something to Aristotelian method and to his hard-edged behaviourism. The preface and the moralizing epilogues to this work seem to be Byzantine. Unfortunately, the works of Theophrastos, though this one less than most, are in need of closer scholarly attention than they have yet attracted. Pasquali suggested long ago that the *Characters* is written with no avoidance of hiatus, so is not formally literature. He believed they were notes for lectures, but they are better and fuller than that. Nigel Wilson has suggested to me in conversation that they may have been entertainments, after-dinner performances. I find this view attractive.

But the new interest in types of weakness and general lines of character seems to reflect the practice of comedy, of rhetoric used in court, or, most likely, both, and this interest does look like an influence on Menander. We cannot be certain of the date of the *Characters*, but if, as is perfectly possible, this or something like it predates almost all Menander's work in the theatre, then the *Characters* is an almost uniquely precise example of the usefulness of the new philosophers to a comic poet. At the least, the *Characters* of Theophrastos indicates a climate and an interplay. The idea that character has consequences which can be acted out was an old theatrical and epic convention, but in comedy there are conversions, and character can change or be revealed late. Both Menander and Plutarch found this fact hard to deal with. The Greeks never got far beyond Theophrastos in character analysis.

But Menander was a poet. He was capable and swift in dramatic verse. As dramatic constructions, his plays are not always more brilliant than what we conjecture about his elder contemporary Philemon, but in range of tones and Mozartian spirit he triumphs even in his fragments. Diphilos, another elder contemporary, was a more boisterous figure, at least as seen through the medium of Latin imitations. In his *Sappho*, Archilochos and Hipponax appeared as the lady's lovers. Menander is smoothly humane, but he can be hilariously funny, not least at his most sententious. Being incomplete, alas, his comedies have seldom been tested on the modern stage, but if they were, they might reveal a Shakespearean movement of eddies and subtleties.

> So much is summary: now the detail
> you shall see if you will it: and you will.

The politeness of tone, the excited formality and the idle-looking word-play of these verses, which Menander used more than once at the end of prologues, do recall the Elizabethan verse theatre, which, of course, inherited something from Menander through the Romans and Italians. The prologue, for example, has some significance. It is usually spoken by a minor god, a constellation or an allegorical figure, and in *The Shield* it is spoken by Chance, or Providence one might almost call her, who enters after the first scene to tell the audience she has things in hand. The apparently dead hero is the most rescued and alive man there ever was. At the end of the first of his five acts, before the choral interlude, for which we never get words or music, Menander always, in the five cases where this bit of the play survives, uses the formula 'But drunks are coming: walk out of the way'. He plays with formality in many ways. The central door can be a shrine door or an inn door and the source of a crowd. The altar has more than one use. Stage movement swirls and eddies between monologues and conversation pieces, characters are formally contrasted, the action spills this way and that between one act and the next.

T. B. L. Webster, in a detailed study, sees in Menander the system of exposition (*protasis*), development (*epitasis*) and dénouement (*katastrophe*), to which later critics refer. Whether or not this rather mechanical skeleton is a useful way to anatomize Menander, it is important that the dénouement seems to begin with the fourth act and the last third of the play, and that the number of verses in an act can vary greatly. One need not follow Webster here in seeking an influence of Aristotle. All that sensible man said was that plays should have a beginning, a middle, and an end. He also said comedy uses probable events and chance names, but this does not mean that when Menander drew his most improbable events from tragedies the audience knew he was thinking of Aristotle. As for names, he appears to use the same name for a similar character from one play to another: a helpful device in a theatre of masks. This and some other features of his staging appear clearly in a mosaic at

Mytilene on Lesbos, which shows how his plays were enacted fifty years after his death, when their characters were already famous.

The moral atmosphere of Menander, whenever he becomes serious, is Aristotelian, and the characters criticize one another from the point of view of Aristotle's common-sense ethics. It is important to notice that Menander's characters are a projection of his plots; the plot is not secondary to them. One character, one stage moment and above all one piece of verse may be more serious than another. The figure of the slave tutor or governor, whose charge has grown up, is an interesting mixture of learned quotations, eloquent and educated sentences, and in certain drastic situations much sharper and more slave-like speech. Slaves in Menander seem to look forward to freedom as virtue's reward, and one at least seems to have pondered in a monologue the slave's duty of loyalty. In general, as W. Ludwig has pointed out, providential chance and moral consequence rule these plays, and poetic justice is victorious. That is the true, everlasting religion of comedy, and no philosopher has improved on it.

Menander is said to have written 108 plays, of which we have ninety-six titles, but he often used two alternative titles for one play. We have almost no idea of their chronology. His first, *Orge*, was produced when he was extremely young, in 322/1 B.C., at the Lenaian festival, and the *Difficult Man* in 317/6; his first victory in the great Dionysia was in 316/5. So at least we can know something about his earliest use of stage conventions. The five-act system, which occurs both in the *Difficult Man* and the *Woman of Samos*, with the dénouement starting in act four rather as the car chase always used to be in the seventh of eight reels of the more exciting films, was adopted early. He is said to have taken care over his plotting, and then fitted verses to the plot rather swiftly. His powers of agility in verse are remarkable, and make him extremely hard to translate even into prose. Characters interrupt one another or at times themselves, and his flair for reported conversation and for parody is like Plato's. One would greatly like to know if that was an influence of comedy on Plato or of Plato on comedy; very likely it was both.

Menander's narratives, his messenger speeches, are virtuoso performances. In his time, comedy has sucked the marrow out of tragic verse and left it dry. Not all his allusions to tragedy are serious by any means, but when he chooses he can use a tragic tension of tone, even though the basic purpose and momentum of his plays are purely comic, and their effect overwhelmingly sunny. If there are undertones of shadow, those are still part of the comedy, as they are in Watteau's paintings or the comedies of Shakespeare himself. Menander's theatre was not one of mixed genres, but he mingled many elements into comedy alone. Not the least of these elements is observation of life. His comedy is not set in a never-never land, but in precise years, in exact places, with special troubles and a distant rumble of politics. Scholars have not neglected this dimension as a dating factor for individual plays, but the fragmentary allusions we mostly possess do not make for secure arguments.

We have the *Difficult Man*, for which I feel more affection than most Menander scholars. We have about 441 lines of the *Sikyonian*, a play of dazzling speed and intricate intrigue, with a splendid messenger speech. We have most of 560 lines of *The Shield*, a swiftly and lightly moving comedy, which once again I value more highly than many scholars. Hugh Lloyd-Jones has deftly sketched its attractiveness, but I like it even more than he does. Critics have been annoyed by its lack of profundity, but comic profundity is an elusive quality, and Menander is funnier and less high-minded than we used to be taught. *The Shield* is a play with a surface texture of shimmering irony and a strong comic impetus.

We have more than seven hundred verses, mostly from a Cairo papyrus, of *Epitrepontes* (*The Arbitration*), a late and mature work of Menander. Its shadows are deeper, and have more of experience of life in them, than those of his earlier, more formal comedies. It is common ground among critics that Menander's plots owe a great deal to his sharp analysis of Euripides, but in this play he calmly transmuted the royal and divine persons of the *Alope* of Sophokles into modern Athenians, for the climax scene. A young man who has been to sea finds that his wife bore a bastard child and abandoned it to die. He moves to a friend's house and tries without success to drown his grief. Shepherds find the abandoned child and quarrel over the trinkets found with it. Intrigues of more than Shakespearean speed and complexity follow. The child is recognized by a ring, the lovers come together, and it turns out that the hero was the child's true father, having made love to his own wife at a night festival, and never loved anyone else. Perhaps it is foolish to transcribe such a plot. But the play most richly embodies it, and it is to the *Difficult Man* as mature Shakespearean comedy is to *Love's Labour's Lost*. It has touches of moral beauty. It is based on a personal morality of compassionate poetic justice.

Unless I misremember, the *Shorn Woman*, another late play, of which we have nearly 450 lines, was once successfully performed in London in a version completed by Gilbert Murray, a scholar whose feelings were too fine for Aristophanic comedy, as his book on Aristophanes indicates, but who felt a strong attachment to Menander. But even here, his English, gentle version was unlike its original. This play is the story of a foundling who knows part of her own secret, and as a colonel's concubine lets a man kiss her because she knows he is her brother. The colonel shaves her head. After the knotted intrigues have swollen and at last been untied, she finds that her father was the next-door neighbour, and she marries the colonel. Some degree of social criticism, shared between Menander and his audience, seems to be implied. The comedy must have been boisterous all the same. It included one of the favourite stock scenes, the siege of a house, uncommon presumably in Athenian life, but most liberating on the stage.

We have substantial fragments of the *Woman of Samos*: as many as 737 lines, though some of them are sadly tattered. It revolves around the usual love intrigues, and has a pleasing comic cook, a stock character the audience clearly appreciated. A huge quantity of comic verse about food was written in the fourth century, and even a lyric poem about it, in the simplified stanzas of the lyric revival, by Philoxenos of Leukas. Poetry of that kind is even harder to translate effectively than Menander, with his sizzling liveliness and changes of tone. It is mostly to be found quoted by Athenaios in his *Deipnosophistai* (*The Dinner of the Savants*).

The *Woman of Samos* also has an old man in senile love, a subject almost more popular on the stage than a miser. The quarrels and love intrigues of comedies like this are scarcely a reflection of everyday life; they are special cases, like those on which young orators were trained for the lawcourts. Menander's most obvious good qualities are his dexterity in manipulating these plots, and his control of tone, pace and momentum in enacting them. But at the heart of his comedy lies a kind of poetry. This is a poetic theatre, even if it were in prose.

One of his most amusing pieces may have been *The Virgin Possessed*:
Krato and Lysias are two old men, the possession is divine.

> KRATO: Is she pretending?
> LYSIAS: You see for yourself,
>   If she really and truly is possessed
>   she'll come leaping out here any minute,
>   full of the Mother or the Wild Dancers.
>   Listen: her flute. Stand at the cupboard doors.
> KRATO: Well done Lysias, Zeus, really well done,
>   this is what I want. Oh good goddess!

The two old men appear to be hiding from the young girl, who
probably lives in the shrine at the centre of the stage. Their cupboard
is a store room of some kind, since the scene has to be out of doors.
There is plainly some comic business about Krato hiding. Krato speaks
again in another fragment.

> If a god came to me and said, Krato,
> when you die you begin over again,
> be what you like, a dog, a sheep, a goat,
> a man, a horse: but you have to live twice,
> that much is fated, so choose what you like;
> make me anything else, I think I'd say,
> except a man ...

Menander at his best is more complex than these fragments show:
his language jumps about like a basket of live fish. But the Virgin
Possessed in contrast with the old men is an admirable comic conception, and the sententious tone of Krato's speech about reincarnation
is comic on more than one level: one laughs more at him than with
him. One might be in danger of exaggerating the virtues of Menander,
because every generation of scholars is specially stimulated by the
freshest discoveries, and the recovery of texts of Menander in the
last hundred years has certainly been dramatic. But Menander repays
close study; he is prismatic and humorous, and his verse has the
same multiple quality, with many levels or facets, a range of tones
and transmutations, that Plato's prose has. The mainstream of Greek
literature in the fourth century passes through Plato and Menander,
and it is still very strong. Late in the century, the best writers in
Greece still came to work in Athens.

The lyrics that survive from the later century are pleasant and sententious at times, but they lack the tension and the brilliance of Menander's performance, and the intellectual pressure of Plato's dialogues. 'No boy child, no gold-wearing virgin, no deep-breasted woman is beautiful, but what is decent by breeding, blossom of modesty grows over it.' The sentiment is charming, and the thought no more than mildly mad. It is minor poetry like Abraham Cowley's, written by obscure Lykophronides. 'I dedicate you this rose ... and my beast-murdering spear; my mind pours out elsewhere, to my dear girl, to my fine girl the Graces love.' This stumbles half-way between drama and epigram; it is Lykophronides again. I mention him not to mock his awkwardness or his facility, which combine in him as in the minor poets of every age, but because the minor poetry of this period offers a viewing-point, a criterion of a kind. Great works unvaried make a dangerous diet for the critic. Lykophronides has a sort of innocence; he is an improvement on rhapsodic Telestes, with his musical verbosity, and of course on ghastly Timotheos.

Aristotle composed what is called an *Ode to Virtue*, though it seems really to have been an after-dinner song commemorating his dead friend and patron Hermeias, and Ariphron wrote an *Ode to Health*:

Health, eldest of the blessed to mankind, may I live my life out with you; be with me in goodwill. If any grace of wealth or child, or kingly rule godlike to men, or wishes we hunt down in Aphrodite's secret boundaries, or what delight the gods have sent, or any breathing-space from pain appears, it flourishes with you, blest Health, and shines by season and by Grace. Without you no one has been happy born.

Combed out into prose, might these words, whose traditional wisdom Plato would have accepted and Sophokles endorsed, not have come from some Platonic dialogue? Or more tautly stated, they could be fitted into comedy. Aristotle's poem has more intellectual power, but no greater charm or lucidity; his language is consciously sublime. Some ray of the dying and milder sun touches Ariphron. Ariphron on Health reminds one of Anyte of Tegea, and the sanctuary of Asklepios, god of health, that she helped to set up near Naupaktos.

Pausanias, at the end of his *Guide to Greece*, tells the story, perhaps in the poet's own words inscribed somewhere at Epidauros.

The sanctuary of Asklepios was in ruins; it was originally built by

Phalysios, a private individual. He had an eye disease and was nearly blind, and the god at Epidauros sent Anyte the poet to take Phalysios a written and sealed tablet. She thought this order was a dream, but she suddenly awoke and found the writing with the seals on it really in her hands: so she sailed to Naupaktos and told Phalysios to take off the seal and read what was written. He felt it would be beyond him to see this writing, because of the state his eyes were in, but hoping for a blessing from Asklepios he took off the seal, and as he looked at the wax tablet he was cured; so he gave Anyte what was written on the tablet: two thousand gold pieces.

We are not far from the theatre of Menander in this story.

BIBLIOGRAPHY

Entretiens Hardt, vol. 16, on Menander, 1970

S. M. Goldberg, *The Making of Menander's Comedy*, 1980

A. W. Gomme and F. H. Sandbach, *Menander*, 1973

A. S. F. Gow and D. L. Page, *The Greek Anthology*, 1965

C. M. Havelock, *Hellenistic Art*, 1970

P. Jay (ed.), *The Greek Anthology*, 1973

H. Lloyd-Jones, 'Menander's *Sikyonios*', *Greek, Roman and Byzantine Studies* 7, 1966

H. Lloyd-Jones, 'Menander's *Aspis*', *Greek, Roman and Byzantine Studies* 12, 1971

J. W. Mackail, *Select Epigrams from the Greek Anthology*, 3rd edition, 1911

F. H. Sandbach, *The Comic Theatre of Greece and Rome*, 1977

C. A. Trypanis (ed.), *Penguin Book of Greek Verse*, 1971

T. B. L. Webster, *Introduction to Menander*, 1974

17

ARISTOTLE AND THEOPHRASTOS

Aristotle lived from 384 to 322 B.C. He was the son of a Macedonian court doctor, but from the time when he was seventeen and Plato was nearly sixty until Plato died and Aristotle was thirty-seven, Aristotle lived as Plato's pupil. He was sharper as a philosopher, at least technically, and went further as a physical scientist than his master, but there is no doubt that he developed under Plato's shadow and as Plato wished and directed. He was closer to Plato than Plato was to Sokrates. When Plato died, Aristotle first lived two years or so with other Platonists at the court of a fellow pupil, Hermeias King of Atarneus in Asia Minor, and married the king's niece; then at forty-one he moved to Lesbos when the king died, very likely to be with his friend and pupil Theophrastos, who was still in his twenties. On Lesbos he concentrated on zoology. A few years later he was appointed tutor to the young Alexander of Macedon.

His earliest writings are lost. They were dialogues and collections of scientific notes, but we have only some stray fragments and lists of contents. He seems to have written on rhetoric, imitating the *Gorgias*, and on the soul, imitating the *Phaido*; also an invitation to philosophy much imitated by later writers, and in Asia a dialogue about the eternity of the world and the development of mankind. He was already criticizing Plato's views about the hierarchy of Ideas, and particularly the tendency to reduce philosophy to mathematics, which Plato's immediate successor and kinsman Speusippos had further exaggerated. It was dislike of Speusippos that made Aristotle leave Athens. But he never finished his wrestle with Plato.

For better and worse, it makes more sense with Aristotle than it does with Plato to speak of doctrines and a system. We are dealing at first with a dogmatic quarrel between disciples. In Asia, Aristotle was already at work on his metaphysical system. But it is not easy to chart his development. His genius is inseparable from his vast curiosity (the zoology on Lesbos, the research on political systems), his ostrich digestion, his Platonic ability or need to organize and sub-divide intellectually, and the sharpness of his questions; these qualities are evident throughout his career. After being tutor to Alexander he moved to Athens, where he set up his own institution for research and teaching.

The Italian Marxist philosopher Gramsci remarks somewhere that there are three reputed kinds of knowledge, common sense, religion and philosophy, that religion consists of isolated, mutually contra-dictory fragments of common sense, and that by philosophy we over-come religion and common sense. It is surely true that philosophers value one another as much for the quality of their paradoxes as for the tightness of their arguments. The ancient philosopher Alkidamas, little if anything of whose authentic writings we have, since he was opposed to written arguments, had maintained a generation before Aristotle that philosophy was a fortress wall against the laws and customs of mankind. He thought God had made all men free, and Nature destined no man to slavery. His predecessor, the sophist Antiphon (not the orator), had dared to hazard the opinion that political organization should be based on consent and cooperation, and that nobles and commoners, Greeks and barbarians, were all naturally equal. But for Aristotle the purpose of philosophy was to rescue the heart of religion and morality from the ruins of belief, to defend common sense and extend it like a scientific method into every kind of human inquiry.

Science is not so easily achieved. Aristotle's political studies were far more widely based than anything known before his time, but his writings on the subject are a curious mixture of empiricism and prejudice: what is new in them is his own moderateness, his iron common sense. As a zoologist and a natural scientist he made his greatest contribution where the collection of a huge number of examples and their comparative study matters most. Among the stars his principles were misleading and his explanations too neat. His universe and his development of mankind were no great improvement on Platonic mythology. But his procedure by division and subdivision and rigorous definition produced great improvements over Plato's metaphysics and his psychology. His early rejection of forms or Ideas of things having separate reality above the quotidian world is an example of his common sense. But in criticizing other philosophers, Plato included, and in handling earlier workers in every field, he was systematically unfair. Scholarship, as a wholehearted, endlessly patient pursuit of the truth about the past, had not really been invented in his time.

But with money from Alexander, Aristotle collected at Athens a museum of natural history and a big collection of maps and manuscripts. He organized the recording of 158 different political systems. Under his direction, Theophrastos worked at botany, and other researchers at the histories of physics, mathematics, medicine and so on. Unfortunately, his rooted sense that reason arose only with Platonic philosophy, and that philosophy penetrated all subjects, made these enterprises less useful than they sound. One of his pupils, Aristoxenos, is almost a parody of Aristotle. He wrote 453 books, some about philosophical biography but most about musical theory. As a theorist, he belaboured the obvious, but he subdivided and defined it with unflagging industry. He was an embittered man, who expected to succeed Aristotle but failed to do so. The sheer laboriousness of Aristotle's collection of facts is impressive always, but he uses them like playing cards, and often with irony. On human happiness for example, and its minimum requirements, 'It is curious to consider the number of different opinions people have entertained on this subject.'

The difficulty of dating his works and tracing his development is a formidable obstacle. Werner Jaeger made a heroic attempt, but the problem is perplexed by Aristotle's habit of revision and addition, and by the nature of his writings. What we have are his private papers, not exactly notes for lectures, but something never elaborated for formal publication. It used to be thought they remained unknown for generations, but that is not quite true. Nor will it ever be possible again to consider them as a single systematic enterprise, an empire of the intellect, although scholars have not ceased to be tempted to do that. But Jaeger's account of Aristotle's development has been forcefully criticized. One can no longer rely on it, and I am not competent to substitute anything better; the article by Thomas Case in the eleventh edition of the *Encyclopaedia Britannica* is said to give the best account. There are no linguistic criteria for dating these writings which a computer could distinguish; some pages and some works seem quite fully written out, others not. Aristotle's knotty and pungent prose style can be thrilling. In his description of courage, for example, on the brave who die young, he ends by saying: 'Therefore those who have the most of what is noblest and best in life are stripped of it soonest; and this is grievous.' But often his work is so compressed as to require the most careful attention and a full-scale commentary before it can be understood. This task was undertaken over a lifetime of patient scholarship by W. D. Ross. Some of the notes to his translations are as invaluable as his fuller thoughts.

Aristotle's style can be preposterously formal. He is the first writer we know on any scale to have used pedantic language for the sake of precision. 'Given the preceding preambles, let us begin from the beginning by saying ...'; 'These distinctions established, one must now state ...' And yet his lucid exactness makes for a fascinating text, even when the argument appears foolish, for example, on musical education, where he pours scorn on the Platonic and traditional teaching of instruments, which he thinks slavish and without moral effect, as if one had to learn cooking to appreciate food. The argument is like an organized snowstorm of logic.

His power of controlled generalization makes him memorable even where he is banal. On the rearing of children, he suddenly interjects 'for nothing young can be quiet'. The multiple resonance of such phrases is second nature to him. Small wonder he has so often been admired and revived. The Aristotle of Thomas Aquinas, on whom I myself was brought up, is less supple than the true Aristotle, though often closer than most people think. The air of Paris in his time was electric with resonant phrases that combined poetry and exactness, and derived ultimately from Aristotle's Greek style. Bonaventure, preaching on Christ at rest in his tomb the day before Easter, suddenly ended 'Omnis enim labor est propter requiem, et omnis motus propter quietem' ('All labour is for rest, and all motion towards quietness').

Aristotle's descriptions of movement disposed of the paradoxes of the early sages. His conception of material and its relation to the forms and substances of things was an enormous advance on every earlier explanation. His definitions of potentiality, of qualities and of the interactions of things, left a new high road open for science. His theory of particles and his astrology were strangely mistaken, though with brilliant insights, partly because he failed to understand light. He believed strongly in process, and that the world is process, but odd as it may seem to us, he was confused by the apparent permanence of the sun into thinking that fire was a permanent substance, and light no more than its appearance: 'For when there is anything fiery in a transparent medium, its presence is light, and its absence darkness ... It is the common property of air to be transparent.' Common sense is not quite enough; or we should perhaps admit that science has gone beyond common sense.

For Aristotle, science of course was part of philosophy. In his book *On the Heavens* he made many fine distinctions, and wove a web of interdependent descriptions and definitions of the physical world too subtle to reproduce in this brief notice. His theorizing was physical and philosophic at once. Solmsen, who started his account of Aristotle's physical theories with an eye to their dependence on the earliest Greek philosophy, was led on into writing a long and most readable book by their constant interplay with the late theories of Plato. Here, as elsewhere, Aristotle combs out Plato's conceptions; he defines and distinguishes and organizes. But he continues to be a physicist. In his work *On the Parts of Animals* he treats the four elemental qualities of hot, dry, moist and cold as the substratum, almost the fundamental material of composite bodies. Is that natural science or philosophy?

It is strange to us that philosophy should have an organizing or generative power over science, still more a controlling and penetrating power. One must not equate philosophy with theology. It is still after all true that the language we use when we think we are talking scientifically has a heavy influence on our inquiries and our truths. If one thinks Aristotle's definitions pedantic, one should consult the history of the word 'entropy' in Murray's Oxford dictionary. The words 'psychotic' and 'civilized' would not stand up well to philosophic analysis; they are both used in areas that interested Aristotle. He would have had something to say about 'random' and 'aleatory', he would have shown intelligent interest in quantum theory, in Einstein and in the speed of light. If science is not still part of philosophy, and seldom generated by it, at least since Whitehead, yet it is still haunted by the ghost of philosophy, a ghost that must be placated.

The central axiom of science is that there are natural laws, that whatever is can be said, that the universe is regular. It is not eccentric to think of that as Aristotle's legacy.

Some of his scientific observations are mistaken, particularly those in the field of anthropology, where he was least self-reliant, and of contemporary politics, where his view of what should be done about the Persians makes one's hair stand on end. But one must note it was sometimes theory, the rational impulse, that misled him. He thought crabs and lobsters failed to know right from left, not having right and left claws of equal size. The truth is that most lobsters at least are right-handed, with overdeveloped right claws, and that left-handedness in lobsters is apparently related to nervous disease. The scientist who demonstrated this spent his last years trying to show something similar about kittens. Such details would have pleased Aristotle, and he cannot seriously be blamed for getting them wrong. It is a more serious fault that his pupil Theophrastos thought lobsters, crabs and oysters in old age could renew their youth. Was it that he found empty shells, and imagined they were like snakeskins? It is indeed true that young lobsters do abandon their shells and then consume them in order to grow a bigger, tougher shell, but Theophrastos has muddled his observations with general theory. For that matter, Xenophon believed hunted hares always ran in circles to the left (they do, but not always) because one ear weighed more than the other.

His political writings are businesslike and stuffed with examples. The method is a little chilling, but it is a genuine attempt at political science. He shows the ways in which oligarchies fall, and the variety of situations that may follow. He goes through the likely causes of revolution. He is conscious of classes and their interests. I have already written that we need a close study of Aristotle's *Politics* in relation to Plato's *Laws*. The *Laws* was full of information about comparative institutions. It entered into great detail. Aristotle appears to have much more of this information than Plato, or to have it better organized. He is like a lecturer with a card index. On the other hand, it is also true that he quotes poetry, evidently by heart and outside any literary context. His memory must have been prodigious and he may well simply have remembered the examples in the *Politics*. But his Political Constitutions are another matter. The fragmentary knowledge we have of them suggests they were a full and thorough record.

The only one we have complete is his *Constitution of Athens*, since its recovery from a papyrus in the last century. There is little or no doubt that this text really is the famous lost work of Aristotle. Wilamowitz, who wrote about Aristotle, perhaps in the heat of that moment of discovery, with warmer excitement even than his pupil Werner Jaeger, based his view of Aristotle chiefly on the *Constitution of Athens*. It certainly does confirm the sense one has elsewhere that Aristotle belongs to the city states, to the old Greek world that hardly outlived him. The branches of literature had concluded their evolution and attained their nature as mankind had done, as the plants and animals in their species had done, as political society and civilization had done, in his mind, in a past age which he recorded and could analyse. His rather loyal and respectful treatment of the development of Athens was thrilling to Wilamowitz and his pupils. Aristotle's account is indeed succinct and most useful and practical. It was written in 329/8 B.C. Historians continue to discuss its details, but it would be hard now to imagine Greek history from any point of view that neglected it. Aristotle and his circle had no quarrel with Athens, and no confidence in the world fantasies of Alexander. They were protected by prejudice from believing in the fusion of nations. It is true as Jaeger claims that 'Aristotle stood over the Greek nation like a troubled physician at the bedside of his patient.'

The ethics of Aristotle are attractively liberal and moderate, and their influence has been a civilizing one. Wilamowitz remarks that what Aristotle did was just to codify a piece of folk-wisdom: the god favours the moderate man. An inscription on the temple of Apollo at Delphi proclaimed 'Know thyself', and 'Nothing overmuch'. But in a series of ramifying definitions and distinctions, Aristotle set up on this foundation a way of life. The *Ethics* is the most readable and moving of his books. If one looks for it, one will find a Platonic element, even an intransigent insistence on contemplation and the Good, but one can live with Aristotle's moral system without much unworldliness or other-worldliness. His definition of the big-spirited or 'magnanimous' man, with his heroic gravity and impressiveness, includes the remark that he offends no one unintentionally; it was oddly transmuted in the nineteenth century into Newman's definition of a gentleman, who gives no offence even by mistake. Aristotle is not at all so meek or emasculated. His *Ethics* read today still seems a most spirited contribution to the subject – a subject that effectively he founded.

Of his contributions to logic I am not competent to express an opinion. Their influence was powerful, and I think fruitful. It persisted into the nineteenth century at least, and the dust has not yet settled deeply or quietly enough on the lively recent history of the subject for this to be a good time to judge Aristotle's logic. Experts have strong views. I have the impression that for Aristotle logic was just a method of organizing reason, organizing one's method, a kind of classification, but I offer even so modest an observation with diffidence.

On the soul, and on the inner structure of human beings, his views have not only been overtaken by science but also abandoned. 'The effective activity of intellect is life' is a thrilling maxim with a typically multiple resonance, but out of fashion as a philosophic precept. Aristotle's analysis of soul is interwoven with his distinction of form and material, and what acts and what is acted on. It looks, if one reads the small print, as if he thought the peak or principle of the soul was some spark of Intellect or Nature, or, as we would say, God. His universe was a hierarchy in which the origin of all motion was an unmoved mover, a muted description of Plato's absolute.

But here we have a problem. In his analysis of the heavens, Aristotle is inclined to employ more than one unmoved mover. Yet at a certain point in his *Metaphysics*, only the supreme one exists, and all motion, all activity, descends hierarchically as if from God. Jaeger's work on Aristotle began from an attempt to sort out the order in which the *Metaphysics* was written, or as he came to believe patched together. I am not clearly convinced that a final solution of this critical problem has been or ever can be attained. That entails agnosticism about how Aristotle's system developed, and about how it fits together. It means that his description of the universe is not quite coherent; it can be fitted together in more ways than one.

He certainly took the same view as Plato, that the ultimate principles must be numerically definite and simple, and certainly

finite in number. He admired the perfection of circular motion, mere
rotation, and used it to explain heavenly bodies. This limited insight
of his was constantly modified by later astronomy down to the late
Renaissance, with more and more complicated mathematical results.
It also had a strange and distant echo in the Church's condemnation
of an opinion of Origen that the risen bodies of the just shall be
perfectly spherical. We know that Aristotle believed the earth was
everlasting, without beginning or end. Even his disciple Thomas
Aquinas thought it would dissolve at the Day of Judgement into its
elements and drift away empty for ever. But Aristotle believed the
world or nature was a god or divine, and the universe was a kind
of pantheon, and he was bitterly sarcastic about whoever thought
otherwise. His world-soul and his first mover are Platonic conceptions, and under the sobriety of his language the same enthusiasm
lurks. For Plato, circular motion was the best image for the movement
of mind. In Aristotle's thinking, nature does most of the work that
soul does in Plato. Hence the importance he attaches to movement.
'If movement is not known, nature is not.' But these jejune sentences
must not be taken for a serious exposition of Aristotle's inter-
locking doctrines. The best treatment of them I know is by Solmsen,
in *Aristotle's System of the Physical World*.

The enormous prestige of Aristotle in the late Middle Ages and
the Renaissance, when Plato never entirely ousted him as a sage,
gave a powerful influence to his writings about literature. He did
open the door to true scholarship by closing the history of literature,
or at least some of its divisions, and making it appear a single,
manageable thing. In this he was more right than wrong. No one
in his time understood that the enormous change in the Greek world
was a matter of economics and monetary inflation, a phenomenon
previously unknown to mankind, money being quite a recent
invention, and banking newer still and rather uncontrolled. The huge
social change that transformed the ancient world reached its crisis
late in his lifetime. It really was closing time in the gardens of the
ancient Muses. The world had altered utterly in its fundamental
political and social conditions. Tragedy was effectively a dead art,
as Aristotle first pointed out, though his abundant quotations make
it clear he was perfectly familiar with fourth-century tragic verse.
He was also the first to point out that Homer, in the *Iliad* and the

Odyssey, was also the end of something, and its flower. They had unity, completeness and greatness. The so-called epic cycle was something different, and lesser. There was nothing perfect about it. 'A cycle is not a circle,' he remarked acidly.

But he never edited a text, and his lost work on Homeric problems, which we know from numerous quotations, particularly from a similar work by the late philosopher Porphyry, did not really study the *Iliad* or the *Odyssey* thoroughly as complete poems. He did very greatly admire Homer, and defended him against sophistic quibbles, even against Plato's quibbles. His defence was characteristic, being based on encyclopedic knowledge. How could Hektor have been dragged around the tomb of Patroklos? He knew a tribe in Thessaly where that was still done to the bodies of murderers. In another context, he appealed to the customs of the Illyrians, who slept on their shields. Early in the *Iliad*, where plague breaks out among the mules and dogs, he rationalized Homer by suggesting the word for mules might be an archaic word for guards. This kind of Homeric criticism is little more than a sophistic defence against sophistry, yet it has often been thought necessary down to our own day. All the same it hardly justifies the time and ingenuity it must have needed.

Aristotle's *Rhetoric* is a full treatment of tricks and devices. It was surely the clearest, most comprehensive and best organized work of its kind. We know of numerous works on the art of oratory, and we know that Aristotle collected them. But apart from his organizing clarity and a constant sharpness over details, this book is valuable mostly for its allusions and quotations. It tells one little else that one wants to know. Aristotle begins with the long-overdue admission that rhetoric and philosophic dispute or dialectic have something in common. The purpose of the activity rests in the listener, he says, as judge or jury of what is past or passing or to come, or else as audience. The apparent implied equivalence of Apollo, who alone knows what is past or passing or to come, with the democratic voter in this last sentence is perhaps not present in Aristotle's wording; it would be a startling intuition, even for him. It seemed to emerge between the lines of his text, and I found it irresistible, though my analogy with Apollo is not really what he intends.

His treatment of rhetoric is based on cynical common sense. The speaker is not to blame for the story he has to tell. 'If you have a proof or demonstration, then speak morally and demonstratively, otherwise just morally. It better fits the decent man to appear honest than for his speech to be sharply calculated.' Moral, in this context, means personal. He gives a long and amusing list of types and characters who may appear in court, and how to treat them. No doubt this was one source of the dramatic *Characters* of Theophrastos. Aristotle's addiction to lists is as remarkable as his passion for classification. He produces a string of examples of the failure of Alkidamas in the use of adjectives, so long that it must surely derive from written notes. Alkidamas says 'wet sweat' instead of 'sweat', and 'covered in timber branches' instead of 'branches'. The criticism is well observed, but the list of examples grinds the subject into the ground. And one does not always agree with Aristotle's judgements. What one likes is his intelligent malice. 'The rich are preoccupied with their own private pleasures, and they believe everyone else envies them, and wants what they want.' Is that not true to life? And 'a juvenile type of exaggeration much used by Athenian orators, unsuitable for the older man'.

The spurious works later attributed to Aristotle went on being written from the time of Theophrastos, perhaps in the master's lifetime, until the fifth and sixth century A.D. They show an increasing woodenness of course, and a failing power of intellectual organization, but they belong recognizably to his school, they are an interesting parody of his style and they offer some indication of the strength of his influence. One might dare to say that the renaissance of science in Europe came earlier than the renaissance of literature, and it was founded on the rediscovery of Aristotle. There is something chilling and bizarre about the spurious work on money-raising (hanging the rich and selling their corpses to the families) and the chapters on sex (why the eyes roll upwards in death and copulation, but downwards in sleep, and do the balls dangle lower in summer), but the level, organizing tone in which the real Aristotle discusses the fall of governments and the tricks of court oratory are as chilling and as bizarre, and the attempt to explain the whole of experience rationally has often the same quality.

Of all the writings of Aristotle the most widely and intensely studied is the *Poetics*. This is a short and in some ways penetrating work, but hardly able to sustain the great weight that has sometimes been put on it. Its influence on such works as the *Poetics* of J. C. Scaliger was lamentable, but no fault of Aristotle's. We should treat Aristotle's *Poetics* a little more fully than the text warrants, if only because it is about the history of literature; it was never meant to be a prescription for poets to produce masterpieces, and when it was so used in Renaissance Europe, the result was a predictable ossification. Even what is often taken for Aristotle's central insight is a vulgar and wrong-headed simplification. He wrote that the effect of tragedy was a purge, like a physical purging of the stomach (that is a removing of excess), of fear and apprehension. It is quite clear from his *Rhetoric* that the usual phrase 'fear and pity' is a mistranslation of his *Poetics*. He means fear and horrified apprehension. Is that really what we experience? If we did feel fear and apprehension in excess, would a tragedy cure us?

The great tragic poets seem to have written without any theory, with a rich humus of conflicting purposes. That is as true of Shakespeare and the Cretan *Sacrifice of Abraham* as it is of Aischylos. Any attempt, therefore, to put fetters on the art, and to demonstrate that its evolution was towards the attainment of its true nature, after which it ceased to develop, must be misguided. Aristotle is forced to ignore late Euripides, and to stop the clock at a tragedy with an iron skeleton. He chooses the *Oedipus the King* of Sophokles, an effectively strong choice. And he has much to say of great interest, some of which scholars still need to relearn.

The study by John Jones, *Aristotle and Greek Tragedy*, which was the outcome of his earlier cooperation with C. A. Trypanis, makes this point admirably. When it first appeared its lessons seemed completely fresh, as if no one had read Aristotle for years, which was certainly not true. The romantic importance of the tragic hero, and the sense that sin must lurk under the word 'fault' or 'mistake', which Aristotle justly remarks is an element in tragic consequences, blind one to the simplicity of Aristotle's description. A tragedy is an enactment of an action, not a presentation of characters: it is an event. All the same, Jones follows Aristotle into what I conceive to be injustice to Euripides. 'Whereas a glaring uncollectedness in argument is found throughout Greek Tragedy, only in Euripides does it give offence, and this is primarily because of the expectation of coherence.' But coherence is not experienced in the theatre as it is in a scholar's study. Aristotle's demands for unity not only extend too far, so that they would disallow for example the *Eumenides* of Aischylos, let alone the whole of Shakespeare; they are really a philosophic view imposed on criticism. For better and worse the criticism in the *Poetics* is the projection of Aristotle's mature philosophy.

I have maintained that the purge effect is not a profound but a banal idea: but Aristotle does promise in his *Poetics* to discuss it later in more detail. He seems to have applied it in some form to comedy as well as tragedy, or so Vahlen argued from a hint in the commentary of Proklos, the late antique philosopher, on Plato's *Republic*. Aristotle went on where our text of the *Poetics* finishes, to discuss comedy as well. No doubt different emotions were purged, and comedy was some sort of reversed mirror image of tragedy. One would greatly like to know what Aristotle said about comic unity. Perhaps he felt that comedy had attained its nature only with one of the immediate predecessors of Menander? But that is mere conjecture. Janko has suggested and others have suspected that Aristotle's views are encapsulated in the *Tractatus Coislinianus*, but that short work offers only hints of the Master; it is a feeble echo. I have no doubt that if Aristotle on comedy is ever rediscovered, we shall be greatly surprised by whatever he said, and made to think again about that art. His *Poetics* are not like his Homeric problems; they are really as their full title, uniquely worded among the catalogue of Aristotle's writings, suggest: a treatment of the art of poetry.

He assumes that poetry, painting, sculpture, music and dancing are all examples of imitation, *mimesis*, a resonant rather than a precise word, an inherited conception from Plato. 'Poetics' really means creative art, or composition of any kind, and it includes in his usage all these branches. He constantly illustrates one from the others. Dancing is a moral expression and therefore an imitation, an expression of character, emotion and life. He seems to have felt something similar about music. Lyric is another matter: he noted it was an element in tragedy, but it was the moods of music he conceived as Plato did as having a moral content, being imitations of life. As for poetry, Simonides was credited with this as with so many pregnant sayings, that painting is silent poetry and poetry is painting that speaks. Aristotle is constantly wrestling with Plato, and it may be that his idea of the purge is meant as an answer to Plato's observation in the *Republic* that indulgence in epic poetry and in tragedy causes moral weakness. But the argument that in the arts, as consumers of art, we get rid of excess emotions, is not a convincing defence against the *Republic*, even if it were true. It has the advantage and demerits of a common-sense suggestion.

There are many details of this short book with which one cannot deal briefly. Aristotle's fascination is in details, particularly here. He believed, as anyone with so strong an evolutionary sense would be bound to do, that the ideal tragedy had to be complex. It had to contain a reversal of expectation or a recognition surprising the characters. As D. W. Lucas pointed out in an appendix to his commentary, even the simplest of Greek tragedies, the *Persians*, depends on surprises, the arrival of unexpected news and the appearance of a ghost. Illusion is dissipated, the truth suddenly becomes clear. One can see why he took *Oedipus the King* as his great example. He felt Prometheus, Ajax and Medeia lacked the true inward complexity that produced the right degree of apprehension and fear in the audience. But he approved the *Iphigeneia among the Taurians* of Euripides, and the middle play of the *Oresteia*. His principle of criticism appears insecure and not very useful, yet detail by detail the criticism itself is of great interest. That is not unique in the history of literary criticism.

Aristotle is a mixture of coarseness and intelligence.

And tragedy has everything that epic poetry has (one is allowed to use metre, for example) and music plays no small part, through which pleasures are most vivid, and also tragedy has vividness even when read, as in performance, and the imitation has its effect in a shorter space (the more compact is more pleasurable than what is mixed into a length of time, as if one put the *Oedipus* of Sophokles into epic verse like the *Iliad*) . . .

The mixture of interesting truth with wrong-headedness here is not easy to disentangle. Aristotle has apparently little conception of economy of means in the arts. Would he have preferred grand opera to *War and Peace*, or even the film to the book, because it took less long and was more vivid and had music? In the evolution of art, tragedy seemed to him an advance on epic poetry, and more complex. Might he have thought the novel an advance on both, as it is in a way, if art is assessed as the imitation of life? He seems to have had little sense that one kind of art excludes another, or that one becomes a substitute for another as the world alters, the new art being a radically new subject of criticism. If poetry itself is one subject, the remark about metre makes it clear that Aristotle had not understood it.

Yet Aristotle loved literature. It nourished his philosophy and all his thoughts. Woe to the philosopher who moves too far from poetry, and woe to the poet who has not philosophized. In Aristotle's will, he left his school of philosophy at Athens, which by then was an established institution like a college, to those who would follow him in the study of philosophy and of literature. It is a delightful will, with an Epicurean tranquillity, and it makes one understand the devotion he inspired. There are some verses from his circle which convey a similar impression, from the Eudemos elegy, quoted by Wilamowitz.

> ... and came to Athens and the famous fields,
> and set up holy Friendship's altar there
> to one whom evil should not even praise:
> who showed alone or first of all mankind
> by his own life and methods of his words
> how one may be happy and virtuous,
> as no man ever shall be in these days.

It is beyond the scope of this history to trace the development of Greek mathematics and astronomy and mechanics. But among the pupils of Aristotle let one stand for many. Theophrastos of Eresos on Lesbos was born about 370, nearly fifteen years after Aristotle, and died in the 280s B.C. He lived with Aristotle until 322, and inherited in the philosopher's lifetime the directorship of the college. His surviving works fill a stout volume, but they are small compared to his lost writings. He wrote encyclopedic lost books on the history of natural science and on the laws of nations, of which we possess fragments, and philosophic books depending heavily on Aristotle's methods. Where he differed from his master was in the still increasing emphasis on empirical observation, both in ethics and in his study of the processes of nature. He is an unjustly neglected writer, and his works on botany and on stones well repay study, not only for such fascinating occasional details as the customs of the Arkadian countryside, and the rituals of the root-gatherers, but for the scope and vision of his own mind.

The botanical books are magisterial. He begins with an Aristotelian analysis of differences, then moves at once into full detail of trunk, root, leaf, seed, fruit, taste and smell of trees, variety of blossom, and the rudiments of classification. 'Some saps are vinous, as vine, mulberry, myrtle; some oily, as olive, laurel, walnut, almond, pines and fir; some like honey, as fig, palm and chestnut; some sharp, as oregano, thyme, cardamom, mustard; some bitter, as absinth and centaury. And there are various perfumes, as of aniseed and cedar.' The combination of sensuality and sharp perception with the classifying, rationalizing urge makes for a remarkable effect. But Theophrastos is also widely informed on such matters as the planting and propagation of palm trees and what the soil where they best grow has in common in Libya, Egypt and Babylonia. He knows that in Crete their trunks are multiple, and that a special variety grows in Ethiopia. From Theophrastos one draws a sense of the late Greek world. He is not above peasant phrases such as 'which they call punishing as it were an arrogant tree', or learned quotations: 'Androtion says olive, myrtle and pomegranate need the most powerful dung and the most watering and cleansing.'

Not long after the lifetime of Theophrastos, books like his began to be illustrated. We know, for example, of an illustrated poetic work on snakebites in which the snakes are identified. Botanical illustration and botany are likely to have advanced together, but it is clear Theophrastos himself did not envisage an illustrated book. Such a luxurious item probably first arose in the courts of Hellenistic kings. They were practical: they were *materia medica*, intended for druggists and doctors. It is interesting that Theophrastos was already concerned to cover that aspect of botany; the herbal as we know it in later antiquity was a by-product of his huge enterprise.

His medical theory was not progressive; his reasoning about why cures worked was still based on the excesses of hot and cold and wet and dry, but the reasoning seems to be secondary to the practice of herb-gatherers. Perhaps this is just another case of the rational classification of a huge collection of information from all over what was then a freshly discovered world. The exploration of America in the seventeenth century had the same stimulating effect on botany and herbal studies that the conquests of Alexander had for the Greeks. 'Strychnus and small-apple mean the same. One strychnus induces sleep, the other madness. The second has a blood-coloured root when dried.' His purpose is clearly practical; he proceeds as Aristotle did, from distinction to distinction.

No doubt the charm of Theophrastos is largely that of his subject-matter. On sweet-smelling plants 'which they use for strewing under-foot' he gives a thrilling odoriferous list, ending in a kind of sigh: 'Some grow everywhere, but all the rarest and most scented come from Asia and the warmer lands: in Europe none of them grow except the iris. That is at its best in Illyria, and not on the sea-coast of Illyria, but in the interior and the north.' He is as interesting on the varieties of wheat, and as empirical: 'There is a two-month wheat that was brought to Achaia from Sicily: meagre and unfertile, but light and delicious in bread. There is another in Euboia, mostly around Karystos.' Yet he has just spoken of some forty-day wheat, though in guarded language, 'as they maintain about Aeneas'. Epic poetry or mythology still rated a mention, but it had lost its hold on empirical science.

Theophrastos on the generation of plants (*De Causis Plantarum*) is even more practical, but still his work is strictly organized on Aristotelian lines. 'Plant theory contains two considerations and two divisions: in the self-born, there is the principle of nature, and in those nourished by thought and industry, nature is aided to her purpose.' But it is not long before he is down to the uses of dung in breaking up and warming the earth, which he observes to be two useful effects for good germination. Practice and theory, in fact, run together. 'Straightness and smoothness make the channel run freer and growth swifter.' One feels that the eighteenth-century walled garden is almost in sight. No doubt so it was. The art of gardening came to the Romans from Pergamon, where the writings of Theophrastos were well known, and even most of our works of Aristotle somehow survived, as manuscripts guarded for their great value.

Among works ascribed to Theophrastos we have books or fragments on *Fire, Smell, The Winds, Fatigue, Sweat, Fainting* and *Paralysis*. I am not clear that enough work has been done on these for many years now to enable one to be confident of their authenticity. Recent work has concentrated on newer fragments. In a book *On Religious Piety*, which is lost, he seems to have disapproved of blood sacrifices and defended the natural kinship of all mankind. He apparently wrote much on rhetoric, something on diction, and something unfortunately irrecoverable on the art of history. Aristotle and his school had been interested in antiquarian knowledge, and issued lists of the winners at the Pythian games and the Olympian games, and the dates of theatrical productions. One would like to know what Theophrastos thought about historical science.

Theophrastos' *On Stones* displays in miniature much of his quality. This short book has fascinating information about the whereabouts of stones, and odd information about their properties. He knew where agates and obsidian were to be found. He scorned magical properties, but noted magnetic ones. He accepted that a certain stone came from the piss of lynxes, and entered into detail about the wild and tame, the male and female lynx. Eichholz, in his useful introduction to this book, suggests that Theophrastos relied on the famous doctor Diokles who wrote about the urinary tract. But that would create an even stranger problem. Theophrastos did think in the Platonic tradition that both earth and stone were elemental earth, but that metal was created by the pressure of underground air and a mysterious kind of water. Aristotle thought gems were aqueous, and Theophrastos does seem to have explained them by the analogy of a stone one might pass in one's water. In contrast to this surprising doctrine, he is ironic about the Egyptian records of the stone smaragdus. His concern throughout the book is process, and the nature and origins of materials, as much as it is geography or empirical knowledge. For hundreds of years after Theophrastos, no one else studied stones for their own sake, or their place in the universe, as he had done, but only for their magical or medical use, or for their value.

How different the sharp-eyed observations of Aristotle and Theophrastos are, and how different the impetus of their attempt to make sense of the world is, from the vague sublimity that was soon to swallow up philosophic religion. Kleanthes (331–232 B.C.), the Stoic and ethical puritan, has left us a hymn to Zeus that was quoted by St Paul. 'Greatest of immortals, many-named, omnipotent for ever, Zeus lord of nature, ruling all things by law, hail! For it is all mortals' right to address thee: for from thee we come into being, and are the imitation of God, we alone of all things that live and move upon earth.' Even the intimate personal sense of the divine as Kleanthes expressed it, moving as it may be, is a falling-away and a failure of freedom after Aristotle. 'Lead me, Zeus, and thou, my fate, whither I am destined to go, so that I follow without fear, but if I do not want to follow and am cowardly, I shall follow all the same.' Aristotle's ethics and the inquiring mind of Theophrastos may well be thought preferable to this solemn nonsense.

BIBLIOGRAPHY

(i) ARISTOTLE

T. Case, 'Aristotle', *Encyclopaedia Britannica*, 11th edition
H. Cherniss, *Aristotle's Criticism of Plato*, 1944
W. Jaeger, *Aristotle*, 2nd edition, 1948
R. Janko, *Aristotle on Comedy*, 1984
W. D. Ross, *Aristotle*, 6th edition, 1955
J. H. Smith and W. D. Ross (eds.), *Oxford Translation of Aristotle*, 1908–52
F. Solmsen, *Aristotle's System of the Physical World*, 1960

(ii) THEOPHRASTOS

D. E. Eichholz (ed.), *Theophrastus, De Lapidibus*, 1965
A. F. Hort, *Theophrastus, Historia Plantarum* (Loeb Classical Library), 1916
R. Pfeiffer, *History of Classical Scholarship*, 1968

18

HELLENISTIC POETS

The Alexandrian or the Hellenistic age took its name not directly from the great conqueror, but from the city of Alexandria in Egypt, and from Greeks abroad and foreigners who learnt to be Greek, who 'Hellenized', as the Macedonians had done. Greek writings from the early third century onwards must be seen against the vast background not of the ancient towns and their tribal territories, but of an extensive world. Philosophers took refuge in its nooks and crannies, but most historians, scientists, even poets, would depend on court patrons or safe centres, first in Alexandria, then in Rhodes and Pergamon, and finally in Rome. Athens became a pleasant backwater haunted by antiquarians, a university town depending even for food on great benefactors.

One of the first lessons of the new age is that when everything else crumbles poetry triumphantly survives. But poetry had never been an exclusively Athenian art. Tragedy and perhaps oratory had almost been, and philosophy, as it now survives, almost was, but comedy had been vigorous in Sicily under Epicharmos and Sophron, and therefore the Doric dialect had its own prestige. Lyric and elegiac poetry had always been international. The history of poetry was more continuous than scholars usually admit, as I have tried to show in dealing with the fourth century, and stressing the sophisticated freshness of fourth-century epigrams. The dialect poetry of Erinna is an almost more significant case.

Still, the new poetry that now emerged was indeed a wonderful and surprising creation. It looked back at the classical achievement from a distance, and far afield for untapped sources of erotic and exotic mythology. It was learned and urban, intended for educated readers. It treated fishermen and herdsmen and even the townspeople of the great cities as if their simplicity was astonishing and moving, and it imitated their magic and their music. It was intensely conscious of the texture of language, and fascinated by dialect. It was influenced by the tone of satyr plays, comedy and mime. It was an amusement. It was profoundly erotic.

The father of this new movement was Philetas of Kos, of whose work we have no more than fragments. His most striking characteristic is a playful sophistication of texture, which I suspect he took over from popular poetry of some kind. It depends on simple word-play and seductive half-rhymes: *deilaion heilen ..., horaion erchomenon eteon, neai aien aniai.* The relationship of this phrasing, which had always although less markedly been a feature of elegiac verse, to music, like that of Thomas Campion's phrasing, is not fortuitous. These verbal tricks of Philetas were imitated in Latin even by Catullus and Virgil, and mechanically by Cicero, a much lesser but not uneducated poet. In very late Greek poetry in the fifth century A.D. they ran riot. 'All the charm of all the Muses often flowering in a lonely word' goes back to Philetas. A little local spring is 'the outpourings of *black-rocked* Byrine', and Phlious is a city 'the beloved son of Dionysos, Phlious himself built, *white-crested* Phlious'. 'Among the prickle-foot and harvest-weed, the white snow-blossom *softly* flowering.' The italics are mine. I have disguised the precise names of the flowers, because their identifications are not secure.

Philetas invented bucolic, or as we say by an English limitation, wrongly excluding the cattle and the goats, pastoral poetry. He was also tutor to the royal family, and attached to the great library of Alexandria, where all available ancient literature was first collected and classified, where serious and thorough scholarship first began, and through which most of our knowledge of the Classics was transmitted to the Romans and to us. The poets and scholars who worked there were priests of a temple, officials of a royal institution, fellows of something like a college. They were one another's first audience and readers. That is the first key to the new nature of Alexandrian poetry. There are others, but that is the first. It implies an intimacy, and a shared culture.

Rudolf Pfeiffer, the editor of Kallimachos and historian of ancient scholarship, makes a most interesting case that scholarship in its first generation was invented by poets, summoned into existence like Frankenstein by poets who needed to understand the history of their own art, until a generation or two later it had become a profession and plodded off into the world with a life of its own. Pfeiffer thought this had happened twice, the first time in Alexandria and the second with Petrarch, and each time, generation by generation, later scholarship lost its creative edge, became encyclopedic, became dusty, showed diminishing returns. It would be thrilling to imagine that in our own day we could start again, receiving through the generation of Pound, Eliot and the art historians and archaeologists a new electric charge. But one can hardly make that claim; poetry has simply continued to live, and scholarship has continued to live, less raided than it used to be by poets, and incomparably less than in that wonderland of Alexandria, when everything that was ancient seemed fresh. I am reluctant to abandon Pfeiffer's majestic conception, though he has been tellingly criticized.

But ever since Philetas, European poetry including that of Virgil and Horace, and the French, English and Spanish poetry of the Renaissance – Ronsard, Shakespeare and John of the Cross – has been to some degree Alexandrian. The exceptions have come from new peoples and untried languages. It is important to realize that freshness in poetry is not confined to primitive performances. The Alexandrian poets often have a sparkling freshness, even when their language is an artificial construction; it is as sweet and clear as honey, they can be moving as only deep and great writers can be, and at times highly amusing as well. Their verse has an abundance of invention and a controlled virtuosity of expression that the world had not previously seen in poems. It is thoroughly literary, more I think for better than for worse.

Philetas was born before 320 B.C. He was tutor to the second Ptolemy, who was born on Kos, and Theokritos was his pupil. He wrote numerous short poems, but also a narrative about the wanderings of Demeter in Kos and elsewhere (she 'will see long-speared Athene's holy city, and see godlike Eleusis'), and another about Odysseus and the incestuous daughters of Aiolos, who lived on a small island near Sicily. It appears from the small amount we know of this poem and its heroine that 'she wept, she cried, she damn near died'. He also wrote poetry, as Theokritos and Virgil did, about the birth of the first honey-bees. It is also of some interest that he compiled a lexicon of obscure and Homeric and dialect words, which his Alexandrian successors will have found all too useful. His own poetry has here and there a heavy sprinkling of archaisms that appealed to him. Pfeiffer has argued strongly that the work of Philetas does not depend on Aristotle. It was a new departure.

Kallimachos was born in Kyrene in about 305, Theokritos in Syracuse perhaps in 300, Apollonios of Rhodes, named from the island where he retired, in Alexandria about 295 B.C. He is supposed to have been a pupil of Kallimachos, and to have quarrelled with him over his preference for heavy, pseudo-Homeric, romantic epic. Indeed, scholars used to organize the poetry of the third century B.C. around the literary politics of this quarrel, but the evidence is slippery, and the quarrel may never have had the significance that has been wished on it. Still, there was certainly a difference, and the great work of Apollonios on the Argonauts, carefully phrased and polished as it is, has little in common with the ideas of Kallimachos, who favoured elegance, wit, and an art that conceals art. Yet Apollonios rewrote some lines by Kallimachos in his own style, and it remains obscure to me why that should represent a feud: it might more easily be a compliment. Apollonios was a director of the Alexandrian library, but in 247 B.C. he retired to Rhodes to compose or to revise his *Argonauts*. (We hear of its being a work of his old age, but also of a public reading as a young man, and an 'early edition' of some kind.) It is certain that it was Kallimachos who was imitated by Apollonios, and not the other way round. But in just the same way Theokritos rehandled material from the *Argonauts*.

Kallimachos was an innovating genius, Apollonios less so, but it will be convenient to deal with the Rhodian at once. The lines of the new poetry were probably first suggested by Philetas and they appear to me to represent something in common between this whole intimately related and competitive generation of poets. Apollonios wrote epic poetry of a highly episodic and ornamental kind. Piece by piece, it is not so very distant from the epyllion, the short narrative poem of the Alexandrians, with its fresh angles and romantic interest, the kind of thing that stands behind Catullus and Ovid, and even behind the romantic, episodic character of parts of the *Aeneid*. Scholars have cast Apollonios in the wicked role of supporter of the most grandiose pseudo-Homeric epic, to which both

Kallimachos and Theokritos objected, but as K. Ziegler pointed out in 1934, the epic won in the end, and things went back to normal. Certainly grandiose literary epic went on being written. And yet in epigrams, in epyllia, and even in the magical touches that bring Virgil and Milton to life, the influence of Kallimachos was life-giving. I believe it already was so for Apollonios.

The *Argonauts*, the voyage of Jason for the golden fleece, is stuffed with geographical curiosities and antiquarian pleasures. Its language is so peculiar that one of its latest editors had radically altered the text, but G. Giangrande has recently demonstrated that most of its linguistic oddities are based on learned and wrong-headed interpretations of the obscurer passages of Homer: they are deliberate. Personally I find Apollonios almost unreadable in quantity, but his finish is exquisite, and the story has moments of passion and beauty. It resembles a Victorian mythological painting, an acquired taste. Metrically, Apollonios follows tradition without the refinements of Kallimachos, but his warmth and sentiment, the aesthetic lethargy of his narrative and of his tedious hero, recall nothing more vigorous than the epic verse style of William Morris. 'She smiled sweet nectar, and her melted heart ...' All the same he has his moments, and they often owe something to visual art. Hence perhaps his tableau quality, and his lack of energy.

> The Nereids from every side swam in
> and Thetis on their rudder laid her hand
> and guided them between the Wandering Rocks.
> As from the sea-deeps dolphins rise and bask
> in flocks and circle round a speeding ship,
> seen leaping now in front and now behind,
> now alongside, and give the sailors joy,
> so leapt, so circled her the Nereids ...

One is tempted to say, as Bentley said about Pope's *Iliad*, 'It is a pretty poem, Mr Apollonios, but it is not Homer.' But it is not meant to be, and one must get that out of one's head. It has a bewitching and lunar beauty of its own. If it had been written in the Renaissance, as many such literary epics were, we would value it highly. Here is Aphrodite seeking out Eros on Olympos.

> She went away through glens of the mountain
> and found him by fruit-laden orchard trees,
> with Ganymede, whom Zeus brought home one day
> to live in heaven with immortal gods,
> having desired him. Now, two boys alike,
> they played at knucklebone with dice of gold ...

The reader must take my word for it that the technical level of these verses is remarkable. But they are claustrophobic, and so perfumed as to be unappetizing. The dice of gold are somehow the last straw (they are more accurately 'golden knucklebones'), and the poem does not improve in the next few lines. 'And sweet upon his cheeks red blossom came.' The scene is typically static, a Hellenistic painting maybe, but the verse is wonderfully musical.

There really are Hellenistic paintings of 'Eros punished' by women, as a naughty boy weeping, and so on. Even in his mythic narrative, the verse style of Apollonios is long and lingering. Boutes is an Argonaut nearly caught by the Sirens. Readers will not be surprised to hear that any sailor of Apollonios who lands on the rock of the Sirens will die 'by a strange lethargy consumed'. Homer creates a perfect calm in this region, but Apollonios paints a more baroque picture. Boutes was a Sicilian herdsman, the lover of Aphrodite of Eryx. When Athens allied with Segesta in the fifth century, an Athenian ancestral hero of the same name got identified with this local herdsman; he was included among the Argonauts to explain how he got to Sicily. Apollonios is pleased with the novelty and the local colour.

> Boutes, heart-pierced at the clear Siren's voice,
> swam through the purple swell and strove for shore –
> unhappy! – and had lost his homecoming,
> but from Eryx, the goddess pitied him
> as he struck through the waves, and rescued him
> and set him on the Lilybeian coast.

This rough translation simplifies the verses and thins their texture.

Kallimachos is refreshingly sharp. Cory's marvellous English version of one of his epigrams – 'They told me, Heraclitus, they told me you were dead' – strays so far from the harder quality of its original that it would, if retranslated into Greek, as Norman Douglas said, have given Kallimachos a stomach-ache. It is not just the sentiment that gets out of hand in Cory's version, but the insipidity of Victorian metre. Kallimachos is the greatest of all the poets of the Palatine anthology and his ear is the finest. By a few subtle adjustments, he so renewed Greek metre that in competent hands it was never the same again, and the Romans, when at last they learnt the trick of adapting Latin to Greek sound-patterns, inherited his finesse. He dares to be as simple as Simonides. 'Philippos here laid away his twelve-year-old son, Nikoteles, his great hope.' He can be passionate and personal: 'There is, by Pan, some fire, by Dionysos, there is some hidden fire beneath this ash. I have no courage, do not embrace me. Often in secret a quiet river eats away a wall. So I fear now Menexenos ...' And he can be frivolously courtly to the queen of Egypt:

> There are four Graces; with the three
> a fourth takes her own place,
> O Berenike, without thee
> the Graces would lack grace.

One could do without poems of this kind, but it is no use being high-minded about Kallimachos. It was the pressure of having many sides to his intelligence and many kinds of things to say, and of seeing many sides of life, that brought about his remarkably versatile poetry. 'What a good piece of magic Polyphemos discovered for lovers: by Earth, the Cyclops was no fool. Philip, the Muses have a cure for love: and their wisdom is an all-healing drug ...'

Of his longer poems we have a huge hoard of fragments, further increased by papyrus discoveries since Pfeiffer's edition. The new bits were recently edited by Peter Parsons and Hugh Lloyd-Jones in their *Supplementum Hellenisticum* (1983). No one who is not a professional scholar is likely to have encountered this, so the point is worth making that it rather raises the already high reputation of Hellenistic poetry. Nothing seems beyond Kallimachos, and he attempted more than one had realized. He has Auden's restlessness, something like Pope's abundance and facility, and yet almost Marlowe's certainty of touch.

As with Menander but more so, the mixture of high quality and complexity makes him hard to translate. The only complete longer poems we have by Kallimachos are his six hymns. They are written in fine, ringing verses, but none of them is without jokes and one or two are extremely funny: in particular *Athene's Bath*. Even to Zeus he remarks 'They say in the Idaian mountains you were born, they say in Arkadia, so who was lying?' But these hymns contain passages of striking beauty, and they have a crispness, a neo-classic resonance, like that of Milton's 'Nativity Ode'.

The style of the hymns is deliberately varied: the first four are in hexameters, the traditional metre, but the first, to Zeus, is full of scholarly jokes, the second, to Apollo, is dramatic and personal, Apollo being the poet's god, the third, to Artemis, is a narrative with humorous undertones. The fourth is a court poem with a prophecy by Apollo in his mother's womb about the birth of Ptolemy on Kos (so Apollo himself had better move on and be born on Delos because Kos has its god), but it also plainly sets out to rival the Delian part of the Homeric *Hymn to Apollo*. The fifth hymn, *Athene's Bath*, is in Doric dialect in couplets, and the last one, to Demeter, is in Doric hexameters. His mania for variety of tone and virtuosity of texture is justified in its results. If we had a full modern commentary on all the hymns we might learn a lot about the art of poetry. The hymn to Demeter is perhaps more beautiful and less quirky than the others. Its texture is a little like that of the first stanza of Matthew Arnold's 'Scholar Gipsy'; it is what we think of as Theokritean; it gives a variety of subtle pleasures, and makes one smile. Kallimachos is an excellent story-teller, and he manages dialogue well. One thinks one is not vulnerable to mere charm, but the pure playfulness of this poem has a memorable power. And he can be serious in an old-fashioned way.

> Apollo prophesied to Battos our deep earth,
> a crow led those who came to Libya,
> on the steerman's right side, and swore to give
> walls to our kings: he keeps his promises.
> O god Apollo called by many names,
> Klarios, Boedromios, I say
> Karneios, as my father's father said: ...

Kallimachos was fond of popular prophecy and magical language, and used it as a comic poet might do. He spoke with classic crispness of 'Kallisto, dry-footed from Ocean's pools', a verse brought to life by the slight, pedantic mockery of the unexpected 'pools', and ends a passage of folk-tale and prophecy with the mocking epic line 'so speaking sleep took one, and listening one: they dozed not long ...' These are among the fragments of his masterpieces, the *Hekale* and the *Aitia*. The *Aitia*, the causes of things, was a poem in four books of seven thousand lines in all, telling a series of tales whose excuse was to explain the origins of rituals and beliefs and customs. His introduction was a manifesto on the art of poetry; his climax was the 'Rape of the Lock of Berenike', of which we have an imitation by Catullus. Its narratives were chosen for contrast and variety, like Ovid's *Metamorphoses*.

He displayed an extraordinary variety of metres and styles in an added iambic book of a thousand lines, which followed the *Aitia* in their revised, final form in his collected works, and his lyrics, of which we have too few fragments, show a correspondingly far-ranging grasp of ancient and modern techniques. The *Hekale* was an epyllion, an amusing, ornamental, non-heavy narrative: a truly modern poem. Hekale was an old peasant woman who entertained Theseus on his adventure against the bull of Marathon. The birds held a conversation, and Kallimachos dwelt lovingly on Hekale's frugal rustic supper. *Hekale* has been called just another Aition, since it explains a place-name, but it was also a show-piece, a deliberately and impudently perfect poem that exploited tones and textures no other poet could command until Virgil's eclogues.

The manifesto that opens the *Aitia* is sadly fragmentary. It defends short and fine poems against long ones; Philetas and the old couplets of Mimnermos seem to be his examples. The fine musicality of the verses of Mimnermos had surely through him, and perhaps at all times among serious poets, a vital influence on poetry. This has to be judged by ear, and one cannot argue securely about it so late in the day, so many sound-values in ancient Greek being confused or lost; yet I imagine that I can hear this influence, as one can hear the influence of Milton's Latin verse in his English poetry, and the influence of Shakespeare in very many poets. 'Nightingales trickle honey ... thunder belongs to Zeus', if one may adapt some stray phrases of this manifesto. He calls his nightingales merely 'sweeter', but the sense of honey is present in the word.

> When I first put my notebook on my knee,
> Apollo Lykios appeared to me:
> Singer, he said, keep your sheep-fleeces thick,
> I like fat sacrifice and thin music.
> Drive down no waggon-rutted and no broad
> highway, but paths untrodden, the lone road.
> And no braying, only the cricket's cry ...

One stumbles awkwardly in English over these dry and sparkling Greek couplets, but the message is clear enough. As Kallimachos wrote elsewhere in a love epigram, 'I hate sub-Homeric poetry and crowded roads and popular lovers and public fountains; I loathe all common things ...' It is hard to know which of his narratives to single out from the fragments; their fieriness and variety are ceaseless. The fragment of folk-tale, how the crow became black, is fine enough.

> ... the crow who now is rival to the swan
> like milk for white, like foam crest of a wave,
> in blue-black pitch will dip his downy wing.

That is from *Hekale*. But the story of Akontios and Kydippe is as narrative more brilliant. The poetry is allusive, and intricately knotted together. Its narrative line twists and flashes like a swimming watersnake. Kallimachos takes a teasing rather than a voyeuristic attitude to sex, but his tongue is in his cheek, he is writing for a sophisticated circle. 'Eros taught young Akontios, when he glowed for virginal Kydippe, his own art ...'; 'Much knowledge is much evil for loose tongues ...'; 'The bulls of dawn will bellow out their lives; they see the blade clear in the drinking trough.' This image is tied carefully into the narrative; it reflects what had seemed an innocent joke which is suddenly serious. The bulls are meant for a wedding sacrifice, and the bride by local custom has slept the night before her marriage with a pre-adolescent boy. The narrative turns on a swift double meaning.

Kallimachos takes pride in the appearance of casualness, and in turning his verse to all possible purposes. He is the precursor of the famous nineteenth-century schoolmaster who put his gas bill into elegiac couplets. He can summon up a statue ('At Samos the vine runs in Hera's locks ...') and fit even its measurements into verse. He is the champion of the view that whatever can be said can be said better and more memorably in verse. But of course that is only the outer edge of his virtuosity, and he is not to be held responsible for Dyer's *Fleece* or the astrological verses of Aratos or Manilius.

Kallimachos is a true poet, and a most fastidious technician. 'The ship that took the only sweet light of my life, I beg of Zeus the guard of all harbours ...' – this comes from a little Doric song: it is mannered, not great poetry, but still in perfect taste. A long poem by Kallimachos might be as dazzling as a sheet of snow, though it would certainly be more varied. As certain modern painters have the unfair advantage of reproducing well as postcards, Kallimachos survives extremely strongly in his fragments. His prose writings should not be forgotten. They included a huge catalogue of literature, a chronology of the Athenian theatre, and a study of the language of Demokritos. He made encyclopedic collections of material about birds, rivers, winds, and about games – a kind of *materia poetica* – and he was an authority on Nymphs.

Theokritos was in at least one kind of poem a perfect poet; he thoroughly exploited the new form of poetry based on herdsmen's songs and conversations, and on their love affairs. We have thirty complete poems said to be by him, even apart from his epigrams; most of this material is genuine. It shows an astonishing freshness and originality, and a much greater range than is often realized. Of course it is the overwhelming success of his pastoral and bucolic poetry that has overshadowed his other qualities, both inside and outside the pastoral convention, and since his are the first full-length bucolic poems we have complete, and among the first ever written, he has become so famous for one thing that his reputation is unjustly limited.

The bucolic poem was never a Platonic Idea: it was a variety of experiments of many kinds, deliberately intended to show changes of tone, differences of approach, modulations of theme, and differences of character. The poems of Theokritos are meant to display, as they do, an abundant variety of different types of friends and lovers. Virgil understood that, and attempted on a lesser scale to imitate the variety of Theokritos. Theokritos has court poetry among his poems and an epyllion, and town scenes and women's scenes and fishermen, and metres taken from Sappho, and more than one kind of language.

... Ye Shepeheards, tell me true, am not I fair as any swan?
Hath of a sodaine anie God made me another man?
For well I wote, before a cumlie grace in me did shine,
Like ivy round about a tree, and dekt this bearde of mine.
My crisped locks like Parslie, on my temples wont to spred;
And on my eiebrowes black, a milke white forhed glistered:
More seemelie were mine eies than are MINERVA'S eies, I know.
My mouth for sweetnes passed cheese, and from my mouth did flow
A voice more sweete than hunniecombes. Sweete is my rundelaie,
When on the whistle, flute or pipe, or cornet I do plaie.
And all the weemen on our hills, do saie that I am faire,
And all do love me well: but these that breathe the citty air
Did never love me yet. And why? The cause is this, I know,
That I a Neteheard am. They heare not how, in vales below,
Fair BACCHUS kept a heard of beasts. Nor can these nice ones tell
How VENUS, raving for a Neteheards love, with him did dwell ...

This anonymous translation of Theokritos, published in 1588, conveys some of his qualities well. The poem, the twentieth idyll, is perhaps not genuine, but it was written under his close influence, and it nicely demonstrates something about his characters. But the twentieth idyll is too sweet and sugary for Theokritos, and its best phrases are stolen from elsewhere in his work. At his best, Theokritos is untranslatable and inimitable. So great a poet as Virgil did not succeed: he smooths and simplifies where Theokritos is rougher, more playful and more various. But no one since Virgil has come so close. The 1588 version has an uncontrolled awkwardness and undesirable prettiness, closer to the twentieth idyll. The original closeness of Theokritos to folk-song and peasant life cannot now be re-invented.

Singing shepherds are real, and his poetry is full of unrecognized truth. The antiphonal singing of shepherds has been recorded by A. L. Lloyd, and I have heard it in the remoter fields of Nuristan. Singing can be a way of exchanging banal information or any snatch of traditional poetry, often with an ironically humorous overtone. Kallimachos also shows an influence of folk-song and a willingness to adapt its special music, but Theokritos takes it over bodily. His metrical refinements may derive from it. His Doric dialect, which gives a modern reader the sense of one unbroken texture of language –

probably a mistaken impression – is not the true spoken language of Sicily or anywhere else. Theokritos makes some mistakes in dialect. His parents were Syracusan, but we first hear of him on Kos or in Alexandria. His language in poetry was adapted and contrived for his own purposes. Even the shepherds and cowherds and goatherds are adapted and contrived in the same way. Singing shepherds may be real, but those of Theokritos are the inventions of a poet.

> Fresh is the whisper goatherd in the pine
> above the water-spring, and your piping ...

The scene is set at once, in two lines as musical as have ever been written by any poet. I have translated 'sweet' or 'pleasant' as 'fresh', because in our world sweetness has lost its old taste, and because the landscape is one where freshness matters. A shepherd is speaking to a goatherd, the lowest of peasant boys: 'And after Pan you shall have second prize.'

He goes on to praise the meat of a young kid before it has given milk. The mention of Pan does not indicate anything unreal. The goatherd replies by reversing the compliment. 'Fresher your music, shepherd, than the falls that run down from the rocks into the pool.' This shepherd is famous for 'the height of herdsman's music', and they sit down together for a performance of the sorrows of Daphnis who died of love. But before we are allowed to hear that, we get a long verse description of a wooden cup, a rustic work of art. Works of art described in verse are a constant ingredient in Hellenistic poetry. The tradition goes back to Homer's Shield of Achilles. This one is a vignette within a vignette, a country landscape with figures: an old man fishing, a boy in a vineyard, and two haggard unsuccessful lovers inside the cup. The vignette has a shimmering, illusory quality. It suggests the familiar world of great art with its stock figures, but it modulates them into a pastoral world more appropriate to this poem, though excessively unlikely on a wooden cup. It is a fantasy, really, a dream in the heat of noon, and this is intentional. The progression of the poem depends on innumerable subtle tensions and variations.

The shepherd starts the story of Daphnis with its refrain, which he uses to separate stanzas of two lines or of four or five. 'Begin

Muses, begin the herdsman's song.' The word I give as 'herdsman's' is 'bucolic': it refers principally to cowherds, and Daphnis was one. But Theokritos uses this word as if it implies a familiar kind of music: a song in stanzas which can be antiphonal, with a refrain. We can come no closer to the folk-song origins of his art. The shepherd begins with his own name: 'Thyrsis of Aitna, and my voice is fresh. Where were ye Nymphs, when Daphnis died of love? In forests of Peneios, on Pindos? Not by the river-stream of Anapos, not on the peak of Aitna, ye were not where Akis pours her holy water down.' The lament for Daphnis is almost a narrative, with dramatic fragments of reported speech in the first person, and a most interesting variety of syntax and of verse texture. Its mythology is allusive and its fauna and flora deliberately contrast the exotic with the simple. 'O wolves, O jackals, lurking mountain bears, farewell. Your herdsman Daphnis comes no more, among the woods, the forest and the grove. Arethusa farewell, and rivers all, ye that down Thybris roll your water fair.' The poem ends when the song is over, with the purest realism about milking and the misbehaviour of goats. But the two herdsmen in the shade are more than a frame: through all the transformations of the poem they are its substantial truth.

The poetry of magical incantation uses refrains in a different way. We know that the subject goes back to Sophron, and we even have a verse incantation 'against headache, by Phyllis of Thessaly', from a papyrus. That is wilder and stranger than Theokritos, though less so than the genuine magical rituals in prose, which survive in quantity. It refers to 'seven wolf-springs, seven bear-springs, seven lion-springs, where seven blue-eyed virgins water drew in jugs of blue and quench the tireless fire'. This is one of the few scraps of verse to cast any new light on Theokritos since Gow published his magisterial standard edition. I take the first line to refer in the exotic language of folklore to the water of pure springs that the witch can summon.

Theokritos, as one might expect, gives us a dramatic performance framed in reality like a theatrical mime or a Platonic dialogue, and his magic is love-magic. The refrain is 'Mark my love whence he comes, thou Lady Moon'. The poem powerfully suggests the passion of an abandoned woman, particularly in its long closing passage when the incantation is over. This is the second idyll. It has nothing to do with bucolic poetry, but it has a similar relation to material from low life, and a smouldering erotic force that was new to literature.

The third and fourth idylls are only fifty-four and sixty-three lines long, as opposed to 152 and 166 for the first and second, but they both include variations of tone. The third is the serenade for Amaryllis. A goatherd speaks. He leaves his goats with a friend, then speaks his love in charming but desperate terms to a girl who lives in a cave, and finally sings a formal love-song of short stanzas about famous lovers.

> My head hurts, you care nothing. No more songs.
> I shall lie here till I'm eaten by wolves.
> May that run sweet as honey down your throat.

The fourth introduces the gossip of Battos with the cowherd Korydon, who grazes the cattle of Aigon. Aigon has gone off to the Olympic boxing 'with a pickaxe and twenty sheep from here'. We are near Kroton in southern Italy. Amaryllis (is she the same girl?) is dead. The calves stray, Battos gets a thorn in the ankle, the entire poem is a peasant dialogue of allusive local gossip, mostly about cattle and about love-affairs. The fifth idyll is another south Italian one. It tells in pure dialogue form a quarrel followed by an antiphonal singing contest between a shepherd and a goatherd. The quarrel includes obscene insults, and the antiphonal singing includes reference to normal and to homosexual passion. The judge is a wood-man, and the prize of a lamb goes to the goatherd. The last line refers to a proverbial goatherd who came to a bad end in the *Odyssey*: a pedantic and rather intrusive joke to our taste, but one the Alexandrians would relish.

The sixth idyll presents two pretty adolescent youths, both cow-herds, singing in turn. This poem is framed in narrative, and addressed to Aratos, probably not the famous poet but some unknown friend. The boys' songs differ greatly in style and tone. At the end they kiss and give one another presents. One might have the momentary feeling, which I express diffidently since Gow does not share it, that this poem presents characters from real life, poets with known styles, in a disguise which is a joke at their expense. But I make this comment hardly as a conjecture, only as the record of a question.

There is no doubt about one or two of the allegorical figures in the richer seventh idyll being contemporary poets. This is a poem of late summer in Kos, a journey on foot to a harvest festival. The first-person teller of the tale is Simichidas, very possibly but not certainly standing for Theokritos himself. The other characters are mysterious: Lykidas seems to be a known poet, but no argument that identifies him has ever been secure. The poets Philetas and Sikelidas, also called Asklepiades, are mentioned by their real names. So are Aratos and apparently some other friends of the poet. This is very like a bucolic poem, yet deeply felt and personal, and its climax is without irony; its landscape and its place-names are real. The poem begins as a Platonic dialogue might, but in the usual Doric hexameters. 'It was the time when Eukritos and I went to the Haleis, out from the city; Amyntas came with us and made a third ...' Theokritos gives us plenty of obscure mythological local colour; but the landscape is green and well watered, and his descriptions of it are among the most attractive of all his poetry. 'Now sleeps the lizard in the dry-stone wall.' His verse is sharpened by contrasting smells, heat and coolness, light and shade.

The friends meet the goatherd Lykidas, 'among all herdsmen and all reapers best' at piping. Simichidas, who tells the story, challenges Lykidas to a singing match. The goatherd's song is educated and allusive. Its first subject is love for a boy, but it modulates into a rustic feast and the poetry of singing shepherds, the unhappy love of Daphnis, whom a king buried, 'but swarms of bees with their blunt faces came out of the meadows to his cedar chest, and fed him with soft flowers of the fields, because the Muse poured nectar on his lips'. Bees do in fact sometimes swarm on the lips of a sleeping man. I have a photograph of a man bearded with bees.

From this strange story Lykidas modulates his theme again to speak of Komatas 'closed in the box and fed with honeycomb'. The sensuous strangeness and the obscurity of these myths are of course part of their deliberate effect. Simichidas replies with a song about Aratos in love with a boy. Once again, the poetry is very beautiful, but its obscurity gives it a surrealist quality – probably intentionally. The idyll ends with the harvest festival itself, plainly and luxuriantly described.

Many a poplar and elm murmured over our heads, and near at hand the sacred water from the cave of the Nymphs fell plashing. On the shady boughs the dusky cicadas were busy with their chatter, and the tree-frog far off cried in the dense thorn-brake. Larks and finches sang, the dove made moan, and bees flitted humming about the springs. All things were fragrant of rich harvest and of fruit-time. Pears at our feet and apples at our side were rolling plentifully, and the branches hung down to the ground with their burden of sloes. And the four-year seal was loosened from the head of the wine-jars.

> And O Castalian Nymphs, O you who keep
> Your revels on the high Parnassian steep,
> Was it such wine as this old Chiron gave
> To Hercules in Pholus' marble cave?
> Was it such wine as this that mid his flocks
> Set Polyphemus dancing, who with rocks
> Like mountains once bombarded Ulysses,
> Drained he such sparkling cups, ye Nymphs, as these
> That you then mixed us from your spring before
> The shrine of Ceres of the threshing-floor?
> Ah, to plant once more in the chaff, my friends,
> The winnowing fan, whilst great Demeter stands
> Laughing, poppies and corn-sheaves in her hands.

These thirteen lines of verse are remarkably accurate in tone to the altering tones of the end of this wonderful poem. They were written by the Aristotelian scholar W. E. Charlton as an undergraduate in the 1950s. Their neo-classic musical quality well recaptures a long tradition which Theokritos himself began.

The eighth idyll is usually thought to be partly or wholly spurious, though the manuscripts and their annotations accept it tranquilly, and Virgil took it often for a model. It may well be genuine. It records an encounter between Daphnis and Menalkas: they sing anti-phonally, with a goatherd for their judge. Daphnis is a cowherd, Menalkas a shepherd: 'striplings both', as Gow puts it, but the Golden Age quality of these poems does not extend far beyond the beauty of the boys. Their conditions of life are not shown as easy. Menalkas loves a boy, and a girl loves Daphnis, and their affairs have an innocent pathos. 'Fresh is thy mouth, Daphnis, lovely thy voice. I'd sooner hear thy song than lick honey.' Daphnis marries the nymph

Nais in the last line. I believe this poem to be genuine Theokritos, but as Gow has suggested, an early work. The ninth idyll really is spurious; it is an incompetent imitation of the all-too-imitable conventions of this style. Virgil appears to have accepted it, but that is not a knock-down argument.

The tenth idyll is a conversation between reapers about the torment of love, with a charmingly ridiculous love-song, and a reaper's song of fragmented couplets. The eleventh, to Nikias, is about Galatea and the Cyclops, one of the finest short poems of Theokritos. 'There is no other remedy for love, no poultice, no ointment, poor Nikias, except the Muses . . .' After the introduction, only the Cyclops speaks; no one answers him. 'So Polyphemos took his love to graze with music, and did well not to give gold.' The twelfth idyll is a passionate love-song to an unnamed boy, written in Ionic dialect, though our version of the poem has had an attack of Doric measles that editors strive to cure. In the thirteenth idyll Theokritos tells for Nikias the story from the *Argonauts* of the boy Hylas whom the Nymphs loved and stole and Herakles longed for in vain. This is a nicely contrived and polished performance, gently erotic and perfectly entertaining as verbal music. Theokritos makes the water-spring where the boy disappeared a thrilling place, and his Nymphs are frightening, 'dancing in mid-water, sleepless'. But this is a mannered poem: like certain works of Pope, it precludes greatness even though it is obviously written by a great poet, or an extremely able one.

The fourteenth idyll is often forgotten. It is a conversation about a party and an unhappy love-affair, by no means sentimentally treated. In many ways this is like a fragment of comedy, but less smoothly observed. 'We're all greying from the temples, and time creeps down our cheekbones whitening hair by hair. We should do something while our joints have sap in them.' If this poem were alone of its kind, it would be no more than a fascinating experiment. Theokritos has an excellent ear for habits of speech, not only for the music of poetry. But the fifteenth idyll is a masterpiece. It describes the visit of two lower-class Syracusan women at Alexandria to the festival of Adonis, with a house scene, a street scene, a brief description of a tapestry, and a fine, rather heavily ornamental hymn to Adonis as its climax. It has 148 verses, but within its short length this is a substantial piece of work, for dramatic observation and sheer constructive ability, as well as some casual touches of mere beauty. Its range of tones from the comfortable, vulgar women's talk at home, through the excitements of the street, to the formal stillness of the tapestry and then the other world of the hymn with its over-civilized aesthetic values, impressively summons up an evening and a city. This is a purely urban poem; in its religious rituals it is utterly true to the new life of Alexandria. And it contrives to be satiric and beautiful at once, or very closely together. The work of Theokritos has a strong dramatic base, but he does far more to convey what Alexandria was than the theatre could do, by mingling so many elements in these rather short poems.

We have a poem Gow admired about Hieron king of Syracuse, which owes something to Pindar. Gow particularly liked the prayer for Sicily which it contains. It is indeed ably written, but there is a frigidity about it. Still, it has both great formal and some personal power, a combination seldom achieved by any poet less than great. The praises of Ptolemy in Idyll 17 are, as Gow would agree, less successful. The wedding-song for Helen is an archaizing exercise; its interest is largely in the strong attraction for Theokritos of early poetry, and the amount he learnt from it. He echoes Stesichoros and Sappho. The poem has no obvious purpose or known context, yet it remains a remarkably successful exercise, if nothing more. When I first read Theokritos it was one of my favourite pieces, perhaps because of its pleasurable phrases, its simple coherence, and its charming subject. We possess a little-known later imitation of this idyll by a certain Niketas Eugenianus, about which nothing is very interesting beyond the fact of its existence; Gow believed our poem was also used by the court orator Himerios, but it remains just as likely that Himerios and Theokritos drew independently on Sappho.

There are some minor and some spurious poems about which I have nothing to say. But the twenty-first idyll has some importance. Theokritos tells a story of fishermen, their poverty and their dreams of wealth. They are types from late Athenian comedy, I suppose, but very fully imagined, and drawn with touches of pathos and irony, and with phrases of seductive music. They are as good in their minor way as his bucolic characters. He begins, as he often does, with a general truth, addressing a friend Diophantos. 'Poverty alone raises up craft, and teaches toil: working men cannot sleep, anxiety and trouble prevent it ...' Theokritos is not often given to such serious moralizing, and Wilamowitz and others have thought this poem spurious. It would be inappropriate to defend it in great detail here, but it has merits as well as difficulties. 'There was no neighbour there, beside their hut the sea swam in against the crumbling land.' Whoever wrote it, this short poem is worth reading. Once there was a whole Hellenistic literature about poor fishermen, but apart from some epigrams and an echo in Plautus, this is all we have left of it. Perhaps that makes one overvalue the poem.

Theokritos treated an epic theme in his long and to my own taste unlovely *Dioskouroi* (*The Heavenly Twins*), which draws on a Homeric hymn, perhaps on Apollonios of Rhodes, and on the *Iliad*. His use of the Homeric hymn is no improvement, his narrative makes more sense than Apollonios, but his *Iliad* material is a dispiriting pastiche. To judge by its length (223 lines) this was an important set piece, a Hellenistic poem in the central tradition. It reads like a prize poem. Thank heaven Theokritos did not waste his whole life on such enterprises. He did waste time enough for an exercise on the infant Herakles, but that is a lighter and more enjoyable tale, a domestic, homely retelling of a story from Pindar. Baby Herakles is attacked by two big snakes, which he strangles. The family are roused, but they then go back to bed, as Legrand memorably observed, as if they had got up to put a cat out of the window. This is an amusing idyll: more than can be said for the thirty-eight verses of his *Bacchai*.

His *Distaff*, which went with a present to the wife of his friend Nikias, is a pleasant and moving occasional piece in an old lyric metre. It gives a stately, almost biblical impression of the position of such a woman, and an unexpected vignette of a temple, 'green, with soft rushes, Aphrodite's house'. His epigrams are wonderfully pungent. 'The dewy roses and the dense thyme-bush ... the dark-leafed bay that grows thick on the Delphic rocks ... the horned white goat who crops the end spray of the terebinth ...' paints a sharp image; the poem ends with the red blood of the goat. Daphnis has some pretty scenes in these short poems. In a sacred garden the nightingales answer to the clear spring-song of the blackbirds. The epigrams each have a touch of wit or sharpness; they are not oversweet. A number deal with poets; the oddest is four verses of advertisement for a banker.

An appalling poem written in the shape of Pan-pipes, called the
Syrinx, a series of pedantic riddles, has often been attributed to
Theokritos, and claims to be by him, but Gow properly finds him
not guilty. One could fill a chapter with the records of bad Alexandrian poetry, but I will not deal with it in this history.

Scholars used to believe that the bucolic world of Theokritos was
as artificial as his dialect, but the mimes of Herodas were a direct
imitation of life written in genuine Ionic dialect. The truth is that
the works of Herodas are literary inventions in every way; their urban
realism reflects the stage, and is convincing by its banality, and less
sharp in some ways than the observant ear of Theokritos. His metre
is a type of iambic, his dialect is based on the eastern Ionic of
Hipponax, but his mastery of it was less than complete, and clearly
not native. He uses common Greek or Attic phrases by mistake,
though his scribes have added more, which editors try to eliminate;
he is fond of rare words from Hipponax, just as all the Alexandrians
were thrilled by rareties and weird interpretations in Homer. The
word in the Theokritean fishing idyll I translated as 'earth' is an
example. But these are the outer conditions of a considerable achievement. Herodas does deserve to be remembered and read as a poet.
He took over the form of the mime, a popular entertainment, and
adapted it to an antiquated metre and dialect with some success.
Kallimachos had used the metre and the language of Hipponax in
his own iambics on new subject-matter. It is usually and probably
rightly said that Herodas was younger than the other great
Alexandrians, though no one really knows his date.

One would like to know about his inheritance from Sophron, but
the evidence is simply inadequate. His scenes are indoors, in a house
or courtroom or shop or temple. The characters are lower class and
urban, but not charmless. The plots are brief and realistic pieces of
life, but the emphasis is always on character, never on a story. And
these are highly literary poems. 'Arise, slave Psylla: how long will
you lie and snore? Drought is tormenting the sow. Waiting until
the sun gets in your skin and warms you up?' That is the beginning
of the *Dream*. It is unoriginal except in its exaggerations, but if one
can make one's peace with the language, it has a charm and the
drawing is certainly strong. '. . . The vision ended. Where's my coat?
Bring it. That was my dream and this is what it means . . .' And

then we are suddenly talking about poems and critics. This is literature about literature. Still, it is not negligible.

The pimp of Herodas is a convincing figure; so are the schoolmaster and the awful mother of the boy who gets beaten. Herodas is a satirist and an ironist. His passages of dialogue are often well observed, and sometimes moving. 'I live a long way off from here, my child, and the mud in the lanes reaches my knees, and I have no more strength than a fly has: age weighs on me, the Shadow stands by me.' This is an old nurse, the go-between in a love-affair. Her habit of speech is earthy, nothing shakes her composure, she is shameless. But the people of Herodas are seldom pleasant, and one feels he despises them. His clients of Asklepios are interesting, but even their prayers are being mocked. 'Be gracious for the cock I offer here, the herald of my house's walls, he'll make a savoury ...'

A friendly chat between women is a typical subject for Herodas. Their gossip is stuffed with historically fascinating remarks about daily life and unofficial attitudes to it. But I find him mostly too acid for my digestion. He is a capable technician of verse, yet neither in texture nor in construction is he a great poet, as Theokritos is. He is however extremely lively, in and out of season. That liveliness was learnt by intimate study of ancient literature, and probably from Theokritos. It is part of the extraordinary renaissance of poetry that took place at Alexandria under the influence of Philetas and Kallimachos, and under the patronage of the Macedonian kings.

One can best judge the reviving depth of the influence, and the flooding volume of this poetry, by the river of epigrams, often the only work we have of poets whose major works are lost, that went on being written from this time on for hundreds of years. The most inventive generation was that of the great Alexandrians, or perhaps as I have suggested, a little earlier. The humorous epigrams translate least well, since they depend on niceties of elegant musical balance or on unexpected progressions not possible in our language. But Leonidas of Tarentum survives at times, particularly in country vignettes.

> Nymphs of water, daughters of Doros,
> flow in to wet Timokles' garden,
> because Timokles always offers you
> fruit from this garden when it ripens.

Whatever Leonidas did, Theokritos did better, but Leonidas remains indestructibly enjoyable to this day. Kenneth Rexroth has caught his tone well in one poem:

> Here is Klito's little shack.
> Here is his little corn-patch.
> Here is his tiny vineyard.
> Here is his little wood-lot.
> Here Klito spent eighty years.

Leonidas could pay beautiful compliments, and his epitaphs are often moving. Nor was his range of subject or style narrow. We know little about his life: he was poor, he travelled, he knew Kos, he wrote in the names of farmers, fishermen and craftsmen, and of women. Gow thought him tedious, but he is a fine poet.

> The sun whirls an axle on fire,
> blackens stars and the moon's holy wheels:
> Homer lifting the clear light of Muses
> has darkened the hymn-sellers in one crowd.

Asklepiades has some merit; so has Anyte of Tegea, as I have suggested; so has Mnasalkes of Sikyon. But the epigrams have to be savoured individually. Asklepiades is intensely personal, but his tone is elegant, even in a drinking-poem, and too mannered.

> Drink Asklepiades, why weep? What is it?
> You are not the only one to be mugged by Love:
> and bitter arrows were not sharpened by
> Eros for you alone. Why lie in dust?
> Let's drink the alcohol of Bacchos, dawn's one inch,
> or shall we wait for lamps brought in again? . . .

Still, Asklepiades has a convincing desperation. Mnasalkes wrote short and crisp war epigrams, an epitaph for a young girl, and a poem about a cicada too good to be easily translatable. 'You will sing no more with the clear voice of your wings, cicada perching on the furrowed spikes, nor delight me lying below shade-leaves, chattering your fresh tune with yellow wings.' Has the season gone by? Or is this death? The brief couplets perfectly express a sadness and a chill that belong to every philosophy of pure enjoyment. One does not need to know more than they say. They are as complete as that famous Theokritean line, 'There is in empty kisses some delight'. Anyte's children's poems and pet animal poems, greatly as Mnasalkes seems to have admired her, have no other message. The Hellenistic epigrams are an endless series of fresh variations, some of them exquisite, and that is all.

They were still being written in the time of Virgil and Horace, and were imitated by them. In the *Eclogues* of Virgil, some of these late Greek epigrams were fed back into the mainstream of Theokritean bucolic poetry. That also had gone on being written, by Bion and by Moschos, a little more sweetly and simply alas. But the style and the convention remained attractive, and as late as Alcuin and Sannazaro and Ronsard and Alexander Pope, Theokritos has had followers. It appears unlikely that the taste for his work will ever quite die, yet his power as a poet is usually underestimated.

The numerous Alexandrian poems wrongly attributed to Anakreon include many pretty, some beautiful and a few powerful ones. Pastiche became a new style. The fragments of lyric verse that came from Alexandria have less power than earlier poetry but great charm. 'The moon is sinking and the Pleiades, the watch has gone by, I lie alone.' The Boiotian dialect poems supposed to be by Korinna are probably a piece of early Alexandrian playfulness; they are no disgrace to the circle of Theokritos. After the third century, and with these important exceptions, there were no great original poets who wrote in Greek until the collapse of the ancient world.

BIBLIOGRAPHY

(i) GENERAL

M. M. Austin, *The Hellenistic World* (historical sources), 1981

A. S. F. Gow and D. L. Page, *Hellenistic Epigrams*, 1965

P. Jay (ed.), *The Greek Anthology*, 1973

P. Levi, *Atlas of the Greek World*, 1980

A. Momigliano, *Alien Wisdom*, 1975

D. L. Page, *Further Greek Epigrams*, 1981

I. U. Powell, *Collectanea Alexandrina*, 1925; H. Lloyd-Jones and P. Parsons, *Supplementum Hellenisticum*, 1983 (the *Supplementum* has an index to both volumes)

W. Tarn and G. T. Griffith, *Hellenistic Civilization*, 3rd edition, 1952
C. A. Trypanis (ed.), *Penguin Book of Greek Verse*, 1971

(ii) KALLIMACHOS
The edition of Kallimachos in the Loeb Classical Library by C. A. Trypanis (1958) has a useful translation and draws on R. Pfeiffer's great and monumental edition of the fragments (1953)

(iii) THEOKRITOS
A. S. F. Gow, *Theocritus* (edition with commentary and translation), 1952

(iv) HERODAS
I. C. Cunningham (ed.), *Herodas*, 1971
W. Headlam (ed.), *Herodas*, 2nd edition, 1966
(It is essential to use both editions of Herodas)

19

HELLENISTIC GREEK

Hellenistic historians flourished in great numbers, and we have a comparatively enormous mass of their writings. But the survival of a particular author and the disappearance of another are not always an indication of which is the more important. To this day we read the Hellenistic historians largely for their subject-matter; few of them were great writers or even good historians. One would like, all the same, to read more than the fragments we have of Philochoros, a scholarly and patriotic historian of Athens who died by assassination about 262 B.C., out of whose ruins Felix Jacoby has constructed an enticing figure. He was not the first Athenian universal historian, but a conservative and solid figure of the 280s, an official interpreter of omens. He wrote on numerous Athenian antiquarian subjects, collected inscriptions and annotated rituals and festivals. He wrote about tragedy and about Alkman. His great work was his Athenian history, both ancient and contemporary. There is no point in treating at any length at all those other writers whose fragments readers of history are unlikely ever to encounter, and still less point in merely listing them. Philochoros must stand for a crowd of ghosts.

Polybios is a fascinating historian, whose life and writings form a bridge between Greece and Rome. He was the last successful Greek historian in the grand style, which demanded notice as literature in the same way as eighteenth-century and some nineteenth-century history does in English. His style was in that same way ossified, and yet it still convinces. We have about a third of his forty books, which followed the close of Timaios (264 B.C.) as Xenophon followed the close of Thucydides. His history took the form of annals after 215 B.C., and reached a climax with the battle of Pydna in 168, but it ended in 144. He has been dismissed as a pragmatic recorder, who lacked the depth of Thucydides, but that is only to say he has learnt a lesson from the real progress of events. He intended to be as universal as Ephoros, and he discussed the fate of states in terms of their constitutions, as Aristotle might have done. But his spur was the reality of the second century B.C.

His father was an important Greek statesman of the last days of Greek freedom. Polybios himself carried the ashes of the last great general of the Greeks, Philopoimen, to their burial in 182 B.C., and served as ambassador and cavalry commander. After the lost battle of Pydna, he was taken as a hostage to Rome. There he became a tutor and friend of Scipio, and it is to his writings that we owe the knowledge of how Scipio wept over the ruins of Carthage. He knew the world and its great actions as few historians ever have done, before or since.

The hostages were set free in 150 B.C., but Polybios stayed with Scipio. The incident at Carthage was in 146 B.C. After that he set out to explore the Atlantic, fruitlessly alas. His history was first intended to trace the rise of absolute Roman power, though his personal dedications engraved on stone have been found at more than one Greek sanctuary. He believed that history might train statesmen, and could help us all to accept disasters with equanimity. He thought of Fortune as a universal providence. My own impression is that he was trying to teach Aristotelian ethics as he understood them, but this is a disputed conjecture. He took from Aristotle the opinion that a mixed constitution is the only way to halt the cycles of instability, and constitutionally the Romans were his heroes. He died by falling from his horse at the age of eighty-two.

F. W. Walbank, the greatest modern scholar of Polybios, has expressed a dislike of his style, and a disbelief in its influence. And yet it has its good moments, and certainly its moments of influence. No one denies his honesty, a rare quality in his day, and a formal style not unlike that of Polybios persisted through Livy, who used him hugely, for a long time among historians. He is the last Greek writer to have some comprehensive sense of the use of particles, an essential element in the noise and the rhythm of Greek as it was once pronounced. But the old pitch accent was dying out, and inflections of the voice, which used to be determined by accentual and musical rhythm even in prose, became available, as they are in modern European languages, for shades of expression, so that the particles of the ancient Greek language, which had once carried so many intimate precisions of meaning, were no longer necessary. In a world where more and more Greek speakers were not native Greeks, that meant that the particles would go out of use. There is a sense in which Polybios was the last old-fashioned prose writer. He was not as agile as Plato by any means, but later writers would either be vernacular speakers of a new tongue, like the evangelists, or brilliant imitators of how language used to be, like Lucian, who was a native Aramaic speaker as the evangelists were. The written accents which used to indicate pitch, as in Chinese, but in medieval and modern Greek indicate only stress accent, were a late device invented for foreigners. The history of literature should not be separated from the histories of languages.

Polybios is more autobiographical, and at times personal, than most ancient historians, yet his history is a grand conception, not a personal essay. It ends not with the Greek catastrophe at Pydna, but with Roman power. It was Polybios, followed by the Rhodian philosopher Panaitios (born in 185), and the savant Poseidonios, both of them influential figures in Roman intellectual life, who appears to have invented the historical inevitability and the divine providential character of the rise of Rome. No doubt other Hellenistic historians had said similar things about other world powers, Athens included, but Polybios had a strong case, and it thrilled his readers. And he was detailed, thorough and truthful. He disapproved of invented speeches; where he felt compelled to use them he attempted to make them authentic at the level of language. He believed, rightly I think, that the known, inhabited world had become one place and had a single history. Separate events in distant places had woven themselves together into a massive unity. The importance of this insight can hardly be overestimated. His sense of Rome depends on it and has less weight.

As a writer he sets out to teach by great examples.

Nearly all the historians of our political constitutions have handed down the famous virtue of the Spartans and Cretans and Mantineans, and even the Carthaginians, and some have left memorials of the Athenian and the Theban state. But I shall leave these aside; I am persuaded that Athens and Thebes require no lengthy treatment, both because they did not keep their winnings as reason dictated, and their achievement was impermanent, and because their transformations were not on any modest scale, but they shone as it were by a stroke of Fortune at a particular juncture, and while they expected to flourish for ever and attended on prosperity, what they experienced was a contrary transformation.

This argument contains some peculiar implications. The Athenians will not be analysed because their success was unreasonable and no process of reason will illuminate it. They failed to attain to Aristotelian stability, and Polybios is dismissive about Fortune in their case, though in principle he venerates Fortune. He is like the German next to a friend of mine at a football match, who as everyone cheered some surprising shot was heard to groan, 'Unwissenschaftlich (unscientific)!'

Polybios was not a deep philosopher; his religious views were conventional, and also not deep, though his observations of Roman religion are interesting. He was deeply penetrated only with the idea of science, of reason, and I think with love of his own country. But he had no motive to feel patriotic about Athens, and the index to his works reveals solid complaints against the Athenians in recent history. It is clear enough that Athens had never quite abandoned her imperial avarice, or at least was never quite believed to have done so by other Greeks. He did of course think that 'At Athens one would find few things bitter, many excellent and awe-inspiringly great, when Aristeides and when Perikles governed the republic.' But those examples belonged with others, among which he places them, in a received repertory of the past already processed by earlier writers. His greatest predecessor, as a universal, analytic historian, was Ephoros, he thought. But it must be recalled that apart from Ephoros, Plato and Aristotle were both concerned with the evolution and development of mankind, and with the rudiments of political science.

Even in his narratives he was neatly analytic, and scornful of all unreason.

Philip marched to the Trichonian lake and, when he arrived at Thermon where Apollo's temple was, ruined and vandalized all over again everything he had formerly left standing of its dedications – evilly indulging his disposition on the second as on the first occasion, because sacrilege against the gods on account of one's rage against human beings is a mark of utter unreasonableness.

Even in battle Polybios gives a precise analysis. His battles are
perfectly intelligible and his trumpets are a tactical signal, not a chant
of defiance. This is true even of a passage (15.13–14) that begins
'The battle being hand to hand and man against man ...' One is
not surprised when the Romans win in the end; it all seems to be
a conjuring trick done with syntax. '... Most were cut down in
formation, but of those who attempted to escape few in the end got
away, as they were in the hands of the cavalry, and the ground
was level. Of the Romans more than one thousand five hundred fell,
and of the Carthaginians more than twenty thousand, and not many
less than that were taken prisoner in addition.'

His sense of history in these huge set scenes is I think tragical;
and that is hardly surprising, since he had experience of war, and
the morning after such a terrifying slaughter must have been unforgettable. The field of Waterloo was a small matter in comparison.
'He put the mercenaries in front, and the Carthaginians behind them,
so as to wear out the bodies of the enemy first, and by the heap
of the dead render the points of weapons useless, and to compel the
Carthaginians, who were enclosed, to stand and fight, as the poet
says, "So that unwilling yet a man must fight".' The line of Homer
is a grim joke, I suppose, but surely it is also a tragical insight. To
identify with Homer was to accept an unhappy destiny. Polybios does
not often quote poetry, but when he does it is usually Homer on
the hell of war. 'Shield thrust on shield, helm helm, man against
man, the horse-hair plumes shook on the glittering crests, nodding
together, so dense was their strife.' He is explaining the deadly effect
of a particular infantry formation.

Polybios is interested in geography, and quite precise about it, however distant. 'The Apasiaks dwell between Oxos and Tanais, of which
the Oxos runs into the Hyrkanian sea, but the Tanais into the Maiotic
lake. They are both of navigable size. There are two accounts of this
matter, one probable, the other surprising but not impossible ...'
His seriousness never quite relaxes, and he genuinely imagines
knowledge can be encyclopedic and science universal. The first addict
of that optimistic world-view was probably Eratosthenes, called Beta,
because he was second best at everything, or Pentathlos, because
of the number of his publications in different fields. He succeeded
Apollonios of Rhodes as head of the library; he measured the earth,

doubled the cube, dated all history, wrote an antiquarian study of comedy, and published some foolish poetry. He died in 194 B.C. when Polybios was a child, but there is no doubt that for all his absurdity he represented enlightenment, and it is essential to Polybios that what separates him intellectually from the circle of Aristotle is the formidable and deadening scholarship of the later Alexandrians.

Although Polybios wrote so much more than we have of his work, we still have more of it than most scholars who are not specialized historians ever read. That is largely due to lack of interest in his period of history, which is a pity, because the lucid flow of his narrative is rewarding even though he is unexciting. And he is not without anecdotes and set pieces. I am fond of the secret message in proverbial terms that was sent to Demetrios ('Night favours all, but favours the brave most' and so on), in which a German scholar in the nineties discovered a hidden acrostic that dry Polybios failed to notice. And yet in this same fragment of a few pages (31.13–15) he tells an adventure story excellently. The more distracting pleasures of history are unknown to him, but his level gaze falls equally on events, and the result is a seemly text. His greatness is usually better understood by Roman historians than by literary scholars; and yet Scipio weeping over ruined Carthage is one of the most revealing moments in the history of the ancient world, and we owe it to Polybios: it was to him it seemed worth recording.

'And when Scipio saw the city as it lay in burnt ruins and the utmost devastation, he is said to have shed tears, and to have made no secret of weeping for his enemies.' He understood that cities and nations and empires must suffer transformation and decline, just as human beings lose their luck, and as Troy did, 'which was once a fortunate city', and the empires of the Assyrians and Medes and Persians, and most recently the Macedonian empire.

And either deliberately or because it escaped his lips, he said, ' "The day will come when holy Troy will die, and Priam and the people of Priam." ' And when he was openly asked by Polybios, who had been his tutor, what he meant, they say that without pretence he clearly named his own country, for which when he considered human fate he trembled. Polybios heard this and records it.

The verses about Troy are from the *Iliad*, of course.

In the lifetime of Polybios, Greek prose was already I think developing in fresh and unforeseen ways. His own severe habit of speech, which one might call the grand conservative style, was continued into Latin. The luxuriant rhetoric that had been cropped but never killed off by the philosophers flourished uncontrolled in the courts of the Asian Greek kings: it became called the Asian style, and it was rivalled and largely ousted in the end by a revived, pedantically precise and crisp Attic or Athenian style. But the theorists, the critics and the later practitioners of rhetoric have very small importance in the genuine history of literature. As for Plutarch, he must have a chapter of his own. What matters even more than famous names is the beginnings of prose fiction, that is of the romance, which in later centuries, under other circumstances, brought forth the novel. In the Greek romances, Eros invaded history and adventure, as in epigrams he had already invaded the epitaph and the dedication. The early Greek romances reek of Theokritos and of the comic stage. But they deserve consideration for their own sake. And they cannot quite be explained away in terms of Menander or the Alexandrian mime.

The first pure fictions known to mankind were surely historical fictions. The style of Ktesias, a highly entertaining writer famous and even proverbial for his untruthfulness, seems to have offered a foretaste. He was a Greek doctor working for the Persian court in the time of Alexander, and his tales were many and marvellous. Semiramis, princess of Babylon, was one of his characters. He had no need to go beyond the Greek cities of Asia Minor for his amiable habits of mind, but no doubt in Ktesias, if no earlier, Asian storytelling entered European literature. The *Alexander Romance*, by pseudo-Kallisthenes, has similar origins; it is a jejune construction, although its progeny in later versions is mighty.

We have already considered the tragic fictions of Agathon, of which we know hardly more than their existence. His master Euripides was a strong influence on the devices and the suspended climax of prose romance. So were the Homeric hymns, with their pirates and travels, and the troubles and triumph of each god. Probably Egyptian sources were important more often than we know. We have the Jewish romance of *Joseph and Azenath*. Come to that, we have even a late Greek tragedy of a kind with a Jewish theme, the *Exodus* by Ezekiel.

Such writings have an exotic appeal for us, but they are marginal to Greek literature. In the Hellenistic period we are suddenly plunged into a wider and very vigorous world, and although we cannot here trace all its interactions, we must at least grasp that the fact that the world is wide is extremely important to the writers of romances.

They belong to the proper history of Greek literature because they have a lively core, they are well written, and when all other arguments have been weighed, the prose romance does seem to have been a Greek invention. In its low form it flooded its way through into Latin, and we hear of an officer of Crassus who carried in his luggage for light reading a Latin version of the *Tales of Miletos*, witty and salacious fictions it would seem. In its high form, the romance was adapted as the *Golden Ass* of Apuleius and the *Satyricon* of Petronius, a fragment of whose Greek original has turned up recently on a scrap of papyrus. But high or low, the form is essentially the same. It inspired Boccaccio, Chaucer and Shakespeare, and of course Sidney, and the *Diana* of Montemayor. The romance is seedlike: whether in a greater or lesser form it can catch the imagination, which it was always meant to do, and seeding in an imagination or a humus of better quality, it can produce even after centuries an astonishing and unstunted tree. That is what happened with Shakespeare's *Pericles Prince of Tyre*.

B. E. Perry, the most convincing writer in English on the ancient romances, speaks of an 'ideal novel' which 'does not come into being until, through the agency of a new class of writers morally and sentimentally inspired by a new middle-class idealism, a complete and sudden break has been made with previous literary practice'. That seems to me too high-minded and too absolute. The 'middle-class idealism' he imagines was lacking. There was a wider literate class to be entertained, that was all. The idealism of late antiquity was philosophic. Their sense of chance and their desire for a finished story and a happy ending were primitive, and go back at least to Euripides and the comic stage. R. Merkelbach has thrown at least a most interesting sidelight, possibly a central light, on those Greek romances which we have complete, and which interest us most, though they are not as early as Polybios, by suggesting an underlying connection with mystery religions, which at least mirror the difficult journeys, the initiation and the glorified ending. If he is right, what he suggests is true only of a late development in which romance stories had 'attained their nature'.

But ancient critics ignored popular stories, and so the genre, the form or kind to which these writings belonged, was never defined. They spilt over unregenerately in many directions. What is worse from our point of view is that they were censored. The earlier and unreformed, short or formless stories have hardly survived. Perry scorns the view that 'attempting to write history, these popular writers stumbled into romance', which for the early period I think remains a possible opinion.

Professor Barns the Egyptologist, who was deeply and widely informed, thought an Egyptian influence was paramount on love stories. That may be true, but erotic narrative was by no means beyond the scope of the earliest Alexandrian Greek writers, or of the popular Greek mime which we know underlies surviving written literature. Those romances that survive in bulk are late, beginning under the Roman empire; they have been intellectually, even pedantically, adapted. Some of the less respectable, more interesting stories we now have are later still. The papyrus texts that have come to light have not been thoroughly studied together, so far as I know; they add to what existed already only an endless and wild variety. Romances are extremely hard to date.

The story of Khaireas and Kallirhoe by Chariton can at least now be shown from papyrus evidence to be earlier than the traditionally accepted dates of the other romances. For many years it was thought to be even later than they were, but it has to be at least as early as the first century A.D. It was written as a historical fiction, the story of the daughter of that famous Hermokrates who defeated the Athenians in Sicily. Chariton is not a great genius, though the papyri and the gibes of a later writer show he was popular in his own time. But in this area we are forced to study the form itself: admirable examples are far to find.

Hermokrates the general had a daughter, a wonder and a miracle of a young woman, the idol all Sicily adored. Her beauty was superhuman, it was godlike, no beauty of a mere Nereid or Nymph in the mountains, but of Aphrodite ... Suitors came pouring into Syracuse ... But Eros wanted a marriage of his own pleasure. There was a young man called Khaireas, surpassing all the youth of his age in beauty; he was as sculptors and painters express Achilles and Nireus and Hippolytos and Alkibiades ... returning from the gymnasium, shining like a star with the ruddy glow of youth, he met Kallirhoe on a narrow path, as the god Eros had contrived ...

The end of the story is introduced like this. 'I think this last chapter will please our readers most: it is a purging of the previous sad events. No more piracy and slavery and lawcourts and war and trouble and captivity, but true love and lawful marriage. Now I will tell you how the goddess revealed the truth, and made the lovers known to one another ...' It would be pedantic to point out in detail the origins of all these motifs in earlier Greek literature. Readers of this history will be aware of most of them. But it is worth pointing out Reitzenstein's analysis in his brilliant *Hellenistische Wundererzählung* (*Hellenistic Miracle Narratives*) in 1906, of Chariton's construction. It is in terms of a five-act play, something well known in the comic theatre. The details are usefully reproduced in English by Perry, but anyone truly interested in this whole area of studies would do well to consult Reitzenstein's book on more matters than one. In most romances, the complications and episodes are so abundant as to defeat such a climactic construction, each episode having a climax of its own, with constant divine interventions. But Chariton hinges his narrative on a trial scene, and his readers have a chance of following the whole plot; it is only his characters who get lost in it, as Shakespeare's do in theirs. I would be a little surprised if Chariton's book did not in the end turn out even earlier than scholars now think.

The richer, denser romances by Heliodoros and Achilles Tatios are to most modern taste somewhat unreadable, but their workmanship is exquisite, and they are thickly stuffed with plums. These survived because they were not popular works swiftly thrown off or carelessly put together; they attracted the mind of the early Byzantines by their sweetness and variety, and many pedantic pleasures; no doubt it helped that Heliodoros was thought to be a bishop. These writings even came close to achieving the status of popular literature, and their European influence has been enormous. The description of a garden by Achilles Tatios passed through a literary version of the Byzantine epic story of Digenis Akritas into what scholars used to believe was a genuine medieval epic tradition – but wrongly, alas.

The best surviving Greek romance is surely the *Daphnis and Chloe* of Longos, whom no ancient critic ever appears to have read, and no papyrus fragment records. It survived by a freak of manuscript history. Indeed we owe even Chariton, who was popular once, as well as Xenophon of Ephesos, to a single thirteenth-century manuscript (Conventi Soppressi 627), first printed only in 1726 in London, when that manuscript had travelled to Florence from a minor monastic library. Longos was from Lesbos, where he set his story; numerous aesthetic and linguistic arguments combine to make it highly probable that he wrote in the second century A.D. The Theokritean aspect of his narrative appears to have descended to him through the paintings that he knew, one of which he describes. Pictures of rustic love-affairs are not uncommon in second-century descriptions of painting, but that art and its patronage did not continue; nor does it seem to have flourished before the destruction of Pompeii in 79 A.D. Such arguments are delicate, but we cannot afford to neglect them.

Longos is now possibly overvalued, as he used to be undervalued, for his powerful erotic charge. My own sympathies are with the overvaluers. He has a voyeuristic streak, and has attracted fine illustrations, as well as some vulgar ones, in modern times. But he is never obscene. His theme is the pleasure and innocence of love, his characters being of such rustic innocence that the pleasure is long delayed. His style sparkles with charm and amusement, and his Greek is attractively readable. He is one of the few ancient writers perfectly at home in a modern Greek translation (by Rodis Roufos, illustrated by Ghika). Of all the late Greek writers, Longos is the one that students most infallibly enjoy. He is a sorbet of literature; he melts on analysis and there seems nothing to him. But he gives great pleasure and has an obscurely deeper resonance.

Nietzsche remarked unfairly that Christianity gave poison to Eros but he did not die, he survived as Vice. What he said is truer of Victorian Europe than of the ancient world, where Eros drank his poison not among Christians, but in places like the brothels of Pompeii. To Longos at least, in the second century A.D., the garden of Eden aspect of paganism still belonged by nature and by inheritance. It was a world of art and literature viewed with the sharpness of an urban nostalgia, but in his pages one can still feel it.

As it was summer, Dionysophanes had couches laid down on piles of leaves in front of the cave, and had all the country-people sit down to a fine feast. Lamon and Myrtale were there, Dryas and Nape, Dorkon's family, Philetas and his sons, Chromes and Lykainion; even Lampes, who had sought and found forgiveness, was not missing. As you might expect with guests like that, the atmosphere was pure rusticity. One sang reaping songs, another the work-songs they use for treading the vintage. Philetas played the flute, Lampes played the reed-pipe, Dryas and Lamon danced, Daphnis and Chloe kissed. The goats were grazing nearby, as if they had their part to play in the feast, something that those who came from the city found by no means to their liking. But Daphnis called out to some of the goats by their names, and gave them fresh leaves, and took them by their horns and kissed them.

And not only that day, but for all the rest of their lives, Daphnis and Chloe passed most of their time at the steadings. For gods, they worshipped the Nymphs and Pan and Eros; they came to possess numerous flocks of sheep and goats, and of all food they always preferred fruit and milk. They gave their son to a nanny-goat to suckle, and put their little girl who was born later to suck a ewe . . .

The story and the style are trembling on the edge of oversweetness and childishness. They have a pantomime quality. Yet they are saved by humour and by a certain sprinkling of saltiness. *Daphnis and Chloe* is well written; it is a beautiful and a unique achievement. Shakespeare would have liked it probably better than we do, but he would have been right. Our appetite has been cloyed by later mishandlings of the same themes.

So late in their history, it is evident that the ancient Greeks had entirely lost neither their virtuosity nor their originality. Dio Chrysostomos was a contemporary of Longos, and capable of a rustic set piece, though it depended on painting. His account of the ruined and overgrown state of Greece has a true romantic melancholy. But many of his writings are literary exercises. The exceptions have a moral and political bite. But they would not survive purely by their literary merit, and they interest us only for their marginal position on the edges of the history of authentic literature. Like many scholars, I have spent happy hours scrambling about among such marginal authors, because they have a reviving quality, but they belong to the history rather of civilization than of literature. The great exception is Lucian, whom I shall discuss later.

I have said relatively little about ancient criticism of literature, because on the whole the subject is disappointing, but one work of criticism in Greek, written in the first century A.D., is itself a real contribution to literature. Whatever may be the origins of his opinions, this author does not belong to any known school of thought; he shows startling originality and freshness. He seems to be called Longinus, though no one now knows who he was or when and where exactly he wrote. His book, which is incomplete as we have it, is called *On the Sublime*, or *On Height*, and it is based both on a detailed and thorough knowledge of style and a clear sense of the importance of simple boldness in works of literature. The modern conception of greatness owes something to the older prevailing notion of sublimity, which was inherited from Longinus. No doubt conceptions like these are always false, or swiftly become false, and yet we do know what they mean, and the idea of sublimity as Longinus defines it has a forceful and immediate appeal. It was in his hands a useful instrument for analysing the work of many different writers. Classical scholars still admire him as a critic, perhaps for his unique directness and lack of pedantry. To the modern general reader, he would seem less surprising, but still interesting. There is a foolish conspiracy to call him pseudo-Longinus, because although no one knows which Longinus he was, if that was indeed his name, we do know a Longinus he was not, but was once thought to be.

Philostratos, who wrote the lives of the men of letters of his own and earlier ages, wrote as these other writers did, late in the day. All the same, his merits are remarkable, and far higher than those of some more centrally concerned historians. Under the Empire every man of letters, with few exceptions like Longos, was a lackey of literature. But Philostratos was well educated, informative and technically able, and even if his best works are pastiche, he retains a real attractiveness. He is much more interesting than what have been called the 'concert-orators', the virtuoso performers of the literary, such as Aelius Aristides, and the famous patron Herod of Athens, a capable imitator of antique styles, both as an architectural patron (his buildings are all over Greece) and as a writer.

Philostratos is a name shared, or so it seems, by four members of a family. The important one, who wrote the *Lives of the Savants* (or sophists) and the fascinating life of a professional mystic and wonder-worker called Apollonios of Tyana, appears to have lived in the late third century A.D., though the strange Apollonios had lived two hundred years earlier. Philostratos plays down the miracles and plays up a kind of divinity or sanctity, but all the same his book offers its readers plenty of exotic excitements, and it is a moving and unique record. Even the rhetorical savants were to him haloed and in a way holy. His extravagant respect for these sometimes tawdry old figures does indeed make them live, and for a moment one feels for them as he does, though his list goes back to Gorgias.

This Philostratos, or someone else of the same name and unknown date, wrote the *Heroikos*, a work that should be prized. This is a conversation, a dialogue between a foreign traveller and a local peasant near the site of Troy. We know that the dead heroes of the *Iliad* received genuine religious worship, and in the *Heroikos* the old peasant tells how their ghosts walk in his fields. This book is not just an excuse for literary nostalgia, but rather a study in the real beliefs of such a peasant. It contains two delightful snatches of lyric verse, which Philostratos seems to have made up, and as a fiction it is arresting and subtly convincing.

The principal heroic ghost is Protesilaos, the first Greek to be killed at Troy, but Philostratos is no more distant from his peasants and the haunted landscape than Yeats was distant from the Irish peasants. His *Heroikos* has perhaps been underestimated and neglected because of its late or uncertain date. Its surface texture is crisp, not soft, though it is essentially a literary artifice, a kind of game. It contains some emendations of Homer, and only a scholar writing for scholars could have produced it. But nostalgic as it is, it stands on its own feet as a book, perhaps because the peasant is so convincing. It deserves to be revived.

Since later Greek writing has drawn us into this wonderland, a little must be said about the New Testament. Jewish works in Greek already existed. I have ignored the religious works of Philo and the history of Josephus only as I have ignored other late philosophers and historians. I believe the history of the Maccabees is a better example of a Jewish work in Greek. The Bible itself was translated into Greek, and at least a sentence of it was admired by a famous

Greek critic. The apocalyptic writings of the Jews interested the Romans, and struck a note familiar to the Greek world since Herodotos, though that note seldom attained the virtues of great literature. In particular the *Sibylline Oracles*, a long and tangled series of verse prophecies of doom or redemption, had a fascination even for Virgil and Horace, at least where they affected the ultimate destiny of Rome.

The documents collected as the *Corpus Hermeticum*, which are broadly speaking gnostic – that is, writings inviting the individual to a mystical revelation, much like the Orphic verses, which are almost all equally late in date – include at least two treatises of interesting merit and beauty. They deserve a place in any history of Greek literature, as the fables of Plato do. The *Poimandres* is a fable about the fall of the soul and its redemption. The background of all these writings appears to be Judaeo-Greek Egypt, with strong Egyptian colouring. They are essentially other-worldly, but the notion that the Greeks were never other-worldly before Plato, or before Christianity, is quite false. The loss of confidence in earthly values that came to a climax under the Roman empire had been maturing for a long time, as the history of philosophy demonstrates.

One could scarcely attain a full understanding even of the official literature of the Greeks, or of the historical process of the ancient world, without looking at least by contrast at the Christian book of *Revelations*, the last work of the New Testament, the intrusion of a fresh and authentic voice both into Christian and into pagan litera-ture. It has very great power. Its condemnation of the world is precipitous, its phrasing terribly memorable. No moralizing Hellen-istic philosophic sermon or verse exhortation can remotely compare with it. This is not a difference of doctrine but of style. The writer of *Revelations* is committed utterly to every image he summons up, and to the overwhelming importance of what he has to say. That sense had been lacking for a long time in Greek. It is like the difference between the best and most authentic ballads and the more literary writings of the centuries when they were written. Yet it implies no lack of construction or of a genuine momentum, as of a poem. The outburst against Babylon the great city, with its deadly climax 'the souls of men', does not deserve its neglect by historians of literature and of the ancient world. Nor is it easy to change a phrase or a word in this entire work without grave loss. It is not written in classicizing Greek, and if it were it would be worth less. In any of its older versions, it is one of the greatest, the most impressive pieces of English prose, as it is of Greek prose.

The Gospels, which may have begun in Aramaic, have something of the same original simplicity and freshness, and therefore the same extraordinary quality of producing in many languages translations almost as fine as themselves. It is difficult to discuss them as literature, almost as if one were otherwise uninterested in their contents, and yet they are books on a shelf among other books, and the time has surely come when we should look closely at their virtue as Greek. The narrative is solemnly simple. The teachings and fables have a strength which is not always precisely literary, but it often is. The Gospel of John, into which poetry and ritual have crumbled, is perhaps the most impressive. What is laconic in these writings is best and most resonant, but here and there some small, apparently unnecessary detail can bring page after page to life, and the fuller phrasing of the discourse of Christ on the night of the last supper has an irresistible depth and completeness. Plato would have admired it very greatly.

The narratives of the judgement and crucifixion of Christ convey a strong sense of tragic inevitability and of appalling climax. They have a grander simplicity, and they are more terrible, than any of those acts of the martyrs which were the residue of the Greek popular romances. There do also exist acts of the Jewish martyrs, with dialogue of question and answer, based partly on Roman legal processes and no doubt on records. Here and there they show a consciousness, or a half consciousness, of Euripides. So it is at least conceivable that filtered through philosophic discussion and example, such as can be found inherited by Horace in his poems, the footfall and progression of tragedy may have influenced the way in which the Passion Narrative was written. I refer chiefly to the dialogues with the Jewish and the Roman authorities, and this remote, conjectural influence presupposes a Hellenized Judaism which was basically Jewish. Certainly, the narratives of the death of Christ had been intensely meditated before they were written down. They have a majestic sobriety.

Having said that these are quite new and authentic voices, it is hard to pass on to others which are less so. But as writing, as something Plato might criticize, Christian literature had already entered with Paul into its long decline. There were fine works to come, and fine passages in Paul, which if this book were to be very much extended one ought to include. But we are considering books on their merits as writing, essentially a secular undertaking, perhaps an impossible task, and it may be some corrective to the excitements of the last few paragraphs to turn to a secular stylist of the second century whose work depends entirely on wit, pastiche and stylish intelligence, a pure intellectual entertainer.

Lucian, Loukianos in Greek, was born around 120 A.D. at Samosata on the Euphrates. He thought of himself as Syrian. He has been thought of as a throwback, but that is a mistake. He is humorous, and quite at home in his own skin. Syria had been Hellenized for a very long time in his day. We owe the first substantial collection which swelled with the centuries into our Palatine anthology to Meleager of Gadara in the first century B.C., one of a number of excellent poets on a small scale from all over the Greek world. These men believed that in spirit they were world citizens, but they also felt that whatever was Greek was their intellectual inheritance. Lucian is thoroughly a Greek writer, from the depth of his soul to his educated fingertips. The diversity of these late Greek writers depends partly, as I have said, on the great size of the Greek world.

Five years before Lucian was born, the last Syrian Macedonian prince of Commagene, whose capital city was Samosata, died and left a monument at Athens. He had served as Roman consul. He was Philopappos, after whom the hill of Philopappou is named, and the gnarled white marble tooth that crowns that hill is his memorial. Seen from a distance it has great charm and a position that makes it romantic, but seen from close it has a crispness of execution and some boldness of conception. In the history of Greek sculpture it has its place. Today it broods above pine trees, meditating the Parthenon. The works of Lucian are just such a monument.

One would be foolish to be dismissive about Lucian. His dialect is educated, not affected, his style is more original than pastiche. His sophistries are jokes, and his verbal simplicity is calculated and varied by phrases as sharp as a bee-sting. He translated well into modern European languages of the seventeenth and eighteenth centuries, but he requires some subtlety: he is never quite as racy or as obvious as he sometimes seems. And he has vigour, he is not living in the twilight of the west where the bat cries to the owl, nor in a mellow afterglow invented by Gibbon. He is a citizen of his world. His identification with Greece and the Classics is a passionate obsession and an identity.

He wrote a long series of short prose works, including ironic treatments of purists and pedants, religious charlatans, philosophy, rhetoric and mythology. He is particularly funny about the gods, in a manner that recalls Aristophanes. In the rather thorough and usefully earnest discussion of him by Albin Lesky, one can scarcely recognize the writer one has read with a lifetime of increasing admiration and pleasure. He learnt his Greek at school, and it has the curious purity of the kind of French that used to be spoken by educated people in the Balkans, a beautiful and sinuous, but slightly refined, unidiomatic language. There is no English equivalent. He was apprenticed to a sculptor who was his uncle, but disastrously. He went through a school of rhetoric, but abandoned a career in that subject at forty. In his *Twice Accused*, he defends himself against the reproaches of Rhetoric itself on the Akropolis of Athens.

But of course he no more abandoned the skills he had acquired than Plato did, and of rhetoric and sophistry as entertainment he is perhaps the greatest master. Some of his pieces are more seriously intended than the *Praises of the Fly*, and more substantial, but what he took seriously was literature and good taste and common sense, not the art of rhetoric. He encountered philosophy but was never a convert, although he was penetrated, as all Greek culture was in his time, and more deeply the deeper it went, by moral philosophy and inherited thoughts. I greatly doubt whether what Lesky calls his early successes 'as a bombastic sophistical orator' are seriously intended. In later age he worked as a literary secretary to an official in Egypt. He criticized writers of history with relish and justice, he parodied romantic fiction in his *True Stories*, and we owe probably to him the first version of the *Golden Ass* of Apuleius, a much more discreet performance than that uncontrolled masterpiece. One of the best qualities of Lucian is his abundance of invention. We know nothing about his death, but he was still writing after 180 A.D. He was not 'an opportunist', nor does his power consist of 'a certain adroitness of appeal to the less reflective side of human nature', as the *Oxford Classical Dictionary* prudishly maintains. In an age in which the best Greek was a pastiche of past language, he is an excellent stylist, and a brilliantly sound and versatile writer who should rank with Diderot.

Under the surface of his writing lies a reverence for the lost greatness of Greek literature. The festival of Zeus had been dropped, there were crowds of absurd new gods, Dodona had been robbed, so had Olympia; statues were broken even in Athens. He is not afraid to argue that Rome is empty and boring, and Athens still a thrilling city. He likes Herodotos and imitates his dialect, but puts him in hell as a liar. He shows interest in Ktesias, who was famous for entertaining lies. He knows the famous ruins, and some obscure ones: not only Babylon and Mycenae but Kleonai as well. He shows much more penetrating knowledge of art than the usual ornamental references to it. He remarks, for example, that Parthian architecture was built to impress and not to give pleasure, he notices what marble comes from Lakonia, and what statues are more ancient than their setting. Indeed, his antiquarian interests make him a useful and rather untapped source for ancient religion and for archaeology. But he is entertaining, not pedantic. One is pleased to hear of oaths sworn by geese and by dogs (favoured by Sokrates) and by plane trees. He remembers or invents verses in more than one style. He is a master of the picturesque, but without lingering too long on it.

His famous dialogues of the gods were pleasantly put into English by Charles Cotton, who oddly chose to put them into verse. They do draw on the comic stage, and theatre and dialogue had been intimately linked since dialogue was invented. Hera berating Zeus about Ganymede has an appropriate sharpness in spite of the relaxed pace. It may be thought more civilized than the loud voice of moral Juvenal, in English as in its own language.

> And yet, for all thy Pranks on Earth,
> (Unfitting for thy Place and Birth)
> Thou hitherto hast ever yet
> Had either so much Grace or Wit,
> Manners, or shame, or altogether,

> As not to bring thy *Trollops* hither,
> As thou hast done this *Dandiprat*
> For all the *Gods* to titter at:
> And all under Pretence the Youth
> Must be thy *Cup-bearer* forsooth; ...

The mere list of titles of Lucian's writings conveys something of his agility and creative abundance: *The Council of the Gods*, *On Dancing*, *The Syrian Goddess*, *The Dream*, *The Donkey*, *On Grief*, *Prometheus*, *Ikaromenippos or Above the Clouds*, *The Long-lived*, *How to Write History*, *The Drinking-party or The Lapiths*, *Zeus Convicted*, *Zeus in Tragedy*, *Loves*, *Herodotos*, *Raising the Dead*, *Pictures*, *Halcyon or Transformations*, *Gout*, *Conversations of Whores*, *Submarine Conversations*. There are many more. Even his treatment of space travel is memorable. He combines the untramelled zest and multiple consciousness of the Renaissance with the crisper solidity of the ancient world. He was widely read in the Renaissance in a Latin translation.

There were Byzantine writers who tried to be as clever as Lucian, but it was impossible for them. That world had died, and it was the death of a world, not the birth of Christianity, that made Lucian's tone impossible for many centuries to come. Christianity might have begotten a Lucian of its own, but the moment passed perhaps, with the generation of More and Erasmus. Still, the ruins of Greece did not pass away without record. Pausanias described everything in loving detail, in Lucian's generation. Their observations often coincide, and where they differ the difference is of great interest.

Pausanias is not a great writer, his prose style is mannered and unacceptable on the whole. We read him only for what he tells us, and because what he describes is lost. But much more than the Augustan Strabo, and the earlier topographic fragments of Polemon and Dikaiarchos which litterati sometimes prefer, he does give one an intense and full sense of what mainland Greece was like, and of its social and intellectual atmosphere. From that atmosphere Lucian stands out as a wonderful firework display. Man cannot live by style alone, but it is at least arguable that Lucian is the last Greek writer one can read simply for his style, for the mere pleasure of his company. With the late writers of brief poems, like Rufinus and Palladas, one can live for only a few minutes at a time.

A more typical member of the generation of Pausanias is the ill and anxious Aelius Aristides, with his ingrowing religion, his admiration of Rome, and his six books of private revelations from Asklepios. He was a pupil of the tutor to Marcus Aurelius and probably of Herod of Athens. His writings are not unreadable, but they are not memorable either. He was admired in his own time for the Athenian purity of his language. He is more read now than he used to be, because he offers a fascinating insight into his times, and into the development of personal religion. But he is not a great or even a very brilliant writer, and we read him rather from curiosity than from appetite. He is hardly fit to be mentioned in the same book as Plato and Homer, or the same chapter as Lucian and St John.

THE DATES OF EARLY PROSE FICTION

Ktesias	4th-3rd centuries B.C.
Romance of Alexander	?2nd century B.C.
Ninus story	1st century B.C.
Spread of 'Miletos stories'	1st century B.C.
Greek original of *Recognitiones* of 'Clement'	1st century B.C.
Joseph and Azenath	1st century B.C.
Chariton, *Khaireas and Kallirhoe*	?1st century B.C.
Xenophon of Ephesos	mid-2nd century A.D.
Diogenes, *Wonders beyond Thule* (parodied by Lucian)	pre-160 A.D.
Lucian (?), *The Donkey*	mid-2nd century A.D.
Iamblichos, *Babylon*	c.165 A.D.
Lollianos, *Phoenicia*	2nd century A.D.
Longos, *Daphnis and Chloe*	2nd century A.D.
Achilles Tatios, *Kleitophon and Leukippe*	2nd century A.D.
Heliodoros, *Aithiopia*	4th century A.D.

Note: The list in the *Cambridge History of Classical Literature* (vol. 1), p. 684, attempts to date some papyrus fragments as well as these works, and is in general inclined to later dates than B. E. Perry's *Ancient Romances* (p. 350). I am inclined to an even earlier date than Perry wherever possible, and even tempted to tie the origins of the whole phenomenon as closely as possible to the generation of Kallimachos and Theokritos or the next. The dates I suggest here are compromises, but do not stray far from received opinion. The dates of the actual papyri that survive offer only a *terminus ante quem*.

BIBLIOGRAPHY

G. W. Bowersock, *Greek Sophists in the Roman Empire*, 1969

Charles Cotton, *The Scoffer Scoff'd*, 7th edition, 1765

E. R. Dodds, *Pagan and Christian in an Age of Eternity*, 1963

A. Momigliano, *Alien Wisdom*, 1975

S. H. Monk, *The Sublime*, 1935

G. Murray, *Five Stages of Greek Religion*, 3rd edition, 1935

A. D. Nock, *Conversion*, 1933

A. D. Nock and A. Festugière, *Corpus Hermeticum*, 1945–54

B. E. Perry, *The Ancient Romances*, 1967

B. P. Reardon, *Courants littéraire grecs de 2e et 3e siècles apres J.-C.*, 1971

D. A. Russell, *Longinus* (translation), 1966

E. S. Shuckburgh, *Polybius* (translation), 2nd edition, 1962

S. Treubner, *The Greek Novella*, 1958

F. W. Walbank, *Polybius* (commentary), 3 vols., 1957–79

J. Winkler and G. Williams (eds.), *Later Greek Literature, Yale Classical Studies* 27, 1982

D. Russell's *Declamation* (1984) appeared too late for me to use it; to have mastered it in time would have perhaps greatly improved this book.

Note: On Jewish history in Greek, readers are referred to the study of Josephus by P. Vidal-Naquet, *Flavius Josèphe, du bon usage de la trahison*, 1975, which is based on the preface to the *Jewish War* of Josephus.

On the other late historians, and on late philosophy, one should consult the *Cambridge History of Classical Literature*, vol. 1, 1985, which has a wider and less precisely literary scope than this brief history.

20

PLUTARCH

Plutarch, or Ploutarchos in Greek, lived from 50 A.D. or earlier until 120 A.D. or later, in the generation of Philopappos not of Lucian. In spite of being earlier than Lucian, he will not fit easily into the same general discussion of late writers; he needs a chapter of his own. He was a mainland Greek from an old local family established at Chaironea between Thebes and Delphi; although he lived there most of his life, he had grand Roman friends in public life and Greek literary friends. He 'did not wish to diminish Chaironea by the withdrawal of even one inhabitant'. For thirty years from his forties until his death he was a Delphic priest. He knew Athens of course, and had travelled at least to Rome as a diplomat and a lecturer, and to Egypt and Asia. He even knew Demetrios of Tarsos, who acted as a diplomat for Agricola in the British isles, and whose tales of the western islands of Scotland he records. He was a deeply and tranquilly passionate antiquarian, and a moral philosopher of humane warmth and undisturbed religion, but without intellectual originality. His works, of which we have a satisfying haystack, include writings sometimes thrilling but sometimes amateurish, on a wide variety of what had become the usual themes, and some unusual.

The exception to all this sympathetic late antique mediocrity, and what raises him to a level of greatness as a writer, is his *Lives*. We have two of his lives of the Caesars, one or two stray lives, and twenty-three in a series of contrasting pairs, always one Greek and one Roman, usually with a summary comparison of their moral qualities. He wished to teach us about the characters of great men, concentrating on their education, morality and moral type, and the way in which character worked itself out. But the result goes far beyond the plan. As a historian he is little better but no worse than the sources available to him, and he was widely read, but his dramatic sense of the past and of the careers and fates of human beings constantly touch his pages with a quality which is more than glamour. The death of Cicero is thrillingly sinister. In Plutarch the disastrous attempt to inject poetry into history has at last paid off, perhaps because it is second nature to him and he seizes it from his sources, and because he applies it almost wholly to the fate of individuals. His *Lives* really are the stuff of poetry, though they read as unpretentious prose. With the alteration of very few words, they transmute into Shakespeare: '"Was this well done of your lady, Charmion?" "Extremely well," she answered, and as became the descendant of so many kings. And as she said this, she fell down dead by the bedside.'

For the relationship with Shakespeare, one should read North's translation of Amyot's French version of Plutarch. It ought not to be used by historians, because Amyot made mistakes here and there, but it retains its gripping power as an English classic. What I quote here is the revised version by the poet A. H. Clough of the translations by various hands edited by Dryden, which as a schoolboy I bought for a few shillings and have an affection for. Clough's introduction to the *Lives* is still the best treatment of Plutarch for anyone but a specialist. What one remembers about his biographies is not moments or sharp anecdotes, or the noble and pungent eloquence of Tacitus, but the progression of scenes and paragraphs towards a climax, the momentum of a life or of a death. Tacitus was ten years younger than Plutarch, and Suetonius was twenty years younger.

Biography had been written in Greek since the fifth century inchoately and the fourth formally; it was given a form and shape by the circle of Aristotle and the Alexandrian scholars. The art of portrait sculpture, warts and all, flourished in the courts of Hellenistic kings and on their coinage, and in Roman republican portraits. It was one of the final attainments of Greek art. But Plutarch has a vigorous moral interest in individuals, and at his best a momentum, a dramatic sense of life, which is not to be found before his time. His Roman lives are the most exciting, because they are the best informed. The Greek examples which stand in the background throw a more useful light than one might expect, since they often raise interesting moral questions, and the parallel lives are structurally so close that a puzzling anecdote in one life will often explain one in another. We hear details we are glad to know about the descendants of Aristeides and Aristogeiton, which are oddly irrelevant to the great man's life, just because Plutarch wants to end his Marcus Cato with a compliment to his great-great-grandson, Cato the philosopher. The Athenian antiquities and the origins of festivals, which are the only interesting feature in his *Theseus*, are meant to balance the Roman antiquities in his *Romulus*. Phokion is recorded for his death, to balance the death of Cato the Younger, who read 'Plato on the soul' before his suicide.

Must I be disarmed, and hindered from using my own reason? And you, young man, why do you not bind your father's hands behind him, that when Caesar comes, he may be unable to defend himself? To despatch myself I want no sword; I need but hold my breath awhile, or strike my head against the wall.

When he had thus spoken, his son went weeping out of the chamber, and with him all the rest ... Then the sword being brought in by a little boy, Cato took it, drew it out, and looked at it; and when he saw the point was good, Now, said he, I am master of myself; and laying down the sword, he took his book again, which it is related he read twice over. After this he slept so soundly that he was heard to snore by those that were without.

About midnight, he called up two of his freedmen, Cleanthes his physician, and Butas whom he chiefly employed in public business. Him he sent to the port, to see if all his friends had sailed; to the physician he gave his hand to be dressed, as it was swollen with the blow he had struck one of his servants. At this they all rejoiced, hoping that he now designed to live.

Butas, after a while, returned, and brought word they were all gone except Crassus, who had stayed about some business, but was just ready to depart; he said also that the wind was high, and the sea very rough. Cato, on hearing this sighed, out of compassion to those that were at sea, and sent Butas again to see if any of them should happen to return for anything they wanted, and to acquaint him therewith.

Now the birds began to sing, and he again fell into a little slumber. At length Butas came back, and told him all was quiet in the port. Then Cato, laying himself down as if he would sleep out the rest of the night, bade him shut the door after him. But as soon as Butas was gone out, he took his sword, and stabbed it into his breast; yet not being able to use his hand so well, on account of the swelling, he did not immediately die of the wound; but struggling, fell off the bed, and throwing down a little mathematical table that stood by, made such a noise that the servants hearing it cried out. And immediately his son and all his friends came into the chamber, where seeing him lie weltering in his blood, great part of his bowels out of his body, but himself still alive and able to look at them, they all stood in horror. The physician went to him, and would have put in his bowels, which were not pierced, and sewed up the wound; but Cato, recovering himself and understanding the intention, thrust away the physician, plucked out his own bowels, and tearing open the wound, immediately expired.

The long night is very well conveyed. Phrases like 'Now the birds began to sing' and 'all was quiet in the port' somehow add to its unexpressed tension. The climax is gory, and yet never loses its awful fascination. The 'little mathematical table', like other details in the *Lives*, the crows cawing on Apollo's temple roof before Cicero's death, and the disappearance of Cleopatra's asp ('only something like the trail of it was said to have been noticed on the sand near the sea'), adds sharply to the realism as well as the symbolism of the narrative. Plutarch's *Lives* present a remarkable gallery of deaths, and it may well be that his ability to portray human beings depends on an attitude to death, as has been said equally plausibly about Republican portrait heads. He liked a heroic or a catastrophic death, and he was avid for its details. But he comes closer to Plato's treatment of Sokrates than to tragedy or the acts of the martyrs. Stoical suicide is important to him.

The comparisons between Greek and Roman great men are usually interesting only as a guide to Plutarch's mind, and to his way of selecting the various constructions of the biographies. Alkibiades is compared with Coriolanus. Plutarch sternly condemns Coriolanus, adding sentence after sentence to point the moral. 'The origins of all lay in his unsociable, supercilious, and self-willed disposition, which in all cases is offensive to most people; and when combined with a passion for distinction passes into absolute savageness and merciless-ness.' Alkibiades just found it 'pleasant to be honoured and distasteful to be overlooked', and acted accordingly. Still, Plutarch takes off his hat to Coriolanus 'for his temperance, continence and probity', whereas Alkibiades was 'the least scrupulous and most entirely care-less of human beings in all these points'.

His reading of character is not morally unsubtle, but the interest to us of these *Lives*, which he thought of evidently as moral examples, admirable or cautionary tales, has long survived any serious interest in his moral standards. He can be too superior, as he is in the case of

Lucullus whom he reports all the same with relish and not without humour. The life of Lucullus is like fifth-century comedy, he says, with action and politics and great issues at the beginning, and then a degeneration into feasting and festivals and sheer entertainment. One feels he had too much respect for the 'great' Aristotelian public man, as if greatness of scale were in itself a great moral example. No doubt that mistake was inherited from earlier historians and from Aristotle himself, and no doubt it was a factor in the survival of Plutarch's writings through the Middle Ages. Part of his interest for Shakespeare was surely that of an alternative moral world to one's own, not an alternative morality like that of Marlowe's version of Ovid's *Amores*, but at least a pagan world in which moral consequences could have free play, and virtues and vices be examined, without the intervention of Christianity. But Plutarch's *Lives* have in that way an impressive moral strength, which is built into their fibre and their impetus. It is not just applied externally or as a final verdict.

The lives of Alkibiades and Coriolanus both contain religious interventions, and it is worth observing how Plutarch treats them. At Athens, before the Syracusan expedition, 'When all things were fitted for the voyage, many unlucky omens appeared.' Women who worshipped Adonis carried out 'images resembling dead men' with 'lamentations and mournful songs'. Statues were mutilated. The paragraph proceeds to its climax, in which Alkibiades is accused. The ominous events have served first of all to show the disturbance of the people. When Alkibiades is falsely accused, the still more dreadful charge of profaning the Mysteries is introduced. The 'lamentations and mournful songs' were merely ominous and symbolic, but not otherwise relevant except to the people's state of mind. In *Coriolanus*, a noble lady has a prophetic fit, and rushes to the house of the hero's mother, to ask her to intercede for the Romans with her son. Plutarch explains here at some length how Homer has been criticized for the interventions of gods, but unfairly, as he usually allows free play to human choice and deliberate action, with phrases like 'But I consulted with my own great soul'. In extraordinary actions, Plutarch maintains that Homer 'does introduce divine agency, not to destroy, but to prompt the human will; not to create in us another agency, but offering images to stimulate our own; images that in no sort or kind make our action involuntary, but give occasion rather to spontaneous action, aided by feelings of confidence and hope'. Man, in fact, for Plutarch's Homer, is an Aristotelian machine, scarcely haunted by any ghost. For such a religious man, Plutarch is an extremely secular writer. He is the historian of moral, as Thucydides was of historical, consequences.

The catastrophic ending is his strongest card. He both foresees it and conceals it. Cicero is compared to Demosthenes. Plutarch felt that Demosthenes was a more serious character and a deadly serious and victorious speaker, but he lacked 'authority and place' and Cicero's integrity. 'Cicero's death excites our pity' by his age and miserable murder. But Demosthenes 'demands our admiration ... When the temple of the god no longer afforded him a sanctuary, he took refuge as it were at a mightier altar, freeing himself from arms and soldiers, and laughing to scorn the cruelty of Antipater.' Plutarch gives the death of Demosthenes in splendidly melodramatic terms. At the last moment he tricks the Macedonians by taking poison, and dies with a noble speech on his lips.

But O gracious Neptune, I while I am yet alive will rise up and depart out of this sacred place; though Antipater and the Macedonians have not left so much as thy temple unpolluted. After he had thus spoken and desired to be held up, because already he began to tremble and stagger, as he was going forward and passing by the altar he fell down, and with a groan gave up the ghost.

At a stroke, Plutarch has wiped out all his ignobilities.

The death of Cicero is like a man being hounded by the furies. The weakness of Cicero is part of it. The life ends in details of baroque horror, though Plutarch is historian enough to hint that they are not true. But he liked to show the barbarity of the Romans. He nursed a particular resentment of Antony, whose soldiers had whipped all the people of Chaironea like slaves under burdens of grain to the sea, at the time of the battle of Actium; Plutarch's grandfather was among them. His Antony out-Herods Herod. 'He commanded Cicero's head and hands to be fastened up over the rostra, where the orators spoke; a sight which the Roman people shuddered to behold, and they believed they saw there, not the face of Cicero, but the image of Antony's own soul.' That is only the beginning of the gore in which Plutarch plunges the end of his story, though in the last few sentences

Antony's name will be disgraced for ever, and Cicero's fame restored. The order of nature means virtue must be somehow rewarded, if only after death. Demosthenes was vindicated and his betrayer punished in just the same way. Cicero's private temple of Apollo corresponds to the great temple of Poseidon on the island where Demosthenes died.

There was at that place a chapel of Apollo, not far from the seaside, from which a flight of crows rose with a great noise, and made towards Cicero's vessel, as it rowed to land, and lighting on both sides of the yard, some croaked, others pecked the ends of the ropes. This was looked on by all as an ill-omen; and therefore Cicero went again ashore, and entering his house lay down upon his bed to compose himself to rest. Many of the crows settled about the window, making a dismal cawing; but one of them alighted upon the bed where Cicero lay covered up, and with its bill by little and little pecked off the clothes from his face. His servants seeing this blamed themselves that they should stay to be spectators of their master's murder, and do nothing in his defence, whilst the brute creatures came to assist and take care of him in his undeserved affliction; and therefore partly by entreaty, partly by force, they took him up, and carried him in his litter towards the seaside.

But in the meantime the assassins were come with a band of soldiers, Herennius, a centurion, and Popillius, a tribune, whom Cicero had formerly defended when prosecuted for the murder of his father. Finding the doors shut, they broke them open, and Cicero not appearing, and those within saying they knew not where he was, it is stated that a youth, who had been educated by Cicero in the liberal arts and sciences, an emancipated slave of his brother Quintus, Philologus by name, informed the tribune that the litter was on its way to the sea through the close and shady walks. The tribune, taking a few with him, ran to the place where he was to come out. And Cicero, perceiving Herennius running in the walks, commanded his servants to set down the litter; and stroking his chin, as he used to do, with his left hand, he looked steadfastly at his murderers, his person covered with dust, his hair and his beard untrimmed, and his face worn with his troubles. So that the greatest part of those that stood by covered their faces whilst Herennius slew him. And thus was he murdered, stretching forth his neck out of the litter, being now in his sixty-fourth year.

This narrative with all its telling details has some pretence to derive from an eyewitness; throughout the Roman lives, Plutarch shows a close knowledge that depends of course on his sources. Cicero in the few pages before his death has done nothing really but dither and panic. How brilliantly therefore what Plutarch sees as his true quality is suddenly apparent in the last sentences, without any dying speech at all. The whole death-scene would lose its meaning if it were not so closely in the context of Apollo's temple, the crows everywhere, and the 'close and shady walks', the soldiers running in the garden. 'And thus was he murdered, stretching forth his neck out of the litter ...' Biography has become suddenly more serious than history, or the most serious part of history. Its devices are those of literary art.

Most of his immediate sources for the Roman lives seem to have been in Greek. His Coriolanus comes from Dionysios of Halikarnassos (? 60 B.C.–A.D. 10). His Sertorius was probably based on a recent translation of Sallust into Greek. But many of his friends seem to have known more Latin than he did, and no doubt he employed secretaries who could translate. Yet this limitation of his stamps his work very strongly with his own personality. He wrote the *Lives* rather late in his own life, Demosthenes and Cicero being among his first subjects. He wrote at home from notebooks, without access to any important scholarly library, and his principal weapon was, as he says, the experience of life itself. He produced what he intended, a masterpiece not of history but of moral portraiture and biography. Even the Emperors Galba and Otho became moral examples in the mind of Plutarch. Tacitus took a severe view of Plutarch's historical short-comings. But the early Roman empire rapidly became a distant, almost unbelievable epoch, and Plutarch's *Lives* were acclaimed long before the end of antiquity as an acceptable guide, and as Plutarch's masterpiece. With the reservations I have expressed, I still see no reason to dispute that opinion.

It has been suggested that 'In making the advent of monarchy the inevitable and desirable outcome of civil strife, Plutarch shows himself, as in his account of Romulus, under the influence of Augustan propaganda.' But as C. P. Jones notices, his sympathies are humanly too wide for any party line. He praises Caesar and Augustus, but also those who opposed them; he honours the Roman general who liberated Greece, but also the Greek general who fought him in the name of liberty. One should remember that the activity of providence in Roman history, and a sympathy with both sides, go back to Polybios; Plutarch's constitutional doctrine goes back in the end to Aristotle and to Plato.

Plutarch did write special works about politics, as about many other subjects. His *Political Precepts*, as they are usually called, are addressed to an Asian Greek; they are more concerned with how one should behave in office than with any deeper philosophic analysis of constitutions. His attitude is frankly upper class, and throws some interesting light on the world of Trajan. His most enthusiastic reader was a Roman knight called Cornelius Pulcher who was also a nobleman of Epidauros. Plutarch assumes the well-born were chosen by providence to rule, and the people are like some suspicious and wayward animal. The virtues of rulers are courage and integrity, their principal aim should be concord and the prevention of civil war. Plutarch in fact was a well-intentioned Whig. He was cultured, experienced and well read, and highly moral, but I do not believe he had ever thought as deeply as even the most erring disciples of Sokrates; least of all about religion.

We have three of his dialogues on theological subjects, all three written with great charm and, in their setting at Delphi, all three touching. There is also an early essay of his on superstition, which takes a young man's uncompromising line about monotheism being the only sensible position. In youth, he rejected the existence of *daimones*, or lesser divine powers, of any kind, but evil ones in particular. Later on, when he was a priest at Delphi, and wrote his dialogues, he was more concerned to interpret the orthodox rituals and beliefs symbolically, and the lesser gods flourished again under his theological umbrella. Indeed, the motive of these fascinating late writings was probably to reconcile philosophic monotheism with accepted theological systems.

Although we are tracing the history of literature, but not of theology, or after the pupils of Aristotle even of philosophy, the dogmatic background of Plutarch's dialogues needs a short explanation. Plutarch was trained by the philosopher Ammonios (not Ammonios Sakkas), a magistrate of Athens and three times general of the local infantry. Plutarch was brought up to detest the atomists and Epicureans as atheists, and Euhemeros (?341–288 B.C.) as a rationalizer, who explained gods as ancient human kings. Euhemeros had little influence; Plutarch must have known his work through Diodoros of Sicily (80–20 B.C.?), who took his fictions and allegories literally. Plutarch was vaguely a Platonist, but extremely tolerant of everything except atheism. He would go far to discover the inner or the symbolic sense of any theological belief. We know Ammonios only from Plutarch's dialogues and a few inscriptions. He was an impressive teacher, not at all charmless or stupid, but no substitute for Sokrates.

It would be nice to be sure about the exact or even comparative dates of Plutarch's Delphic dialogues, but the arguments about them are mostly weak. The dialogue *On the Delphic E* seems to have been written late in life, a little before the one on the Pythian oracles, about 120 A.D. One may well accept the view of J. Gwyn Griffiths that the related treatise dedicated to Flavia Clea, a famous Delphic lady, on Isis and Osiris, is as late; I conceive it to be later, partly on feeble and merely theological grounds, *Isis and Osiris* being even wiser in tone, and containing even worse nonsense about *daimones*. 'Not even the crocodile has received honour without a cause: it is said to be the only tongueless creature and thus a likeness of God.' *On the Dying Out of Oracles* is perhaps the earliest in the true Delphic series. *On the Final Vengeance of the Gods* is also set at Delphi, but this is not precisely about Delphic religion; it might have been the beginning of the entire literary device of the Delphic setting.

The Delphic E was a symbol of mysterious and in Plutarch's day long-forgotten significance. He recalls a conversation with Ammonios and some others at the time when Nero was in Greece. and one may assume at Delphi. The dialogue is dedicated to Serapion. who sounds like an Egyptian Greek priest, although he was in fact an Athenian and a poet. 'I send you some of my Delphic writings but only in the hope of getting more and better books in return, which is only natural as you live in a great city and have more means of study and abundance of books and all kinds of lectures'; '... Apollo is, as Ammonios said, as much philosopher as prophet ...' Plutarch describes how he sat one day on the temple terrace with his sons and 'certain foreigners due to leave', and remembered an earlier dialogue in the same place, when Ammonios played Sokrates to Plutarch's brother and their circle.

The dialogue setting is pleasant but cursory. The quotations from poetry give some pleasure, but the intellectual pressure of the whole work is not great. Still, Plutarch does understand the Platonic habit of opening out the argument into deeper and deeper waters, and to advance by definitions to or towards the reserved truth. He can always produce pleasing sentences on such a subject as the quincunx (if E is read as 5), on the freshness of Apollo in art, the transformations of Dionysos, and so on. Dionysos in this theology is a daimonic natural force, constantly dying and reborn, but Apollo is a true god. The thoughts of Ammonios on the Delphic E have a powerful religious force, and they had an influence as late as Montaigne. The giant ghost of Plato is in the background of course. It is charming that Plutarch so loved Apollo and Delphi, but in this dialogue his most remarkable achievement is his lucid transmission of something beyond his own talent.

On the Delphic Oracles, or *Why the Delphic Oracle No Longer Uses Verse*, is a straight conversation. 'You have drawn out the evening, Philinos, conducting the stranger round the dedications. I gave up waiting for you ...' But the setting is perfectly drawn, and we hear comments in detail of some aesthetic precision – 'the patina of the bronze ... a sombre and gleaming blue' – which gave him a joke about the statues of the Admirals where the visit began: 'From the colour of their skins they really do look underwater.' Conversation turns for some time on the techniques of bronze-workers and the effects of the special climate of Delphi. This subject is then abandoned, like the role of the crows in the death of Cicero, but it has a similar symbolic effect, as the quality of Delphic verse comes up for discussion. 'No, said Serapion, we are weak-eared and weak-eyed, and through our luxurious living and the softness of our taste we find everything beautiful and noble which is sweet ...'

Plutarch respects Serapion as a conservative and a Stoic, but he also thinks him absurdly extreme. The arguments are elegantly nourished by the famous Delphic show-pieces, one after the other. Discussion widens into the value of prophecy and the nature of inspiration, and ends in a Sokratic admission of ignorance. Plutarch appears to reserve his own positive belief. Serapion is nicely balanced by an Athenian Epicurean. The final momentum of this dialogue is towards reformed religion, with a compliment to Hadrian on the last page. 'In the old days ... people were stupid and childish: children get more pleasure out of rainbows and haloes and comets, and love them more, than seeing the sun and the moon, and they miss the riddles and allegories and metaphors of the old oracles ...'

The dialogue *On the Dying Out of Oracles* is a disturbing and moving piece of writing, not only because of its strangeness and sadness and obvious honesty, but to us because one of its characters, Demetrios of Tarsos, has been in the British islands. He seems to have travelled to Mull or Skye, in the time of Agricola, and Plutarch has him call in at Delphi on his way home. Demetrios was a grammarian and maybe a geographer, but he travelled 'with an imperial escort'. This same Demetrios left inscribed dedications at York, which are still to be seen, to the god and goddess of Ocean, and the local military gods. The philosopher Ammonios plays a part in this dialogue, but a briefer one than usual, and his victorious opinions are barely outlined. Plutarch's brother and Ammonios are hosts to Demetrios and a Spartan called Kleombrotos, another traveller, a man of unseemly credulity and a theological appetite amounting to greed. But this is a dialogue of strange information, not of solutions. It borrows ideas from all philosophies except Epicureanism. Its latest editor, Robert Flacelière, wants to put it comparatively early in Plutarch's religious development, at the beginning of his Delphic priesthood. It was certainly not meant for a final statement, though it is the longest Delphic dialogue and the most literary.

At the top of the sanctuary, Ammonios and his party meet other friends in a famous building with ancient frescoed walls. With these friends is a Cynic, a philosophic wild man, drawn with pleasing gusto. Plutarch may have been no philosopher, but life he understood. The Cynic disrupts the polite texture of the dialogue, and then, alas, he vanishes. But one is left musing about why this interruption occurs. He is not present for local colour or as an alternative way of life. Maybe we should think again of the crows, and the texture of the bronzes. Demetrios is a little too exquisite, with his pedantic and charming jokes. The Cynic is extremely serious. 'Not only Conscience and Shame have quit mankind, as Hesiod said, but divine Providence as well, with all the oracles in her luggage.' He makes a well-mounted attack both on the practice and the theory of Delphi. I do not think Plutarch is without some sympathy with the Cynic. This man is like the ruder adversaries of Sokrates: he needs answering and he raises difficulties in a sharp form. Ammonios continues, 'Be careful what we are doing ... for fear we reduce the god's role to nothing.' The dialogue proceeds at the end of all its examples to daemonic intervention, underworld exhalation, and 'spirit'.

At these words Herakleon began to meditate something in silence. Then Philip said, But Herakleon, it was not only Empedokles who left evil *daimones* to survive, it was Plato as well, and Xenokrates and Chrysippos, and Demokritos too, when he made that prayer to encounter only 'happy apparitions', because he showed he knew of other kinds, evil ones and harmful ones ...

As for the death of beings of that kind, this is something I heard said by one who was no fool and no liar; Aemilianus the orator, whose courses some of you have followed, was the son of Epitherses, my own fellow-countryman and my professor in literature. He used to say how one day on the way to Italy by sea, he was on a ship that carried goods, and she also carried a number of passengers. In the evening, when they were already somewhere near the Isles of the Echinades, the wind suddenly fell, and the ship was carried by the current towards Paxos. Most of the people on board were awake, and many of them still drinking after dinner. Suddenly a voice was heard shouting out from the Isle of Paxos, calling for Thamous. They were amazed. This Thamous was an Egyptian pilot, and very few passengers knew his name. He heard them call him twice without saying anything. Then the third time he answered whoever cried out: and the voice roared out to him, When you get up to Palodes, tell them there great Pan is dead. They were all frozen with horror. They were discussing what to do about it, whether to follow orders or forget it, but Thamous decided if the wind blew he was going to pass up the coast and say nothing. Only if it was dead calm when he got there, he was going to say the words. So when they got up by Palodes, there was not one breath of air, not one wave. Thamous stood on the poop and faced the land, and called out the message, Great Pan is dead. He hardly finished when a mighty lamentation rose up, not one person but many, mingled with cries of shock.

This curious story could have numerous explanations, all of which have been suggested. But it has a residual strangeness. If it is true that romanticism is always nourished by particulars, this is in more ways than one a romantic story. The story of the British isles follows it almost at once.

And Philip saw his story confirmed by several of those present; they had heard Aemilianus tell it in his old age. Then Demetrios said there are a number of desert islands scattered around Britain, and some of them are named after demons and heroes. He said he was sent himself by the Emperor on a mission of reconnaissance and exploration, and landed on the island that lay nearest the deserted ones; it had few people, but they were sacred, and in sanctuary from the British. When he arrived there had just been a great storm in the air with a lot of thunder and lightning flashes and the winds were let loose and the storm broke heavily. When it grew calm, the islanders said it was the end of one of the rulers of the world. Just as a lighted lamp does no harm, they said, but when you put it out it can be troublesome to many, so these great souls are friendly and harmless alight, but when they go out and perish, they often breed high wind and tempest like this. Sometimes they poison the air with plagues.

There is one island there where Kronos is a prisoner guarded by Briareus in his sleep. Sleep was the fetters designed for Kronos, and many *daimones* lie around him as servants and followers.

Once again there are various interpretations equally possible. The 'rulers of the world' seem to be gods, but the language of this passage constantly suggests astral magic. I am not at all clear whether the 'rulers' are gods in the air, *daimones* more likely, or something else. We might even be talking about a solstice or the seasonal disappearance of a star. But it is agreeable to think of Plutarch at Delphi impressed by British superstitions. Briareus in the story had a hundred hands, and Kronos, the father of Zeus, seems to mean a kind of earth-father and ancestor worshipped by the Gauls. The true reason for Plutarch's interest is suggested at once by Kleombrotos. 'I have many such tales to tell, but for the argument we need only say that nothing is against them, nothing prevents their being true. And we know the Stoics among the multitudes of the gods admit only one, incorruptible and eternal, and they believe the others had a beginning, and will have an end.'

This dialogue being a long one, at least by Plutarch's standards (about sixty-five pages), it has room to imitate the form and argumentation of a real Platonic dialogue. Plutarch was at heart a serious Platonist. It is surprising how much he understands about dialogue construction, parody and irony, and the sublime, reserved message. But it is better not to pry too closely into his reasoning, which is no more than a respectable product of the age of Trajan and Hadrian. Yet his Platonism is by no means an affectation. He seriously believes in the educative and spiritual power of eros, though homosexuality gets swept under the carpet in his restatement of these famous themes. It would be a mistake to value Plutarch only for his *Questions* and *Table Talk* and his infinite fund of gossip. His information is always attempting to serve some moral or Platonic purpose; he is not ignoble in his intellectual strivings, and without those we would have missed the lives, the Delphic dialogues, and everything about Plutarch that our own worldly wisdom prefers.

Perhaps one should pay some closer attention to his lives of Galba and Otho. It has been suggested, over-cleverly as I believe, by Bowersock, that his role, like that of the much less interesting Dio Chrysostomos (Dio Cocceianus of Prusa, ? A.D. 40–112), was essentially to reconcile the Greeks to their fate. He seems to me to have been just as interested in how Romans ought to behave, and as Johnson in reporting Parliament 'never let the Whig dogs have the best of it', so Plutarch paints Greek glories in special colours. As for patriotism, his city is not Athens, only Chaironea, but to that he shows extreme loyalty. The late historians' rumour that he once governed all Roman Achaia is rather unlikely, but it would be no disgrace. It does not however affect the moral seriousness of his writing, which Bowersock's imputation I think does. His *Galba* contains plenty that Roman propaganda would not wish Greeks to think or to know, even apart from the ultimate assumption that practical wisdom is Greek.

And Plato, who can discern no use of a good ruler or general if his men are not on their part obedient and conformable (the virtue of obeying, as of ruling, being, in his opinion, one that does not exist without first a noble nature, and then a philosophic education, where the eager and active powers are allayed with the gentler and humaner sentiments), may claim in confirmation of his doctrine sundry mournful instances elsewhere, and in particular the events that followed among the Romans upon the death of Nero, in which plain proofs were given that nothing is more terrible than a military force moving about in an empire upon uninstructed and unreasoning impulses. Demeuades, after the death of Alexander, compared the Macedonian army to the Cyclops after his eye was out, seeing their many disorderly and unsteady motions. But the calamities of the Roman government might be likened to the giants that assailed heaven, convulsed as it was, and distracted, and from every side recoiling as it were upon itself . . .

. . . Forthwith a senate was convened, and as if they were not the same men, or had other gods to swear by, they took that oath in Otho's name which he himself had taken in Galba's, and had broken; and withal conferred on him the titles of Caesar and Augustus; whilst the dead carcasses of the slain lay still in their consular robes in the market-place . . .

The *Life of Otho* follows at once after the end of *Galba*, as soon as heads have been thrown into sewers and so on, and a brief didactic paragraph has cleared the air. 'The new emperor went early in the morning to the Capitol . . .' and we are off. But Otho's career was brief and violent. Plutarch's account of him has no interesting set pieces except for a quick and noble death scene. Plutarch intended to continue with lives of later emperors; we have an ancient catalogue reference to a series from Augustus to Vitellius. Whatever is touched by the experience of life in Plutarch's writings is always fascinating.

They placed the remains of Otho in the earth, and raised over them a monument which neither by its size nor the pomp of its inscription might excite hostility. I myself have seen it, at Brixillum; a plain structure, and the epitaph only this: To the memory of Marcus Otho. He died in his thirty-eighth year . . . if he lived not better than Nero, he died more nobly.

It is not possible to go through the whole works of Plutarch very thoroughly here. Some are ridiculous. His pamphlet on the prejudices of Herodotos is a good idea that turns out badly. History had to be close to contemporary if Plutarch was to criticize it competently. His *Spirit of Sokrates* is well thought of, but it is unhelpful. His writings of consolation after a death have been much praised, but I have never found such compositions very comforting myself. On the other hand, Plutarch on exile is nicely stuffed with examples and quotations; it is a cheering pamphlet. His *Eroticus* is a dialogue set locally. I find it moving even apart from its neo-classic colouring. A large proportion of his work is the merest antiquarian amalgam, suavely set out. It is the Greek equivalent of writers like Aulus Gellius. Some of the works attributed to Plutarch are spurious, though among those the *Lives of the Ten Orators* are more interesting than one has any right to expect, and so on a lesser level are the *Love Stories*. Among the stranger themes that attracted Plutarch now and then – relics, I suppose, of sophistic playfulness about science – the *Man in the Moon* (*De Facie in Orbe Lunae*) gives the most pleasure. My own favourites among his shorter works are possibly *On How to Read Poetry*, and certainly his *Gryllos*, the story of the sailor of Odysseus who refused to be turned back into a man, because he preferred being a pig.

No doubt there would be a moral in a history of Greek literature that ended here. But it is really impossible, once literature has begun, to draw a clear line between the end of one movement or period and the beginning of another. There is no doubt at all that between Homer and Plutarch, literature was even more utterly transformed than life: and yet one can draw no clear line in 400 B.C., or with Alexander, or between Menander and Theokritos for example. After Plutarch and Lucian, Greek books did not cease to be written, though mostly they were poetry intended to entertain, or history intended to beguile. *Hero and Leander* is a beguiling poem of the fifth century A.D., though to read it is to drown in honey and word-play. Short poems like the Greek originals of 'I sent thee late a rosy wreath . . .' and 'Drink to me only with thine eyes . . .' went on being written. Baroque poems whose mere length and the weight of their ornamentation are achievements of a kind went on appearing.

The only really great writer who might be called classical in some sense, the only one to be thrilling for his style as well as his message, and to have conferred by his writings an enormous benefit on readers of Greek, whom I have excluded from this survey, is Plotinus. He wrote so late in time, and has so little in common with the others, and his philosophy and his Greek are so technically hard, that I must leave him alone. Ancient Christian sermons are often better than modern ones, though they seldom rise to the heights of Donne. But the general truth sadly remains. Most of the fathers of the Church, of those who wrote in Greek, continued and enlarged the decadence of literature.

Of course, the Middle Ages also produced written Greek, some of it wonderful. It is like a scatter of islands in a barren, blue sea. Indeed there should really be written a simple and clear account in English of later Greek literature, from the end of antiquity to George Seferis. The Greek language is perfectly continuous, from that day to this, and in every hundred years there has been something or other written in Greek of great interest and some beauty. Wherever one draws a line will be the wrong place. The Middle Ages in Greece had started before the classical age ended. Revivals began earlier still. In the classical period, the constant rebirth of Greek is amazing; the sheer vitality and variety of it is amazing. But artifice withers. In the later classical period one begins to get, as with no other language, a sense of the undertones and the continuous power of the Greek language itself, which underlies prose and poetry alike. The principal hero and the *deus ex machina* of late classical literature is the Greek language.

BIBLIOGRAPHY

G. W. Bowersock, *Greek Sophists in the Roman Empire*, 1969

A. H. Clough, *The Dryden Plutarch*, 1864 (the Everyman edition reprinted Clough's revision of Dryden's *Plutarch*)

R. Flacelière (ed.), *Plutarque, Dialogues Pythiques* (with French translation and notes), 1974

J. G. Griffiths (ed.) *Plutarch, Isis and Osiris* (with English translation and commentary), 1970

C. P. Jones, *Plutarch and Rome*, 1971

D. A. Russell, *Plutarch*, 1973

A. Wardman, *Plutarch's 'Lives'*, 1974

G. Wyndham (ed.), *Plutarch's Lives by Sir James North*, 1895

INDEX